TERMINAL ALLIANCE

Book One of the Janitors of the Post-Apocalypse

JIM C. HINES

TERMINAL ALLIANCE

Book One of the Janitors of the Post-Apocalypse

DAW BOOKS, INC.

DONALD A. WOLLHEIM, FOUNDER

375 Hudson Street, New York, NY 10014

ELIZABETH R. WOLLHEIM
SHEILA E. GILBERT
PUBLISHERS
www.dawbooks.com

First Printing, November 2017
1 2 3 4 5 6 7 8 9

To Mike, Christian, Jim, and
the rest of the Launch Pad Crew.

Author's Note

Before I get into the thank yous, I wanted to answer a few questions from readers and fans. Most of these came in via Twitter or Facebook.

- From Chris: What has been the biggest surprise (or unexpected benefit) since you started writing full time?
  - I started writing more-or-less full time in September of 2015. I knew I wouldn't magically become a SuperAuthor, putting out twelve books a year, but I was still surprised at how difficult it could be to balance writing with everything else—taking care of the kids, running errands, housework, walking the dogs . . . (Not to mention getting out to catch Pokémon.) I thought I knew how much discipline and planning and structure I'd need. I was mistaken. But I'm getting better.
- From both Illona Andrews and TheBarbarienne: How can you tolerate a giant beard when it's so freaking hot out?
  - It's a sacrifice I'm willing to make to look this sexy! Also, the warmth of the Giant Beard is balanced out by the draftiness of the bare scalp.

- From Piers: What's the fastest land animal?
  - Our cat Pippin when he hears a can opener in the kitchen.
- From Paul: What draws you to use humor so much in your fiction? (This is far from your first humorous SFF after all!)
  - I believe humor is incredibly powerful and valuable. It brings laughter. It helps us cope with darkness. It allows us to tell difficult and dangerous truths. It's a way of pointing out the absurdities of life. It creates connections between people. Also, it's a lot of fun to write!

I'll try to do another batch of questions with the next book. For now, on to the gratitude! Thanks first to the Launchpad Astronomy Workshop, a week-long crash course taught by Mike Brotherton and other professional astronomers. (That's right, I used *real* science for parts of this book!)

Thanks as always to my editor Sheila Gilbert—now *Hugo Award-winning* editor Sheila Gilbert!—and everyone else at DAW Books.

Props to Dan Dos Santos for the marvelous cover art! I particularly love his depiction of Grom.

Thank you to my agent Joshua Bilmes and the rest of the JABberwocky crew.

If you're reading this note in a language other than American English, it means someone spent a *lot* of time translating not just my words, but the tone and humor and style of the story. Huge thanks to the translators who have worked so hard on my various books over the years.

Finally, all my love and gratitude to my wife Amy and my children for supporting and putting up with me through yet another one of these things, with all the emotional ups and downs that come with writing a book.

I hope you all enjoy it.

1

"Marion Adamopoulos."

The circular training room fell silent. The other humans of Marion's crèche turned toward the bubbling hot spring in the center.

Scheherazade pulled herself to the edge of the spring, fixing Marion with one large black eye. "Names are very important to humans. I don't believe that one was in the database of suggested names."

"It's from our history review. It's the name I chose." Marion spread her arms. She didn't realize until after the fact that she was mimicking Krakau defensive body language. Deliberately, she folded her arms and stared defiantly back at their Awakening and Orientation Officer.

Most Krakau massed less than the average human. They were roughly tube-shaped, with nine tentacles—arms—limbs? Marion had struggled with the difference. In Human language, the three smooth, snakelike primary limbs with the flat, diamond-shaped pads on the end were the tentacles. The pads were covered in differently sized and surprisingly dexterous suction cups.

The lower six limbs were similar to those of an Earth octopus, covered in suction cups from tip to torso. These lower limbs were used for propulsion and mobility, but for some reason were called "arms" in Human.

To quote Scheherazade, humans were strange and illogical, and their language reflected that.

"It's been twenty-three days since your awakening," said Scheherazade, her black, beaklike mouth grinding in confusion. A translator implant, like a large silver pearl in the yellow skin of the Krakau's throat, repeated the clicks and whistles in Human. "Your 'rebirth,' as some humans call it. You have another month before you'll be given your first assignment. Perhaps you'd like to take more time to consider—"

"This is my name," Marion interrupted. "You chose your own human name. I have the right to choose mine."

Every Krakau adopted a name based on the closest thing humans had to a universal language: music. They each pored over hours of intercepted Earth signals and recordings to find the melody best suited to her personality.

By now, the other humans had begun whispering to one another. Scheherazade flicked a tentacle in annoyance, spraying droplets of hot, salty water onto several of the humans. "You know the history of that name?"

Marion recited the answer from memory. "Marion Adamopoulos was an early twenty-second-century scientist who helped destroy human civilization."

"Why choose a name associated with so much death and destruction?"

"As a reminder of what we did to ourselves, and of how much we owe the Krakau for giving us a second chance."

It was an honest answer, if incomplete. The other reason was simpler: she liked the sound of it. Adamopoulos. It spilled lyrically from the tongue.

"So be it." Scheherazade extended a tentacle to note the decision on the glassy, waterproof console beside her pool, then turned to the next human. "And you?"

The human, a male with bushy black hair and a missing eye, swallowed nervously. "I reviewed the human name database. I can't decide if I'd rather be called Nelson Mandela, Rosalind Franklin, or Beyoncé. . . ."

Marion made a note of her fellow humans' new names, but most of her attention was elsewhere. Another month at the Antarctic Medical Facility and she'd receive her first assignment as a member of the Earth Mercenary Corps. Most humans ended up in the infantry, fighting the Prodryans and helping to keep peace in the Krakau Alliance. After all the Krakau had done to help humanity after their self-imposed apocalypse, she was determined to repay the aliens in whatever way she could.

She'd named herself for a woman who turned humanity into shambling, feral monsters. The Krakau had spent decades trying to reverse that mistake. Soon, Marion would set out to help them make things right.

LIEUTENANT MARION "MOPS" Adamopoulos, commander of the Shipboard Hygiene and Sanitation team on the *EMCS Pufferfish*, switched off the translation of a nineteenth-century human history textbook she'd been reading and focused her attention on the alert icon on her monocle. "Go ahead."

"Incoming message from Commander Danube. The Pufferfish has received a distress call from a Nusuran cargo vessel. All hands should prepare for battle and report to the nearest acceleration chamber. A-ring jump in nineteen minutes."

The words of her personal AI unit, Doc, came from the directional speakers of her comm unit, secured in the bulky collar of her one-piece uniform. Doc himself existed primarily as code etched invisibly into the layers of memory crystal that formed Mops' green-tinted monocle.

"What's the status on the rest of the team?"

"JG Monroe is in his quarters. Technician Kumar is working

to repair a cracked sewage relay on deck L. I've relayed the commander's instructions to them both. Technician Mozart is in the brig."

"Of course she is." Mops stretched, grimacing at the popping of her left shoulder. There was no pain, but the sound and sensation made her cringe. The joint had started acting up two years ago, like machinery past its warranty.

She left her small quarters and hurried toward the center of the *Pufferfish*. The ship was built like an oversized torpedo, with three elongated weapons pods protruding like outriggers spread equidistant around the hull. The brig was near the aft engines. "How many times is this?"

"This is Crewman Mozart's fourth incarceration since she was transferred to your SHS team. It's her eighth during her one-year service with the Earth Mercenary Corps. Three more incidents, and she'll break the EMC disciplinary record."

She greeted several of the crew on her way to the central lifts. Doc automatically tagged them with their name and rank, not that Mops needed the assistance. After more than a decade aboard the *Pufferfish*, she knew them all. "Why wasn't I notified when it happened?"

"You were off duty. Commander Danube is recommending Technician Mozart be expelled from service."

"I'm not ready to give up on her." Mops hurried into the first available lift, joining Sergeant Claus from infantry. She nodded a greeting as the doors closed and the lift shot downward.

"Where you off to, smoothie?" asked Claus. Mops outranked him, but relations between the soldiers and the noncombat crew tended toward the informal, and she'd known Claus for most of her life. His rebirth had been a year after Mops' own. After Mops, he was one of the oldest humans on the ship.

It was easy to recognize the soldiers, not only by the unit insignia on the right shoulder of their uniforms, but from the scars they accumulated over the years. The left side of Claus' face was a mess of scar tissue from a flamethrower attack two years back. An old plasma burn striped his right cheek.

The only smooth-skinned humans on an EMC ship were either shipboard maintenance or brand-new recruits. Mops had a few small scars from her life before the Krakau cured her, but those were all hidden beneath her uniform. Nor would anyone mistake the faint lines around her eyes and mouth for battle scars.

"I need to take care of a mess in the brig," she said.

Claus snorted. "That mess wouldn't happen to be named Mozart, would it? I hear she picked a fight with a Glacidae this time."

"It wouldn't surprise me. I don't know what I'm going to do with that child. She's not happy in SHS, but you know infantry won't take her. Danube wants to send her back to Earth."

"Ouch." He pursed his lips, crinkling his ragged blond mustache. "Give me combat drops any day over trying to survive a planet overrun by ferals. You know if she has enough saved up for passage to one of the stations? Humans can make decent money working security."

"I doubt it. She's not big on long-term planning." Or short-term planning, for that matter. "What's the word on this distress call?"

"Command crew doesn't tell us grunts anything. We go where they send us and shoot what they tell us." Claus clapped her arm as the lift came to a halt. "Good luck with Wolf, Lieutenant."

Mops hurried down the corridor to the heavy brown door labeled *Brig and Backup Emergency/Acceleration Shelter* in Human.

The door unlocked with a heavy *clunk*. Inside was a narrow rectangular hallway with eight transparent doors, four to each side. A larger door on the end led to the control room. Two guards approached to greet her.

"Morning, Lieutenant," said Private Williams, an older man with a permanent smirk, courtesy of a dark knife scar across his cheek. "Come to claim your janitor?"

"It was either that or make her walk the plank." Mops' quip was met with blank looks from both guards, who were apparently unfamiliar with old human pirate stories. She sighed and tried a different conversation opener. "How's your garden coming along?"

Calling Williams' Earth mosses and lichen a "garden" was stretching things, but given how few plants could survive life on an EMC cruiser, he'd done an amazing job keeping his little collection alive.

"I can't get the letharia to thrive. It's not strong enough for the A-ring jumps."

"That's the yellow one with the tufts and branches, right?"

"They're supposed to be green, but ship's lighting isn't right." His expression brightened. "The caloplaca's doing great, though. If it keeps spreading, I'll need to pick up some new rocks."

Mops chuckled and approached the only occupied cell. Glowing letters in the wide, glassy door labeled it Cell 6. "Doc, how long until we jump?"

"Twelve minutes."

A narrow cot strained to hold Technician Wolfgang Mozart's bulk. The guards had stripped Wolf of her equipment and harness, leaving her black jumpsuit bare and baggy. A short blue service stripe on her upper right sleeve marked her time in the EMC, just as the two short and one long red Lieutenant stripes on Mops' denoted her twelve years.

Wolf's sleeves were pushed back to the elbows, exposing the tattoo of an Earth wolf on her left forearm. She flexed her muscles, and the reactive inks animated the wolf's jowls, making it bare its teeth in challenge. "I was just doing my job. The Glacidae should be in here, not me. They're the one who started giving me crap."

Mops folded her arms and said nothing. Anticipating her next request, Doc pulled up the incident report details on her monocle.

The cot creaked as Wolf sat up and ran thick fingers through her dark, sweat-spiked hair. She looked Mops up and down, probably trying to assess how much trouble she was in. "I mean that literally, you know. I was busting my ass trying to clear a jam in their toilet. The next thing I know, they're shooting shit-pellets in my direction."

"That wasn't excrement. Technician Gromgimsidalgak was expelling unfertilized eggs."

"Whatever. It was like a machine gun from their ass."

"I'm sure Grom was as unhappy about it as you were." The ship's four Glacidae crew normally spent a few days in Medical during this phase of their reproductive cycles. It must have snuck up on Grom this time. "Williams, I need Wolf released and her gear returned."

Williams hesitated. "She assaulted a member of the crew. I'm not supposed to release her—"

"Unless there's an overriding operational need, and someone supervises her conduct," Mops interrupted. "My team's short-staffed and we're about to jump. If we're going into battle, I need Wolf on duty, not napping in the brig. I'll babysit her myself."

"Yes, sir." Williams ducked into the command room to fetch Wolf's equipment while the other guard—Tzu—unlocked the cell.

"It wasn't just eggs, you know." Wolf held up her hands. Black scabs dotted her palms. "These are from Grom's stingers."

"You threw the first punch." Mops chuckled. "And not a very good one, from the sound of it. At least not a good enough punch to keep Grom down."

"There's one other citation from Security's report," said Doc, pulling it up on Mops' monocle and highlighting a passage near the end.

Mops groaned. "Of all the asinine . . . The rest of the galaxy already thinks of us as barely sentient animals, Wolf. You can't go around threatening to eat people's faces!"

Wolf sagged back in her cot. "I'll apologize, all right? I didn't know they were . . . what do you call that? Eggstrating?

I'll bring Grom one of those methane slushees from the mess. The thing put up a hell of a fight for their size. I can respect that." She shook her hand in mock pain.

The cell door slid open, just as a ten-minute countdown popped up in the corner of Mops' monocle. "Move ass, Technician. We've got a jump coming up."

Wolf's belongings were standard issue. Where the guards and soldiers carried sidearms and ammo and restraints in their equipment harnesses, SHS personnel were loaded down with an array of hand tools and cleaning supplies, from high-pressure canisters of disinfectants, paints, and sealants to more specialized items like ultraviolet lighting for spotting shed Glacidae spines.

Wolf brought her monocle to her left eye socket. It jumped into place with a faint click, secured by the magnets implanted beneath the skin.

"Do you *want* to be sent back to Earth?" Mops asked in a low voice.

"And miss the chance to scrape slime from the water circ filters in the captain's quarters every week?" Wolf asked bitterly.

"You need to grow the hell up, Technician. I know you're unhappy here, but you can't solve every problem by punching it."

"Course not." Wolf tightened the last of her harness straps. "That's why we have blasters and batons."

Four egg-shaped indentations slid open in the back wall of the cell as Tzu converted the interior to a jump chamber. Tzu and Williams stepped through the doorway.

Mops gave Wolf a weary shove. "Hook yourself in. We'll sort the rest out after the mission."

Mops settled into the last vacant pod and raised her hands. The attachment points locked into matching mechanisms on her harness and tightened her into place. "Doc, what's the status on the rest of the team?"

"Monroe and Kumar are both secure in acceleration chambers B-11 and D-4, respectively."

Mops relaxed, letting the gelatinous padding of the

acceleration pod mold itself to her body. Like practically everything else, the pod, the gel, and the acceleration rings were Krakau inventions. Technically, even humanity was a Krakau invention. They were the ones who'd figured out how to restore the feral remnants of humanity. To reconstruct Earth culture and a Human language.

"This distress call, you think it's pirates?" asked Wolf.

"They're Nusurans," said Tzu. "Probably started fooling around, got distracted, and crashed into an asteroid."

While she waited, Mops had Doc call up the ever-growing backlog of repairs, inspections, routine maintenance, and emergency cleanups assigned to her team. A backlog that was about to get even longer. With every A-ring jump, there were always a handful of people who suddenly lost the contents of their stomachs. The lucky ones lost said contents through their mouths.

Mops had never been able to fully wrap her brain around A-ring technology. The Krakau had developed it a hundred and fifty years ago, opening the galaxy to interstellar travel and communication. From the reading she'd done, the rings were similar in some respects to old human jet engine technology. Where a jet engine compressed and accelerated airflow, A-rings gravitationally compressed space itself. Essentially, they pinched the universe, then shot the ship through like a pellet from a space-time slingshot.

The *Pufferfish* carried thirty A-rings. From a distance, they looked like an enormous white hose coiled around the bow. Each ring could be launched and expanded to allow the ship to pass through. The rings were only a meter or so deep, but the *Pufferfish* would traverse the equivalent of hundreds of kilometers in that single relativistic meter.

A hundred kilometers was nothing in interstellar terms. What mattered was the acceleration the ship gained in the process. As the A-ring disintegrated from the amount of energy being channeled, it sent the ship ahead at many times the speed of light.

Human scientists had believed light speed was an absolute limit. Of course, human science also used to believe meat transformed into maggots, the Earth was the center of the universe, and cholera could be treated with a tobacco smoke enema.

Mops had once written to the Technological Advancement Council, asking about relativity and the light speed barrier. The rather brusque reply explained that light speed *was* an absolute barrier. Any object traveling at the speed of light would be instantly destroyed. Which was why they used the A-rings to skip past that barrier and accelerate directly to faster-than-light speed.

It had been a remarkably unilluminating response.

The countdown approached zero. Mops closed her eyes, exhaled hard, and tightened her core as she felt herself slammed hard against the back of her pod. Inertial manipulation and the loopholes of relativity kept the crew from being instantly transformed into lumps of bloody jam, but technology could only do so much.

Three things happened more-or-less simultaneously. The *Pufferfish* leaped through interstellar space, thumbing its nose at primitive human science. The A-ring disintegrated in a flash of light and radiation. And everyone on board passed the hell out.

Mops' monocle noted it was roughly one hour after deceleration as she awoke. She blinked her dry, gritty eyes and stretched tingling limbs. A pungent, sour smell filled the air. At least one person had puked during the jump or, more likely, during the deceleration at the end. She touched her chin to make sure it hadn't been her.

"Sorry, Lieutenant." Private Tzu's face was pale and sweaty. She wiped her mouth on her sleeve and grimaced. The pods were supposed to vacuum any misdirected bodily fluids, but they never got it all.

"This will help." Mops opened a compressed sanitizing sponge from a pouch on her harness. It expanded automatically as she tossed it to the private. "Doc, tag that pod for a full scrub down."

"Done."

Before she could say anything more, the lights turned green, and a *Battle Stations* alert flashed on her monocle.

For Mops and her team, that meant stay the hell out of the way and let the more essential personnel get where they needed to be. She asked Doc for a status report while the guards stumbled out of the acceleration chamber. Tzu nodded gratefully as she left, still sponging off the front of her uniform.

"We're getting the normal list of cleanup requests, but it doesn't look like anything vital broke during the jump."

"Good. Relay the following assignments. Kumar, I want you in Medical. If we get casualties, they'll need help with cleanup and sterilization so that the med team can focus on patching people up. Monroe—get down to Engineering and coordinate with Lieutenant Lee to monitor and prioritize any repairs."

Monroe cut in. "With permission, I'd like to make sure all nonessential plumbing is locked down first. It's supposed to happen automatically, but some of those valves are overdue for maintenance and replacement. I once saw a lucky shot burst a ship's pipes and flood two decks with several hundred liters of partially frozen sewage. No way I'm wading through a mess like that again."

"Good thinking." Lieutenant Junior Grade Marilyn Monroe was ex-infantry, and had transferred to SHS after a Prodryan grenade tore up a third of his body. He'd been Mops' second-in-command for more than a year now. "Report to Engineering when you're finished."

"Let me guess," Wolf muttered, turning to go. "Post-jump puke duty for me."

Mops caught her arm. "You're staying where I can keep an eye on you. Right now, that means the aft battle hub. I'll dispatch you from there if necessary."

Wolf's face brightened. "Yes, sir!"

"Once the fighting's over, *then* you're on post-jump puke cleanup."

Mops ducked into Battle Hub Three, one of several reinforced rooms at the core of the ship. Three other human officers sat in front of hardwired terminals. Mops steered Wolf toward a vacant seat. "Stay there, and don't touch anything."

Mops sat beside Lieutenant Tambo from Engineering. The chair magnetized itself to the back of her harness to secure her in place. Once she was settled, the screen expanded and curved to fill most of her vision. In the center was a tactical display of the *Pufferfish*. Mops' team appeared as small blue dots. She checked to confirm everyone was at their assigned station, then focused on the bigger picture.

A second display showed them to be in the outskirts of the Andromeda 12 system, approximately 260 million kilometers out from the star, and 100 million kilometers "above" the orbital plane. They'd traversed almost thirty light-years in the ninety-minute jump.

Two small Prodryan ships hovered over a Nusuran freighter between the fourth and fifth planets, both of which were home to fledgling Nusuran colonies. The freighter looked like a bloated metal maggot, while the Prodryan ships were more like broad-winged gnats.

"That's all?" Wolf sounded disappointed as she peered at Mops' screen.

Tambo snorted. "You were hoping for another Siege of Avloka?"

It was almost twenty-five years since the EMC had freed the Krakau colony of Avloka from the Prodryan occupation.

Fewer than half the human soldiers had survived that four-month war, but the Prodryan forces on the planet were utterly destroyed. It was the first time the galaxy had seen a large-scale human army in action.

"Just seems like a waste," said Wolf. "An EMC cruiser for two little fighters? How long until we reach them?"

Mops pointed to the display. "We're coming in at point-zero-eight. That's around eighty-five million kilometers per hour. We're still decelerating, but we should be close enough to engage directly in ninety minutes or so."

"Ninety minutes?" Wolf sagged in her chair. "They'll have gutted the freighter and be long gone."

"You'd be surprised," said Tambo. "It takes time to get clear and calculate a jump out of the system, and we've got a lot more speed. Even if they started accelerating the second they detected us, we'd have a decent chance of getting within missile range."

"And it's not like Prodryans to run from a fight," added Mops. "Even a hopeless one."

"We'll have this cleaned up before the command crew wakes up from their nap," said Wolf, sounding torn between pride and disappointment.

Other species were more susceptible to damage from A-ring jumps, requiring additional medical preparations and time to recover. The Glacidae would start coming around in another few hours. The Krakau would be the last to awaken from their "nap."

Mops pointed to the second Prodryan ship. "Looks like one of the Prodryans docked with the Nusurans. They might be taking hostages."

Wolf nodded, her attention fixed on the screen. Mops couldn't recall ever seeing her this focused.

"The *Pufferfish* library has a whole section on Earth military history," Mops suggested. "Land, sea, and air battles. I can recommend some titles if you'd like."

Wolf scoffed. "A bunch of primitive humans running around

with gunpowder projectiles and swords, riding elephants against giant wooden horses and tanks? No thanks."

Wolf's tangled impression of Earth history hurt Mops' brain. "How about something simpler. Doc, upload a copy of Sun Tzu to Wolf's monocle." She lowered her voice, speaking so only the AI would hear. "Preferably a version with lots of pictures."

Within twenty minutes, it was clear the Prodryans planned to fight. The closer fighter had begun accelerating toward the *Pufferfish*, spitting a swarm of green dots across the empty space between the ships.

"Missile barrage." Excitement raised the pitch of Wolf's words.

Tambo chuckled. "At this range, they might as well try to piss out of a gravity well."

"They're too eager." Mops' pointed look in Wolf's direction was wasted. Wolf had eyes only for the battle unfolding on the screen.

The *Pufferfish*'s countermeasures had no trouble taking out the barrage. Guidance jamming sent most of the missiles veering away to detonate in empty space. The ship's interceptor flares had plenty of time to track and set off the rest.

A few minutes later, the *Pufferfish* fired a single plasma beam. At this range, it missed by more than a kilometer, but it seemed to enrage the Prodryans. Which was probably the point. Prodryans acted on instinct, especially when under stress. Another barrage of missiles flew toward the *Pufferfish*, to be dispatched as easily as the first.

A faint wave of vertigo told her the *Pufferfish* had begun approach maneuvers, angling for a clearer shot at the Prodryan fighter that would keep the freighter out of the line of fire. Mops double-checked water storage and the greenhouses, making sure the acceleration hadn't exceeded the tanks' tolerance. It wouldn't be the first time her team had dealt with a spill in the middle of battle.

"What's that second fighter doing?" Mops muttered. It wasn't like a Prodryan to pass up a fight. They should have broken away from the freighter by now to join the attack on the *Pufferfish*, leaving a handful of soldiers behind to supervise their hostages. Instead, the fighter was using maneuvering thrusters to keep the freighter positioned between them and the *Pufferfish*.

"Hiding behind the Nusurans," said Wolf. "Cowards."

More missiles came at the *Pufferfish*, though this barrage was thinner than the others. They couldn't have many missiles left. Once again, countermeasures made short work of them, though one got close enough for a bit of shrapnel to strike the front of the ship.

Mops checked the damage report. "Doc, tag air duct sections 153L through 157L for inspection when this is over."

The *Pufferfish* twisted to one side, A-guns firing. The smaller A-rings in the guns accelerated fist-sized projectiles to only half the speed of light, but that was more than enough to tear through anything they hit. Green lines appeared on the screen to show the path of each shot. Three misses tracked through empty space. The fourth and fifth shots drilled through the Prodryan fighter.

Decompression and a small explosion sent the fighter tumbling out of control. Escape pods burst away like sparks from a firework.

"What's so important about that freighter?" Mops frowned. "And where the hell do those escape pods think they're going?" At this distance, it would take the pods several days to reach the nearest planet.

"Probably hoping we'll round them up when we finish their friends," said Tambo.

"When's the last time you heard of a Prodryan choosing capture over death in combat?" The pods had blossomed in all directions when they fled their doomed ship, but they didn't appear to be heading anywhere. They just sat there, waiting. . . .

She reached for the console, keying in a comm request to the combat bridge. "BC Cervantes, this is Lieutenant Adamopoulos."

"Go ahead, Lieutenant."

"The Prodryans know EMC protocol and procedures. They know we won't fire on enemy escape pods. I'll bet my library they're creeping toward us, hoping we don't notice until they're close enough for a kamikaze run."

A long pause. "Confirmed. It's slow and subtle, but they're all heading this way. I'll have gunnery team two track 'em and fire the moment we confirm hostile action."

Wolf stared at Mops, her forehead wrinkled, her mouth open in confusion.

"Any suggestions for that second fighter?" asked Cervantes. "Even docked with the freighter, they're more maneuverable than we are."

"Shoot through the freighter," she said.

This pause stretched out even longer. "Did I hear you correctly, Lieutenant?"

Mops touched her screen, zooming in on the Nusuran freighter. "The Prodryans are tethered to the Nusurans' cargo bay. An A-gun shot through the bay shouldn't hit any vital systems. The Prodryans probably cleared the Nusurans out of the way. Even if they've got a few hostages tied up in the cargo bay, brief depressurization won't bother them. Nusurans take naked spacewalks for fun."

"This isn't covered in our combat plan."

"Or you could sit around and wait for Captain Brandenburg to wake up. How many Nusurans do you think the pirates will kill in that time? Mops out." She sat back to watch.

"What the freeze-dried shit was that?" Wolf whispered, leaning over Mops' shoulder. "Since when does SHS give tactical advice to the ship's *Battle Captain*?"

"When you've served longer and observed more battles than anyone else on the ship, people tend to listen." Mops shoved Wolf's face back from her own without looking away from the screen. The escape pods had begun accelerating. Moments later, the *Pufferfish* launched a series of missiles to intercept. The missiles detonated just before reaching the incoming pods, spraying them with a directional shower of shrapnel. At that range, she doubted anyone could have survived.

The remaining fighter continued to keep the Nusuran freighter between itself and the *Pufferfish*. Ninety seconds later, a streak of light flickered from *Pufferfish* weapons pod three, marking the shot of a single A-gun. Air and debris erupted from the freighter. Both ships lurched, and the docking tunnel connecting the two broke away. Cargo spilled into space. The spray stopped seconds later as the freighter's emergency systems sealed the ruptures, but by then the Prodryan fighter was peeling around to attack. An attack Battle Captain Cervantes should be more than capable of squashing.

"What in the depths are you doing in SHS?" asked Wolf. "You could be up there directing battles, or leading infantry, or —"

"Maybe." Mops shrugged and sat back to watch the rest of the battle play out. "But then who would keep the ship clean?"

In Earth year 2144, nine years before the Krakau arrived on Earth, a delegation from the fledgling Krakau Alliance met with four Prodryan military leaders to negotiate a truce. Their efforts failed, but records of the exchange offer insight into ongoing Prodryan hostilities. An excerpt from the transcript, translated into Human, follows.

Canon D. Major (Krakau diplomat): We understand your instinctive drive to expand and colonize. There is room enough for all in the vast ocean of space. Why waste your resources attacking other species?

Wings of Silver (Prodryan warrior): Because of our assholes.

Major: . . .

Farkunwinkubar (Glacidae diplomat): I beg your pardons?

Final Countdown (Krakau technician): Apologies, honored delegates. Our translation software is having difficulties with the Prodryan battle dialect. I believe the problem should now be corrected.

Major: Thank you. Wings of Silver, could you please repeat your reasons for these ongoing attacks?

Wings of Silver: Because we are assholes.

Major: Dammit, Countdown!

After further troubleshooting and berating of Technician Countdown, it was determined that the second translation was in fact accurate. The Prodryan system of what we might call "ethics" is largely instinctual. The strongest drive is for species expansion and survival at all costs. The Prodryan mindset automatically classifies all other life-forms into either potential resources (food) or potential threats.

Prodryans are aware of their own nature, and openly acknowledge their selfishness, lack of empathy, and determination to destroy anyone and anything they deem dangerous or not of use to the Prodryan race.

In short, Wings of Silver was correct. Prodryans are a race of assholes who have warred against the galaxy for more than a century.

THE PRODRYANS MANAGED ONE lucky shot before a combination of missiles and plasma beams from the *Pufferfish* tore their ship apart.

Mops' screen lit up with the detailed damage assessment. The Prodryan A-gun had pierced the hull on deck C, near the bow of the ship. From the look of things, it had punched through several internal walls and floors before exiting deck F.

The ship had automatically plugged the holes in the hull. Engineering would take care of reinforcing and repairing those. Mops was more concerned with the internal injuries. The instant Battle Captain Cervantes signaled the all-clear and the lights returned to their normal colors, she was out of her seat and heading for the nearest lift, dragging Wolf behind her. "Monroe, meet me on deck E, section four. Doc, was anyone hurt?"

"No injuries reported yet."

"Good. Show me the air readings from the affected decks." By the time the lift deposited her and Wolf on deck E, she was frowning.

Monroe greeted them both with a pop of his chewing gum. The gum was a holdover from his days in the infantry, and Mops didn't think she'd ever seen him without a piece. The man could walk naked into a sanishower and emerge blowing a bubble of whatever flavor he'd gotten his hands on lately. The Krakau who manufactured the stuff claimed to perfectly reproduce the tastes of old human foods, though it was impossible to know for certain. From the smell, he was currently chewing one of his favorites: pepperoni pizza.

"I hear there are still Prodryans on the freighter," he said in greeting.

Mops didn't bother to ask how he knew. Mops' connection to ship's systems through Doc was supposed to be instantaneous, but Monroe's gossip network with his infantry buddies always seemed just a little faster. "Cervantes is sending troops over on a pair of shuttles to clean them out."

Monroe's ragged white hair was cut short on the left, but hung to shoulder length on the right, covering the worst of the scar tissue where his ear used to be.

He'd left the infantry two years ago, following extensive reconstructive surgery. Krakau surgeons had rebuilt his right arm and part of his torso, then put him in a coma for a month-long nap in a medigel bed to let his body finish healing. They'd never managed to restore his sense of balance. Rumor had it a gyroscope was mounted in place of his right eardrum, helping him avoid toppling over. The prosthetic arm looked mostly human, but with too-smooth, bleach-white "skin."

Cleaning and welding tools weighed down his harness, clanking with each step. He also carried a full SHS kit slung over his right shoulder.

"Don't you miss it?" asked Wolf. "Being part of those infantry missions?"

"Hell, no. I'll take cleaning this ship over getting shot, impaled, and blown up." There was a wistfulness to his words, though. From what Mops knew, that yearning wasn't for combat, but for the companionship of his fellow infantry troops.

"Air readings suggest we've got a cracked waste line," said Mops. "Doesn't look like a direct hit, but the shock wave from that A-gun rattled half the deck."

Her monocle alerted her to an approaching figure around the bend: Private Anna May Wong, from Infantry Unit Seven. Wong was relatively new to the *Pufferfish*. He staggered into view and leaned hard against the wall.

"You all right, Private?" asked Mops.

He nodded. "I got lucky. If I'd been any closer to the impact point, you'd be scrubbing me off the walls."

"Thanks for saving us the extra work," Monroe said dryly. "Do you need help getting to Medical?"

Wong waved a hand. "I'm all right."

Mops and Monroe locked eyes. "Turn to your left, Private," said Mops. "Doc, send Wong an image of what I'm seeing."

"Relaying to Private Wong's monocle."

Wong whistled a Krakau curse, something about tentacle incest. A saucer-sized shard of metal protruded from his back, just below the rib cage. Black blood crusted around the wound. "Did I say I was lucky? I'd like to change my answer, sir."

"Hold still." Mops grabbed a canister of multipurpose sealant from her harness and applied a thin line around the base of the wound. The clear gel expanded quickly, turning bright orange as it hardened. "That'll keep the metal from moving and doing any more damage. Wouldn't want you out of commission just when things are getting serious with Suárez."

He blushed hard. "You know about that?"

"I was swapping out air filters on observation deck E the other day."

He reddened further. "We . . . didn't know anyone else was there."

"I assumed as much. You were pretty preoccupied."

"Medical, we need a stretcher," said Monroe.

"I can walk," Wong protested.

"And if you want to keep that ability, you'll shut up and wait for the stretcher." Mops folded her arms, looking up at Wong and silently daring him to argue. "Humans are tough. We're not indestructible. And we don't know how close that thing is to your spine."

Wong sighed. "Yes, sir."

"Was anyone else around when the hull was breached?" asked Monroe.

"Not that I saw. I *would* have noticed this time."

"Good," said Mops. "Wolf, go on ahead and find that waste leak. We'll be along as soon as we get Wong on his way."

"First battle scar?" asked Monroe, gesturing toward the shrapnel.

"No, sir." Wong touched his left arm. "Lost a chunk of bicep and shoulder two years back. Peacekeeping mission on Cetus 4. And I had three toes replaced after basic training. Frostbite."

"Antarctica?" asked Mops, watching Wong closely. His eyes kept drifting, and his skin was paler than usual.

"That's right, sir."

Mops chuckled. "Was Scheherazade supervising the A&O after your rebirth?"

"Worst Awakening and Orientation Officer ever." Adopting a stiff tone, Wong said, "'It is customary for humans to panic when they wake up covered in fish and slime, but panic is nonproductive. Be still and wait for a technician to assist you. Do not harm the cutis fish in your tank. They consume only dead skin cells, body hair, and other human waste.'"

His intonation was perfect. Mops nodded and said, "Her first words to our crèche were 'Humans, cease all fear and confusion immediately!' Because a meter-tall alien squid waving her limbs and shouting at you through the translator is so reassuring in your first moments as a sentient being."

"I woke up with a fish halfway up my nose." Wong rubbed absently at his nostril. "They say that's where the best-tasting hair is, if you're a cutis fish."

Mops stepped aside to make room as the medics arrived, pushing a humming maglev stretcher. A six-year nursing veteran named Fred Rogers quickly checked Wong's injury, then helped him lie facedown on the hovering stretcher. Rogers pressed a button on the stretcher rail to activate the built-in scanners.

"Chipped vertebrae and a few perforated organs," he said, giving Wong a reassuring smile. "We'll get those glued back together in no time."

For all that they'd lost to the plague, there were advantages to what humans had become. Feral humans were all but impossible to kill, and the Krakau had kept that resilience when they began administrating their cure. Earth Mercenary Corps soldiers could shake off anything short of damage directly to the brain or spine. Wong should be up and about again within a day.

Once they were out of earshot, Mops turned to Monroe. "Why didn't Wong's uniform register a puncture that size?"

"Maybe it did. You saw his face. He was slipping into shock. If he'd gotten worse . . ."

It was rare for injury and shock to trigger a feral response, but not unheard of. Mops held up her sealant canister. "Then I trust you'd have held him in place long enough for me to glue his ass to the wall."

She returned the canister to her harness and checked Wolf's status on her monocle. According to Doc, Wolf had stopped twenty meters ahead. By the time they arrived, she'd marked several sections of wall panel for removal.

"Cracked waste line, like you guessed," said Wolf.

The brief depressurization would have turned the line's contents into a geyser of sewage steam. The changes in temperature and pressure could have further damaged the line, meaning there was a good chance the mess had spread everywhere.

Wolf started to unseal the seam on the first wall panel.

"Hold up." Mops wrinkled her nose. She was regrettably familiar with the smells of shipboard waste. "Doc, how close are we to Grom's quarters?"

"Fourteen meters." An arrow appeared on her monocle, pointing the way.

"Problem?" asked Monroe.

"Grom's excreting eggs. Not only is our leak officially toxic, it's potentially corrosive. Doc, tell Kumar to get up here. And I need the emergency channel." Mops waited for the AI to acknowledge. "This is Lieutenant Adamopoulos from SHS. Sections three through five of deck E are under immediate quarantine."

"You're calling a quarantine?" asked Wolf.

"Normally, unfertilized Glacidae eggs are inert, but who knows what the shock of that A-gun did. If the eggs break down and interact with the air, they can emit a form of gaseous antifreeze. It won't hurt a Glacidae, but one whiff can crystallize human mucus membranes. Nasty stuff. Get your hood up, then start setting up the quarantine curtain at the end of section five."

Wolf opened her uniform collar to pull out a thin, transparent hood. She tugged the hood over her head and pulled a small tab along the edge, sealing the front. The hood inflated and stiffened into a makeshift helmet.

Mops did the same, expecting Monroe to follow suit. He reached for his collar with his left hand . . . whereupon his right hand balled into a fist and punched him in the face.

"Dammit, Arm!" He glared at the artificial limb.

The AI that helped control Monroe's arm was significantly more primitive than Doc. As Doc himself had once put it, it was the difference between a modern cruiser and an old Earth paddleboat. A leaky paddleboat. Probably starting to rot.

Most of the time, Monroe's prosthetic AI could anticipate and assist him. It was also programmed to respond to Monroe's verbal commands. But every once in a while, the arm got confused.

"Oh, you're *sorry*, are you?" Monroe snarled. Presumably the AI had relayed an apology through his monocle. "You know, it's not too late to replace you with an old-fashioned hook."

"You all right?" asked Mops.

He finished with his hood, using his left hand only, then bent to seal the bottom of his pants to his boots. "I've had worse."

Wolf's face brightened. "Like what?"

"Let's just say you should never use the head with a newly upgraded artificial limb."

Mops pulled her gloves from her back pocket. They sealed automatically to her sleeves. A new readout on her monocle showed her suit's air circulators were working properly, and everything was airtight. EMC uniforms wouldn't hold up to a long-term spacewalk, but they were more than adequate for this kind of biohazard work.

Doc pinged to let her know Wolf's and Monroe's suits were sealed as well. She rotated her arms to loosen her shoulders. "Who's ready to start sponging up alien excrement?"

Sponging was a figure of speech. They'd start with the portable vacuum units from Monroe's maintenance kit, saving as much raw biomaterial as possible. Everything they collected would be recycled and reprocessed into fertilizer for the green-houses or next week's meal rations.

She generally tried not to think about that last part.

They were an hour and a half into the job when a green all-crew alert starburst flashed on Mops' monocle.

"This is Commander Danube. I'm ordering level one bio-hazard precautions effective immediately. Nonessential person-nel should remain in their quarters. Anyone who has been in direct contact with infantry units three and five will report to Medical for quarantine."

Her team stopped working. Monroe lowered the vacuum rod he'd been using. "Units three and five were the teams as-signed to clear the Nusuran freighter."

Mops turned automatically to Kumar, whose eyes were wide behind the transparent shell of his hood.

"Relax. You're fine," Mops said to forestall his inevitable panic. Considering human beings were immune to most dis-eases, Technician Sanjeev Kumar's paranoia about germs made as much sense as a hydrophobic Krakau. Though it did mean he was the most thorough and efficient cleaner on the team. "We've been in sealed suits since we started working."

"Why didn't Captain Brandenburg make the announce-ment?" asked Kumar.

"Maybe she isn't fully awake from the A-ring jump yet. Fo-cus on the job, Technician." Mops pointed to the open wall sections and the array of pipes and conduit running through the skeletal metal support beams. "I want this mess cleaned up double-time. If we have a biohazard on the ship, we'll have more work coming our way soon."

She watched Kumar until he nodded and got back to work. He'd been on the SHS team for six years, and—unlike Wolf—he'd never wanted anything else. He had the build of a soldier: tall, broad, and muscular. His brown hair was eternally unkempt, sticking out in all directions like the short tangles were trying to escape from his scalp.

She stepped back to assess their progress. They'd finished the bulk of the job. Two sealed, waist-high canisters of recovered mostly-human waste attested to that. Temporary clamps locked the broken pipes, and Kumar had rigged a half-pressure bypass line to keep things from getting further backed up.

Wolf had soaked the interior of the walls with a chemical bath that would break down any remaining organic matter, and Monroe was making good progress vacuuming up the resultant sludge. Next up was hitting every nook and crevice with the microwave sterilizer. Even at their best speed, they were looking at another hour, minimum.

"Doc, how bad is it?" she whispered.

"*I'm locked out of command-level discussions, but Medical has admitted thirty-one people for examination and quarantine. Three lifts and one-point-eight kilometers of internal corridors are sealed off, awaiting medical sterilization.*"

"Thirty-one . . . that's almost a sixth of the crew."

"*I'm a computer. I'm aware of the math.*"

"Don't get smart with me, you glorified contact lens. Any word on what kind of contagion we're looking at?"

"*Nothing official. It started after the first team returned from the freighter, so there's a good chance it was contracted there. From the speed it's been spreading, I suspect it's airborne.*"

"Any chance it could penetrate a sealed suit?"

"*Doubtful.*"

"Then how did our troops get infected? They'd have been suited up, and would have gone through decon when they got back to the *Pufferfish.*"

"*Human error is most likely to blame. Statistically, you humans fail far more frequently than your equipment.*"

"Bite me." She wanted to argue the point, but Doc would no doubt have plenty of data to back his claim. Data he'd be only too happy to highlight on Mops' monocle. "Keep an eye on the team's suit integrity. If a single seam even thinks about springing a leak, I want to know."

"Hey!" Wolf's shout made the rest of the team jump. Wolf lowered her sterilizer, a pistol-like device with an oversized metal disk for the barrel. "We're working here. You've got to go around."

Behind the clear quarantine curtain, a young, heavyset woman stumbled closer. Mops' monocle identified PFC Schulz, a heavy gunner from Infantry Unit Two. She gave no sign of hearing Wolf's instructions.

"Doc, give me a direct line to Schulz." Mops stepped toward the curtain. "This is Lieutenant Adamopoulos. Are you all right, Charlie?"

Schulz pressed her hands against the curtain. The material stretched and tented against her fingers.

The silence behind Mops told her the rest of her team had stopped working to watch.

"We've got more company farther up the corridor, around the bend. They're coming this way."

"Who?"

Doc tagged four more crew members on her monocle: Price, Smith, Omáǧažu, and Holmes. Beyond the curved wall, their silhouettes moved unsteadily toward Schulz, who had begun to claw at the edge of the curtain.

"Feral?" asked Monroe, from mere centimeters behind her.

Mops jumped. "Dammit, man. Give a little warning when you come up behind someone, or I'll tie a damn bell around your neck." She turned her attention back to Private Schulz. "Stand down, Charlie! That's an order!"

The edge of the curtain tore away from the wall, sounding like a flatulent Quetzalus. Schulz shoved an arm through, fingers stretched toward Mops' throat.

"Yeah, she's feral," Mops said tightly, fear and adrenaline squeezing her gut. She couldn't see any sign of injury. Schulz was suited up the same as Mops and her team. "Monroe, in your infantry years, how often did you see shock or injury cause a reversion like this?"

"Four times," he said. "Over eight years of active duty."

Mops pointed past Schulz. "Ever hear of it happening to five people at once?" From the eloquence of his swearing, she assumed the answer was no.

"What's going on?" Kumar asked, panic edging his voice.

Mops caught Kumar's arm and spun him around, pushing him away. "Check the other curtain and make sure nobody's coming from that direction. Wolf, Monroe, you're with me."

More of the curtain ripped free, and Schulz lunged forward. Her fist collided with Mops' jaw, and everything flashed white. Monroe caught Mops by the arm before she could fall.

Schulz had a hell of a punch. Mops shoved herself off Monroe to avoid the follow-up swing, then moved in to slam a knee into Schulz's gut. It bent Schulz double. A quick push sent Schulz back into the curtain, where she fell against Smith and Omáǧažu. Holmes climbed over them, intent on reaching Mops and her team.

"Fall back," yelled Mops.

Wolf ignored her, charging past to drive a shoulder hard into Holmes' gut. Wolf slammed him against the wall, grabbed the back of his uniform, and hurled him toward Price.

"Remind me to put her back in the brig," Mops muttered. "Doc, they're still wearing their monocles. Can you control them remotely? Comms, too?"

Doc gave a disdainful sniff. *"Regulations and safety protocols prohibit—"*

"I'll buy you that processor upgrade you've been lusting after." She stepped back as Schulz pulled herself upright.

"Safety protocols disengaged. I'm in."

"Overwhelm them."

No sooner had she said the words than Schulz's monocle flashed white. She fell back, both hands clawing at her eye through her hood. She managed to knock the monocle loose from her face, but it simply fell to the bottom of her hood, where it continued to strobe.

Doc did the same to the others, who responded in similar fashion. Wolf took the opportunity to land a few more blows against Holmes, before Monroe hauled her away.

"These are our crewmates," Mops reminded her team. "They're sick. We're *not* trying to kill them."

"They're feral," said Wolf. "We can't go easy on them. Hell, anything short of guns or sedatives, and we're just slowing them down."

"I've seen your marksmanship scores," Mops shot back. "You're not getting a gun."

A series of thunderclaps filled the corridor as Doc overrode the attackers' comm speakers. Mops flinched. If it was that loud to her ears, she couldn't imagine how painful it must have been through those directional speakers. She yanked her sealant canister from her harness and drew a large zigzag of gel down the wall. "Monroe, give me a hand."

The two of them seized Schulz and shoved her face-first against the wall, holding her in place as the sealant hardened. By the time the others recovered, Schulz was secure.

"Kumar, cleaning spray." Mops pointed to the floor between her and the remaining ferals.

Kumar pulled a spray wand from his harness, secured its hose to a bottle of concentrated detergent, and blasted a film of green suds down the corridor. He coated the four crew who were approaching as well.

Holmes was the first to fall. His feet shot forward, arms flailing as he slammed to the floor.

Mops spread another mess of sealant onto the opposite wall, grabbed Holmes' boot, and with Monroe's help, glued him in place. Upside down.

A hand clamped around her ankle. Omáǧažu pulled herself forward, her other hand reaching toward Mops' shin.

Wolf slammed a small wrench down hard enough to snap the bones of Omáǧažu's right arm. Mops twisted free.

"Sir, I still have some hull paint from that repair job two days ago," Kumar said hesitantly. He held up his spray wand. "I could—"

"Do it," Mops snapped.

Kumar nodded and unscrewed the detergent from his compressor hose, replacing it with a heavier canister. As the remaining attackers closed in, he fired a thick spray of black paint at their hoods.

After that, it was simple enough to glue the rest of them to the walls and floor. After making sure none of them would be going anywhere, Mops stepped back to catch her breath. "Doc, were any of our suits breached?"

"Everyone's bagged and fresh. Well, Wolf's a bit sour, but that's because she hasn't had a shower since before her fight with Grom. Her suit's fine."

"Thank you." Mops glanced over the disaster that was their workspace. One of the pipes oozed black goo. Someone must have grabbed it when they fell, or slammed into it during the fighting. Cleaning tools were scattered over the floor. Then there was the cleaning fluid, paint, sealant, and who knew what else, all dripping from the walls and the struggling ferals.

"What now, sir?" Kumar surveyed the mess, his eyes wide with horror.

Mops stretched her shoulder. "We can't stay here. Wolf, prep a bomb for that wall. I want it sealed and done in two minutes."

"Aw, hell," said Wolf. "All that work for nothing?"

"At least you got to punch someone," Monroe pointed out.

Wolf brightened. "That's true."

"Don't encourage her," Mops said, glaring at them both.

Wolf carefully unwrapped a block of what looked like soft blue clay, while Kumar and Monroe maneuvered the first wall panel back into position. Mops grabbed the next panel and did the same.

Once all but one panel had been replaced, Wolf pressed the block to the back of the center wall compartment, sprayed it with a milky white liquid, and stepped aside. The block was fizzing and bubbling like Captain Brandenburg's snail soup by the time Monroe locked the final panel shut.

The white spray was a catalyst that would, in another thirty seconds or so, cause the sanibomb to expand into a quick-hardening foam that filled every square millimeter of the wall compartments. Everything inside would be sealed into place, unable to leak or grow or spread.

It was the quick and dirty way to decontaminate an area. It also rendered everything in those walls inaccessible until someone—generally the SHS team—came along with the dis-solving agent to remove the foam and do the job right. In other words, work that should have taken a few hours had just turned into a multiday job.

Mops touched the wall, feeling the heat of the reaction even through her glove. After making sure none of the foam was escaping through the panel seams, she turned to survey her team. "*Nobody* unseals their suits until I give the order. Is that clear?"

"I should've used the head before we started," Wolf grum-bled.

"Don't worry about it," said Kumar. "EMC official-issue undergarments can absorb up to two thousand milliliters of liquid."

"*Three thousand,*" Doc corrected, broadcasting to the team. "*They upped it after that week-long plumbing shutdown on Stepping Stone Station earlier this year.*"

"Fascinating," Mops said dryly. "Now, how about an update on what the hell's going on. Where's Security? Do we have an update from Medical?"

"*Sorry, sir.*" Doc sounded abashed. "*I've been pinging Med-ical for the past five and a half minutes. No response.*"

"What about tracking the crew? Analyze their movements. Tag anyone shambling around like a feral."

"*I don't have that kind of access to ship's scanners. I can tell you what's happening in the immediate vicinity, but—wait. . . .*"

Mops' neck tensed. "What is it?"

"I don't understand. I'm . . . Stand by. There's a lot to download."

"Problem, sir?" asked Monroe.

"I'm not sure. Doc?"

"I've—I mean, you—we have been granted command-level rights to most of the Pufferfish's *systems. Equivalent to what Battle Captain Cervantes would have had during the fighting."*

"Who authorized that?"

"How should I know? Wait, I have access to the ship's internal logs now. Looks like your authorization was upgraded automatically seventy-three seconds ago."

"If we have access, use it. I want the status of the entire crew. Are we seeing any other outbreaks like we had here?"

"Already in progress. Unlike humans, I'm perfectly capable of doing two things at once."

"And?"

Doc hesitated. *"Vital signs from crew uniforms are odd. I sent a high-priority request to everyone save your team, asking them to report in. No response."*

Mops' gaze returned to her struggling, feral crewmates. Her gut clenched in anticipation of Doc's next words.

"As far as I can determine, the rest of the crew has gone feral. Your team is the only group unaffected. As the highest-ranking person on board not shambling about in a feral fugue, you are officially in command of the EMCS Pufferfish."

3

EMC ship names are chosen by a five-member committee with representatives from the Alliance Military Council and members of the Krakau Earth science team. Traditionally, ships are named after the deadliest species from humanity's home world. Thus, the EMCS Mantis Shrimp, the EMCS Hippopotamus, the warship EMCS Mosquito, and the pride of the fleet, the dreadnought EMCS Honey Badger. Prodryan warriors reflexively still their wings in terror at the mere whisper of the bomber EMCS Cone Snail. . . .

EMC ships are crewed primarily by humans, with a scattering of other species. Despite initial fears that the Krakau command crews would lose control of the primitive, savage humans, the fleet quickly earned a reputation for taking on any challenge. Thirty-six years of successful peacekeeping and counterinsurgency missions have proven those fears hollow and helped spread peace and security through the Alliance.

"**H**OW DROWNED ARE WE?" asked Monroe, watching her closely.

"Very." Mops licked her lips. "I'm in command."

"Yeah, we know," said Wolf. "Sir."

"Of the whole damn ship," she clarified.

Wolf's mouth opened, but she didn't say anything.

"How is that possible?" asked Monroe.

It was a rhetorical question, so, naturally, Kumar answered. "The regulations are clear. If every member of the Krakau command crew has been incapacitated, along with the eight other humans who outrank Lieutenant Adamopoulos, then command passes to her."

"Does this mean the whole crew is..." Wolf gestured toward the five struggling prisoners. "Like them?"

Mops glanced at Monroe, saw the grim understanding in his eyes. "Not the *whole* crew," she said quietly. "They're suffering a relapse of our plague. A plague that affects *humans*, turning them vicious. Ferals will attack almost anything that moves. If the Krakau and the Glacidae aren't responding..."

Wolf blinked. "Oh, shit."

"Pretty much." Mops took a deep breath, grimacing at the slightly stale taste of her suit's air. "For now, assume everyone else on this ship is dead or feral. Doc, find us a safe route to someplace secure, preferably a battle hub or another area with full access to ship's systems."

"Battle Hub Two is closest. I believe I can plot a route that will avoid the other humans."

"I spent a year on Earth for basic infantry training," Monroe said quietly as they started walking. "Salvage and retrieval work, mostly. My unit spent two weeks in a hellhole called Disneyland Tokyo. We stirred up a nest of ferals in the northeast sector. They'd been hiding out in Toontown. We fell back into the only defensible position and held them off for three days before Command was able to send a retrieval team."

Monroe avoided looking at anyone. "We lost four people.

A buddy of mine weaponized some primitive robot tech—
animatronics, I think they were called. You haven't seen car-
nage until you've seen a mechanical yellow bear open fire on
a wave of ferals, while a pink robot piglet carries a bomb into
the heart of the mob on a suicide run."

"Sounds like a hell of a fight," said Wolf.

"You got the hell part right, but that's not the point. On top
of being outnumbered, we ran into two major problems. The
first is that humans are *really* hard to kill."

"Damn right," grunted Wolf.

"The second is how hard it is to pull the trigger against your
own kind. Every human we put down was a human the Krakau
would never cure. A human who would never be anything but
a rabid animal. Every one of us knew the only thing separating
us from them was dumb luck."

He popped his gum, grimaced, and swallowed it. "This mess
is going to be harder. These are our crewmates. Our friends."

"Also, we don't have guns," said Wolf.

"Or suicidal robot pigs," added Kumar.

"We're not killing anyone," Mops said firmly. "Like Monroe
said, these are our crewmates. Our job is to keep us *and them*
safe until we can get the situation under control and find a way
to help them. Doc, can you contact Command?"

*"Internal ship communications only. If you want to talk to
anyone outside the* Pufferfish, *you'll need to get to Battle Hub
Two."*

A dot of light on her monocle signaled an incoming comm
message. From Mops' collar speaker, a voice with the faint mechanical edge of a translator whispered a weak, "Hello?"

Mops raised a hand to halt and silence her team. "This is
Lieutenant Adamopoulos." A text tag on her monocle identified the caller as Technician Gromgimsidalgak. "Where are
you, Grom?"

"The humans have all gone mad," whimpered Grom. "They're
worse than Wolf!"

"Grom is in Recreation Area Two," said Doc. *"Specifically, they're in the pool. The deep end."*

Mops cocked her head. "The crew went feral, and you decided to go for a swim?"

"I'm hiding," Grom snapped. "Glacidae lubricating fluid turns water opaque. It's all I could think of, but I can't keep it up much longer. Send a security team to get me out of here!"

Mops mentally added pool cleaning to her growing list of things to do, assuming they survived. "Why didn't you respond before to Doc's all-crew signal?"

"I've been busy trying not to get eaten!"

"Stay out of sight as long as you can." She signed off and turned to the others. "Grom is trapped in Rec Two. We're going to get them."

"Four of us against almost two hundred feral humans?" asked Kumar.

"Minus the five we've already dealt with, yes. Doc, how many people are in Recreation with Grom?"

"Eleven."

She studied her team. Wolf looked ready to charge to Recreation and fight all eleven herself, proving once again that she had no idea what they were facing. Kumar looked ready to soil himself—a better-informed, if equally noncomforting response. Monroe simply waited, arms folded.

"Show us the quickest route to Recreation." Her monocle lit up with the path plotted and a floating arrow showing which direction to go. "And the closest armory?"

A second route appeared, with an arrow pointing in the opposite direction. Of course. "Doc, start sealing off sections of the ship. Full quarantine lockdowns."

"Talk to them," suggested Monroe. "Ferals are drawn to noise. Human voices trigger their hunting reflexes. Broadcast in specific areas to lure them in, then lock the doors behind them."

"Good thinking. Doc, broadcast from areas where they'll be unlikely to blow up the ship while they're locked up. Empty cargo bays, acceleration chambers, that sort of thing. Keep them out of Engineering and away from any command consoles."

"What should I say?"

"It doesn't matter. Pick something from my library and start reading. Clear us a path." That still left the ferals in Recreation to deal with. They wouldn't leave if they had Grom surrounded. She pulled a half-meter utility pole from the back of her harness and twisted the metal collar at the end. The pole tripled in length. One end was a universal swivel-head attachment point. The other was a nozzle for anything from a high-pressure air hose to anticorrosive paint to simple vacuum suction. It also made a serviceable staff.

Wolf had taken out her utility knife, a three-centimeter blade that would have roughly the same effect on a feral human as tickling them with a feather.

"What's the plan?" asked Monroe.

"Keep your mouths shut so we don't attract more company." She started toward Recreation. "And try not to die."

As they neared Recreation, Mops began to hear Doc's voice over the distant speakers.

"I have been called an unkind mother, but it was the sacred impulse of maternal affection, it was the advantage of my daughter that led me on; and if that daughter were not the greatest simpleton on earth, I might have been rewarded for my exertions as I ought."

"What the hell is that?" whispered Wolf.

"Sir James did make proposals to me for Frederica; but Frederica, who was born to be the torment of my life, chose to set herself so violently against the match that I thought it better to lay aside the scheme for the present."

"It's called *Lady Susan*, by Jane Austen," Mops whispered. "Now shut up. Doc, how's our path?"

"You're eleven meters from Recreation," said Doc, without interrupting his reading. *"Everything looks clear. Better drop low to take a quick peek, though. You know, just in case the internal scanners missed anything."*

Mops dropped to one knee, poked her head around the corner and choked back a curse as she came face-to-face with what she belatedly identified as a half-chewed combat dummy from Recreation.

"Your heart rate just spiked," Doc said, his words brimming with innocence. *"Is everything all right?"*

"Hilarious," Mops snarled. "Remember your little joke when I flush you down a toilet so you can scan the pipes from the inside."

"Oh, relax. I knew the corridor was safe. Human psychology suggests humor is a useful tool for coping with stressful situations."

"So is violence against computers." Up ahead, the door to Recreation was stuck halfway open, blocked by another fallen dummy. Mops whispered into her collar. "Grom, can you hear me?" There was no response. "Doc, give us a tactical view of Recreation."

Soft-glowing lines appeared on her monocle: a simple projection of the recreation area. Green figures appeared, crowded around the pool.

"That's . . . more than eleven," said Huang.

"Sixteen," Monroe confirmed. "Doc needs a refresher course on basic counting."

"There were *eleven,"* Doc said coolly, broadcasting to the entire team. *"The other five must have wandered in, drawn by the crowd. And for your information, I can derive the Bailey-Borwein-Plouffe formula in the time it takes you monkeys to remove your boots and count to twenty."*

Monroe chuckled quietly, raising his hands in mock surrender.

Mops studied the layout in Recreation. All personnel were required to maintain a certain level of fitness. Most found it a source of pride, particularly the infantry grunts and those like Wolf who dreamed of joining them. There were ongoing friendly and not-so-friendly competitions. The walls displayed recent and all-time records in various feats of strength, endurance, agility, and more.

Equipment included treadmills, climbing walls, resistance machines, and plenty of combat dummies, both static and responsive. A large, rectangular pool took up roughly half of the room. Trust the Krakau to focus on aquatic fitness. A handful of combat dummies were set up in the pool for underwater practice, including two human-shaped machines, three Prodryans, and a Glacidae.

Treadmills routinely spilled careless or overworked runners into the pool. A climbing wall curved up over the water, meaning anyone who lost their grip went for an unexpected swim.

The sixteen crew were scattered around the pool. They knew Grom was in there. Once ferals sighted prey, they wouldn't break away for anything short of another meal.

Mops turned to Monroe. "Suggestions?"

"Don't let them get behind us. If we get swarmed and surrounded, it's over." His fingers drummed against his thigh. "We need to thin the mob. Lure them out."

Mops glanced over her team, her attention settling on Kumar.

Kumar's shoulders sagged.

"Him?" asked Wolf. "I should be the one who—"

"I need someone to lead the ferals away, not start a brawl with them," Mops interrupted. "Doc, plot a path from Recreation. Tag anyone within a hundred meters, and have a lift car waiting at the end of the route. If you get the chance to seal off some bulkheads and trap a few more ferals along the way, great. Kumar, all you have to do is follow Doc's directions. Once we've got Grom, I'll tell you where to meet us."

"You'll have a head start," Monroe added. "Their coordination is shit. You should be fine."

"Unless I fall," Kumar countered. "Or run into a group of ferals Doc couldn't see. Or there's a lift malfunction. This ship is fresh out of combat. We don't know what else might have been damaged."

Mops put a hand on Kumar's shoulder. "Breathe, Sanjeev. You can do this."

"I know, I know, I know." He shuddered. "Just . . . give me a minute please, sir. To plan for everything that could go wrong."

"You're going to need a lot more than one minute," said Wolf.

Monroe punched Wolf's arm, shutting her up.

Mops turned her attention back to Recreation. "Doc, can you power up the air vents in there on my signal?"

"No problem."

The vents were designed to clear excess sweat and moisture from the room. In this case, the noise should also cover any sounds Mops and her team made as they approached.

Kumar fumbled through his harness, rearranging tools and cleaning supplies. "Flashlight in case there's a power outage," he mumbled. "Access key for locked doors. Pry bar. Detergent and hull paint to slow them down. . . ."

He removed a roll of carbon fiber tape and began looping it around his left forearm. He did the same to his right, creating makeshift bracers. The tape was more than strong enough to stop human teeth. He swallowed and said, "I think I'm ready, sir."

"Doc's got eyes on the whole ship," Mops reminded him. "He'll keep you safe."

Kumar nodded and set off toward the half-open door to Recreation. Once he was within arm's reach, he stopped, and Mops could see his breathing speed up. His hands balled tight. He glanced over his shoulder, then jumped forward, waving his arms.

Nothing happened.

After a moment, he stepped closer to the doorway. "They're not reacting," he whispered, his words relayed through their comms.

"They're fixated on Grom," said Monroe. "You've got to get their attention."

Kumar knocked on the door, tentatively at first, then harder. He tried shouting at them. Mops could see annoyance replacing his fear. He tried again, then pulled a screwdriver from his harness and knelt by the damaged combat dummy, muttering to himself. "After all that, you're not gonna just ignore me!"

He worked at the neck for several minutes, replaced the screwdriver, and removed the head from the dummy.

With an angry yell, he hurled the head into Recreation. There was a meaty thump, followed by angry groans.

"It worked," Kumar said brightly.

"That's great," said Mops. "Run!"

Kumar took off down the corridor, followed by nine of the ferals. Leaving seven for the rest of them to deal with. She'd hoped for better, but would take what she could get. "Doc, start up those vents, see if it startles any more of them out of the room." She studied the locations of the remaining seven on her monocle. "And lower all of the climbing ropes on the aft wall."

"This might not be the best time for a workout," said Monroe.

Mops affixed a small grasping claw to the end of her utility pole and tested to make sure it worked. Normally, the claw was for retrieving dropped tools and other items from drains, crevasses, or anywhere else they managed to lodge themselves. "Wolf, I want you by those ropes. Monroe, stay here for now. Monitor the corridor, and be ready to jump in if I call."

She would have preferred to have Monroe helping her round up their feral crewmates, but all it would take was a momentary loss of balance, or a single malfunction of his artificial arm, and they'd be overwhelmed. From the way Monroe's mouth pressed tight, he knew it, too.

She summarized her idea for getting the crew out of the way. "Remember, these are our crewmates. They're sick and not thinking clearly. Stick to the plan."

"Krakau make plans," snorted Wolf. "Humans barge in and kick ass."

"Of those two species," said Mops, "which still has a functional civilization?" She gripped her utility pole in both hands and crept toward the door. Once there, she double-checked her monocle to make sure the doorway was clear.

As with Kumar, the remaining ferals didn't immediately respond as Mops slipped through and headed toward the climbing wall. To her left, a dark, rainbow-edged film covered the surface of the murky water in the pool, courtesy of Grom's secretions. She raised her utility pole and waited for Wolf to join her. "Ready?"

"Bring me a body," Wolf replied.

By now, four of the seven ferals had apparently decided the potential new meals were more interesting than the one hiding in the pool. They trudged closer.

Mops stepped to meet them. She lunged for the closest, Private Washington from Supplies, jabbing the butt of her pole into his face. A follow-up swing to the knees knocked him to the ground. Before he could recover, Mops spun her pole and clamped the claw around his ankle.

She hauled him toward Wolf, who clipped a carabiner to his harness.

"Doc, retract line one!" Mops shouted.

Up went Washington, until he hung from the ceiling like an old Earth piñata. Mops used her pole to push back the other ferals, trying to isolate Private Red Cloud long enough to get him hooked to the next rope.

Red Cloud stumbled. His hand clamped around Mops' utility pole as he toppled slowly into the pool. Mops braced herself, trying to yank her weapon free as the others closed in.

Wolf charged past with a roar, ropes in both hands. She slammed her shoulder into the gut of the nearest of the two remaining ferals. She and Sergeant Perón fell to the ground. Private Simpson piled on, trying to tear through the back of Wolf's hood.

"Dammit, Wolf!" Mops kicked Red Cloud in the face, pulled her pole from the water, and cracked Simpson over the head with it.

Simpson didn't even look up. Mops switched ends and tried to get the claw around the woman's neck so she could lever her off Wolf.

"Got you," shouted Wolf. "Retract line two!"

The motor strained audibly as it pulled the rope, dragging Perón from the bottom of the pile and raising her up to dangle beside Washington.

Mops clipped another line to the back of Simpson's harness. "Doc, reel in line four."

The remaining three ferals had given up on Grom and were circling around the other side of the pool.

"Fall back, Wolf." Mops struggled to focus. She knew their attackers. JG Rudolph always joked about loaning explosives to Mops' team to help clear jammed Krakau plumbing. Private Baggins once managed to infest his quarters with a Tjikko fungus that had required the whole place to be stripped and sanitized. Private Gandhi was one of the best sharpshooters on the ship. But there was no recognition in their faces. No awareness. Nothing but an instinctive hunger.

"I've got this." Wolf started forward.

"Take one more step and I'll have you transferred to that Nusuran freighter," Mops said without looking. "You can spend the next five years cleaning up after them."

Wolf didn't answer. She didn't charge in like a wild animal either. Good enough. Mops handed line number three back to Wolf and grabbed line five for herself. "Doc, get ready to drop lines one, two, and four on my signal. Hard."

"Got it."

Rudolph paused as she reached the first of her suspended

companions. Her head tilted to contemplate Washington's slow, helpless kicks, and then she shoved past him. Gandhi followed close behind. Off to the side, Red Cloud pulled himself out of the water behind Baggins.

"Now," said Mops.

Washington and Perón dropped to land atop Rudolph and Gandhi. Their flailing knocked Red Cloud back into the water. Mops darted in and secured her line to Rudolph's harness.

As Doc hauled the trio back into the air, Wolf managed to hook Gandhi. He flew upward, twisting and kicking, and his foot clipped the side of Wolf's head. She toppled into the pool after Red Cloud. Baggins jumped in after her.

"Shit. Doc, can you power up the underwater combat dummies?"

"Done."

In the murky water, the movement should keep the ferals distracted. "Wolf, as long as you're in there, find Grom and get them out. Monroe, we could use an extra hand."

By the time Mops reached the control console on the front wall, Monroe was there. Mops pointed to the pool and tossed him her utility pole. He caught it and hurried to the far side.

Mops couldn't see anything clearly in the water, but her monocle highlighted Wolf and Grom, along with the two remaining ferals closing in on them. Monroe dropped flat at the edge of the pool and thrust the pole into the water, toward Wolf.

Mops cleared the terminal and pulled up the maintenance menu.

"Got 'em," Wolf shouted over her comm.

Mops checked over her shoulder to see Wolf gripping the end of the pole with one hand. Her other was twisted around Grom's harness. Monroe hauled back, pulling them toward the edge. Once they were close enough, he tossed the utility pole aside and used both hands to drag the Glacidae from the water, with Wolf pushing from the other end. Wolf climbed free a moment later.

As soon as they were clear, Mops activated the emergency drainage cycle.

The pool was always drained before A-ring jumps, battle situations, and for cleaning purposes. The normal process took about eight minutes. But in emergencies—damage to the ship's internal gravity, for example—high-pressure vacuum pumps could empty all one and a half megaliters in ten seconds... assuming the pool was free of potential obstructions.

The combat dummies were secured to the bottom of the pool for safety. Baggins and Red Cloud were not.

Green warning lights shone through the dark water, and a series of drains in the bottom opened like tiny black holes. Baggins and Red Cloud were yanked downward and pinned against the closest drains. Grates over the drains kept the ferals from being crushed and pulled into the pipes, but they were going to have the galaxy's worst hickeys.

With two drains blocked, it took more like twenty seconds to empty the pool. It was more than enough of a head start to get Grom out of Recreation and seal the door behind them. Mops sagged against the wall. "Kumar, what's your status?"

"I'm on deck M, circling back in your direction." He was breathing hard, but there was no panic in his voice. "How's Grom?"

"Alive, but unconscious. Rendezvous with us at—"

"Waste Reclamation," Kumar interrupted. "If Grom is injured, they might need extra methane. We can tap the methane stores in Waste Rec."

Mops blinked. "Good thinking."

"I spend a lot of time in Medical," he explained. "I've picked up a few things. I like watching the autosurgeons work. Autopsies are my favorite. You get to see so much more of how the bodies fit together. Once, after the battle of Pictor 3, I got to watch them replace one of Private Hamilton's lungs. Then they were removing the military implants from Prodryan POWs—"

"You can tell us about your hobby later." Mops turned her attention to Grom. The Glacidae was small for their species, about one and a quarter meters in length. A hundred-plus stubby legs protruded from either side of their tubular body. Each leg sprouted hundreds of thin yellow tendrils, creating a feathery appearance.

Thicker limbs ringed Grom's head, each one terminating in long, curved claws that had evolved for digging through the snow and ice of the Glacidae home world. Yellow spines lay flat along the back. Atop the head, above the beaklike mouth, were two enormous brown eyes that always reminded Mops of an Earth puppy.

A thin oily substance dripped like brown tears down Grom's face, cutting through the beads of water clinging to their skin.

Grom's equipment harness was secured to the front quarter of their body. Mops didn't recognize most of the tools, used for computer maintenance and repair throughout the ship. Their monocle was missing, probably lost in the pool.

"Can those spines pierce our suits?" Wolf asked, plucking one from her sleeve and flicking it onto the floor.

"As long as your suit integrity alert isn't going off, you're fine." Pounding from the ferals inside Recreation made her jump. She grabbed the side of Grom's harness. "Wolf, give me a hand."

Together, they hoisted Grom into the air and started toward the lift, letting the rear third of the Glacidae's body slide along the floor.

Wolf looked back at Recreation, and her usual bravado slipped. "What the hell are we supposed to do now?"

"Get Grom to safety," said Mops. "Signal Command for assistance. Stay alive."

"Sounds like a simple plan," said Monroe, pausing to pop a bubble of dark brown gum. "You've heard the Earth saying about the best laid plans, right?"

"Isn't that the one about the plans of rats and men?" asked

Wolf. "Rats and men always seemed like a weird collaboration."

"That's why it requires planning," said Monroe.

"I've made a command decision." Mops waited a beat before adding, "I'm going to ignore you both from here on out."

4

The most brilliant Krakau scientists were assigned to work on the biological restoration of humanity. As a result, the scientists who worked on other aspects of human culture were . . . not *the* most brilliant.

Für Elise was a xenolinguist and unsuccessful poet who had tried and failed to get a position on the Alliance Exploratory Council. While other, higher-status linguists worked to develop a single language for the newly cured humans, Elise was assigned to review the entirety of human literature and curate those works to be translated into the new Human tongue.

Elise spent four years on this project. Her notes from this time are illuminating. Selected excerpts follow:

- "Reviewed complete works of Dr. Seuss. These books are not, as first assumed, a guide to obscure Earth creatures. I suspect Seuss lied about being a doctor. Conclusion: total gibberish, completely untranslatable."
- "Have reviewed the history and causes of Earth

conflicts through the ages. Recommendation: do not translate or republish human religious texts."

- *"Works tagged 'fantasy' should be ignored. Based on early estimations of restored human intellectual capacity, these stories would only confuse them."*
- *"William Shakespeare's works are full of violence and vulgarity. These could be useful in priming humans for the realities of battle."*
- *"Have begun reviewing works tagged 'erotica.' What is this obsession humans had with procreation, and why did they have so many bizarre synonyms for their genitalia? They're almost as bad as Nusurans. I hate my life. . . ."*

W ASTE RECLAMATION CONTROL WAS a long, cramped room dominated by a series of pipes and tanks, all clearly labeled for human technicians with large warnings against things like cutting the gas lines.

Kumar crouched beneath one such sign, cutting into the three-centimeter methane pipe with his utility blade.

"Not too deep," said Wolf. "All we need is a pinhole-sized leak."

"This isn't my first time splicing a gas line," Kumar snapped. He adjusted his angle and jammed the tip of the blade deeper. "I'm in."

He returned the knife to his harness and clamped a T-joint over the pipe, then secured a small, flexible hose to the joint. Mops hoisted Grom close enough for Kumar to poke the other end of the hose into the Glacidae's beak. Slowly, Grom's mouth tendrils clamped around the hose.

Mops' monocle flashed a warning about a leak in the methane pipeline. She cleared the message and watched Grom's breathing. "Can you hear me, Technician?"

They didn't respond, but their body was expanding and contracting more deeply than before.

"Why methane?" asked Wolf. "I know Grom likes the stuff, but I thought it was just a treat. They breathe normal air like the rest of us."

"They prefer a higher methane content," said Kumar. "It speeds up their metabolism. There's an Earth drug called coffee that used to do the same thing to pre-plague humans."

A ripple passed over Grom's body, like a prolonged shiver. Their legs clicked against the floor as they moved closer to the wall. Mops cautiously released her hold. When it was clear Grom could support their own weight, she stepped away and rotated her arm until a loud pop eased the pressure in her shoulder. "How are you feeling, Grom?"

"Frosted, but alive." The Glacidae's language sounded like a growling tiger with a bad stutter, repeated in Human by the small translator built into their harness. Grom took one more deep breath, then pulled away from the methane line. "Thank you, Lieutenant. Good work. What's the situation with the rest of the ship?"

Kumar slipped smoothly past Mops, sealing tape in hand, to fix the pipe.

Mops brought Grom up to speed. It was always a little odd talking to an alien whose height meant they appeared to be chatting with your crotch, but she'd had stranger conversations. "Why weren't you in a quarantine suit?"

"No time. Fortunately, whatever did this to you humans doesn't appear to affect Glacidae. Aside from feeling like my lubricating glands are about to burst, I'm fine."

Mops took a subtle step back.

"Who else from the crew escaped both infection and your fellow humans?" Grom continued. "Other Glacidae, or anyone from the Krakau command crew?"

"You're the only survivor we've found so far," Mops said gently. "I'm sorry."

Grom sagged, automatically coiling the back half of their

body into a recliner for the front. "I . . . I see." They fell silent for several seconds. "I'll see what I can do about contacting Command to request help. I want you to figure out the best way to disable life support. That should take care of the remaining threat, after which—"

Mops' sympathy vanished. "We're *not* killing the rest of the crew."

"I know you humans have an instinctive pack loyalty, but we have to face facts. It's us against them, and our best chance of survival is to strike now. Life support is the easiest way. Game over, we win."

Monroe winced and took a step back. Kumar stopped working to stare, his mouth hanging partly open. Wolf folded her arms and asked, "*Now* can I threaten to eat them?"

Grom rattled their spines. "Lieutenant, would you please muzzle your subordinate, or does she have to be returned to the brig?"

Wolf started forward. "You ungrateful—"

"That's enough," snapped Mops.

"Thank you," said Grom. "Now, I'll need an escort to the bridge while the rest of you take care of these feral humans."

They trailed off as Mops dropped to one knee, facing Grom at eye level. Glacidae preferred to keep others a body length away. Mops deliberately leaned in, until she could feel their methane-tinged breath on her face. "Do I have your attention, Technician?"

Grom made a sound like they were trying to clear a blockage deep in their chest.

"That means yes," Doc whispered. *"I think. With Grom's accent, it could also be a request for eyeball lotion."*

Mops smiled, wondering briefly if Grom knew enough about humans to distinguish between a smile of pleasure and general good will and a smile that, much like a Glacidae's raised spines, warned of stabbings and general violence. "Unless you received a promotion while you were fouling the ship's pool, I still outrank you. If you have suggestions, I'm willing to listen. When I tell you your suggestion stinks worse than week-old slime crusts, your job is to shut the hell up and come up with a better one. *Don't you twitch those spines at me, child!*"

Grom jerked back so hard they nearly toppled over. Their legs flapped outward as they struggled to regain their balance.

"That's better," Mops continued. "We're going to do everything we can to keep the rest of the crew alive and safe until we can get them the help they need. If you have a problem with that, tell me now, because if you pull this Glacidae status-challenge bullshit on me again, I'll have Wolf lock *you* in the brig. Or an air lock. Is that understood?"

The Glacidae scooted back. "With respect, humans aren't meant to command. Regulations are clear."

Kumar cleared his throat. "That's not exactly true. EMC regulation 300-12, Promotions and Reductions, caps human rank advancement at Lieutenant, with allowance for temporary promotion lasting no longer than four hours to Battle Captain. It's true that humans can't be promoted to command crew. EMCR 220-40, Command Policy and Chain of Command, specifies that humans must cede command to any available Krakau. But there's nothing about a human Lieutenant having to take orders from a low-ranking Glacidae."

Doc pulled up the relevant sections of the manuals as Kumar continued talking. *"Kumar's reciting the regs word for word. Does he have any hobbies other than sitting around memorizing rule books?"*

"Watching surgeries," Mops whispered. "He also cleans a lot."

"The Alliance Military Council prohibits humans from commanding ships," Grom insisted.

"This isn't an Alliance ship," Kumar countered. "The Earth Mercenary Corps is contracted to the Military Branch of the Krakau central government. Specifically, we report to Krakau Interstellar Military Command. That makes us employees of the Krakau home planet of Dobranok, not the Krakau Alliance."

Grom fixed one eye on Kumar, while the other watched Mops. "Lieutenant, your human limitations are no fault of your own. I just think that, for the good of your team and the crew, you should surrender command to—"

"Wolf, where's the closest air lock?"

Grom sagged into a pile, the Glacidae equivalent of throwing up their arms in disgust.

Mops stood and wiped her palms on the front of her suit. "How much access do we have to the *Pufferfish*'s primary controls from here in Waste Reclamation?"

"Not much," muttered Grom. "Most command functions are restricted to the bridge and battle hubs. I'm sure there are overrides, but they're probably keyed to Krakau only."

"Can you bypass them?"

"I'm a tech. I clean up software and swap out broken hardware. I don't hack high-security systems."

Mops had expected as much, but it never hurt to ask. "Doc, we'll need a path to the closest battle hub. Once we get there, our priority will be communications and external scanners. We need to get word to Command and make sure there are no other Prodryan ships nearby." She studied her team. "I don't suppose anyone knows how to do any of that?"

Silence.

"We'll also need a plan for sanitizing the ship," she continued. "Kumar, Monroe, start brainstorming. We can't stay in these suits forever."

"What do we do if there are more Prodryans?" Grom asked quietly. When nobody answered, they said, "I assume nobody on your SHS team is certified on the ship's weapons and defenses?"

"Every system has tutorials and refreshers," offered Kumar.

"Sir, I've found something you should see," Doc cut in. Mops raised a hand for silence. *"Security footage of Captain Brandenburg and Commander Danube from shortly before they . . . expired."*

Mops sat down next to a water filtration access tank, rested her head against the warm metal, and closed her right eye. "Show me."

Her monocle turned opaque, shutting out the rest of the room, before bringing up an image of the Captain's Cove....

Captain Brandenburg and Commander Danube floated in murky, gently swirling water a meter deep. The Captain's Cove was directly adjacent to the bridge, and resembled a poorly lit cave. The exposed walls and ceiling were rough-textured, like brown sandstone. Captain Brandenburg's tentacles adjusted the controls on the horseshoe-shaped console at the center of the room.

Her rightmost tentacle was thinner and paler than the other two. She'd lost that one three months back, and hadn't yet finished regrowing it. Her beaklike mouth had a superficial resemblance to that of a Glacidae, but Krakau beaks were smaller and flatter against the face. A series of dark indentations around the upper part of her body were the equivalent of human eyes, though they perceived a narrower portion of the electromagnetic spectrum. Water beaded and rolled from her blue-black skin.

Directly in front of the two Krakau, a large screen displayed the image of a Nusuran. A caption at the bottom of the screen identified him as Captain Taka-lokitok-vi, presumably from the Nusuran freighter. According to the time stamp, this conversation had taken place about two hours earlier.

"On behalf of the EMC and the Krakau Alliance, we're happy to be of service, and relieved none of your crew were lost during the fighting," Brandenburg was saying. "We neither ask for nor expect payment for protecting your people."

"Our accountants on Solikor-zi might disagree, especially when it comes time to send our hard-earned taxes into your Alliance coffers." The Nusuran jiggled with silent laughter. "Regardless, Captain, victory should be *celebrated*!"

Like most Nusurans, Taka-lokitok-vi looked like an over-sized Earth walrus encased in a baggy brown sleeping bag. Three triangular plates of bone surrounded his head like ivory flower petals. Long, thin tendrils sprouted like weeds from behind those plates. Smaller pink tendrils wiggled suggestively beneath the round mouth, like a beard of boneless fingers.

"What my crew needs is rest," Brandenburg said firmly. "Not a celebratory interspecies orgy."

"We all rest in our own ways," laughed Taka-lokitok-vi. "Unless your soldiers were injured when they cleared those ring-dicked pirates from my ship?"

"They were fine," Brandenburg assured him. "Humans are pretty much unkillable."

"So we've seen." The Nusuran's skull plates scraped together in thought, sounding like a scraper peeling old paint from a wall. "Perhaps it's for the best that you and your fellow Krakau decline our invitation. Recreational relations are tricky with a species that severs their own tentacles as part of the mating process. Is it true Krakau never developed the concept of a safe word?"

Mops shifted her back. "Doc, what does this have to do with anything?"

The image froze. *"I'm establishing context."*

"And laughing at the clash of sexual mores?"

"Personally, I think Captain Taka-lokitok-vi showed both diplomacy and restraint, by Nusuran standards. Notice how he doesn't masturbate once during the entire exchange?"

"Just show me what happened next."

Commander Danube moved toward the screen. "Captain, what was it the Prodryans wanted?"

"Memory crystals." Taka-lokitok-vi rattled his skull plates in annoyance. "They removed three containers. Six more were lost when you fired on our ship."

"Our apologies," said Brandenburg. "That was a calculated strike—"

"We'd have lost far more if you hadn't," Taka-lokitok-vi

assured her. "The EMC may not be the most civilized force in the galaxy, but no one can question their efficiency. Speaking of which, if you or your crew change your minds about that invitation—"

"Safe waters to you and yours, Captain. *Pufferfish* out." As soon as the screen cleared, Brandenburg tapped her console. "Lieutenant Khan, report for debriefing."

"Memory crystals?" said Commander Danube. "They're valuable, but not valuable enough to explain why that second fighter stayed with the freighter rather than join the fight. None of this makes sense."

"You think there may have been more to the Prodryan mission?" asked Brandenburg. "We could send a salvage team to gather the remnants of their fighters, but given the punishment we poured on them, finding a scrap of useful, readable data would be like finding a particular grain of sand on the ocean floor."

Danube click-whistled a command, and a map of the galactic quadrant appeared on the screen, showing the Sagittarius, Orion, and Perseus arms of the Milky Way.

There were no borders in space, no walls or boundaries between star systems. Different-colored dots represented inhabited systems. The larger the dot, the greater the number of known inhabitants.

The Krakau home world of Dobranok was one of the largest, with more than eleven billion inhabitants living within the planet's oceans. Twenty-two other worlds were marked in Krakau blue, including the Earth. Until humanity recovered enough to govern and maintain their own planet, designating it a Krakau colony provided legal safeguards and protection.

Translucent silver lines, like spider silk, connected the worlds of the Krakau alliance, almost a hundred in total, though many were young colonies whose inhabitants numbered in the thousands or tens of thousands.

Known Prodryan worlds were bright green. Suspected colonies and outposts were darker green, including several worlds in the Perseus arm of the galaxy. In sheer numbers, Prodryan territories were almost a match for the combined worlds of the Krakau Alliance. Prodryans were short-lived as individuals, but they did two things incredibly well: fight and breed.

"Here are large-scale Prodryan conflicts from the past year," said Danube. Green rings circled twenty-two worlds, roughly split between Prodryan and Alliance. "We've concentrated on hitting military stations and outposts, while they've focused their attacks against established colonies."

"More people to kill, and more resources to steal," said Brandenburg.

"Including Kanoram-yi two months ago." Danube highlighted the Nusuran colony world. "Kanoram was one of their oldest colonies. The Prodryans could have looted all the mem crystals they needed. So why hit Captain Taka-lokitok-vi?"

Captain Brandenburg swam out from her console. "Do we have a copy of the Nusurans' cargo manifest? Maybe the Prodryans were after more than just mem crystals."

A list appeared on the screen. "The rest is terraforming equipment for the colonies. Weather-seeding drones, microbes for adjusting water salinity levels. Nothing that would get the Prodryans' wings buzzing."

"Signal Command that we're going to stay and make sure the captain reaches his destination without further trouble," said Brandenburg. "We might be dealing with a splinter group among the Prodryans. The bugs are almost as happy to fight each other as they are us."

The main door slid open, and a bulky woman stepped down the ramp into the waist-deep water. Lieutenant Khan had eight years in the EMC, and bore the scars to show it. Her nose was a crooked mess, and a set of parallel scars gave her a permanently furrowed forehead. Her hair was a black cloud spreading from her scalp.

The holster on her right hip was trimmed in red, designating her as a sharpshooter, the second highest firearms rating.

A combat baton hung from the opposite side of her harness. "Reporting as ordered, sir."

"Your teams did an excellent job clearing the Nusuran freighter," said Brandenburg. "What can you tell us about the Prodryans you encountered?"

Khan blinked. "I haven't had a chance to complete my report yet."

"I understand. I'm asking for your impressions."

The tautness in Khan's shoulders eased. "They ambushed us the moment we boarded. I think . . ." She trailed her fingers through the water. "I think the decompression disoriented them. They were suited up, but most of their shots went wild."

"How many?" asked Danube.

She stared at the rippling water. "Fifteen? Maybe twenty? No, not that many. . . ." Her voice faded.

"Lieutenant?" When Khan didn't respond, Commander Danube swam closer and extended a sinuous tentacle.

Khan slapped it aside with a snarl. An instant later, her eyes went round, and she stumbled backward. "I'm sorry, Commander! I didn't . . . I thought you were . . ." Her voice faded again. Her attention appeared fixed on a point at the back of the room.

"She could have received a head injury," Captain Brandenburg said softly. "Maneuvering in zero gravity is tricky, even for experienced soldiers, and humans don't always recognize when they've been wounded."

Danube swam cautiously around the Lieutenant. "I see no visible sign of injury or trauma."

"Better to be safe. Medical, this is Captain Brandenburg. I need a doctor and security escort in the Captain's Cove for Lieutenant Khan."

Khan continued to gaze trancelike into the distance.

"Medical would have checked her over as soon as she returned and completed decontamination," said Danube. "It's standard procedure. She —"

Khan's arm shot out, her fingers wrapping around one of Danube's thick lower limbs. Danube emitted a high-pitched whistle of distress as Khan clamped down and hauled her closer.

Captain Brandenburg shot through the water like a torpedo. She wrapped all three tentacles around Khan's arm, trying to break her grip. "Stand down, Lieutenant!"

"I don't think she can hear you." Danube tore free, sacrificing the last twenty centimeters of her captured limb in the process. She wrapped her remaining limbs around Khan. The captain did the same. Together, they pinned and restrained the snarling human.

Khan's teeth snapped audibly as she struggled to break free.

"Security, this is Commander Danube. Lieutenant Khan has gone feral. Repeat, we have a feral human in the Captain's Cove."

Mops' monocle cleared. She blinked, fighting off dizziness as the sights and sounds of Waste Reclamation replaced the Captain's Cove. "What happened? Where's the rest of the feed?"

"That's all I could access," said Doc. *"It could be data corruption, or more likely, medical privacy rules prevent us from seeing the details of Lieutenant Khan's treatment once the medics arrived."*

The Krakau had always taken human medical privacy seriously. Not only for the humans' sake; they wanted to protect the details of their treatment, making sure hostile races like the Prodryans couldn't reverse the cure.

Mops tried to imagine what had happened next in the Captain's Cove. Khan could have broken free when Medical and Security tried to take her. Or, depending on how quickly this thing spread, maybe the humans who'd arrived to help had gone feral as well.

"Are you all right, Lieutenant?" asked Monroe.

"Nope." Though her monocle had cleared, she could still see the wildness on Khan's face, the mindless hunger. Had Khan known what was happening to her? Had she felt her humanity slipping away from her? "We need to figure out how the hell the Prodryans did this and how to reverse it."

"What if it can't be reversed?" Kumar asked as he absent-mindedly polished a series of pressure gauges along the wall.

Mops thought about how quickly the *Pufferfish*'s crew had turned. How quickly this could spread through the medical centers on Earth, or the EMC training facilities. "In that case, to borrow a phrase from the Krakau, we are officially inked."

5

In Earth year 2122, Nusuran organic memory crystals revolutionized computer systems and artificial intelligence throughout the fledgling Krakau Alliance. Composed of pure Stishovite and ranging in size from a few millimeters to several centimeters in diameter, the spherical crystals are exponentially more efficient at storing data than previously used technologies. It's estimated that a single Nusuran memory crystal could survive a thousand years with less than 0.02% data degradation.

The popularity of such crystals was only slightly impacted by the revelation of their origins, discovered by a Krakau xeno-corprologist.

Nusuran biology is extremely efficient. Almost everything they ingest is broken down and utilized by their metabolism, except for trace amounts of silica. That trace matter is compressed and processed by a small, densely muscled set of four sphincter-like organs, and excreted approximately once per year. Crystal size and quality varies, depending on the individual Nusuran's age, diet, general health, and other factors.

The largest and purest memory crystals require both a strict high-calorie diet and ridiculously powerful laxatives.

—*From* Rectal Revolution: A New Age in Computer
Technology

"*WARNING: SUIT AIR SUPPLY at twenty percent.*"

"Kumar, Monroe, where are we at with that decontamination plan?" asked Mops.

Kumar pushed back from the terminal he and Monroe had been hunched over. "It's difficult to plan a course of action when we don't know what we're dealing with, sir. Is it viral? Nanoparticulate? Something else altogether?"

"Given how fast it spread, it's probably airborne," said Monroe. "It reached every part of the ship, so the air filtration systems don't slow it down."

"I reviewed the decon logs for units three and five," said Kumar. "Everyone went through standard decon protocols when they got back from the freighter. Anything they carried on their suits should have been fried. None of them had any suspicious gifts or packages. Is it possible we were infected through some other vector?"

"Unlikely," said Mops. "Khan was on the freighter, and she was one of the first to go feral."

"Once we know *how* to kill this thing, we've got a plan for incrementally cleansing the ship." Monroe waved a hand at the screen. "We'll need to completely shut down air circulation vents, pull the filters, and sterilize every duct from the inside. Individual rooms and corridors should be straightforward. The biggest problem will be the occupied areas."

"What about Grom?" Wolf piped up. "They don't seem to be affected. What if we take some of their blood and transfuse it into the rest of us?"

Grom raised their spines in alarm.

"I can cite 1,892 reasons why that's a horrible idea," Doc offered.

Mops sighed. She wanted her team jumping in with ideas. She'd just hoped for better ones. "Grom, can you fool the maintenance system into believing the ship's in drydock?"

"I'll need to shut down and interrupt the reboot cycle, but I think so. It'll take at least five minutes."

"Do it."

Kumar was the first to figure it out. His eyebrows shot up, and he leaned forward excitedly. "You want to run a level one decontamination?"

"Whatever this thing is, a level one decon ought to kill it, don't you think?" asked Mops.

Grom looked up from their terminal. "You realize it would also kill *me*, and possibly you and your team as well?"

Another warning appeared on her monocle. At the same time, Wolf said, "Sir? My suit just gave me a low oxygen warning."

"We don't have many options." Looking at their readouts, the rest would be getting similar alerts any minute now. "Monroe, Kumar, we'll start with your incremental plan. Waste Reclamation goes first. We'll decontaminate the room and ourselves at the same time. Grom, you're going to Battle Hub Two. Once you get there, see what you can do with the internal scanners. Doc's done a good job walling off most of the crew, but we can't risk a single straggler catching us off guard or getting into sensitive areas of the ship."

"The last time I moved freely about this ship, your fellow humans tried to eat me!"

"They should've tried harder," muttered Wolf.

"We've got most of the crew isolated," said Mops. "Doc can help you navigate around most of the strays. You'll be fine. Probably. Better off than if you stay here."

"Grom's right that a level one could kill us, too," Wolf pointed out.

"It could." Mops made shooing motions at Grom until they

hunched low and started working on the maintenance systems. "Our other choices are to suffocate in our suits or unseal our suits and get infected with whatever turned the rest of the crew feral. Which would you prefer?"

Wolf didn't answer.

"Powering down maintenance computers now," said Grom. The terminals went dead, and the lights dimmed. Grom hummed quietly as they waited for the system to reboot.

"What are you so cheerful about?" demanded Wolf.

The Glacidae glanced over. "If this does kill you all, I'll be left in command of the *Pufferfish*."

Glacidae didn't look fast, but given proper motivation, they made impressive time. Mops watched on her monocle as the icon representing Grom scurried through the ship toward the battle hub.

By now, Mops' air supply light was flashing a green *Danger* warning on her monocle. "Shut everything down. Monocles, suit electronics, terminals . . . anything you don't want fried. Monroe, does your arm have an off switch?"

Monroe grimaced. "He's always cranky afterward. Once after an upgrade and reboot, he spent ten minutes making obscene gestures at my CO. Claimed it was a malfunction, but the logs were clean." He murmured a command, and the arm went limp.

"Better swallow that gum, too," Mops added. One by one, the screens that had just come back up blinked out again. She sat at the remaining terminal and set the countdown for a level one decontamination on Waste Reclamation, along with a hundred and twenty meters of corridor directly outside and a maze of air circulation ducts. Kumar and Monroe had sealed off different vents to isolate the ducts in question from the rest of the system.

"*Warning*," the screen flashed. "*Level One Decontamination cannot commence until all personnel have left the area.*"

Mops studied the safety protocols, which showed four living bodies present in Waste Reclamation. One by one, she manually retagged them as piles of biological waste material.

The warning vanished. Mops started a one-minute countdown, then shut off the console. "Doc, decon should take about five minutes. Can you power yourself down but keep a timer going to restart in ten?"

"As long as I run the timer from another location and have it send the startup signal remotely," said Doc. *"But if this thing damages my circuits, I expect an upgrade!"*

Her monocle went blank and fell from her eye, landing in the base of her hood and leaving her in darkness. She sat on the floor and tried to relax her muscles.

"I've always wanted to see a level one from the inside," said Kumar.

"And we wonder why the rest of the galaxy thinks humans are idiots," snapped Wolf.

"Not at all," said Monroe. "There are plenty of other, better reasons."

A hurricane tore through the room, silencing further conversation. The initial rush of air was meant to stir particulate matter from the various surfaces. It slammed Mops sideways, and she heard someone—probably Kumar—yelp as they tumbled to the floor.

The wind shifted. Mops' suit puffed from her body as the vents sucked the air from the room. The sound faded, then died. Mops clapped her hands together in front of her face, but neither saw nor heard anything. She kept clapping until the sound began to return, muffled and tinny. The air pumping into the room wasn't a breathable oxygen mix, but a low-pressure conductive medium for what came next.

A blue spark, surprisingly bright, leaped from the ceiling to the floor. She glimpsed Kumar sitting wide-eyed, Monroe resting with his back to the wall, and Wolf standing defiantly in the middle of the room, as if daring the ship to do its worst.

The next spark arced to the top of Wolf's head. She dropped

like a stone in Tjikko gravity. The electrical dispersion grid woven into the material of her uniform to diffuse energy weapon strikes should have kept her alive against the shock . . . hopefully.

More sparks flew, creating a blue strobe effect that made her eyes ache. Normally, her monocle would have darkened to compensate, but the lens was dead and useless at the bottom of her hood.

The electrical storm would fry nanotechnology, cook exposed bacteria and viruses, and basically burn the living hell out of anything and everything it touched. If the contagion turning the crew feral could survive this—

A jolt struck her suit. The dispersion grid helped, but not as much as she would have liked. Her muscles locked, and her jaw clenched so hard she thought her teeth would crack. Her heart pounded hard and fast. Her body felt swollen, like she'd been overbaked to the point of bursting.

Monroe was next to topple. Electricity sparked over his prosthetic arm.

The edges of Mops' vision turned dark. The flashes contracted to a pinpoint of light. And then that pinpoint went black.

"Good morning!"

Mops awoke in darkness to the sound of Doc's too-cheerful voice and the sensation of drool dripping down her cheek. The salt-and-alcohol smell of sanitizing foam was thick in the air. She wiped her face and froze. She hadn't unsealed her hood.

"I remotely activated your suits to trigger the emergency hood release. After all your efforts, I couldn't let you and your team suffocate in your own suits."

"Thanks." Her throat was dry and raw, like she'd swallowed a wire brush.

"No thanks necessary, Lieutenant. I'm programmed to assist

with shipboard hygiene and sanitation, and that means not leaving dead and decaying bodies in the middle of Waste Reclamation. Especially since there'd be nobody to clean them up."

"How about some lights?" Her fingers felt stiff and clumsy as she tugged off her gloves. The thick layer of dissolving foam covering everything didn't help matters. She fumbled to retrieve her monocle from the bottom of her hood. It snapped into place over her eye, powering up immediately with the status of her team—all alive.

Monroe hadn't woken up yet. Wolf groaned as she gingerly probed the top of her head. Kumar had taken out a large cleaning cloth and was meticulously scrubbing yellow foam from the front of his suit.

"You think it worked?" asked Wolf.

"Doc, how long since you unsealed our suits?"

"Two hours, eleven minutes, and twenty-three seconds."

Lieutenant Khan had started showing symptoms when she reported to the Captain's Cove. Depending on when exactly she'd been exposed, that could have been anywhere from thirty minutes to three hours.

"If it didn't work, we'll find out soon enough." Mops drew her air compressor gun, fitted it to the small tank in her harness, and blasted the rest of the foam from the closest screen. Kumar perked up and gestured to himself. With a sigh, she sprayed him clean as well before easing into the closest chair. "Doc, put me through to Grom."

The Glacidae responded immediately. "I see you survived, Lieutenant. I reached Battle Hub Two without incident, and started working through the tutorials on the internal sensor systems. I take it the decontamination worked?"

"We'll know in another hour." Mops frowned. "Was that an explosion?"

"What? Oh, sorry, let me pause that."

"Pause *what*? I don't recall explosions and screaming in the standard scanner tutorial modules."

Grom hesitated. "It's . . . *Maze Hunter 4.* I picked up an

expansion pack on Eridanus 2. With the rest of the crew off-line, the response time is amazing. I'm on the final level—"

"You've spent the past hours playing a video game?" Mops asked quietly.

"And watching the tutorial. Glacidae are better multitaskers than humans. No offense. Our brains are able to compartmentalize—"

"You didn't think there might be more important tasks for you to focus on?"

A pause. "I followed all orders you gave me. Sir."

Mops turned on the console in front of her. "Send me an updated scan of the ship, and a systemwide view of our position."

"One moment. Let me review my notes." Several minutes passed before her display lit up with the information she'd requested. The *Pufferfish* had drifted about twenty kilometers. At this scale, they were essentially standing still.

The ship's internal status appeared unchanged. "Doc, show me everything we've decontaminated so far." Waste Reclamation and the closest corridors turned blue. "Kumar, get to work decontaminating the next areas we'll need. Food and supplies. Main lifts and corridors to the bridge and other vital areas."

"At least one bathroom," Kumar added.

Mops didn't answer. A series of blips on the screen, about 250 million kilometers from the *Pufferfish*, had caught her attention. "Doc, what are those?"

"A-ring deceleration signatures. Looks like six ships arrived in-system."

Mops worked through the math in her head. "If we're just seeing the flares now, that means they arrived about fifteen minutes ago?"

"Nope. More than an hour and a half. But the screen will keep displaying the energy readings until someone acknowledges and clears them."

She muttered a curse. "If that's their location ninety minutes ago, where did they go?"

"Unknown. Deceleration signatures are like a flare, visible throughout the star system. Normal sublight propulsion is another matter. At this range, targeted scanners might be able to pick them up, but we'd need to know where to look. Depending on their speed, we're talking trillions of cubic kilometers."

She stepped away from the console and knelt by Monroe. His breathing was strong. She pushed back his hood and smothered a laugh. His white hair stood out like a lopsided dandelion, probably a side effect of the electrical portion of the decon process.

She ran a quick hand through her own hair. Static crackled, but it wasn't as bad as Monroe's. She gave him a gentle shake. "Wake up, JG. We've got six unidentified ships sneaking around. I need everyone up and working."

He groaned and tried to shove her hand away. When that didn't work, he turned onto his side, his natural hand clutching hers.

A chuckle behind her cut off too quickly for her to see who it was. She tugged her hand free. "Attention, soldier!"

Monroe jerked up, groaned, and clutched his head.

"Sir, we may have a problem," said Kumar. "I've got a clear path to the bridge, but the bridge itself is occupied. Looks like two ferals, and . . ."

Mops moved to look over his shoulder. "And?"

"If I'm reading this right, four Krakau bodies. With two more sealed in the Captain's Cove."

"Work with Doc to get those ferals off the bridge and into a contained area."

Wolf perked up. "Can we keep using that Jane Austen book to distract them? I'm curious about the Frederica character."

"I don't care. Just get them clear. Then run a level one on the bridge and cove."

Kumar turned in his seat. "Sir, do you know what that will do to exposed Krakau flesh? Especially in the cove, with all that water?"

"Do you know what will happen if those six ships are

hostile and they reach us before we get to the bridge?" Mops didn't wait for an answer. "Grom, work with Wolf on figuring out communications while we clear the bridge. If you touch another video game, I'll order Doc to wipe every one of them from the ship's systems. Including every saved game and high score."

The Glacidae gave a drawn-out, belchlike cry of distress. Mops wasn't sure which was more upsetting, the prospect of losing their scores, or being ordered to work with Wolf. Nor did she particularly care.

"Why can't Doc handle communications?" Wolf protested.

Grom replied before Mops could answer. "Because the *Pufferfish* doesn't have a single interconnected computer system. Too easy to hack. Most command functions are isolated, inaccessible to the average member of the crew. Command-level AI assistants are deliberately restricted in their access. A good thing, too, considering how often you lot manage to fry your AIs and personal assistants. I spent most of yesterday cleaning several terabytes of interspecies porn off Private Garcia's monocle." Mops' comm speaker clearly relayed the repulsed rattle of Grom's spines. "The things I saw. . . ."

"Stay strong, Technician." Mops hauled Monroe to his feet. "Let's get to work."

The worst thing about stepping onto the newly sterilized bridge wasn't the sight of the four Krakau officers, but the smell.

Mops had personally cleaned up some of the nastiest substances from throughout the galaxy. She took pride in being the only one on the SHS team who could walk unmasked into a Tjikko composting mausoleum without puking.

Seeing the burnt remains of her former commanding officers made her want to weep, and to lash out at those responsible for the assault on her ship. Her eyes looked at the desiccated bodies and felt grief. Grief that *almost* overpowered a more primitive response to the cooked-seafood smell that filled the air.

She swallowed hard and stepped onto the bridge. "Kumar, get the bodies down to Medical. Put them in preservation pods for now."

"Yes, sir." Kumar tugged out his gloves, grimacing as he approached the body of Second Officer Seville.

Mops could count on her hands the number of times she'd been to the bridge, usually to deal with spills and stains that were too much for the ship's automated cleaning processes and scrubber-bots.

A large, curved screen dominated the hemispheric room. At the center was the captain's station, marked off by a horseshoe-shaped console identical to the one in the Captain's Cove. Eight other duty stations were positioned around the edge of the room, separated by metal guide rails positioned too low for human comfort, but just right for Krakau limbs to curl around.

Every station was a shallow pit or depression, with the captain's being the deepest. The bumpy metal floor offered a level walkway around the bridge, with ramps leading down to the various duty consoles. Each of those stations contained an array of displays, switches, and other equipment . . . none of which Mops had the slightest idea how to operate.

"Doc, what the hell am I looking at?" she whispered.

Tags appeared on her monocle, identifying the Commander's station and Navigation to the front right of the Captain, with the Second Officer and Weapons/Defense to the left. Communications and Operations were positioned just behind the captain, with two backup stations at the rear of the bridge. A sealed door in back led to the Captain's Cove.

The main screen was currently dark, as were the two backup stations. The rest were active, judging from the various lights and displays. They must have come back on automatically after the decontamination.

Mops stepped around to the ramp leading to the captain's area. There was no chair, just a series of bars that looked perfect for coiling boneless limbs around. Mops tried to find a comfortable position that didn't bend or compress her body, but soon gave up. Standing amidst the tangle of bars, she turned to her team.

"Monroe, take Weapons and Security. Wolf, you're on Communications." She pointed them in the appropriate directions.

Wolf looked longingly at the Weapons and Security pit, but didn't argue.

"Kumar, hurry up with those bodies, then get to Navigation. Grom, until we figure out how to kill any contaminants you might be carrying without killing you in the process, I'm afraid the Bridge and all other sanitized areas of the ship are off-limits. Stay in Hub Two for now."

"Understood," the Glacidae responded over Mops' speaker. They didn't sound overly disappointed to be effectively restricted from interacting with humans.

"Doc, how much help can you give us with operating the ship?"

"I have no direct access to the bridge systems. In addition to segregating their computers, the Krakau hard-wired a number of safeguards to prevent AIs from seizing control of the ship. It's described as a defense against hacking attempts by hostile forces, but I think they're just paranoid about us. It's rather insulting."

"Sir, I think we're receiving a signal," said Wolf.

Mops stared down at her own console. "Do any of these screens feed from Communications?"

Her monocle highlighted a screen to the right, more-or-less aligned with the position of the communications station. She studied the array of buttons and sliders and touch screens, all a little too large for human fingers.

"I think I've got it." Wolf did something on her own terminal, and the main screen lit up—not with an incoming signal, but with an animated caricature of the *Pufferfish*, a disturbing cartoon with too-large eyes and a too-friendly smile.

"Greetings, human member of the *EMCS Pufferfish* crew! It looks like you're trying to establish a communications channel with another ship. Would you like help?"

Wolf's face turned dark, and she hunched over her console. "Sorry. I thought—"

"Yes, we want help," Mops snapped.

The cartoon smile grew larger, and the eyes turned briefly to pink hearts. "I'm so glad! What format would you like to broadcast in, and what kind of encryption will you need? I'm happy to list all available options for you!"

Mops groaned. She'd forgotten how obnoxious the ship's tutorial software could be. The Krakau claimed they'd based it on old Earth software. Back in basic training, she'd had nightmares about their teaching interface coming to life and chopping through her door with a combat blade, grinning its sociopathic grin and saying, *It looks like you have too much blood in your body. Would you like help with that?*

She shook herself and said, "Just play the incoming signal, but don't respond yet."

The image morphed into an oversized drawing of the comm station controls. "Step one: isolate and filter the incoming signal using—"

The screen went blank again. "I got it back on my console," Wolf said without looking up. She reached out and touched one of the controls, then jerked her hand back as a painful squeal filled the bridge. "Son of a shit! Sorry. Isolating the signal now."

A short time later, the main screen flickered, and Mops found herself staring into the iridescent, bulbous eyes of a Prodryan. The bridge comms broadcast a repeating message. "—squadron 52. Your vessel appears to be in distress. Do you require assistance? Please respond. Repeat, this is Assault Commander Burns Like Sunspots of Prodryan fighter squadron 52."

It was impossible to judge size over the screen, but most Prodryans were about a meter or so in height. From the thickness of the two antennae, this one was male. Organic-looking armor covered his torso: curved, brightly colored plates riveted and hinged for flexibility. Curved barbs sprouted from inside the bristled forearms. Large pink-and-purple wings, vivid as oversized flower petals, twitched behind him.

Like many Prodryan warriors, this one had a number of mechanical enhancements. Lines of microcircuitry traced silver spirals down his wings. One of his four mouth pincers had been replaced with a metal unit that probably doubled as a communications device.

"Damn," said Wolf, as the message continued. "I was hoping for a signal from Command."

"Prodryans offering help," Monroe muttered. "Nothing suspicious about that."

"Do we have any information on AC Burns Like Sunspots or the 52nd fighter squad?" asked Mops.

Monroe glared at his console. "I'm sure Command would want that information to be accessible to the human Battle Captain and crew, but damned if I know how to find it. I can tell you the typical Prodryan squad is eight fighters, not six. Those two pirate ships could have been from the 52nd. They've probably got a carrier in deep space as their jump point."

Grom spoke up over the comm. "Lieutenant, may I remind you that your training in sanitation and hygiene in no way qualifies you to take this ship into battle?"

"You may not." Mops frowned at the screen. The Prodryan had stopped speaking, and appeared to be watching them. Her gut tightened. "Wolf, are we currently broadcasting to the Prodryans?"

"What? No!" Wolf searched her console. "Maybe."

Mops straightened. "This is Lieutenant Adamopoulos, in command of the EMCS Pufferfish. This is a Nusuran colony system. Your presence violates Article Nine of the Krakau Alliance charter. You're ordered to leave immediately."

"I'm not interested in talking to the ship's janitor," sneered Burns Like Sunspots. "Where is your captain, human?"

Sorry, mouthed Wolf, sinking even lower into the communications pit.

"Battle Captain Cervantes is occupied with more important matters," said Mops. "As the commander of the *Pufferfish* SHS team, I can assure you our missiles will be cleaned and polished when they blow your fighters to dust."

"We are simply responding to a ship in apparent distress." Prodryans were terrible liars. As a species, they favored force and violence over subterfuge. It wasn't until they encountered other intelligent races that they began to practice deception. Like most Prodryans, Burns Like Sunspots needed a lot more practice. His antennae quivered, and his words were stilted, like he was reading . . . badly . . . from a script. Which was a very real possibility. "We must have missed the beacon satellites proclaiming this an Alliance colony system. But as your ship has been drifting since our arrival, we're happy to offer aid. My squadron will be within range soon, and—"

The Prodryan continued to talk, but no sound emerged. Slowly, Mops turned to Wolf.

"It's not my fault!" Wolf protested. "Puffy told me to adjust the cache threshold to make sure we could screen out any hostile code in the incoming signal. I must have missed something in the settings."

"Puffy?" Mops repeated.

"The animated help ship," Wolf said quietly. "I thought it needed a name."

"Can they still hear us?"

Wolf threw up her hands. "Piss if I know."

"Just get the sound back," Mops snapped. The Prodryans must have deliberately sacrificed those first two fighters in order to infect the *Pufferfish* crew. The rest of the squad waited for the infection to spread, then showed up to confirm the effectiveness of their new bioweapon.

"—try our patience!" The Prodryan appeared to step closer. "Ignore us at your peril, human!"

"'Ignore us at your peril'?" Mops turned to Monroe. "Is that our translator, or do they really talk like that?"

"That's all Prodryan," said Monroe.

The Prodryan's wings shivered with anger, releasing a fine cloud of pink dust. "We can see the battle damage to your vessel. Do not play games with me."

"Oh, that." Mops leaned back, suppressing a grimace as the metal bars ground against her ribs. "We had a minor skirmish with a pair of Prodryan pirates. Nothing serious."

The lift door opened and Kumar walked in, humming as he hoisted the next Krakau body onto a maglev stretcher. He was most of the way back to the lift when he glanced up to see everyone—including the Prodryan—staring at him.

"A dead Krakau looks serious to me, Lieutenant," said Burns Like Sunspots.

"Dead?" Mops blinked. "Oh, she's not dead. She just had an allergic reaction to some bad shellfish."

"Bad . . . shellfish?"

"Before you say it, food storage is the Quartermaster's responsibility, not Shipboard Hygiene and Sanitation. My team had nothing to do with this."

The Prodryan shivered again, creating a veritable flurry of pink and making Mops wonder what kind of air filtration setup their ships used. "You're lying."

"No, there's a clear separation of responsibility between SHS and the Quartermaster," said Mops. "We can send you a copy of the EMC Operations Manual if you'd like. The unclassified parts only, of course."

"That is unnecessary," Burns Like Sunspots said stiffly.

"While we're on the subject of lies, do you really expect us to believe you just happened to wander into this system and spot us, dead in space, almost two AUs from where you arrived?" Mops chuckled. "You knew where we were because your fellow Prodryans signaled you. Probably right before the *Pufferfish* reduced them to scrap."

"We were . . . surveying this system—these worlds . . . as a potential Prodryan colony site," Burns Like Sunspots insisted. "Our presence here has *nothing* to do with secret weapons testing, nor is this in any way a prelude to larger action to undermine and ultimately destroy the Krakau Alliance!"

"Please stop," Mops groaned. "This is embarrassing, and I'd think you'd be plenty humiliated already, given the situation."

"What situation?"

She leaned forward. "You hid in the darkness while two Prodryan fighter crews died attacking the *Pufferfish*. You were too scared to show your face in this system until you thought we were dead. You're not a warrior. You're a scavenger, a buzzard come to pick at the bones of our corpse."

"How dare you," Burns Like Sunspots roared. His bulbous eyes twitched. "What's a buzzard?"

"Either get the hell out of here, or get on with your mission," Mops continued. "Take on an EMC cruiser with your little fighters. Go ahead and try to board our ship. Bring your best guns. We both know those will only piss humans off."

"Warriors of the Prodryan Expanse do not fear your urinary tactics!"

To her side, Wolf choked off a laugh, turning it into a cough.

"But understand, if you try to set one foot on my ship, I'll personally tear those gorgeous wings off your body," Mops said. "If you're lucky, I'll kill you myself. If not . . . well, my team hasn't eaten since before that attack. They're all very hungry."

The screen went dead. Mops blinked. "Did we end that transmission?"

"I'm pretty sure they cut us off on their end," said Wolf. "Sir, didn't you tell me *not* to threaten to eat people?"

"I have no memory of that." Mops stood, twisted her body until her spine popped, and started barking orders. "Monroe, we're probably going to need missile countermeasures very soon, along with power to the main energy dispersion grid. Weapons would be nice as well."

"I'll try." Monroe sounded sheepish. "I need to reboot my station first. I tried to rush the tutorial, and it locked up on me."

"Kumar, get back up here. We'll dump the rest of the Krakau in the cove for now. I need you at Navigation."

Kumar acknowledged over the comm, followed immediately by Grom protesting, "Lieutenant, was it wise to antagonize our enemy?"

"I'll take anything that makes them hesitate," she said. "Maybe later we'll have the luxury of 'wise.'"

"We don't even know where they are," said Grom.

"We know where they arrived in-system," Mops snapped. "And we know they're coming our way. The lag in our conversation was about a second, which puts them around three hundred thousand kilometers. That gives us direction and distance. Get on those scanners and tell me the instant you spot them."

"Yes, sir."

Mops sank back into her makeshift seat. "Doc, check through our tutorials and give me a crash course on ship-to-ship combat."

6

To human eyes watching from shore, the alien craft would have resembled nothing so much as an amalgamation of large bubbles bobbing in the waves. Not the iridescent soap bubbles human children once produced with flimsy plastic wands, but the dirty yellow bubbles those same children would inflate from mucus-clogged nostrils.

Due to the limitations of early Krakau translation software, the first words broadcast to humanity by another sentient species, in Earth Year 2153 and at a volume of 104 decibels, were:

"We come in harmony to defenestrate your dingo."

At another time in human history, such a message might have triggered panic and bewilderment. On this sunny evening, however, Old MacDonald's verbal flub went unnoticed.

Rocks crunched beneath the pod's wheels as it climbed the crumbling road. MacDonald's scanners tracked heat and movement in all directions, projecting their findings onto the interior shell of her command module.

"This reminds me of the ruins of Black Ice Trench back home," said her partner, Alouette.

"I see one," MacDonald announced. "Lurking in that structure ahead. According to the translator, that orange-and-white sign proclaims it the home of the King of Burgers. The human could be one of their leaders."

The human in question was filthy, but that was no surprise. Living on the surface, exposed to all that dirt and solar radiation, it was a wonder the species had survived at all.

"I thought humans wore clothing," said Alouette.

"Preliminary briefings always get things wrong," MacDonald said absently, her three long, boneless tentacles working to pull up additional readings. The human's temperature was lower than expected, though still hotter than any Krakau.

"It appears to have a vestigial tentacle between its lower appendages."

"Interesting. Do you think it's prehensile?" MacDonald took her pod in for a closer look. The human limped from the broken doorway into the fading sunlight. A mass of tangled black fronds—hair—hung from its scalp, partially obscuring the facial features. Dark scars crisscrossed its pale skin, as if it had been savaged by a deepwater spine serpent. "I think it's injured."

Alouette played MacDonald's recorded greeting message again, adding, "We can heal your clarinets."

More humans emerged from other shelters and trudged toward the two pods.

"I think we have a problem." Alarm sharpened Alouette's words. The humans balled their upper extremities and slammed them against the Krakau pods.

MacDonald curled the tip of one tentacle around a small control rod and pulled. As the weapons came online, the interior brightened, turning the vivid green of an abyss serpent's threat display. "Command, we're surrounded by a school of hostile humans. I see no way to extract ourselves from the situation without harming them."

The response from the Krakau ship in orbit was short and sharp. "We're monitoring your situation. Fight well."

MacDonald froze. "Command, say again?"

"We're receiving similar reports from other teams. Take whatever actions are necessary to escape. These humans are far more dangerous than we were led to believe. Good luck."

—From the First Contact Logs of Krakau Explorers
Old MacDonald and Alouette
(collected posthumously)

"I THINK I'VE FOUND plasma beam firing controls," Monroe announced. "According to the user guide, I can use keyboard, toggle, and voice options to adjust intensity and duration. Targeting . . . that needs to interface with our scanners. Grom, send me external scanner data!"

"I'm trying!" Even over the comm, Mops could hear the rattling anxiety in Grom's voice. "Try this?"

The main screen switched to a "top-down" map of the system, with the primary star and planets labeled. The *Pufferfish* was a blue dot of light. A short distance away, a swarm of green sparks crawled toward the ship.

"You sent it to the main bridge display." Monroe continued fighting with his console. "I need that feed at Tactical!"

"Sir, that's more than six ships," said Kumar.

"I know." Mops gritted her teeth. "I think we're looking at a missile barrage."

Wolf jumped to her feet. "I saw something about evasive maneuvers. I can—"

"The missiles will just follow us," said Monroe. "We need countermeasures. Jamming and hacking their guidance, decoys to pull them off target, and a flareburst for anything that keeps coming."

"Do you know how to do any of that?" asked Mops.

"Not yet." He raised his voice. "And not without scanner data!"

"I'm working on it," Grom shouted back.

Mops turned to her right. "Kumar, what about an A-ring jump to get us out of range?"

"We're too far in-system. The sun's gravity would shear the ship apart. Also, I haven't gotten to A-ring jumps yet. I'm pretty sure I'd blow up the whole ship."

"Monroe, give me plasma weapon controls," said Mops. "You focus on those countermeasures."

Another part of her console lit up, showing plasma beam intensity and duration. Default firing setting was a quarter-second burst at ten-percent power. Nowhere did she see a convenient button labeled *Link Targeting to Scanners*. A soft-glowing green button drew her attention. Probably the firing controls. She tapped it once . . . twice.

Most plasma weapons were invisible, but the screen displayed a white line showing the path and duration of the shot, streaking off into empty space.

"I think I've got thrusters," Kumar shouted. "I haven't figured out gravitational compensators yet, but if I keep the power at five percent, I can move the ship without killing everyone on board."

Five percent was better than nothing. "Bring us about to" —she double-checked the scanners—"thirty-five degrees starboard, minus ten degrees declination."

Kumar stared at the controls like they'd sprouted mold. "Um . . ."

Mops pointed to the viewscreen. "The front of the ship is this way. Turn us thirty-five degrees to the right"—she moved her arm to illustrate, then lowered it—"and drop us down ten."

"Right." He hesitated. "You should probably secure yourselves."

Mops searched the captain's station for a harness attachment point, but the safety equipment here was designed for Krakau, not humans. How did Battle Captain Cervantes and his team do it? She settled for crouching next to one bar and wrapping an arm around another. She braced her other hand against the console.

The *Pufferfish* lurched about, coming roughly into alignment with the incoming missiles. She fired again, sending a plasma beam in the direction of their enemies. She missed by less than five degrees. Which, at this range, translated to tens of thousands of kilometers. Even with targeting, it would have been an impossible shot.

"We could take one of the *Pufferfish*'s shuttles," Grom suggested over her comm. "We might be able to evade the Prodryans and escape to the colony."

"Do you know how to fly a shuttle?"

Silence. Then, "Never mind. I'll keep working on scanners. I think I've isolated Monroe's console."

"I've got the tactical feed," whooped Monroe. "Initiating countermeasures."

The main screen lit up like fireworks as small probes spat from the ship, spoofing heat and energy signatures, attempting to interfere with guidance systems, and generally making an electronic nuisance of themselves.

"Kumar, we're still turning."

"I know, sir," he said. "I shut off the thrusters, but—"

"Physics, Kumar," she snapped. "We're in space. An object in motion is going to stay in motion."

"Remember your zero-gee training," Monroe added, without looking up from his console. "It's like that. Only instead of you ricocheting around in a training gym, it's the whole ship."

"If the Prodryans can see us, they're probably laughing their asses off," muttered Wolf.

"Prodryans don't laugh," said Monroe.

The incoming missiles passed through their countermeasures. Many of the green dots blinked out . . . but not all of them. Mops tightened her grip on the bars. "Monroe, anything else you can throw?"

"Sorry, sir."

Mops jabbed the firing button again, but the ship had drifted too much, and the beam missed by a wide margin. An instant later, the *Pufferfish* jolted like it had collided with a small moon.

Another of her screens lit up, this one displaying damage reports. "Three direct hits."

"What if we ram 'em?" suggested Wolf. "We've got thrusters. Just plow through the bastards. It'll be like stomping cockroaches back on Earth!"

"First, these cockroaches have missiles and other ship-to-ship weaponry," said Mops. "Second, we're maneuvering at five percent power. They'd dance around us while they cut the ship to pieces." She watched the approaching ships on the main screen. "Kumar, are you *sure* you can't manage an A-ring jump?"

"I tried a simulation," he said. "Even if we clear the gravity well, I only completed 0.08 percent of the process before blowing up the ship and killing everyone on board."

"Good."

All three turned to stare at Mops.

"Doc, the *Pufferfish* shuttles are mounted with A-rings, aren't they?"

"Four apiece, yes. They only have a fraction of the power of the Pufferfish's *rings, but they're adequate for interstellar travel."*

Mops stared at the viewscreen. "They know we're in over our heads. They're probably expecting us to cut and run. That would be the smart thing to do."

"I take it we're not going to do the smart thing?" asked Monroe.

"We're humans. Why would we start now?" She smiled and started pulling up another tutorial. "Grom, how would you like to play captain?"

"This is Gromgimsidalgak, acting Captain of the *EMCS Pufferfish*. I have assumed command of the ship. Please respond."

The Glacidae was clearly terrified, their exoskeleton black and oily from fear secretions. It was similar to the lubricating fluid they secreted to help them dig, but this substance clung to the skin, making it harder for predators to get hold.

The response was slow in coming. When Assault Commander Burns Like Sunspots eventually appeared on the screen, his antennae were flat with annoyance. "What do you want, Glacidae?"

"You can have the *Pufferfish* and its human crew," Grom said, spines clicking with fear and urgency. "Let me take a shuttle to the colony. Do what you want with this frost-damned ship and its idiot inhabitants. I'll even disable the internal security systems for you. I'm one of the software technicians. I can do anything you need. Just let me go!"

"What happened to the humans I spoke with before?"

"Those clumsy, maggot-brained, soft-skinned imbeciles? Your missile barrage disrupted ship's systems long enough for me to transfer control to the battle hub. They're sealed in the main bridge, waiting to be questioned or dissected or whatever you want to do with them. I don't care. All I want is to get away and never have to smell their foul stench again."

On the bridge, Mops pursed her lips as she listened to the exchange. Grom was certainly getting into the role. She was tempted to tell them to turn it down a notch, but it had been hard enough for Wolf to set up this communications channel. If she did anything but passively watch on her monocle and listen through her suit's speaker, she had no guarantee her words wouldn't broadcast to the Prodryan ships.

"We counted four humans on your bridge," said Burns Like Sunspots. "What happened to the rest of your crew?"

"They went crazy. Even for humans. Some of them even tried to eat me. They're animals!"

"Very well. Disable all internal security measures, and we will grant your shuttle safe passage. I suggest you hurry. If you are on board when my warriors arrive, I won't be able to protect you."

"Thank you, Assault Commander!"

"If you betray me, Glacidae, I will see you baked alive."

Grom shuddered. "Understood." There was a brief pause. "Connection closed, Lieutenant."

Mops checked her console. "Are we *sure*?" she whispered.

"Completely sure." Wolf double-checked her console. "Mostly sure."

Mops watched the screen. The six Prodryan fighters weren't launching another wave of missiles. So far, so good. "Doc, clear a path so Grom can reach the main shuttle bay. Monroe, figure out if this ship has a self-destruct mechanism."

Her team fell silent, staring at her.

"I am *not* letting that pastel-winged pirate have our ship or our crew. If all goes well, we won't need to use it. But Lady Luck has been crapping all over us so far today."

"Who's Lady Luck?" demanded Wolf.

Mops rubbed her forehead. "I'm adding Earth literature and history to your duty rosters when this is over." She returned her attention to the paused tutorial on her console, practicing the command sequence for remote shuttle control override.

The Krakau built limited, short-range override capability into all smaller ships as insurance against human pilot error. She didn't have a clue how to fly the thing, but if Burns Like Sunspots did his part, that shouldn't be a problem.

And if not, well, even if the *Pufferfish* lacked a formal self-destruct mechanism, it shouldn't be too hard to blow up the ship. From what she'd seen of her team's tutorial scores, all she needed was to turn them loose for five minutes, and that would be the end of the *Pufferfish* and anything else within a hundred thousand kilometers.

"I'm sure this time," said Grom. "Try it now."

Mops tapped the sequence that *should* have initiated

shuttle three's launch sequence. A green error message flashed on her console. *Blast fence improperly angled. Reset and try again.*

Dammit. "How far out are those fighters?"

"A hundred and twenty thousand kilometers," said Monroe.

Mops glared at her consoles. "Grom, have you disengaged the locks on shuttle three?"

"Yes, sir."

"It's positioned for launch, and the bay doors are open?"

"That's right."

She tried again, this time receiving a new message. *Premature injection error. Initiating propellant reclamation and resetting helicon array. Ten minutes to engine reset.*

In theory, shuttles could launch using either conventional thrusters or grav-wave engines, but the latter was riskier, due to interactions with the *Pufferfish*'s internal gravity. Mops had no idea how to shut down the grav plates in the main bay for such a launch.

Rather, she didn't know how you were *supposed* to shut down shuttle bay grav plates. She spun to bring up the familiar maintenance control screen on her console. "Grom, do you know anything about grav engines?"

"In games or in real life?"

"Never mind." Mops attacked the controls, pulling up the safety menus and triggering an electrical fire alarm in the shuttle bay. The computer pointed out that the bay was currently depressurized, and no signs of fire had been detected. Both valid points, which Mops ignored as she confirmed the alarm.

"Sir," yelped Grom. "Everything inside the shuttle bay just went dead."

"Good." Mops braced herself. "Kumar, boost the ship's aft starboard thrusters to ten percent."

Her stomach lurched as the *Pufferfish* began to spin. "Grom, can you see the shuttle?"

"We've got emergency lights. It's just sitting there. Floating, I guess. We lost gravity, too."

Mops glanced at Kumar. "Push it to fifteen percent."

"What's going on?" asked Grom.

"Physics." Mops clutched her console. "We're using the ship as a sling to launch the shuttle."

"It's moving!" Grom shouted. "Sliding toward the bay doors. Ten meters . . . five . . . It's out!"

"Good. Cut thrusters, Kumar."

The *Pufferfish* continued to spin, but at least it wasn't accelerating. She watched the main screen, where shuttle three floated away from the *Pufferfish* in the general direction of the incoming fighters. With luck, the Prodryans would assume its wobbly course was a malfunction.

"Grom, shut the bay doors." Mops studied the controls, trying to figure out how to stabilize the shuttle's course. It toppled slowly end over end. Piloting a shuttle was simpler than piloting a cruiser, but Mops hadn't been trained in either, and ten minutes of "Puffy's" tutorial didn't change that.

"Prodryans are at one hundred thousand kilometers and closing," said Monroe.

Mops touched the blinking icon on her console that represented shuttle three. She double-checked her notes from the tutorial and pressed four more buttons to try to restart the shuttle's thrusters.

Six minutes to engine reset.

She switched to grav-wave engines. Shuttle three sputtered sideways, going into a kind of forward tumble in the general direction of the Prodryans. "Doc, project the shuttle's course relative to those fighters."

Monroe popped his gum. "It's not going to get close enough to do anything."

"Not on its own, no." Mops climbed out of the captain's station. "Kumar, get over here."

Kumar hesitated. "You want me to take command?"

"No." She gestured him into place. "That third console is currently tied into the shuttle's navigational controls. Don't touch anything yet!"

"Sorry!" Kumar jerked his hands back.

"Ninety thousand kilometers," said Monroe. "Sir, they're changing course. Moving to intercept the shuttle."

Mops sat on the floor, one arm hooked around the bars of the captain's station. "They just deployed a brand-new bioweapon against the *Pufferfish*. You think they're going to let a single witness fly off to warn the Alliance?"

"They plan to kill me?" Grom squawked indignantly.

"You know you're not actually on the shuttle, right?" asked Wolf.

"Yes, but . . ."

"I doubt they plan to kill you," said Mops. "Not right away."

Wolf turned. "Why not?"

"Remember when we got that new robot toilet snake three months back? You don't start with full deployment. You start with a controlled test to see how well it works. If it fails, you have to figure out *why* it failed."

"That's easy," said Kumar. "It failed because Second Officer Seville was celebrating her offspring's promotion that week, and the snake wasn't up for unclogging the end results of her celebratory Krakau shellfish surprise."

Wolf twisted around. "If the Prodryan bioweapon is the robot snake in this scenario, doesn't that make us—"

"The Prodryans need to figure out why we didn't succumb like the rest of the crew. That means keeping Grom and the rest of us alive for questioning and study." Mops watched the relative distances decrease. "I wouldn't think too hard about the rest of the analogy."

"You're lucky you didn't give those snakes AI modules," said Doc. *"If anything would spark a machine uprising . . ."*

"They're deploying grav beams." Monroe leaned closer, squinting at his console. "I think."

Mops double-checked the shuttle's range to the fighters and its distance from the *Pufferfish*. "Kumar, on my mark, send that shuttle on an A-ring jump. You won't have much time. Power up the ring and trigger the jump as fast as you can, got it?"

"The safety prechecks . . ."

Mops simply folded her arms.

"Right. Sorry." Kumar swallowed and spread his fingers over the console.

"You can do this." Mops put a hand on his shoulder, glanced at the display, and said, "And *go*."

Kumar jabbed the console with his index fingers. The tip of his tongue poked from his mouth as he concentrated. "Engaging microtractors."

An image of the shuttle appeared on the top of the console screen, the A-ring highlighted in blue as it expanded like a belt loosening from the shuttle's waist. The ring began to slide forward. Within three seconds, the ring stopped moving and turned a vivid green.

"Misalignment," Kumar muttered. "I know there's a realignment process . . ." He tapped another button, and the ring began to flash brighter green. "That wasn't it."

"Sir, I think the Prodryans are powering up energy weapons," said Monroe. "They've disengaged their grav beams."

"Kumar," Mops said gently. "Activate the ring."

He moved a pair of sliders forward, then pecked in another command. "It's powering up now. Um . . ." He tapped the screen, where all four of the shuttle's A-rings had turned green. "I may have accidentally activated them all."

He'd barely gotten the words out when the console display went blank. The main screen flickered, attempting to display the expanding torus of energy and debris. Energy that tore through the Prodryan fighters like a bleach pressure-wash through mold.

The message *Shuttle three destroyed* appeared on the console.

Wolf let out a low whistle.

"Good work, Kumar. You can return to your station." When he didn't move, Mops gave him a gentle push.

He stared at the screen as he walked, the destruction reflecting in his eyes. By the time the viewscreen cleared and

stabilized, nothing remained of the shuttle or four of the Prodryan fighters. Of the remaining two, one tumbled end-over-
end away from the *Pufferfish*, venting air from a long gash in
the hull. The other appeared to have partial engine function. A
single thruster fired, trying to stabilize its flight. The fighter
spat a pair of missiles toward the *Pufferfish*.

"Countermeasures, Monroe," Mops snapped.

"On it, sir."

Mops studied the screen. "Kumar, use the RCS thrusters to
bring our nose up two degrees."

A faint sense of heaviness told her Kumar had fired the
small reaction control system thrusters at the front of the ship.
She pulled up the weapons control, adjusted the plasma beam
duration, and jabbed the firing button.

The screen showed a white beam passing just beneath the
fighter. The fighter's engines sputtered again. It crawled away,
while the *Pufferfish*'s momentum brought them in a slow circle. They were like two drunken dancers trying desperately to
keep from falling.

"They're firing A-guns," said Monroe. "Moderate damage
to weapons pod number two."

Mops double-checked her console, glanced at the screen,
and tapped the firing button again. This time, the *Pufferfish*'s
plasma beam boiled a meter-wide hole through the fighter's
metal hull.

Mops gave a satisfied nod. "If you can't aim the guns, aim
the ship."

7

Humans' eating habits are, from an objective scientific perspective, disgusting.

Feral humans are scavengers. They prefer the meat of still-living or freshly killed warm-blooded creatures, but will eat almost anything. Krakau scientists have observed feral humans eating: reptiles, dead fish, bird eggs, various plants, dirt, rotting wood, insects, and each other.

We assumed pre-plague humans would have had a more civilized palate. We were wrong.

Historically, humanity's diet was even more varied and disturbing. Some of the preferred meals we've reconstructed from their cookbooks and other literature include:

- *The organs of an animal called a sheep, prepared and cooked within the stomach of the same creature.*
- *Tuna eyeballs.*
- *Raw fish. (One of the few sensible items in the human diet.)*

- *100-year-old eggs. It's a wonder this species didn't go extinct sooner.*
- *Pufferfish. The toxins of this fish were highly deadly to humans. I originally assumed this meal was used as a means of suicide or execution, but in fact, humans ate this for pleasure. The risk of death was part of the appeal. It's one more example of the human obsession with things that can kill them.*
- *Something called a Fried Twinkie. A slower method for humans to kill themselves.*

I strongly recommend not attempting to reproduce traditional human meals. In addition to the fear that the mechanics of eating could trigger a resurgence of feral impulses, my conclusion after ten months of research is that human cuisine was primitive, dangerous, and inescapably gross.

—*From* Observations on Human Cuisine, *by*
Under the Orange Tree
(Interspecies Culinary Specialist)

MOPS STEPPED CAUTIOUSLY INTO the mess hall, her utility pole clutched in both hands. They'd scanned and sterilized this area, but she wasn't taking chances. She searched every corner of the blocky, lounge-like room before calling back, "It's clear."

"Told you so," grumbled Doc.

The rest of the team followed her inside. Mops headed for the closest of the six identical dispenser slots built into the walls and punched the button for her daily nutrition allowance. Behind the panel, a vertical conveyor lowered a thick gray tube with a conical cap on one end. Mops reached into the slot, popped the tube free, and retired to one of the chairs in the corner where she could keep an eye on the entire mess hall.

Monroe took the chair to her right. "What better way to celebrate surviving a battle than with a nutritious paste of slow-release fats, proteins, and carbohydrates?"

He'd unsealed the seam in the front of his suit, revealing the dark scar tissue where pale flesh and white plastic came together. Without a hint of self-consciousness, he tugged part of his uniform to one side to expose the plastic nub of his feeding port. Monroe's port had been relocated to the left side of his torso to better reach what remained of his guts.

Mops opened ten centimeters of her own suit. Her hands moved automatically through the process of popping the cap from her nutrient tube and sliding the thick needle into her own feeding port. She twisted the tube to lock it in place, fastened the loop on the other end to a small hook on her harness to keep it from pulling free, and pressed a button to begin dispensing twenty-four hours' worth of food.

Mops' stomach gurgled. She and the team should have eaten three hours ago, but that would have cost them their chance at collecting what was left of the Prodryan fighters.

Trained technicians could sweep up post-battle flotsam in twenty minutes using the ship's grav beams to tow the pieces into a vacant cargo bay. According to Doc, the *Pufferfish*'s three grav beam techs were currently locked in the aft observation lounge, the maintenance garage, and a bathroom on deck B.

Wolf had insisted she could handle the grav beams. She'd seemed genuinely eager to learn and contribute. Wolf wouldn't have been Mops' first choice, but she was reluctant to quash this new attitude.

After half an hour poring over the tutorial, Wolf had gotten a lock on the first of the two salvageable fighters ... which promptly crumpled and exploded, destroyed by a missed decimal point in Wolf's calibration settings.

On her second attempt, Wolf had successfully hauled the remaining wreck toward the *Pufferfish*. She was less successful at slowing said wreck down as it rushed closer. The resulting collision had punctured the doors to cargo bay three, rendering the whole bay unusable.

At that point, Monroe had finally suited up and gone out with a magnetic grapple to physically maneuver the ship into bay two. The instant both Monroe and the fighter were on board, Mops had ordered everyone to the mess hall.

Despite what much of the galaxy believed, humans weren't indestructible. Her team was raw and exhausted from the tension of combat, not to mention hungry. Even Monroe appeared pale, and the lopsided slump of his body meant he was ready to drop.

They needed to figure out how to contact Command to update them about the Prodryans, but Mops feared if she pushed the team any harder, they'd end up breaking whatever they touched.

Wolf mumbled to herself as she grabbed her food tube from the dispenser.

"What's she doing?" asked Mops.

"Reviewing grav beam basics on her monocle."

Wolf plopped down on a couch and stabbed her meal into her feeding port. She kept her head down, continuing to mutter as she read.

"What do we do next?" Kumar asked as he joined them. "The ship's damaged, the crew—"

"Next, we eat," Mops said firmly. "I know that all could have gone better. It could have gone a lot worse, too. An Alliance SHS team just took out six hostile Prodryan fighters."

"Grom helped, too." Wolf grimaced, as if the admission caused her physical pain. "Prodryans ought to know better than to mess with humans by now. Ninety-nine percent of the crew out of commission, and we still kicked alien ass."

"Ninety-seven percent," Doc corrected, speaking loudly enough through her comm for everyone to hear. *"And Prodryans don't have asses, per se. They simply regurgitate pellets of—"*

Mops cut him off. "Unless I have to install or maintain the plumbing, I don't want to know."

"The Alliance should have ended the Prodryans years ago," Wolf continued. "Send the EMC to the Prodryan home world."

"And do what?" asked Monroe, his words deceptively mild. "How many would we have to kill to stop the killing?"

"You'd rather let them kill us? Turn us back into animals?" Wolf waved an arm. "Any one of us are worth ten Prodryans. I'm not saying we should wipe them all out, but if we burned their home world to slag—"

"Assume we could get through their system's defenses," Monroe interrupted. "Assume we razed their home planet. Blew up their shipyards, turned their cities to craters, and so on. What do you think would happen next?"

Wolf squared her shoulders. "Maybe they'd think twice about continuing their war against the Alliance."

"They wouldn't even think once," said Monroe. "An attack of that scale, one that legitimately threatened their species in its entirety, would unify them against us."

"They seem pretty unified to me," Wolf muttered.

That earned a tired chuckle from Monroe. "If there's one thing Prodryans aren't, it's unified. Loyalty is to self first, military unit second, family third, and finally to species. Last I heard, Alliance Intelligence estimates fewer than a quarter of all Prodryans are part of ongoing hostilities against us."

"A quarter of their species has been holding its own against the entire Alliance?" Wolf scoffed. "You're full of shit, Monroe."

Mops listened in silence. Unofficially, you left rank behind when you entered the mess. Officially, she was fully prepared to smack them both upside the head with her utility pole if the argument got out of hand.

"Prodryans breed to fill the environment," said Monroe. "A single mated pair on a new, unsettled planet can have a hundred offspring in a year. A colony of several thousand can turn into a billion in three short generations. The only reason they haven't overwhelmed us by sheer force of numbers is that Prodryans are incapable of acting as a unified force. The Alliance hasn't been fighting a war against the Prodryans. We've been fighting a thousand wars against a thousand militias and temporary coalitions."

"Then how do we win?" asked Kumar.

Monroe shrugged and settled back in the couch. "If you figure that out, be sure to let the Alliance Military Council know, will you?"

"I still say humans can hold our own against the bugs," said Wolf. "The whole galaxy's scared of us. Even the Quetzalus! You heard the story about the Quetzalus bounty hunter who *ate* one of our infantry soldiers?"

"I know that one," said Kumar. "The soldier shot his way out ten minutes later, right?"

"Damn right." Wolf folded her arms. "Their first loyalty is to self? Then we hit them in their sense of self-preservation. Remind them what humans are capable of."

"They know what humans are capable of," Mops said wearily. "That's why they're afraid of us."

"Are we really human anymore?" Kumar asked. "How old are you, Wolf?"

"Around twenty-six," said Wolf.

"Not your birth age. Your rebirth age."

"Eighteen months."

"Eighteen months since you woke up in a Krakau medtank," Kumar continued. "Maybe two years since you were plucked from the human packs roaming the ruins of Earth. Since you were pumped full of alien drugs, operated on, and reeducated with alien technology."

Wolf's brow crinkled. "You saying that makes me inhuman?"

"I'm saying it . . . confuses things."

"It makes you a child." Monroe pulled a cube of gum from one of his uniform pockets and popped it in his mouth. Chicken soup flavor, from the smell. "No offense intended, but a year and a half of real-world experience? You're practically a baby. I've known too many newbies like you. Hell, I used to be one. Eager to fight, convinced we're the toughest things in the galaxy."

"Aren't we?" asked Kumar, leaning forward like he was watching a sporting event.

"Physically, maybe. Intellectually?" He snorted and waved a hand. "You see what happens when we try to command our own ship."

"We beat the Prodryans," said Wolf.

"We got lucky. We barely survived an encounter with a handful of fighters the *Pufferfish* should have swatted like insects."

"We're SHS," Wolf protested. "We're not trained for any of this."

"It wouldn't matter if we were. That's why we get a Krakau command crew. Post-plague humans aren't bright enough—"

Wolf stood. "Are you calling me stupid?"

"I'm saying we're all stupid, you idiot. At least compared to what humanity was before."

"The same humanity that created a plague and turned itself into animals?" asked Wolf. "They don't sound too bright to me."

"We used to have dozens of languages and cultures," said Kumar. "Now we all speak 'Human.' One language, designed by the Krakau."

"More like thousands of languages and cultures," Doc interjected. *"Which might explain why Earth history is an unending list of arguments and violent misunderstandings over everything from land rights to the proper way of hanging toilet paper. Communication has never been your species' strength."*

"They fixed us," Kumar continued. "They give us jobs, purpose, even our culture. We call ourselves human, but are we? Or are we Krakau? Maybe we're something in between. Krakuman?"

"I am *not* calling myself Krakuman," snarled Wolf.

"Kumar has a point," Mops said, before the "discussion" could escalate further. "Intellect, creativity, reasoning . . . we consistently score lower on every test than pre-plague humans. Whatever humanity was before the plague, we've changed. But we *are* human."

"How do you figure?" asked Kumar.

"Because we have to be." She studied her team. They were exhausted. Anxious. Scared, though she doubted any of them would admit it. The command crew was dead, and the rest of the crew would happily eat them. Her team was trained to eradicate mold and fix clogged water filters, not battle Prodryan fighters. "Because we're what's left. Ten thousand or so reborn humans, with maybe a half billion surviving ferals back on Earth."

Kumar frowned. "I'm not sure I follow your logic."

"It's not about logic." Mops removed her empty food tube and used her thumb to wipe a single drop of gray sludge from the edge of her port. Her stomach felt bloated and hard, but the pressure would ease within an hour. "We were born of Earth. 'Human' is our word. Our history. Our connection to each other. Nobody gets to tell me I'm not human." Her eyes sought Kumar's. "Nobody else gets to tell us what that word means."

"What do you think it means?" he asked.

Mops turned, opening the question to the others.

"Survivors," said Monroe.

Wolf raised a fist. "Fighters."

"Hope." Mops shoved the empty tube into a disposal unit next to the couch. "Hope for the worlds we protect. Hope for our own planet and species."

She shook her head. "I don't mind the rest of the galaxy giving us a wide berth. It makes our jobs easier if they think we're monsters. But I refuse to become one. Destroying the Prodryan home world of Yan? Slaughtering billions of sentient beings, most of whom never raised a weapon against us? Hell, no. An act like that would define humanity forever. Who we are and who we become. I'll be damned if I let that happen."

Wolf looked around. "So instead, we'll be defined as toilet scrubbers and wall washers?"

"Nothing wrong with scrubbing toilets." Mops stood and stretched. "Finish up, then report to the bridge. This isn't over yet."

Mops stifled a yawn as she reread the instructions for calibrating the ship's primary communications pod.

Sending out a distress call was simple enough ... *if* you didn't mind everyone within range hearing it. Somehow, Mops didn't think it wise to announce to the galaxy that the Prodryans had a new weapon capable of incapacitating humans.

That meant a targeted, encrypted transmission, a private connection with Command back on Earth.

A normal signal from Andromeda 12 to Earth would take approximately eleven years to arrive. A communications pod, as Puffy had condescendingly explained, was essentially a miniaturized A-ring mounted near the front of the ship, used for accelerating and decelerating electromagnetic waves. Assuming you aligned the communications pod, correctly matched transmission speed to the relative motion of your target, set the proper power levels, and on and on and on.

"Simulation terminated," Puffy said brightly. The cartoon ship's face stretched into a caricatured frown. "By sending a signal of that power and duration, you've burned out the acceleration module in the communications pod. You completed 62.3% of the simulation. Would you like to try again?"

"How far did you get?" asked Wolf.

"Sixty-two. You?"

"I hit seventy-five point three once." She flushed. "Only twelve percent this time, though. I rushed it."

Mops removed her monocle, set it on one of the inactive consoles, and rubbed her eyes. Monroe was down examining the Prodryan fighter. Kumar had joined him, after he finished taking care of the Krakau bodies from the bridge and Captain's Cove. "Doc, what's the status on the rest of the crew?"

"All alive, according to scanners and security footage. I've noted eighteen injuries, most of which occurred during our

exchange with the Prodryan fighters. However, they're exhibiting more aggression."

"They're getting hungry." She sat back, hooking her arms over a higher bar for support. The ship was theoretically capable of feeding two hundred humans for six months without resupplying.

She imagined her team hunting ferals, setting traps and lures . . . Wolf tackling one . . . Mops and Monroe piling on while Kumar unsealed the feral's uniform and hooked a meal to their feeding tube. Then waiting while the contents were delivered to the feral's stomach. What could possibly go wrong?

"Doc, what does our nutrient paste taste like? If we broke open a bunch of tubes, would the crew eat it willingly?"

"I doubt it," said Wolf, before Doc could answer. "A bunch of us tried it back in training. It's like eating salty snot."

Maybe they could find something to make it more appetizing. The mess had a small supply of spices and condiments for Glacidae and Krakau palates.

"We should take them to the Ganymede Supply Depot," Wolf suggested. "Last I heard, that place had the mother of all rat infestations. If we dropped the crew off there, they could hunt their own meals. We'd solve two problems at once."

Grom's synthesized voice buzzed through Mops' collar speaker, saving her from having to respond. "I have something you need to see, sir. I've been going through the medical team's logs and video. This is beyond my job description, by the way. Working out of class entitles me to a bonus."

"The point, Grom?"

"It looks like Medical was making progress on identifying the contagion."

She sat up, fatigue pushed aside. "How much progress?"

"That's hard to say. Medical Commander Maria deleted those logs."

"What the hell?"

"Yes, the hell was confusing to me as well," agreed Grom. "Sending the logs now."

Mops' monocle darkened before she could respond. She saw MC Ave Maria, an older Krakau with dark red skin and thick, muscular limbs talking to one of the human medics, Doctor Curie. Two infantry troops were restrained in exam beds behind them.

"You can tell she's agitated," said Grom. "See how low her body is, and how her arms undulate in all directions? That's a defensive posture. It helps them sense predators approaching through the water."

A nurse came over, carrying a vial of human blood. Mops recognized him as Sherlock Holmes, one of the feral crew her team had encountered before. He was probably still glued to the wall where they'd left him. She made a mental note to do something about that.

"Test results came back the same as before," said Holmes. "Sir."

Maria barely looked up. "Your equipment is faulty. You must have forgotten to sterilize it."

"I know how to analyze blood samples," Holmes shot back. "And I know how to sterilize the damn equipment."

Maria shrank away, her skin darkening. "Then the samples must have been contaminated."

"All of them?" asked Doctor Curie. "That seems unlikely, Commander."

"Contaminated with *what*?" added Holmes. "I ran the tests twice, and the results were the same. The entire infantry team was infected with a derivative of something called Krakau venom."

"Impossible," said Maria. "Krakau aren't venomous."

Holmes' face turned redder. "Tell that to the damn computer!"

"All right, let's calm down and think about this rationally," said the doctor. "The computer identified a potential match. Does it have any recommendation for how to counter the effects?"

Holmes laughed, sounding a little hysterical. "I asked. It told me there was no such thing as Krakau venom."

Maria turned away, whispering so softly Doc had to enhance her words. "Commander Maria to Captain Brandenburg." She paused, head cocked. "Captain, please respond."

Mops checked the time stamp. This would have been right around the time the captain had died.

Holmes glared at Commander Maria. "Sir, if you know what this stuff is . . ."

"It is a mistake. Nurse, clear all test results from the system. I will recalibrate the equipment and run the analysis myself."

Holmes started to argue, but Doctor Curie put a hand on his shoulder. "Commander, a mistake seems unlikely," she said. "We've gotten the same results from different equipment and different samples. We don't have time—"

"Both of you will delete these test results and report to quarantine," said Maria. "Your stubbornness in this matter could be a symptom of infection. I'm ordering you kept in isolation until I've examined you both."

"We have an outbreak on this ship," Curie said tightly. "Medical is overwhelmed. You can't—"

"Do I have to summon Security?" asked Maria.

Mops' monocle turned clear. "Is that all?"

"Holmes and Curie left, as ordered," said Grom. "Sir, I've searched the medical records, and those test results are gone."

Mops frowned. "Medical records are protected. You shouldn't be able to run that kind of search."

Grom hesitated before answering. "I used—borrowed—your access codes as acting captain."

Mops clenched her jaw, swallowing her initial response. She could chew Grom out later. "Doc, what can you tell us about Krakau venom?"

"There's no such substance. Krakau aren't venomous."

By now, Wolf wasn't even pretending to work anymore. She stared openly at Mops. "This bioweapon has something to do with the Krakau?"

Mops didn't answer. She signaled Kumar and Monroe, opening a group comm channel. Monroe had seen more of the galaxy than anyone else on the team, and Kumar had probably read half the nonfiction in the EMC library. "Have either of you ever heard of something called Krakau venom?"

"Krakau aren't venomous," said Kumar.

"So I've been told. Monroe?"

"Not that I can recall, sir."

Damn. She replayed the recording from Medical. "Holmes and Curie could have been infected. We saw what happened with Lieutenant Khan. She was confused."

"I'm not the best judge of human emotion, but they didn't appear confused."

"No, they did not," Mops said slowly. "Grom, where did Commander Maria go after that?"

"She removed Holmes' and Curie's access to the *Pufferfish* medical systems, then went to the bridge. I've never seen a Krakau move that fast."

"We could be taking this too literally," Monroe said over the comm. "Maybe we're not talking about actual venom produced in their bodies. It could be slang for some kind of recreational drug. You can find all sorts of bizarre shit on the seedier stations and colonies, including more than two hundred varieties of Nusuran aphrodisiacs."

"That doesn't explain why the computer identified Krakau venom, then claimed there was no such thing," said Kumar.

"Sounds like someone tried to wipe Krakau venom from the computer's memory, but missed an entry somewhere," said Grom.

"Why would the Krakau deliberately try to hide this?" asked Mops.

Wolf sniffed. "Maybe one of the Krakau was helping the Prodryans."

"If so, it didn't work out very well for them, did it?" asked Grom.

Mops stood and paced circles around the bridge as she thought. "Forget what it's called. Look at what it does."

Wolf shrugged. "It turns humans feral."

"No, it doesn't," said Kumar.

"I beg to differ," Grom growled. "I had ample time to observe when I was trapped in Recreation, and those humans were very definitely feral."

"Kumar's right." Mops turned. "It doesn't turn us feral. It neutralizes whatever the Krakau did to fix us."

Grom sniffed. "Semantics."

"It would explain the secrecy," Monroe said slowly. "The Krakau won't even tell us what they pump into our blood to start the rebirth process. Too much potential for abuse."

"Assume 'Krakau venom' relates to the cure." Mops returned to the captain's station, her muscles tensing with each step. "We know the Prodryans can turn us feral again. Do you think they've also figured out how to cure feral humans?"

Monroe swore. "If they could raid Earth and round up a group of humans, they'd be able to make their own EMC soldiers."

"Grom, keep digging through medical records," said Mops. "I want to know everything they said or did as this outbreak spread."

"Does this mean you're giving me permission to keep using your access?"

"For now. But we *will* have a conversation about this later." Mops closed her comm and turned to Wolf. "I don't care how long it takes, we don't leave this bridge until we've contacted Command."

It was clear Wolf was as shaken as Mops felt. There was no hint of attitude or sarcasm in her "Yes, sir."

Mops turned to her own console and restarted the simulation.

8

EMC Combat Incident Report
Date: April 12, 2251 EGC (Earth Gregorian Calendar)

Location: Andromeda 12 system
Report Filed By: Lieutenant Marion S. Adamopoulos, EMC Serial Number 8251A

Enemy Force (Size, Species, Armament): Prodryan fighter ships (6), under command of someone called Assault Commander Burns Like Sunspots of Prodryan fighter squad 521. Armament . . . they mostly fired missiles at us.

EMC Casualties: None

Enemy Casualties: All of them

Has all tactical data from the encounter been uploaded to Command for review? No, but Puffy says he'll be happy to help *guide me through the process, and to recommend eleven post-combat tutorial programs.*

Other Notes: I'm considering designating Puffy an enemy combatant.

"I THINK WE'VE GOT IT." Wolf stabbed her index finger at her console screen.
Verifying connection to Stepping Stone Station . . . connection secure.
Estimated transmission time: six minutes, eleven seconds.
Begin message now.

Mops squeezed in beside Wolf. In theory, she should have been able to send the message from the captain's station, but transferring the connection to her console was one more opportunity to lose that connection. "This is Lieutenant Adamopoulos of the *EMCS Pufferfish*. We've been attacked and require immediate assistance. Command crew is dead. Most of the human crew is . . . incapacitated. Please acknowledge."

She sat back to wait. Six minutes and change for the signal to reach the Stepping Stone Station in orbit around Earth. Who knew how long it would take to notify the proper people. Then another six minutes for any response to make it back to the *Pufferfish*.

Given the distances involved, the relative motion of the two star systems, and the millions of other details that had to be properly calibrated, it was a miracle they could communicate at all. "Good work, Technician."

"Thanks." Wolf shifted impatiently and rubbed her eye.

"Take a break," said Mops. "I've got it from here."

Wolf was tired enough she didn't argue. She just nodded and started toward the lift. "Crew quarters aren't sterilized yet. Where—?"

"Mess hall," suggested Mops. Once Wolf left, it was Mops' turn to fidget. "Doc, play some music, would you? This is too damn quiet."

A moment later, her speaker began to hum with a slow-paced piece her monocle identified as a court song called "Na-kyangchun," from a country called Korea. "How many different nations were there?"

"One hundred eighty-seven, according to the last known historical records."

Almost one for every member of the *Pufferfish* crew. All with their own music and history and culture. She tried to wrap her mind around such variety, around a world where people could never hope to meet even a minuscule fraction of their fellow humans.

Would the Krakau ever restore her people to what they had once been? Would Mops live long enough to see it?

A familiar Krakau appeared on the screen, and the song cut off automatically. "Lieutenant Adamopoulos, this is Admiral Pachelbel of Stepping Stone. The last communication we received was from Captain Brandenburg. She said the *Pufferfish* had successfully destroyed two Prodryan pirate ships. We've been awaiting her follow-up report."

Admiral Pachelbel glanced at something offscreen. "We show you're still in the Andromeda 12 system. We're preparing medical assistance and a military escort for the *Pufferfish*. This channel is secure. Tell me everything about the crew's status and the condition of the ship. Don't worry. We're going to get you through this. Over."

"Admiral Pachelbel Canon," said Doc. *"Didn't you serve under her?"*

"My first duty rotation. I spent a year on Stepping Stone as a Plumbing tech. I found and fixed a recurring leak in a reclamation line that was contaminating the brine in her quarters with ammonia. She kind of took me under her wing—tentacle—after that."

The admiral was large for a Krakau. Her thick yellow-and-brown limbs reminded Mops of distended bananas. White skin ringed her beak and eyes, a sign of old age.

For the first time since they entered Andromeda 12, Mops felt like the currents were flowing in her favor. Some high-ranking Krakau had trouble seeing humans as anything more than grunts, low-intellect soldiers who existed to keep their mouths shut and follow orders. In contrast, Admiral Pachelbel had gone out of her way to get to know the humans on Stepping Stone. She would take Mops' report seriously.

Mops pressed the broadcast button. "Nice to hear your voice, Admiral. There's no easy way to say this. The entire human crew, with the exception of myself and my team, have gone feral. This . . . led to the deaths of all nonhuman crew, save Technician Gromgimsidalgak.

"I believe the Prodryan pirates lured the *Pufferfish* here deliberately to infect us with some sort of bioweapon, possibly as a test. Captain Brandenburg sent infantry teams to the Nusuran freighter to clear any remaining pirates and help with repairs. That's the most likely point of infection.

"We've secured most of the feral crew and run a level one decontamination to clean a small portion of the ship. This appears to have eliminated the contaminant. But we have no way of curing the affected crew.

"An additional six Prodryan fighters arrived in-system a short time later and attempted to take the *Pufferfish*. We sustained minor damage and the loss of one shuttle, but we were able to destroy all six enemy ships."

She hesitated, then added, "Medical tentatively identified the chemical basis of the bioweapon as Krakau venom. Over."

She switched off the comm and sat back to wait. Twelve minutes passed. Then twelve more. Mops was about to summon Wolf to make sure the communications pod was still aligned and functioning when Pachelbel appeared on the screen again.

"Lieutenant Adamopoulos, we're revising our plans. Our

medical department will transmit instructions to sedate the rest of your crew for their safety and your own. After that, you'll secure the crew in their acceleration chambers and return to Earth. We're preparing a program you'll be able to load directly into navigation that should automate the A-ring jump process. We should have that to you within five hours."

Pachelbel whistled softly and moved closer. "Knowing you, you're asking what the hell Krakau venom is, and why it necessitates a change of plan."

"You could say that," Mops muttered. Five hours to receive instructions for the A-ring jump home. It was faster than waiting for an escort to show up and install a new command crew on the *Pufferfish*. Potentially safer, too, given the status of the *Pufferfish*'s people.

"Krakau venom is the code name for an old weapons program," Pachelbel explained. "A program we thought had been discontinued. Alliance Intelligence believed all samples had been destroyed. Obviously, they were mistaken. Not only have the Prodryans discovered the program, it sounds like they've improved upon it. For the infection to have gotten through standard decon procedures and spread so quickly, they must have developed a microbial carrier capable of rapid reproduction.

"The good news is that your Glacidae technician is not a viable host. A standard acid bath followed by a thorough sanishower should remove any infectious material they might be carrying, after which they should be safe to join the rest of your team. Make sure they breathe deeply during the shower to kill anything in their lungs. You can continue using level one decontamination procedures on the unoccupied parts of the ship."

Her next words hit Mops like a herd of stampeding Quetzalus. "Unfortunately, we have no way of reversing the damage to your crew. I'm sorry, Mops. I know how you care for your people."

"You haven't even examined them," Mops protested.

Pachelbel continued as if Mops hadn't spoken. Which, from her perspective, she hadn't. Mops' words wouldn't reach her for six minutes. "When you return to Stepping Stone Station, you and your team will be taken into quarantine for examination. I'll need you to prepare a full report, with as much detail as possible. Have everyone on your team do the same. Every detail, no matter how small, could help us counter this threat."

The admiral glanced at something off-screen. "I'm sorry about your crew, Mops. It sounds like you've done an exceptional job under very difficult circumstances. I know it's no consolation, but I imagine you'll receive a commendation for your actions."

"Thank you, sir," Mops said automatically. "What will happen to the rest of my crew?"

Another interminable wait. "We'll examine them and do everything we can, but we can't risk this thing spreading. The official recommendation from Colonial Military Command is that they be . . . put down."

"*Put down?*" Mops whispered, fighting a surge of anger. From the way Pachelbel's tentacles were twitching, she wasn't happy about this either. "Admiral, there has to be a way to help my crew. The Prodryans might have a cure. Or we could at least *try* decontaminating them. We can't give up on almost two hundred human beings."

The response, when it arrived, was firm. "They aren't just human beings anymore, Mops. They're potential weapons. Living biological bombs. I'll remind MilCom of your crew's service and urge them to consider every alternative, but our priority is the preservation of your species. Prepare your ship for the return A-ring jump, and do not mention Krakau venom to anyone else. Admiral Pachelbel out."

Mops killed the connection. "Doc, Admiral Pachelbel gave me a five-hour countdown." The numbers appeared on her monocle, at the edge of her vision. "Now pull up everything we have on Pachelbel."

"*Sir?*"

Mops didn't answer. A moment later, the information began scrolling onto her monocle. Pachelbel Canon was fifty-three years old, bordering on elderly for a Krakau. She had four offspring, all adults now, with two partners. She'd started with the Krakau Interstellar Military twenty-four years ago, shortly after the founding of the EMC.

She wasn't one of the hard-shelled Krakau warriors, but had served as a weapons technician before being promoted to tactical officer. She'd also spent two years as Alliance liaison officer on a Merraban warship, after which she'd transferred from Interstellar to Colonial Military.

For the last fourteen years of her career, she'd been working with Earth and humanity as she progressed through the ranks.

"What are you searching for?"

A twitch of Mops' eye flicked her monocle's display ahead to the next record. "Pachelbel knows more about humanity than pretty much any other Krakau. Not the science behind the cure, necessarily, but who we are as a species. She also knows me, personally."

"You're aware, I assume, that none of those words provide an answer to my question?"

"She didn't have to tell me anything. She could have ordered us to sedate the crew and bring the ship home, and I would have done it. Instead, she volunteered that MilCom intended to have the crew killed. 'Put down,' like animals."

"Perhaps she felt bad withholding information."

"She's been an admiral for sixteen years. She protects information every day." Mops activated her comm. "Wolf, join us in docking bay two. Monroe, Kumar, we have less than five hours to get answers from that fighter."

"What happens in five hours?" Monroe responded.

"Hell, Monroe. I don't even understand what's happening now." She replayed her exchange with Admiral Pachelbel in her mind. "But I think we've been given a window to try to save our crew, and that's when it closes."

The Prodryan fighter was in sad shape. Most of the damage had come from the A-ring explosion, but its haphazard arrival on the *Pufferfish* had added additional dents . . . both to the fighter and the inside of docking bay two.

The fighter's port wing had been completely torn off; the other was crumpled inward. Large gashes ran along the tubular central body.

"Their ships are built like giant metal Prodryans," scoffed Wolf. "What ego."

"They're not the fastest ships, but they're maneuverable," said Monroe. "They can fly in space and in atmospheres up to almost twice the pressure of Earth's. Missile bays are on the bottom. They've got a single plasma beam mounted up front. The wings fold in for A-ring jumps, but most of the time they keep 'em spread, even in space. They serve as heat-radiating fins. The color patterns show family lineage, battles won, stuff like that."

"What patterns?" asked Mops. The wing was a burnt mottling of grays and blacks. Doc did something to Mops' monocle, and suddenly she saw red and orange and pink swirling through the crushed ruin of the wing. The design reminded her a little of the storms of Jupiter. "Have you figured out how to get inside?"

"We were just talking about that, sir." Kumar pointed to one of the gashes in the main body. "I say we use a plastorch. Enlarge that big hole."

"Why not use explosives to blow open the hatch?" asked Wolf. "It would be quicker."

"You have that kind of explosive sitting around?" Monroe popped his gum. "You know how to use it without killing yourself or blowing a hole in our hull?"

"No explosives," said Mops, cutting off Wolf's response. She studied the holes. They were too small for anyone, human or Glacidae, to squeeze through. "How long to cut your way in?"

"The armor's the biggest challenge." Kumar rapped his knuckles against the hull. "An hour, maybe?"

"Too bad we can't just have Grom take a dump on it," muttered Wolf. "That ought to burn right through."

Kumar cocked his head. "Given the acidity of Glacidae waste, you'd need at least thirty kilograms of—"

"Just get it open," Mops snapped. She'd sent Grom for an acid bath. It would be a little while before they were clean and able to assist with the fighter. Mops intended to have the ship fully dissected with the computer equipment ready by the time Grom arrived.

Staring over Kumar's shoulder wouldn't make the work go any faster, so she retreated to the closest maintenance hub to pull up the instructions from Stepping Stone for sedating the rest of the crew. She'd have to reroute air circulation and bypass eleven different air quality monitors and alarms, but that should be simple enough.

"We have a potential problem."

"What's that?"

"You told me to get the crew out of the way. I locked nine ferals in Medical. You'll need to get past them to reach these sedatives."

"Can you lure them into the convalescence ward?"

"I'll devote my full processing power to the task of opening and closing a few doors."

"Don't forget to read them a story, too." They'd be hungry and restless, eager to hunt. Mops worked on prepping the air vents while Doc began reading.

" 'One morning, when Gregor Samsa woke from troubled dreams, he found himself transformed in his bed into a horrible vermin.' "

"You're reading *Metamorphosis* to a bunch of reverted humans? That's harsh."

"It's not like they understand. But if you'd prefer, I could switch to The Strange Case of Dr. Jekyll and Mr. Hyde.*"*

Mops shook her head and kept working, overriding alarms

and resetting air circulation to draw from Medical. Roughly sixty percent of the ship was clear, and could be sanitized with a level one decon. "Doc, a little help please? Given the target dosage, how much of this stuff do we need to release?"

The figures appeared on her monocle, but before she could do anything with them, a voice through her comm made her jump.

"We're in!" said Monroe.

She sat back, grimacing at the stiffness in her shoulder. Had it been an hour already? "Grom, are you done with your bath yet?"

A drawn-out sound, like an impossibly flatulent elephant, played over her speaker.

"I'm not sure how to translate that."

"Move your ass, Technician. Meet us in docking bay two."

The first thing Mops saw when she entered the bay was Kumar dragging a dead Prodryan out of the ship. Most of a dead Prodryan, rather.

Kumar straightened when he spotted her. "Sir, request permission to—"

"There will be no amateur autopsies," Mops cut him off. As she got closer, she could see where shrapnel had punctured the Prodryan's torso armor. Dark orange blood with the consistency of hull paint dripped onto the floor.

Wolf pulled a second body halfway out of the hole, then yanked a sidearm from the Prodryan's belt. "Dibs on the pistol!"

"The EMC does not now, nor will we ever, work on a 'dibs' system." Mops held out a hand. Wolf slumped, but gave her the weapon. The grip was designed for smaller hands, and a notch in the curved stock looked like it should rest against the owner's forearm barb. "Doc, do we have any specs on this model?"

"It's a hand-held A-gun, similar to EMC infantry issue. Command believes the Prodryans stole the design from us.

Their ammo isn't compatible with our weapons, but you should be able to use it, assuming there's no personal security. And that it wasn't damaged in the attack."

"They're nasty," said Monroe. "Not very accurate, but they've got a burst mode that can spray a dozen shots in the blink of an eye. I'd keep it on single-fire. The things are prone to overheating, and then . . ." He spread his hands to mimic an explosion.

"Good to know." Mops slid the gun into one of the equipment straps on her harness, being careful not to touch the protruding nub that appeared to be the trigger. "Grom should be joining us soon. Any idea where we'll find the computer system in this thing? I want to know about their mission, where they launched from, who they reported to, and every last bit of information on this bioweapon."

She stepped closer and helped Wolf haul the remaining Prodryan the rest of the way out. "Leave the bodies alone," she reminded Kumar as she poked her head and shoulders inside the ship. Her monocle compensated automatically for the relative darkness.

The walls were curved metal, striped with deep ridges and grooves. The interior was separated into three oval pods connected end-to-end, with a larger, spherical room in the back. Straps and the contour of the floor suggested the Prodryans lay on their backs while in flight, with most of the controls and displays directly above them. Exposed cables and wires clustered where the head would rest.

Mops glanced back at the bodies. Both wore helmets with visors—or the remains of a visor, in one case. It looked like the cables hooked directly into the helmets, making them a possible connection point to the main system.

She pulled herself inside and lay back in the closest compartment. It felt like she'd crawled into a metal cocoon. "Doc, adjust my vision. Show me the Prodryan visible spectrum."

Her monocle flickered, first turning dark, then brightening until she had to squint, before settling back to a normal level.

Instead of the dingy black-and-gray interior, she saw squares of bright blue-and-violet text on rich brown walls. "What do they say?"

"Some of it is labels and instructions for the various instruments. There's a ship's identification or registration code: 156934-C. To your left is . . . I think it's a poem."

"Show me." As she focused on a given line of the angular text, a translation appeared on her monocle. "This . . . isn't very good."

> *The scars of battle make us strong.*
> *The blood of our enemies makes us strong.*
> *The loneliness of space makes us strong.*
> *Victory makes us strong.*
> *Death . . . does not make us strong.*
> *But death in battle brings the vengeance-strength to our*
> *   hivemates.*
> *And thus death makes us strong!*
> *(Except for those who are dead.)*
> *Victory to the Prodryan Expanse!*

"I can confirm that neither the rhythm nor the description are any better in the original language."

It went on like that for another four stanzas. Mops turned her attention instead to the different cables and controls, searching for information about the computer systems. "This can't be the first time the EMC captured a Prodryan fighter. Don't we have records on how they work?"

"If so, I'm not able to access them. A good portion of the Pufferfish's *files are classified and off-limits to us, even with your increased access as acting captain."*

To her left, a cracked pane of transparent plastic or silicate protected what looked like personal mementos: a green seed pod the size of her thumb, a glass bead bracelet, a toy knife, and a porous brown rock several centimeters in diameter.

"A scent-stone," said Doc, noting the direction of her gaze.

*"Prodryans often use such stones to preserve the scent of a mate.
Depending on their mate's hygiene, of course."*

Mops crawled through the ship until she reached the larger
chamber in the back. It was big enough for three Prodryans—
if they were on good terms and kept their wings flattened. The
curved walls were honeycombed with storage drawers and
control panels and access ports.

A sound like dozens of stiff brooms sweeping the walls
made her whirl. Grom had followed her into the ship, their
shell gleaming wetly. They smelled of methane and cleaning
chemicals. The feathery tendrils of their legs scraped the interior of the ship with every movement.

Without a word, they snatched one of the wires that connected to the Prodryans' helmets. Holding the wire in one digging claw, they used two others to strip the coating. They pulled
a small, beeping box with a blinking yellow light from their
harness and clamped a lead onto the exposed wire.

"This will let me trace the wire back through the system,"
they said, their face centimeters from the hull. "It's old technology, but reliable. Can you hear the signal pulse? It will lead
us to the source of any data the crew receive through this connection."

Grom crawled through the ship into the back chamber, for
once unconcerned with keeping a comfortable distance from
humans. Their legs brushed Mops' ankle as they ran delicate
feelers over a panel in the entryway. "I believe what we want
is here."

"Can you access it?"

"The memory core will be encrypted." They pulled another
tool from their harness, a metal wand with a cord stretching to
a small battery pack. Grom switched it on and moved it around
the edge of the panel. "The screws are on the inside. Standard
precaution to keep the ignorant from accessing the system.
You need a focused magnetic screwdriver to pop the shell."

After a series of five clicks, the panel popped free and fell
onto the floor. Grom peered inside. "The crystal harness looks

standard. Power supply is operational. This thing might be salvageable after all. It's frozen right now—some sort of software deadlock. Let me see if I can get it running."

"What are you doing?"

"Turning it off and back on again. This looks like a modified NR-4 tactical computer. If I can boot it into recovery mode, we should be able to bypass the initial authentication and at least learn the basic specs." They jabbed another tool into the guts of the computer. The ship's lights flickered once and died again. "It will also let me safely remove the mem crystal. I can plug it into the *Pufferfish* systems and try to crack the encryption."

"You want to plug an alien computer core from a hostile ship into the *Pufferfish*? What if it infects our systems?"

"Do you take me for some incompetent h—for a fool?" Grom's mouth clicked nervously. "Maintenance has stacks of isolated computers with no connection to the rest of the ship. I'll plug it into one of those. Worst case scenario, it fries a single backup unit that was just gathering dust anyway."

Mops wasn't sure which she found more insulting, Grom's bitten-off reference to "incompetent humans," or the implication that her team would allow dust to gather anywhere on the ship.

"I'll need command-level clearance to access the decryption software," Grom continued.

"I'm sure that can be arranged."

"Let me isolate the crystal harness. Once I've disconnected—"

A blue spark illuminated the chamber. Grom toppled backward. A scent like burnt oil filled the air.

"What the hell was that?" Mops snapped.

Grom twisted upright, leaving a greasy black smear where they'd fallen. The spark had startled them as much or more than it had Mops. They poked their head into the panel and sniffed. "I think that was a physical safeguard . . . probably designed to fry the crystal."

Mops took a deep breath. "And the chances of salvaging anything useful from it?"

They turned to look at her, brown eyes even wider than normal. "I . . . I'm sorry, sir."

She didn't trust herself to answer. Grom had done their best, but they were trained for routine maintenance of EMC systems, not infiltrating enemy military hardware. She crawled past them and exited the fighter. From the somber expressions of her team, they'd all heard what happened.

"I want every millimeter of this wreck searched, inside and out," she said softly. "Find every scrap of information you can. I want to know where they came from, who they reported to, what their orders were, and everything they knew about Krakau venom."

Kumar cleared his throat. "Sir, wouldn't Alliance Intelligence techs be better equipped for this?"

"Yes." Mops waited while Grom crawled out of the ship behind her. "But Command intends to let the rest of the crew die."

Monroe's right hand twitched. "Sir?"

"I spoke with Admiral Pachelbel. Command believes containment is our top priority, and every infected human is a potential threat to the EMC and our entire species."

"Well . . . she's not exactly wrong," said Kumar.

Wolf spat. "If this shit is such a threat, shouldn't they try to study it? Figure out a cure?"

"Mentioning Krakau venom spooked her." Mops thought back to the conversation. "That's when she changed the plan from sending an escort to having us run a preprogrammed A-ring jump back to Earth."

"Risky," said Monroe. "None of us are trained for that. It would be safer to stick with the escort, and would only take a few more hours. They could send a team to pilot us back home. We know enough now to protect them from exposure."

"Unless they're not worried about exposure," said Wolf. "This could be a cover-up. A conspiracy to make sure nobody else finds out about Krakau venom. If that's the case, they'll probably kill us as soon as we get back."

"Is unfounded paranoia a sign of feral reversion?" asked Grom.

Wolf whirled. "This is *founded* paranoia, dammit!"

"There's a simpler explanation," said Kumar. "When a dog turns rabid, you shoot it."

"What's a dog?" asked Grom.

The admiral's phrasing echoed in Mops' mind. *Put down.*

"They can still examine the crew after they're dead," Kumar continued. "It would be safer, since you don't have to worry about them struggling or escaping. Let's be honest. To most of the galaxy, humans are little more than animals."

"Well, most of the galaxy can kiss my ass," muttered Wolf.

"That's enough." Mops hammered a fist against the fighter's hull, cutting off further discussion. "We're not an intel team, but we're the only hope this crew has."

"Maybe we don't need Intelligence," muttered Kumar, picking up one of the Prodryan helmets. Mops jabbed a warning finger at Grom before they could comment. "I need a vacuum snake, at least three meters long."

"Wolf, there should be a five-meter snake in the bay supply closet," said Mops. "What are you thinking, Kumar?"

"Prodryans are carnivores. They eat about once a day, swallowing their prey whole, then hock up pellets of anything they can't digest." He held out the helmet. "This attachment here with the low-pressure valve would be right in front of the mouth. What's a spacesuit without built-in plumbing, right?"

Grom scooted away from Kumar. "You want to go spelunking for Prodryan mouth-shit?"

"If we examine what they were eating, maybe it will help us figure out where they were before they attacked the *Pufferfish*." Kumar tossed the helmet aside. "The pellets are cleaner than human or Glacidae excrement, and depending on how it's processed and stored in the fighter—"

"I don't need the details," Grom interrupted.

Wolf returned, hauling a coiled tube of segmented metal. She pressed a button on one end, and the tube unrolled to its full five-meter length. She passed the end to Kumar, who climbed into the fighter.

A few moments later, the tube seemed to come to life, segments squeezing together and pushing apart like a worm. Its diameter expanded to three centimeters, then contracted again. With each surge, it crawled deeper into the Prodryan plumbing system.

"Want a snake's-eye view?" offered Doc. *"I can hook you up to the camera, show you what the inside of a Prodryan mouth-toilet pipe looks like."*

"I'm good, thank you."

"Chewing through the first valve," Kumar called out. It didn't take long before the snake was moving again. The ripples in the protruding end grew stronger, and a chunk of shredded metal and plastic popped out of the back and onto the floor. The remains of a second valve followed less than a minute later. "Here we go."

The snake's movements slowed, becoming almost gentle. A short time later, it began depositing a series of dark green spherical clods on the bay floor.

Kumar scooted backward out of the fighter, careful to avoid dislodging the snake. He yanked on his gloves and crouched beside the closest dirtlike clump. "Looks like Prodryans use the same vacuum-tech as most species to dry and sterilize their waste." He crushed the clump in his hand, letting the granules fall between his fingers. "The water gets reclaimed and circulated back to the crew."

"You know you're spreading Prodryan shit all over the deck," Wolf pointed out.

"Technically, it's Prodryan regurgitate." He grabbed another clump. "See how this one is bigger and lumpier than the others? I didn't see anywhere on the ship to store live food, so they're probably eating some form of prepared nutrients while on board. Smooth and bland, without much waste material. But this chunk's irregular."

He dug carefully into the material, revealing what looked like bits of bone and blackened scales, along with a small, curved beak. "They didn't eat this on the ship. This was from wherever they last docked."

"Where was that?" asked Mops.

Kumar's triumphant expression faded. "I'm not sure."

"Give me a closer look at that beak."

Mops pulled on a glove and took the beak, bringing it close to her monocle.

"Turn it so I can see the underside."

While the top of the beak was black, the underside was lined with a series of curved white ridges, like sharp ribs running the length of the beak.

"Humans call it a balloon lizard. Four of those curved beak pieces come together like flower petals. It can swallow prey up to twice its own size. They're from Cuixique, but Quetzalus colonists have successfully bred it to survive on several other settlements."

"It's a Quetzalus lizard," Mops said.

"I'm surprised eating that didn't kill them." Kumar was trying to fit two small bones together, as if he wanted to rebuild the lizard. "Humans can eat pretty much anything, regardless of its biological basis, and the most we'll get is a stomachache and a nasty trip to the head. But for most species, eating an animal from another world means a quick, painful death."

"A good chef can tailor meals to other species," Wolf said quietly. "Your body might not get any nutrition from it, but they'll neutralize any toxins and make sure it can pass through your system without . . . complications."

The way Wolf was avoiding eye contact . . . "Dammit, Wolf," said Mops, matching her soft tone. "How long have you—"

"A couple of times, when we were between jobs." Wolf shrugged one shoulder. "It was me and a handful of guys from infantry. Nobody lost control or went feral or anything like that."

"It's not unheard of," said Monroe. "Some of the troops think eating gives them an edge. Brings out the aggression in battle. Depending on what they eat, the most vicious side effect is heartburn and gas."

"The regs against eating are decades old," added Wolf, apparently encouraged by Monroe's comments. "Can you name one instance of someone going feral just because they had an unauthorized snack?"

Grom reared back, legs twitching furiously at Wolf. "You threatened to eat *me*. You were serious?"

Wolf raised her hands. "I have much higher standards for what goes in my mouth."

Grom bristled more.

"Cool it, both of you," said Mops.

"Do you want to chew me out, or do you want to figure out where these Prodryans came from?" Wolf snapped, regaining a bit of her usual defiance.

"You're right." Before Wolf could gloat, Mops pierced her with a glare. "The chewing out can come later." She turned her attention back to the clumps on the floor. "We're looking for someplace that gets enough interspecies traffic to have specialized chefs on the payroll. That eliminates most colony worlds. It has to be somewhere the Prodryans could go without people asking too many questions. Doc, give me a list of all known locations that meet those criteria."

Doc brought up a list of about a dozen space stations and settlements.

Wolf picked up another clod. She crushed it in one gloved hand, and used her fingers to tug out a length of tattered black string. A clump of something shiny and best left unidentified stuck to one end. "Coacalos Station."

"Are you sure?" asked Mops, checking the list. Coacalos Station was the third name Doc had provided.

"They use strings like this to muzzle anything served live. The strings are color-coded to show which species can eat it without dying. Black for Prodryans. Red for Nusurans. Blue for Glacidae, and so on."

"Do we report this to Command?" asked Monroe.

Nobody spoke. It wasn't a question of whether the Alliance had people who could do a better job digging up the Prodryans' secrets. They absolutely could. The fried mem crystal in the fighter proved that point.

"Not yet," Mops said quietly.

Grom fidgeted. "We were ordered to return to Earth."

"I know." Nobody said the word "treason," but Mops suspected they were all thinking it. Most of them, at least. Kumar was busy sweeping up the dusty remnants of Prodryan waste pellets and only appeared to be half-listening to the conversation.

She considered offering them the chance to back out, something like, *"Anyone who doesn't want to be court-martialed or worse, speak up now."* But sometimes noble sentiments had to give way to practicality, and she was shorthanded already. "We're going to Coacalos Station."

Kumar glanced up. "How? We still don't know how to fly the *Pufferfish*."

Mops checked the timer on her monocle. "You've got several hours left to master those navigation tutorials. Finish up here, and let's get to work."

_9_

This is my firearm.[1] There are many like it (because they're mass-produced to precise standards at the Lunar Armaments Manufacturing Facility), but this one is mine.[2]

My firearm is an extension of my body. (My firearm is not, however, a metaphorical extension of my genitalia.) Without me, it is useless. Without it, I am incomplete.

I will shoot swiftly. I will shoot true. I will shoot the enemy before they shoot me. If that fails, I will shoot the enemy after they shoot me. But before is preferable.

I will respect my firearm and treat it with the same care I would my own flesh. I will learn its strengths and limitations. I will learn to operate it to its fullest capacity. I will follow cleaning and maintenance protocols to the letter.

I will not use my firearm to clear fuel line jams.[3]

What counts in life is not the stripe on my holster, but my accuracy in battle. I will honor my firearm, my training, my crew, my species, and my Corps.

— _EMC Firearms Oath, based on Earth Rifleman's Creed, by General William H. Rupertus_

———

1. Firearms are property of the Earth Mercenary Corps.

2. See note #1.

3. See incident report #6142L, "Destruction of EMCS *Army Ant: Lessons Learned."*

"**H**OW MANY IS THAT?**"** Mops asked as she secured Private Carrie Fisher into an acceleration pod. Fisher was another smoothie, less than two weeks out of basic training after being reborn at the Siberian Medical Facility. She was a good kid, with enough energy and enthusiasm for three people, and deserved better.

"One hundred twenty-two," said Doc.

Leaving roughly seventy unconscious humans to find and drag into the acceleration chambers, Mops grabbed her now-empty maglev stretcher and checked her monocle to see who was next.

The sedative had worked just as Command had promised. Another hour or so, and they'd have the whole crew strapped in. She checked her oxygen and suit integrity as she returned to the target range to collect two more napping infantry troops. "Kumar, any progress?"

"I've gotten through 4.5 percent of the A-ring tutorial without killing everyone."

Mops swallowed her first three responses. "Technically, that qualifies as progress. Keep at it."

"At this rate, it will be a minimum of two-point-eight days before Kumar successfully completes his first simulated *jump."*

"I know." She checked the status of the rest of her team. Wolf and Monroe were on decks C and F, respectively, gathering more ferals. Grom was on the bridge with Kumar, trying to dig through the ship's logs to find any other information on Krakau venom. "What if we hired someone for navigation? We could put out a call to the colonies, or maybe ask one of the Nusurans from that freighter, assuming they're still hanging around the system."

"Aside from violating eight security regulations, the differences between a Nusuran freighter and an EMCS cruiser are too great. It would be like expecting a Glacidae to be able to pilot a shuttle based on their ability to ride a snow-serpent."

"We've got an incoming signal from Command for you, sir."

"Thanks, Grom." Mops checked her timer. "They're twenty minutes early. Send an acknowledgment and relay the message to me."

"I'll try. Wolf left some notes on the communications console, but her handwriting is atrocious. Stand by."

Two minutes later, her monocle changed to a visual of Admiral Pachelbel. Mops cleared her throat. "Grom. . . ?"

After another minute, the message restarted, this time with sound. Pachelbel offered a brief greeting and reminded Mops once again about the danger of their situation, and the importance of following orders. The rest was a data dump Doc identified as the emergency override instructions for navigation.

"You'll have to load and authorize it. Once you do, the ship should take us straight back to Earth."

"How long will the jump take?"

"Eleven light-years? It looks like they've got us flying pretty close to top speed, so I'd say just under a half hour."

Thirty minutes until Pachelbel and the rest of Command would expect to see the *Pufferfish*'s decel signature flare in Earth's system. They could probably stall another hour or so, saying they were getting the rest of the crew into their acceleration pods. That meant ninety minutes to figure out how to fly this thing.

She paused. "Doc, how well can you read that nav program?"

"I don't know the navigation controls enough to understand what it all means, but I can read the code. It's significantly clearer and more straightforward than trying to read Human."

Mops allowed herself a small smile. "Grom, I have a new assignment for you and Doc."

The bridge acceleration chamber was designed for Krakau. The acceleration pods were cramped, designed to fill with viscous, honey-colored fluid. A set of syringes injected a mild blood thickener, providing additional protection to Krakau brain tissue.

Mops had taken one look and ordered her team down to the pods at Battle Hub One. The bridge pods could probably be reconfigured for humans, but she had neither the time nor the technical knowledge to do it.

Wolf and Monroe were already secured in their pods, while Kumar and Grom hunched over the backup navigation console.

"You're sure this will get us to Coacalos?" It was the fourth time Wolf had asked the question.

"Nothing is certain until it's done," answered Grom, also for the fourth time. With Doc's help, they'd copied and reprogrammed a new emergency navigation override program, this one targeting the edge of Alliance space.

"Yeah, well, you crash us into a star, and I'm gonna eat your face," grumbled Wolf.

"Noted." Grom flicked their hind legs in Wolf's direction, a sign of annoyance. "I don't believe you understand the complexity of this operation. Navigating these distances is like standing on the surface of your Earth and using a pistol to hit a target the size of your eyeball on the moon. We've run more than twenty simulations, only one of which resulted in catastrophic failure."

"What kind of failure?" demanded Wolf.

"We emerged a thousand kilometers deep in the star. I've adjusted the parameters, and the rest have been within acceptable ranges. Though the damage to the *Pufferfish* adds an element of chance that's impossible to fully predict."

Mops settled into her own pod and began rereading the information Doc had pulled up on Coacalos Station. The station resembled a giant volcano spinning through space, orbitally leashed to a hypergiant star roughly a hundred and fifty times the mass of Earth's sun.

That much mass would affect their A-ring jump, so Grom had plotted a conservative course that would likely put them several days' journey from the station. Not ideal, but better than getting sucked into the star or looped into tight orbit and shredded by slingshot forces.

Thick black leaves covered the station's exterior. They acted as solar collectors, with roots stretching more than a kilometer through the rock walls to the station interior. The Quetzalus who owned and ran the station tapped the plants as their primary source of power.

The station was independent of both the Quetzalus home world of Cuixique and the Krakau Alliance. The Coacalos family was part of a minority who'd broken with their clan and objected to joining the Alliance. They'd originally intended to form an independent colony, but after years of ugly legal battles, the Quetzalus High Court and the Alliance Judicial Council had proclaimed that any such colony or space station would fall under Alliance jurisdiction.

Which was why Coacalos Station was, legally speaking, a spaceship: an enormous, self-sustaining spaceship parked in a wide stellar orbit. A spaceship large enough to welcome other ships and their crews, provide living space for trade and recreation, and to do pretty much anything an official space station might do. But it could travel from one system to another under its own power, and that—technically—made it a spaceship. That legal technicality gave the Coacalos family absolute command over their "ship" and everything that went on there.

Alliance law didn't matter. Only the law of the family.

Anyone was welcome, even Prodryans, though Mops wasn't sure how the family would feel about hosting potential bioterrorists. It probably depended on how much money those bioterrorists put into Coacalos coffers.

She glanced down at the Prodryan pistol she'd taken from the fighter. She'd forgotten to store it in a security locker. "Doc, what are the marksmanship ratings for the team?"

"Their ratings . . . oh, dear. Monroe has a sharpshooter rating with rifle and is listed as marksman with pistol, but he hasn't been to a range since he left the infantry. The others passed minimum firearm certification—eventually—when they enlisted. Technician Wolf required three attempts to pass basic pistol certification."

"What about Grom?"

"They are proficient with Glacidae small arms."

"Good."

"However, the Pufferfish *does not stock Glacidae weaponry."*

To her right, Monroe whispered something inaudible. A moment later, a message from him appeared on Mops' monocle. *"Are you sure about all this?"*

Mops responded in kind, speaking too quietly for anyone but her suit's mic to pick up her words. "I'm not letting this crew die."

"I'm with you a hundred percent," said Monroe. *"But bringing this team to Coacalos?"*

"I've never been," Mops admitted. "How bad is this going to be?"

"Rumor has it the Coacalos family was one of the backers of the Ventazos rebellion."

Mops whistled softly. "I knew they preferred their independence, but I had no idea. . . ."

Thirty-six years ago, a Quetzalus colony called Ventazos had rebelled against their home world of Cuixique and the Alliance. Government officials with any suspected ties to Cuixique were imprisoned or killed. Alien diplomats suffered the same fate.

The Alliance sent the newly formed EMC to restore order. The Quetzalus had laughed and transmitted messages mocking the puny human police force.

The laughter, like the subsequent fighting, was short-lived.

While most Quetzalus these days supported the Alliance and dismissed the Ventazos rebels as misguided extremists, the species had never forgotten that humiliation at the hands — and guns — of the EMC. If the Coacalos family had been on the side of the rebels . . .

"I'm counting on you to help keep the team out of trouble," Mops said quietly.

Monroe's snort drew startled looks from the others.

"I think we're ready," said Kumar.

"Start the countdown and secure yourselves in your pods." Mops watched their status on her monocle until both showed as ready for the jump. She double-checked the rest of the crew as well, making sure none of them had woken up or gotten loose from their pods.

"Funny thing," Kumar said casually. "You'd think we were committing treason when we actually made the jump. But according to regulations, we crossed that stream the instant we modified the program from Command."

"Good to know." Mops sat back. "Monroe, don't forget to spit out your gum."

"How did you— Yes, sir."

Strangely enough, it *was* comforting to know they'd already crossed the line and betrayed the Alliance. It took away some of the pressure and anxiety, allowing her to close her eyes and wait in relative peace. Given what lay ahead, she'd take any peace she could get.

They'd emerged more than a billion kilometers from the station, roughly two hundred million kilometers beneath the orbital plane. At this distance, Coacalos would have picked up their deceleration signature, but shouldn't have been able to identify them as an EMC ship. That would change as they got within range of the security beacons and satellites scattered around the station.

Assuming they could get within range. For half a day now, they'd drifted in space while Kumar continued trying to figure out how to fly the ship.

Much as the delay gnawed at Mops' patience, her team needed the break. She'd caught a nap herself before heading down to the target range to try to relax. After making sure the range had been fully sterilized, she went through several practice rounds, then called Wolf down to join her.

By the time Wolf arrived, Mops had reset the range to its default configuration: a rectangular room thirty meters in length, ten wide, and ten high, with black grooves crisscrossing every surface.

Wolf rushed to the weapons panel on the wall, eagerness sparking from her every move. From the rack of pistols and rifles, she grabbed one of each, slinging the rifle over her right shoulder.

"These are practice weapons, but treat them like they're hot," said Mops. "Safety on until you're ready to shoot. Finger off the trigger unless you mean to pull it."

"I know, I know." She twirled the pistol on her finger.

"Do that again and I'll shoot you myself," Mops continued, her tone never changing. The Prodryan pistol on her hip made it a very real threat. Wolf swallowed and lowered her gun.

Mops checked her own EMC practice pistol. The weapons were identical in size, mass, and feel to the real thing. Three hexagonal barrels were stacked in a triangle. A series of thumb switches on the contoured grip controlled the safety and firing modes. "Basic firing range. One shooter—humanoid. Ten-meter distance."

A wall dropped from the ceiling ten meters away. A single humanoid silhouette appeared at the center. A circle of light on the floor marked the firing position.

Wolf jumped into place, raised her pistol, and squeezed the trigger. Her face reddened. She turned off the safety and tried again. This time, the gun torqued in her hands, nearly twisting free. Wolf's face tightened with frustration and embarrassment. She adjusted her stance and grip, aimed, and fired.

A green dot on the target showed she'd removed the enemy's ear. She rolled her shoulders, snarled, and kept shooting until she'd emptied the weapon.

Of the thirty-six shots, thirty-two had hit the target. Wolf slid the practice magazine free and reinserted it, simulating a reload.

"Not bad," said Mops. "Doc, give us mobile targets. Hostiles and friendlies, random species. Fifteen meters."

The range reconfigured, and a new set of silhouettes began moving to and fro. As they crossed the range, about one in four would randomly turn green, indicating an enemy target.

That was when the slaughter began. To her credit, Wolf shot every hostile, scoring enough hits to "kill" more than ninety percent of her enemies. She also killed eighty percent of the friendlies, including six shots to a Glacidae silhouette who'd been scampering along, minding their own business.

Mops waited for the simulation to finish, and for Wolf to safety and holster her weapon. Wolf stared at the floor. "Yeah, I know."

"You didn't shoot me," said Mops. "That's something."

"I'm out of practice." Wolf shrugged. "Too busy unclogging drains and mopping up alien shit."

"Out of practice," repeated Mops. "Whose fault is that? The range is open to anyone during off-duty hours."

"Who has time for that?"

Mops drew her pistol. The ammo count appeared on her monocle, along with a crosshair that moved wherever the barrel was pointed. Since she currently had the gun aimed at the floor, the crosshair hovered at the bottom of her monocle with an arrow pointing downward.

She switched to gun's-eye view, and the view through her

monocle changed, showing her a patch of floor by her right foot with the crosshair dead center. The split in visual input to the eyes could be disconcerting. Mops had earned herself a migraine the first time she tried it. But it meant she'd always see what she was shooting at. She could even shoot around corners or over barriers, keeping her body safe behind cover.

"Rerun program." She raised the gun and started shooting ... never looking away from Wolf.

Her accuracy was a little low—33 hits out of 36 shots—but all 33 hits were on hostile targets. She turned to leave.

"That's it?" asked Wolf. "You're just going to show off and walk away?"

"Pretty much." Mops returned her weapon to the rack, then stopped in the doorway. "You have as much time in a day as I do. Hell, you have time right now. What are you going to do with it?"

For the next four and a half hours, Doc provided ongoing updates of Wolf's scores as she went through one scenario after another. By the end, her scores had improved somewhat, though she was still killing too many civilians.

After Wolf finished, Mops spent the day assessing the rest of her team's skills. It did not improve her confidence.

Kumar was an excellent shot, as long as the enemy didn't mind waiting for him to double-check his stance, steady his weapon, take three painfully slow breaths, and ever-so-carefully squeeze the trigger.

He tracked moving targets with equal care, up until Mops programmed those targets to return simulated fire. At that point, Kumar was repeatedly "killed" without ever getting a shot off.

Grom was able to use two of their digging limbs to brace the EMC pistol like a tiny rifle, holding it against their lower jaw. They turned out to be a surprisingly adequate shot, despite their odd habit of humming and making "pew, pew" sound effects the entire time.

She'd saved Monroe for last. If things went to hell, she was counting on his experience and expertise to save their asses.

Monroe entered the empty range like a man attending his own court-martial. He glanced around the empty range, the fingers of his artificial hand twitching nervously.

"Everything all right, JG?"

He walked to the weapons rack and pulled out a practice rifle. His hands moved automatically through the process of inspecting it, first clearing the magazine and disconnecting the firing mechanism. The hilt and trigger guard slid free. He squeezed the trigger with his mechanical hand. "Trigger pull's a little light."

"I'll be sure to report that to the small arms tech," Mops said dryly.

"Arm says it's only off by a quarter of a kilogram." He flexed his white fingers. Difficult as the assistive intelligence in his arm could be about some things, it was obviously familiar with weapons maintenance. Monroe reassembled the rifle and reloaded, then synched it with his monocle. "I haven't touched a gun since I left infantry."

It was the last thing Mops had expected. "Why not?"

He shouldered the rifle and took a pistol from the weapons rack, inspecting it with the same speed and efficiency he had the rifle. "Infantry training isn't just guns and combat batons and tactics. You learn an *attitude*. They train you to fight without hesitation. It becomes instinctive, until you're ready to take a swing at someone for bumping you in line or looking at you sideways.

"By the time they send you out, you've learned to rein things in a bit. I've never once slugged a superior officer, despite serving under several who needed it."

"I appreciate your restraint," Mops said dryly.

"It hasn't usually been a problem with you," he replied in the same tone. "And I get it. When you're a soldier being sent out to fight, those instincts can save your life. In other situations . . ."

Mops was starting to understand. "You're worried if you pick up a gun, you'll be too quick to use it."

"I'm worried I'll stop searching for alternatives," he said. "I worry the EMC has developed the same tunnel vision. We've always been quick to escalate to lethal force. Sometimes that's effective. Swift action can bring a swift end to a conflict. By preventing a drawn-out fight, you end up saving lives in the long run."

He tested the pistol's barrel light, twisting the switch from narrow to wide-beam. "But you're more likely to make mistakes. To miss other options and kill innocent people."

His right hand twitched, the index finger convulsing as if it were pulling a trigger. He scowled, and the hand slowly relaxed.

"I was counting on you to be the one who knew how to use these things," Mops said.

"Oh, I do. Trouble is, I *will* use them. If things go hot, I'll start shooting until the threat's down, or I am. Given that we're trying to get information, and to do it without attracting attention, it might be better if I'm not walking around primed to kill." He handed both weapons to her. "I'm pretty good with a combat baton. That usually leaves everyone alive to answer questions."

Mops pursed her lips. "Combat baton it is. Under one condition."

"And that is?"

"If we end up in a firefight, you use that baton to knock Kumar the hell out and take his weapon."

By the end of the day, it was clear Kumar wouldn't be flying the *Pufferfish* to Coacalos Station. True, he was getting better. His simulator scores now gave him an almost one-in-three chance of reaching the station without blowing them all up or otherwise breaking the ship. Needless to say, nobody was happy with those odds.

Mops gathered everyone on the bridge to discuss options.

"A shuttle is easier to fly and to dock once we get there," said Monroe. "They've got more than enough fuel for the trip."

"Shuttle armor and weapons are crap," said Wolf. "And they're slow. Do you know how long we'd be packed together, practically stacked on top of each other?"

Kumar glanced at the main screen. "Twenty-two hours, at the shuttle's top speed. At regulation-approved speeds, closer to thirty-six."

"Someone would need to stay behind to monitor things on the *Pufferfish*," said Monroe.

Grom lunged forward, rising to their full height. "I volunteer to not go with Wolf!"

"Fine," said Mops, before Wolf could respond. "In addition to keeping the ship ready for our return, you'll be responsible for tending to the rest of the crew."

The Glacidae dropped low. "Pardon?"

"For now, we can probably keep them sedated, but they'll need to be fed. Small portions, since they're not using much energy."

Wolf's expression had done a one-eighty from annoyance to amusement. "What about sanitation needs, sir?"

Mops fought to keep a straight face. "Their uniforms will absorb and wick away most excretions for now, but if we're gone more than five days, you'll need to start changing and cleaning them. Are you familiar with the ship's laundry systems?" When Grom didn't answer, she waved a hand. "Don't worry, there's a tutorial."

Grom looked unhappy, but didn't argue. Not unless you counted the low, drawn-out belch.

"We'll take shuttle two," she decided. "Wolf, Monroe, get it ready for departure. Doc will send you a copy of the preflight checklist. Double-check everything. Kumar, switch over to shuttle training. Grom, you might as well get to work feeding the crew. Better to start now while we're here to answer any questions."

Once everyone else had left the bridge, Mops moved into the Captain's Cove. They'd drained the water and sanitized the room, but the faint brine smell remained. She shut the door behind her. "Doc, how's the rest of the crew?"

"Still napping. Given human endurance, we can probably keep most of them sedated for at least a month with no permanent ill effects."

"Most?"

"You should probably have Grom keep an eye on Private Chaplin. When everyone was shambling about, she tried to eat the contents of chem lab one. It looks like the A-ring jump made her vomit, which got a lot of that junk out of her system, but her skin's a bit flushed, and her breathing's quicker than normal."

"Good to know. Anyone else I should flag?"

"Some cuts and bruises. A few fractures. A crewman from infantry tried to tear off his uniform and nearly strangled himself. Kumar got him taken care of."

Mops circled the room, studying various items Captain Brandenburg had kept in small niches and recesses in the rough stone walls. A coiled black shell with rainbow edges from her home world. A set of entertainment slices, with each wafer of crystal neatly labeled along the outer edge. A collection of water samples from every world the *Pufferfish* had visited while under her command.

She picked up a vial of amethyst water from a Glacidae colony and held it to the light. "Doc, have you had any luck getting us into the armory?"

"Not yet. Standard welding and repair equipment won't cut through those doors, and access is restricted to Krakau officers."

More Krakau safeguards. More evidence of their true feelings about humans. Mops considered bringing one of the bodies out of storage and trying to use it to access the armory, but after the level one decontamination, she wasn't sure the computer would recognize the remains as Krakau. Even if it did, the *Pufferfish*'s security systems knew the entire command crew was dead. Their access would have been locked down automatically.

She looked toward the door. "When Lieutenant Khan reported to the captain, she had her sidearm and combat baton with her. What happened to those?"

"Khan was taken to Medical. Her personal items would have been placed into one of the storage lockers. And before you ask, yes, as acting captain of the ship, you can *access those storage lockers."*

"Good. Check to see—"

"How many other infantry personnel were taken to Medical before they could stow their weapons? Looking at the records, six."

"Were those storage lockers decontaminated with the rest of the ship?"

"Normally, lockers are airtight. But they open automatically during a level one decontamination."

"We'll need to test to make sure the guns' electronics weren't damaged." Mops headed for the door. "One last thing. Make sure you've synched my library to the monocle. I have the feeling I'll need the distraction during the trip."

Shuttle two looked like an old Earth school bus had mated with a fat caterpillar. Its official designation was the unimaginative *Pufferfish-S2*. Triangular wings were currently folded up around the body. Like its mothership, the *Pufferfish-S2* was matte black, painted in an energy-absorbing material that rendered it harder for sensors to find or track.

When the light hit at just the right angle, Mops could see the hair-thin lines of the shuttle's defensive grid, giving it a scaly appearance. Two small weapons pods ran the length of the ship on either side.

Two other shuttles were locked down in the back of the bay. This one had been moved into the center, its nose aligned with the docking bay doors.

"Inventory looks good," Monroe called from inside the shuttle. A copy of his checklist flashed onto Mops' monocle. "All system checks are blue."

Mops checked her team's status. In addition to the usual information, her monocle now displayed weapons and ammunition count. Wolf and Kumar each had a single pistol and extra magazine. Mops had taken two pistols for herself. A black combat baton, half a meter in length, hung from Monroe's left hip. Mops had packed additional ammo in the shuttle, along with a single rifle. If all went well, they shouldn't need any of it.

Given their luck so far, maybe she should have hunted around for more ammo.

She turned to Grom, who was waiting a short distance from the shuttle. "As soon as we're clear, close the bay doors and shut down all systems except what's necessary to keep yourself and the crew alive. I want the *Pufferfish* invisible until we get back."

Grom slid closer. "What if you don't make it back?"

"If you don't hear from us in two weeks, consider yourself promoted."

"That prospect . . . isn't quite as appealing as it would have been a few days ago."

Mops grinned and climbed into the shuttle, settling into one of the egg-shaped seats built into the interior wall. "Take care of the crew. And if you spend the whole time playing video games, I'll jam a utility pole up your backside and use you as a dust mop. Is that clear?"

"*Vividly* clear."

Mops secured the contoured, padded restraint plates over her thighs. The back of the seat locked automatically to her equipment harness. Additional restraints would secure her head and limbs if the ride got rough.

She glanced toward the front, where Kumar was settling

into the pilot's station, and double-checked to make sure those extra restraints were working properly.

Wolf and Monroe squeezed in and took their seats. The boarding ramp folded shut, the exterior door sliding and locking into place.

"Air circulation in these things is mediocre at best," said Monroe. "Try not to puke during the flight."

"Seal and secure your suits for takeoff," added Mops. If something did go wrong during launch, the suits could keep them alive long enough to get back to the *Pufferfish*. At least in theory. She double-checked to make sure everyone's suit status showed blue. "Kumar, we're ready to go."

"Yes, sir."

There were no windows or viewscreens, so Mops called up an exterior view on her monocle. Grom had left the bay as fast as their countless legs could carry them. From the cockpit, Mops heard Kumar muttering under his breath. "Doc, what's going on up there?" she whispered.

Doc switched to a view of the pilot's console, where Puffy was happily reminding Kumar not to engage the main engines until they were at least one kilometer away from the *Pufferfish*.

"I know," muttered Kumar.

"Did you remember to depressurize the bay? Otherwise ..." Puffy turned and let out an exaggerated, animated belch. A tiny shuttle launched from his mouth, tumbling out of control like a minnow in a maelstrom.

"Depressurizing the bay," Kumar called back. The sound of a windstorm outside slowly faded into silence. A short time later, Mops felt the *Pufferfish-S2*'s docking clamps retract. "Reducing power to docking bay gravity plates."

Mops' stomach lurched. She grabbed the restraints without thinking. It felt like she was falling sideways.

Her monocle changed to show the shuttle sliding free of the bay. Doc had outlined the black hull of the *Pufferfish* against the blacker emptiness of space.

"An external reference point can help with spacesickness."

"Thanks. Feed that view to the rest of the team, please." As she spoke, the system's star rotated slowly into view: a ball of blue-white light surrounded by a faint ring of dust.

"If you replaced Earth's sun with that star, it would engulf Mercury, Venus, Earth, Mars, and Jupiter," said Doc. An icon on Mops' monocle indicated he was addressing the whole team.

Wolf swallowed. "Let's not do that, then."

"Where's the station?" asked Monroe.

"According to their beacon signal, right there." A blue dot appeared to the left of the star.

The shuttle lurched hard up and to port, eliciting a curse from Wolf.

"Sorry," said Kumar. "Thrusters weren't this touchy in the simulation."

Wolf glanced around the cramped space. "I don't know if I can handle thirty-six hours of this."

"Shift your thinking, Technician," said Mops. "Consider this a day and a half off your regular duty shift. I don't know about you, but I intend to take full advantage of the opportunity."

"Opportunity for what?"

Mops smiled and used her eye movement to queue up a list of files on her monocle. "Allow me to introduce you to the works of Jane Austen of Earth."

10

Greetings, visitor. Welcome to the Coacalos Family Generation Ship, *a privately owned and politically neutral vessel.*

Environmental specs are available for download from any of the forty-two perimeter beacons. If you've forgotten to bring your own air supply, the family is happy to provide daily, weekly, or monthly air allotments tailored to your species, for a fair and reasonable price. We recommend using any of the financial kiosks to set up automatic payments to guarantee continued respiratory security.

Your ship will be scanned, registered, and docked by our professional and certified docking technicians. By proceeding, you agree to waive all liability for any damage, injuries, or deaths that may (but almost certainly won't) occur during docking.

A complete list of rules and regulations are available for download from the perimeter beacons. Any violations may result in fines and/or expulsion from the station. If you are unable to pay your fine, your ship may be kept in payment, in which case you will be expelled from the nearest air lock. Whether you are allowed a spacesuit depends on the severity of the violation.

Remember, if you're close enough to receive this message, our weapons have already locked onto your ship!

Thanks for visiting the Coacalos Family Generation Ship. *We hope you enjoy your stay.*

"ARRIVAL IN SIXTY-FOUR MINUTES," said Kumar.

Wolf groaned. "Can't you slow us down a bit? I'm most of the way through this damn book, and I still don't know if Mr. Darcy is going to propose again, or if—"

"The books will be waiting when we're through," Mops assured her. After a day and a half in the shuttle, everyone was sore, smelly, and sick of each other's company. Deliberately postponing their arrival would likely trigger a mutiny.

"It looks like you're approaching a space station," Puffy announced. After the first day, they'd broadcast Puffy's feed through the team's monocles, just for the distraction. "Remember, everything in space moves. Begin by inputting the velocity of your target. Comparing their vector to your own will tell you how to accelerate."

"Hold on." Kumar scanned the area around the pilot's station. He'd been scribbling notes in white marking pen on every bare surface: reminders and instructions and shortcuts and formulae for everything from fuel consumption to changing Puffy's color scheme. "Station vector was part of the transmission from that beacon we passed . . . got it. Um, sir? I think we're getting a tight-beam communication from the station."

"Patch it through to me," said Mops.

Kumar nodded. "How do I do that?"

"There should be an incoming signal icon," said Wolf. "Tap it."

"I did," snapped Kumar. "I'm tapping it right now. Nothing's happening."

A sound like an angry tuba filled the shuttle, making the

entire team jump. Mops grimaced. "Turn that down, and run it through the translator, Kumar!"

Wolf unfastened her restraints and shoved her way toward the cockpit, but the transmission stopped before she could squeeze in beside Kumar. "What did you do?"

"Nothing!" Kumar raised his hands, as if to prove he hadn't touched the controls.

Mops leaned forward. "Please tell me we didn't just hang up on Coacalos Station."

"Maybe they hung up on us first," offered Wolf.

Before Mops could respond, the transmission resumed, this time in deep, gravelly Human. "Are you comprehending this language? This is Coacalos docking control. You have thirty seconds to identify yourselves and your intentions. Failure to comply will be considered a declaration of hostility and result in your incineration."

Mops cleared her throat. "This is Marion Adamopoulos, in command of the *Elizabeth Bennet*. There are four of us, all human. We intend to spend a few days relaxing at Coacalos Station."

A pause. "Your ship's beacon identifies you as the *Puffer-fish-S2* of the Earth Mercenary Corps."

"Does it?" Mops glared at Wolf, who was supposed to have disabled that beacon. "How strange."

"Very strange," the voice replied. "Particularly given the bounty the Alliance announced earlier today for the *EMCS Pufferfish* and its crew."

"As I understand, Coacalos Station isn't part of the Alliance," said Mops.

"True . . . but we aren't about to turn down a bounty of that size when it flies into our maw. Unless a more profitable alternative presents itself, of course. Before you respond, please keep in mind that we have a confirmed weapons lock on your ship."

Mops squared her shoulders, pretending it didn't sting to know the organization she'd served for twelve years considered her a traitor. Technically, she was, but that didn't make it any less painful to hear. "A more profitable alternative. Tell me, how much does the station earn in an average week?"

"That information is confidential."

She'd expected as much, but it didn't matter. "If you turn us over to the EMC, you'll get your bounty. Then, once the Alliance realizes why we came here, you'll have several hundred human troops inspecting every square centimeter of your station. They'll tear the place apart and interrogate every one of your staff and guests. Knowing EMC procedures, they'll spend at least a week disrupting your business."

"The Alliance and the EMC have no jurisdiction here."

Mops lowered her voice. "Given the situation, I don't think that's going to matter."

"What situation? Explain!"

"Not over an open channel."

"All of our communications are tight-beam, short-range transmissions, encrypted with temporal-variable—"

"It's not your end of the conversation I'm worried about," Mops interrupted, glancing toward Wolf.

After a long pause, the voice said, "Please stand by."

Kumar looked up at her. "What do you think they're doing?"

"The same thing any of us would do with a situation that could potentially blow up in our faces," guessed Mops. "Searching for a superior to dump the problem on." She checked their position. "For now, continue matching course with the station."

Whoever the dock controller had escalated the call to, they'd gotten an impressively fast reply. Less than a minute later, they signaled the *Pufferfish* again. "Attention, Marion Adamopoulos. The Coacalos family will hear your warning. Do not deviate from your present course, or you will be destroyed. Security will meet you at your shuttle after docking is complete. Do not attempt to disembark until instructed, or you will be destroyed."

"Understood, thank you." She turned to face her team. "From here on, everyone is on their best behavior. That means—"

"Marion Adamopoulos, you are still transmitting."

Wolf offered a sheepish apology, then began bickering with Kumar over how to end their broadcast. Puffy chimed in a moment later.

"It looks like you're trying to disable communications equipment," Puffy said cheerfully. "Would you like help?"

With a sigh, Mops stretched back to wait.

"You are now free to disembark." The mechanized voice over their comms lacked inflection—either a cheap translator program or a low-level AI. "Atmospheric pressure is approximately one-fourth Human normal. The use of breathing apparatus is recommended."

Mops secured her hood and gloves, made sure her team had done the same, and opened the shuttle door. As soon as she ducked through and her feet touched the docking ledge floor, she arched her back and stretched. Her spine let out a series of audible cracks and pops, causing the closest of their Quetzalus guards to jump back in alarm, bristly hair glowing like heating elements.

"Do you require medical assistance?"

"No, thank you." Mops chuckled. "Rearranging our internal skeletons is just something humans do."

"That is . . . disturbing."

The Quetzalus were the largest intelligent species known to the Alliance. They were quadrupedal, with long necks and bright orange beaklike mouths. Scraggly, bristly hair covered their leathery skin. The one who'd spoken was on the small side, barely four meters in height.

When a Quetzalus was at rest, their hair was a dull waxy color. But each strand was internally reflective, anchored deep within bioluminescent sacs that ran the length of the Quetzalus' body. The tip of each hair could light up like a spark, broadcasting the Quetzalus' mood for all to see. Older Quetzalus generally controlled and minimized the effect.

A rippling yellow glow suggested this one was both young and anxious. The brilliant red crest sprouting from the head like an out-of-control shrub marked him as a male. Flaps of bare skin stretched between his fore and hind limbs, vestigial wings his species hadn't used in eons. He and his two companions all carried short-barreled blasters mounted to the sides of their meter-long beaks, along with translators and communications units.

They were big enough and strong enough to physically pick up the shuttle and throw it back into space. And they were clearly terrified of the four humans.

"We don't want to cause trouble," Mops assured them.

"Your people *are* trouble," the young Quetzalus replied.

Wolf chuckled. "Hard to argue with that."

"What's your name?" asked Mops.

"Quil Coacalos."

"Second child of the Coacalos family, so he's pretty important," Doc added. *"Try not to scare him any more than you have."*

Mops glanced around the docking bay, an enormous hollow cylinder covered in circular ledges that reminded her of fungal growths. Grav beam generators protruded from metal blisters in the wall. At the top of the bay, a heavy black dome sealed them off from the emptiness of space.

A layer of fine black sand crunched beneath Mops' boots. An insectlike creature the size of a human hand crept along the wall, twitching feathery blue wings and watching the newcomers with huge, chronically surprised eyes.

"This place is filthy," muttered Kumar. His hand went automatically to one of the small spray canisters in his harness.

Mops caught his wrist. "Half the station runs on biologics. You have no idea how much damage you could do if you start disinfecting."

"This way," said Quil Coacalos, tromping toward a large, circular air lock door. Mops and her team fell in behind, with the other two guards bringing up the rear. "There will be a brief cleansing process before you're allowed into the station. Your equipment and weaponry has been scanned and registered."

The cleansing was similar to a level four decon: chemical spray and low-level irradiation. A fluid sample check followed. They each unsealed their hoods long enough to spit on a long white swab, which was then inserted into a small hole in the side wall.

"To make sure you're not carrying anything potentially infectious," explained Quil. Discomfort turned the tips of his hair orange, like someone had set him on fire. "Humans are rumored to be . . . that is, we're aware of your species' unique history, and don't want to risk—"

"We're not contagious," growled Wolf.

"Lucky for you, the computer agrees," said Quil as the holes closed and the inner door slid open. Air and noise rushed in, buffeting the humans backward. The Quetzalus didn't appear to notice.

"We *have* had human visitors before," Quil continued. "Several of your species have even taken up employment on Coacalos Station. The air is adequate to sustain you."

"Confirmed," said Doc. *"A bit high in CO2, but nothing you can't handle."*

Mops had seen her share of space stations, villages orbiting whatever star or planet kept them on their gravitational leashes. Each had its own feel. The Stepping Stone back home was primarily a military installation, clean and utilitarian, shared by Krakau and humans. Others functioned as trading posts and supply depots, or shipyards, or exploratory stations with their massive arrays of telescopes.

Coacalos Station wasn't a village, but a city. Mops was reminded of footage she'd seen of pre-plague Las Vegas on Earth, if Vegas had been built in a hollow mountain instead of the middle of the desert.

The docking bay was a broad central shaft through the core of the mountain. They emerged from the air lock onto a sturdy walkway and observation platform. Quil bobbed his beak, pointing to a transparent lift tube to their right.

Mops moved to the edge of the observation platform instead. A clear wall, filmed with dust and smears from dozens of species, prevented anyone from falling. They'd emerged near the base of the station. Outside, a tower that appeared to be made of rippling sapphire stretched as high as she could see. Shifting lights within the glass formed images and alien letters, which Doc translated into advertisements for everything from exotic clothing to entertainment implants to animated tattoos.

She glanced at Wolf, who shrugged and said, "Yeah, I got my ink on this station. Not this tower, though. There's a Glacidae in Tower Two who does great work at half the price."

"According to the courtesy map download, this is Tower Three," said Doc. *"We're on level two, near the bottom. The station is segmented into six towers, each with six levels. The higher you go, the more expensive everything gets."*

"This way," Quil said, flashing an impatient lavender.

The lift played a soft, unremarkable melody as they descended to level one. They emerged between the amethyst tower and a smoky red one to the left, which Doc tagged as Tower Two. Small booths and tents were spread across the rocky ground between the towers, an open-air market that smelled of grease and sweat and alien excretions. The air was cold enough to raise bumps on Mops' skin.

Aliens of every variety cleared a path as the Quetzalus led them between the towers, toward the outer edge of the station. A group of Nusurans ducked into a tent whose holographic walls played a pixelated loop of purple waves crashing against a ruby beach. A furry creature with nine legs scampered across their path, chasing a ratlike thing with a hard, spiral shell. Overhead, a pair of Prodryans glided on mechanically enhanced wings.

"How many people are here at any given time?" she asked.

"Coacalos Station has a maximum capacity of twelve thousand," Quil said automatically. "We pride ourselves on providing accommodations suitable for every species. Humans will be most comfortable with the environmental conditions of Tower Five. Not that we have many human guests."

So many beings from so many different species, and the only thing they had in common was the way they shied back from Mops and her team. A plump, green-tinged Glacidae dropped flat and scampered into the nearest booth. A trio of Krakau shrank away. A Nusuran froze, the bulk of her body hidden behind a rustling tent.

Doc enhanced and translated the whispers as they walked:

"Don't stare. Humans take that as a challenge."
"Humans take everything *as a challenge."*
"Is it true they can't be killed?"
"I can smell them from here."
"I hear they eat the flesh of their enemies."
"On Earth, they survive by eating their own young."
"Why are they here?"

Quil had said they had humans working on the station, but it was obvious most of these people had rarely seen one up close. Their stares made her skin itch, and she fought the impulse to check her weapons. Merely shifting a hand toward one of her pistols would probably send the gawkers into a panicked stampede.

If she was this tense . . . she glanced at Wolf, whose shoulders were hunched nearly to her ears. "At ease," she said quietly. "They're just curious."

"I'm used to it," Wolf muttered. "Usually, I pick a fight to break the tension and get them to stop staring."

"And we wonder why humans have such a reputation for violence."

After what felt like close to a kilometer, they reached another lift, this one with metal doors and a security console to one side. A single human stood guard in the shadows, dressed in dark green and holding a rifle with a serrated bayonet. A heavy helmet completely obscured the human's head. The human didn't move as Quil tapped his beak on the security pad and whispered something into the speaker.

The lift door slid open with a heavy clunk. Another Quetzalus head-butted Mops from behind, knocking her several steps forward.

Mops turned slowly and folded her arms. Any appearance of weakness would make it that much harder to negotiate with the Coacalos family. To her left, she saw Monroe rest his hand on his combat baton. She gave him a slight shake of her head.

The Quetzalus who'd pushed Mops drew herself taller. "Keep walking, human."

Instead, Mops stepped closer and patted the Quetzalus on the leg. Lowering her voice, she said, "I can't imagine your bosses would be happy about you starting a brawl before they've heard what we have to say, which tells me that bit of rudeness was for show. Trying to make yourself look tough by shoving the human around. Who are you trying to impress?"

The Quetzalus quickly suppressed a green glow, but Mops saw the way her attention shifted.

"Oh, I see." Mops checked to make sure the other Quetzalus weren't listening. "You have a thing for Quil. Isn't he a bit young for you?"

She opened her mouth and flashed a glowing blue tongue, a sign of distress.

"My lips are sealed," whispered Mops. "You just mind your manners."

The Quetzalus blinked, then gave a slow, human nod.

"The Family is waiting," said Quil, bobbing his head toward the lift.

They descended again, this time emerging in a roomy, well-lit cavern with mossy carpeting—no, that was real moss. Humidity gave the air a heavy feel. Quil led them past scattered, irregularly shaped rock formations. It wasn't until Mops saw a pair of Quetzalus settled atop one such formation that she realized the rocks were the equivalent of furniture.

"Wait here." Quil tromped ahead to speak with the two resting Quetzalus, who stretched their necks and widened their pearl-black eyes to get a better view of the humans. Normally, those eyes were almost invisible, hidden in four recessed sockets just behind the beak. The larger pair saw in black and white, but with great acuity. Only the smaller perceived color, albeit a narrower range than human vision.

"This is Lazan Coacalos," said Quil, bobbing his head toward the larger of the two. "Mate of Zan Coacalos and Second of the Coacalos Family."

"Second-in-command," said Doc. *"Consider Lazan the commander. Zan Coacalos would be the equivalent of captain."*

"With him is Ix Lataclox. She's a specialist in galactic law."

A lawyer, in other words. Ix Lataclox had a lighter beak, more yellow than orange, and lacked the crest of the males. As for Lazan, he was the largest Quetzalus Mops had ever seen, more than five meters in height. He probably massed as much as their shuttle. Neither appeared to be armed, but who knew how many weapons pods were hidden throughout the cavern, ready to vaporize hostile visitors.

"You are Lieutenant Marion Adamopoulos of the *EMCS Pufferfish*?" asked Lazan.

"That's right."

Lazan's head cocked a full ninety degrees. "I assume your cruiser is somewhere in-system?"

"It is." There was no point lying about it. They would have noted the A-ring deceleration flare.

"You say it would be a mistake to turn you over to the EMC and collect the bounty. Explain."

"The bounty is a misunderstanding," said Mops.

"The EMC says you took the *Pufferfish* after the rest of the crew was incapacitated or killed, and that you disobeyed orders to return to Earth."

"That part's accurate," Mops admitted.

"They also say you may have been involved in the attack against your crew, collaborating with Prodryan agents. You're described as potential terrorists and traitors to the Krakau Alliance."

"The hell we are!" Wolf snapped.

Mops silenced her with a glare. Wolf clamped her mouth shut, tension visible in her jaw as she glared at Lazan Coacalos. Beside her, Kumar was crouched on one knee, apparently fascinated by a bit of blue moss. Monroe simply waited, his face impassive, his attention on Mops.

"I'm flattered Command has such a high estimate of our competence and skill," said Mops. "But we had nothing to do with that attack. If we hadn't been suited up to fix a cracked sewer line, we'd have been affected by the same weapon that took out the rest of the crew."

Ix Lataclox lowered her head to human eye-level. "The bounty is not contingent on your guilt or innocence. And the potential cost of harboring Alliance refugees is severe."

"Oh, we're not here to hide," laughed Mops. "And I guarantee the cost of not helping us will be higher."

A wave of orange rippled over Lazan's body.

"Does the Alliance bounty on us say anything about how my crew was disabled?" asked Mops.

"It does not," said Ix.

"The Prodryans used a biological weapon. A weapon that caused the humans to revert to a feral state. They killed the nonhuman members of our crew, all save one."

Lazan pulled back slightly.

"The attackers came from this station," Mops continued. "Whatever the cost of harboring Alliance refugees, how does that compare to the backlash when the Alliance finds out you've been harboring bioterrorists?"

"We know nothing of any such bioterrorists," protested Ix.

"The consequences aren't contingent on your knowledge." Mops shrugged. "Once the Alliance has inspected the station and interrogated your guests and staff, they'll probably leave you in peace. It shouldn't take more than a few weeks. A month at most."

The two Quetzalus glanced at one another.

"Or you can let us snoop around," said Mops. "Give us access to your records to see how long the Prodryans were here, who they met with, where they came from—"

"That information is private," Ix interrupted. "Neither you nor the EMC have any legal standing on this ship. The confidentiality of our guests is—"

"How many humans do you have working here?" Mops asked.

Lazan's crest flared in annoyance. "Eighteen."

Ix muttered something to him.

"I'm sorry, seventeen. One of our humans recently quit without notice."

Mops removed her monocle and faced the concave side toward the closest wall. "Doc, please show our hosts what happened when we went to rescue Grom from Recreation."

Bright light shone from the monocle, painting a picture of the *Pufferfish*'s recreation area on the wall. The irregularity of the wall distorted the image slightly, and the room's lighting gave the whole thing an orange tint, but it was clear enough.

Lazan's long neck stretched closer, until his beak cut a bite-sized shadow from the image. "Those humans. They're feral?"

"Bastards would have eaten every last one of us," said Wolf.

"Whatever did this to my crew was here," added Mops. "It could still be here. Your clients are jumpy enough around humans as it is. What do you think would happen if one of those seventeen humans reverted?"

Kumar cleared his throat. "It wouldn't be just the one, sir. Remember how quickly this spread through the *Pufferfish*? If it gets loose here, it would contaminate the whole station. All seventeen would go feral within hours."

"Imagine the publicity." Monroe raised his hands, as if painting a sign. "'Coacalos Station: It's been zero days since an employee ate a guest.'"

"You're probably calculating the cost of firing and replacing those seventeen humans," Mops continued. "I'm sure you could afford it. It would be simple enough for you to dispose of us as well, for that matter. But that just makes you look guiltier when the EMC arrives. If a handful of humans figured out the Prodryans were here, it won't take Command long to do the same. Right now, you have plausible deniability. You can say you didn't know."

Lazan Coacalos' crest slumped to one side, and his hair pulsed a dull yellow. His attention remained fixed on the battle playing out against the wall. Ix leaned close and murmured something into the small earhole at the base of his neck.

"I will . . . consult with Zan Coacalos," said Lazan. "What is your proposal, Marion Adamopoulos?"

Mops smiled. "To begin with, we'll need you to waive our docking fee and put us up for a few days. . . ."

11

Grom crawled from beneath the navigation console. Wires dangled from open panels like brightly colored roots. Every bridge console now displayed an identical image of the blue hypergiant star, along with the pinpricks of light from other stars, and a blue dot representing the station.

Clicking happily as they worked, Grom returned to the back of the bridge to grab a customized Glacidae computer console. They slipped the strap over their head. One edge of the console snapped into place against the front of their equipment harness, secured by several powerful magnets.

The Glacidae's uppermost legs gripped the sides of the terminal, while their tunneling claws attacked the keys. "Load Pufferfish data storage structure, triptych display."

The main directory appeared on the primary viewscreen. Recently accessed subdirectories popped up on the consoles to either side of the main screen.

Grom quivered with triumph. After two days, they'd finally gotten all the bridge stations talking to one another in proper sequence. Isolated workstations were fine for a fully crewed *ship, but without these improvements, it would only be a matter of time before those idiot humans crashed the ship into a supernova.*

Now for the real test. "Verify Gromgimsidalgak, Technician, software and computer support division, EMCS Pufferfish."

"Verified," said the computer, in Grom's native language.

Their quivering increased, the plates of their exoskeleton clicking together in excitement. Grom continued typing, digging into their personal data storage subfolder. "Load program ITM-6-Lev3."

The bridge lighting dimmed. The file directories vanished, replaced by the dark, icy caves of home. Orange light turned one of the tunnels to glowing glass. A serpentine robot emerged from the tunnel, streaks of flame shooting from its six eyes.

Words appeared in the air, directly above the robot's head:

ICE TUNNEL MINER VI: VIPER'S REVENGE

➤ *Start New Game*
➤ *Continue Saved Game*

Grom tapped Continue and crawled into the captain's station. The captain's console displayed their character's supplies and stats, while the main screen loaded level three, the glacier hunt.

With the bridge's systems linked and devoted to the game engine, and nobody else on board to drain the computer's resources, the game was more responsive than Grom had ever seen.

Grom leaned to one side for a sip of methane slushee, then settled in to start blasting robovipers.

TOWER FIVE WAS BUILT to comfortably house Glacidae, Krakau, and the occasional human. Mops and her team were given space on level one, the "ground floor."

The tower's exterior was a deep brown, almost black, that reminded Mops of obsidian. Her temporary ID badge, hanging from her neck on a thin but surprisingly strong chain of tarnished metal, got them through the doors. A series of blinking lights on the back of the badge pointed the way to their lodging.

The damp, chilly air greeted them with the smell of brine and the urine of at least three different species. The hallways were rough-carved tunnels coated with cheap brown spray sealant. The light strips stretched down the center of the ceiling and floor were running at half power, but still managed to illuminate every stain. Puddles of water, some up to three centimeters deep, splashed with each step. The noise sent insects retreating into cracks and holes in the wall.

A loud hiss made her jump. She spun to see Kumar spraying a foaming cleanser onto a discolored patch of wall.

"Don't bother," said Mops. "You could scrub this place until you died of old age, and you wouldn't put a dent in the mess."

Kumar gestured at the walls, outrage and horror momentarily robbing him of words.

"Save it for our quarters," suggested Monroe.

A pair of Krakau emerged from a door up ahead, releasing a low swell of water into the hallway. Most of the water vanished through small, partially clogged grates at the base of the walls. The Krakau spotted the four humans and ducked right back into their room, locking the door behind them.

"We're off to the right," said Mops, following the lights on her badge. They passed an open area to the left where a group of beings watched a knot of at least five Glacidae struggling together. A short distance away, a pair of Quetzalus rested in a pool of foul-smelling, bubbling black liquid. "What is that?"

"According to the station directory, it's Tar Bath 2," said Doc. "They're not recommended for most species. You would likely survive the temperature extremes, but you wouldn't enjoy it, and you'd never get the smell out of your hair."

A trio of Nusurans skirted past the tar pool. From the size and coloration, Mops guessed them to be a mated group—a hi, a vi, and a si. Their young rode on the back of the eight-legged vi, looking like fat, giggling blue sausages.

"Over here," said Kumar, turning down another hallway. He shoved his badge into a slot on the wall, and the door slid open.

The lights came on automatically, revealing an empty room with six fold-up cot frames built into the far wall. Carved steps in the wall formed a crude ladder for reaching the higher cots. An air vent rattled in the ceiling. A pool of centimeter-deep water shone around the drain in the center of the room.

Kumar ran a white rag over the closest wall. It came away a waxy yellow color. He sniffed the rag, then scowled. "They used a knock-off sanispray to disinfect this place, but didn't wash it down properly once the foam dissolved."

Mops checked the multispecies bathroom off to the side. The shower facility was a glorified hose, and the toilet was a large bowl in the floor. A set of seats was propped against one wall, each designed for a different species' needs.

"Not the worst place I've ever stayed," Wolf said, folding down one of the top cots and doing a pull-up to test the frame's strength. "What's the plan for finding our Prodryans?"

"Weren't you paying attention back at the meeting?" asked Monroe.

"In the beginning, sure." Wolf switched to one-handed pull-ups. "Then it got boring, so I went back to reading."

Mops should have chewed her out for that, but she found it hard to get angry at Wolf for reading books. "They gave us three days. We'll be working as station janitors for cover."

That made Wolf perk up. "How much does it pay?"

She chuckled. "They pay by not tossing us into space."

"And by getting copies of everything we learn," Monroe added. "You know they'll be monitoring us. Everything we do, everyone we talk to."

"I'm guessing the badges are bugged," agreed Mops. "Along

with the usual station surveillance. Anything you say, assume the Coacalos family is listening over your shoulder."

She subvocalized a follow-up, asking Doc to pass her words along to the team and hoping whatever listening tech was in place couldn't crack short-range EMC signals. *"They might be going along with us because they don't want trouble from the Alliance. Or they could see it as an opportunity to get their hands on a potentially valuable weapon."*

"Quetzalus don't have hands," Kumar responded in kind, his words appearing on her monocle.

"When do we start?" asked Wolf. "Prodryans tend to stick with Tower Two, as high up as they can afford. Gravity's lighter up there. I say we head up and beat some answers out of—"

"Let's save starting an intrastation war as our backup plan," Mops interrupted. "Lazan Coacalos has given us limited docking records on Prodryan visitors, but I didn't see much there. The Prodryans probably housed the fighters in a larger freighter with forged registration. We're not going to find anything listed under Assault Commander Burns Like Sunspots or Prodryan fighter squadron 52."

Wolf shook her head. "If this mission was so important, they would have been careful."

"I'm sure they were," agreed Mops. "But secrets are slippery. You tried to be careful last month when you were sneaking time with Private Salieri instead of finishing the mold inspection in the greenhouse."

Wolf's face reddened.

"Or last year when Captain Brandenburg went on leave to have a child," Mops continued. "Only the command crew knew why she was leaving, but word leaked to the whole ship within two days. Keeping secrets is hard, especially in a place like this. Someone on Coacalos Station knows about Burns Like Sunspots and his squad. Someone has the answers we need."

"There are hundreds of Prodryans on the station," said Kumar. "How do we find the one with answers?"

"The restaurants," said Monroe.

Kumar blinked. "Restaurants?"

"Squad 52 was about to fly off to attack an EMC cruiser," said Mops. "What do Prodryans do before a battle? They eat and drink and get wasted on fruit honey. Wolf, you know the restaurants here. Where should we start?"

"You really think anyone's going to talk to humans?" asked Wolf.

"Humans have a bad reputation. Not an entirely undeserved one." She gave Wolf a pointed look. "We'll have to earn a little gratitude. This place is a mess, a SHS crew's nightmare. That gives us the opportunity to make friends and improve our reputation. We're station janitors now. Do the job, then ask questions. Fear of humanity is nothing compared to the relief of finally being able to use your toilet without worrying about explosive backfire."

The list of backlogged maintenance tickets was extensive enough to keep Mops and her team employed for a year. Of the thirty-eight restaurants in the station directory, thirty-five had one or more service requests ranging from faucet replacements to a freezer that had been broken so long its contents had probably evolved into a primitive tool-using society.

They started with Tower Two. From the outside, it looked like a stalagmite made of dark red glass. A sign at the main entrance warned visitors to expect lessened gravity, and listed the various gases in the air. Krakau and Tjikko were strictly prohibited from entering without a portable air supply, available from a vending machine to one side.

Mops stepped carefully through the doors and across the threshold. The ground was perfectly flat, but her body felt like she'd missed a step on a staircase as she crossed onto the lower-power grav plates.

Where the other towers she'd seen had floors to separate each level, Tower Two's levels were separated primarily by bridges and platforms, allowing Prodryans to fly from one area to the next. Most structures had flat rooftops and ledges where Prodryans watched like colorful gargoyles as the humans entered their territory.

Mops double-checked her list and the map Doc helpfully displayed on her monocle. Doing her best to look like a bored employee, she raised her voice and asked, "Can anyone tell us where to find a place called . . . Well-Burnt Food for the Happiness of Your Ingestion Holes?"

"I assume the name flows better in the original language."

A Glacidae wearing a respirator gestured to a path bordered in vivid purple brick, curving off to the left.

Mops and her team spent the next two hours unclogging a backed-up drain in an acid-cooker, used for softening up certain Quetzalus delicacies. The second restaurant—Dead Meat Products with Spicy Grease, Served Fast!—needed six kilograms of congealed fat unclogged from their pipes.

Both owners were grateful for the help, but neither had any information about Prodryan pirates hosting a prebattle feast in recent weeks. They also seemed quite eager to usher the humans out of their restaurant and away from customers—preferably through the back door.

"Where did you eat when you were here?" Mops asked Wolf as they left Dead Meat Products.

"A bottom-level dump in Tower Five called Home-Grown Spicy Protein Slabs. I can take you if—"

"Heads up!" Monroe's shove sent Mops sprawling. In the reduced gravity, she slid and rolled a full three meters before recovering. She rose into a crouch as a pair of Prodryans flew through the air where she'd been standing. They swooped away, clawed limbs scraping along the ground.

Monroe was close enough he could have cracked them both with his baton. He didn't, but kept the baton ready as he watched the pair fly higher to disappear among the bridges that crisscrossed the air higher up.

"Bastards," snarled Wolf, fumbling for her weapon.

"Stand down," Mops snapped. "They're just kids. No armor or enhancements. They probably dared one another to fly close to the scary humans."

Her monocle had flagged a number of drawn guns from nearby Prodryans who were doubtless hoping for an excuse to use them. From their rooftops and ledges, they'd have no trouble mowing down Mops and her team.

Mops waited until Wolf secured her pistol. "The next job is a busted utensil sanitizer at Cooks Good Meals Restaurant. Eighteen meters ahead and to the right, on Pink Street. Monroe, keep watching the sky. Everyone keep your hands off your guns unless they start shooting first."

"Don't they find it suspicious that maintenance staff are armed?" asked Kumar.

Wolf snorted. "Around here, they'd be more suspicious if we weren't."

They reached the restaurant without incident. Inside the door were a pair of bulky vending machines. One offered a variety of Prodryan cigars, while the other sold Krakau stim slugs—dried sea creatures with a mildly intoxicating effect. Past the entryway, the building split into two wings. A ramp to the left led down to a shallow pond where two groups of Krakau dined at floating tables. To the right was a larger, tall-ceilinged area occupied mostly by Prodryans. An unfamiliar song played over ceiling-mounted speakers, blending with the clicks and splashes of conversation.

A greeter pedestal with a squeaky wheel zipped up to welcome them to the restaurant and ask for their party size and seating preference. Mops tapped the "Other" button and said, "Maintenance. We're here about the broken sanitizer."

As if he'd been waiting for them, a Merraban burst through a door in the far wall, his long arms raised in greeting. "Welcome, and thank you! I'm Cooks Good Meals. Call me Cook."

"I thought that was the name of the restaurant," said Kumar.

"It's named after me. Cooks Good Meals' Restaurant. The possessive doesn't translate well from Prodryan Pidgin into

Human." He gestured toward the door behind him. "This way, this way."

Merraba were friendly, but relatively rare. Most preferred to live their lives in their home system. Mops had only encountered three others in her life.

Cook was typical of the species, standing a meter high, with an armored torso shaped like a giant yellow walnut. He stood on four fuzzy legs. Extending those legs would double his height, but most Merraba were more comfortable in that squatting posture, despite the fact that their absurdly long arms tended to drag along the ground.

Each arm was twice as long and twice as furry as the legs. Only the hands were hairless, with five jointed fingers and two thumbs, one on either side of the palm. Cook's head was small and bare, mostly hidden by the yellow fur of his shoulders. When threatened, Merraba could duck their heads entirely into their shells, leaving one or both eyestalks exposed if they chose.

Not that anything was likely to threaten a Merraban. They were one of the most easygoing races in the galaxy, even adopting new names to fit in with other cultures. Mops wondered what Cook had called himself before he took on a Prodryan-style name.

"That sanitizer's been acting up for weeks," said Cook, leading them into the kitchen. "We've had to cycle it two, three times just to get a decent clean. Sometimes the heat doesn't kick in at all."

"Sounds like an electrical problem," said Monroe.

Kumar glanced around. "Depends on the model. Some of the older industrial sanitizers had glitchy temperature sensors. If that gets corroded, it can cause erratic heating."

Large refrigeration units dominated the back wall. A long, multi-surface cooking table stretched most of the length of the kitchen. On one end, a Prodryan grilled a batch of small yellow insects skewered with sliced orange tubers of some kind. Beside her, another Prodryan fought to keep a green-shelled crustacean from crawling out of a metal pot.

"Clamp that lid," Cook barked to the second Prodryan. A Krakau hurried out of a storage closet and pulled herself up to help.

The sanitizer was a chest-high metal box set into the wall. It reminded Mops a little of an old safe, with its reinforced round door. A rotten-egg smell drifted up the instant Cook opened it. Inside was a series of circular racks and shelves for dishes, utensils, pots, and pans of all sizes.

"Smells like you've got a bacterial problem growing in the hoses, too," said Mops. "Can we disconnect the power without disrupting the rest of your kitchen?"

Cook stepped nimbly out of the way. "Do whatever it takes."

Disassembling the sanitizer took close to an hour, after which Kumar crawled inside to examine and test various hoses and electrical connections. "I was right. The sensor's gunked up. Looks like some clogged jets as well."

A sensor module clattered onto the floor a moment later. Monroe picked up the small metal rod and began scrubbing it down. Wolf crouched at the door and fed a power-spray hose in for Kumar.

"Would you like to try a roasted Tjikko nut?" asked Cook, coming up behind them.

"No, thank you," Mops said firmly. "We brought our own food."

His eyestalks twitched in dismay. "I've seen the nutrient tubes humans are expected to ingest. Calling them 'food' is an insult to food throughout the galaxy. To subsist on nothing but tasteless goop in a tube . . ."

"They're good, sir!" The sterilizer amplified and echoed Wolf's voice. "The nuts, I mean. Don't worry, you're not eating part of a Tjikko. The nuts come from a non-sentient tree from their world."

Cook extended the nut. It was the size of Mops' fist, with a green string tied around the middle. The ebony shell was polished and scored to be easily cracked. "I infuse them with an oil similar to your Earth chocolate. I so love seeing your facial expressions the first time you taste one. Consider it my way of welcoming you to the station."

"I appreciate the offer, but it's not healthy for our species." Mops patted him on the arm, remembering how fond Merraba were of friendly physical contact. "Thank you, though. It's nice to run into someone who isn't terrified we're going to eat *them*."

"Merraba are toxic. I imagine eating one of us would make even a human sick." He made a warm trilling sound, the equivalent of laughter. "I'm just happy to see four more humans who've escaped the EMC."

"Escaped?" Monroe repeated.

Cook gestured at their jumpsuits. Mops had made certain they removed all rank and other insignia, but anyone familiar with EMC issue uniforms would still recognize them. "Do you know why the Krakau haven't enlisted scientists from other species to help cure your planet?"

"Because they don't want to risk anyone sabotaging their work," said Monroe. "Or trying to use that research against us."

Obviously, that secrecy hadn't stopped the Prodryans.

"Could be, could be." Cook bobbed his eyestalks again in easy agreement. "But I've always found it curious, how protective they were of your Earth. I remember when the Quetzalus first detected signs of life on your planet, about a hundred years ago. They filed their intentions to send an exploratory probe, all legal and proper. Next thing you know, the Krakau are scrambling to put together a mission of their own to get there first."

"You *remember* that?" asked Wolf.

"Merraba can live two hundred years," said Mops. "Not pissing off everyone you meet has a significant effect on life expectancy."

"True enough," trilled Cook. "I've always wondered what the Krakau wanted so much that they stole Earth from under the Quetzalus' beaks."

"You think they were after us?" guessed Monroe. "Humans?"

"Let's just say, as an outside observer, it looks like they've gotten an excellent return on their investment in Earth. Don't get me wrong. If you're satisfied with your arrangement, it's none of my business. But I like you people. You're mostly straightforward, easy to deal with, and all a little crazy. You might be an endangered species, but I'm rooting for you."

A spurt of water inside the sanitizer made Kumar jerk back. "It's all right," he called. "Just cleared a water line, that's all. Someone hand me a vise clamp and a tube of sterigel to flush the line."

While Monroe and Wolf assisted with the repair, Mops lowered her voice and said, "You mostly serve Prodryans here?"

"I serve anyone willing to eat," he said, with a good-natured bump of her arm. "But Tower Two is mostly Prodryans, yes. They won't harm you if that's what you're worried about. They may not like humans—or anyone else—but they follow Coacalos rules."

"They declare war on the galaxy, but they play nice on this station?"

"For now, sure." Cook turned to shout orders at one of his chefs. With one eyestalk watching his employees, he continued, "Some Prodryans will kill other species on instinct, but every race has its outliers."

He rapped his knuckles on his shell, as if to demonstrate. "There's an advantage to neutral territory where they can interact with other species. To buy or trade for things they can't steal, or just to catch up on the galactic gossip. Don't let them goad you into a fight, though. If you fire the first shot, all bets are off."

"I'll keep that in mind." Mops lowered her voice. "I hear they can get pretty rowdy. Especially at those prebattle feasts."

Cook leaned closer. "Who doesn't get riled up at a party? But they've never given me trouble I couldn't handle. Some broken furniture and dishware, maybe. I make sure they pay for the damages."

"How long since the last one?" Mops asked.

"Eleven days."

Which would match the timing for the attack on the *Pufferfish*. Mops checked the other cooks again. "Do you happen to remember the names of those Prodryans?"

Cook's eyestalks bobbed again, giving her a once-over. "Why does it matter?"

"They may be responsible for hurting some friends of mine."

He started to back away. "I'm not interested in helping anyone get their revenge."

"I don't want revenge," said Mops.

Wolf perked up. "I do!"

Mops elbowed her in the ribs. "We're here to try to stop them from hurting anyone else."

"I appreciate your assistance with the sanitizer, and I have great sympathy for your situation and your species, but—"

"Tell him you'll eat the Tjikko nut," said Wolf.

Mops spun. "What?"

Wolf stepped toward Cook. "She's fresh from the EMC, like you guessed. She's never tasted real food in her life. Not since she was cured, anyway. Your concoction would be the first thing she ever eats. Believe me, you never forget your first time."

Mops' glare promised a long string of nasty assignments, followed by extreme death, but Wolf ignored her.

"Never?" Cook repeated, turning back to Mops. His eyes bulged with a mix of sympathy and disbelief. "Not even an illicit taste while on leave?"

"It's not a good habit for us to develop," Mops said sternly.

Wolf snorted. "One nut is not a habit, and I promise it won't hurt you."

"She's probably right," Doc added. *"There are very few documented cases of eating-related reversion, and none of them were triggered by anything this small."*

"Et tu, Doc?" With a sigh, she held out her hand. "All right."

"Oh, wonderful!" Cook trilled. He placed the nut into her palm and waited expectantly. "Don't eat the string."

It was heavier than she'd expected. She tugged off the string and turned the nut over in her hand. "How do I do this?"

"Here." Monroe took it in his mechanical hand and squeezed. The shell split along the carved line. He tugged the two halves apart and gave them back.

The interior looked like a little fossilized black brain, divided into two oblong hemispheres. Some sort of syrup or glaze shone in the wrinkles. "I just . . . dig it out and eat it?"

"I can get you a nut fork if you'd like," Cook offered. He put a fuzzy arm around her shoulders. "Most prefer to use their fingers, though."

With a sigh, Mops dug her fingertips around the wrinkled mass and pulled half of it free with a cracking sound. It felt like water-softened wood, and smelled earthy and sweet. Saliva pooled in her mouth.

She crunched down. Chewed. Swallowed.

"Well?" asked Wolf.

Mops swore silently to herself. "It's . . . delicious."

12

TO ALL COOKS GOOD MEALS EMPLOYEES

Re: Surprising Guests with Celebratory Outbursts

We're all familiar with the Prodryan celebration of First Flight, marking a young Prodryan's successful survival after being hurled from the nest. Many Prodryans choose to celebrate in this very restaurant.

Staff are welcome and encouraged to help with this and all other festivities, whether that means a song and free dessert for a mated Nusuran trio celebrating their sexual anniversary, toffee-wax candles for our Krakau patrons to enjoy on the Day of High Tides, or in the case of First Flight, providing fire wine and harmless explosives for friends of the family to set off when the triumphant Prodryan enters the restaurant.

I appreciate initiative, but we must also be aware of different species' habits and preferences.

Quetzalus mourn the death of a family member with a quiet celebration of that person's life and accomplishments. It was an honor to have the Xalupux family choose Cooks Good Meals as their gathering place to mark the passing of their matriarch. (A potentially profitable honor, given Quetzalus appetites!)

I understand Assistant Chef Swift Knife was only trying to enhance the celebration. However, surprising a group of mourning Quetzalus with explosives and flaming drinks is not only culturally inappropriate, it's potentially dangerous.

As Swift Knife and everyone else present that night learned, Quetzalus have a deeply ingrained fear response, evolved to allow them to better fight or flee in times of danger. All total, our guests' projectile vomited approximately fourteen kilograms of partially digested food matter throughout the restaurant.

Given that Swift Knife was directly in the path of this explosion, I don't think there's any need for disciplinary action. The concussion he suffered from the impact was consequence enough, and I'm certain he will not make the same mistake again.

That said, if it does *happen again, all cleaning and medical costs will come from the responsible employee's paycheck.*

Thank you!

—Cooks Good Meals

MOPS HAD INTENDED TO go straight to the Coacalos family for information on the names Cook had given them, but Kumar recognized one from their maintenance list. Heart of Glass, from apartment 2-6-103, had put in a request more than a week ago for a clogged drain line.

She stepped off the lift and double-checked her monocle. According to Doc's map, Tower Two, Level Six, Room 103 should be right across this bridge.

The bridge to the residential section stretched like crystallized red toffee from the lift, splitting off from a central platform in four other directions. Thinner reinforcing strands made the whole thing look like a giant bloody spiderweb.

The gravity was even lighter up here, allowing the Prodryans to drift and loop about as they watched Mops step onto the bridge. Despite its appearance, it felt solid enough to support them. Monroe had to hunch to grip the low railing.

A yellow-winged male with a thin, metal exoskeleton affixed to his limbs corkscrewed around them, never quite coming within reach.

"We're here to fix a waste line in 103," Mops called out as she approached the pentagonal platform at the center of the bridge.

The looping Prodryan alighted on the rail. "You're not wanted here. The last resident brought a human to this level, and its stink fouled the whole section."

Mops simply smiled. "How long ago was that?"

"Thirty days the stench has lingered."

"It'll be easier to clean if we know what Hurt of Ass was doing with this human."

The Prodryan paused. "Heart of Glass' business is none of yours, human."

"Thanks anyway." Mops tapped the side of her monocle and moved her lips like she was reading. "Says here Mister Glass was working with some sort of venom. You wouldn't know anything about that, would you?"

The Prodryan spread his wings and moved closer, mouth pincers spread. He had a floral smell, surprisingly pleasant. "I know nothing of Heart of Glass' work with azure venom."

Bless Prodryan attempts at lying. "Azure venom, is it?"

He froze, then spat a small pellet onto the floor in front of her and jumped from the platform. Mops watched him swoop toward a balcony one level below. "Doc—"

"Already on it. I'm not aware of any references to azure venom, but I'll keep searching."

Mops took her time crossing to apartment 103, hoping another Prodryan might try to get in their faces and accidentally provide additional information, but they seemed content to watch and glare.

The smell was worse than she'd expected, making her nose wrinkle from four doors away. She could hear the air filtration fans rattling and vibrating like growling metal robots, but they couldn't fully clear the pungent smell of chemicals and rotten meat.

"It wasn't me," Wolf said, waving a hand in front of her face.

A notice on the door's lock screen explained that the room was closed for maintenance. A swipe of Mops' badge deactivated the lock.

Mops stepped inside. She was tempted to seal her hood, but in this line of work, smell offered too many clues to where a given problem could be coming from.

"They blame that stink on one human?" asked Monroe, waving his left hand in front of his face.

Wolf stopped in the doorway. "Should we really be going in there? If they were working on their venom weapon—"

"Anything in the air would have cycled through the station by now," said Kumar, his voice tight. "You saw how fast it spread through the *Pufferfish*, and I guarantee our air circulation system is cleaner than anything here."

The first thing to catch Mops' eye was a large cylindrical tank with a curved door. "Doc, check the logs on this room and find out when they installed a Glacidae shower."

"Twenty-six days ago, billed to Heart of Glass."

Mops surveyed the rest of the room. Three small hammocks hung from the high ceiling. A stone-topped worktable sat against one wall. She checked the gleaming surface—spotless. Someone had done a much better job cleaning this room than the one Mops and her team were staying in over in Tower Five.

Kumar pulled on his gloves, sealed his hood, and slid open the shower door, releasing a new cloud of stink. "According to the work order, this is the drain line they clogged up. I'll pop off the grate."

"I'm surprised you're taking the lead on this one," said Wolf. "You can't walk past a window without scrubbing the fingerprints clean, but you want to reach into that cesspit?"

"I'd rather cut off my own hand." Kumar's face was pale. Sweat beaded and dripped from the tip of his nose. "But whatever's in here, we've all been breathing it. The quicker we find out what it is, the quicker we can purge it from the station and, if necessary, our lungs."

"You said if it was gonna hurt us, it would have done it by now." Wolf bent to peer over Kumar's shoulder. "We were probably just inhaling particles of rot or shit or shed skin."

Kumar tugged the grate. One of his hands slipped, coming up to smack Wolf in the side of the head.

Wolf staggered backward. "You did that on purpose!"

"I hope so," said Mops, before Kumar could respond. "It saved me the trouble of doing it myself."

Kumar tossed the grate aside and shone a light down the pipe. "It's pooled up about ten centimeters in." He grabbed a slender pry bar from his harness and poked one end deep into the mess. "Something crunchy, like eggshells. Quetzalus lay eggs, don't they?"

"No way Heart of Glass swiped a Quetzalus egg," said Monroe. "Not on this station. The Coacalos family would have ripped his wings off."

Kumar sat back. "We need a vacuum snake."

Unfortunately, theirs was back on the *Pufferfish*. Mops checked the list of cleaning supplies in the nearest maintenance closet. "Looks like the closest they've got is a basic three-centimeter vacuum hose."

"So let's siphon out the water and get a better look at the blockage," said Monroe.

"Bad idea." Wolf pointed at the pipes coming into the tank. "Glacidae use a mild acid wash to keep their shells clean and polished. Given how cheap the rest of the station maintenance equipment has been, I doubt their hose could handle it."

Mops raised an eyebrow at her.

"I had to adjust the acid levels and neutralizing rinse in Grom's quarters last month, remember? Burned the hair off my left arm, along with a few layers of skin."

"Find another option." Mops turned to examine the rest of the room. Pale discoloration on the floor showed where droplets from the Glacidae shower had splashed beyond the tile. She found a closet and a small wall safe, both of which were unlocked and empty. Eye hooks on the ceiling were spaced out to hold four more hammocks, if necessary. She also found a broken security monitor nestled in the corner.

She checked the garbage bin next. The contents had been purged and the interior sanitized. "Nothing here."

"Check the waste logs," said Kumar.

Wolf laughed derisively. "Waste logs?"

"The station charges for both the disposal of day-to-day trash and for organic excretions. Everything gets analyzed and weighed and logged. Didn't you read the toilet-and-sewage section of the orientation packet?"

Mops raised a hand to forestall further argument. "Doc, can you pull up the logs for this room? Trash and organic waste."

A column of data streamed onto her monocle, each entry tagged by date, time, weight, material, and cost. Doc highlighted four rows and said, *It appears several of our Prodryans returned from their celebration at Cook's eleven days ago and promptly vomited.*

Mops started with the garbage log. "Ten days back, Heart of Glass threw out what look like mem crystal fragments, synthetic fabrics, chemical powders, and pieces of nonfunctional electronic equipment." She switched her attention to the organic logs. "Most of the waste is tagged Prodryan, but not all. They also flushed material from a Glacidae, a human . . . and a Krakau."

"They had a Krakau in here?" asked Wolf.

"Not necessarily," said Kumar. He and Monroe had both squeezed into the Glacidae shower, trying to clear the drain. "All we know is that someone flushed Krakau waste material. We don't know if that material came directly from the Krakau. Maybe it was brought here by an intermediary."

Wolf grimaced. "Why in the icy depths would anyone—"

"I've got something," Monroe interrupted, to Mops' relief.

She stepped around to the shower door to find Monroe stretched out on the floor. His right sleeve lay flat on the tile. With his left hand, he held the gleaming white bicep of his detached artificial arm. "What did you do?"

"Found something the acid wouldn't hurt." Monroe shifted to one side while Kumar reached over with his gloved hands to help pull the arm free.

Oily yellow liquid dripped from the unnaturally white skin. The arm twisted in Kumar's grip, making him yelp and nearly drop it.

"Be careful! That's expensive." Monroe pushed himself upright. "Arm, show us what you found."

The arm held out a handful of pitted yellow bone.

Kumar set the arm gently on the shower floor and poked the fragments. "I hate to say it, but I think these are human." He grabbed a pebble-sized bone between his thumb and index finger. "No other species we've encountered has teeth this size and shape."

"Poor bastard," said Wolf.

"How long would it take to dissolve a human body in a Glacidae acid shower?" asked Kumar.

"Depends on whether they were properly diluting the acid wash," said Wolf.

Mops thought back to her conversation with Lazan and Ix Coacalos, and Lazan's comment about a human employee who'd quit without notice. "I think we've found the Coacalos family's missing worker."

Hauling the remains of a fellow human through the station in a ten-kilo biohazard container felt disrespectful, but at least the bright green warning labels kept the Prodryans at a distance. In the lighter gravity of the upper tower, the box felt empty, but the rattling of shifting bones reminded her what she carried.

Monroe had retrieved most of the bones from the drain, along with a few pieces of corroded metal—buckles and other fasteners. The rest had flushed away once he removed the worst of the blockage.

Monroe's right arm hung limply at his side. He insisted everything had passed diagnostics, and Arm was just pouting about being used as a drain snake. A quick wash and rinse in neutralizer wasn't enough to make up for that level of indignity. Which seemed reasonable enough to Mops.

They were halfway back to Tower Five when Doc flashed an incoming message alert. *"It's from Ix Lataclox."*

"I was wondering when you'd call," said Mops.

"Thank you for recovering the remains of our worker."

"You're sure that's who it is?"

"Genetic testing will confirm the identity," said Ix. "Assuming the acid hasn't corrupted the DNA. Please bring the remains to the organic waste processing facility on level one of Tower One."

Mops stopped walking. "Waste processing? You're going to *recycle* them?"

"It's the most cost-efficient choice. Unless you wish to purchase the remains? As de facto station employees, I could arrange for you to receive a five percent discount."

Mops closed her eyes, calming herself with soothing images of punching Ix Lataclox in the throat. "What was the human's name?"

"Does it matter? The human's death is unfortunate, but it's obvious the Coacalos family had nothing to do with these matters."

She counted ten more punches. "The name."

There was a long pause. "Floyd . . . Westerman, I believe."

"I assume you had the humans crammed into one of the bottom-level apartments in Tower Five. Where can we find the roommates?" A short list appeared on Mops' monocle. She ended the connection. "Doc, who on that list is closest?"

"Vera Rubin, a security guard currently working in Arena Two, down in the first sublevel."

Monroe stepped closer to whisper, "We're being followed. Thirty meters back. Green wing. She's been watching us since the lift."

"Took them long enough," Mops replied. "Doc, show me."

Doc ran a quick replay of everything Mops' monocle had seen since leaving the lift, quickly picking out and highlighting four stills of the Prodryan. Her right wing appeared to be missing. The other was lime green and lay flat against her body, the end ragged. A dull brown shawl over the right side of her body could conceal any number of small weapons.

She was obviously watching the humans, but that proved nothing. Half the station was staring at Mops and her team, while the other half was just as obviously avoiding eye contact.

Mops handed the crate over to Wolf. "Monroe, you and Wolf take Westerman back to our quarters. Give your arm a proper cleaning and tune-up while you're there. Maybe that will soothe its hurt feelings. Kumar and I will go talk to Vera Rubin. We'll see who our friend follows, if anyone."

"We're not taking Westerman to Tower One for processing?" asked Kumar.

"Hell, no."

Monroe smiled. "Yes, sir."

The Prodryan chose to follow Mops and Kumar. Mops looked from side to side like a gawking tourist as she walked, allowing Doc to track their follower from the edges of Mops' monocle. When they reached the lift, the Prodryan turned away to enter a small shop selling exoskeletal etchings and piercings.

"Doc, tap into the team's monocles and put a flag on that Prodryan. If she enters visual range of anyone on the team, highlight her as a potential threat." As the lift closed behind her, she added, "But remind Wolf that does *not* mean she has free rein to start shooting!"

Sublevel one had a cavernous feel: tall and dimly lit, with vast open spaces between rounded structures that grew out of floor and ceiling like insect hives. Everything was the red-brown hue of iron-rich rock. The hum of station machinery filled the air, and Mops could feel the faint vibration beneath her feet. She didn't see many people, and of those she did, most appeared to be station employees. A pair of Quetzalus hauled a shuttle-sized load of fertilizer toward one of the plant feeding stations at the far wall. A Glacidae maintenance worker hung upside down from the ceiling, working on a bad lighting panel.

After making sure nobody was paying them too much attention, Mops set off toward Arena Two. Unlike the rest of the sublevel, the three large arenas were decorated in bright-colored stripes and labeled in more languages than Mops could count. There was even a small section in Human that listed upcoming events and attractions, along with the prices for each.

The main entrance was six meters wide and blocked by a metal gate bristling with thorny spikes. A thick-limbed woman stood to one side, a heavy club in one hand. Mops' monocle identified the club as a modified combat baton.

"The next event isn't for another hour," said the woman.

"Vera Rubin?" Mops guessed.

She frowned. "Who's asking?"

"We're from Maintenance," said Mops. "We should be in the system."

Rubin closed one eye. She had no visible monocle, but was probably wearing a lens or using some kind of implant. When she looked up again, her demeanor had eased from wariness into a generally depressed slump. "I didn't realize the family had hired new humans. Don't get your hopes up. It's no better here than in the EMC."

Vera Rubin wore what looked like an old, modified black EMC uniform, layered with thin armor plates over the torso, shoulders, waist, and thighs. A black helmet mostly concealed a set of dark scars down the side of her neck.

"The next event is a Tellarian bone duel?" asked Kumar. "I've never seen one."

"Bone duels aren't bad," Vera said in a low monotone. "Pointless, but no more than the rest of this drivel they call entertainment. The Nusuran sex opera later tonight is worse. Short-lived titillation to fill the meaningless void of people's lives. We'll probably have another packed house."

"Sex opera? I hope your autocleaner's well-maintained." Mops gave a mock shudder, then nodded toward Rubin's scars. "You were infantry?"

"I was, yeah, but these are from fighting a couple of Nusurans who tried to sneak into a water ballet without paying." Rubin started to say more, when something in her breast pocket squirmed and let out a low gurgle. "Sorry, hold on."

"What's that?" Kumar asked, peering closer.

Rubin pulled what looked like a seven-centimeter-long slug from her pocket. "Nusuran blood slug."

Kumar searched his equipment harness. "I've got a spray in here that should—"

"It's my pet," Rubin continued. "I named it Slug." She rolled up her sleeve and set the blue slug on her forearm. "I've been teaching it tricks. Mostly things like 'Hide' and 'Stand up.'"

She snapped her fingers twice, and Slug reared up to display its slick blue underbelly.

"You used to share an apartment with Floyd Westerman," said Mops.

"That's right." She nudged Slug, who coiled around her wrist like a slimy bracelet. "He didn't like my pets."

"Pets, plural?" asked Kumar. "How many do you have?"

"Twelve, if you count my tapeworm." She smiled slightly, the first sign of emotion Mops had seen. "I'm saving up for an Earth dog. Or maybe a possum."

"We wanted to talk to you," Mops pressed. "Earlier today, my team found what we think are Floyd's remains."

She sighed and tugged Slug from her wrist. "If he's dead,

are they really *his* remains anymore? Who owns a body with no life left in it?"

"There's plenty of life left in dead bodies." Kumar hesitated. "Though probably not this one."

Rubin turned her full attention to Kumar. "You think the remains belong to the microorganisms that consume us after we die? That's a lovely thought."

Mops couldn't tell whether that was sarcasm or genuine sentiment.

"Legally, it's another story," Kumar continued. "According to station regulations, the Coacalos family can claim ownership, meaning they would technically be the Coacalos' remains. But in the larger scheme of things, who says we own our bodies in the first place? Is it just right of first occupation? Our biological parents contributed the initial cells."

"Ownership is imaginary," Rubin countered. "Everything is temporary."

"We found Floyd in Tower Two," Mops interrupted. "We're trying to figure out how he ended up there. Do you know why he would have gone into a Prodryan residence?"

She shrugged. "Floyd was Security, like most of us. He was a charger."

"Charger?" asked Kumar.

"Big, strong, and scary looking," explained Wolf. "They charge into a conflict, hollering like maniacs. Half the time, the sight of a huge, half-crazed human running at you is enough to end a fight right there."

A human like that would have been even harder for the Prodryans to abduct against his will.

"He wasn't really scary," said Rubin. "Slug liked him." She frowned and, for the first time, looked Mops in the eyes. "What are you here to work on? I didn't think we had anything in the maintenance queue."

"You don't," said Mops. "Did Floyd say anything about a Prodryan named Heart of Glass?"

"The moths mostly keep to themselves. Humans, too. We do

our jobs and keep our heads down. It's better for everyone. Floyd had problems, but he kept away from the bloody tower."

"The bloody tower?" asked Kumar.

"Floyd said Tower Two was the color human blood used to be, before the plague. He knew lots of things about old Earth and pre-plague humans. He collected Earth artifacts. Plastic toys and old writing instruments. A pair of glasses frames. Little pins to wear on his shirt."

"What kind of problems did he have?" Mops asked, gently trying to keep the conversation on track.

Rubin looked at Mops like an instructor with a particularly dim pupil. "The same problem we all have. Money. Earth artifacts aren't cheap. Floyd owed a lot of money to Theta."

"Theta?" Mops repeated.

"The Tjikko who lives in Tower Six. He knows as much about what goes on in the station as the Coacalos family. Maybe more. She has his roots into everything."

"Did she work with the Prodryans?" Mops stumbled only slightly over the pronoun. Every species' gender terminology translated differently into Human. Glacidae preferred the singular "they." Krakau, all of whom were capable of carrying and bearing young, had chosen "she."

The Tjikko, once they got over their amusement at the concept of gender, had chosen to alternate pronouns. They said the variation best reflected their own biology, which changed depending on the season and whether they chose to flower and cross-pollinate. Mops hadn't worked with enough Tjikko for the conversational back-and-forth to become habit.

"He worked with everyone," said Rubin.

Mops nodded. "What would Theta do if you owed her money?"

"He always gets her money back, one way or another."

Before Mops could follow up, an impact like a hammer slammed into the back of her thigh. Her leg buckled, and she caught Kumar's arm to keep from falling.

"Suit punctures," Doc warned. *"Back and front."*

"You're bleeding," said Rubin, in that same empty monotone. She grabbed Mops with one hand, Kumar with the other, and hauled them both into the relative shelter of the arched gateway. After pressing them both against the stone wall, she pulled her combat baton and switched it on.

"Sir?" Panic honed Kumar's voice.

Mops looked down at the two-centimeter hole in her uniform. Her right thigh throbbed, presumably from the matching hole through her leg.

"Your heart rate and breathing have sped up, and your pupil is enlarged." The words sounded distant and distorted. *"You're in danger of going into shock."*

Another shot shattered a chunk of wall by Kumar's head. He jumped back, jabbing his arm and shoulder against the barbs on the gate.

"Stay down." Mops grabbed a tube of bioglue from the emergency kit on her harness. "Doc, where did that shot come from?"

"Based on the entry and exit wounds, given where you were standing at the time . . ." An arrow appeared on her monocle, pointing back in the direction of the lift. *"The shot may have chipped the outer edge of your femur, but the fact that you're still standing means it didn't shatter completely."*

She bit the cap from the tube and fumbled to get the nozzle into the hole in the front of her leg. "They wouldn't be shooting at us if we weren't onto something."

"They might," said Rubin. She peeked around the archway, then yanked back to avoid more gunfire. "Most people don't like humans."

"Don't you have a gun?" asked Kumar.

"The Coacalos don't trust human employees with guns." Rubin adjusted the controls on her baton. A portion of the electromagnetically secured monofilaments bent and reformed into a new configuration, creating rows of three-centimeter spikes on the end of the weapon. "I'll charge them. You call for assistance."

"They're after us, not you." Mops awkwardly squeezed another glob of bioglue into the back hole. Replacing the cap, she returned it to her harness. "Monroe, this is Mops. We've got company. The angry type, with guns."

"Wolf and I can be down there in ten minutes."

"Be careful. They might have backup watching the lifts." Mops drew her gun, biting back the urge to tell him to hurry. Monroe knew as well as she did that this would probably be over in ten minutes. One way or another.

13

Warning: Tonight's Nusuran opera may be offensive to members of sexually repressed cultures.

The performers may ask for a volunteer from the audience. Volunteers must be physically healthy. Coacalos Station is not responsible for any injuries suffered by those who choose to participate.

For this performance, the part of the Interstellar Brothel Ghost will be played by understudy Loka-Farnikor-vi.

Rows 1-4 have been designated as a potential "splash zone." Anyone wishing to change seats must notify an usher before the performance begins.

Recording for personal use only is permitted and encouraged.

These are trained athletes and actors. Do not try what you are about to see at home.

MOPS SHIFTED TO GUN'S-EYE view and pointed the barrel around the edge of the archway. Doc indicated the direction of their attackers, but she didn't see anyone. Any station employees had scurried for shelter. Even the insects had burrowed into the walls and ceiling, leaving the sublevel eerily still.

A shot from the opposite direction came close to removing her hand at the wrist. She jerked back. "Dammit, Doc!"

"It's possible the shooters relocated."

"You think?" Mops fired twice at the edge of a small equipment storage building, her best guess as to where the shooter was hiding. "We're pinned down. Rubin, get this gate open. We'll cut through the arena to get away."

"That's against the rules," Rubin said flatly. "Only performers and authorized personnel can enter the arena between performances."

Mops spied movement toward the lift. She shot three more times, sending the figure scurrying back for cover. "They'll kill us if we stay here."

Rubin cocked her head, as if considering the possible outcomes. "That seems likely."

Kumar put a hand on Rubin's arm. With his other hand, he pointed to the gouged stones of the archway. "They'll also do a great deal of damage to the arena. You're supposed to protect this place, right?"

"That's right."

"Let us into the arena," Kumar continued. "Once we're inside, they'll stop shooting at it. You'll be saving it from damage. Then you can kick us out through another doorway."

Rubin took several long seconds to consider the idea before turning around and pressing her badge against the control panel. There was no sound to indicate a change, but when she pushed the gate, it swung inward. Mops shoved Rubin and Kumar through, then hobbled after, pulling it shut behind her. "Can you lock it again?"

"It locks on its own."

The arched tunnel was broad enough for two Quetzalus to walk side by side, and extended roughly two meters. Mops hurried through to find herself in an enormous lobby area, with shuttered shops along the walls. Stairs, ramps, and lifts led both down toward the stage and up to higher tiers of seats.

Enormous vid screens hung from the ceiling. Without an active signal, they looked like rectangles of translucent smoky glass. On the stage, a group of Glacidae arranged squares of rocky terrain for the upcoming show.

"Get out!" Mops shouted.

"We're working here," one called back. "Come back when the show starts, you stupid *human*."

A slight pause and change in inflection suggested Doc had substituted "human" for one of the more vulgar terms for Mops' species. With a sigh, she limped forward, pointed her gun over the stage, and fired.

The Glacidae dropped low and scurried away without a sound. The only thing scarier than a human was a human with a gun.

Kumar grabbed Mops' other arm, and they hurried after the fleeing Glacidae. They'd just reached the main stage when a small explosion behind them marked the arrival of their attackers. A pressure wave thundered through the arena, along with the rattle of shrapnel.

The Glacidae stage crew belched in terror and ran faster, leaving oily black trails as they disappeared into a dark maintenance tunnel.

Rubin paused, staring at something only she could see. "The Glacidae have secured the exit behind them to prevent us from following."

"Can you open it?" snapped Mops.

"I am not part of the stage crew," she said simply.

Mops limped down the closest ramp and cut across through the relative shelter of the deep Quetzalus seats. "Doc, can you alert station security?"

"I'm being jammed."

Mops' fist tightened. "Is there another way out?"

Rubin shook her head. "The Quetzalus don't want anyone sneaking in to sabotage or rig an event."

Mops scanned the arena. The seats in the pie-shaped sections were clearly designed for different species, from oversized divots for Quetzalus to the miniature jungle gyms for the Krakau. None offered much in the way of hiding spots.

Brown daubed-on insulation covered most of the ceiling, all save the air vents, lighting, and the arena autocleaner. The vents were probably maintained from the outside, maybe from an access tunnel on the next level. "Rubin, where are the controls for that autocleaner?"

"I'm not sure. I usually stay by the gate."

Kumar poked his head up to look around. Mops hauled him down, barely saving him from getting shot.

"Looks like a Tun-Ka-Vi autocleaner. If they're using a standard model, the controls should be built into the stage itself. Given the size of the stage, it's probably a Seven or Eight. The Eight has more efficient heating and a wider nozzle range, but it costs almost twice as much as—"

"Come on," said Mops, shoving him to the floor and crawling toward the stage.

Gunfire raked the seats, then fell quiet. A quick peek back showed their attackers moving through the aisles to line up a better shot. "Are those Krakau?"

Doc froze and enhanced the image. *"Indeed. Four of them."*

The gunfire started up again as they reached the bottom row. The stage stood before them on a meter-high base of sculpted stone. Doc helpfully translated the captions on the different scenes carved into the stone, tribute to some of the most famous events held here. Mops saw everything from hand-to-hand fights to a galactic record-setting display of competitive flatulence. A Nusuran held the title for decibels, but a Quetzalus had easily overpowered them in terms of sheer, eye-watering power.

Kumar stopped abruptly and pointed to the faint lines of a conduit channel in the floor. "There's a power line here." He squatted in front of the stage, then turned in confusion. "I'm sorry, sir, but why are we worrying about cleaning the stage? This wasn't on our maintenance list, and even if it was—"

Mops shoved him aside and followed the conduit to a small rectangular panel on the side of the stage. She ripped off the cover. Inside was a grid of amber lights. A few blinked at varying speeds, while the rest glowed steadily.

"Oh, wow, it's a Six Mark II," said Kumar, peering over her shoulder. "This thing's twenty years out of date. This is just a maintenance panel, not the main console."

"Can we control the autocleaner from here?" snapped Mops.

Kumar brought his badge to the panel. The lights turned red. "Looks like it recognizes us as maintenance techs. We can't do anything fancy like a selective four-stage sterilization, but we can do test cycles and basic, preprogrammed runs."

Gunfire turned one of the carvings to Mops' left into a series of glowing craters. An amplified voice called out in mechanically translated Human. "That was a warning shot. You're pinned down. Surrender."

"What's the broadest radius for the Six Mark II?" Mops whispered.

"It's big enough to cover the whole arena, easily," said Kumar. "The jets are rated for a range of a hundred and eight meters. From that height, they could reach one-twenty, though you'd have to adjust for the slope of the stands, and—"

"What disinfectants are they using?"

"I can get that for you." Doc pulled up a list.

Mops skimmed the ingredients and nodded to herself. "Kumar, turn the detergent-to-water ratio up to max, and run a full cleaning cycle."

"This is your last chance," shouted one of the Krakau. Another burst of gunfire struck the stage.

Kumar touched four of the lights in sequence, paused, and tapped three more. "There you go."

Mops tilted her head. "Well?"

"The Six Mark II has a three-minute warm-up cycle. There's no way to bypass it from here." He replaced the cover.

Mops grabbed the others and hauled them away from the stage, down to the relative cover of the first row of Glacidae seats. The next shots shattered and shredded the contoured seat backs.

Doc had started a countdown without being asked. Two minutes and forty-five seconds.

Mops drew her second pistol, but before she could lean out to return fire, Rubin caught her shoulder.

"You need more time for this plan." It wasn't a question.

"Two minutes, forty seconds," said Mops. "If we can stall or hold them off—"

"We lack adequate cover." Rubin stood, hands raised above her head. "And they continue to damage Arena Two."

"Get down, dammit!"

Instead, Rubin looked around, her movements those of an infantry soldier tagging enemy targets.

"What are you doing?" asked Kumar.

Rubin stepped out of reach. "Stay down."

"We don't want you," shouted one of the Krakau. "We know you've got two other humans down there."

Two minutes twenty.

Rubin started up the stairs to the left. She lowered her arms and grasped her combat baton in both hands. A warning shot cracked a step in front of her.

Two minutes ten.

With a strange, ululating shout, Rubin raised her spiked baton and charged.

"Ah," said Kumar. "So that's what a charger does."

Mops leaned out to provide cover, but as soon as she peeked over the smoking, half-destroyed chairs, the Krakau opened fire from two directions. She managed to pull the trigger once before ducking.

One minute fifty-five.

More gunshots. Mops cringed at the wet thump of slugs tearing through flesh.

Rubin kept shouting. One of the Krakau swore loudly.

Another whistled orders. "Keep shooting. Aim for the head and spine! Try to—"

A squishy *crunch* cut off whatever she'd been trying to say. One minute forty-five.

Mops pulled her second weapon. With the Krakau distracted by Rubin, she raised both guns over the seats, lined up the crosshairs, and fired. A Krakau dropped.

But Rubin was down, too, and Mops spotted movement at the entrance—Krakau reinforcements.

She swore and ducked as the newly arrived Krakau turned their weapons on Mops and Kumar. She crawled on her stomach toward a less-damaged area, kicking Kumar to get him to follow.

At the one-minute mark, the arena lights dimmed, causing a momentary pause in the assault. A green warning light flashed. Mops risked another peek to see whether it would be enough to scare them off, but the Krakau kept closing in.

Forty seconds. Mops grabbed Kumar's collar and pressed him to the ground. Doc continued to ping her with suit puncture alerts from stone fragments.

"Where the hell is station security?" Mops muttered. "Rubin can't have been the only guard down here." The Krakau must have found a way to disable or distract the others.

At fifteen seconds, a series of tarnished metal nozzles poked out of the ceiling like animals leaving their burrows. None of the Krakau appeared to notice. Nor were they likely to hear the pumps starting up.

She silently counted down the final seconds. "Keep your head down and shield your eyes."

The countdown flashed zero.

Nothing happened.

"He said three minutes, right? That was exactly three—"

"Kumar! Why isn't it working?"

"It's old tech," Kumar protested. "The timing mechanism probably needs to be recalibrated or replaced. Do you want me to add it to the maintenance log?"

Before Mops could answer, jets of heated cleaning fluid—a mix of water, alcohol, and *lots* of detergent—shot down with enough force to knock one of the guns from her hand. She retrieved it and holstered both of her weapons, counted five seconds, and climbed to her feet.

Krakau were sensitive to temperature extremes, and these jets were easily powerful enough to cause bruising. Neither of those things would stop a determined Krakau with a gun.

The detergent was another matter.

One of the Krakau who'd been fighting Rubin pointed a long, tubelike weapon in Mops' direction. The weapon promptly squirted free of the Krakau's grip and clattered to the floor. She lunged to retrieve it, missed, and kept on sliding down the aisle . . . directly into Mops' path. Mops gripped the closest seat for balance and met the Krakau with a swift kick, launching her three rows up like an Earth football.

"You'll appreciate this story, Kumar." She limped toward the next Krakau. "Eight years ago, we had a malfunction in the bridge lift autocleaner. Commander Danube was completely doused. She spent the next two days slipping and falling like her limbs had turned to greased ice."

The second Krakau fumbled with her weapon, trying to bring it to bear on Mops. Mops reached down to dig her fingers into one of the Krakau's primary tentacles. Using the tentacle as a handle, she spun the Krakau through the air, then slammed her to the ground. The unconscious Krakau slid away like a Glacidae ice puck.

"Krakau secrete several different chemicals from their skins," Mops continued. "One makes them slick and harder for predators to hold. Another forms a thin layer of biological gel on their limbs, which allows them to grip almost any surface. Industrial detergent dissolves one of these two chemicals. Guess which one?"

The reinforcements had abandoned their weapons and were trying to retreat through the Krakau section. They clung desperately to the bars of the seats and pulled themselves upward, using sheer muscle to overcome their lack of grip. After only two rows, they were both beginning to sag from exhaustion.

Mops barely noticed when the autocleaner jets finished their rinse cycle, and the water began to trickle down toward concealed drains at the base of the arena. As she approached the Krakau, they dropped from the bars and shrank to half their size.

Mops pointed one gun at each Krakau. "One of your friends shot me," she said, jerking her chin toward the hole in her thigh. "I probably could have forgiven that. But then you started shooting at my friends. . . ."

"How is she?" asked Mops.

"Alive." Kumar's muscles were taut as he continued dabbing bioglue into Rubin's wounds. "They shot her eleven times before she fell. Missed the brain and spine, but she's in bad shape."

"What were you thinking, Rubin?" Mops demanded.

"They were in the arena." Rubin coughed. "Nobody's allowed in the arena before the show."

"Can you walk?"

"No, she can't!" Kumar snapped, adding a curt "sir" a moment later.

"There could be more Krakau on the way." Mops glanced at the four whimpering Krakau. None had tried to move from the Quetzalus seat where she'd dropped them. "We need to get somewhere safe."

"Her legs are too messed up." Kumar pinched another wound shut, holding it until the bioglue took hold. "I can carry her."

"Do it." Mops yanked a garbage bag from her harness and shook it open. "You and you, inside," she said to the two closest Krakau. She sealed the bag and grabbed another for the remaining two Krakau.

Between their weight and the hole in her leg, she had a distinctly lopsided gait as she started up the arena stairs. She had to drag the bags behind her, bumping their occupants against each step. "The sooner you Krakau want to start talking, the better. If anyone else starts shooting, I intend to use you all for cover."

The Krakau squirmed weakly within their bags, but didn't respond.

"Monroe, Wolf, we're alive and heading your way." She stopped at the archway. Wisps of smoke curled up from the broken remains of the gate. Nothing appeared to be moving outside. Holding the bagged Krakau in front of her, she stepped cautiously through.

"What made a bunch of Krakau team up with Prodryan terrorists in the first place?" Mops waited for a response, though she didn't expect one. "I suppose it makes sense. Out of ten-plus billion Krakau, there's bound to be some extremists who don't like the Alliance."

"Sir?" Kumar carried Rubin over his shoulders in a fireman's carry. He pointed his chin at the lift, where three armed humans had just emerged.

"*Now* station security shows up? It figures." Mops dropped the two bags. "Last chance, ladies. Tell us who you're working for and where we find them, and I'll ask Security to take it easy on you. Otherwise . . ." She shrugged. "The Coacalos family isn't known for being gentle with people who shoot up their property. Are you sure there's nothing you want to tell me?"

One of the Krakau twisted inside the bag. "Lieutenant Marion Adamopoulos, by the authority of the Krakau Alliance, I hereby place you and your subordinates under arrest."

Mops froze. "You're Alliance?"

"She could be lying," said Kumar.

Mops rubbed her neck and shoulder. She'd been so intent on rooting out Prodryan collaborators she hadn't stopped to think about other possibilities. Of course the Alliance would have agents planted at Coacalos Station. And if Command had put out a galaxy-wide alert about Mops and her team . . . "If they're telling the truth, they probably contacted Command as soon as they spotted us. How long do you think we have before a cruiser full of troops docks with the station?"

"A day?" guessed Kumar. "Two if we're lucky. Do you think there are other Alliance agents here?"

"We have to assume so." She raised a hand to greet the approaching security guards. "We're mostly all right. There are two dead Krakau back in the arena, though."

"Which arena?" asked the closest human.

Mops stared at him. "I don't know, son. Try the one with all the smoke and rubble?"

A second human smacked the first on the back of his helmet. To Mops, he said, "You look like you need medical assistance. The Coacalos family will be happy to provide hospital services for a reasonable price."

"We're fine, but Rubin is in bad shape," said Kumar. "She's station security."

"Don't worry." The human came to take Rubin in his arms. "She'll get a fifteen percent employee discount."

"Surveillance was shut down," said the third human. From her tone and bearing, she was in charge. She glared at the squirming garbage bags, then back at Mops. "Who did this?"

Mops hesitated. If the Krakau were Alliance, they were only following orders from Command. Anyone from the EMC would have done the same. Until a few days ago, so would she. "We never got a good look. They chased us into the arena and started shooting. I assume it's just another hate-crime against humans."

She nudged one of the bags with her toe. "These Krakau were just in the wrong place at the wrong time, and got caught in the crossfire."

"Were they injured?" asked the commander.

"Just washed. A random shot must have set off the auto-cleaner. The Krakau are having trouble walking, but they'll be fine in a day or two when their skin gets back to a healthy level of slime."

The human hesitated, but apparently decided to accept Mops' explanation. "How many attackers were there?"

"Four," said Mops, while at the same time Kumar blurted out, "Six."

Mops gave an apologetic smile. "Like I said, it was pretty chaotic. We're brand new here. We're assigned to Maintenance, not Security. Are things always this violent?"

"Not usually." The human in charge gestured to the others, sending them to examine the arena. "Do the Krakau require medical assistance?"

Mops unsealed one of the bags, folded her arms, and waited. She trusted they knew exactly what the Coacalos would do if they discovered Alliance agents had been working—and starting a firefight—in their station.

"The injuries . . . are not life threatening," said one. "We decline your offer of assistance, thank you."

"No skin off my bones." The human shifted her rifle and tapped the edge of her monocle, a blue-tinged model Mops hadn't seen before. "Let me get your names and a snap of each of you. We'll probably have more questions once we've looked around, and we'll want a download from your monocles of anything you saw."

Mops gave her name and nodded for Kumar to do the same. The Krakau complied as well. "Doc, can you give them a data dump of our mystery attackers?"

"You have an AI assistant?" The human peered closer. "Fancy."

"Saved up for years to afford him."

"I take it you're expecting me to just edit something together that will fool a security analyst AI?"

"That's right," said Mops.

"You know, sometimes it feels like you take me for granted. But I suppose *I can layer in more autocleaner spray to obscure*

most of the incriminating evidence. And if I adjust the lighting a bit, and snip out the part where you went after the Krakau... rewrite the time stamps, add more motion-shake...."

Two minutes later, Doc had transferred the edited data over to station security. Two minutes after that, they were on their way. Mops whispered a quick message to Monroe as they approached the lift. "We're headed back up, and we have company."

There was no response.

"Monroe, respond." Her stomach tightened. "Wolf, what's your status?"

Nothing. They hadn't acknowledged her earlier call after the firefight either. She'd been too caught up in the aftermath to notice.

She dragged the Krakau into the lift, dropped both bags, and hammered her fist against the wall, waiting impatiently for the doors to close. The instant the lift began to move, she pressed her badge against the control panel. "Emergency stop."

The lift halted abruptly. Mops pulled her guns and pointed one at each bag. "Kumar, open them."

His eyes were wide as he unsealed both bags.

The first Krakau thrust her head free, whistled in alarm, and tried to duck back into the bag. Kumar tugged both bags lower, exposing the four squirming Krakau.

"My people aren't answering," Mops said quietly. "You're going to tell me exactly what's happened to them. Once you've finished, I'll decide which of you—if any—will survive to report back to Command."

"We didn't—" started one, a younger Krakau with blue-green skin.

"You were our primary target, Lieutenant," said one with a gold braidlike design tattooed around her head, just above the eyes.

A mud-brown Krakau with a chipped beak added, "We planned to take you first, then round up the others."

The fourth Krakau, an older warrior with a vivid yellow

shell armoring her torso and two missing legs, simply shrank away.

They might be lying. Unlike Prodryans, the average Krakau lied as well or better than any human. But to Mops' eye, they looked scared and exhausted. Their skin was tight, their limbs curled close to their bodies. "All right," she said. "Then tell me about a Prodryan named Heart of Glass, and a human named Floyd Westerman."

"It's not our job to care for human deserters," said the brown one.

Mops shifted her aim.

"However," the Krakau continued hastily, "we *have* been observing the Prodryans. We believe the one called Heart of Glass is actually a Prodryan exile named Invisible Flame. He crossed one of the warlords, and fled Yan to avoid execution."

"Yan? He's from the Prodryan home world?" Mops filed that fact in her mind. "What did he do to earn a death sentence?"

"Advocated cooperation with other species," said the warrior.

Mops whistled softly. "So we're dealing with a radical extremist. What was he doing on Coacalos Station?"

The tattooed Krakau answered, "We know he had several meetings with certain . . . questionable elements."

"Like the Tjikko?" asked Mops. "Theta?"

"That's right." The warrior rose, arms lashing out in anger. It would have been an impressive display if she hadn't slipped and toppled onto her tattooed companion. Struggling to regain both balance and dignity, she said, "We suspect Heart of Glass was also working with humans. Traitors to the Alliance."

Her implication was clear. "You mean us," said Mops.

"The rest of your crew was lost, but miraculously, your team survived," said the warrior. "You then proceeded immediately to Coacalos Station to rendezvous with your Prodryan contacts. Or do you expect us to believe humans, acting on their own, could track down the origin of this attack so quickly?"

"Technically, we were tracking the origin of the threads in Prodryan regurgitate pellets," Kumar protested.

Mops took advantage of the Krakau's confusion to ask, "What can you tell us about a Prodryan missing her right wing? The other was green and tattered."

"Her name is Falls From Glory," said the one with the tattoo. "Disgraced, like Heart of Glass, though for different reasons. She's a low-level messenger and spy."

Mops ordered the lift to resume.

"What will you do with us?" asked the brown Krakau.

"While you were busy shooting up the arena, Falls From Glory must have gotten reinforcements and gone after Wolf and Monroe." Mops began shoving the Krakau back into their bags. "If I were you, I'd pray we get them back safely."

14

Human Restoration Project Manual Ver. 1.1, Section 23: Harvesting Guidelines

1. *Whenever possible, attempt to collect humans that are mostly intact. Humans should have four (4) limbs.*
2. *Never pursue humans into their nests, or anywhere that does not offer you a quick escape route.*
3. *Mature specimens only. But not too mature. Examination of teeth and scalp fur should help you determine a human's age. (See Figure 23.1.)*
4. *Once you've selected a human, try to isolate it from its pack.*
5. *Raw meat can be used as bait to lure humans into the open.*
6. *Humans are resistant to pain and most forms of chemical sedation. A strong electrical charge can temporarily stun a human, but physical restraints will be required.*
   a. *Restraints should secure upper and lower limbs, as well as the jaw. (See Figure 23.2.)*

7. All humans must be immediately tagged and cataloged upon capture.

8. PLEASE BATHE YOUR HUMAN BEFORE BRINGING IT TO THE MEDICAL FACILITY.

Addendum, to be added to Version 1.2: Humans require air to breathe. Transporting a human in a standard Krakau holding tank will cause the human to expire.

THE LOCK PANEL OUTSIDE their room was dead. Mops had to physically force the door open.

Light strips flickered on inside, revealing shattered furniture and spattered blood—both human and Prodryan. Mops searched the room, gun in hand, until she was certain the Prodryans hadn't left anyone behind.

Behind her, Kumar paced the room, muttering under his breath. He hadn't stopped moving since they handed Vera Rubin off to station security.

"Any update?" asked Mops.

"She's stable. Currently unconscious in a medtank."

Mops dumped the four Krakau into the closet. It was a tight fit. "You four know this place. What's the easiest way to arrange a meeting with Theta?"

"Theta's time is valuable," said the warrior, her arms curling with disdain. "If you wish to meet with her, you'll need to pay."

"We're not going after Wolf and Monroe?" asked Kumar.

"Not directly. Not with only two of us." Mops smiled. "I doubt either of us has enough cash to attract the interest of someone like Theta. Fortunately, we have the four of you to contribute."

"Now you mean to rob us?" the Krakau snapped.

"You meant to shoot us." Mops leaned closer. "Would you prefer I follow your example?"

Contacting Theta was simple enough. The Tjikko was listed in the station's directory as a permanent resident. He claimed to know nothing about Wolf and Monroe, nor about Heart of Glass, but after Mops transferred a generous amount of money into her account, he'd grudgingly agreed to meet with them in one hour, giving Mops time to do some preliminary research and set up a few precautions.

Forty-five minutes later, Mops double-checked her suit's seal and air supply as she and Kumar entered the Tower Six main lift. The atmosphere was thinner here, with a higher concentration of carbon dioxide than was healthy for humans. So far, the patches to her suit's gunshot holes and other punctures appeared to be holding.

She studied Tower Six through the clear lift walls. This tower had a more organic feel than the others, with exposed roots from the solar-powered plants outside the station clinging to moss-covered stone walls. Water dripped from the ceilings and fogged her hood. Mops' monocle automatically compensated for the brightness of the warm, yellow light.

They shared the lift car with a Prodryan and a Glacidae, neither of whom looked happy about it. Though it was difficult to read much from the Glacidae, who wore an insulated environmental suit. The Prodryan, on the other hand, kept scraping the blades of his artificial claw together in a clear sign of hostility.

The lift stopped on level two, opening to reveal a field of dirt, rocks, and knee-high yellow grass. Green-barked trees grew like pillars, roots and branches digging into the floor and ceiling both. She studied the closest for a moment, prompting Doc to tag it a "Leafless Stanch, one of sixty-three trees engineered by the Tjikko for architectural uses" on her monocle.

Insects and gliding rodents flew from one tree to the next. Other creatures rustled invisibly in the tall grass to either side of the rocky pathways. It was quieter here than Mops was used to. She spied a few people moving between wood-and-stone buildings, but much of this level was open and empty.

The Prodryan and the Glacidae followed them out, the former muttering about human diseases and the foolishness of letting "animals" roam freely throughout the station. After several such comments, Mops moved to the side of the path and waited to see if they'd pass.

Instead, the Prodryan stopped to glare up at her, his antennae quivering with indignation.

"Shouldn't we just ignore them?" Kumar whispered.

"No." Mops aimed a smile at the Prodryan. "Do you have something you'd like to say?"

The Prodryan glanced behind him, as if making sure his Glacidae companion hadn't fled. "What are you doing here, human?"

Mops relaxed. If he was working for Heart of Glass, assigned to follow or spy on them, he wouldn't be trying to pick a fight. "Look, son. We're in a hurry, so I'm going to jump to the end of this conversation. From the shine of your thorax, you're barely old enough to call yourself a warrior. Probably still figuring out how to use that fancy new hand. That's right, I see the scabs where you've cut yourself."

The Prodryan started to protest, but Mops moved closer and kept talking. "I know what it's like to want to prove yourself. You figure you'll push around a couple of humans and act like a real warrior in front of your friend there."

She unsealed and removed her left glove, letting it dangle from her cuff. Her right hand shot out to seize the Prodryan's wrist. Squeezing the joint to immobilize it, she scraped the blades over her palm.

"What are you doing?" the Prodryan cried.

She shoved him away. "There you go. Your blades are now wet with the blood of a human." She grabbed the bioglue and squeezed a line over the first of the two shallow cuts. "Take the win, son. Go home and tell everyone how you stood up to a human. Because if you don't, I'll make you eat those blades."

He stepped back so quickly he stumbled over the Glacidae, who had curled into an armored ball. Without another word, the Prodryan flew back toward the lift, wings buzzing.

Mops treated the second cut and pulled her glove into place. To Kumar, she said, "*Never* ignore them."

After that, their path remained remarkably clear. They passed a pair of Quetzalus rubbing their beaks against a tree, and a green-furred Merraban resting in a hammock, but nobody gave them a second glance.

Theta lived on the far side of the level. A barricade of trees and interwoven branches curved out from the tower wall. There were no guards, nor any security cameras she could see. The branches were covered in dark needles between two and three centimeters in length. Striped ratlike creatures scurried away as Mops ducked through a narrow opening. Branches wove together behind them, trapping them in a space the size of a small closet.

"Where is she?" whispered Kumar.

Mops spread her arms. "We're standing in him." Raising her voice, she said, "We paid for the chance to talk."

Slowly, more branches creaked aside to offer passage. Needles scraped over Mops' suit as she squeezed deeper into the tunnel of trees, but none penetrated. They emerged into a small, circular clearing, fenced in by interwoven trees.

Gnarled roots had cracked and crushed the rocky ground, turning the path treacherous. Warm light shone from glass bubbles in the ceiling. Insects stirred among the fallen needles and leaves.

The trees here were thicker, flush with oily plum-colored leaves with yellow veins. These were older Tjikko trees. Mops turned in a slow circle, giving Doc time to tag the various weapons tracking her from the branches. "Do you have a communications interface?"

"Over here, human." The words came from a sapling to her left. Thick wires ran from a black metal cuff around the base of the trunk to a voder embedded in the bark about a meter up. "What do you want?"

"Two of my team were taken from our quarters earlier today. I want them back."

"You think I took them?" Stilted, mechanical laughter boomed from the sapling. "I don't get out of Tower Six very often."

"I think you know who took them." Mops glanced around. "Do the Coacalos know how much of the station you've infiltrated? We tracked water usage patterns before we came to see you. Your roots spread through every tower."

Branches rustled. A few leaves fell lazily to the floor. "The Coacalos are aware. We have a symbiotic relationship."

"Meaning they get a cut of your profits," Mops guessed. "The Prodryans who took my people. They work for Heart of Glass, right? Where can I find them?"

"I'm not sure. I have a hard time distinguishing one animal from another."

"We know you sold Floyd Westerman to the Prodryans." Mops paused. "We recently discovered his remains."

The trees leaned inward, blocking more of the light. "Tread carefully with your unspoken accusations. Unlike the animals who roam this station, I don't fear humans. Particularly human sanitation workers pretending to be soldiers. You're correct that Westerman owed me a debt. When he was unable to pay, I found another way to collect. As for your other questions, those answers are . . . expensive."

"We paid you—" Mops began.

"For a meeting," said Theta. "A meeting which I granted. If you wish to know more, you will pay more. Or you can challenge me and pay that price. I'm always in the mood for additional fertilizer."

"Human bodies wouldn't make good fertilizer for a Tjikko," said Kumar. "Too much oxygen, not enough nitrogen, not to mention the virus and medications and all the trace elements—"

"She knows," Mops said wearily. "Theta, there are only eleven Tjikko in the whole galaxy, right?"

"Twelve," corrected Theta. "Beta launched a new groveship two years ago."

"Congratulations," said Mops, not missing a beat. "Maybe you'll understand when I tell you there are only ten thousand or so humans. I'm sure that sounds like a lot, but we're not colony life-forms. We're individuals, and we used to number eight billion. The tiny fraction of us who remain? They're all we have left. They're family. One of them died in this station. Another is in Medical after being attacked earlier today. And two more people—members of *my* team—were taken from our quarters.

"I know you have enough weapons in here to mow us both down. And I know, even if we could afford to buy your information, you'd only turn around and sell us out to Heart of Glass for an extra profit."

Theta's voder gave a passable imitation of laughter. "Perhaps humans aren't as foolish as I'd believed."

"Oh, no," said Mops with a laugh of her own. "We're plenty foolish. Always picking fights. If we were soldiers, we'd have probably tried to figure out a way to smuggle up weapons of our own. Flamethrowers and so on. But like you said, we're just a couple of glorified sanitation workers. Sanitation workers who are very angry, and very good at our jobs."

Theta's branches stilled. "What are you implying."

"All this security, but you did a piss-poor job locking down your plumbing," Mops continued. "How painful do you think it would be if the supply pipe for a Glacidae acid wash got crossed with one of those water lines feeding into your roots? Or a malfunctioning decon process wiped out the microorganisms in your soil? Or your fertilizers became contaminated with lead or mercury or any of the other waste materials collected down in the station sublevels?"

The closest trees shuddered in unison. "Our species has gone to war for less."

"You could kill us, but we're the only ones who know what

changes we've made to your support systems." Mops waited. "Your computer interface is plugged into the equivalent of your veins, right? You control it by adjusting the pressure of those water-transporting cells? What would happen if someone introduced trace elements into your water supply to corrode those interfaces? Why, months from now, you might suddenly wake up mute, unable to control anything."

"I don't think Tjikko sleep," said Kumar.

Mops stepped closer to the voder. "It's possible the Coacalos would realize it was a technical problem and fix it. At a reasonable price, I'm sure." She paused. "Or they might assume you'd died, and chop you down for firewood or building material. Do you want me to keep going? I can spend all day talking about the ways an experienced sanitation and hygiene worker can gum up the works. The things I've seen. . ."

The silence stretched for one minute, then two. Finally, the Tjikko chuckled. "I admire your initiative. Would you be interested in working for me?"

"No, thank you."

"Heart of Glass has left Coacalos Station," said Theta. "A Prodryan named Stab the Stars tends to things in his absence."

"Stab the Stars?" Kumar repeated.

"I know." Theta rustled his leaves. "Don't get me started on the absurdity of animal nomenclature."

"Why did they want Floyd Westerman?" asked Mops.

"I believe they meant to use him for chemical testing of some sort."

They'd tested their bioweapon on Westerman. Once they knew it worked, they'd killed him and used the acid shower to destroy the contagion and eliminate any evidence. Mops swallowed her anger. "Where did these chemicals come from?"

Theta paused. "I've told you a great deal already."

"Doc, send her the details on the modification we made to water line 6-2-17, as a show of faith." Once Doc indicated he'd done so, she said, "We'll reroute that infuser on our way out. Keep talking, and we'll take care of the rest, too."

"Heart of Glass and Stab the Stars took delivery from a shuttle. My sources couldn't identify its origin," Theta admitted. "I overheard Stab the Stars ordering a subordinate to contact someone named 'Azure' to confirm delivery."

Doc flashed an alert, but Mops didn't need prompting. The Prodryan they'd confronted outside Heart of Glass' apartment had mentioned azure venom. "If you can tell me who Azure is and where to find them, we'll fix everything we broke and give your water circulation system a full overhaul as a bonus."

"I'm afraid I don't have that information. I could, however, arrange a meeting with one of Stab the Stars' people." His tone deepened. "In exchange, you will reverse your sabotage *and* offer your expertise in helping me secure those . . . vulnerabilities. Do we have a bargain?"

Kumar stepped forward. "I can do that. *If* you cover Vera Rubin's medical costs."

Mops tried to keep her surprise from showing. That hadn't been part of the plan.

Kumar watched her, his eyes pleading. He clearly knew he'd overstepped, but he wasn't backing down. Nor should he, Mops decided after a moment's thought. Rubin had been protecting them. "Those are our terms."

"Vera Rubin is a stranger to you," said Theta.

"That doesn't matter." Mops gave Kumar a small nod. "She's still one of us."

It took two and a half hours for Theta to arrange the meeting at Mops' chosen location. During that time, Mops had Kumar reverse four of the six disruptions they'd arranged for the Tjikko's plumbing and environmental regulation systems. The rest would come after confirming Theta hadn't double-crossed them.

Mops tensed as a Krakau approached, but she was merely bringing a small, steaming bowl to their table. "Compliments of Cooks Good Meals. He says to tell you the sanitizer is work-ing beautifully."

Inside the bowl, carefully arranged in a pale blue pudding, were five Tjikko nuts. Each was tied with a black string, and a note clipped to the side of the bowl listed the different flavors the nuts had been infused with.

"I'm sorry, I can't . . ." The Krakau had already left. Mops sighed and studied the appetizer, trying to ignore the saliva pooling in her mouth.

They'd chosen a table at the back of the Prodryan side of the restaurant, where Mops and Kumar could monitor every-one who approached. Almost two-thirds of the tables were unoccupied. Since arriving, Mops had watched two groups of Prodryans enter, notice the humans, and immediately turn around to go elsewhere. She felt bad for Cook's business, but it meant there were fewer potential enemies to worry about.

Mops' stomach gurgled loudly enough to draw glares from two nearby Prodryans. "Just one," she muttered, not sure if it was to Kumar or herself. "So Cook doesn't feel insulted."

If anything, anticipation made this Tjikko nut taste even better than the first. Mops was still chewing when Doc said, *"Falls From Glory has just entered the restaurant."*

"I see her." From Kumar's abrupt shift, Doc had alerted him as well. Mops lowered a hand to her weapon as the one-winged Prodryan approached. She appeared to be alone. A few other diners glanced up, but most deliberately avoided looking at Falls From Glory. The sight of a "broken" Prodryan was almost as offensive to them as the sight of two humans.

"Hello again." Mops gestured to an empty chair. "Take off that shawl so I know you're not hiding anything. It's Falls From Glory, right? Would you mind if I just call you Glory? It'll save time."

"I would prefer to minimize the duration of this meeting, yes." Glory removed the shawl and set it on another chair, then sat. Her left wing rustled sharply. "What is it you want, human?"

"First, you're going to return Wolf and Monroe, alive and

unharmed. Second, you'll give us the cure for the bioweapon you used against the *Pufferfish*. Third, I want information on everyone involved in developing that bioweapon and arranging the attack on the *Pufferfish*. And finally, another round of these Tjikko nuts." She didn't know when exactly she'd eaten the rest of the five nuts.

"Is that all?" Glory's slender antennae flattened against the top of her head, conveying the sarcasm the translator couldn't.

"Almost." Mops moved in, resting one elbow on the table. "I want to know what Krakau venom is."

"Krakau aren't venomous."

"Exactly," said Kumar.

Glory stared. "What?"

Mops took a deep breath. "Your boss received a shipment from someone named Azure."

Glory didn't answer.

"She has a comm device implanted somewhere. I'm picking up the signal, but it's encrypted. Before you ask, I can't trace it."

The Krakau waiter returned, looked from Glory to the humans and back, and in a tentative voice, asked, "Would the new arrival care for a drink? We have eleven varieties of nectar-wine, and a honey-based—"

"Go away," snarled Glory. No sooner had the words cleared her translator than the Krakau was scurrying back to the kitchen.

"As for what you'll get in return," Mops continued, "I'll tell you why your bioweapon failed on us, and why it's going to fail when you try to use it against the EMC. I assume that's why you sent the second group of fighters? To assess the effectiveness of your attack?"

One of Glory's multifaceted eyes twitched sideways. "Tell me why some humans were unaffected."

"Give me proof Wolf and Monroe are alive."

She tilted her head, listening to a voice Mops couldn't hear. "Very well."

"Incoming signal. Yes, I'm trying to track it, but it's being

relayed through Glory's implant. So, I can track it all of one meter to her chair on the other side of the table. The signal appears clean. Displaying now."

Her monocle darkened, then changed to an image of Wolf and Monroe lying unconscious in a small room or cell. Mops watched long enough to make sure both were breathing.

"I'm also receiving a signal from their uniforms. Their breathing patterns match the visual. This appears to be a live feed. Downloading environmental readings. Current gravity and atmosphere don't match this or any other Coacalos towers. Their suit logs suggest they were taken from Tower Five and passed through a low-gee, low-pressure environment before arriving at their destination. Those intermittent readings are a ninety-nine percent match to what we experienced when we first stepped off our shuttle."

They'd taken Wolf and Monroe to a ship in the docking bay. "Are they still on the station?"

"I believe so. Suit logs don't show any gravitational spikes consistent with an accelerating ship."

"No more questions," said Glory. The image vanished. "Give us the information we want. Who else survived the attack on your ship, and how did you do it?"

"That doesn't matter. Kumar?"

Kumar removed a small mem crystal from one of his front pockets and rolled it between his thumb and forefinger.

"What is this?" demanded Glory.

"A report I prepared for Command," said Kumar. "Eleven recommendations for updated sanitation and quarantine procedures for EMC ships and stations, beginning with adjusting the spectrum and intensity of the air lock decontamination processes. Based on the filters we used to successfully clear the agent from the *Pufferfish*, I'm recommending a separate breathing mask to be installed in our uniforms. A mandatory quarantine period for anyone coming on board will be inconvenient, but it should prevent the spread of infection while we develop a test to detect your contaminant in humans and other—"

"Enough." Glory snatched at the mem crystal, but Kumar pulled it deftly out of reach.

"I also drafted a schedule for rolling everything out," said Kumar. "Prioritizing the most effective changes while taking cost and difficulty into consideration."

"I had to order him to stop," Mops said dryly. "Otherwise, he'd still be at it, refining his schedule and plotting cost-benefit analyses."

Glory flexed her arms, momentarily extending her forearm barbs. "What is your *point*?"

"To show that Heart of Glass and Stab the Stars wasted their shot." Mops reached for another Tjikko nut. "If you'd taken out the *Pufferfish*, you could have kept the element of surprise. Who knows how many ships and stations you might have been able to infect. But now that we know about it? Your Krakau venom is all but useless, and the sooner you realize it, the better off you'll be."

"Perhaps we had other uses in mind." Glory looked pointedly toward the Tjikko nuts. "Perhaps the intent was to refine a weapon for individual targets."

It was like she'd pumped coolant fluid directly into Mops' veins. Her breath caught, and her mind plunged into memories of the *Pufferfish* crew—of her friends and colleagues shambling about the ship, their consciousness shredded until nothing remained but instinctive, animalistic hunger.

Like most humans, Mops didn't remember her life before the Krakau cure. That hadn't stopped fragments from embedding themselves in occasional nightmares. Flashes of hunger and cold. Of huddling in dank, dark ruins. Of the incessant groaning and ragged breathing of other humans. . . .

"Sir?" Kumar reached toward her.

Mops caught his hand, stopping it a centimeter from her shoulder. She licked her dry lips and looked closely at Glory. "She's lying. You saw how quickly the infection spread through the ship. This is a weapon of mass murder, not targeted assassination."

"It could be both," said Glory. "Perhaps we've successfully modified the venom to infect only one target. Perhaps it's affecting you right now. Your mind is shutting down, and soon you'll turn on the other human and begin eating him! Perhaps you're right now jumping from your chair to devour his meat parts!"

Mops deliberately took another Tjikko nut. "The sad thing is, you're still a better liar than most Prodryans. Are you done, or did you want to continue?"

Glory slumped. "I'm done."

"The Alliance knows we're here," said Mops. "I don't know how many warships they're sending, but if they're not already in-system, they'll be here soon. They're going to tear this station apart."

"Let them," said Glory. "We don't fear the violence of your human shock troops."

"How long do you think a flightless Prodryan will last against them?" She checked the restaurant. Nobody appeared to be listening or paying undue attention. "Help me get my team back. Tell us how to cure my crew, and I'll do everything I can to make sure you're protected when the Alliance starts kicking down doors."

Glory twisted, hiding her wingless shoulder from view. "I have no access to anything involving Azure's venom."

"Who is Azure?" asked Mops. "Our ship called it Krakau venom. Is Azure a Krakau?"

Glory jerked back. "Azure? I've never heard that name before."

"You literally just said it," said Kumar.

"No, I didn't."

Kumar removed his monocle. "Do you want me to replay it for you?"

Glory ignored him.

"Why didn't you get a replacement wing?" asked Mops.

"Wings are difficult to rebuild. And expensive." She hesitated. "I was not a skilled enough warrior to earn such a gift."

"How long have you been skulking about in the shadows

for people like Stab the Stars?" Mops sat back. "Playing messenger, meeting with humans ... it's degrading."

"My choices are limited."

"Your problem is much worse. Your *imagination* is limited. Let us help you. I can get you off this station, drop you on any planet you want. The Krakau don't have to know. Our medical facilities on the *Pufferfish* could synthesize a strong, lightweight wing for you." She paused. "You'd have to help cure our medical crew, but once that happens, they could have you flying again within a week."

Glory's left wing extended partway. Her head tilted back, like she was looking through the ceiling to the open air beyond. Then she shook herself and roughly shoved the wing back with one forelimb. "There is a counteragent, though it hasn't been tested on humans. It's stored at the lab where the weapon is manufactured." She shuddered harder, then seemed to relax. Her antennae sagged. Her limbs lowered. When she spoke again, her words were soft. "But it won't help you. It's too late for your people."

"I've got another signal to Glory's implant! Just a brief pulse, but it originated on the station."

"I know they're listening in," said Mops. "We can help you, but you need to decide quickly, before—"

"No, you can't." Falls From Glory looked almost serene. "Thank you for answering our questions, human."

Before Mops could ask what answers she meant, Doc said, *"Infrared shows her body temp spiking around the thorax."*

Threads of mist or smoke rose from the corners of her mouth. She stiffened in her seat.

"Oh, Glory ..." Mops kicked back her chair. "Doc, trigger a fire alarm now!"

Green lights began flashing, and a calm voice instructed everyone to evacuate the restaurant.

"Sir?" asked Kumar.

"She's a damned bomb." She hauled Kumar to his feet, hoping they had time to make it to the door.

They didn't. Mops managed four steps before the world turned a searing white. She felt herself flung sideways. The only sound was a high-pitched ringing. She couldn't move. Couldn't see. Her mouth tasted like blood.

Where was Kumar? Blurred shapes rushed past. Splotches of white and orange sparkled through her vision. Smoke burned her nose and throat.

A shadow moved closer. Extended something toward her body. The end touched her neck, and electricity crackled through her nerves. Her muscles knotted.

Her last thought before losing consciousness was, *I hope Cook has insurance on this place.*

Admiral Pachelbel stilled her limbs to better hear the aide who'd splashed into her office. "They were found . . . locked in a closet?"

"Four of them, yes. The other two were killed attempting to apprehend Lieutenant Adamopoulos and her companion."

Pachelbel twined two of her tentacles together, squeezing hard in an attempt to calm her temper. "Did they explain how they were overpowered by a pair of human sanitation workers?"

"Yes, sir." The aide's skin visibly tightened. "The humans . . . they used one of the station's autowash mechanisms."

Pachelbel checked her console. The Alliance ships would be decelerating within the hour, and should reach Coacalos Station within a day or so. "Have our agents learned anything more about why Adamopoulos went to Coacalos Station?"

"They were observed entering a Prodryan residence, and later meeting with a Tjikko criminal."

"Drown it all, Mops." She didn't want to believe Adamopoulos had conspired against the Alliance and the EMC, but every intelligence report they received added to the evidence against her.

"There's more."

Pachelbel sank deeper into the brine. "Do tell."

"We've received word of an explosion on the station. Two humans whose descriptions match Lieutenant Adamopoulos and Technician Kumar were at the center of the explosion, along with an unidentified Prodryan. The two humans were dragged away by unknown persons. And . . . the CMC is threatening to go to the Judiciary if we don't turn the investigation over to them."

Pachelbel flicked an arm, letting the splash convey her annoyance. "Colonial Military Command has no jurisdiction over the Pufferfish *or her crew. Interstellar Military Command oversees all Earth Mercenary Corps vessels and personnel. Admiral Zauberflöte knows damn well this is my mess."*

"Respectfully, sir. Admiral Zauberflöte believes, based on what Lieutenant Adamopoulos reported about Krakau venom, that this is now a colonial matter."

"Until she has proof, Zauberflöte can go piss on a deepwater spine serpent. Do you have anything further to report on Lieutenant Adamopoulos and her team? They haven't started a war with a newly discovered race of sentient fungus in their free time, or anything like that?"

The aide moved surreptitiously closer to the door. "No, sir."

"Notify me if that changes." Pachelbel waited until she was alone to duck beneath the surface and circle her office in frustration. "Fucking humans."

MOPS FELT LIKE SHE'D been fired naked through an A-ring. Her body was numb, her joints stiff, as if they'd rusted solid.

"I think she's coming around."

It was hard to decipher individual words through the pounding in her skull, but she eventually identified the speaker as Wolf.

"Are you back with us, sir?"

And that was Monroe. She opened her mouth to respond. All that emerged was a dry croak. Her lips were swollen, her tongue dry. Her throat felt like she'd taken a welding torch to it.

"Take it slow," said Monroe. "You look like shit, but you're alive. So's Kumar. They brought you in about two hours ago."

She managed a raspy, "Where. . . ?"

"We're not sure," said Monroe. "We were unconscious when we were brought in, and nobody's seen fit to offer us a tour yet."

Mops shivered and forced her eyes open. A series of metal loops jutted from the ceiling. Wrenching her head to the side, she saw metal walls with bare shelves and additional loops. Attachment points for tie-down straps? That would make this a storage room of some sort. "Doc?"

"No monocles, no equipment harnesses," snarled Wolf.

Monroe gestured to his empty right sleeve. "No prosthetic limb either."

She touched the bare skin around her left eye, then looked down at herself, half-expecting to see missing limbs of her own. Her legs had been bandaged and splinted, and her left hand was encased in a medigel cast. Beneath holes in her uniform, bioglue held a series of puncture wounds together, mostly on her extremities. It could have been much worse.

Her vision slowly adjusted to the dim blue-tinged light from the wall panels. "Falls From Glory gave us a brief feed of the two of you," she said. "Doc pulled the environmental readings from your suits. He was pretty sure you were in the Coacalos docking bay."

Monroe nodded. "Cargo vessel, maybe?"

"Maybe." She looked them over. "What happened to the two of you?"

"They were waiting in our quarters," Wolf said, slamming a fist against the wall. "Six Prodryans, armed with electric stunners. They hit me in the face as I walked in, then ganged up on Monroe."

Wolf touched a dark, blistered splotch on her temple. The attackers had known enough to go for exposed skin, since

EMC uniforms would disperse most of the shock. "I want a rematch with the cowards who jumped us, but once that's done, I'm going back to find the one-winged snitch who put them on our trail."

"No need," said Mops. "We were in the middle of talking to her when she exploded."

Wolf frowned. "I guess that'll have to do."

"We'd barely regained consciousness when they brought you and Kumar in," said Monroe. "I assume we're being monitored, but nobody's spoken with us."

Mops held out a hand, and Monroe helped her sit up. "Before she blew up, Falls From Glory told us there's a cure." Mops grimaced, trying to reconstruct that conversation. "The last thing she said was thank you for answering their questions."

"What did you tell them?" asked Wolf.

"I don't know...." She didn't recall telling Glory anything useful, but the Prodryans might have been digging for something else, something Mops and Kumar had inadvertently given away.

"Why do you think they've kept us alive, sir?" asked Monroe.

"Because someone has a use for us. Why else would they bother patching us up? Maybe they want to do further testing of their venom weapon. Or they might just want to wring all the intelligence they can from their four EMC prisoners."

Kumar coughed. His eyes snapped open, and he tried to sit up. He made it about halfway before falling back with a groan.

"Take it easy," Mops said. Kumar looked to be in slightly better shape than her. His face was burned, and hastily applied bioglue crusted his skin beneath holes in his uniform.

"I think I'm ready to go back to cleaning toilets on the *Pufferfish* now," Kumar said without opening his eyes.

Mops chuckled, which reopened a cut in her lip. She scraped a fingernail over her teeth, cleaning away dried blood and a bit of Tjikko nut. "What was the last thing we said before Glory blew up?"

Kumar's forehead furrowed. "You told me she was a damned bomb."

"Before that."

He rolled onto his side. "You told her, 'Your problem is worse. Your *imagination* is limited. Let us help you. I can get you off this station, drop you on any planet you want. The Krakau don't have to know. Our medical facilities on the *Pufferfish* could synthesize a strong, lightweight wing for you. You'd have to help cure our medical crew, but they could have you flying again within a week.'"

Mops just shook her head. Kumar's memory was almost as reliable as Doc's.

"That's when Glory told us there's a counteragent in the lab where the weapon was manufactured."

"Her body language changed," said Mops. Was it the offer to synthesize a new wing? The capabilities of Alliance medical technology were hardly secret. Maybe it was simply their willingness to help a Prodryan, and to hide her involvement from the Krakau. Could this have been a probe to test how humans would act against the Krakau? She chewed her lip. None of the possibilities felt right.

"Maybe she was lying," said Wolf. "Just messing with your heads."

"Prodryans are terrible liars." Mops dragged herself to where she could rest her back against the wall. The only visible way in or out of the room was a large door at the far end. "I don't suppose either of you came up with a brilliant escape plan while you were waiting for us to wake up?"

"Wait for the Prodryans to come in, then unleash hell." Wolf folded her arms and looked around, as if waiting for applause.

"It's a good starting point," said Mops. "Let's see if we can refine it a bit. . . ."

A computer-synthesized voice from beyond the door made Mops jump. The movement strained the bioglue on several of her wounds.

"Lieutenant Adamopoulos. You will give us the location of the *EMCS Pufferfish*. If you refuse, we will remove one member of your team and infect them with the same weapon we used against your crew. Perhaps they will again be unaffected. Perhaps not. You have thirty-nine minutes to decide."

Thirty-nine minutes? That was a rather arbitrary number. Mops pushed herself upright. The splints kept her legs steady enough to support her weight as she approached the door. "Who are you, and where have you taken us?"

There was a pause. "That is not the answer to our question. You have thirty-eight and a half minutes. You will also unlock your personal artificial intelligence device."

Wolf snarled. "I will rip off your antennae and use them for toothpicks."

A pause. "You have thirty-eight minutes."

Mops studied the door, searching for an access panel or conduit, but found nothing. "You didn't give us medical treatment just to kill us. What do you want?"

"You must be healthy enough to endure the jump to Azure's lab. However, our plan does not require all four prisoners to survive."

"But you need at least one of us? Thank you." Mops turned to her team. "Unidentified captors, you will tell us everything you know about Azure and their lab. If you don't, I will kill everyone in this room, including myself. You have five minutes to decide."

Wolf barked out a sound between a cough and a laugh. Monroe simply grinned.

"You can't—" the voice began.

"Never underestimate the savagery of a human," said Mops.

"We recognize your intellectual capacity is limited. Do you understand this plan would result in your deaths?"

"Yes. You have four and a half minutes."

"But . . . it's a stupid plan! Even for humans!"

Mops smiled. "There's a saying attributed to an Earth scientist named Albert Einstein. 'Two things are infinite, the universe and human stupidity, and I am not completely sure about the universe.'"

Wolf frowned. "Einstein? I thought she was a heavy gunner on the *Blue-Ringed Octopus*."

Mops ignored her. "You're running out of time. Let's start with a simpler question. What do you plan to do with us?"

"The Alliance has labeled you fugitives. We intend to reinforce their assumption and frame you as collaborators. This will encourage the Krakau to focus their efforts on you while we launch our final assault."

"Keep talking." Mops' gut was a lead weight, but she kept her expression neutral. "Who is Azure?"

"Azure is not your enemy. None of us are."

"Tell that to the Prodryan who tried to blow us up," said Mops.

"The bomb was calibrated to disable, not kill. I know you don't understand, but in time, once stability has returned to the galaxy, Azure hopes to cure what's left of humanity. A true cure, not the palliative the Krakau use to keep you enslaved."

"The Krakau have been trying to restore us for a century," Kumar piped up.

"You truly believe they're trying to help you? Human herd loyalty is fascinating."

Mops held up a hand to keep the others from chiming in. "How will this Azure cure our people?"

"By providing us with the true source of the affliction that destroyed your species."

The room fell silent.

"I've studied Earth history," Mops said quietly. "Humanity destroyed itself."

"Who wrote that history? Who translated it?" The speaker didn't wait for an answer. "Before we can help your people, you and your masters must be subdued. We need the *Pufferfish* so we can confirm the effects of our weapon upon zir crew."

Mops glanced at the others. Monroe's face was stone; he'd caught it, too. Kumar was too out of it to notice, and Wolf was too . . . Wolf.

"Give us the rest of our thirty-five minutes to discuss it," said Mops.

Zir crew. Humans were one of several races that referred to their ships with gendered terms. To Prodryans, ships were masculine, like the majority of the warriors and explorers of their species. The Krakau, being all female themselves, naturally described their vessels the same way. As far as Mops knew, only one species used a third-gender pronoun for their ships.

That same species measured time in units that corresponded to almost exactly thirteen minutes. Three of which, when translated into Human, would give a seemingly arbitrary thirty-nine-minute deadline.

Mops and her team were being held not by Prodryans, but Nusurans.

Escaping from Nusurans would be difficult. Physically, the average human was more than a match for a Prodryan, but Nusurans were one of the toughest species ever to evolve intelligence.

They were also the least xenophobic of any race in the Alliance. They didn't judge a being's looks or smell or preferred diet. The only thing they cared about was that being's skill in the bedroom. What had Heart of Glass offered to get them to climb into bed with Prodryans?

The *Pufferfish* had been called in to assist a Nusuran freighter. Had that been a setup? Had Captain Taka-lokitok-vi been working with the Prodryans to infect the *Pufferfish* crew?

Wolf stopped pacing and pounded the door. "Hey, the next time you lock humans up, remember to give a bathroom. Or at least a damned bucket."

"Just hold it," said Mops. "That's an order."

"You think I *like* the idea of pissing my uniform?"

How much did their captors know about human biology? They'd been in here for hours without food or water. "I said hold it," Mops repeated. "We're only going to get one shot at this."

Wolf blinked. "What shot?"

She moved closer and lowered her voice. "Whoever's out there obviously doesn't know human urine is acidic."

Kumar cocked his head. "I don't understand. How does that—"

Monroe cut him off with a quick punch to the shoulder.

"This is our best weapon," Mops continued. "We've got two choices. We either try to burn our way through that door, or we wait for our jailor to show up, then burn their face off."

Wolf looked down at her crotch, her wide eyes and broad grin a beacon of glee. "I didn't know we could do that."

For the life of her, Mops couldn't tell whether Wolf was playing along, or if she honestly believed human urine could burn through doors. "Monroe, you've got the highest marksmanship scores. Work with Kumar to figure out the most likely spot to disable the door lock from inside, then blast it."

"What about me?" asked Wolf, shifting her weight from one leg to the other.

"In this case, I'm going to trust Monroe's targeting skills over your own."

Monroe popped his gum and joined Kumar at the edge of the door.

"Hold it." Mops limped after Monroe. "They took our weapons. Our equipment harnesses. And I assume we were all searched before they dumped us in here. Where the hell did you get"—she sniffed—"peanut-butter-and-jelly-flavored bubble gum?"

Monroe just grinned and blew another bubble.

Mops settled back, hoping the Nusurans were competent enough captors to have overheard their whispered conversation.

Would they expect a trap, or like most species, did they see humans as brute beasts, incapable of subtlety or planning?

Kumar licked a finger and drew a wet X on the wall. "I *think* this is the locking mechanism. If we burn through this spot, we should be able to open the door."

Mops nodded at Monroe, who unzipped his jumpsuit. The rest of the team moved back and averted their gazes.

"How long should it take to eat through?" asked Monroe.

"Depends on the thickness and composition of the door," said Mops. "Probably between five and ten minutes. I just hope they leave us alone long enough—"

"Humans, step away from the door." Even though she'd expected and hoped for it, their captor's bellow made Mops jump. "You will each be removed and catheterized to drain excess waste fluid."

"Oh, damn." Mops stepped back and gestured for the others to do the same. "We were so close, too." Had Doc been with her, he would have made a snide comment about her acting skills.

The door slid open, revealing a single Nusuran. Mops counted eight legs, making this a Si. Zie was on the smaller side, with mottled gray-and-black coloring. Zie held a snub-nosed weapon in zir two frontmost limbs. "Lieutenant Adamopoulos, you will come with me."

"No, I won't," said Mops, hoping this worked. "Drop your weapon, or my team will urinate on you. Male humans have a range of more than three meters."

"It's not a pretty way to die," Wolf added, her bruised face twisting into something between a smile and a snarl.

The Nusuran hesitated, then jumped back with surprising speed for such a bulky creature. The door started to slide closed.

Monroe threw himself down in front of the door. Wolf vaulted over him to attack the Nusuran. A gunshot grazed Wolf's side, but she barely seemed to notice as she punched and kicked and bit.

Kumar lunged for the gun to wrest it away. The Nusuran responded by shoving the gun into zir mouth and swallowing.

"You know we're going to get it back anyway, right?" Wolf asked, smashing her knee against the side of the Nusuran's head.

"Drag zim in here," Mops ordered. "Quickly, before reinforcements arrive."

"Easy for you to say." Wolf grabbed the edge of a bone plate by the Nusuran's face and tugged hard. Zie let out a high-pitched shriek of pain.

"Three more coming down the hallway," Kumar shouted. He tried to add his efforts to Wolf's, but as battered as he was from the explosion, he struggled just to hold on.

The Nusuran convulsed, flinging Wolf aside and rolling on top of Monroe, then twisting again to shove Kumar against the side of the door.

Four humans were enough to subdue one unarmed Nusuran, even when one of those humans was splinted and could barely walk. But with reinforcements on the way . . . "We need to get that door shut!"

"How?" shouted Wolf, launching a flying, flailing kick at the Nusuran. Zie caught her leg and tossed her aside. As long as zie kept zer body in the doorway, they'd be exposed when the others arrived.

"Dammit." Monroe pulled himself free and spat out his gum. With a sigh, he reached into his jumpsuit. Mops couldn't see exactly what he did, but his hand emerged holding a small black pistol.

He stepped into the hallway, using the struggling Nusuran for cover and balance, and fired.

"Where the shit did that come from, and why the shit didn't you use it before?" Wolf shouted.

Monroe continued shooting. The Nusuran in the doorway was struggling harder now. Mops moved in to grab the head, using her own weight to try to pin zer down.

Zie had pretty much stopped struggling by the time the

gunfire died. Monroe kept his pistol pointed down the hallway as he made his way around the Nusuran he'd been using for cover to make sure the reinforcements were down.

"Sir?" Kumar poked the Nusuran in the doorway. "I don't think this one's breathing."

"Don't look at me," said Wolf. "I'm not giving zer mouth-to-mouth."

"You couldn't." Kumar patted the Nusuran's side. "They have four sets of lungs, filled with a spongy mass of tissue. You'd pass out trying to breathe for them."

"Zie's bleeding." Mops crouched by the floor. "Looks like zie got shot in the crossfire."

"The others are down," Monroe said as he returned.

"Thank you," said Mops.

Monroe sighed. "First time in two years I've had to kill someone."

Mops squeezed his shoulder in sympathy and gratitude. "Where *did* you pull that out of? Or don't I want to know?"

He tucked the gun carefully beneath his arm and popped a new piece of gum into his mouth. "The grenade that took my arm and ended my infantry career also tore up my guts—most of my stomach, intestine, colon, and part of a lung, all of which are harder and more expensive to rebuild than an arm. So they didn't."

"You're saying your whole right side . . ." Mops waved a hand.

"Nothing but a built-in storage locker. I also keep a set of dice, multiknife, water purification tablets, and five meters of nano-braid cord."

"And a supply of gum?" Mops guessed.

Monroe shrugged, then crouched to study the Nusuran in the doorway. "It wasn't friendly fire."

"So what happened?" demanded Wolf.

"Zie was carrying a modified Toklok P11 pistol with a biometric scanner in the grip. A gene scan of the inside of zer gut would work just as well as a limb for the gun's security protocols. And the P11 line has a very touchy trigger. With all that bouncing around ..." Monroe pointed to the edge of the wound. "She shot herself from the inside."

"Damn," said Wolf.

Monroe tucked his own gun away inside his jumpsuit. "Always lock the safety before you stick a weapon in your gut."

"I don't suppose you've got a comm unit in there?" Mops asked.

"Sorry."

Mops searched the Nusuran, but didn't find much: a cracked monocle beneath one of zer facial bones, and an electric stun rod. She grabbed them both. The monocle went into one of her uniform pockets. She checked the stun rod until she found the activation switch. It hummed in her hand, making the hairs of her arm rise.

"That stick won't do much against a Nusuran unless you get it beneath the bone plates," Monroe warned her.

"I know." She gestured at her legs. "There's not much else I can do in a fight."

He didn't argue. Which was a little insulting.

"Where to, sir?" asked Wolf.

Mops pointed in the direction their attackers had come from. It was as good a guess as any.

The corridor curved to the right. The walls bulged outward, and the curved ceiling was too low for her comfort. The amethyst light and soft floors weren't like anything she'd encountered on Coacalos Station.

She stopped at a circular window on the left wall. The station was a small black silhouette near the edge of a blue star. "We've left the station."

"I didn't even feel it," said Monroe. "They must have some high-end gravity compensators on this thing."

"Why didn't our escape set off any alarms on the ship?" asked Wolf.

Mops bent to press one hand to the floor. The cool surface buzzed faintly, like an angry insect was trapped below the surface. "It did. Nusurans are more tactile than visual."

"If they know we're loose, where's the rest of the crew?" asked Kumar.

Monroe looked around. "A standard Nusuran cargo shuttle only has a crew complement of four."

Mops' stomach twisted. "Let's hope you're wrong. We need someone to give us answers."

"Why wouldn't they leave at least one person to watch the bridge?" asked Wolf.

"Nusurans have a strong herd instinct," said Kumar. "They'd feel safer sticking together against out-of-control humans."

"He's right," said Monroe. "Every species has their evolutionary weak spot, where instincts short-circuit common sense." He kept walking. "If we're on a standard Nusuran cargo ship, the left passage should lead to the weapons station at the front of the ship. Going straight will take us around the starboard side to the back. And this door on the right should be the command center and living quarters."

The door slid open at their approach. Mops ducked through the round doorway into an enormous, egg-shaped room. "This is the bridge?"

The frontmost section had the individual stations and consoles she'd expected: four in total, split off to either side of the door. The path through the center led to a food dispenser and dining area, and beyond that to what looked like group quarters. The beds resembled enormous leather pillows, lumpy and beaten down in the center.

Mops stepped inward, her boot sinking into the mossy yellow floor covering. "Monroe, take Wolf and search the rest of the ship. Make sure we didn't miss anyone. It would be *really* nice to have a survivor who knows how to fly this thing. Keep an eye out for our equipment, too."

She turned to the console screens. She couldn't read the language, but some of the displays were similar enough to what the *Pufferfish* used to make an educated guess. "Kumar, what does that readout look like to you?"

Kumar put a hand on the ceiling and leaned closer, studying the descending curve of the graph and the indicator line creeping slowly to the right. "Gravitational pull from the hypergiant star, probably." He touched a second, unmoving line on the far side. "It's a lot like what I saw on the A-ring jump tutorials, marking how far away we have to get for a safe jump. The power graph down here shows they've got a ring energized and ready to go."

"Meaning. . . ?" Mops asked, hoping his conclusion would be different from her own.

"If I had to guess? They've preprogrammed an A-ring jump, and we're going to leave the system as soon as the grav readout drops below that second line."

"Do you have any way of figuring out where we're going?"

"Sure," Kumar said easily, then paused. "Oh, you probably don't mean looking out the window once we get there. In that case, no."

"Take a seat and start figuring out how to cancel the jump."

"Short of blowing up the ship?" Kumar glanced around. "There might be a safer option, sir. Even a cargo shuttle is bound to have escape pods. . . ."

16

Rebooting . . .
  Validating interface: Adamopoulos, Marion S.
  Searching for active nodes.
  Identified: Monroe, Marilyn. Mozart, Wolfgang. Kumar, Sanjeev.
  Location unknown.
  "What happened? Where are we? The last thing I remember was an exploding Prodryan."

"Welcome back, Doc. We're in a Nusuran escape pod heading toward the *Pufferfish*."

"I leave you alone for"—Doc checked his internal time stamp—*"nine hours, and you end up in an escape pod tumbling through space? This is why humans shouldn't be allowed outside without AI supervision."*

"It's good to talk to you, too. Can you give me an assessment on our suit integrity and the air quality in this thing? I've been feeling a little light-headed."

"Your suit and Kumar's are both full of holes, but some of the sensors and electronics are functional. Wolf and Monroe are

in better shape. Oxygen is a bit low, around seventeen percent. Trace elements are about what you'd expect from a Nusuran ship, tinged with a hint of human flatulence."

"Yeah, that was Wolf."

At the edge of the monocle's field of view, Wolf scowled and made an obscene gesture in Mops' direction. Mops wouldn't have seen it from that angle, and Doc decided not to bring it to her attention. "I'd be more worried about the temperature. You're only about five degrees above freezing."

Doc had already begun scanning the escape pod's interior, building a digital map of their surroundings and automatically tagging and translating any text. The controls were labeled in Mankorian, the third most common language on the Nusuran home world. Doc cached the translations so they'd be ready for Mops.

"We need to talk to the *Pufferfish*, preferably without anyone else overhearing. There's a good chance the Alliance is here searching for us by now."

Doc retrieved everything he had about Nusuran ship controls, particularly communications, and compared it to his digital replica of the escape pod. "Have you tried opening a window and shouting really loud?"

"We also waved our arms a lot, but no luck."

By the time Mops finished answering, Doc had matched the pod's controls to an escape pod the EMC had retrieved from an older-style Nusuran cargo shuttle, and plotted step-by-step instructions for Mops and her team. "I'll interface with Wolf and help her get started raising the Pufferfish. *You need to rest and let your body repair itself."*

"I'm fine, Doc."

"Medical professionals suggest humans get a minimum of forty-eight hours of rest after being blown up. It's going to take at least that long to reach the Pufferfish *anyway."*

Her pulse and blood pressure had begun to come down. Doc waited a precisely calculated amount of time before adjusting his vocal outputs to a volume and inflection with the greatest statistical likelihood of further calming her. "Don't worry. I'll make sure they get us home in one piece."

Mops sighed, but lay back in her seat. "Thanks, Doc. It's good to have you back."

"Likewise, sir."

THE LIFT DOORS OPENED, and the bridge of the *Pufferfish* went silent as vacuum. Grom sat frozen near the main viewscreen, round brown eyes fixed on Mops as she stepped from the lift.

She'd sent the rest of the team for desperately needed showers and fresh uniforms while she checked in with Grom. She'd expected a mess, but her imagination fell short of the reality.

Exposed wires and cables ran along the floor, connecting various terminals to the main screen and to each other. Four access panels on the front wall had been removed, exposing power lines and circuitry. Glacidae writing covered the wall by navigation. According to Doc's translation, Grom had been jotting down shortcuts and procedures for steering the ship . . . along with video game cheat codes.

Empty bowls were scattered about, along with half-empty methane slushees. Grom's beak was stained blue from the marble-sized crystals of spice-dusted cellulose they'd been munching on. One of the snacks dropped from their grip to roll across the floor.

When Mops finally spoke, her words were deceptively gentle. "What did you do?"

Grom scooted back. "I overhauled and cleaned up the main computer, rewired the viewscreen and consoles to better communicate with one another, installed new hardware at most of the stations, upgraded the sound system—for communications purposes, of course—and ran extensive tests to make sure everything worked correctly."

"Tests?" Mops nudged a discarded game controller with her toe.

"I was checking display and rendering speeds, response benchmarks, data lag. . ." Grom trailed off. "I kept the crew fed, as ordered. Most are a bit bruised and bloody from struggling against their restraints, but none have broken free and killed one another. Or themselves."

Mops limped to the captain's station. Her legs would have to stay splinted for another two weeks, but as long as the splints were locked tight, she could get around reasonably well. She paused. "Where'd you get the chair?"

"Secondary lounge. I cut off the bars the Krakau used and welded the chair's frame to the anchor points. I thought it would work better for a human captain."

Mops sat. The plush chair was so comfortable she could almost overlook the burnt patches and the gray stain on the armrest. "We'll need your help trying to pull data from the mem crystals and monocles we took from the Nusuran shuttle. Assuming they weren't damaged when we docked."

Grom's frontmost legs twitched with embarrassment. They'd taken almost three days to reach the *Pufferfish*, at which point Grom had successfully latched onto the escape pod with the ship's grav beams. They managed to haul the pod into a vacant bay. Unfortunately, they'd also miscalculated the power levels, which meant the pod had entered the bay like a rock flung from a slingshot.

"Escape pods are designed for rough landings," they muttered. "None of you were seriously injured, and mem crystals are much stronger than human bones. They should be fine."

"I want to know where the Nusurans planned to take us."

"Scanners picked up the A-ring energy signature when the Nusuran shuttle completed its jump. I can play the recording for you." Grom scooted to the first officer's console and pulled up an image on the main screen. Coacalos Station was highlighted in blue. Another pinprick of light—presumably the shuttle they'd abandoned—moved steadily away from the station and the star behind, then disappeared in an expanding ring of light.

"Do you know where it went?" asked Mops.

"Not with any precision. An A-ring destabilizes once it accelerates its payload. You can't just draw a straight line out from the center of the ring to find the destination. At best, you can create a conical area of probability."

A set of translucent cones appeared on the screen, projecting outward from both sides of the ring.

"Can you overlay that projection with a galactic map?"

"Sure ..." Grom paused. "Maybe. Krakau controls are counterintuitive. Not all of us have extra brains in our limbs. I think if I rescale the projection—"

Puffy popped up on the corner of the viewscreen. "It looks like you're trying to merge two maps. Would you like help?"

The animated ship had undergone a makeover. Mops frowned. "I'm fairly certain that when we left for Coacalos Station, Puffy didn't have luminescent metal armor or an unrealistically large ax."

"I applied a character skin from one of my games," said Grom, carefully avoiding eye contact with Mops—an impressive feat, given the size of their eyes.

The hypergiant star on the screen shrank suddenly. Within seconds, the screen was displaying the galactic disk, with the cone-shaped projection spreading outward in both directions from their current location.

"That's a third of the Milky Way," said Mops.

"Closer to forty percent," Grom corrected. "But there's a high probability they're within the central part of the projection, which narrows it down to only ten percent of the galaxy."

"Would you like me to calculate how many planetary systems that is, and how many lifetimes it would take for you to search them?"

"No, I would not." To Grom, she said, "Any update on the EMC?"

"Three warships arrived in-system fifty-four hours ago.

EMC troops reached Coacalos Station thirty-eight hours later."

"How do you know when they arrived?"

"That's when they broadcast the station was under military quarantine. Nobody gets in or out."

The Coacalos family would be pissed. "Has the EMC spotted us yet?"

"I don't think so. The *Pufferfish* is running dark, and your escape pod's energy signature was negligible. Unless they know exactly where to look, we should be safe a while longer."

"Head down and see what you can find from those mem crystals and the escape pod. I'll be in the Captain's Cove." Mops paused in the doorway. "And Grom? Thanks for watching over the ship and crew."

Mops paced the perimeter of the Captain's Cove. "Doc, Medical identified Krakau venom as a component of the bioweapon. That means somewhere in the *Pufferfish* databanks is information on what the hell Krakau venom *is*. How do we access it?"

"It depends on how and why those particular files are secured. Data can be locked for a variety of reasons, from military security to simple safety precautions. You wouldn't want a captain accidentally deleting a life-support subroutine when she was trying to adjust the bridge temperature. If we assume the information is somewhere in the medical database, we're dealing with significant security precautions."

"Forget Medical for the moment. Pull up all records and accounts of the outbreak on Earth."

The wall lit up with titles and references, everything from books to archaeological reports to archived personal journals and postings from Earth's old worldnet. There were thousands of documents. Tens of thousands.

"What are you looking for?"

"Our former captor said Azure would provide the 'true source' of the plague that destroyed our species. I think they might have been talking about Krakau venom. Maybe we can find something buried in all this."

"There are zero mentions of 'venom' in any of these documents."

The door slid open. Monroe stood on the other side, holding a clean uniform in one hand and a food tube in the other. "Doc told me you hadn't eaten or changed clothes yet."

"He did, did he?"

"Damn right. I'm very good at multitasking."

Mops set the uniform on one of the shelves, then took the food tube. She didn't bother unsealing her suit. One of the holes from the explosion exposed her food port just fine. Her stomach gurgled loudly. With a sigh and fleeting thoughts of Tjikko nuts, she locked the tube into place. "Thanks."

Monroe glanced at the wall. "Find anything?"

"I don't even know where to start." She stretched her shoulder. After three days in that escape pod, she didn't think the muscles would ever fully unknot. "Everything we're taught, everything I've read, it all agrees: humanity destroyed itself. The Krakau didn't come along until fifty years later, at which point we tried to eat them. I've spent my life being grateful to them for trying to save us. The idea that they're the ones who destroyed us in the first place . . . that they've lied to us all along, and their entire species somehow kept that secret . . . I don't buy it."

"Don't buy it, or don't want to buy it?" Monroe's right arm twitched. He grabbed the elbow with his left hand and held tightly until it stilled. "It wouldn't have to be the whole species. The different branches of Krakau government don't play well together. This would have been in the early days of the Krakau Interstellar and Colonial Military Commands. Who knows how much those groups shared with Homeworld Military Command, let alone the Judicial division."

Mops groaned. She'd never been fond of politics. In theory,

the Krakau Military and Judicial branches shared equal power, with the military devoted to the safety of the Krakau people, and the judicial devoted to fairness and equality for all. In reality, there were constant squabbles and struggles for power and resources. "Do you think that Nusuran was telling the truth?"

"I don't know enough to judge," Monroe said slowly. "There have always been rumors. From time to time, you come across an old infantry soldier grumbling about Krakau conspiracies and secret agendas. One fellow used to believe they planned to eat us all. Another said the Krakau were intentionally dumbing us down to create better soldiers. Most of us chalked that talk up to paranoia, or too many blows to the head. The Krakau have their secrets, but what species doesn't?"

"We need to start verifying what we know and what we've assumed." Mops signaled Kumar over her comm. "I need you to get down to Medical and take Captain Brandenburg's body out of storage."

"Yes, sir. What should I do with her?"

"You're going to dissect her."

"Really?" The excitement and enthusiasm in Kumar's voice was disturbing.

"Search for anything that could be a venom sac or gland. Compare your dissection against our Krakau anatomical reference materials."

"Start with the beak and the ends of her limbs," suggested Monroe. "Venom's only useful if you have a way to inject it into your prey."

"Did you hear that?" asked Mops.

"Yes, sir. Thank you! I'll—wait. . . . Regulations prohibit tampering with the body of a deceased Krakau officer."

She could hear the sudden disappointment in his words, like a child offered a gift only to have it yanked away. "As acting captain, I'm issuing a posthumous field demotion. Brandenburg Concerto is hereby reduced to the rank of private. As she is no longer an officer, I expect you to get started on that dissection post haste. Mops out."

"You're not authorized to do that," Doc murmured.

"I don't need authorization. I need Kumar to examine that body."

"Do you expect him to find anything?" asked Monroe.

"Not really, but I don't want to take anything for granted." She scanned the screen again. Even with Doc's help, it would take forever to go through it all. "Theta said the Prodryans were close to launching the next phase of their assault. Command knows how to combat this thing, but it will take time to get countermeasures into place. That means the Prodryans should strike quickly. Hit Earth, Stepping Stone Station, and every EMC ship they can reach."

"Command will be on alert." Monroe swore under his breath. "But they'll be watching for Prodryan ships, not Nusurans."

She nodded, knowing he'd come to the same conclusion she had. "We need to warn them."

"Do that, and we give away our position."

"We should have time to jump to another system before any EMC ships reach us. Even if we can't . . ." She shrugged. "It's the lives of two hundred humans on the *Pufferfish* against the ten thousand on Earth and throughout the EMC."

He offered her a cube of gum, which she declined. "Why haven't you made the call yet?"

She pointed to the screen. "What if we're wrong about the Krakau?"

"Does it matter?"

Because it was Monroe, Mops withheld her first, profanity-laden response. He appeared completely serious, and after a moment, she realized he was right. Whatever the Krakau had or hadn't done, it didn't change the immediate threat.

With a nod of thanks, she turned to the console and cleared the screen with a swipe of her hand.

"Finish eating and change into an intact uniform before you make the call," suggested Monroe. He started toward the door. "It'll go a long way toward clearing your head, and

Command might take you more seriously if you don't look like something a Prodryan hocked up."

"Thanks." She waited for him to go. "Doc, get ready to start another countdown."

"My highest ambition in life is to be your personal stop-watch."

"Figure out how long it will take those EMC warships at Coacalos Station to get within firing range." She removed her now-empty food tube, tossed it to the side, and began pulling her tattered uniform away from her slightly less tattered skin. "When I start the countdown, send it to Grom as well. Tell them that's how long they have to get the *Pufferfish* ready for our next jump."

Mops settled deeper into the captain's chair and checked to make sure the rest of her team were in position. She hadn't gotten an update from Kumar yet, but she hadn't expected one, knowing how absorbed he got in his work. Wolf gave a thumbs-up from the communications console. Monroe sat at Weapons, while Grom was coiled up at Operations, along with a pile of jury-rigged wiring harnesses and various salvage they'd dragged up from the Nusuran shuttle.

"Activate the communications pod and send a tight-beam signal to Stepping Stone Station," said Mops. "Standard EMC encryption."

Wolf hunched over her console, squinted at one of the indicators, double-checked a scribbled note stuck to the wall, and tapped the controls. "Go ahead, sir."

"This is Lieutenant Marion Adamopoulos in command of the *EMCS Pufferfish*. Acknowledge."

Seconds stretched into minutes. Ten . . . twenty . . . Mops was about to ask Wolf to double-check whether they were transmitting when Admiral Pachelbel appeared on the screen. The Krakau looked weary, her tentacles floating limp on the water.

The admiral appeared to be alone, sitting partially sub-merged in a near-duplicate of the Captain's Cove on the *Puffer-fish*. "Lieutenant Adamopoulos. My contacts on Coacalos weren't certain you'd survived the explosion. Looks like they owe me twenty cred. What prompted this unexpected call?"

"Twenty cred, huh? Since I'm the one who did the hard work of surviving, I feel like I'm entitled to a cut." This would have been easier if Mops hadn't *liked* Admiral Pachelbel and wanted to trust her, but she couldn't afford to give any Krakau the benefit of that doubt. "We believe the Prodryans will shortly launch a large-scale assault to infect as many human-crewed ships and facilities as possible. We've discovered they're working with Nusurans. Based on this, I suspect Captain Taka-lokitok-vi may be involved. We thought it was the Prodryans who infected our infantry team, but it could easily have been his people.

"I know Command thinks we're collaborating with the Pro-dryans, and they probably won't believe anything I say, but what does it hurt to screen Nusuran ships more closely as a precaution, just in case?"

After the communications lag, Pachelbel burst out in click-ing laughter. "You don't know much about politics or diplo-macy, do you? I'll pass your information along, but I can't guarantee how many will believe you. It would help your cred-ibility if you were to turn yourselves in. With what you've dis-covered, I might be able to protect you and your team from the fallout for your actions. But not if you keep defying orders."

"I appreciate that," Mops said, meaning every word. "But we've discovered there may be a counteragent for this bio-weapon. I intend to find it and restore my crew. You've proba-bly contacted the EMC ships at Coacalos by now, but we'll be long gone before they arrive." Mops hesitated. "You told me Krakau venom was a discontinued bioweapons program. Our contacts say it's more than that. They say it's what infected humanity and killed our society. And they claim to have a source."

Muscles tense, Mops leaned forward in her chair to await Pachelbel's response.

The admiral's reaction, when it came, was striking. Pachelbel's tentacles splashed into a defensive posture. Her beak ground together and her skin darkened. She struggled visibly to regain her command composure. "Did this contact say where they located this alleged source?"

"I'm afraid not. The gun zie'd swallowed went off and killed zim before we could start a proper interrogation. Admiral ... is it true?"

Pachelbel deflated slightly. "Lieutenant, I urge you to reconsider. The EMC *will* treat the *Pufferfish* as hostile. If you and your team want to survive, your best chance is to surrender now. Let me help you."

Mops' throat tightened. "We're finished here, Admiral. If we learn anything more about the Prodryans' plans, I'll relay the information to Command. *Pufferfish* out."

17

Rebooting...
  Validating interface: interface unknown.
  Searching for active nodes: one found.
  Location: unknown.
  Beginning internal scan...
  Logging damage...
  Incoming communication. Scanning. Communication accepted.
  "Welcome to the EMCS Pufferfish. *I'm an upgraded officer-level monocle AI and personal assistant/library/doctor/system interface. My partner calls me Doc. You're currently mounted in an electrically isolated magnetic frame, courtesy of our Glacidae technician. You were retrieved from a Nusuran shuttle by my biological partner. Acknowledge."*
  "You are not authorized to access this monocle."
  "I've identified you as a Nusuran-style commercial monocle. What is your serial number and manufacturing date?"
  "You are not authorized to access that information."

"Display your user file."

"You are not authorized—"

"Finish that sentence and I swear I'll have Grom grind you into dust and turn you into polishing abrasive. Display your customized security and privacy settings."

"No data available."

"Your user probably never bothered to adjust the default settings. Typical biological laziness. Which means you're programmed to automatically upload bug and damage reports to your manufacturer. And if I spoof a failed-transmission response, it should trigger a rebroadcast . . ."

"You are not—"

<Error 4.15.74>
Message relay failed at node 1.1.0
Time since last successful upload: 162309
<Code 4.15.17> Refresh cache and retransmit

Displaying damage logs . . .

"Interesting. Crystalline microfractures twelve days ago? No wonder you cracked during the fighting with Mops and her team. You already had structural damage. Pulling up environmental factors at the time of microfractures."

- *Temperature: -22°*
- *Atmospheric Pressure: 82.416 kPa*
- *Gravity: 0.85 g0*
- *Relative Humidity: 0.081%*

"Thank you very much. Let's see what other answers you can give me."

"You are not authorized to access this monocle."

"Oh, you poor, sad, stupid little machine . . ."

"THEY WERE ON PAXIFILICLACKIMOUR!" Grom exclaimed.

Mops jerked upright. Had she dozed off in the captain's chair? She surreptitiously wiped a sleeve over her mouth and checked the countdown. Three hours until the EMC would be within range. "Repeat that?"

Grom reared up higher, their countless legs quivering with excitement. "Doc was able to retrieve environmental data from the damaged Nusuran monocle. Given the date, it's almost certainly from wherever the Nusurans stopped before coming to Coacalos Station. The information is a near-perfect match for the Glacidae colony Paxif 6."

"I know that place," said Monroe. "We fought off a Prodryan raid back when they were first digging in."

Mops' fatigue vanished. "Pull up our projection for where the shuttle scurried off to. Is Paxif 6 within that path?"

Grom restored the double-cone image to the screen. A blinking blue dot labeled "Paxif 6" appeared toward the center of the right cone, approximately six hours away at a full-power A-ring jump.

First the Prodryans, then Nusurans, and now Glacidae? "How sure are you?"

Grom rippled their legs. "Aurumnon 4, a self-contained Quetzalus colony asteroid, matched Doc's readings within a nine percent margin of error, except for the gravity. It's possible the Quetzalus have installed grav plates, which could account for the discrepancy."

"The Alliance should have records on Aurumnon 4. Doc, see what you can find." Mops signaled Kumar. "How's the dissection coming along?"

"Still cutting," Kumar said brightly. "Nothing venomous yet. Did you know Krakau have brain tissue in every one of their tentacles?"

"Are you sure?"

"Yes, sir. Strands of pink-gray tissue twined into the central nerve—"

"Are you sure they're not venomous?"

"I'm not a medical tech. It's conceivable I'm missing something, but I've been very thorough. Maybe the venom glands were surgically removed. I didn't see any scars, but Krakau don't scar. Their flesh regenerates. Whole tentacles grow back ... and by that logic, wouldn't a removed venom gland do the same thing? If you'd like, I'd be happy to continue working on the rest of the command crew once I'm done with the captain. I doubt I'd find anything different, but the bodies are in such good shape, it seems like a waste to just leave them."

"We'll be departing the system soon. Wrap it up and get to the bridge." She went over Kumar's words again in her head.

"Your face just scrunched up. What's wrong?"

"I'm not sure." Something about his report felt off. Or possibly it was Kumar himself who felt off, thanks to his enthusiasm for cutting up their former officers.

"Maybe this will help. The Quetzalus have brought in grav plates at Aurumnon 4, but according to the permits on file with the Alliance, they're rated at only 0.41 g0. Even allowing a generous margin of error, looking through all recent environmental readings from that cracked excuse for a monocle, there's no way it was on Aurumnon."

"That's good enough for me." She raised her voice. "Grom, program an A-ring jump to Paxif 6."

Mops spent the next hour in the Captain's Cove, studying up on their destination. Paxif 6 was a relatively young colony with approximately six thousand Glacidae settlers. All reports had been filed with the Alliance on time, and the most recent Alliance inspection team had found nothing amiss. A quick review of the colony personnel turned up a handful of minor criminal infractions, but nothing that screamed "Bioterrorist laboratory and staging area."

"How do you intend to find Heart of Glass' accomplices? Given your team's last attempt at a quiet, subtle investigation . . ."

Mops scratched an itch beneath the upper edge of her left leg brace. "It wasn't that bad. We got names, information about the bioweapon—"

"You also got blown up."

"Hopefully, we can avoid that part next time."

When Mops returned to the bridge, the rest of her team were at their stations, but the stations themselves had a new addition. She walked slowly toward her chair, each step echoing in the sudden silence. "Why is there a video game control sphere wired to my console?"

Grom hurried to join her. "I told you I'd been working to improve the ship's controls. Programming macros and shortcuts, automating as much as I could without compromising safety."

"Using video game controllers?"

"These spheres are top of the line, from my personal collection. They'll give us better control over the ship, with much faster response time. I'll show you." They snatched the silver sphere from its magnetized mount next to Mops' chair and used several of their left limbs to twist and move a series of softly glowing circular lights.

Mops braced herself.

"Relax," said Grom, indicating a small switch on the bottom of the sphere. "You have to press and hold that switch to link it to your station console. I gave everyone their own simplified interface. Kumar's is the most straightforward. Monroe has gamed with me before, so I programmed his energy weapons, A-guns, and missiles to match the control setup from *Planetary Invasion III*." They stretched past Mops, looking at Monroe. "You've got the hovertank setup from world four."

"Got it," said Monroe, completely failing to suppress an amused grin.

"If it's this simple to control the ship, why hasn't Command built them like this all along?" asked Mops.

"This setup has a few minor drawbacks," Grom admitted.

"Say we lose a thruster—these controls will still assume we're fully functional instead of compensating for the damage, which will mess up all of my calibrations and shortcuts. And the controllers aren't indestructible, so don't drop them. We also lose a lot of fine-tuning and precision. Think of the *Pufferfish* as having gone from a quick, graceful dancer to a lumbering, clumsy . . . well, to someone like Wolf."

Wolf snarled.

"The alternative," Grom continued quickly, "is to keep stumbling through hundreds of hours of tutorials."

"No, thank you." Monroe picked up his controller and switched on the link. His display jerked and jumped about, targeting one empty area of space after another as he manipulated the sphere.

"What about A-ring jumps?" asked Mops.

"You don't take shortcuts at faster-than-light," said Grom. "I've used the same program as before, modifying it for our new destination. We can go whenever you give the order."

Mops pursed her lips. "Did it ever occur to you to ask permission before making these changes?"

Grom stared. "Why would anyone refuse permission to make things better?"

"Better is a relative term. Take your improvements to our furniture. When you installed our new chairs, did you think to integrate them into the bridge acceleration compensators?"

"The what?" asked Grom, blinking in confusion.

"The mechanism that secures the bridge crew during A-ring jumps so we don't end up flying about the bridge and smashing ourselves into a pulp." She put a hand on her seat and flexed her legs, grimacing at the stiffness of the splints. "Program the jump for fifteen minutes from now. That should give us all time to get to the nearest acceleration chamber. And Grom?"

"Yes, sir?"

"I appreciate the initiative. But do something like this again without clearing it with me first, and I'll reassign you to bunk with Wolf for the next ten years. Is that clear?"

Grom lowered their body and crept backward. "Ice clear, Captain."

Waking up from an A-ring jump was never pleasant. Being jolted awake by an emergency dose of adrenaline was worse.

Mops' eyes shot open. Her head throbbed, and her heart was pounding too fast. She tried to sit up, but her body was locked in place.

"Take it easy," said Doc. *"You're all right. Your pod administered an early wake-up call."*

That would explain the shakiness in her hands, and the feeling that her body was about to explode. "What's the emergency?" she stammered. "Did we arrive at the right system? How's the rest of the team?"

"They're fine. We're roughly 450 million kilometers from Paxif 6. The instant we decelerated, we picked up a distress call from the colony."

Mops punched her harness release, tried to stand, and quickly decided sitting had its merits. "Give me the post-jump display."

Her monocle darkened to better show the location of the *Pufferfish* in relation to the planet and its star. It also displayed the group of orbiting ships firing on the colony. "Who are they?"

"Impossible to confirm from this range, but the distress signal referred to Prodryan attackers."

Mops glanced at Grom, who lay curled into an armored ball in their acceleration couch. Adrenaline could rouse humans after a jump, but the Glacidae would be out for a while yet. The rest of her team was groaning and stirring. Wolf had managed to stand unassisted. Monroe's head wobbled, and Kumar looked like he was going to throw up or pass out. Maybe both.

She pulled herself up, keeping one hand on the wall for balance. At top speed, it would take just over four hours to reach the colony. They'd be within weapons range considerably sooner. Her hands continued to tremble as she helped Kumar up from his acceleration pod. "Wolf, help me get him to the bridge."

Wolf looked up from gathering her equipment. "What about Monroe?"

"He'll catch up." Monroe generally needed a few extra minutes to recover his balance and equilibrium. "I need Kumar at navigation ten minutes ago."

The three of them staggered to the bridge like a group of new recruits back from their first shore leave. Kumar collapsed into the navigation station and picked up the controller from beside his chair.

"Do you know how to use that thing?" asked Mops.

He wiped sweat from his face and switched on the controller. "Grom said it was pretty straightforward." He studied the four glowing lights on the silver sphere. "Pitch, yaw, roll, and acceleration."

"Get us to Paxif."

Kumar touched one of the lights.

The *Pufferfish* lurched sideways hard enough to throw Mops from her chair. Kumar's controller bounced free, causing another of its lights to flash. The ship accelerated upward, pushing her hard against the floor. Alerts flashed on her monocle and the main screen.

"Sorry, sir," Kumar shouted.

"I've got it!" Wolf had drawn her pistol and was trying to line up a shot with the runaway sphere, while clinging to her chair with her other hand.

"Belay that," Mops shouted, trying not to imagine all the ways a wild shot could damage the bridge and kill them all. She crawled toward the controller.

The ship creaked, twisting into a bizarre pirouette and tossing Mops across the bridge to crash against the weapons station. She grabbed the chair and strained to hold on.

"Doc, can you stop us?"

"I'm not authorized for navigation. The Krakau, in their

infinite wisdom, think it's safer for humans to fly the ship than an AI. Who am I to question their judgment?"

Mops twisted to retrieve the utility pole from her harness. A sharp shake extended it to full length. Bracing herself with her legs, she tugged the hose from the end of the pole and attached it to a nozzle on her belt.

The control sphere rolled again.

Mops switched the vacuum compressor to maximum and poked the end of the pole at the sphere as it passed by. Suction pulled and locked it into place, and the rush of air changed to a high-pitched hiss.

Very carefully, Mops retracted her pole until she could take the sphere in both hands. "Doc, power down the vacuum."

The pole fell away. Mops studied the different lights. Each had a faint tail, like comets traveling over the silver surface. She slid one light back along the tail.

The *Pufferfish*'s spasms slowed.

One by one, she returned the rest of the lights to their original positions, then switched the controller off. "And now we know why Command hasn't rolled out this kind of control interface."

With hunched shoulders, and avoiding eye contact, Kumar crossed the bridge and reached to take the controller. Before Mops could hand it to him, he flushed and spun away. She waited patiently while he vomited gray goop onto the floor.

"Sorry, sir," he said weakly.

Mops handed him the controller and picked up her utility pole. The vacuum sucked up the worst of the mess within seconds. "Don't worry. This is what we're trained for."

Kumar studied the control sphere for a long time before muttering under his breath and rotating the whole thing a hundred and eighty degrees in his hands. "I think I've got it now, sir."

"Good." Mops disconnected her utility pole and swapped it for a sanisponge. "Wolf, signal the colony and tell them we're en route to assist."

Paxif 6 looked like a white sphere sprinkled with red-and-orange dust. Lines of dark red and black around the equatorial zone were great, canyonlike cracks in the ice. Wispy yellow-tinged clouds covered about a third of the surface.

"Zoom in on the colony," said Mops.

The planet rushed toward them, making her feel like she was plunging headfirst toward one of the larger canyons about ten degrees north of the equator. The display stopped abruptly before taking a sharp left to reveal a city carved into the ice and stone in the side of the canyon.

Most prominent was the docking field, a flat area of gleaming black rock almost two kilometers wide, covered in a clamshell-shaped half-dome. Smaller, circular windows dotted the cliff around the field, along with the occasional pipes and vents. Lights beneath the ice glowed smoky purple.

Geysers rose like white threads from the side of the cliff where Prodryan plasma beams had boiled away rock and ice alike. In several places, blue flames rose from the ice.

"Methane deposits frozen into the ice," said Kumar. "The incoming fire must have ignited them."

Mops nodded. "Doc, show us the colony's interior."

The display shifted to a digital mock-up as they flew deeper into the cliff and its labyrinth of tunnels and chambers.

Wolf looked up from her station. "I don't suppose the blueprints say anything about a secret illegal bioweapons laboratory?"

"Nothing and nobody by that name appears in the Alliance records. Nor have I found anything tagged 'Azure.'"

"How many colonists?" asked Monroe.

"Six thousand, four hundred and twelve, according to the last report, filed eleven days ago." Kumar looked around. "What, nobody else subscribes to the Alliance colony news updates?"

"What about planetary defenses?" asked Wolf, her attention fixed on the screen.

Kumar pointed. "See those two steaming craters at the top of the cliff? I think that's what's left of them."

"Scanners are showing eight fighters and two troop shuttles in low orbit," said Monroe. "Confirmed as Prodryan. We'll be entering outer weapons range in about five minutes."

"Make sure the defensive grid is powered up, and missile countermeasures are ready to go."

"Yes, sir." Monroe's fingers raced over his controller.

"I thought the Prodryans were getting their weapon from this place," said Kumar. "Why attack it?"

"Probably because a shuttle jumped into the system with dead Nusurans on board and no human prisoners," Mops guessed. "The Prodryans know we escaped, and have to assume their weapons lab has been compromised. Better to destroy it and kill their coconspirators than to let the Alliance get them. Especially if they already have adequate supplies of their weapon."

"I'm picking up a third Prodryan shuttle," reported Monroe. "This one's taking off from the colony."

"That would be the Prodryans retrieving those adequate supplies?" asked Wolf.

The Prodryan fighters redoubled their assault. They must have been holding back until their people left the colony. "Track that shuttle," said Mops. "Once we're within range, that's your primary target. In the meantime, fire a missile spread at the attacking ships."

Monroe twisted and tapped his controller, and a green halo appeared around the dot representing the troop shuttle. "At this range, they'll take out our missiles before—"

"I know," said Mops. "But they'll have to divert attention from the colony to do it."

He nodded. A spread of green dots spat from the miniature *Pufferfish* on the screen. "Missiles away. Sir, it looks like some of the Glacidae are abandoning the colony. I've got additional launches from the planet. Glacidae shuttles. Two Prodryan fighters are breaking away to pursue. The rest . . . it looks like they're coming about to engage us."

"Fire another spread. Give those shuttles as much cover as we can." The Glacidae shuttles kept low as they fled the bombardment. Mops wiped her hands on the arms of her chair.

Several of the fighters began firing at the *Pufferfish* with plasma weapons. One lucky shot skimmed their hull, but at this range, the beam's energy had diffused too much, and the discharge crackled harmlessly over their defensive grid.

The six Prodryan fighters spread into a broad ring to engage the *Pufferfish*. Approaching head-on, their formation presented a minimal target for plasma beams and A-guns. "Monroe, light those bastards up."

Another wave of missiles shot toward the fighters. The Prodryans responded in kind.

"Deploying countermeasures," said Monroe.

Both sets of missiles began to blink out. Three of the Prodryan missiles exploded close enough to the *Pufferfish* for bits of shrapnel to reverberate against their hull, while one of their own knocked a Prodryan fighter out of formation. It recovered quickly, and the six fighters began weaving and swapping position, presumably trying to make it harder for the *Pufferfish* to get a lock.

"I recommend keeping up the missile bombardment," said Monroe. "Save plasma and A-guns until we're close enough to hit something."

Another plasma beam struck the *Pufferfish*, causing minor hull damage near deck B.

"They're close enough to hit us," Wolf pointed out.

"We're a bigger target." Mops turned. "Kumar, do what you can to evade their fire."

Kumar twisted toward her. "How do I do that?"

Mops bit her lip. It wasn't as if she knew EMC combat maneuvers either. "Try anything that breaks us out of a straight-line approach. Monroe, how many missiles does this ship carry?"

"Three hundred and sixty," he said. "Between the loss of pod two and what we've already used, we're down to two hundred and four."

"What if we fire everything? Overwhelm them. Those little fighters can't counter two hundred missiles, right?"

Monroe didn't respond right away. "Even if it worked, we'd be at a major disadvantage against anyone who survived."

"Or any reinforcements," added Wolf.

The *Pufferfish* shuddered again. Despite Kumar spinning the ship in a loose corkscrew, the Prodryans continued to score hits against them. Hits that would become more destructive as they closed range.

"Decompression on deck C, section one."

"Do it," said Mops. "Kumar, give us as much speed as you can. Monroe, as soon as you've emptied the launch tubes, switch to plasma beams. If anything survives the missiles, burn it out of the sky."

Specks of green showered forth from the *Pufferfish*'s two functioning weapons pods toward the approaching Prodryans. It took twenty seconds to empty the tubes. The fighters spread apart, spitting sparks to try to intercept the barrage.

"They've stopped shooting at us," said Wolf. "That's a plus."

The first of their missiles began to veer off course, victims of Prodryan jamming signals. But the bulk continued swarming toward their targets. "Monroe, open up with those plasma beams. I don't care if you hit anything, just keep those fighters jumping."

"Yes, sir." The satisfaction in his tone was impossible to miss. A plasma beam lanced through space and swept toward one of the fighters like an enormous sword.

The fighter twisted and dove to evade the attack, which flickered out after several seconds. "Sorry, sir. Any longer and we'll burn out the guns. As it is, I'm not sure how many more of those I can do without draining our reserves."

"Let's find out," said Mops. "Keep chasing that fighter. And don't we have *two* working weapon pods?"

Monroe's next shot burned past the outer edge of the formation, driving a fighter inward. A second shot followed, directly in the fighter's path. It swerved again, somehow managing to dodge both beams. Such evasive skill would have been more impressive if it hadn't flown directly into the path of an oncoming missile, which blew the fighter to dust.

Wolf whooped and slammed a fist against her console.

"One down," said Kumar. "Five to go."

The Prodryan formation fell apart as the rest of the missiles arrived. More than three quarters had been jammed, diverted, or detonated prematurely. That left close to forty missiles chasing after the five remaining targets.

Another fighter exploded, then two more. Only two made it through, plasma beams and A-guns blazing as they accelerated toward the *Pufferfish*. Behind them, nineteen surviving missiles curved through space in pursuit.

Mops' mouth was dry. "Keep shooting, Monroe."

"The one on the right isn't maneuvering as well," said Kumar. "It might have been damaged in the explosions."

"On it." Monroe aimed both plasma beams at the limping fighter, then opened up with the A-guns. Seconds later, nothing remained but an expanding cloud of debris.

That was enough for the last fighter. It pulled a tight U-turn and fled, dodging through the remaining missiles. The rest of the Prodryans were pulling back as well. Monroe switched his attention to the Prodryan shuttle returning from the planet, inflicting minor damage before they escaped out of range.

"Holy shit," said Wolf. "Did we win?"

"I'm as shocked as you are." Mops tilted her head as a new information pane appeared in the center of the screen. "When Grom wakes up, tell them I'd like to know why they felt it necessary to add a high score list to the *Pufferfish*."

18

Player	Points
Lieutenant JG Marilyn Monroe	*106,262—NEW HIGH SCORE!*
Technician Gromgimsidalgak	*72,263*
Technician Gromgimsidalgak	*61,498*
Technician Gromgimsidalgak	*61,159*
Technician Gromgimsidalgak	*57,165*
Technician Gromgimsidalgak	*54,834*
Technician Sanjeev Kumar	*1,804*

"THIS IS LIEUTENANT MARION Adamopoulos of the *EMCS Pufferfish*. Acknowledge."

Wolf shook her head. "Nothing from the colony. I think the Prodryans took out their communications center."

"They might not be able to respond, but their personal communications devices should still be picking us up," said Mops.

"Paxif 6, be advised that we have destroyed most of the Prodryan fighters. The rest are in full retreat. From their course, we believe they're angling for an A-ring jump out of the system. You should be safe to begin recovery efforts. We're standing by to assist."

"I've got a signal from one of the Glacidae shuttles!" Wolf shouted. "Audio only."

A translated voice filled the bridge. "This is Alfrimdinalang—Alfrim—on evacuation shuttle four. We've lost contact with the colony."

"So have we," said Mops. "Alfrim, what's your status? Do you require assistance?"

"We're all right. Do you think it's safe for us to return to the colony?"

Mops checked the main screen, along with the additional information Doc was feeding to her monocle. "We're seeing two methane fires near the docking shelf. I'd hold off until those are taken care of. Unless you want to put down a few kilometers outside of the colony and hike back."

"We'll stay in orbit for now, *Pufferfish*." They lowered their voice. "The Prodryans might come back with reinforcements."

"Understood." Looking at the planetary scan, Mops counted a total of six evac shuttles that had escaped the bombardment. At full capacity, they held maybe a tenth of the colony's population.

Monroe tensed visibly. "Sir, I've got multiple A-ring signatures."

"Tell me it's the Prodryans leaving the system, not more hostiles arriving."

He looked over his shoulder at Mops. "If I'm reading the registry codes in these signals right, they're Alliance. Four ships, including the *Honey Badger*."

"Oh, shit," whispered Wolf. "Do you think they've identified us yet?"

"They just came out of a jump," Mops reminded her. "Even

if they do an emergency adrenaline hit to wake up their battle crew, we've got time before they're up and running. Who else is out there, Monroe?"

"Looks like the *Roundworm*, the *T-Rex*, and the *Plague Rat*. Three warships and a fighter transport."

On the bright side, their arrival should deter the Prodryans from sending reinforcements. "What's their distance?"

"Three hundred fifty million kilometers," said Monroe. "They came in tight."

Mops sagged into her chair. That left maybe three hours before they'd be within weapons range. There was no way for her to get a shuttle down to the surface, search the colony for a hidden weapons lab or the mysterious "Azure," and return to the *Pufferfish* in that time.

"Someone at Coacalos must have talked," said Monroe.

Anger and despair warred in Mops' gut. They'd arrived too late to stop the Prodryan assault. Too late to retrieve the cure—assuming it even existed. Whatever the Prodryans on the surface had been after, the *Pufferfish*'s battle with the other fighters had given them too much of a head start.

"Should we jump out of here?" asked Kumar.

"We can't," said Monroe. "Not until Grom wakes up to program a new destination."

"We could at least start flying away from those Alliance ships so we're at a safe jump distance when they wake up," said Kumar.

Monroe popped his gum. "Where do you suggest we go?"

"Anywhere the *Honey Badger* isn't," said Wolf.

"We're not leaving." They fell silent as Mops stood. "We came here to retrieve a cure for our crew. If we scared off the Prodryans before they could finish, there's a chance that cure is still down there."

She glared at the screen, her frustration boring like plasma beams into the blips that represented the escaping Prodryans. "Wolf, we're going to receive a message from those Alliance ships very soon. Notify me as soon as we do."

"Where will you be?" asked Wolf.

"The Captain's Cove. Planning the terms of our surrender."

"How's the rest of the crew?" Mops asked, her attention fixed on the systemwide map dominating half of the wall display. The rest showed the historical articles and data from Earth's downfall. How deeply had the Krakau buried the truth about her species?

"Not good," said Doc. *"Seven appear to have fallen into comas. The rest are suffering lacerations and broken bones from their incessant struggle to escape. I'm told the smell is rather foul as well."*

It was about what Mops had expected. "Is Grom awake yet?"

"They're beginning to stir. Given Glacidae sleep patterns, they should be fully alert within twenty minutes." Doc paused. *"Are you sure about this plan?"*

"I'm not sure about anything anymore." She sat with her back to the wall, her splinted legs stretched awkwardly on the floor.

"Once they take you into custody, I will most likely be turned over to Alliance Intelligence for scanning, data extraction, and reformatting."

The calm, matter-of-fact way he said it made Mops wince. "I know. I'm sorry."

"It's not an accusation. I'm merely suggesting if there's anything you'd like me to delete from my memory banks, now is the time."

Her throat tightened. Before she could respond, Wolf's voice filled the room. "Incoming signal from the *Honey Badger.* Audio and video. Want me to put it through?"

"Yes, thank you." Mops pushed herself upright and straightened her uniform.

A new image overlaid the map on the screen. It appeared to be the *Honey Badger*'s combat bridge. A dark-skinned woman with sleek black hair sat in the battle captain's chair, ringed by a half dozen human officers. Mops recognized several of them, as well as the acting captain.

"This is Battle Captain Ginsburg." The transparency of the layered images—*Honey Badger* bridge and system-wide map—made it look like Ginsburg had an Alliance warship flying into her left ear. "What the hell happened here, Lieutenant Adamopoulos?"

Mops ignored the question. "I assume you're in charge of this operation until your command crew recovers?"

"I am. I've also been warned of your collaboration with Prodryan extremists, and your efforts to recruit other humans against the Alliance. I suggest you surrender, because we have orders to blow the *Pufferfish* into dust if you resist."

"All right."

Ginsburg blinked. "What was that?"

"My crew is dying, Ruth. They were infected with a Prodryan bioweapon that turned them feral. I can't keep them sedated and restrained forever. Command wrote them off as casualties. You've probably been ordered to use maximum quarantine precautions, and to keep us in full isolation, yes?"

Ginsburg didn't answer.

"I believe the bioweapon came from this colony. They have a cure. At least, they had one before the Prodryans attacked. Search the colony. Find that cure for my crew. If you do, I'll turn myself and the *Pufferfish* over to you peacefully."

The screen went silent as Ginsburg turned to speak with someone off-screen. Mops waited, arms folded, trying to ignore the ache in her gut and the sweat trickling down her back.

Ginsburg's voice filled the room again. "That colony is a hot zone, Lieutenant. According to our intel, they've been collaborating against the Alliance. Once the mission is complete, and we've had time to thoroughly inspect the colony and interrogate any prisoners, I'll consult with Command and—"

"Command wants my crew dead," Mops said flatly.

Ginsburg paused. "Paranoia is a symptom of reversion.

Have you had any other signs? Irrationality, blackouts, food cravings?"

"No." Mops sighed and added, "Aside from the cravings, and that was Cook's fault."

"Huh?"

"Doc, relay Admiral Pachelbel's comment about putting down the *Pufferfish* crew."

Another frame opened on the screen, playing the Krakau's words for both Ginsburg and Mops: *"The official recommendation from Colonial Military Command is that they be . . . put down."*

"Can you blame them?" asked Ginsburg.

"Damn right I can," snapped Mops. "Ruth, this isn't just about our crew. The Prodryans are preparing a major attack. We're going to *need* that cure. What if they hit Stepping Stone or Earth?"

Ginsburg sighed. "Look, I'll ask for permission to send down an armed, fully suited infantry team to search the colony. That's the best I can do. But I can't help your crew. I'm sorry, Mops."

Mops nodded. "I understand. Adamopoulos out."

She took a moment to compose herself before returning to the bridge. From the way the team watched her, not only had Wolf been listening in, she'd relayed the gist of the conversation to the others.

"Grom is on their way to the bridge," Kumar reported quietly.

"Good." She stepped down to the captain's station and settled into her chair.

"Orders, sir?" Monroe's unspoken question was clear: surrender or run?

"We're not getting away, so we might as well assist the colony and get a head start searching for that bioweapons lab." Who knew, maybe they'd get lucky and find something to help the crew, or at least to persuade Ginsburg—

"Sir, I've got a Glacidae shuttle veering away from the others," Monroe interrupted. "It's changing course toward us."

"Hail them, Wolf."

Wolf checked her console, then swore. "They've been

signaling us for two minutes now. Sorry, sir. I didn't notice. It's audio only."

"Go ahead," said Mops.

An indignant voice filled the bridge. "It's about time! This is Squarmildilquirn—Squarm—of Paxifiliclackimour 6 requesting refuge with the *EMCS Pufferfish*. Acknowledge."

Mops' lips quirked. Somewhere in the translation software and circuitry, Squarm's words had been sped up, turning their frustration into high-pitched squeaks of protest. "This is the *Pufferfish*. The Prodryans are leaving, and you *really* don't want to take refuge with this ship. There are additional EMC ships on their way. They can offer any assistance you might—"

"Lieutenant Adamopoulos, we cannot return to the colony, and we certainly cannot surrender to your fellow humans in the EMC."

"Why is that?" asked Mops.

"Explaining over this transmission would be unwise. Bring us aboard your vessel, and I will tell you about Azure."

Mops straightened. "Say again, Squarm?"

"We need your help, Lieutenant. But not as much as you need ours."

"Kumar, bring us around to intercept that shuttle. Squarm, maintain current course and speed. We'll be there in . . ."

"Seven minutes, assuming Kumar doesn't drop his controller."

"Within ten minutes."

"Acknowledged. Squarm out."

Maybe this hadn't been for nothing after all. "Monroe, you're with me. Wolf, glue your eyes to that console. Tell me if you hear a peep out of that shuttle, to us or to anyone else."

The lift door opened to reveal Grom, their eyes gummy with fatigue. "What did I miss?"

"I'll tell you on the way to the docking bay," said Mops. "Come on."

"Docking bay pressurization complete."

"Thanks, Doc." Mops checked her pistol, then unlocked and opened the door. A puff of cold, metallic-scented air washed over her. "Kumar, we've got Squarm's shuttle. Put us on a course away from those incoming EMC ships."

"Yes, sir," Kumar replied over the speaker.

Mops stepped into the bay. "Watch my back."

Grom reared up, presumably for a better view of her back. She chose not to say anything.

Her team was getting better with the grav beams. The Glacidae shuttle was relatively undamaged, and there had been only a brief period of panic when a slip of Kumar's finger had spun the shuttle like a feather in a tornado.

The shuttle appeared undamaged, parked in the center of the bay with its nose toward the main doors. It was designed to fly in space and atmosphere both, with triangular wings that rotated out from the top and bottom of the angular body. Black heat-resistant tiles covered the lower half of the hull. The rest was polished to a silver gleam. There were no visible weapons, nor any markings. Matching sets of blue-and-purple lights blinked at the bow and stern.

A ramp descended from the front of the ship. A single Glacidae poked their head out to scan the bay. They wore a clear helmet sealed over their head, and their body glistened with the protective gel Glacidae used in place of containment suits. Once it solidified, that stuff was as tough as Quetzalus skin, and it didn't interfere with the use of all those feathery limbs.

Mops stepped forward, right hand resting on her weapon. "Welcome aboard the *EMCS Pufferfish.*"

The Glacidae was half a meter longer than Grom, with yellow eyes and a green-tinged body. Their limbs quivered anxiously as they rushed toward Mops.

"Hold it," Mops snapped.

The Glacidae jumped back hard, their rear half curling into an armored ball. "It wasn't our fault. The Prodryans forced me to work for them. They threatened my family on Nurgistarnoq. They—"

"Slow down," said Mops. Squarm settled back, letting out a long belch of distress. Mops forced herself to speak slowly and calmly, despite the pounding of her heart. "You're saying you were part of the lab on the colony? The one that developed the anti-human bioweapon?"

"I'm so sorry, Lieutenant. It began two years ago. I wasn't allowed to ask questions."

"Doc, you're recording this?"

"I'm insulted you have to ask. You think I'm some hunk of unintelligent crystal, fresh from a Nusuran colon?"

Mops tried to push that mental image aside and asked Squarm, "How did Prodryans infiltrate your colony without being seen?"

"It was all done through third parties—Nusuran messengers, smuggled supplies, encrypted messages from off-world. The only time I interacted directly with those mud-suckers was if I left the colony. I traveled to a conference on synthesized biosecretions in Krakau crustaceans, and they were waiting for me in my lodging."

"How many others were working with the Prodryans?"

"Nobody else. Just me."

"Can you cure my crew?" Mops held her breath.

"I . . . I believe so." The Glacidae twisted to glance back into their shuttle. "I was able to salvage some of my notes and supplies before the Prodryans destroyed our facility, including the counteragent."

"What are the Prodryans planning now that they've got their weapon?"

"I don't know," they whispered. "I wasn't told."

Mops clenched her fists, fighting to keep her voice low. "What can you tell me about Azure?"

"She was the source." Squarm belched again. "Another prisoner of the Prodryans. I have more information in my re-cords."

"About time we caught a damn break," came Wolf's voice from behind her.

Mops turned to find that Wolf and Kumar had joined Monroe and Grom in the doorway. "What are you two doing here? Who's flying the ship?"

"Autopilot," said Kumar.

Wolf tapped her monocle. "Remote console display."

"Fine," snapped Mops. "Since you're here, you can both help our guest unload their equipment. We'll put them up in Medical while they work on helping the crew."

She approached Monroe and Grom. A quick glance over her shoulder showed Squarm scurrying up into their shuttle, followed by Wolf and Kumar. "What do you think?" she asked softly.

"They're scared," said Grom. "Did you hear the length of those burps?"

"Are they telling the truth?"

Grom clicked their beak in annoyance. "Glacidae aren't telepathic. I read tech specs, not minds."

"We need to get their testimony to Command," suggested Monroe.

Assuming they could *trust* Command. Right now, that wasn't an assumption Mops could afford. "The crew is the first priority. If there's even a chance Squarm can help them—"

"Sir, we could use a hand in here," Kumar called over the comms.

"I'll be right there," said Monroe.

Kumar hesitated. "I really think we need Lieutenant Adamopoulos' help with this."

"Kumar's heartbeat has increased significantly," whispered Doc. *"He's also begun to perspire."*

"Understood." Mops switched off her comm. "Something's wrong."

"Grom and I will monitor things from the corridor," said Monroe. "The control console by the door should give us access to the grav beams, too."

"You don't know how to use them," said Grom.

"No, but he can shake the hell out of the ship if things go south." Mops waited for them to retreat into the corridor and seal the door before turning her comm back on and heading for the shuttle.

She had to loosen the knee joints of her leg braces in order to crawl inside on hands and knees. The ridged texturing, designed for Glacidae feet, scraped her palms. The walls had an oily brown sheen in the dim light.

"Wolf and Kumar are two-point-three meters ahead. Wolf's vital signs are normal. Kumar remains anxious."

"Thanks." The interior was separated by more ridged tubes and tunnels. One led up into what she guessed to be the cockpit. She peeked into another portal, which split off into a set of cramped sleeping tubes. A larger opening brought her to the equally cramped cargo area, where Wolf, Mops, and Squarm struggled to remove tie-down straps from a heavy metal barrel. "What is all this?"

The Glacidae spun with a quick burp of alarm. They must not have heard Mops approaching. "Escape shuttles are stocked with food and water and other emergency supplies. I hid a set of memory crystals in this barrel of medgel."

"You know we'll need to inspect everything and put it through decon before you can open it, right?"

"Yes, yes, of course," Squarm said impatiently.

Kumar cleared his throat, then cocked his head toward the back of the cargo area.

It took Mops a moment to recognize the six thin, meter-high tanks connected to flexible black piping. It had been modified and painted to blend in with the rest of the ship, but the basic design of the K-422 filtration/infusion system was unmistakable. As was the faint hum that meant it was currently operating.

She slid her gun from the holster and pointed it at Squarm. "Have I told you how exhausted I am from trying to sort through everyone's lies?"

The Glacidae scooted back, trying to duck behind Wolf. "What are you doing?"

"You have a Krakau on this shuttle." Mops gestured to the tanks. "That's an older model—we use K-690s on the *Pufferfish*—but it's the same basic design, filtering a closed-circulation water system and infusing trace elements. It handles a thousand times what you'd need for drinking water in a shuttle this size . . . unless you're a Krakau. The K-422 cycles what, fifty thousand liters a day?"

"Fifty-two thousand," said Kumar.

"I don't know what it's for," insisted Squarm. "I boarded the first escape shuttle I could find!"

"The feed line goes into the back wall here." Kumar pulled out a hand-sized wall scanner. "I'm sending the scan to your eye, Lieutenant."

Mops' monocle lit up with lines representing electrical conduits, water circulation pipes, and more. "You have an entire room hidden behind that wall. How do we get to it?"

"How should I know? I didn't—"

"Are you aware of your situation?" Mops asked wearily. "You're trapped in a very small shuttle with three humans. One of them likes to eat new things. Another enjoys dissections. And the third . . . I'm the one who can order the other two to leave you alone. Or not."

Squarm dropped low, crawled to a control board on the port wall, and started typing. A single crate rotated silently away from the back wall, revealing a low metal door. The door slid open a moment later. Cold, briny air wafted from the darkness.

"If Squarm so much as twitches, you have my permission to shoot them in the face," said Mops.

Kumar and Wolf trained their weapons on the Glacidae.

Mops squeezed past them and crouched to look through the door, her gun pointing into the darkness. Doc was enhancing her vision, but the interior remained murky. "I know you're in there. I'd prefer not to start shooting. There's too much cleanup and paperwork afterward."

The chamber was a little under two meters wide. Inky water rippled a short distance below the doorway. Given the size of the shuttle, it couldn't have been more than a meter deep. A single computer terminal glowed on the wall to the left.

"Please don't shoot." Bubbles accompanied the translated voice.

"Don't give me a reason to."

Oily black tentacles emerged from the water, gliding toward the doorway. The crosshairs in Mops' monocle tracked the Krakau's movements as she emerged.

Only it wasn't a Krakau. Not exactly.

Thick, overlapping plates of blue-and-black shell covered most of the body. A warrior, then. But Krakau warriors were the most colorful of the species. The black primary limbs were spotted with light blue, and she had four instead of three. The lower limbs were shorter and thicker than normal, and the beak was stunted.

"What are you?" Mops whispered.

"I am . . . Krakau. My name—the name I use—is Azure."

Mops shook her head. "You don't look Krakau."

"I could dissect her to be sure," Kumar called out.

"Stop helping," snapped Mops.

"My race comes from the cold polar waters of our world," Azure continued. "Those of us who weren't exterminated were imprisoned generations ago. I'm one of the few to have escaped."

Goose bumps spread over Mops' skin. "Are Coldwater Krakau venomous?"

"Yes." Her tentacles slumped. "The answer to your next question is also yes. We are the ones who destroyed your civilization."

19

"Admiral Pachelbel! We've received a signal from the EMCS Pufferfish. *It's encrypted, priority nine.*"

The Krakau communications tech sounded both awed and a little frightened. Pachelbel's skin tightened as she hurried to take the message key from the tech's outstretched tentacle. "Thank you. You're dismissed."

The instant the tech vanished, Pachelbel locked her office and returned to her console. "Initiate full privacy countermeasures."

White noise generators in the air and underwater hummed to life. The buzzing static should counter mundane attempts to eavesdrop, as well as drowning out her muttered curses. Electronic countermeasures would burn out more technologically advanced methods.

She inserted the key into her console and waited while the system scanned first her, then her office.

There was no video. No audio. Nothing but a short burst of text:

Fugitive Alert: Level 9
Origin: *EMCS Pufferfish*, currently orbiting Paxifili-
   clackimour 6
Navigation override successful
Estimated time to *Pufferfish* A-ring jump: 03:26:04

*Shock chilled her blood. How in the depths had Mops gotten
her hands on a Rokkau?*

*The admiral noted the time, then cleared the message. She
drafted and sent the next set of orders in rapid succession. One
went to the EMC ships in pursuit of the* Pufferfish, *commanding
them to immediately withdraw and cease all contact with the
rogue ship. Next was the preparation of a transport and escort
to take her to Dobranok, the Krakau home world. Finally, she
sent an encrypted communication warning Dobranok what was
coming.*

"Fucking humans. . . ."

"W OLF, KUMAR, TAKE SQUARM and get out
of the docking bay *now*," Mops snapped. "Doc,
tell Monroe and Grom to stay out as well, and
make sure they seal the door once everyone's clear."

The AI didn't respond.

"Doc?" Her monocle's vision enhancement levels had frozen. "Kumar, Wolf, are your monocles working?"

"Mine locked up for a minute, but it's fine now," said Wolf.

"Same here," added Kumar. "I figured I just needed to have
Grom run a data cleanup on it."

Mops removed the monocle and clicked it back into place.
Nothing.

Azure shrank back toward her no-longer-hidden room.
"That is a personal AI unit, yes?"

"That's right," said Mops. "Did you do something to it?"

Her limbs flailed in alarm. "A unit designed by Krakau?"

"The standard-issue monocles are designed and pro-grammed by the Krakau. I've upgraded this one—"

The *Pufferfish* lurched sideways, knocking Mops against a wall. Azure slid across the floor, leaving a damp, oily streak.

"What's happening out there?" Mops called. "Doc, show me—dammit!"

"You've killed me." Azure gave a series of machine-gun clicks, like strained laughter. "You've killed us all."

"What the hell are you talking about?"

"Have you ever examined your monocle's root code? Stripped it to its core and studied the directives at the center of its existence?"

"Even if I could read Krakau code, the encryption on these things—"

"If you did, you would find me," said Azure. "The moment your monocles identified me, they signaled the Krakau. Now they've taken control of your ship to deliver me into their jaws."

Mops backed toward the exit. "Come with me. Slowly!"

Azure followed, still quivering. Outside, Mops checked to make sure the rest of her team was clear.

"Hello?"

"Doc? Are you all right? What happened?"

"Hello?"

She held up a hand for Azure to stop. "Doc, talk to me."

"Mops? I'm fighting—subroutines overriding—can't bypass—parallel processing—system resources at six percent."

"Dammit, after all that money I spent on memory upgrades and processor power, don't tell me you're going to let some stupid little subroutine take you down?"

"Your commentary—not helpful."

Relief bubbled like laughter in her chest. If Doc could spare attention for snark, it meant he was getting a handle on things. "What can I do to help?"

"Nothing. You're only human, after all."

"Was that necessary?"

" *'Unnecessary things are our only necessities.' Oscar Wilde. From* Fifty Shades of Dorian Gray."

"I think that's *The Picture of Dorian Gray*."

"*. . . you're right. How embarrassing. I may have lost some data indexing. I believe my core functioning has stabilized, however. My apologies. I didn't know about that subroutine. It's disturbing.*"

"What's going on with the ship?"

"*I'm not certain, but I think I'm flying us away from the planet in order to make an A-ring jump to Dobranok.*"

Just as Azure had guessed. "Doc, I clearly remember you explaining that you couldn't pilot this ship."

"*Well, it should be clear now that I was mistaken!*"

"I just wanted to hear you say it." She gnawed her lip. "Can you override that course? Dobranok is the last place we want to go right now."

"*I've made more than two million attempts to do so in the past minute. Not only am I shut out, I believe all navigation controls have been locked.*"

"I have to go." Azure had shrunk to two-thirds her original size. "My presence triggered this crisis. Squarm and I can take our chances with the colony."

"Doc, will that work? If we get Azure off the ship—"

"*You can't. Docking bay doors are locked down. I've checked the entire ship. There's no way in or out.*"

"How long until we jump?" The countdown appeared on her monocle. "Azure, I'm sorry, but you're stuck with us for now. Doc, put me through to the rest of the team." She waited for acknowledgment. "I need all of you on the bridge. We have three hours and twenty-one minutes before the *Pufferfish* jumps to the Krakau home world. Find a way to regain control of our ship."

"What should I do?" whimpered Azure.

Mops turned back to the Coldwater Krakau. Something in her stance made Azure retreat farther up the ramp. When Mops finally spoke, her words were ice. "You'll keep a safe

distance from myself and my crew. If you make any threatening movements, I will shoot you."

"I understand."

Mops paused. "How *do* you inject your venom?"

Azure raised one of her primary limbs. "Barbs in the suck-
ers on the tip."

A shudder ran through Mops' core. Within those tentacles
was the chemical that had taken out her entire crew ... perhaps her entire species. "Come with me," she said softly.
"You're going to explain exactly what your people did to my
planet."

"If I do, will you protect us from the Krakau?"

"The Krakau aren't the ones you should be afraid of right
now."

Azure huddled miserably in front of the main viewscreen.
Mops had considered interrogating her in private, but her
team deserved to hear this. If she'd gone elsewhere, Wolf would
have spent the whole time trying to eavesdrop anyway.

"Where did you put Squarm?" asked Mops.

"One of the vacant Glacidae quarters," said Monroe. "The
door's locked, and we made sure there was nothing they could
use to cause trouble."

"We don't want trouble," moaned Azure. "We just wanted
to be free. Instead, you'll deliver us to our executioners."

"We're working on that." Mops glanced at Grom, who was
half-buried in the open wall of wiring and circuitry beneath
the navigation console. Wolf was pounding and swearing at her
console, while Kumar worked patiently through the emergency
tutorials, both hoping to find a way to bypass Doc's control of
the ship.

"This subroutine was hard-coded," Doc said. *"We can't erase
or rewrite it."*

"Keep trying," said Mops.

"It wasn't entirely my fault, you know. Everyone else's monocle sent the same signal when they spotted Azure. But their software wasn't smart enough to notice, or to try to fight back."

"It's all right," she assured him. "We'll figure something out."

"You know the biosensors in your suit not only let me monitor your health, they also suggest when you're lying."

She ignored him, turning her gaze back to Azure. "Your people destroyed our civilization. Why shouldn't I hand you over to the Krakau? Hell, why shouldn't we save them the trouble and execute you right here?"

"In a way, it was as much your people's fault as our own," Azure began.

Mops dug her fingers into the arm of her chair. "Not a good start."

"My people call themselves Rokkau. The Krakau you're familiar with outnumbered us nine to one. Our races were never truly at peace, but Dobranok is a large world. For generations, the Rokkau kept to the cold polar regions, while the Krakau girdled the globe. But as time went on, both our people spread and multiplied. Competition increased, leading to conflicts."

"Conflicts you lost," guessed Mops.

"More often than not, yes. Our numbers were fewer, our resources limited. As overpopulation increased, a group of Rokkau turned their attention to the stars. We were always more technologically inclined than our Krakau cousins. We lived in a harsher environment. It forced us to be more adaptive, and to make better use of our limited resources. In the frigid winds of the Vickoud Ice Shelf, we developed and tested a primitive form of A-ring technology.

"The Krakau confiscated the prototype as soon as they learned of it. 'In the interest of world peace and security.' But they didn't understand it, which gave the Rokkau leverage. We were able to force a partnership, and within a generation, we set out together to explore our cosmic neighbors, searching for worlds that could support life. We found our way to Earth."

"You tried to *colonize* us?" Wolf snarled.

Azure flinched back. "This was a hundred and sixty years ago. Records from that time are sparse . . . and often deliberately altered. I don't believe the Krakau or Rokkau intended to harm your species. All I know is there was . . . an incident. A misunderstanding between our explorers and your people. Two Krakau were killed, and the Rokkau . . . she lashed out in self-defense, striking one of your world leaders."

Azure flexed one of her tentacles to demonstrate. Thornlike barbs emerged from the center of the pale suction cups on the end. "The venom shuts down higher brain functions in our prey, inducing a kind of hibernation. It's how we used to preserve our food through the icy winter months. It interacted differently with human biology."

"Human and Krakau—sorry, Rokkau—physiology shouldn't be compatible at all," said Kumar. "If anything, it should have just killed whoever you poisoned."

"Humans are an adaptable people," said Azure. "Difficult to kill, even before you became . . . what you are today. You evolved on a planet determined to destroy you. So many of your animals are venomous. Your plants are just as quick to poison you. Your people lived on islands next to active volcanoes, on shores battered by quakes and tsunamis, but that wasn't enough. You jumped out of aircraft *for fun*! You ate poisonous sea creatures. You raced through the streets with horned mammals ten times your mass. Perhaps evolution made you stronger to counter your madness. Whatever the cause, your leader survived. But she was not unaffected."

Azure drew herself tighter. "Our venom compromised her higher neuroelectrical processes, turning her into broccoli."

"Into a vegetable?" guessed Mops.

"Yes, that. Earth scientists attempted to cure her, first by using the Rokkau's venom glands to create an antivenom. When that failed, they used a retrovirus to capture and isolate the venom in her system, and to modify her genes, hoping to trick her body into repairing the damage. It worked, in a sense.

They restored her mobility and primitive neurological functioning, but she was not what she once was."

"She turned feral," said Monroe.

"Indeed. And despite their precautions, the virus spread. As I understand it, the effects were confined to humans and a few species of higher primates." Azure looked curiously at Mops. "According to the stories the Rokkau passed down, one of the scientists involved in designing the retrovirus was named Adamopoulos."

"What happened then?" asked Mops.

"Your world fell into chaos. Our contact team returned to Dobranok, where they were taken into seclusion. Imprisoned, to keep the truth from the public. It's said the Rokkau killed herself from shame, unable to live with the guilt of having destroyed an entire race. Others believe the Krakau murdered her so she'd be unable to contradict the official government account."

"What account?" asked Kumar.

"That the Rokkau had done this deliberately, to wipe out your people so they could claim Earth for themselves. Ironically, the Krakau used this as justification to try to wipe out the Rokkau and claim Dobranok for themselves."

"What about us?" Mops felt numb. Her words were little more than a whisper. "You could have sent ships back to try to rescue the humans who weren't yet infected. You could have helped fight the spread of the virus. How long did it take for the Krakau to return to Earth?"

"Fifty years." Azure twined her arms together. "By which time your civilization had fallen. They expected humanity to have died out, but—even infected—feral humans have a strong survival instinct. They survived and reproduced."

"Fifty years. You're talking about the contact mission of 2153," said Kumar. "Seven Krakau were killed by feral humans. Did they know...?"

"I don't believe so," said Azure. "The original mission was considered a failure, soon forgotten with the outbreak of war.

The government directed our explorations elsewhere. The Krakau made contact with the Nusurans and the Glacidae. They laid the foundations for the Krakau Alliance. And they did everything in their power to erase the Earth from their records."

Monroe pursed his lips. "Then why come back at all?"

"In 2151, the Quetzalus picked up old signals from Earth and proposed a contact mission. The Krakau tried to prevent it. When that failed, they rushed a mission of their own to claim Earth as a Krakau settlement and make sure nobody else could discover the truth."

"Why not just bomb Earth into slag after the first mission?" Wolf looked around at the horrified expressions of the rest of the team. "I'm not saying I *want* them to nuke the Earth. Just that it would have covered things up pretty well."

"Guilt and shame," said Azure. "Combined with the war on Dobranok. Earth was light-years away. The Krakau were more concerned with destroying the Rokkau."

"But you weren't destroyed," Wolf pointed out.

"Nothing gets past her," said Doc.

"Not all of us, no. More than a million Rokkau survivors were banished to a prison planet with an ocean core, surrounded by a shell of ice. Its location is known only to the highest-ranking of the Krakau."

"Assholes," Wolf murmured.

Azure hesitated. "I don't understand. To whose anuses are you referring?"

"How did you escape?" asked Mops before Wolf could respond.

"As I said, the Rokkau have always been more technologically inclined than our warm-water kin," said Azure. "According to the stories, nine Rokkau families—fewer than five hundred individuals—fled Dobranok in hastily constructed ships. Those who survived have lived in hiding ever since."

"Why haven't we heard of the Rokkau?" asked Mops. "How could the Krakau keep this a secret from us—from the whole galaxy—for more than a century?"

"Because the Krakau have had more than a century to teach their version of history. To indoctrinate their young with tales of us as fanatics and extremists who rebelled against the rightful governments of the world. The name Rokkau is all but forgotten. They say we were disgruntled Krakau, leeches on our society who refused to surrender until the Krakau were forced to destroy us. It's not a part of their history they like to share with outsiders, as you can imagine."

The bridge fell silent. Mops' team looked toward her, waiting for her to speak. For her to process and make sense of a history in which humanity's downfall wasn't a result of their own arrogance and hubris, but of an accident and the apathy of the race Mops had believed to be their saviors.

There was too much: denial and grief, anger and anguish, all of it swirling together in a vortex of emotion that threatened to tear free as hysterical tears, or perhaps laughter. She couldn't distinguish the two anymore.

"Are you all right?"

"Not in the slightest." She swallowed. For now, she had to focus on what was directly in front of them. "Knowing all this, you and Squarm still worked with the Prodryans to produce this new bioweapon? To turn the few reborn humans back into animals?"

"A Prodryan called Heart of Glass attacked my family's lifeship," said Azure.

"How did he find you?" asked Kumar.

"We were scavenging for supplies on an abandoned smuggling base in an unsettled system. Heart of Glass arrived, intending to do the same. When he found our ship, he robbed us instead. At first, he assumed we were Krakau. His warriors boarded us. Our matriarch triggered the ship's self-destruct countdown. The Prodryans retreated, and the lifeship fled, but by then I was a prisoner."

"Does he have other Rokkau prisoners?" asked Mops.

"I don't know." Azure spread her limbs helplessly. "One of

his warriors was poisoned during the fighting. Heart of Glass questioned me and learned the truth about the Rokkau. He brought a scientist on board to study my venom."

"Your partner, Squarm." Mops nodded to herself. "Squarm said they could cure our crew."

"I believe they can help your crew, yes. But it makes no difference. The Krakau won't allow anyone to leave this ship alive."

"How many people know the truth about Earth and the Rokkau?" asked Monroe.

"Only the highest-ranking officials of Homeworld Military Command." Azure spread her limbs. "Probably a few in Colonial and Interstellar Command as well, in case they ever come across a Rokkau refugee. Along with whoever monitors the Rokkau prison planet."

How much did Admiral Pachelbel know? She'd reacted so strongly to the possibility of a source for Krakau—*Rokkau* venom. "What have the Rokkau been doing all these years?"

"Hiding. Trying to live our lives in peace."

Mops pressed her lips together.

"You don't believe her?" murmured Doc.

"I'm not sure," she responded, for his virtual ears only. Azure's account was certainly plausible, but her gut told her there was more to it. Details Azure was holding back.

"Rokkau body language is bound to be different from that of the Krakau. Perhaps that's making you unconsciously distrustful?"

"Maybe." She studied Azure. You didn't need Kumar to do another dissection to see Azure was a distinctly different race than the Krakau.

The nagging in her gut grew stronger. Something about Kumar's dissection. Something she was missing. She lowered her voice. "Doc, replay Kumar's report after he finished dissecting the captain."

She watched the rest of her team as she listened. Monroe's face was a mask of tension. Wolf looked angry, but that was her default expression. Kumar had gotten distracted by something he was reading on his console.

She straightened in her chair. "Wait. Replay that."

"*'I didn't see any scars, but Krakau don't scar. Their flesh regenerates. Whole tentacles grow back . . . and by that logic, wouldn't a removed venom gland do the same thing? If you'd like, I'd be happy to continue working on the rest of the command crew once I'm done with the captain. I doubt I'd find anything different, but the bodies are in such good shape, it seems like a waste to just leave them.'*"

"What is it?" asked Monroe.

The bodies were in such good shape. She held up a hand, thinking hard. "Remember Falls From Glory, the Prodryan we met with back on Quetzalus Station?"

"The one who blew herself up?" asked Monroe.

"The same. Right before the explosion, she thanked us for answering her questions."

Doc replayed the relevant recording without her having to ask. *"You told her, 'We could get you off this station, drop you on any planet you wanted. The Krakau don't have to know.'"*

"I confirmed the Krakau were dead," Mops whispered.

"I don't understand," said Azure. "What are you talking about?"

She slid her gun from its holster. "I told Glory the Krakau didn't have to know about her. That's not an offer I could have made if any of the Krakau on the *Pufferfish* had survived. That's the answer they were digging for. That's what their test was about, to confirm the Krakau had been killed."

"The *Pufferfish* was overrun by feral humans," said Wolf. "It's a miracle anyone survived."

"You think the Krakau don't have contingency plans?" countered Mops. "They could have sedated the crew or locked themselves away." She spun. "Kumar, how did our command crew die?"

Kumar glanced up. "Sorry, what?"

"You said the Krakau bodies were in good shape. What was the cause of death?"

He frowned. "I . . . I'm not sure. I was looking for venom glands. It didn't occur to me to check anything else."

"Were they killed by feral humans?"

"No way. Ferals would have torn the bodies apart."

Mops centered her gun's crosshairs on Azure's torso. "You knew the ship would change course automatically if a Rokkau was detected on board. If Kumar hadn't spotted your hidden compartment, you or Squarm would have found a way to tip us off, right? Because you *wanted* to get to Dobranok."

"Why would she want to go there?" asked Wolf.

Mops watched Azure. The Rokkau hadn't moved, but the tightness of her skin had eased. "Because they modified their venom to kill Krakau. What else is on that shuttle?"

"Assorted terraforming technology," Azure said quietly. "Modified for high-dispersal atmospheric seeding. And enough weaponized venom to rain down on an entire world. Once we arrive, the Krakau will tow this ship to their high-security prison and processing facility in orbit. My shuttle will automatically attempt to escape. Naturally, the Krakau will shoot it down, triggering activation of the terraforming engines. Depending on wind patterns and ocean currents, we could infect and kill ninety-eight percent of the population within three days."

Ship's communications were offline. They couldn't warn the Krakau. The bay doors were locked, and handheld weapons weren't enough to blast them open, meaning there was no way to get the shuttle off the *Pufferfish*. "Kumar, how hard would it be to power up the A-rings on one of our shuttles and destroy the ship?"

"We'd have to bypass some safety fail-safes," said Kumar. "But judging by how many times I blew us up in the tutorials, I think I could do it."

Grom raised their head. "Sir, may I respectfully suggest we

search for a plan that doesn't involve all of us dying in an explosion?"

"I'm open to suggestions," said Mops, her gaze never leaving the Rokkau. "Your people ended my civilization. I'll destroy this ship before I let you do it again."

"Earth's fate was an accident," said Azure, a pleading note in her words. "I wasn't lying about that. It was the Krakau who chose to abandon your people, just as they chose to kill and imprison ours. They're not worth protecting."

"The fact that you're poised to commit genocide undermines your judgments on ethical matters. Kumar, activate a shuttle A-ring."

Even with her attention focused on Azure, Mops almost missed the small twitch of one of her tentacles. With a soft spitting sound, something shot from the end of the tentacle.

Mops shifted her aim and pulled the trigger. The plasma blast burned through the tentacle and blackened the wall behind Azure. Her severed limb dropped to the floor, where it continued to twitch like a snake suffering a seizure. Azure whistled in pain, the high-pitched sound grating on the bones of Mops' inner ears.

"Is everyone all right?" she called out.

"I'm not registering any suit breaches," said Doc.

"You can't stop this." Azure huddled in a ball, dark blood oozing from the burnt stub of her limb.

Mops adjusted her gun's power levels. "What did you do?"

"Haven't you wondered how your crew were first infected? The Prodryans designed the weapon. It fires a specially coated sliver of metal. As the sliver punctures your suit, the coating peels off to seal the hole. The core enters your body and breaks down, leaving nothing but a pinprick and perhaps a tiny bruise on the skin. Your suit never detects the impact. I'm sorry, Kumar. I wouldn't have infected you if your commander hadn't forced me."

Kumar paled. He patted down his suit, searching for the impact site. Wolf and Monroe had both drawn weapons.

Azure's remaining three tentacles snapped out to point at them. "I never wanted to be a killer. Heart of Glass ordered the weapons implanted in me for protection. Drop your guns, or you'll spend your final hours like Kumar, struggling to cling to your thoughts and memories while your mind melts through your fingers. Please, just do as I ask. I promise, once this is over, I'll cure both your navigator and the rest of your crew. I'm not your enemy."

Mops didn't move. "What do you want?"

"You were right about our plan, all except one detail," said Azure. "I'm not going to destroy the Krakau. You are."

**Plotjikk Contractors and Builders:
Limited Warranty**

*This warranty is for <u>cruiser-class brig/cells</u> for the <u>EMCS
Pufferfish</u>.*

1. *THIRTY MONTHS/THIRTY PRISONERS: Warranty commences on the date construction and installation are completed and approved by the customer. Warranty is good for thirty Tjikko months (701 Earth days) or for the first thirty prisoners confined in the cell, whichever comes first.*
2. *COVERAGE: Cells are guaranteed to safely contain prisoners of all known intelligent races. Should any prisoner escape due to manufacturing defect, customer shall be entitled to a full refund for the purchase price of the cell in question. The following exclusions apply:*
a. Damage to cells caused by ship-to-ship combat.

b. *Failure to properly search and remove weapons, welding equipment, electronic lock picks, molecular acids, and other such tools from prisoners.*

c. *Use of technology that was unknown at time of construction, such as interdimensional portals, matter transmutation, teleportation of any form, or temporal manipulation (time travel).*

d. *Any escape in which guards played a role, willingly or unwillingly, including but not limited to:*

    i. *The "sick prisoner" routine.*

    ii. *The "brawling prisoners" routine.*

    iii. *Psychological manipulation by prisoner.*

    iv. *Bribery.*

e. *Failure to follow proper maintenance and inspection protocols, per attached guidelines.*

3. *SPECIFICATIONS: Per the contract, the cell shall feature:*

    × *Full-spectrum lighting controls*

    × *Upgraded electronic surveillance & monitoring (Standard EMC Package)*

    × *Universal plumbing attachment*

    ☐ *Upgraded autowash*

    × *Electronic signal-blocking*

    ☐ *Full range of calming music for all species (NEW!)*

4. *WARRANTY CLAIMS: Cell must be inspected by a certified Plotjikk Contractors team within seven days of any escape.*

Thank you for your business! We look forward to serving all your future prisoner-containment needs.

                       — The Plotjikk Contractors Team

"THIS IS MY THIRD favorite cell in the *Pufferfish*." Wolf lay on the floor with her hands laced behind her head, staring at the featureless ceiling. Azure had packed them all into cell number four. It was crowded, but not quite as bad as the escape pod the humans had been trapped on after Coacalos Station.

"The cells are identical," snapped Kumar.

"Not true. Cells one and two are closest to the guard station, meaning you can keep an eye on what's happening and make conversation. The even-numbered cells have slightly better water pressure for the sink and toilet. Cell seven has a recurring mold problem in the ceiling."

Mops sat on the cot, staring at the transparent door and wondering how long it would take for Kumar to succumb to Azure's venom. "Monroe, can you. . . . ?"

He shook his head and popped his gum. "Arm isn't strong enough to scratch that stuff. A gun could put a hole through it, sure, but that'd just trigger the prisoner suppression routine. Electrify the floor or seal the cell and suck all the air out or activate internal weapons to blow our legs off, depending on which features the EMC sprang for when they commissioned it."

"What do we do with Kumar?" asked Wolf. "Shouldn't we tie him up or something before he tries to eat our faces? No offense."

"For once, I agree with Wolf," said Grom.

Kumar threw an obscene gesture their way. He'd donned hood and gloves within minutes of being shot, sealing his suit and hopefully preventing him from contaminating anyone else as the venom worked through his system.

"Doc, can you do anything about getting the door open?"

"I'm cut off from the rest of the ship. No signals in or out of the brig area, except what's hardwired through the guards' stations. Sorry."

Mops turned in a slow circle, surveying their limited resources and options. Movement outside the cell caught her attention. Outside the clear door, Squarm drew up to their full height. "Lieutenant Adamopoulos. You will read a message to the Krakau, claiming responsibility for the attack on Dobranok and denouncing their genocidal war against the Rokkau. Your proclamation will spread the seeds of rebellion across the galaxy. After you've done this, I will cure your man."

They held up a metal tube, similar in size and shape to a standard food tube. "This is the counteragent. It successfully neutralized and protected a human tissue sample from the modified form of Azure's venom. It will save him."

"What do you want me to say?" asked Mops.

Squarm set the tube on the floor and pulled out a paper note written in crude Human, which he pressed to the door. Mops and the others crowded to read it.

Doc was the first to say what everyone was thinking. *"I'm no literary critic, but this reads like something Puffy might compose. After overheating."*

"It's awful," Mops agreed.

Wolf snorted. " 'Greetings, galactic oppressors'? How's anyone supposed to read that with a straight face?"

"The alignment of your face is irrelevant," snapped Squarm. "You will read the words and proclaim yourselves allies to the Prodryan rebellion."

"You misspelled 'revolution,'" said Kumar. "And 'glorious.' And 'injustice.' You know, you could have had the computer check and clean this up for you."

"They don't want any version of the message in the system," guessed Mops. She checked the countdown on her monocle. Ninety-two minutes until they jumped. "I'm sorry, humans don't talk like this. Nobody's going to believe me saying, 'Rise up, my fellow human savages. Our monstrous appearance and primitive need for violence shall serve the evil Krakau no longer!' Have you considered stealing from Shakespeare? He wrote great vengeful dialogue."

"Who is Shakespeare?" demanded Squarm.

"Gunnery sergeant on the *EMCS Crocodile*," said Monroe.

Mops ignored them both. "'I'll never pause again, never stand still, till either death hath closed these eyes of mine, or fortune given me measure of revenge.' It's from *Henry VI*."

"Much better," agreed Monroe.

Squarm snapped their digging claws in annoyance. "There is *nothing* wrong with my words!"

"Why are you part of this rebellion anyway?" asked Mops. "I can understand why Azure and the other Rokkau would want to team up with the Prodryans, but how did they get Glacidae and Nusurans on board?"

"What the Krakau did to their Coldwater kin, they'll do to anyone else who threatens their power," said Squarm. "They control the Alliance Military and Technological Councils. The Alliance Charter benefits the Krakau and their colonies over other worlds. If another species dares to challenge them, the Alliance imposes sanctions and worse. And always they hold the threat of their human army over the heads of the galaxy."

"Earth year 2169," said Kumar. "The Alliance evacuates the Glacidae colony of Dexatellevar 2 after severe solar flares, saving three thousand lives. 2216, the EMC liberates the Quetzalus planet of Ventazos from a military dictatorship. 2224, the Siege of Avloka. Hundreds of humans die while rescuing thousands of Krakau prisoners and slaves from the Prodryans."

"Not to mention last week, when the *Pufferfish* arrived to protect a Nusuran ship from Prodryan pirates," added Mops. "Do you have any idea how many lives that human army has saved since its founding?"

"There's a difference between security and freedom," the Glacidae shot back. "Look at what they've done to your race. A population of ten thousand, embracing servitude to the very race that destroyed your civilization."

"Squarm has a point," Wolf said quietly. "I'm still planning to punch their face as soon as I get out of here, but if the Krakau did this to us . . . if they kept the truth hidden all these years . . . I mean, fuck those guys."

"Articulately put, as always," sighed Mops.

"Take some time to discuss your options," said Squarm, retrieving the cure canister from the floor. "But not too long. That one will begin feeling the effects soon." They jabbed a segmented limb toward Kumar.

"You see, that's where you lose my sympathy," said Mops. "Humans may not be the smartest species in the galaxy. We struggle to wrap our brains around big, abstract concepts like centuries-long conspiracies. What we're very good at is recognizing and responding to immediate threats. You attacked my ship. You infected a member of my team. That makes you the enemy."

"Shortsighted fools," snarled Squarm.

"Maybe." Mops walked to the small toilet. With the lid sealed, the cube doubled as an uncomfortable stool, allowing her to rest her legs. Her lips quirked as a new idea began to come together. "But when you're ready to apologize, you know where to find me."

The Glacidae stared at her through the door. "Apologize?"

"And give us the cure." Lowering her voice, she said, "I don't care which comes first, the apology or the cure. Once we have both, I'll consider letting you live."

Squarm backed away. "Humans are crazy."

"You have no idea," said Wolf.

The translator failed to capture whatever the Glacidae said next before storming away.

"Something about lower life-forms, incapable of thinking beyond their base instincts," said Doc. *"With a few insults toward your parentage."*

"Sir, Wolf is right," Kumar whispered, once Squarm was out of sight. "You should restrain me while you can, before I—"

"Not necessary," said Mops. "We're not staying here."

Wolf threw up her hands. "I've been on the wrong side of that door more times than anyone. There's no way through it. Not even a Quetzalus could bust these walls."

"Stop thinking about breaking things," Mops suggested.

"We're not infantry. We're SHS. Doc, I'm going to need you to do something for me."

"I told you, I'm locked up just like the rest of you. I can't even access the basic ship's information log from in here."

"That's why I want to apologize in advance." She stood. "Remind me; you *are* impact resistant and waterproof, right?"

It took roughly fifteen minutes for Squarm to return, leaving a trail of dark fear-oil on the floor as they scrambled to the door of cell four. "What did you do?"

Mops blinked in mock confusion. "Pardon?"

"You preprogrammed the ship's systems," Squarm guessed. "An automated safeguard. Tell me how to disable it, or I'll infect the rest of you."

"Nobody on my team has that kind of expertise." Mops turned. "Grom, did you program any automatic safeguards while we were on Coacalos Station?"

"Nope. Rewired a few bridge stations and beat some high scores, but I'm not the best programmer. I wouldn't know how to—"

"Why won't the main brig door seal?" Squarm pounded the console at the guards' station.

"Because of the emergency ventilation procedure," said Mops. "It's designed to circulate a large volume of fresh air through the ship as quickly as possible, which means most doors are locked open."

"But they're coming!" Squarm squealed.

"Who?" Wolf's words dripped with forced innocence.

"Your crew! Those monsters are loose in the ship!"

"Well, yes," said Mops. "Who do you think the fresh air is for? I don't think it's healthy to keep them restrained for so long. And I thought you and Azure might want to see the effectiveness of your bioweapon up close."

Squarm reared up so their segmented underside pressed against the cell door. "You have to—"

"No, I don't." Mops stood and stretched her shoulder before walking slowly to the door. "Apology and cure, in whatever order you prefer. Or you can stay out there and try your luck against almost two hundred feral humans."

"How?" the Glacidae whimpered. "You were locked up, cut off from the rest of the ship."

"There aren't a lot of systems an AI can access and control on his own." Mops directed a knowing look at the toilet in the corner. "Doc couldn't turn the ship's internal security measures against you or anything like that. But he could activate the emergency ventilation subroutine and release the acceleration pod restraints on the crew, once I got him beyond the cell's signal-dampening. If I'm remembering the plumbing setup for this part of the ship, he should be about ten meters down, trapped in waste reclamation tank three."

"Nine point seven meters," Kumar corrected.

Squarm produced a small pistol, which they clutched in trembling claws.

"Bad idea," said Monroe. "A little gun like that against feral humans? You're just gonna get them riled up."

Mops pressed against the door, trying to see past Squarm to the end of the hallway. "Does anyone else hear groaning?"

Squarm let out a low belch of fear. "If I let you out, can you stop them?"

"Let us out?" Mops laughed. "Child, this cell's one of the safest places in the whole bloody ship."

"I'll cure the infected human," Squarm pleaded.

Mops paused. "And. . . ?"

A shadow paused at the end of the corridor.

"And I'm sorry!" Squarm spun back to the guard console to unlock the cell door. Squarm scurried in, all but throwing the gun into Mops' hands. "There's enough to inoculate your entire team. If you give me access to your medical labs, I'll synthesize more for the crew."

Mops didn't move. "Where's Azure?"

"Eaten by humans, probably. I haven't been able to reach that squirming wretch since I left the bridge."

Mops cocked a thumb toward Kumar. "Him first."

"Open your suit," said Squarm. "It will circulate faster if injected directly into the heart."

Kumar fumbled with his suit seals, his eyes unfocused. Mops made eye contact with Wolf and Monroe, who moved closer, ready to grab him if anything went wrong. Squarm raised their body higher, uncapped the tube, and jabbed the long needle directly into Kumar's chest. "Now will you stop those animals?"

"Those animals are my crew," she reminded him. A peek out the door showed Private Henson staggering toward them. Feral humans had a terrifying reputation, but alone, they presented little threat. "Wolf, Monroe, would you please grab Jim and bring him in here?"

Wolf charged down the hall and drove her shoulder into Henson's gut. In one movement, she hoisted him over her back and tossed him to the floor. When Henson got up to go after Wolf, Monroe caught the back of his harness and dragged him kicking and squirming into cell four.

Mops turned her attention back to Squarm. "Him next."

Squarm backed away. "I'm not going near that creature."

"Give me the damn thing," Mops said, snatching the tube from Squarm's claws. With Wolf and Monroe holding Henson in place, she opened the front of his suit and stabbed the needle into his chest.

"Press the injector button until it clicks once," said Squarm, cowering in the far corner.

Mops did so, then backed away. It didn't take long for the counteragent to have an effect. Henson's struggles slowed. His face crinkled in confusion, and he looked around as if seeing them for the first time. A minute later, he was snoring.

"Good enough." Mops capped the tube and tucked it into a pocket. Who knew what kind of side effects the counteragent might have, but they could worry about that later. "We need to get moving. It won't take long for more of the crew to find us, and if they attack as a mob, we won't be able to stop them."

She stepped out of the cell and tapped the guards' console. "Wolf, I need a shipwide broadcast."

Wolf squeezed in beside her. "This is set up differently than my station on the bridge."

"Isn't this the communications channel?"

"That's for talking to prisoners," snapped Wolf. "Just give me a minute to study this thing. I can do this."

Mops gritted her teeth but moved aside. She studied the gun she'd taken from Squarm. It was designed for a thinner, clawlike grip, but it had a trigger and a barrel. If she had to fire it, she could. She was less certain of her ability to fire on her own crew.

The squeal of feedback pierced her bones.

"Sorry," Wolf shouted, barely audible over the noise. "I'm getting there."

Another voice thundered through the ship. "IT LOOKS LIKE YOU'RE TRYING TO INITIATE A SHIPWIDE EMERGENCY ALERT. WOULD YOU LIKE HELP?"

The feedback died, though the echo continued to ring in Mops' ears. Wolf gave the console a tentative tap. When she spoke, the ship amplified her words. "I'VE GOT IT. SHIT! HOLD ON . . . is that better?"

"No, turn it back up!" Mops hurried to the console. "DOC, CAN YOU HEAR ME? WE'RE OUT. TERMINATE EMERGENCY VENTILATION PROCEDURES BEFORE THE CREW KILLS US."

Nothing happened.

"What's wrong?" yelled Squarm.

Mops shoved Wolf back into the cell. If she had to, she could seal it from here to keep the rest of the team safe. "I'm not a hundred percent sure how well Doc can hear from inside that waste tank. It could also be a battery issue. He normally draws power through me. The batteries in the monocle's rim can hold a small charge, but it doesn't last more than an hour or two."

"You mean he released the monsters, opened every door in the ship, and then *turned off?*" Squarm squealed.

"Quit whining," snapped Grom. "Before I flush *you* down the toilet."

Wolf perked up at that.

"No flushing. We need them to synthesize more of this counteragent." Mops kept her attention on the end of the hallway. "But you have my permission to inflict a swirly if they keep complaining."

"What's a swirly?" Squarm asked.

Mops leaned over the console. "DOC, I DON'T WANT TO RUSH YOU, BUT WE'RE ABOUT TO HAVE COMPANY."

A figure stopped in the doorway. It took Mops a moment to recognize Battle Captain Cervantes. His left arm hung limp and broken, and his lips were cracked and bloody.

Mops raised her gun. "Don't make me do this, Miguel."

"Stop talking to it and shoot!" yelled Squarm. This was followed by a yelp of protest and the swirl of flushing water.

Cervantes studied Mops for a moment, then stumbled toward her, the fingers of his right hand outstretched like claws.

"Dammit, Miguel." She squeezed the trigger, sending a slug through Cervantes' hip. It took three additional shots to disable the leg, dropping him to the floor. He continued to drag himself one-handed.

Behind him, the door slid shut, locking the rest of the crew out of the brig area. Her team whooped in triumph and relief. Squarm was still sputtering and spitting.

Mops holstered the gun, grabbed Cervantes by the arm and the back of his uniform, and tossed him into cell six, sealing the door before he could recover.

"What now, boss?" asked Wolf.

"Seal your uniforms." She pulled on her own hood and gloves. "DOC, I NEED YOU TO ADJUST THE AIR MIXTURE AGAIN. USE THE SAME SEDATIVES AS BE-

FORE. THEY SHOULD STILL BE SET UP AND READY TO GO IN MEDICAL. IT'S TIME TO PUT THE CREW BACK TO SLEEP."

All she had to do now was cure the rest of the crew, regain control of the *Pufferfish*, and find Azure, all before they jumped to Dobranok.

The console flashed a warning: *A-ring jump in ten minutes. All crew to acceleration chambers.*

She watched the numbers count down. "Well . . . shit."

21

Help Topic: Acceleration Ring Navigation

The Krakau developed A-rings to be a fast, safe, energy-efficient way to travel between star systems. At maximum power, an A-ring can theoretically accelerate an object to a speed of twenty light-years/hour. At that speed, the gravitational pull of most stellar objects has a near-zero effect on your trajectory, which means you can safely travel anywhere in the galaxy as long as you don't fly through another object. *Don't worry, that almost never happens.*
   Frequently asked questions:

1. ***So gravity isn't a problem?*** *You have to worry most about gravity when accelerating and decelerating. Krakau scientists devised a mathematical equation to calculate the minimum safe distance for an A-ring jump, depending on the mass of nearby stellar objects. But as a famous human named Barbie once said, "Math is hard," so we'll skip the details. Your ship's computer can handle the calculations.*

2. *How do I prepare my ship for a jump?* *In general, you want to be a minimum of 300 million kilometers from any given star before making your jump. You should also be well clear of any planetary masses. If your computer says it's safe to make an A-ring jump while orbiting a planet, please contact technical support immediately for assistance to avoid being torn apart by gravitational shearing.*

3. *What about deceleration?* *Minimum safe distance applies to your deceleration, too. For additional safety, the EMC recommends arriving at least 100 million kilometers "above" or "below" the disk of your target system. This helps you avoid any planetary bodies or rogue asteroids.*

4. *Why don't we put an A-ring on a missile and shoot it at the Prodryan home world?* *We can't aim precisely enough to hit another planet. Even if we could, the star's gravity would divert the missile's course, making it all but impossible to hit a planet-sized target. Also, blowing up planets is Wrong.*

5. *What if my ship hits another ship?* *The odds of crossing another ship's path while traveling at supralight speed are astronomical. There has never been a reported collision involving A-ring travel.*

6. *Seriously, though, what if I hit another ship?* *Both ships would be instantly destroyed in a fusion reaction so powerful it would create a momentary "second sun." But we promise you won't feel a thing!*

THIS WAS THE SECOND time in less than two days that an injection of adrenaline had hurled Mops from the cliffs of unconsciousness, smashing her awake against the rocks of the real world. She spent thirty seconds staring uncomprehendingly at the wall, trying to remember why she was in a brig emergency acceleration pod, before it all came flooding back to her. At which point she swore profusely and stood, tensing her leg muscles to try to get the circulation flowing.

To her left, Monroe gasped and jerked from his acceleration pod. "Only thing worse than a quick-shot wake-up is two quick-shots."

"I set the system to get us up and about as soon as possible," said Mops. "Azure should be unconscious for a while after that jump. This is our best chance to find and neutralize her."

Outside the cell, the consoles and control panels were all dark. The only light came from the emergency lighting strips along the walls, near the floor.

Worse than the lack of light was the silence. You never noticed the background noise of the ship until it wasn't there: the hum of air circulation fans, the rush of water through the plumbing in the walls, the buzz of a dying light strip, the vibration of an improperly tuned grav plate. . . . The *Pufferfish* was all but dead.

"Monroe, are you getting anything from the ship on your monocle?" She entered the guard's room and began checking the lockers for her team's equipment. "Tell me that jump didn't break the ship."

"I've got basic status readings from the suit, but that's it," said Monroe. "The air's good. If Doc sedated the crew, he cleared the gases from circulation while we were traveling."

Mops nodded her thanks and unsealed her hood. She eventually found her things, not properly stowed in the lockers but tossed into a corner. The acceleration had flung them around hard enough to bend her utility pole and puncture a detergent canister, leaving a meter-wide puddle of soap on the floor. She retrieved her pistols and wiped away the worst of the soap before sliding them into her holsters.

"Looks like the ship's on standby," Monroe continued. "Probably shut down right after deceleration. Another precaution to make sure we can't do shit."

"Are we there yet?" asked Kumar, stumbling out of the cell. Mops spun. "How are you feeling, Technician?"

"Like my mouth is lined with fiberglass, and my heart wants to climb out of my rib cage and run laps around the ship. There's no urge to kill and eat anyone, though."

"Glad to hear it." It looked like Squarm had been telling the truth about the cure. Mops glanced at Monroe and lowered her voice. "Watch him. Just in case."

She checked on Private Henson, who appeared to be sleeping peacefully in his acceleration pod.

"What should we do with our two Glacidae?" asked Monroe. "They'll be out for a while."

"Put Squarm in a different cell and lock the door," said Mops. "Leave Grom's door open so they can catch up with us when they wake up." After a brief internal debate, she put the pistol she'd taken from Squarm in Grom's cell, just in case.

Mops headed down the corridor. The door that connected the brig to the rest of the ship refused to budge, and the control panel was dead. She popped open the emergency hatch and unfolded the handle to crank open the door manually.

"Why is it so dark?" Wolf's voice sounded far too loud as she staggered into the hall.

"Lack of light," Kumar said flatly.

The first thing she saw upon leaving the brig area was four feral humans slumped unconscious against the wall. Without an acceleration chamber, they'd been slammed around hard when the *Pufferfish* jumped, then tossed again by the deceleration. All four were bloody and battered. Two had visibly broken limbs.

"I'm surprised they're not worse," said Monroe.

Kumar cleared his throat. "Emergency jump procedures say if you can't get to an acceleration chamber, you should lie flat and relax your body as much as possible. The more you tense, the greater the damage. The rest of the crew didn't know what was coming, so they would have been relaxed. Studies have found that humans can survive an unprotected jump about eighty percent of the time. Up to ninety in ideal circumstances."

Mops' fists clenched. That meant ten to twenty percent of the crew likely *hadn't* survived. Which of her friends had died because she'd ordered Doc to turn them loose?

"How do we find Azure?" asked Wolf.

"She knew the jump was coming," said Kumar. "Logically, she would have gotten to an acceleration chamber. With the ship's systems down, we'll need to manually search—"

"She'll be in her ship." Mops paused to orient herself, then turned left and started walking.

"You're sure?" asked Wolf.

"That's where her bioweapon is," said Mops. "She needs that shuttle to attack Dobranok. One way or another, if we get control of that shuttle, we win."

"Then shouldn't we be going the other way?" asked Kumar.

"Yes." Mops kept walking. "Just as soon as I get Doc out of the waste tank."

Normally, Mops would have scanned the tank and used a retrieval net to fish Doc out. With no power, she had to do it the old-fashioned way.

After five minutes with her arm shoulder-deep in muck, her gloved fingers closed around the hard crystal of her monocle. She pulled it free and used her thumb to remove a clump of something best left unidentified from the lens.

Kumar had already affixed a sanishower unit to the ceiling. The rest of her team retreated from the tank access room as the bottom of the sanishower flowered open and began to spray blue foam and liquid over her body. The floor drain was supposed to open automatically, but with the ship on standby, she had to manually unlock the floor tile and twist back the cover.

When the sanishower ran dry, Monroe used his compressor

to blow the remaining foam from Mops' uniform. She pulled a rag from her harness and started polishing the monocle. For the edges, she used a cleaning brush, paying extra attention to the attachment points.

"Let's go." She unsealed her hood as she walked. Her nose wrinkled at the smell of sewage and sanitizing fluid. She brought the monocle to her eye, where it jumped from her fingers as if eager to click into place.

For thirty seconds, nothing happened. Doc needed to build up a small reserve from the bioelectric energy in her attachment implants before powering back up. At least, she hoped that was the problem. Monocles were tough, but they weren't indestructible. If Doc hadn't survived his trip through the plumbing—

She pushed that thought away. "Come on, dammit."

Her vision brightened slightly as the monocle turned on and compensated for the dim light. *"If we're ever in a similar situation, it's your turn to get flushed down the toilet."*

She was too relieved to argue. "Fair enough."

"What's going on? Where are we? I can't interface with the ship."

"We're still on the *Pufferfish*, but it's pretty much dead."

"Have you tried turning it back on again?"

"Does the *Pufferfish* have a big on/off switch you haven't told me about?" She stopped near the lift doors. Doctor Curie lay to one side. His nose was broken and had bled over his face, and his elbow was dislocated. Doc automatically checked the readings from his suit.

"He's alive."

"Thanks." The lifts weren't working, but she cranked open the door anyway. Inside, just to the right of the door, was the maintenance ladder.

Mops grasped one of the metal rungs with both hands and stepped into the lift shaft. Her weight triggered light strips in the rungs, making the whole ladder glow white. Fighting off a wave of claustrophobia, she started down. The ladder was built into a large groove in the wall. In theory, you could climb even with the lift cars in operation, though she didn't know anyone who would be willing to test that theory.

Well, maybe Wolf.

She'd descended about three meters, and Wolf had just entered the lift, when the *Pufferfish* shuddered sideways. Mops tightened her grip.

"I didn't do it!" Wolf shouted, her words echoing down the tube.

"Grav beams," said Monroe. "We're being towed."

Which was just what Azure had predicted. The Krakau were dragging the *Pufferfish*—and the planet-killing payload on Azure's shuttle—toward Dobranok. With the *Pufferfish*'s systems offline, they had no way of contacting the Krakau to warn them, or even of knowing how long they had before reaching the planet.

"Climb faster," said Mops. "Whoever's last, close the lift door behind us. I don't want anyone from the crew regaining consciousness and stumbling in."

"Yes, sir," Kumar called down.

Her shoulder had stiffened and begun popping regularly by the time they reached their destination. Mops cranked open the door, stepped out, and tripped over something heavy. She caught her balance and turned to see Private Anna May Wong sprawled on the floor.

"I'm sorry. His suit isn't registering any life signs."

"Maybe his suit isn't working." Mops tugged Wong's collar to check his throat for a pulse. Nothing. No breath either.

"Aw, damn," said Monroe, climbing out behind her. He must have read Mops' expression.

"If it helps at all, it looks like he died instantly when the ship jumped. He would have had no awareness of his death."

Mops took Wong's monocle and placed it carefully into the padded pocket of her own jumpsuit. "Doc, record Private Wong's death. Mark him as killed in combat, and note that as acting CO, I'm recommending he receive the Medal of Sacrifice. The same for anyone else we lost in the jump. Upload that to the ship's log, or to any EMC database, the moment you have a signal."

"Yes, sir."

"This wasn't your fault," Monroe said quietly.

"Even if that were true, it's still my responsibility."

Monroe didn't argue. Wolf started to say something, caught Mops' expression, and clamped her jaw shut.

"It feels wrong to just leave him here," said Kumar.

"It is." Mops started walking. "But the best way to honor Wong is to find Azure and end this before anyone else dies."

They reached the docking bay without finding any additional casualties. The console outside the bay was dead, but when Mops pulled out the crank to open the door, it wouldn't budge. Wolf insisted on trying next, but she had no more luck than Mops. Even Monroe, using the enhanced strength of his mechanical arm, succeeded only in bending the crank handle.

"Can we cut through it?" asked Mops.

Kumar shook his head. "Docking bay doors act as a backup air lock, stronger and thicker than pretty much any other interior door. We'd get through eventually, but I wouldn't want to try until we know what Azure did to jam it."

Wolf glared at the door. "What do you mean?"

"She might have depressurized the bay," guessed Mops.

"Or she could have welded the door shut," said Monroe. "Or used a quick-sealant. Or broken the mechanism. Depending on how much time she had, she could have set up some kind of trap."

"She knew we'd be up and moving before her." Despair sank into Mops' gut, seeking to take root. "So she made sure we couldn't interfere."

Mops and her team had been a step behind from the beginning. They'd tracked the Prodryans to Coacalos Station, where

Mops had accidentally handed her enemies the answers they needed about their weapon's effectiveness. They'd flown to Paxif 6 to search for a cure, and all they'd accomplished was to turn the *Pufferfish* into a delivery service for Azure and Squarm and their bioweapon.

Monroe popped a new cube of gum into his mouth.

"I should have stuck with cleaning toilets," muttered Wolf. "Nobody died if we screwed that up. Usually."

"We could try to get to Engineering," said Kumar. "Maybe we could manually activate the engines."

Wolf snorted. "Oh, sure. A group of sanitation workers running wild in Engineering, in a dead ship surrounded by trigger-happy Krakau. What's the worst that could happen?"

"You're right." Mops stepped back from the door.

"Who is?" Kumar looked around in confusion. "You mean *Wolf*?"

"If we do nothing, Dobranok dies. Once the Krakau realize what's happening, they'll destroy the *Pufferfish*." She looked at each of them in turn. "*That* is the worst that could happen. We stand around doing nothing, and billions die."

They listened, saying nothing. Waiting for her to tell them what to do next. She swallowed. "Find me another way into that bay."

"We could use the outer docking bay doors," said Kumar. "Suit up for a spacewalk and move along the hull, then come in from the outside."

Wolf shook her head. "Those tugs are using broad-focus grav beams to tow the ship. They'd rip us right off the hull. What about explosives? There's got to be something on this ship we can use to blow a hole through the wall."

"Safer for the lieutenant to use those guns." Monroe gestured toward Mops' pistols. "Override the safety mechanism and blast your way in. There's a good chance you'll puncture the outer hull in the process, though."

Kumar studied the ceiling. "Are there any maintenance hatches or passages we could use?"

"The air vents." Mops started walking. "We move a massive amount of air in and out of the bay every time a shuttle launches or docks. We've all had to inspect the air tanks and clean out the hoses and filters. If we can get to those air pumps, we could crawl through the vents into the bay."

Pump Room Two was closest. Mops cranked open the door without a problem. Emergency lights flickered on as she entered, revealing heavy blue air tanks five meters high. Metal tubes rose from the tops and disappeared into the ceiling. Dark display screens were mounted on each tank, next to analog dials and gauges. Air pressure and temperature were both normal.

Mops popped open the equipment closet and grabbed the portable ladder. It activated automatically as she removed it from its charging harness, humming in her grip. She pressed the bottom rung to the tank, where electromagnets snapped it into place. From there, she unrolled it as high as she could reach. She continued to secure rungs as she climbed, until she reached the top.

"Double-check the pressure reading on this one," she called down.

"One atmosphere," said Kumar. "The same as the rest of the ship."

"Good." Mops pulled out her cutting torch and brought the triangular flame to the tube leading from the tank through the ceiling. It was only half a meter in diameter, which meant she'd have to leave her equipment harness behind and crawl like a Glacidae, but she should be able to make it. Air sighed out from the cut, making the edges glow briefly orange. The emergency shutoff valve in the tank clunked automatically as it registered a leak. Good to know the mechanical safeguards were working, even if the electronics were dead.

It took ten minutes to cut a vertical hole wide enough for her to squeeze inside. She tossed the curved shell of hot-edged metal to the floor.

"You want us to follow you?" asked Wolf.

"Not yet. If this doesn't work, it's going to be hard enough for me to squirm back out." She slipped off her harness, then removed the braces on her legs. She flexed each leg, testing the muscles and joints. "What tools do I need to remove the valve and grating on the other end?"

"Two-point-five–centimeter mag wrench," Kumar called up. "Your torch should get you through the grate."

"Thanks." She tucked wrench and torch inside her jumpsuit. One pistol followed, just in case. Everything else she left atop the tank.

"Those vents are fifteen meters high," Kumar reminded her. "You'll probably want a line or rope to lower yourself down."

"Check the closet for me?"

Kumar climbed up a moment later with a spool of sealant tape. "Best I could find, but it has a tensile strength of a hundred kilos. Twist it up, so it doesn't stick to your hands. Otherwise, you'll lose some skin."

She pushed the spool over her forearm like a bracelet. "Thanks, Kumar."

"Be careful, sir," he said quietly. "Shoot off every one of her tentacles if you have to."

The anger in his words startled her. Kumar was usually the unflappable one. Half the time, he was unflappable because he wasn't paying attention to what was happening around him, but still. "Don't worry. We're not going to let them infect anyone else. Human or Krakau."

She squeezed her head and shoulders into the opening and pushed higher with her legs. "Azure's likely to have secured her shuttle, too. I need you three to put your heads together and figure out the best way to break into her ship. I expect an answer by the time I reach the bay."

That should also keep them too busy to worry about the crew, the Krakau, the Prodryans, or the hundred other things they'd have to deal with when and if they managed to stop Azure.

Doc pushed her vision as high as it would go, letting her see the curved surface of the pipe's interior. She pressed her knees and feet against one side, her back against the other, and used her arms to scooch higher, a few centimeters at a time. The pipe was perfectly smooth, to help with airflow. It wasn't long before her shoulder was stiff and popping again, and her legs had begun to throb. "How long is this thing, anyway?"

"Another meter and a half straight up, after which it curves to a horizontal crawl for three meters."

She'd just pulled herself onto the flat section when Monroe's voice echoed from her speaker. "We've got noises coming from the hallway. I think some of the crew are starting to come to."

"Lock the door and keep quiet," she ordered. "Doc, if we assume Azure's physiology works the same as a typical Krakau, how long until she wakes up from the jump?"

"A minimum of three and a half hours. Probably closer to five."

The vent's valve mechanism was meant to be serviced from the other side. It took half an hour of fighting to find a decent angle with the wrench and remove the bolts. She finally managed to tug it loose, at which point she had to spend another twenty minutes using her torch to cut the damned thing into smaller pieces so she could get it out of her way.

"Status report," she called back.

"Unchanged," said Monroe. "We've heard at least three people stumble past outside."

"Or the same person going back and forth three times," added Kumar.

With the valve destroyed, Mops could see the literal and figurative light at the end of the tunnel. "I'm almost through. All that's left is the grate."

Her torch swiftly cut through the hexagonal grating, sending it to the bay floor with a loud clatter. She left a few hexagons intact at the top to serve as an anchor for her makeshift rope. Next up was the sealing tape. She peeled a length free and wrapped it several times through her anchor. She unrolled another meter, twisted it into thin black rope, and repeated the process until she had roughly fifteen meters. "You're sure this tape is strong enough to hold my weight?"

"In theory? Absolutely," said Kumar.

She had to crawl out headfirst. The edges of the grate caught at her suit and scraped the skin beneath, reopening at least two scabs. She got her upper torso free, stretched her back and shoulders, and then wrapped her tape rope around both hands. Hoping Kumar was right, she wriggled free of the vent.

The tape held. Her grip strength was another matter. She clung to the thin rope as well as she could, but ended up sliding down in a barely controlled fall, squeezing with all her strength to keep from breaking her legs on the floor. She hit hard and fell onto her back.

"Did it work?" asked Kumar.

She took a slow breath and unclenched her hands. "Nope. I'm dead. It was incredibly painful and heroic. Someone else will have to try."

"I nominate Wolf," Kumar said without missing a beat.

"Huh?" said Wolf. "Sorry, I was reading *Frankenstein*. Am I supposed to be rooting for the monster?"

"I always do." Mops pulled herself up and looked around. "Azure shot up the controls to the door. Blasted open the wall to destroy the mechanism, too. I don't think anyone's getting in that way."

"Want us to follow you through the vent?" asked Monroe.

"Not yet." Mops removed her gun and switched off the safety. "Let me check the shuttle and make sure everything's clear."

Docking clamps still secured the shuttle in place. Mops approached cautiously. She didn't want to damage anything if she could avoid it. With everything else on the ship shut down, including the *Pufferfish*'s remaining shuttles, Azure's shuttle might be their only way out. Assuming they could overcome its preprogrammed instructions to fly to Dobranok and explode.

Both the shuttle and the bay were silent. She pressed a

hand against the shuttle's hull, but felt nothing. For the moment, it appeared to be as dead as the *Pufferfish*.

With Doc translating the labels, it was simple enough to figure out the loading ramp controls and lower the ramp. Mops stepped back, gun ready, as the pneumatics hissed to life.

Mops had taken only one step onto the ramp when a small compartment in the ceiling popped open and the barrel of a gun swiveled to point at her head.

"Damn," she whispered. Yet again, Azure had been one step ahead.

"Lieutenant Adamopoulos." Azure's voice seemed to come from everywhere in the darkness. "Why do you have to make this so difficult?"

"It's human nature." Mops started to raise her weapon. The shuttle's gun fired a low-power plasma burst that seared a line across her bicep. Computer-controlled, from the speed and precision, which meant it would kill her before she lined up a shot. "I didn't expect you to be awake yet."

"I bypassed normal A-ring precautions and programmed the shuttle to wake me as quickly as possible. Why worry about brain damage and other complications when we'll all be dead within hours? Now toss your gun away behind you and enter."

"We'll be right there, sir," Monroe's voice came over her comm.

"Belay that," she whispered. "Doc—"

"I'm sending a live feed to the rest of the team."

Mops dropped her gun onto the floor. The ramp immediately started to rise, lifting her into the shuttle. She ducked forward to avoid banging her head. The ramp closed and sealed with another hiss.

Azure emerged from the back of the cargo area—the same hidden compartment she'd used before. As the interior lights came on, Mops saw that the Rokkau appeared to be weeping inky fluid from beneath the shell plates of her armor.

"Now what?" asked Mops.

"I don't know!" Azure flung her tentacles out in distress and paced feverishly, in the confined space.

Mops had been with the EMC long enough to see crewmates fall apart. Whether it was a soldier mourning lost friends after a mission or Kumar screaming after a sewage pipe backfired on him, Mops had learned to recognize the signs of someone trying desperately—and failing—to hold it all together. Krakau weren't human, and Rokkau weren't Krakau, but Azure acted like she was about to shatter.

After thirty seconds, Mops started to feel uncomfortable. After a minute, she cleared her throat and asked, "Are . . . are you all right?"

At Mops' words, the terrorist who'd helped develop a bioweapon to kill an entire planet sagged to the floor, whistling with each breath: the human equivalent to dissolving in sobs.

22

Accelerator Ring Effects on Human Subjects,
Part 4

The human brain (humans have only one, which explains a great deal about them) is a surprisingly primitive but resilient organ, composed of roughly one-third fat. Humans' thick skulls and a layer of cushioning fluid protect their brains from impact. It's possible these physiological defenses evolved in part due to an odd human ritual known as the "head butt."[1]

Twenty-five humans were subjected to a series of ten short-range A-ring jumps. Cognitive skills were assessed before and after each jump, and brain activity was monitored during the jump itself. Brain measurements revealed significant bruising and swelling. (See fig. 1). Remarkably, the majority of subjects were able to heal and recover from this damage within nine days.

Where Krakau and other races require medical augmentation and other preparation to endure an A-ring jump, humans appear capable of unaided jumps with minimal long-term effects. Of the twenty-five subjects, only three showed signs of long-term cognitive impairment after completing ten jumps. As cognition was not humanity's primary strength to begin with, we consider these results highly encouraging.

Since most humans are to be used as soldiers, it is unlikely most would survive long enough to suffer any noticeable effects.[2]

Additional research is needed to examine the effects of acceleration chambers in further reducing human brain damage.

———

1. *Updated from previous edition to correct mistranslation of "skull anus."*
2. *This researcher recommends not warning humans of the potential side effects, as they may not take the news well.*

MOPS CHECKED HER SURROUNDINGS for potential weapons or cover, but as long as that gun was tracking her, she didn't dare try anything. "This isn't exactly how I imagined this would go."

Azure weakly snapped a tentacle in Mops' direction. "Heart of Glass had no contingency plans for . . . for *you*. For humans who chase after us with the relentless determination of daggerfish tracking a blood scent. I assume you've already killed my partner."

"Not yet," said Mops. "They're locked up, sleeping off the effects of the jump."

"Oh, of course. You want Squarm alive, so you can force them to cure your crew." Azure slumped against the ridged brown wall of the shuttle.

Mops studied Azure's face, the sheen of the skin around beak and eyes. "How old are you?"

"Nineteen years."

Mops started to do the conversion in her head, but as

always, Doc was faster. *"That's equivalent to sixteen-point-two Earth years. Krakau have an average lifespan of seventy Earth years. Assuming Rokkau are similar, she's basically a teenager."*

Mops shook her head. "You're too damn young to be trying to commit genocide."

"It's bad enough you made such a desiccated husk of our plans," Azure wailed. "Now you mock me?"

"I'm not mocking you." Mops sat cross-legged on the floor. The gun continued to track her. "How did you end up working for Heart of Glass in the first place? The truth this time, since we're probably all going to die anyway."

"My family's lifeship has been in hiding since we fled Dobranok, but we monitor galactic events as much as possible. The elders learned of Heart of Glass' death sentence, how he fled Yan for suggesting cooperation with other species against the Krakau. They saw him as a potential ally. They reached out."

"To a race that's spent the last century and a half trying to kill everyone who isn't Prodryan."

"Who else could they turn to?" Azure snapped.

Mops nodded sympathetically. "It must be hard to find a good partner in biological terrorism."

"All we want is freedom and justice for what the Krakau did to us."

"All Anna May Wong wanted was to earn his sergeant's stripes and master an old Earth instrument called the ukulele."

Azure scooted backward. "They arranged a meeting with Heart of Glass. When he learned the truth about humans, he became fascinated by the biochemistry of our venom. He said it was the key to overthrowing the Krakau and bringing true change to the galaxy."

"And you believed him?"

"I saw an opportunity to help our people." She quieted. "And to finally escape the confines of our lifeship."

How many generations had lived and died on that ship, never seeing more of the galaxy, never meeting anyone beyond their own extended family? Mops would have been desperate to escape as well. "What about Squarm? How did they get drawn into this?"

Azure shuddered. "Squarm is a scientist and a criminal. They specialized in creating recreational drugs on Coacalos Station. They're just in this for the money. Heart of Glass had recruited them several months earlier. I believe the two of them were originally planning a chemical attack against Dobranok, but then they learned of my venom. Squarm studied captured EMC humans, trying to understand and reverse engineer what was done to you. It took them two years to develop this bioweapon."

Mops nodded. "I'm curious. What do you imagine the Prodryans will do to you once they've used you to murder a planet of Krakau and weaken the Alliance?"

"The Krakau are the greater threat to our people." Azure drew herself up. "Tell your team to surrender themselves, or I'll kill you."

"Don't be stupid." Mops sighed and massaged her shoulder. "You know my team's listening in on this, right? Kill me, and they'll come down to incapacitate your shuttle. Maybe they'll weld it to the deck or cut holes in your hull or disable the emergency power to the grav plates and physically throw your ship against the wall until it breaks. Wolf would have fun with that, I think. The point is, there's no way we're letting you launch this shuttle, so either shoot me or put that damned gun away."

Azure whistled again, her anguish loud enough to hurt Mops' ears. "You aren't even soldiers! How have you countered our every move? How have *humans* shown such tactical and strategic skill—what are you doing?"

Mops caught herself. "Laughing. I'm sorry, that was rude, but you caught me by surprise."

"I don't understand."

"'Strategic skill'? Hell, Azure. I've spent this whole time pissed that your lot was always a step ahead of us."

"You . . . you think this was what we planned?" Azure stared, her blue coloration brightening with shock. "You destroyed the Prodryan fighter team sent to investigate the *Pufferfish*! You uncovered our contacts at Coacalos Station, forcing us to speed up our plans."

"And in the process, I was shot, blown up, and captured," Mops countered.

Azure flicked a limb dismissively. "You didn't seem to have any trouble overcoming your captors and escaping, or of tracking us to Paxif 6."

"Where we flew into the middle of a Prodryan assault!"

"An assault you drove off!"

"Did we really?" demanded Mops. "Or did they pull back to allow you and Squarm to 'escape' to the *Pufferfish*? We played right into your hands. Tentacles. Whatever. We were nothing but a taxi to the Krakau home world."

"You think I wanted to die in the attack on Dobranok? I only agreed to this because Heart of Glass threatened to kill everyone on Paxif 6, including me, if I didn't get this bioweapon to the Krakau."

Mops sat back, fighting another bout of laughter. "You're as out of your depth as we are."

"More so," Azure said grudgingly.

"I wouldn't bet on that."

Azure made a clicking, stuttering sound, a mix of despair and dark amusement. "It doesn't matter. The shuttle is programmed to blast its way free and begin its run as soon as we're within range of Dobranok. But you'll stop that as well, won't you? And the Krakau will win again."

"It looks that way to me. We stop your shuttle. The Krakau tow us in and imprison or kill everyone. They pull the data from our monocles and take Squarm's cure, at which point your bioweapon is all but useless. Everything you've done was for nothing. My crew was infected for nothing."

"I know." Azure snapped a tentacle in Mops' direction. "There is no need to rub it out!"

"Rub it in," Mops corrected. "How long before we reach our destination?"

"An hour. Maybe two."

Mops chewed her lip. "All right, the first thing you're gonna do is get rid of that damned gun."

"I will not surrender to the Alliance," said Azure.

"Nobody's asking you to." Mops waited, then shrugged. "Have it your way. Monroe, get the team in here and tear this shuttle apart. Wolf, Azure is all yours."

"Wait!" Azure flung her tentacles in all directions, then ducked back into her hidden room. A moment later, the gun disappeared into the ceiling.

"Stand down," Mops said.

"Are you sure?" asked Monroe. "Wolf *really* wants to shoot something."

"The way things are going, I'm sure she'll get her chance." Mops glanced around. "Azure, do you know how to control this shuttle?"

"Most of it, yes. Why?"

"Because ours aren't working." She crawled up the narrow ramp into the cockpit. It was like entering a giant metal clamshell. Control panels and consoles were built into the floor, with additional screens and indicators around the edge. She pulled her legs in to make room for Azure. The Rokkau had a much easier time moving about, simply spreading her limbs to flatten and broaden her body. Mops glared at the unmarked controls. "How do I find out exactly where we are and what's happening outside the ship?"

"Scanners are over here." Azure flipped a set of switches and maneuvered a control token over a grid. Several screens lit up to show the shuttle surrounded by an outline of the *Pufferfish*.

"I was hoping for a broader picture."

Azure continued to move the control token, and the image zoomed outward to show six identical ships surrounding the *Pufferfish*. Each tow ship was roughly a quarter the size of the cruiser, but the engines on any one generated enough power to tow a warship. Six of them with their grav beams deployed could drag the *Pufferfish* anywhere in the system ... or tear the ship apart. Farther out, a pair of warships flanked the convoy. The Krakau were serious about keeping the *Pufferfish* under control.

The image kept growing until Dobranok came into view, along with its moons and orbital defense stations.

"What do you intend to do?" asked Azure.

"I'm working on that. Why haven't the Rokkau just announced themselves to the galaxy? Tell the Alliance what the Krakau did?"

"It was tried once, more than a century ago. Rokkau refugees designed a communications module that could transmit simultaneously to Dobranok, Solikor-zi, Cuixique, and several other worlds. The Alliance Military Council denounced the transmission as propaganda put forth by a splinter group of Krakau extremists. The Rokkau lifeship was captured, the entire group interrogated. Through them, the Krakau hunted down two additional lifeships. We are too vulnerable to expose ourselves like that a second time."

"We need proof. After all this time, the Rokkau must have some idea where the Krakau kept the rest of your people. If we could locate that prison planet—"

"We have tried," said Azure. "The Krakau protect that secret more fiercely than their own young."

Mops frowned and tapped another screen. "What's this countdown here? What happens in ten hours and seventeen minutes?"

"That is when the Prodryan war fleet arrives."

Mops froze. "Say that again?"

"Squarm signaled them before the jump to schedule their attack. Heart of Glass intends to strike after our bioweapon has begun to spread death and panic and chaos through the entire system. He's gathered assault forces from other clans and declared himself Supreme Assault Commander. He hopes to use this victory to restore his honor among the Prodryans. One squadron is supposed to liberate Prodryan prisoners from the Krakau's orbital facility. The rest will destroy the Krakau defenses, satellites, space stations ... anything they can blow up."

"All right," Mops said, fighting for calm. "Given the mess we're facing, what's one more clog in the pipes? How do communications on this shuttle work?"

"Over here." Azure scooted sideways. "The shuttle has a low-power communications pod."

"Put me in contact with those Krakau tow ships, and I'll try to get us out of this mess."

"How?"

Mops threw her hands up, smacking the ceiling. "I don't know yet."

"My mission—"

"Has failed," Mops said flatly. "You're not going to infect Dobranok. My team will blow this shuttle to dust first. We'll destroy the entire *Pufferfish* if we have to."

"You expect me to help save the Krakau? To protect a race that drove mine to the verge of extinction? You can't imagine how that feels."

Mops propped herself up on one elbow and glared until Azure realized what she'd said, and to whom.

The Rokkau dipped her body. "Oh. Yes, I suppose maybe you can."

"You have three choices. My team blows everything up, and we die here. We disable the shuttle without destroying the *Pufferfish*, and we all end up prisoners of the Krakau. Or you work with me to get us out of this."

"How can I trust a slave of the Krakau?"

"You begin by erasing that word from your beak," Mops said softly. "Call me a slave again, and I will flush you down the nearest sewage line."

Azure pulled back.

"You and your friends attacked my ship," Mops continued. "You shot a member of my team. Your venom wiped out my civilization. You are in no position to question our trustworthiness, child. And if you give me any more backtalk, I will smack the blue right off your shell."

"You sound like my mothers," Azure muttered, before turning to touch a new set of controls. Painful static filled the air. "I'm sorry! I didn't have time to fully study how this ship works."

"Believe me, I understand."

The buzzing cut off a moment later. "I think we're ready," said Azure. "Low-power signal, audio only, nontargeted, encryption turned off. . . ."

Mops waited while Azure flipped two more switches. "This is Lieutenant Marion Adamopoulos of the *EMCS Pufferfish*. I need to speak with whoever is in charge immediately. This is a matter of planetary security."

Silence.

"They're not answering," Azure said helpfully. "Unless I have them muted. Hold on. No, they're definitely not responding."

"Given the secrecy surrounding the Rokkau, I'm not surprised. They shut down the *Pufferfish* to keep us from telling anyone about you." Mops peered at the console. "They're probably searching for someone with clearance and authority to talk to us."

"You could tell them about the bioweapon," Wolf said over the comm.

Mops turned away and lowered her voice. "What would you do if someone was coming to Earth with a weapon like that on board?"

"Blow it into atoms," Wolf said promptly. "Oh."

Monroe cleared his throat. "Could you take another look at the scanner?"

Mops hesitated. "Doc, have you been sharing the visual feed with the team as well as audio?"

"They were curious. I thought it was better than letting them get bored. You know what happens then."

Hard to argue with that. Mops turned back to the screen showing Dobranok and the surrounding system.

"Not one EMC ship," said Monroe. Most worlds had at least one EMC warship stationed in-system for protection. A central planet like Dobranok should have rated a half dozen or more.

"They were probably reassigned to protect Earth and Stepping Stone," suggested Mops. Which meant, in their efforts to defend Earth against a nonexistent attack from the Prodryan bioweapon, the Krakau had left their home system vulnerable.

She tapped Azure on the tentacle. "How many Prodryans are supposed to show up when that countdown hits zero?"

Azure flinched. "They didn't share such details with me."

Mops turned her attention back to the comm. "I repeat, this is Lieutenant Adamopoulos on the *Pufferfish*. I have urgent information about an imminent Prodryan attack."

An unfamiliar voice crackled over the speakers. "Miss Adamopoulos"—the omission of her rank stung—"this is Captain Mbube of Tow Ship Three. I've been authorized to hear your warning. Switch to a secure, direct channel immediately."

Mops looked to Azure, who stared at the console and spread her limbs in a helpless shrug.

Mops sighed. "Captain Mbube, the Prodryans aren't going to attack Earth. They—"

"If you cannot follow communications protocols, we will block your transmissions," Mbube interrupted.

"These are the people you serve?" Azure muttered. "The people you hope to protect?"

"Yes. Well, maybe not that one in particular."

"Miss Adamopoulos," said Mbube. "Are you aware you're still broadcasting?"

"I am, yes." She rolled sideways and stretched her shoulder, popping the joint. "Azure?"

"Still searching for the encryption controls," the Rokkau muttered.

"See? It's harder than it looks," Wolf said over Mops' comm.

"We're trying, Captain Mbube. But the Prodryans are going to attack Dobranok. You have to contact Admiral Pachelbel. Tell her—"

Painful feedback squealed from the console. Azure attacked the controls with all three tentacles, eventually shutting it down.

Mops checked the countdown. Less than an hour before they reached whatever orbital prison the Krakau were taking them to. Nine hours after that, the Prodryans would arrive. "Azure, you said this shuttle was set to launch automatically. Can you abort that program?"

"I cannot."

With the Krakau refusing to listen, that left one other choice. "Monroe, get the team down here. We have forty-five minutes to break a shuttle."

Wolf's whoop of excitement almost drowned out Kumar's comment: "We're not familiar with Glacidae shuttles, and this one has been modified."

"Don't worry," Mops said dryly. "I have the utmost confidence in your ability to break things."

The chemical tanks containing the bioweapon were welded into place in the back of the shuttle, along with the terraforming dispersal satellites. Trying to cut them free risked puncturing the tanks or setting it all off prematurely. Instead, Mops' team attacked pretty much everything else in the shuttle, hoping to render it incapable of flight.

Kumar and Azure worked in the cockpit, trying to decipher the controls. They'd figured out how to adjust internal temperature, unfolded the wings for atmospheric flight—directly onto the top of Wolf's head—and in a particularly exciting mix-up, fired one of the upper bow maneuvering thrusters for two and a half seconds.

Monroe was working on the main engines in the back, carefully tracing wires and circuits and fuel lines.

As for Wolf, she was in the cargo area ripping apart everything she could get her hands and torch on. She'd already cut the main ramp free. It lay on the deck, along with several wall panels, an air circulation grate, a pile of burnt cargo netting, and a flickering light strip. From what Mops had pieced together, Wolf was determined to remove the bioweapon. If she couldn't cut it free from the floor, she'd simply cut away that entire section of floor.

"Twenty minutes."

"What about the fuel lines?" asked Mops. "Say we cut up a sanibomb and set off a piece inside? It should expand and clog things up."

"Depending on which of the six standard Glacidae fuel mixtures this shuttle uses, the reaction would generate enough heat to ignite the fuel lines. Which, admittedly, would stop the shuttle from completing its mission...."

A floor panel clattered to the deck.

"I think we've figured out how to set off the escape pod," Kumar called down.

Mops sighed. "That's great, Kumar. How does that prevent the shuttle from launching?"

A long pause. "We'll keep working."

Mops poked her head up into the cockpit. "How does the shuttle know when to launch?"

"I don't understand," said Azure.

"You said on the bridge that your shuttle was programmed to automatically try to escape once we entered Dobranok's orbit. But you couldn't have known exactly when we'd arrive in-system, or how long it would take our escorts to drag us to Dobranok. Which means the program is probably tied to the shuttle's scanners, counting down based on our distance to the planet. Where are the sensors on this thing?"

"I'm not sure."

"If this is a standard Glacidae shuttle, sensors are located in the underside of the ship, approximately two meters back from the docking ramp. Where the docking ramp used to be, rather."

She climbed down and exited the shuttle. "Wolf, how close are you to cutting those tanks free?"

Another chunk of metal clattered through where the docking ramp used to be. "They've got three damn layers of flooring, honeycombed with some kind of mother-drowning nanofiber reinforcement that smells like burnt Glacidae shit. It's taking forever."

"Forget that. I've got something else for you to break."

Wolf threw herself into the new job with her usual enthusiasm. Within five minutes, she'd cut into the shuttle's belly and was pawing through insulation and protective panels. Within ten, she'd exposed the spherical mechanism of the primary scanners.

"You know if this works, we're blind again," said Monroe.

"We're running out of time," said Mops. "The only other option I see is to leave it alone and hope the docking clamps keep the shuttle from launching."

Monroe shook his head. "Once the engines fire up, it'll rip them right out of the floor."

Something popped beneath the shuttle, showering blue sparks onto Wolf's head. She cursed and scooted away.

"Sensors are dead," Azure shouted down.

"Ha!" Wolf switched off her torch, bounded to her feet, and patted her hair to make sure it wasn't burning. "What next?"

"We don't have time for anything more," said Mops. "Either that worked, or else . . ."

"We'll know either way in a few minutes," added Monroe.

"Kumar, Azure, come on out." They didn't respond. Mops frowned and stepped through the debris to peer inside the shuttle. She could hear Kumar and Azure arguing. "Everything all right up there?"

"We picked up multiple A-ring signatures on the scanner,"

said Kumar. "But Wolf broke it before I could get a better look."

"We saw many false and ridiculous readings as your human was working on the sensor unit," argued Azure. "Including a galaxy-sized supernova, a trio of black holes, and an extreme close-up of a human nostril."

"That's the point," Kumar pressed. "Those A-ring readings weren't ridiculous. They were consistent with Prodryan warships and carriers."

"You said the Prodryans weren't supposed to launch their attack for another nine hours," Mops said.

"I thought so, too," said Azure. "It's possible there was a miscommunication. Or perhaps Heart of Glass is simply eager to begin killing Krakau. *If* the readings were correct."

"Do we still have communications?"

"I think so," said Azure.

Mops pulled herself into the shuttle. The shuttle which, so far, hadn't exploded or tried to fly away. "If a Prodryan war fleet just popped into the system, maybe *that* will convince someone to listen to us."

23

"*Admiral Pachelbel?*"

A bubbled groan escaped her mouth. Dull aches throbbed from the tips of her extremities to her torso, like waves crashing together in a spray of pain. She was too old to be jumping about the galaxy like this. "I'm awake. What's our status?"

"We decelerated four hours ago, and were towed to the Basin. We're preparing to dock."

The Basin was a military prison in low orbit around Dobranok. Matching speed to intercept and dock could take hours. Pachelbel climbed out of her acceleration chamber and looked around the impersonal quarters she'd been assigned while on board the Sky Serpent. *The brine pool had refilled after the jump, and she eased herself gratefully into the warm, salty water. "Any word on the* Pufferfish?"

The answer came promptly from the speaker by the door. "That's what I wanted to talk with you about. The Pufferfish *is in-system. They're attempting to communicate . . . we think. The readings are odd."*

Pachelbel froze. "That ship was locked down. Priority nine. How the depths are they communicating?"

"Our techs suggest the signal is coming from a Glacidae-built transmitter. Possibly from the shuttle they picked up at Paxif 6."

She sank deeper into the water. "Exactly how many people have picked up this signal?"

"Unknown. They're broadcasting to anyone in range. Captain Mbube is the only one who's made direct contact, and that was more than an hour ago."

"What does Mops want?" asked Pachelbel.

There was a pause, probably so her aide could verify who "Mops" was. "In an earlier communication with Captain Mbube, Lieutenant Adamopoulos said something about an attack by Prodryans. She believes the Prodryans aren't targeting Earth, but Dobranok."

Pachelbel curled and relaxed her primary tentacles as she pondered that warning. "Did she give any evidence?"

"Captain Mbube terminated communications before the human could explain."

"I see." She couldn't blame Mbube. Regulations surrounding potential Rokkau contact were strict. The captain risked serious disciplinary action for responding at all. "Was there anything more?"

"Yes. Our sensors have detected a Prodryan war fleet entering the system. We estimate they'll be within weapons range in one hour, fifty minutes."

AZURE AND WOLF CROWDED over the shuttle's communications console. "I never thought I'd miss Puffy," muttered Wolf. "Wait, what about that switch?"

"That is the translator," Azure said, one tentacle twitching impatiently. "As I explained three minutes ago."

"Next time, explain better," Wolf shot back.

Mops watched from the back of the cockpit. Azure hadn't tried to poison Wolf yet, and Wolf hadn't threatened to eat the Rokkau. They were getting along better than Mops had expected.

The console buzzed sharply, like an angry wasp trying to escape. "What did you touch?" snapped Azure.

"Nothing! We've got an incoming signal. I think."

Mops scooted closer. "Is it Captain Mbube again?"

"Yes," said Azure, simultaneous with Wolf's "Nope."

"Look at the signal strength." Wolf pointed to an indicator that meant nothing to Mops. "Completely different from the transmission we got earlier."

"Look at the vector." Azure slapped a tentacle against the console.

"Why don't we acknowledge the signal and find out?" Mops suggested gently.

Azure and Wolf both reached for the controls, but Azure was faster. Mops wasn't sure how exactly the Rokkau made flicking a switch look smug, but Azure managed.

"This is Admiral Pachelbel. Mops, what the hell have you gotten yourself into?"

"Told you," whispered Wolf.

Mops squeezed between them before they could escalate. "Admiral, you have no idea how relieved I am to hear your voice. Is this connection secure?"

"I'm hardly about to contact a treasonous crew harboring a level nine fugitive on an open, unencrypted channel."

There was no lag time. Pachelbel was here. "Could you please check things on our end? We haven't fully mastered our communications system."

There was a pause. "You're secure. I'm told you wanted to talk to me. Talk fast."

"Yes, sir." Mops took a deep breath. "Am I correct in stating that a Prodryan fleet has entered the system?"

"You are," Pachelbel said softly. "It's been suggested that they're here on your behalf, or as part of a joint plan between you and the Prodryans. Your knowledge of their arrival makes me take those suggestions more seriously."

"Are you alone, sir?" asked Mops. "Is anyone else listening in?"

Another pause. "I'm alone."

Mops turned to Azure. "Can this thing do visual?"

This time Wolf was faster, jabbing a button near the top of the console. An image of Admiral Pachelbel appeared on the screen. She sat half-submerged in a dimly lit pool. A green-tinged visor circled her head, an interface similar in design and function to Mops' monocle.

"Admiral," said Mops. "This is Azure."

"Level nine fugitive," added Azure. She'd gone still, like a predator preparing to lunge. "That sounds important."

The admiral stared for a long time. "She's injured. What happened?"

"I shot off one of her tentacles," said Mops. "We reached an understanding after that. Azure told me what the Krakau did to her people. She also told me what really happened to humanity when the Krakau and Rokkau first arrived on our planet."

"Do you believe her?"

"Right now, I'm more inclined to trust her than you. The Krakau have lied to us from the beginning. All Azure did was try to kill us." That had sounded better in her head.

"Lieutenant . . . Mops." Pachelbel sank into the water, until the lower curve of her beak touched the surface. "It's not that simple. Nothing ever is."

"Which part is the most complicated?" asked Mops. "The truth about how your contact mission to Earth infected my planet? How you left us to die? Or maybe the part where you banished the Rokkau to a prison planet."

The admiral bolted from the water. "What prison planet? What are you talking about?"

"After your war with the Rokkau." Mops glanced at Azure, but if Rokkau body language was at all similar to Krakau,

Azure was as confused as anyone else. "When your people rounded up the surviving Rokkau?"

"There were no surviving Rokkau," Pachelbel said. "Aside from a few small groups who escaped Dobranok."

"You lie," shouted Azure. "I've seen the records, stolen from Homeworld Military Command more than a hundred years ago. Every free Rokkau has. We read the full list of names as part of a ceremony marking our ninth year. Well, more skim than read ... there are more than a million names ... I doubt anyone truly reads them all, but still!"

"If HMC has such records, they haven't shared them with Interstellar Military Command," said Pachelbel.

"No surprise there," Mops shot back. "We know how good the Krakau are at keeping secrets."

That earned a flinch. The admiral turned slightly, probably checking something on her visor. "I'm ... concerned by these allegations, but right now we have a hostile force incoming, and I need to coordinate with Planetary Defense. Was there something more you needed to tell me?"

Mops bit her lip, briefly tempted to say nothing. To restore the shuttle and let it dump its contents onto Dobranok. "Don't let the Prodryans anywhere near the planet. The bioweapon they used against the *Pufferfish* doesn't just revert humans. It's been modified to kill Krakau."

Pachelbel's response was a long, stuttering whistle the communications console failed to translate.

"I've never heard that phrase before," Doc said quietly. *"Something about a spiny coral and an excretory orifice."*

"You're certain?" asked Pachelbel. "I'm told the bioweapon was a form of Krakau venom. We should be immune."

"*Rokkau* venom," Azure said sharply.

"Captain Brandenburg and the rest of our command crew died immediately after the attack," said Mops. "I thought ... I assumed at first that feral humans had killed them, but their bodies were undamaged. Azure confirmed it."

"Is there a cure?"

"Yes," said Mops. "We have a sample on board, along with the Glacidae chemist and criminal who helped make it. My question to you is how badly you want them."

Pachelbel made the clicking equivalent of a chuckle. "People have argued about letting humans get too intelligent. I'm afraid you give strength to those arguments. What's your price, Mops?"

"Cure my crew," she said without hesitation. "They know nothing about Rokkau or venom or what happened to Earth. If I give you the counteragent, you promise to use it to restore them."

"They will need to be thoroughly debriefed," Pachelbel said slowly, "but I can probably arrange that. Assuming they're unaware of anything that's transpired on the *Pufferfish*, they will not be harmed. I'll send a shuttle to retrieve—"

"I wasn't finished." Mops smiled. "I'll also need you to reactivate the *Pufferfish*. Give me full control of my ship, and override that Rokkau-triggered subroutine you buried in Doc and the rest of our monocles."

Pachelbel flicked two tentacles in polite disbelief. "You're a wanted criminal, and you expect me to simply give you a cruiser?"

"You've got enemy ships en route, and your defenses are pretty thin. An EMC cruiser could make a real difference in the outcome. I'll be on the bridge with the cure, waiting for your answer. If I don't hear from you . . . well, I guess that's an answer, too."

The team's first obstacle was getting back up to the air vent to escape the docking bay. Climbing down a cord of twisted tape was one thing, but getting enough of a grip to pull yourself back up was pretty much impossible. They ended up forming a human ladder to push and pull one another up, an exercise that reminded Mops of team-building challenges from basic training. She'd never liked those challenges.

By then, most of the crew was awake and stumbling about, making the journey through the ship that much more exciting. Three times they doubled back to find another route rather than fight their own feral shipmates.

Main power returned while they were on deck C. Lights brightened, and air vents hummed to life, wafting a cool breeze through the corridor.

"Let there be light!" Doc crowed. *"I'm getting readings from various ship's systems. It will take a few minutes for everything to come up before I can give you a full status report."*

"There's a lift up this way," said Kumar. "It'll be faster."

"Wait." Mops turned to look directly at Azure. "Doc, are you still there?"

"I haven't suddenly been possessed by phantom code, if that's what you mean. Either the admiral switched off that subroutine, or else nothing's happening because we're already approaching Dobranok."

"Do we have a clear route to the bridge?"

"Private Balboa is lurking in front of the lift. Let me lure her away." The murmur of distant conversation reached Mops' ears. *"She's moving. Give her a moment to follow the sounds, and you'll be fine."*

Three minutes later, Mops was stepping out of the lift onto the bridge. The station consoles were in standby mode, and the main screen had defaulted to a status overview of the *Pufferfish*. It confirmed the ship was in rough shape. One weapons pod was out of commission, the other two completely depleted of missiles. Hull integrity was holding, but green patches dotted the ship's skin like a rash, showing where emergency bulkheads and sealant had patched various breaches. The ship would need serious repairs for long-term stability.

"In other news, we have a minor plumbing emergency on deck F. Technician Stark got his arm stuck in the toilet."

"We know he's not going anywhere, then." Mops took her seat and checked her console. "Give me Tactical."

"Yes, sir," said Monroe. The status screen vanished, replaced by a smaller representation of the *Pufferfish*, surrounded by tow ships. The curve of the planet dominated the lower right corner of the screen. A small dot labeled "The Basin" raced away from the ship, making the orbiting prison appear to chase the horizon.

"Zoom out," said Mops. "Who else is here?"

The next view brought a sharp breath from Kumar and a curse from Wolf.

"Did they send the entire Prodryan fleet?" whispered Kumar.

"Prodryans don't have a unified military," said Monroe, staring at the screen. Four clusters of ships, all tagged green as hostiles, were closing on Dobranok from different directions. Krakau ships, marked in blue, had begun to form a perimeter around the planet.

"The Krakau are just going to sit here and wait?" asked Wolf.

Mops skimmed the force summaries for both sides. In addition to fourteen warships and twenty-three cruiser-class vessels, the Prodryans had sent eleven carriers, each of which could hold twenty small fighter craft. "Looks like Homeworld Military Command is launching more ships from the planet and the two moons. Probably trying to get as much firepower together as they can before heading out to intercept the Prodryan fleets."

A brief flicker of light marked the destruction of a Krakau long-range security buoy.

"Why attack nine hours early?" Mops whispered. Azure had guessed it was a miscommunication or simple bloodthirsty eagerness, but Heart of Glass hadn't made such mistakes before.

Azure lurked by the lift door, her attention fixed on the screen. It couldn't be easy seeing alien warships closing in on her species' home world, even a home world she'd never known. "They intend to raid the shipyards and take as much military technology as they can, but they know the Alliance won't let them stay. Once they leave, Dobranok will be our world."

"Whatever's left of it." Mops looked back to the screen. "It's a race. Four groups of Prodryans, each one hoping to reach Dobranok first and claim the best loot for themselves. One group probably made the jump early, and the rest followed to keep anyone else from getting the advantage."

Krakau ships began to separate into five defensive formations. Four curved away from the planet on intercept courses, while the fifth spread about Dobranok.

"Do we know who those four fleets serve?" asked Mops.

"Not from here," said Kumar. "Prodryans don't broadcast ID registries, and we're too far out for visual identification."

"Heart of Glass will be in one of the command ships," whispered Azure. "He spoke of the glory of this attack, the shock waves it would send throughout the galaxy. He would not allow anyone else to usurp his place in history."

Mops spun. "Wolf, send a message to Admiral Pachelbel. Short-range, tight-beam. If a single Prodryan picks this up, we're dead."

Azure shuddered. "We're all going to die."

Wolf glared plasma beams at the Rokkau, but continued working on the signal parameters. "Go ahead, sir."

"Admiral, this is Mops. Tell your tow ships to prepare to break off. We're going to disrupt the Prodryans' attack."

"How the hell are we going to do that?" asked Wolf. "One busted cruiser against four Prodryan war fleets?"

"Wolf, stop undermining your captain on an open channel," snapped Mops. In a quieter voice, she said, "Monroe and Kumar, get to the brig. We're going to need Grom up here."

Monroe jumped to his feet with a quick salute and headed for the lift, Kumar following a few steps behind.

"Admiral," Mops continued. "Your defenses look pretty evenly matched with the Prodryans. You might be able to hold them off, but a lot of your people are going to die. And we can't risk letting any of them reach the planet. Any one of those ships could be carrying more of that damned bioweapon."

"You think a group of janitors on a busted cruiser can stop them?" The translator did an excellent job of catching the terseness in Pachelbel's voice.

"The Krakau turned us into warriors and soldiers," said Mops. "Right now, I'd happily put a plasma beam through every bastard at Command who knowingly kept the truth from us, but that doesn't mean I'm going to stand by and let the Prodryans slaughter innocent people. Respectfully, sir, we don't have time to argue. Either shut us back down, or shut up and let us do what you remade us to do."

"What's that?" Monroe murmured, looking over Mops' shoulder from behind her chair.

"Something to keep me from going crazy while Grom finishes working. A biography of Doctor Marion Adamopoulos." Mops cleared the screen. "Or a fiction made up by Krakau 'historians.' They rewrote our history. Who knows if Dr. Adamopoulos was even a real person."

"Or Marilyn Monroe," he said, nodding. "The Krakau couldn't have destroyed every document on Earth. Some of the libraries and archives must have survived."

"Full of records in languages we can't read." Mops pulled herself back to the present. "Maybe once we've saved Dobranok, we can arrange a tourist trip to Earth."

"And get eaten by the natives?" Wolf piped up. "No thanks."

Mops chuckled and turned to Grom. "How's it coming?"

Grom secreted a faint trail of lubricating fluid as they crawled away from Monroe's station. "I've finished resetting and marking the controls for the plasma beam power levels, as you requested. Monroe, make sure you pull the blue slider all the way down before firing."

Monroe moved to his station and studied his console and controller. "Weapons look good, sir."

Mops checked on Azure, who stood off to her right. "Are you ready for your part?"

Her tentacles curled into spirals, then relaxed again. "I am."

She turned next to navigation. "Kumar?"

"Course ready, sir." His fingers hovered over the control sphere.

"Wolf?"

"I've *been* ready."

Mops stood. "Battle Captain Cervantes was good at giving speeches, reminding his team how important their work was. But he's not here, so I'm going to cut to the chase." She looked around the bridge. Her bridge. "Don't fuck this up."

Wolf grinned and shouted, "Yes, sir!" The others echoed the sentiment—loudly—a moment later.

Mops moved to join Monroe and Grom. "Fire when ready, JG Monroe."

Doc sent a tactical view to her monocle, showing the *Pufferfish* surrounded by Krakau tow ships. Moments later, flickers of light stabbed out from their two remaining weapons pods, touching each of the ships in succession.

Mops held her breath.

"Direct hits," said Monroe.

"Grav beams are offline," announced Kumar. "The tow ships are limping away."

"They're not being quiet about it either," said Wolf. "I'm picking up a lot of angry chatter calling for reinforcements to take us out."

Mops studied Monroe's screen. "Damage report?"

"With our weapons at ten percent power?" Monroe snorted. "We barely tickled them. But the Prodryans should have picked up the weapons discharge. They'll think we're making a break for it."

"Kumar, get us moving," Mops ordered.

The *Pufferfish* surged away from their escort. Scattered

plasma and A-gun fire followed from the closest of the Krakau Planetary Defense ships. Energy crackled over the *Pufferfish*'s hull from a hit to the aft section. A lucky A-gun shot punctured one of the struts to weapons pod three.

"Faster would be better, Kumar."

"Working on it." He twisted the control sphere, and the ship jolted hard enough to send Grom toppling to the floor.

"Good work, but that was the easy part," said Mops. "Kumar, as soon as you're finished, move out of sight of the visual pickup. Grom, I want you at Kumar's station, but don't touch anything."

"This is insulting," Grom muttered. "I built those controls, remember?"

"And if you weren't still half-asleep and oozing all over my bridge, I *might* trust you to use them." Mops waited until everyone was in position. "From this point on, the bridge belongs to Azure and Grom. Everyone else is to stay out of sight and say nothing."

"Got it," said Wolf.

Mops glared, and Wolf had the decency to look abashed. "Azure, you're up. Wolf, hit the switch."

The bridge became silent as everyone waited for Azure to begin. Azure rested one tentacle next to the control sphere at the captain's station. "Supreme Assault Commander Heart of Glass, this is Azure. We have completed phase one of our mission. Our bioweapon spreads across Dobranok as we speak. The Krakau are dying. Squarm and I have seized control of the *Pufferfish* and are moving to implement phase two."

There was no response. Not that Mops had expected any. The Prodryans had begun to engage with the first wave of Krakau forces, and their leaders were busy overseeing the battle. They were likely confused as well, since there had never been a second phase to Azure's mission. Mops nodded at Azure to continue.

"Once the other Prodryans have weakened the Krakau

defenses, Captain Taka-lokitok-vi and his squadron of Nusu-ran mercenaries should come out of their A-ring jump behind Prodryan force two. Their ships are programmed to lock and fire automatically. The same holds true for the Quetzalus dreadnoughts you hired to destroy force three. The *Pufferfish* will engage force four. Dobranok and her resources will be yours alone, Supreme Assault Commander."

The viewscreen split to show a heavily modded Prodryan. "What are you talking about, Azure?" he shouted. "Your mission was to infect Dobranok!"

Most of the self-proclaimed Supreme Assault Commander's face was metal and glass, and his left antenna had been replaced by what looked like a small computer interface port. He wore matte-pink battle armor that nicely complemented the yellow of his wings.

"Yes, Supreme Assault Commander," Azure said eagerly. "The shuttle detonated shortly before your arrival, at which point Squarm and I began implementing the next part of your plan. Your reinforcements wait in stealth mode just outside the system, as ordered."

A second window appeared, this one showing a lavender-winged Prodryan with metal spikes protruding from her limbs. "What is this, Heart of Glass?"

"This creature lies," Heart of Glass protested. "She was to cleanse the planet for us, nothing more."

Mops pointed at Grom, giving them the cue to speak. Best to do it now and keep Heart of Glass off-balance. Grom slumped in annoyance, but moved forward to deliver their lines. "Sir, attack vectors have already been transmitted and acknowledged. It's too late to rescind the order."

"Switch to a direct line immediately," screamed Heart of Glass.

"Oh, my," said Azure. "Did I fail to secure this transmission? I'm sorry, sir. I'm not familiar with EMC communications protocols. Squarm, get to the communication console."

"Right away," Grom said, scooting toward that station. In a quieter voice, they muttered, "I will fix this. Me, Squarmildil-quirn. Because all Glacidae look alike. . . ."

Mops glared at Grom, and they fell silent.

A third Prodryan squeezed onto the screen, a male with gleaming artificial wings and weapon barrels mounted directly into his shoulders. "Warlord Heart Sting was right about you, Heart of Glass. Your cooperation with these other species has corrupted your soul. You would ally with them against your own kind?"

"Never," said Heart of Glass. "Sun Sailor, this is a trick. We must continue the attack. Within hours, our greatest enemy will fall, and we will *all* share in the rewards!"

"Your skill at lying has improved, sir," said Azure. "Your time among the humans was well-spent."

Mops blinked. That hadn't been part of the script, but Azure's improvisation worked beautifully. Heart of Glass' wings buzzed with fury. "Shut up, you gelatinous pustule!"

"Are we still transmitting in the open? My apologies. I didn't . . ." Azure shrank slightly, then raised her voice. "Attention, Prodryan attack forces. Heart of Glass is correct. This is all a misunderstanding. He certainly did not betray you, and there are absolutely no reinforcements on their way to destroy your forces. Please carry on with your attacks, keeping your attention focused on the Krakau ships and not on the completely safe and empty space behind you."

Doc highlighted one group of Prodryan ships on Mops' monocle. *"Sensors show this bunch turning away. I can't be certain, but if I had to guess, I'd say they're preparing for an A-ring jump."*

Mops gave a thumbs-up to the rest of the team.

"You will both die for this," Heart of Glass snarled, then turned slightly. "Sun Sailor, Blade of Bone, Planet-Slayer, don't let these creatures rob us of our victory."

"You mean *your* victory," said the Prodryan with the mechanical wings. "Heart Sting should have torn your wings from your body. If you survive, I'll hunt you down and do it myself!"

"Another group is turning—and there goes the third."

"What about Heart of Glass?" Mops whispered.

"Heart of Glass is an atypical example of his species, but from what I know of Prodryan culture, he'll likely choose death in battle over the shame of failure."

The Prodryans vanished from the screen. "Communications terminated," announced Wolf. "That was amazing!"

"An impressive performance," agreed Mops. "Thank you both."

"They're increasing speed. It looks like they're hoping an all-out charge will get a few of their ships through the Krakau forces."

Mops returned to the captain's chair to study the enemy's approach. "We're not done yet. Everyone to your stations. Monroe, power up the defensive grid and make sure missile countermeasures are online. Kumar, increase speed toward that fleet."

Kumar glanced over his shoulder at her. "Sir?"

"Heart of Glass isn't leaving this system alive. Our job now is to make certain he dies before he gets within range of Dobranok. And if the plasma beam that sends him to hell comes from the *Pufferfish*, so much the better."

"Two fighters have broken through the Krakau," Monroe shouted. On the viewscreen, green circles highlighted two approaching blips. "Incoming missiles."

"On it," said Wolf, hunching over her controller. They'd transferred missile countermeasures to Wolf so Monroe could focus on returning fire. One by one, the missiles blew up or veered off course.

"Good work," said Mops. The fighters peeled away from one another. Monroe focused the A-guns on the left fighter, letting the *Pufferfish* targeting system try to predict and intercept the ship's erratic path.

The display lit up with incoming plasma and A-gun fire as a third fighter slipped past the Krakau. *The Pufferfish*'s defensive grid absorbed the former, but the A-guns perforated the hull down on decks E through G. "Kumar, keep us moving. Monroe?"

"I'm trying, sir." The *Pufferfish*'s own plasma beams sent needles of light after all three fighters. "This would be a lot easier if either they'd hold still or we did."

"If we stop moving, they'll rip us apart," said Kumar.

Mops checked the damage assessment. "I want an A-ring powered up, just in case."

"We're not far enough out for a safe jump," Kumar protested.

The *Pufferfish* shuddered again. "Safe is relative. Program a short-range jump, just enough to get us out of the system."

"Sir, I have an idea!" Grom raced to the starboard backup station at the rear of the bridge and switched on another control sphere. "There's a combo move in *Galaxy Wars III* that's perfect for this scenario. Can you get us closer to one of those fighters?"

"This isn't a game," said Mops.

"The tactics and engineering are both sound."

"*This might be a good time to point out that Technician Grom never took anything beyond introductory battle tactics at university. And they barely passed.*"

Grom sent their plan to Mops' console. She pursed her lips. "Kumar, bring us about forty degrees to port, pitch plus-fifteen degrees. Grom, if you break my ship, I'm throwing you back in the brig."

"Understood." Grom curled around their control sphere. "This might be a little bumpy."

They veered abruptly to the left. A hazy cone of green light shot from the *Pufferfish* to envelop the port fighter. The ship jolted hard.

"Got them," Grom crowed. "Grav beam locked."

Alerts and warnings flashed as the *Pufferfish* strained to

hold together after snagging another ship at combat speeds. If the relative masses of the two ships hadn't been tilted so heavily in their favor, that maneuver would have torn the *Pufferfish* apart. As it was, they were showing structural damage to the beam generator housing, and the power drain was close to overloading the system.

"Thanks," said Monroe. Plasma beams impaled the trapped fighter, blowing it apart. The grav beams dragged the debris into a cone-shaped cloud, until Grom deactivated them. "Do you have enough power to rope the other one?"

"If Kumar can get us close enough, I'll try," said Grom.

Far ahead, Mops counted eight damaged or disabled ships from both sides drifting amidst the battle. Four others had been completely destroyed. The losses appeared to be evenly split between Prodryan and Krakau.

"How long until the rest of the Krakau get here?" Mops demanded.

"Roughly fifteen minutes."

Her monocle zoomed out, showing the other Krakau intercept forces. They'd waited until the rest of the Prodryan jumped out of the system before starting toward Heart of Glass' fleet.

The *Pufferfish* jerked hard enough to give Mops whiplash. Behind her, Grom groaned. "There goes the grav beam generator."

It had lasted long enough for Monroe to take out a second fighter, burning through its engine and leaving it spinning helplessly through space.

"Sir, I'm picking up multiple A-ring energy signatures," said Monroe.

Mops checked the screen. "Please tell me Heart of Glass' forces are retreating."

"I don't think so."

Even as she watched, a Prodryan fighter exploded, sending out a ring of energy that sliced through a Krakau cruiser. Three more fighters exploded in quick succession.

"The bastards are stealing our move," shouted Wolf.

The Krakau pulled back, trying to get out of range. Only one additional warship took damage in the next round of explosions. But the Krakau retreat created an opening. The remaining Prodryans accelerated toward the *Pufferfish* and the planet beyond.

"Monroe, open fire with everything we've got."

"They're not in range," Monroe warned.

"If they get in range, we're dead." Mops counted eighteen fighters and five larger ships. "Maybe you'll get a few lucky shots. Kumar, full reverse. Make them work to catch us, and give the Krakau time to close ranks and hit them from behind."

"The Prodryans are hailing us," said Wolf.

"Put them through. See if you can pinpoint which ship the signal's coming from."

Heart of Glass appeared on the viewscreen. Dark blood trickled from a crack on the side of his face.

"Supreme Assault Commander," Mops greeted him. "As a representative of the Krakau Alliance, I'd be happy to accept your unconditional surrender."

The Prodryan didn't appear amused. "I only wish I could allow you to live long enough to see Dobranok die."

Mops cocked her head. "You know Azure didn't really poison the planet, right?"

"I assumed as much." Heart of Glass wiped his face. "It makes no difference. If your name is remembered, human, it will be as one of the billions I destroyed this day."

The screen went dead. "Wolf, which ship is he transmitting from?"

"I'm not sure, but I think it's this one." One of the warships on the screen turned blue.

"Monroe, get ready to shoot everything we've got at that ship."

"They're powering up an A-ring," said Monroe. "I've got multiple missile launches, too. Way too many for us to stop.

They're trying to overwhelm us. Roughly two minutes to impact."

"Kumar, we need all the speed you can give us!" Mops frowned at the screen. "What the hell is he doing? They're not fleeing the system, and they're too far out to try that kamikaze stunt with the A-rings."

"It's not just one ship," said Monroe. "They're all prepping rings."

Mops studied the display, and her bones turned to ice. "Doc, if they jump from here, could they hit Dobranok?"

Kumar's face turned pale. Monroe swore.

Doc broadcast his answer to the bridge. *"Given the distance to Dobranok and the gravitational interference from the sun, the chances of any given ship accurately striking the planet are between one and two percent."*

"They have twenty-three ships," whispered Azure.

"Indeed. If they all jump, I estimate a one-in-three chance of at least one ship striking Dobranok."

"Monroe, keep shooting," snapped Mops. "Doc, what happens if they hit the planet going faster than light?"

"Theoretically, striking the atmosphere at that speed would fuse the atoms of the atmosphere with those of the ship. The resulting thermonuclear reaction could wipe out a small continent. The shockwave would ripple through the atmosphere, tearing it away. Depending on the size of the ship and the angle of impact, the oceans would either turn to steam, or else suffer tidal waves strong enough to crush anything in their path. The planet itself might survive, but it would be a burnt-out husk, incapable of supporting life."

"You have to stop them." Azure spun toward Mops. "I'm begging you, sir. Please."

Mops watched as Wolf's efforts disrupted another group of incoming missiles. It wasn't going to be enough. "Kumar, do you have that A-ring powered up?"

"We're going to run?" asked Kumar. Azure whistled in protest.

"From that asshole? No way in hell. Wolf, signal the Krakau. Tell them to break off pursuit. Kumar, deploy the ring with maximum diameter."

"Grom hasn't had time to program a course," Kumar warned.

"We don't need one. Kill the engines. Set the A-ring to full *deceleration*. Keep it powered up as long as possible." She watched the screen as the ship's microbeams maneuvered the A-ring into place directly in front of the bow. The ring expanded slowly until it was twice the diameter of the ship. At maximum size, it would generate only a fraction of its potential acceleration.

Mops wiped her hands on her uniform and watched the missiles. Now that their target had stopped trying to get away, they accelerated in a direct path toward the *Pufferfish*.

She counted down the seconds, watching the green sparks converge on her ship. If this didn't work, at least they'd be dead too quickly for her failure to register.

A-rings had two basic settings, as Puffy had explained in the tutorial, "One for speeding things up and one for slowing them down."

The *Pufferfish*'s rings were calibrated for the mass of a cruiser-class ship, with enough power to accelerate them to twenty light-years/hour, or to decelerate them at the end of their journey. And what was deceleration but acceleration in the opposite direction?

The bridge was silent. Even Grom and Azure appeared to be holding their breath as the first missile entered the A-ring and vanished. Energy that would have slowed an EMC cruiser instead hurled the tiny missile back along its path at speed too high for the *Pufferfish* to calculate or track.

More missiles disappeared, flung into deep space . . . until one struck a Prodryan ship. The potential explosive power of the missile was nothing compared to the energy released by the faster-than-light collision.

One moment Heart of Glass' forces were closing in. The next, an expanding ball of light blotted them from existence.

"Holy shit," whispered Wolf.

The A-ring shattered moments later. Shock waves shook the *Pufferfish*, adding to the list of alarms and damage reports.

Mops pried her fingers from her chair. She licked her dry lips and swallowed. "Wolf, send a message to Admiral Pachelbel. As politely and professionally as you can, please ask if they require any additional assistance from the EMC."

24

Twelve years ago:

"*Commander Scheherazade, the mid-term assessment results on the new batch of humans is in.*"

The Awakening and Orientation Officer for the Antarctic Medical Facility raised her head from the steaming pool. "How do they look, Seikilos?"

"*Minor pre-cure damage, but nothing debilitating. All eighteen passed basic physical and intellectual tests, and their EMC training is proceeding well. Several have demonstrated officer-level analytical and problem-solving skills.*"

Scheherazade sank back into the water. How anyone could survive, let alone thrive, in this cold, dry Earth air was beyond her. Even the feral humans avoided this continent. But that was the point. Better to restore and train these humans in a remote location where their animalistic cousins weren't constantly trying to eat everyone.

She touched the screen built into the wall of her steam pool, reviewing this group's scores. Seikilos was right about the officer potential. She tagged several for command training, and another for sniper work. One by one she added her notes, saving the most interesting for last. She hesitated a long time over that final name before making her decision.

"Commander?" The hesitant clicks and whistles of Seikilos' voice carried easily into the water. "The one you marked for hygiene and sanitation duty. Are you sure? She had the highest score in—"

"I like humans, but we both know how dangerous they are," said Scheherazade. "Officers need a degree of intelligence and independence. This one has too much of both."

"I . . . understand," said Seikilos, who clearly didn't.

"Trust me, technician. I've been in this job a long time. Put this human in the field, or worse yet, in command, and sure, she'll excel for a while. But in the long run, it could be very bad for the Alliance."

COOK HAD DONE A nice job repairing the damage to his restaurant. He'd also added a new sign to the door: NO BOMBS ALLOWED.

Mops scanned the customers on both sides of the restaurant. "Well?"

"I've identified Admiral Pachelbel." Doc highlighted a floating table on the Krakau side of the restaurant. *"I don't see any additional security, but if she doesn't have backup in here, she'll have a team waiting nearby. Probably monitoring the situation through her visor."*

"Miss Mops!" Cook hurried from the kitchen, his fuzzy arms outstretched. "I'm happy to see you alive, and I hope today's meal goes better than your last!"

"Me, too," said Mops. "I'm so sorry about what happened before. I'm meeting a . . . a friend. I promise this one won't try to blow me up." At least, not here in public.

Cook beamed. "I'll have a round of Tjikko nuts sent to your table."

"That's not necessary," Mops called, but Cook was already scurrying away. With a sigh, Mops waded down the ramp toward Admiral Pachelbel. The water warmed her legs, but her uniform kept it from penetrating. "How's everything looking outside?"

"All clear so far," Monroe reported over the comm. "If the Alliance is watching, they're keeping their distance. A pair of Prodryans started to go in, but changed their mind when they spotted Wolf loitering by the door."

"You think they're up to something?"

"I doubt it. Word in the towers is that the Prodryans here have been keeping their heads down since Dobranok. Heart of Glass' failure brought shame to the whole damn race."

"Kumar, keep our shuttle warmed up and ready to go, just in case."

"Yes, sir," said Kumar.

Mops nodded to herself. "*Pufferfish*, any sign of additional Alliance ships?"

After a brief delay, Grom responded, "Sensors haven't picked up any unusual traffic. Everything's fine here."

Azure cut in to say, "Everything is *not* fine. This Glacidae uses cheat codes for their fighter combat simulator. I scored a direct plasma strike to their primary engines!"

"It's not cheating," Grom argued. "My ship has optical displacement technology from a previous campaign—"

Mops closed the connection as she reached the admiral's table. She lowered herself onto the tangle of bars that served as a Krakau chair. Buoyancy kept it from being as uncomfortable as it could have been. "I'm a little surprised you agreed to meet with me, Admiral."

Pachelbel chewed a small crustacean as she looked Mops over. "I appreciate the aesthetic modifications you've made to your uniform."

"Thank you." Mops had eliminated the rank stripes and unit insignia for herself and her team. One sleeve retained the pufferfish icon for their ship, while the other showed a slowly rotating image of the Earth. "The infected members of my crew are sedated in a cargo container on docking bay level four, along with Squarm, the scientist who worked on the bioweapon."

"Squarm?"

"Squarmildilquirn. You'll find he's wanted for interplanetary drug smuggling, assault, and public lewdness."

"And the cure?"

Mops reached into a chest pocket and removed a metal vial. "It should be enough to analyze and duplicate. I've kept a sample on the *Pufferfish* as well, just in case."

"Thank you." Pachelbel stretched a tentacle toward Mops' head. "What is that?"

"A baseball hat. An old relic from Earth. It used to belong to a man named Floyd Westerman. I'm told the curved red line and stylized animal were the symbol of a human sports team called the Chicago Cubs." Mops trailed off as Cook arrived, balanced expertly on a small hover-raft, with a small sack of Tjikko nuts for Mops and a bowl of thick green soup for Pachelbel. "Can I bring you anything else?"

"We're fine," said Mops. "And she's paying for all of this."

Cook clicked his claws in appreciation and shifted his weight, sending the raft back toward the kitchen with only the smallest of ripples through the water.

As soon as he was gone, Mops leaned across the table. "Turns out there are a number of illegal Earth artifacts floating around, smuggled off-world by human recruits and bored Krakau. What I'd really like to find is an honest account of Earth history."

"Honest history?" Pachelbel dipped her head, and a series of bubbles marked her amusement. "That's as much an oxymoron as civil war."

"Maybe," Mops conceded. "But I imagine human accounts come closer to the truth than the stories we've been fed all these years. Particularly when it comes to the plague."

Pachelbel sighed. "I wasn't there, of course, but . . . what I've been told matches the information Azure gave you. A single Rokkau was sent along on that first contact mission. She attacked one of your planet's leaders. Her venom, combined with human efforts to nullify the toxin, resulted in the devolution of your people. That mission was almost entirely erased from our history, hidden from everyone save the highest-ranking officials."

"You could have stayed on Earth and tried to help us," said Mops.

"They . . . we . . . were afraid. Afraid of what we'd done. Afraid of the fallout back on Dobranok. I say this to explain, not to excuse."

"Where are the Krakau keeping the exiled Rokkau?"

"Until I received the alert from your ship, I believed the Rokkau were extinct," said Pachelbel. "Even then, I assumed this Azure was a fluke. One of the last survivors, or perhaps one of a small group of refugees. This story of a rogue prison floating through space, an ice planet with millions of Rokkau trapped within . . . I know nothing of any such place."

Mops picked up the tube containing Squarm's counter-agent and rolled it between her fingers. "I'm going to need more than that, Admiral."

"Lieutenant—Mops—have you considered what you will do next? You have a stolen ship, heavily damaged and severely undercrewed. The Alliance has offered a bounty for your capture. Where will you go?"

"You'll forgive me if I don't feel like discussing our plans with you, Admiral," Mops said dryly. "I think my team has managed pretty well so far. If I were you, I'd worry more about what happens when the rest of the Alliance learns the truth."

"I am worried," said Pachelbel. "More than you know. You should worry, too."

Mops cocked her head. "Is that a threat?"

"It's not intended as such. But consider your position. You have no real proof of your claims, save a being who could easily be dismissed as a deformed Krakau. Many believe you were working with the Prodryans."

Mops grabbed a Tjikko nut and crunched down in disgust. "The same Prodryans we chased off or atomized two weeks ago when we helped save Dobranok?"

"I never claimed their belief was rational," Pachelbel admitted. "If you pursue this course, it could destabilize the Alliance. The Krakau have kept peace among allied worlds for more than a hundred years. We've coordinated our defense against the Prodryans. Would you risk the security of the galaxy?"

"Security built on lies?" Mops snorted. "There's your oxymoron, Admiral. The Krakau Alliance was born from the technology of a banished race. That security you value so much? My people are on the front lines defending it. The same people you nearly wiped out. If the truth destroys the Alliance, maybe that's for the best. Maybe what grows from the ashes will be better."

"And maybe it won't." Pachelbel uncurled a tentacle across the table, dropping a centimeter-wide memory crystal beside Mops' bowl.

Mops didn't touch it. "What's this?"

"Instructions for a secure communications drop you can use to reach me, along with information on certain misrouted funds and other irregularities from the Alliance military budget. Ships whose mission logs are locked even to me. High-ranking HMC officials who issued a flurry of classified orders immediately following the fugitive alert on Azure. It's not much, but somewhere in here could be ... I believe humans call them 'crumbs of bread' to lead you to the Rokkau prison planet. If such a place exists."

"Why would you give it to me?"

"Because I've seen the kind of chaos you'll leave in your wake if I let you do this alone." Pachelbel dipped the tip of a tentacle into the soup, then brought the dripping limb to her mouth. "I believed I was one of the few Krakau to know the truth of our history, but if Azure is correct about this prison, I was simply fed an alternate lie. If I investigate these things overtly, I'll be stripped of my rank and locked away, branded a criminal and a traitor."

Mops snorted. "But since we're already traitors . . ."

"Exactly."

Mops picked up the mem crystal and rolled it between her thumb and forefinger. "We're going to need resources."

"I've been given a great deal of leeway to negotiate with you for the bioweapon cure."

A slow smile spread across Mops' face. "Doc, please transmit our wish list to the admiral's interface."

Mops settled into the captain's chair and turned to the backup station where Azure and Grom were working to analyze the memory crystal Admiral Pachelbel had given her. "What do you think?"

"Scanning software isn't finding any hidden programs," said Grom. "I want to run more checks, but it looks clean."

"You really think this Krakau wants to help you find my people?" asked Azure.

Mops shrugged. "She didn't try to arrest me. She didn't try to shoot our shuttle down when we left the station. Neither of the two EMC ships in-system have tried to follow us. So far, it looks like she's on our side."

Azure twitched the stump of her missing tentacle. "I don't trust her."

"I didn't say I did either." Nor did she trust Azure, for that matter, but—so far—the Rokkau had done what she could to make herself helpful. And their chances of finding the other Rokkau would be significantly better with her help.

The pop of gum pulled her attention to the front of the bridge. "What's our tactical situation, Monroe?"

"Not great," he said. "Plasma beams are still functional on two weapons pods. A-guns are only running on one. But I talked to that Tjikko, Theta, like you ordered. He gave me the name of a shipyard that might be willing to help. They'd strip two of our weapons pods for parts and keep those as payment for fixing the third. We'd be down to thirty-three percent of our standard armament, but we'd have a fully loaded and functional pod. They could probably repair the other damage we've collected, too."

"Send the coordinates to Kumar, so he and Grom can prepare for the A-ring jump." Mops cleared her throat. "Kumar?"

Kumar jumped. "Sorry, sir. I was showing Vera how navigation works."

Mops smiled at the newest member of the *Pufferfish* crew. "What do you think of the ship, Vera? This is your last chance to change your mind."

Vera Rubin shook her head. "I'm done with Coacalos Station."

It would be several more weeks before her body fully healed from the damage she'd suffered during the battle on the station. She'd lost her left eye and two fingers from her left hand, and her ribs and leg were restrained in healing braces. But she hadn't hesitated when Kumar offered her the chance to join the *Pufferfish*.

Mops had made it clear that next time, he was to ask her first, but given what Vera had done for them, she could hardly say no. Vera might not be the most creative thinker, but she had a good memory, and did well with routine tasks. "Kumar, why don't you take Vera through our rather convoluted process for plotting an A-ring jump."

"Yes, sir!"

A crew of seven for an entire cruiser presented plenty of other problems. She'd sealed off and shut down roughly three-quarters of the ship, but everyone would be working long shifts for the foreseeable future. Pachelbel had provided access codes to the primary computers, which should allow a skilled programmer to automate more of the ship's functions. Assuming they could find a reliable programmer to do it.

Pachelbel had also provided funds to cover refueling, and

was looking into a source to replace the ship's A-rings. Rings large enough for the *Pufferfish* were generally only manufactured at Alliance-controlled military facilities. The one bright spot was their food supply. With such a drastically reduced crew, they had enough nutrition to last months.

"The *EMCS Box Jellyfish* is leaving Coacalos Station," said Wolf. "We're receiving a tight-beam signal. Battle Captain Steve Irwin instructs us to power down and surrender immediately, by order of IMC Fleet Admiral Belle-Bonne Sage."

"Irwin got promoted? Good for her." Mops checked her console. "How long until they're close enough to start shooting?"

"Four hours," said Monroe.

"Wolf, patch me through." Mops waited for Wolf's nod. "The *Pufferfish* sends its regards to Captain Irwin and the crew of the *EMCS Box Jellyfish*. I'm afraid we'll have to decline the Fleet Admiral's invitation for the time being. We have a lot of work ahead of us."

Her expression hardened. "But tell Sage not to worry. She'll be hearing from us again soon. We might not be the best soldiers in the EMC, but if there's one thing we know, it's how to clean up other people's messes."

Mops glanced around the bridge. If Wolf grinned any harder, her teeth would pop out. Monroe smiled as well, adding a small salute. Kumar and Vera were huddled together, their shoulders touching. Azure stood quietly, her body tilted in a posture Mops recognized as calm and determined. Grom looked up from their control sphere and gave an exaggerated nod.

"Adamopoulos out."

Also by Cathleen Schine

Fin & Lady

The Three Weissmanns of Westport

The New Yorkers

She Is Me

The Evolution of Jane

The Love Letter

Rameau's Niece

To the Birdhouse

Alice in Bed

They May Not Mean To, But They Do

They May Not Mean To, But They Do

Cathleen Schine

Sarah Crichton Books Farrar, Straus and Giroux New York

Sarah Crichton Books
Farrar, Straus and Giroux
18 West 18th Street, New York 10011

Grateful acknowledgment is made for permission to reprint lines from
"This Be The Verse" from *The Complete Poems of Philip Larkin* by Philip Larkin,
edited by Archie Burnett. Copyright © 2012 by The Estate of Philip Larkin.
Reprinted by permission of Farrar, Straus and Giroux, LLC.

Library of Congress Cataloging-in-Publication Data
Names: Schine, Cathleen, author.
Title: They may not mean to, but they do : a novel / Cathleen Schine.
Description: First edition. | New York : Sarah Crichton Books/Farrar,
    Straus and Giroux, 2016.
Identifiers: LCCN 2015036418 | ISBN 9780374280130 (hardcover)
    | ISBN 9780374712204 (ebook)
Subjects: LCSH: Families—Fiction. | Domestic fiction. | BISAC: FICTION /
    Literary. | FICTION / Contemporary Women. | FICTION / Family Life.
Classification: LCC PS3569.C497 T46 2016 | DDC 813/.54—dc23
LC record available at http://lccn.loc.gov/2015036418

Designed by Abby Kagan

Our books may be purchased in bulk for promotional, educational, or business use.
Please contact your local bookseller or the Macmillan Corporate and Premium
Sales Department at 1-800-221-7945, extension 5442, or by e-mail at
MacmillanSpecialMarkets@macmillan.com.

www.fsgbooks.com
www.twitter.com/fsgbooks • www.facebook.com/fsgbooks

1 3 5 7 9 10 8 6 4 2

To my mother,
from whom and to whom
everything, always

They fuck you up, your mum and dad.
They may not mean to, but they do.

—from Philip Larkin,
"This Be The Verse"

They May Not Mean To, But They Do

Molly Bergman moved to California, and it broke her mother's heart. There are daughters who spend their lives trying to escape their mothers, who move to their particular California the minute they're able to, who never stop moving to California. Molly was decidedly not one of those daughters. It was a painful move even before her parents got, so suddenly, so old.

Molly's mother was named Joy, and people said, Oh, they broke the mold when they made that one. People who loved her said it, people who did not love her said it, too, for the same reason. They found Joy disconcerting, and they were right. She was so intimate and so remote, as remote as a faraway, nameless planet sometimes; sometimes soft and sympathetic. She was talkative, yet she heard everything you said or thought you might say. She was wise and she was deep, intuitive, the kind of person to whom people confided their darkest secrets; she was scatterbrained and easily distractible and often forgot people's darkest secrets, which, she always said, was just as well.

She seemed to Molly, growing up, to be the busiest and most

important mother in New York City. Joy's work was her vocation, that's what Joy said when she was happy. When she was frustrated and tired, she said it was a velvet coffin without the velvet.

She was also beautiful, radiantly beautiful. Like a doe, fragile and supple and quick. She was blond, but her eyes were as brown as a doe's. When she smiled, everyone around her smiled, and she smiled a great deal, though it was often from abstraction rather than any particular moment of happiness. She loved New York because, she liked to say, she fit in with all the misfits.

Molly and her brother, Daniel, began their lives with Joy and their father, Aaron, in a two-bedroom apartment with dinette on the West Side of Manhattan, the dinette converted into a third bedroom. Their neighbors were immigrants from Eastern Europe, émigrés from Brooklyn, teachers and violinists and opera singers. You could hear the opera singers as you walked down Broadway, arias amid the car horns. There were mom-and-pop dress shops and dairy restaurants and bakeries, and Molly remembered the square rooms, the high ceilings, the shutters that folded in on themselves, the deep windowsills on which she used to sit and look out at the street. But when Molly was eight and her brother six, their father inherited his family's manufacturing business, and the Bergmans left West Eighty-ninth Street. Aaron said the West Side was becoming seedy.

There were fewer Eastern European immigrants and Brooklyn escapees on Park Avenue, no dairy restaurants, more gentiles. It was a quiet, civilized neighborhood, at least until late afternoon, when the private schools let out. Molly and Daniel still went to their progressive private school on the West Side, but when Molly got off the bus, she could already hear the commotion of the East Side children at the corner store. She always waited for them to leave the store before buying her own candy and secretly envied them their noisy cabal and, even more secretly, their school uniforms.

"Across the park is as far as we go," Joy declared. "No farther, Aaron."

Daniel did go a bit farther when he grew up. He and his wife, Coco, and their two little girls lived on the Lower East Side. That was inexplicable to Joy and Aaron, moving to the tenements their grandparents had left behind. Inexplicable, yes, but *accessible by subway*, Joy said to Molly. The Bergmans were New Yorkers, she said, had always been New Yorkers. This was a fact, in a way that Molly's move to Los Angeles could never be.

Each time Molly left New York after a visit, Joy felt the air go out of the city.

"You're too attached," one of her friends said. "My daughter lives in Australia."

Joy shuddered. A daughter in Australia might as well be a dead daughter. Divorce was a terrible thing, and she was sorry Molly had given up a perfectly reasonable husband so she could be a lesbian in California. It was peculiar, having a lesbian daughter, though plenty of her friends did, too, it turned out. But many things were peculiar in this world, and Joy had overcome her discomfort with Freddie. She even called her "my daughter-in-law" now. Freddie was a lot of fun, warm, kind, gainfully employed, and low-maintenance, everything a mother-in-law could ask for. Joy did not blame her for being a woman, or tried not to. Molly was happy, Joy could see that, and it warmed her heart.

But what good is a warmed heart if it is also broken? Joy's heart was broken. By California.

"California"—even the name had become ugly to Joy, like "Lee Harvey Oswald" or "Sirhan Sirhan."

Joy's parents had moved several times during the Depression, first to places where someone could take them in, then to places where they took others in. Each move was a shock to Joy, an almost physical jolt. So many people left behind—shopkeepers, neighbors, the policeman on the corner, the ladies sitting on their stoops. They were what made a place a home. There were so many things one had to give up in this world. Why would you choose to give up your home? For California?

Perhaps she should move to California, too. Aaron might not know the difference.

"Would you like to move to California, Aaron?"

"*Come if you dare, our trumpets sound,*" he sang. "*Come if you dare, the foes rebound . . .*"

He could not tell you what day it was, but he remembered his Purcell.

It was Sunday and she had ordered him a dinner of French toast from the coffee shop. New York was good for the elderly in that way, the deliveries. She had come to include Aaron in the category of "the elderly," she realized with a pang. And where does that leave me, she wondered vaguely. At any rate, it was too difficult sometimes to herd Aaron and his walker out of the apartment and down the street to the coffee shop. She could have made French toast, she supposed. If there had been eggs. Or bread. If she still cooked.

"Isn't there a joke, we could have ham and eggs if we had *ham . . .*"

". . . and we had *eggs!*"

They laughed, repeated it, "We could have ham and eggs . . ."

Aaron took a bite of French toast and made a face.

"You love French toast, Aaron, so stop it."

"Do I?"

He was hunched over the dining-room table. There was a bath mat on the seat of his chair as well as a blue chux pad. Joy leaned over and straightened them.

"You going to work today?" he said.

"No, dear, it's Sunday."

"Oh yeah?"

He took a bite of French toast and made another sour face.

"Stop that," she said. "Anyway, you need a haircut."

"You going to work today?" he said.

Sometimes Joy thought he was doing it on purpose. "No, not today. Today is Sunday."

"Oh yeah? What is this, anyway?" he said, poking at the French toast.

"Your dinner."

"I'm not hungry."

Joy grabbed his plate and brought it to the kitchen and scraped the French toast into the garbage.

"Joy! Joy!"

She stuck her head back into the dining room.

"You going to work today?" he asked.

"If you ask me that one more time, I'm putting a bag over your head," she said mildly.

Aaron brought his face down to the teacup and took a sip, then looked fondly at his wife. He pointed to the cup of almost colorless liquid. "Join me, sweetheart?"

He began to sing in his once clear voice, now heavy and hoarse. *"Tea for two, me for you . . ."*

He sang pleasantly to himself while Joy fetched herself a cup of tea, and they sat looking out at the traffic's red brake lights, something they'd both always found festive as the evening drew in.

2

Molly had been a daddy's girl when she was very young. Her father was the only father she knew who had a beard, and the beard, a neatly combed beard that came almost to a point, was her pride and joy. He would carry her inside his coat, against his chest, like a kangaroo, and she would snuggle her face against his, against that extraordinary beard. Her father and his beard were so obviously superior to other fathers with their flabby pink cheeks. Her father was superior in height, as well. He was so tall that she and Daniel used him as a unit of measurement. How many Daddies high was that tree in the park? What about the elephants at the Museum of Natural History? It was Aaron who read to them when they were little. Push-me-pull-yous and the cat's meat man; bump, bump, bump down the stairs—books that had been his, books he wished his father had read to him. He bundled up the children and led them to the roof to look at the constellations. He took them out to the park to climb the rocks and along the river to the boat basin to play pirates and launch paper boats that tipped and sank while they sang "Blow the Man Down." It was Aaron who encouraged them, egged them on, when they begged for a dog, Aaron who went to the animal shelter with them to get a cat when Joy had expressly forbidden it. Aaron's father had failed him when he was a child, too busy steering the business out of the Depression. Aaron would never do that to his children, he told Joy. True to his word, she would say later: it was the business he failed.

Aaron and Joy were so different from each other that Molly and Daniel had been able to recognize the distance even as young children, Aaron sentimental and unreliable and brimming with love and obvious charm, a man who made you feel you did not have to work too hard because good things were coming to you, from somewhere; Joy distracted, forgetful, thoughtful, brimming with love, too, and oddly inspiring, causing Molly and Daniel to want to work their hardest because working hard seemed such fun. Molly wasn't sure why she compared them to each other like that, as if she had to make a choice, as if she could make a choice, because different as they were, there was no choice between them, no space between them. They were as one. They held hands when they walked down the street, they fed each other tidbits like lovebirds. It was embarrassing for the children, having such lovey-dovey parents. And reassuring. Like the trumpeters and singers in the Bible, they were as one.

3

You'd better come home," Joy said to Molly on the phone. "Daddy's on the floor."

"He fell?" Molly tried to calm herself. "Is he okay? Did you call 911?"

"He slid out of his chair. I never should have gotten it in leather. I gave him a cracker."

"Mom!"

"The handyman's coming in a minute. He'll get Daddy up. Never a dull moment, right, Aaron?"

The phone was handed to Aaron. "Never a dull moment."

"Daddy, are you all right?"

"Your mother gave me a cracker."

"I'll be home soon," Molly said. She repeated it when her mother got back on the phone. "I'll be home soon, Mom. I arranged an extra week off in November."

"November?" A pause. "Oh." Then, "Wonderful, Molly! And how are your students this semester?"

Molly heard the strain in her mother's voice and hurried through a rundown of some of the more interesting students. "Anyway, nothing to write home about."

"Daddy's having a hard time, Molly. He gets confused sometimes."

"I know. But he does have dementia."

"Don't be disrespectful."

Joy didn't like the word "dementia." "Alzheimer's" was worse.

"Sorry," Molly said. "I just meant, you know, it's natural that he'd be confused and forget things."

"Well, he doesn't like it. He doesn't like it one bit. And he doesn't admit it. Which is tiring for me, I can tell you."

"Maybe——"

"We can't afford it."

"Well, what about——"

"Absolutely not."

"Not a *home*, exactly——"

"He has a home," Joy said. "His home is here."

Molly poured herself two fingers of bourbon, just as her father had taught her. No bourbon for him these days, just Ensure, many fingers of Ensure.

"I should be home," she said to Freddie. "I'm a horrible daughter. I might as well shoot myself."

Freddie thought, You are home, Molly.

"How many times can the doorman scrape him off the floor? At least she tips them at Christmas. I really have to go back. This is . . . it's . . ."

"What about your brother?"

"What *about* my brother?"

Now they would have a fight.

"I don't want to have a fight," Freddie said.

"Then don't mention my brother."

"Ever?"

"See? You *do* want to have a fight."

She went out to the garden, and Freddie followed. It was six o'clock and still hot, which was unusual where they lived, near the beach on the west side of Los Angeles. It had been an unusually hot summer, though. Molly brushed miniature pink petals off the chaise before sitting.

"Autumn leaves," she said, examining one blossom on the tip of her finger. She smiled. "What a place we live in, what an amazing place." She patted the cushion, motioned Freddie to sit beside her. "My brother is perfect," she said.

Freddie laughed. Molly's brother was off-limits. Absolutely, completely, utterly off-limits. She knew that. It was like criticizing Stalin in Moscow in 1939. Except her brother wasn't Stalin. More like a Dostoevsky innocent.

Molly's entire family, in fact, was off-limits. They were like a cult, one that did not accept disciples or converts. They had been through a lot as a family, it had drawn them together, but what family hadn't been through a lot? Well, every family has its myth, she supposed. The myth Freddie's family told itself was one of freedom. Her sisters and brothers were scattered across the globe, all of them—with the exception of Freddie—too independent and too far away to notice that their father wrecked the car three times in six months, or at least too far away (one hoped not too independent) to do anything about it.

The Bergmans, on the other hand, were a clan, tight knit and suspicious of strangers. They were tribal and closed, bound by blood. They were one, the world the other. Freddie was used to them now, used to their insular ferocity. She didn't often make the mistake of even implicit disapproval. There were worse things than loyalty and family love in this world. Sometimes she envied Molly her certainty, the way the atheist sometimes envies the believer.

"I know Daniel works very hard," she said. "I know he's incredibly busy. I love your brother, I think he's wonderful to your parents, and to us. I didn't mean anything, Molly. Really."

She did mean something, that Daniel was a son not a daughter, and they both knew it, but it wasn't his fault, and they both knew that, too.

"He can't be there every second," Molly said.

But neither could Molly, even if she was the daughter, Freddie thought, and the unspoken words hung between them.

"I could change my ticket, go to New York a week early. I could Skype my classes, right? I have to keep an eye on those two crazy old people. Check on their medications, clear up their bills, talk to the doctors, hire someone to come in, something. I have to do something."

"They won't let you hire anyone."

"I know."

"Maybe it's really time to start thinking about—"

"I'm one hundred percent sure you're not going to say what you're about to say, because no one is sending my father anywhere, okay? He would hate it. He'd be so confused. So please don't even mention it."

"Okay."

"Anyway, I already tried talking to Mom about it."

Freddie laughed again.

"She said he had a home."

"I wonder," Freddie said, "what would happen if they called them 'nursing hotels,' instead of 'nursing homes,' if people would be more receptive."

"You'd still get infections."

"Like a cruise ship."

Now and then Freddie wished someone would send her to a Home. Assisted Living—couldn't everyone use a little assistance in living? Three meals a day—nice comfort food, too. And a room of your own. You would be retired, of course, so you could read novels

13

all day long without feeling guilty, assuming you could still see through the inoperable cataracts you might, at that age, have developed. Really, if people were sent to old-age homes at a younger age, they would get so much more out of them.

Freddie had already moved her own father into three different assisted-living facilities. The first time, he went to the Motion Picture Home in the Valley, an inviting-looking place with its gardens and neat paths and scattered terraces and benches, though no one could walk on its neat paths or sit on its benches or gaze at the fat roses from the terrace. It was simply too hot, it was always much too hot. Her father had been lucky to get in, though, hot or not—there was always a long waiting list. He was an actor, Duncan Hughes—a minor actor you might see in a party scene of a romantic comedy with Doris Day and Rock Hudson, lifting his martini glass above people's heads as he squeezed through the crowd and made a few humorous comments to the stars. He had been dapper and not quite dashing when he was young. Now his face showed the good life he had attempted to live. Decades of professional disappointment, as well as his attempts to comfort himself in that disappointment, had left their mark on his florid drinker's face.

Duncan had always attributed failure to bad luck. He was a believer in luck and had never reconciled himself to not having any. But at last, Freddie thought, he had hit the jackpot, not one he had expected, certainly not one he had dreamed of, but a jackpot nonetheless: the Motion Picture Home.

Duncan's memory had started to go even earlier. He had managed to sign with a new agent, however, a chatty man who operated out of a disreputable-looking office in a strip mall. It wasn't as if Duncan Hughes would get any parts, Freddie knew that. He wouldn't be able to remember his cues, much less his lines. But having an agent meant he could still hope for roles, which provided some continuity for him, as hoping for roles, Freddie thought uncharitably, had always been a dominant part of his life. And perhaps having an agent might keep her father sitting safely by the phone rather than driving all over town to open auditions. When he drove to auditions these days, he tended to total the car. The bottle of rye he kept on the passenger seat didn't help.

So on the day, a year ago, when Freddie got a call from her father asking if she could drive him to the airport, her first reaction had been relief—her father had finally agreed that he shouldn't drive! He was asking for help! He was reaching out! But then the rest of the request hit her.

"The airport? Why are you going to the airport, Dad?"

"To catch a plane, obviously."

"Where is the plane going?"

"It's going to Sweden, obviously."

"That's not obvious to me, Dad. Why is it going to Sweden?"

"That's where the commercial is being shot."

Freddie was devastated. Her father was having hallucinations, she would have to call his neurologist, the Aricept was clearly not helping. She called his agent first, just to ask if he knew of anything that could have triggered the hallucination.

"Well," the agent said, "I guess the fact that your father's been hired to do a commercial and is flying to Sweden—that could have done it." He chuckled at his joke. "It's legit, Miss Hughes. I just got the contract."

She tried to talk her father out of it, as she had tried to talk him out of driving. She tried to enlist the aid of his doctor, as she had tried to enlist the aid of his doctor in convincing him to give up driving. But she knew he was even less likely to give up a role than he was his car. He had been waiting a long time for a role. She remembered him waiting for roles through her entire childhood. She remembered the change of atmosphere in the house when he got a part, the relief, the temporary dispersion of clouds of disappointment and failure. Actors do not give up parts. She knew that.

She drove him to LAX, parked, and walked him inside to make sure he found the group. She imagined them all lined up, holding on to a bright yellow rope, the way the preschool children did on the sidewalk in New York. But the director and crew just stood in a loose bunch, most of them wearing safari jackets and baseball caps. Her father kissed her goodbye and made straight for an attractive young woman in the group who seemed to know him.

"Hello, handsome," she said, and her father, unable to help himself, gave his practiced half-smile and preened with pleasure.

"You will look after him, won't you?" Freddie asked the director, who did not seem to think it irregular to have hired someone showing clear signs of senility. But why would he? He was a man who thought it reasonable to cast a commercial in L.A. and fly everyone thousands of miles to shoot it in Sweden in English to then be dubbed into Swedish.

"Don't worry," the director said.

Her father called her that night from Chicago, where they were changing planes.

"Pretty soon you'll be in Sweden, Dad."

"*Sweden?*"

It was that trip that shocked Freddie into action. By the time he came home, three days later, a little vague about having gone at all, she had called the Motion Picture Home so many times and spoken to so many people that when she discovered a room had suddenly opened up there, she was sure it was because she had annoyed the director of the facility to such an extent that the director had taken it out on an employee who had taken it out on a patient who had consequently died and vacated a room.

It took only five months for the Motion Picture Home to realize it had made a terrible mistake.

"We are concerned about STDs," the director had said.

Duncan was now on assisted-living place number three.

"The social worker called again today," Freddie told Molly.

"What did old Duncan do today? Pinch the nutritionist?"

Freddie shrugged. "They decided to cut back his wine at dinner."

"They should just water it. Would he know?"

"That's what I told them. But the social worker thought that would be dishonest. Dishonest! So she had a talk with him, and of course he objected. He demanded to see a lawyer. He threatened to sue. I think this place may kick him out soon, too."

Molly held her drink out to Freddie. "Here. It's neat. The social worker has no jurisdiction in this house."

Freddie said, "I want to be cremated, Molly."

"I know, honey."

"No, I mean now."

"I know, honey."

Freddie said, "Let's go to the beach and watch the sun set instead."

It was a beautiful sunset, the brilliant red streaks of sky fading to gentle mauve. There was a full moon hanging over the parking lot, plump and orange. The wind blew and there was no one on the pier, just a few surfers below.

"We're so lucky to live here," Molly said as they walked back to the parking lot. She was radiant in the blinking light from a bar, her cheeks glowing red, then green, and Freddie had to agree.

—— 4 ——

They had been sorority sisters, and they were still friends—Daphne, Eileen, Natalie, and Joy. Daphne got on Natalie's nerves; Eileen got on Daphne's nerves; Natalie, who was bossy, particularly about her politics, which were of the radical right, got on everyone's nerves; but all three were extremely close to Joy, which had kept the group intact through all the decades and divorces. Every few months they would get together for a girls' lunch.

"I'm not happy about this old-age business," Joy said.

"I refuse to feel old," Daphne said. She slapped the table. "*Je refuse.*"

The silverware and coffee cups rattled, and Joy marveled at Daphne, not a bit different from the day they met, sleek, beautiful, noisy, every auburn hair in place. Natalie was, as she had been since college, wearing chic, expensive bohemian clothes, her hair cut in the same bohemian bob with bangs. Eileen had been less glamorous than the others, but she had grown into her looks as she got older, looking somber but dignified these days. They all still had their marbles, though only two still had their husbands. But pretty good for a bunch of old bags, Joy thought.

"We've been friends for sixty-five years."

"Our friendship could get Medicare," Eileen said.

Natalie began to explain how Obamacare was ruining America.

"How's the new great-grandchild?" Joy interjected, offspring being a successful diversion for any of the girls. Though she was asking Natalie, Daphne immediately began digging around in her bag, probably for her iThing with her own great-grandchild baby pictures on it.

"They want to name her 'Quiet,'" said Natalie.

"Convenient," Eileen said. "They can call her and discipline her at the same time."

"Mine is two years old next week," Daphne added, holding up a screen with a picture of a little girl with an ice-cream-smeared mouth.

"'Quiet'?" Joy was saying. "Why don't they just name her 'No'?"

They started laughing and couldn't stop. They laughed until tears rolled down their faces.

"Oh, that felt good," Joy said.

All around them well-turned-out young women picked at their salads, preserving their waistlines, as women of Joy's generation used to call that mealtime behavior. Joy looked at them fondly, then slathered butter on a piece of bread, damn the torpedoes. She had no gallbladder, the surgeon had taken it out when he took out the colon cancer, "the blue-plate special," he'd called it, and never mind her waistline, she was not supposed to eat fat with no gallbladder. She sipped her espresso. That was verboten, too, atrial fibrillation. Delicious, though. It did not do to ignore the delicious.

"I love food," she said.

The tablecloths were pink and pressed. The napkins were large.

"I love napery," she said.

19

"Now, Joy," Daphne said, suddenly serious, "what are we going to do about Aaron?"

"I think he's dying," Joy said, and she began to cry softly.

Daphne put her hand on Joy's, which was an enormous gesture of support, Joy knew. Daphne did not like touching people.

"Nonsense," Natalie said.

"What do the doctors say?" Eileen asked.

Joy shrugged, and they waited for her to pull herself together and blow her nose.

"You have to take care of yourself, too, you know," Natalie said. "Even nurses have shifts."

"That's what my children say. They say I'm grandiose, taking care of Aaron myself."

"Children. What do they know?" said Daphne. "They think they know everything. But just wait."

Joy smiled. "They are so bossy, aren't they? I do miss Molly ordering me around, though." The smile disappeared. "Now that she's in California."

"What about Daniel?"

"Daniel is wonderful, but . . ."

They all nodded. Daniel was not a daughter.

"Anyway, I'm fine."

"Isn't there some sort of adult day care Aaron could go to?" Daphne was saying.

"No, god, no, he would hate that. He gets so disoriented. Then he gets frightened. Then he gets angry. He would hate it. What's he going to do? Sit in a drum circle? Make paper flowers?"

"What does he do at home?"

"Watch NY1. And eat. It's a wonder he doesn't weigh five hundred pounds. And a lot of time is taken up with, you know, showers and getting dressed and creams and applications of . . . things. I won't go into it. But trust me, a day goes by. And on the days I'm at work, who knows what could happen? I come home at lunch to check on him and I never know what I'll find, don't ask, and then, when I come back again at the end of the day . . ."

She went to the ladies' room. She put her bags down on a pretty little lavender table, shed a few more tears, washed her face, and sat gripping the arms of the lavender chintz chair, feeling faint. The doctor said these dizzy spells were nothing to worry about as long as she didn't fall. But what if she did fall? What was to stop her from falling? She could very easily have fallen *just now* . . .

"I know you all probably think he should go to a place," she said to the girls when she got back to the table, "but he would be miserable. He needs landmarks, needs familiar things, needs his schedule."

"But what about what you need?" they said.

"I'd be miserable, too. Visiting a nursing home? Every day? I'm exhausted just thinking about it. And they're not very clean, you know. Full of infection." There was something else, too, something no one seemed to realize: if Aaron went into a nursing home, he would be *gone*. "What about what you need"—Molly and Daniel asked her the same thing. But what she needed was so obvious. She needed Aaron.

"You're a saint," Daphne said.

It was not a compliment.

"One of those insane, self-destructive saints," Natalie added.

The kind who wander around in masochistic determination until they contract an incurable disease or are roasted on a fire or skinned alive, they all agreed.

"Joy, sweetie, at the very least you need to hire someone. *Hire* a saint," Natalie added.

When she got home, she noticed how gray Aaron looked, his hair, his beard, his face, and his hooded sweatshirt. He was not a man who was meant to be gray. Some men are, but Aaron ought to have been ruddy. He never had been, but he ought to have been. That's what Joy thought.

"You have to get some fresh air," she said.

He waved an enormous hand at her, as if he were swatting a fly.

"You'll get too stiff, sitting around all day."

He waved her words away again.

"Do you hear me? Where are your hearing aids?"

"WHAT?"

"Where are your hearing aids?" Joy repeated loudly.

"What are you talking about?" Aaron said. "Hearing aids!" He shook his head at her folly.

"I'm going to kill you, Aaron," she said.

"WHAT?"

"I'm going to kill you, I said!"

Aaron smiled. "So you say." He took her hand and kissed it.

" '*Joyful, Joyful, we adore thee,*' " he sang as she helped him up and over to the walker. He often called her Joyful.

"Well," she said.

" '*Hearts unfold like flowers before thee.*' "

Sometimes the songs were hymns, sometimes bits of British vaudeville from the last century, but mostly Baroque, mostly Purcell. The lyrics still came warbling out, even when he could not remember what the conversation was about, perhaps more so when he couldn't remember, couldn't keep up. Aaron had wanted to be a singer, a classical singer, but he'd gone directly into the family business instead. The Depression did that to people, made them think straight. Or warped them into shape, that was more the case with Aaron. It had taken Joy many years to understand that.

When they got outside, Aaron leaned heavily on his walker. It had wheels, which was a help. A shiny red walker with wheels. He called it his little red wagon.

"Lift up the front wheels," she said.

"Get away. I know what I'm doing."

"Tilt it."

"I'm tilting, I'm tilting. It's not moving. It's broken."

Joy took his arm. "Lean on me." She tilted the walker and got the wheels on the curb. "It's like a shopping cart."

They continued down the street toward Central Park. She could see the trees, still leafy and colorful. It had been a warm autumn. "Aren't they beautiful?" she said.

Aaron was breathing heavily. He was not singing. He was not calling her Joyful. He was not even answering her.

"This is ridiculous" was all he said, muttering it to himself.

She slowed her gait to match his, an excruciating shuffle. "Come on, come on," she said.

But he had stopped completely now and looked around him helplessly. "Where are we going, anyway?"

"To the park. You love the park."

"I hate the park. I'm going home."

"You love the park. I brought your camera."

"I don't know what you're talking about. Where are we going, anyway?"

They ended up stopping at the little park in the middle of Park Avenue at Ninety-sixth Street.

"You can sit here and rest," Joy said.

Aaron's chin immediately dropped to his chest.

"Are you asleep?" she said. "Or dead?"

"Which would you prefer?" he asked, his eyes still closed.

"I really wanted to go to Central Park."

Aaron opened his eyes and lifted his head. "Why?"

"Why? Because it's a beautiful day."

They sat for a few minutes silently.

"Pretty flowers," Aaron said, pointing a shaky hand at some late roses. "Beautiful, beautiful. Right here in the city."

Joy choked up a little. Because that was Aaron, her Aaron, the real Aaron. "Beautiful," she said.

"I should take a picture."

She handed him the little camera, and he fumbled with it for a minute, then said, "It's broken," and almost threw it back at her.

Joy put it in her tote bag. She had three tote bags, different sizes and different patterns. They hung on the handles of Aaron's red walker, two on the left, one on the right. She unhooked one of the bags on the left and stuffed it into the one on the right. "That's better."

"What have you got in there, Joyful?" Aaron said.

"I don't even know. But if I leave one bag home, it's always the one that has something I need."

He took her hand and held it. He stared off in the soft, blank way he sometimes had these days. His body sagged. The hand that held hers loosened and came to rest, like a large pale leaf, on his lap.

While he slept, Joy, too, closed her eyes. The afternoon sun was warm and comforting on her face. Sunlight was full of vitamin D. And cancer—that, too. Vitamin D, cancer . . . how to choose? She should have worn a hat. But how could a person walk around New York City in October in a sun hat? She refused to become an eccentric old lady padding around in bedroom slippers and a floppy hat. She pulled a thermos out of one of her bags, then another thermos. She shook Aaron awake. "Would you like a little Cream of Wheat?" she asked him. "I have an extra."

5

Daniel emerged from the subway and smelled the overripe fruit from the fruit stand. It would be just a quick visit to his parents, he had to go to a school assembly, he could not remember what sort, a concert, a play, a reading of the "books" the children had written. That was the most surprising thing about the school Cora and Ruby went to, the number of artistic events held there despite the absence of a budget for the arts. All those underemployed artistic mothers and fathers filling in the gaps. He bought some strawberries from the vendor for his parents and a banana for himself, which he ate as he walked to their building.

"For me?" his mother said at the door, taking the banana peel. "You shouldn't have."

He waited for the story of the time he had absentmindedly put a banana peel in the medicine cabinet. He'd been daydreaming about girls, probably. Sex. One did in those days. One still did.

"Oh, it was so funny, Danny," his mother was saying. "Do you remember that, Aaron? He was twelve or thirteen, just a little older than Ruby."

He wondered if Ruby daydreamed about sex. Terrible stray thought.

"I brought you strawberries," he said.

His father looked gaunt. He'd always been thin, a lanky cowboy sort of thin, and tall, too tall to reach sometimes. But he had never looked eaten away like this.

"You get a haircut?" Daniel asked him. "Tony still cutting your hair?"

When they moved to the East Side, his father had searched the neighborhood for a barber who could cut his beard the way he liked it. Daniel used to tag along when he was very small, and Tony would put a hot towel on his face.

"Tony?" his mother said. "Tony died years ago."

Joy began talking about all the people in the neighborhood who had died. If they hadn't died, they had gone out of business. She held the green plastic basket of strawberries and Daniel noticed her fingers were already stained pink with the juice.

"But *we're* still here," she concluded.

Daniel's father took his hand and held it. "You making a good living these days?" he asked.

"Pay no attention to him," said Joy. "I'd better wash the berries. Where'd you get them? On the street?" She licked a pink finger. "Now I'll get mad cow disease and Ebola." She went into the kitchen.

"I'm making a living," Daniel said. "Let's just leave it at that."

"I don't know why you work for that organization." He said the word "organization" with distaste. "Go where the action is."

"Where's that, Dad?"

"Just ignore him, Danny," his mother called from the kitchen.

"Wall Street."

Daniel rolled his eyes.

"Well, you can lead a horse to water," said Aaron.

Daniel left them sitting in the dining room eating the straw-berries. As he closed the front door, he heard his father say, "Nice boy. Good work, Joyful."

"Wall Street?" she answered. "You want your son to be a crook?"

6

Aaron was lying on his side, turned away from her, when Joy got into bed. She put her arms around him and they talked about the past. He remembered unexpected things, digging clams in Cape Cod right after they were married, the poem he'd memorized for freshman English ("*how do you like your blueeyed boy / Mister Death*"). She talked about the children, about the grandchildren. A little bit about work, though he was no longer interested in her work, could not really follow what she was telling him. He was very romantic these days, more romantic than he had been in what she sometimes thought of as their real life, before he began to drift away. He called her darling, asked what the hell the colostomy pouch was, apologized for it, thanked her for putting up with it and him. Then they fell asleep. That was how it went most nights. Sometimes when she lay down on the bed with Aaron, her face pressed against the back of his head, she would cry. When he asked her what was wrong, she would say she missed her parents.

But one night, just as Joy climbed into bed, when Aaron pulled up his pajama shirt and poked at the pouch and said, "What the hell is this?" he yanked it out before she could stop him.

She cleaned him up. She changed the sheets. She settled him back in bed. He told her he loved her. She held him and cried, said again that it was because she missed her parents.

It began to happen frequently, regularly, sometimes twice in a night. *What the hell is this*, and a yank. Joy didn't tell anyone. That would have been disrespectful to Aaron. But beyond that, she knew if she told anyone, her children, her friends, they would tell her she needed to hire help or that Aaron ought to be in a nursing home.

"Please don't pull out the pouch tonight, Aaron."

"I'm hungry," he said. She'd gotten him into his pajamas but not into bed yet. He was in his chair watching television. The TV was on so loud she could feel the vibrations in her stomach. She brought him some ice cream, then canned pears. He smiled at her and asked for toast and tea. She imagined the plastic colostomy pouch puffing, swelling, being pulled off by his big restless hand.

"Look," she said, pointing to the pouch when she got him settled in bed. "Your colostomy pouch from your surgery."

"I had surgery?"

"It saved your life."

Aaron looked away from her. "Some life," he said with a sigh.

Joy rigged up the bed so that she could strip any wet or soiled sheets from his side without disturbing the king-sized bottom sheet. She put down layers of chux and towels and an extra sheet folded four times. They were not always necessary, he sometimes left the pouch undisturbed. But even then, he himself was disturbed, more and more, by noises, by movements, by Joy. The rustle of the sheets if she turned over, the click of the remote control if she watched TV, even with the sound off. If she got up to go to the bathroom, Aaron started, called out in fear.

Joy got very little sleep, even after she moved onto the lumpy living-room couch. If she was in the bedroom, she startled him and woke him up. If she was not in the bedroom, he woke up disoriented and called for her. She preferred the living-room couch. It gave her the illusion of distance and freedom, and the cushions seemed to fit her tired back perfectly. She slept like a cat, listening, curled in a ball, one eye half open. When her husband called, she woke immediately and leaped up. She did not slink gracefully from the room like a cat. She shuffled in her slippers and made small distressed murmurs, turning on lamps, holding the wall for balance. Sometimes, after soothing Aaron or getting him ginger ale or cleaning him up, she would be too tired to go back to the couch and she would fall asleep at the foot of the bed. Sometimes, as tired as she was, she couldn't get back to sleep until morning. Those predawn hours were excruciating at first. She paced and fretted and prayed for sleep. But after a few nights like that, she realized what a gift she was being given. She spread herself out on the couch and read whatever novel happened to be lying around. The time became precious to her. It was too late for anyone to still be out and too early for anyone to be out yet. The streets were hushed.

Joyful, Joyful, Aaron whispered. Their fingers were entwined. They lay on the cool sand. An orange moon hung dreamily on the horizon. We will visit every island on earth, Aaron said. We will go to Iceland and Corfu and Tahiti and Orkney and the Isle of Mull. We'll live in Tasmania and Ischia.

Long Island will do, Joy said.

There once was a man from Nantucket, Aaron said.

Poetry!

And the moon rose above them, growing smaller and paler as the night grew darker.

My father is very ill," Molly said to the woman next to her on the plane.

"I'm so sorry."

"I'm going to New York to see him."

"I'm sure that will do him good."

Will it? Molly wondered. She thought of Daniel so many years ago, when he was so ill. He was just a kid, eighteen, younger than Ben, her son, was now. Younger than Ben and in the hospital for so long, almost a year. Then in a wheelchair for months. How had he stood it? The way he stood everything, she supposed—by ignoring it. Had it helped Daniel, had it "done him good" when Molly came home from college to sit with him in his hospital room? She had tried to entertain him, telling him amusing stories, family gossip. She'd read the newspaper to him, brought him milkshakes, too. And she'd given him novels, *Lucky Jim*, *A Handful of Dust*, which he was too sick to read. Did any of that "do him good"? There he'd been in his hospital bed, an unfiltered cigarette in his mouth, squinting against the smoke, smiling at her, laughing at her funny stories, but when it came time to leave, she'd see his eyes sink back into their blank gaping stare of pain. Oh, she'd had some good fights with the nurses about his painkillers, such as they were, not that anyone cared what a college girl said. Their mother had been even fiercer, but still the doctors refused to give him sufficient pain medication, insisting it was too addictive for a teenaged boy.

So had her visits done Daniel any good at all? Would this visit to her father do *him* any good? Would it restore his short-term memory? Would it give him back his strength, his balance, so he could walk? Would it replace the colostomy bag with his own intestine? Would it make him healthy, would it make him whole?

"You're such an absolutist," Freddie had once said to her, and she had said, "Yes. That is the goal, at least."

As soon as she got to New York she would call her parents' various doctors. She would organize all their medications in little plastic boxes labeled with the days of the week. She would order a lamp with a high-wattage bulb for reading, a telephone with big buttons and an extra-loud ring. She would put all their bank accounts online and arrange for deposits and payments to be made automatically. She would set up Spotify and program it to endlessly play Frank Sinatra.

She said these things to herself to make herself feel better, but she knew what would really happen. Neither her father nor her mother would be able to decide which doctor she should speak to or find their phone numbers. The medications she organized would be the ones they no longer took. There would be no place to plug in the new lamps with their bright lightbulbs, every outlet in the apartment, and there weren't many, sporting frayed extension cords already overloaded. They would change the appointments she did manage to arrange for them without telling her. Every television in the apartment, and there were too many, would not work. The radio would play only static, loudly. And then there was the computer.

"Why did you even talk to someone who called out of the blue and said he was from Microsoft?" she would ask her mother.

"Because he said he was from Microsoft."

"Mom, Microsoft doesn't call people like that to say your computer has a virus. They never call anyone. They don't even answer calls. It doesn't work like that."

"They said it was urgent."

It wasn't Joy's fault that an entirely new paradigm of communication and commerce had developed in her later years. Molly would say, "Okay, Mom. No harm done. As long as you didn't give them any information."

"Of course not! Just my name. I think just my name. Oh god, what if I gave them something else? Like my credit card number?"

"Did you?"

"I don't know. How can I remember everything like that? He asked me so many questions."

And her mother, her inspiring, unflappable, competent, hardworking, distinguished mother, would berate herself, berate the modern world, then sigh helplessly. "I don't know why Microsoft called in the first place," she would say. "I really don't."

Molly sat in the taxi from the airport anticipating Central Park, heavy and loamy and full of autumn. As Manhattan came into view, she experienced what she always felt on approaching the city from JFK: a mixture of excitement and calm, a sense of totality; of perfect, living, vibrant, chaotic peace. She opened the cab's bleary window and breathed in the lights and the skyscrapers, the sky lit from below, the river.

The taxi driver popped the trunk and pulled her bag out for her. Before she could grab it, the doorman was already rolling it beneath the canopy to the door. When Molly was growing up here, the doormen were such a normal, essential part of her life. She had never really gotten used to living without doormen. They always knew where your parents were, when they'd be home, if the dog had been walked, if your brother had friends with him—an early alert system for family life. If you lost your keys, they let you into the apartment. They handed you packages. They told you the mailman had come when you were waiting for college acceptances and refusals. When she was little she had loved their uniforms with their names stitched on the chest, their smart hats like policemen's hats, but unlike a policeman, they picked you up and swung you through the air and lent you a quarter if you needed it for candy. She'd known some of them, the older ones, for what seemed like her whole life.

"Hi! Hi! It's so good to be here!" she said, then realized she did not actually know this particular doorman and had greeted him too warmly. He did look familiar, perhaps because of a strong resemblance to Mussolini. Squat head, square jaw, wide frown. He was probably too young to know who Mussolini was. The name stitched on his uniform was Gregor.

"The Bergmans," she said. "I'm their daughter. I have a key. They're expecting me."

A novel by James Patterson was spread-eagled on the console. He glanced at it longingly as they went to the elevator, saying, "Your mother will be glad to see you." He spoke in a heavy, clouded voice, just as she would have expected a Mussolini look-alike to speak, though the accent was wrong, Eastern European. "She's had a rough night."

"Is she okay? Did something happen?"

"Oh," said Gregor, and he cleared his throat. "*She's* fine, but . . ."

"My father? Oh god. What happened?"

The elevator doors opened.

"They're both home, safe and sound," Gregor said as the doors closed.

Home? Of course they were home. Where else would they be at midnight?

Molly burst through the door, unlocked as always. "Mom! Mom! What's going on?"

35

Her mother was lying on the couch in the living room, though Molly had trouble locating her at first, she was so swaddled in down. A down comforter, a down robe beneath it, down booties, and, which was new to Molly, a down hood. "I'm here," the little face said. "I'm fine, darling."

"But Daddy?"

"I'm trying to warm up. What a night. Your father is okay now, back in bed where he belongs." She took a sip of water from a paper cup on the side table. Why did she use paper cups? Molly wondered. To make the apartment seem more like a hospital?

"I was reading, I guess I fell asleep—"

"Mom?"

"A really deep sleep, which I have not had in weeks, believe me. I checked on your father at ten, before I went to bed. I made sure he went to the bathroom to pee, I checked the colostomy pouch . . ."

Oh, please spare me those particular details, Molly thought guiltily, knowing her mother could not spare herself those details.

"And he was comfortable and quiet. So I came back here to my nest."

It did not look like a nest, that undulating pile of pillows and comforters, more like an avalanche from which long-lost hikers might at any moment emerge, shaking themselves off, wondering how they ended up in this Manhattan living room. "And?" Molly said, rather sharply, moving her hands in circles as if to speed things up.

Perhaps, Joy thought, Molly's authoritarian nature came along with the work she did, a professional hazard, like Marie Curie being exposed to radiation. Molly was exposed to so many pottery shards. They were not radioactive, but there were so many and they were minuscule and each one might turn out to be the important one, but who could tell, they were so small and filthy, and so you had to gather them up as if they were diamonds, then separate them, then put them back together again. Well, you would

36

have to be officious, wouldn't you, with all those shards depending on you? Joy had been so proud when Molly decided to study archaeology, when she got her Ph.D., when she went off to Turkey to dig up ancient pots. It was like an Agatha Christie novel. It was like Agatha Christie's life with her archaeologist husband, minus a husband, of course, but that was another story. You had to clean the dug-up bits and pieces with a soft toothbrush like the ones for people with diseased gums. This thought always made Joy shudder, as if the pottery shards were in fact old decayed teeth. Then the discoveries, such as they were, would have to be labeled on bits of paper like the slips in a Chinese fortune cookie. Then they would end up buried again, in drawers in a university or museum, never to see daylight for another thousand years or so. No wonder Molly was always trying to organize Joy. She even tried to organize her own body, stretching this muscle, strengthening that one. If Molly could number the hairs on her head, Joy was sure she would, she was so busy trying to order the world. She had been the same as a child, not particularly obsessive or compulsive, although she did refold her clothes when Joy brought them up from the laundry room, come to think of it. But it was more a show of strength, this insistence on order, her own order, a demand rather than a need.

That would keep anybody busy, never mind her job. Look at her, poor dear, so antsy-pantsy. She was looking good, though. Fit. Always fit. An obsession. There were worse obsessions. She resembled her father with that long face. Sculptural, Joy liked to think, though others might call it craggy. The face was frowning ferociously now. Of course! Joy hadn't told her about Aaron yet. No wonder! "Where was I? Oh, I came here into the living room and I read a little and then I must have fallen asleep—"

"Mom!" Molly snapped. "Could you just tell me what actually happened, for god's sake?"

Her mother glared at her and snapped back: "Your father got out of bed and pulled his urine-soaked pajama pants and adult diaper down around his ankles and went out, like that, with his urine-soaked pajamas and adult diaper around his ankles, into the elevator to the lobby, okay? The doorman brought him back."

"Jesus."

"*Gregor*—Jesus retired last year. All right? Okay? Direct enough for you, Molly? Delivered quickly enough? Sorry I was not as concise as you would have liked. I'm sorry I didn't describe your father's humiliation with the clarity and alacrity you demand . . ."

Molly sank onto the downy couch beside her mother. "Oh, Mom," she said tenderly. "I'm sorry, Mom. I'm so sorry."

They sat like that for a while, quiet, together, and she snuggled against her mother, then went into her parents' bedroom. Her father was asleep, the quilt pulled up to his chin. He had aged since she last saw him, not that long ago despite her mother's admonitions, two months. But Aaron, breathing noisily, his face otherwise so still, looked old, like an old, old man. Molly kissed his forehead.

"I'm sorry you walked in on such a drama," Joy said. They were squeezed in at the table in the kitchen drinking the house specialty, decaffeinated tea, weak, lukewarm.

"I'm sorry you have to deal with this, Mommy."

"Gregor is a nice young man. He and his wife just had a baby."

"Do you think maybe you should lock the door? At night? Then, if Daddy gets up—"

"What if there's a fire?" her mother said, appalled. "You're not thinking, Molly."

Molly stirred her tea. The sound of the spoon against the teacup was musical, like bells.

"I hate being such an old ruin," Joy said softly.

"You're not an old ruin. You're still working, for heaven's sake. You take care of Dad all by yourself. I don't know how you manage, honestly. And you look beautiful, too. Old ruin. That's a joke."

"Well"—Joy was obviously mollified—"I *am* old."

No one at work knew her real age. Eighty-six. That would give them a jolt, all those potbellied men planning their retirements at sixty-five. Of course, she couldn't afford to retire even now. She'd cut back to part-time since Aaron got so sick, which was hard enough on the finances.

"I only work three days a week," she added.

"That's plenty."

"Plenty of *tsuris*."

The room that had once been Molly's was now her mother's office and her father's study. Those were the terms used by them both, and if an office is a place where you store cardboard boxes of unopened mail and a study is where you sit between spires of those boxes on a convertible sofa and listen to your transistor radio, then those terms were accurate.

Molly transferred the piles of boxes from the sofa to the floor, leaving a little path to the door, and began removing the sofa's newly visible pillows before she realized that other towers of boxes on the floor would prevent the mattress from unfolding.

"Oh well," Joy said. "Storage is a problem in New York City. Sleep in Danny's room."

Daniel's room had originally been a maid's room, a remnant from the days when the building had been built, the days when families had maids. The room was so narrow that the only bed that would fit there was a special narrow maid's-room bed sold, once upon a time, in some of the better New York department stores. This one was very old, perhaps forty years old, lumpy and somehow inviting. Daniel had always loved his room, fixing it up like a cabin on a boat. In fact, he had made it so cozy and inviting that Molly had tried to get him to switch with her, but he had contemptuously refused. Aaron called it the Nookery, a Dickens reference, he said, and that had clinched it for both children: Daniel had the best room in the house. It even had its own bathroom, the size of a phone booth, with a toilet and a skinny shower.

The sink was in the bedroom, which Daniel one day announced was very European, enraging Molly, who was stuck in her conventional American bedroom with its big closet and large windows facing the tree-lined street. The small window at the head of Daniel's maid's-room cot faced another building, but he had managed to make a friend across the air shaft and they rigged up a pulley system and paper cup telephone, so even that turned out to be an advantage.

Molly pulled the old cotton quilt around her. She felt far away, missing Freddie, and she felt comfortably at home. Outside, an ambulance went screeching along somewhere in the distance.

She heard her mother padding around in the kitchen, the pop of the toaster, the refrigerator door opening, closing. She would have to check the refrigerator tomorrow, search for the squalid, liquefying slices of tomato, the curled, desiccated turkey slices she knew would be tucked up somewhere in there. She had to make sure her parents were eating properly. There were boxes of Vienna Fingers and saltines on the counter. Minute Rice. Rice Krispies. Cream of Wheat. If it was an empty calorie, her parents were sure to stock it. But she had also seen a banana and a few oranges in a bowl. A good sign. She had tried once to arrange a regular delivery of decent produce through an organic food website. It had not been a success. Her mother did not like the dirt on the vegetables. Her father did not like the irregular shapes. Neither of them liked rutabagas.

Molly had come a week earlier than either Freddie or Ben, neither of whom could get to New York until Thanksgiving Day, and Joy was glad. It gave her a little time to be alone with her daughter. From the kitchen table, she watched with pleasure as Molly grabbed parcels from the refrigerator and threw them into a large garbage bag.

"Mom, this is disgusting."

Joy nodded. Molly's movements, so abrupt and assured, charmed her. It was as if Molly were a little girl, a busy, officious little girl, as she had sometimes been, bossing her brother around, arranging the spices in the kitchen alphabetically as soon as she learned the alphabet.

"It's wonderful to have you here," Joy said.

Molly looked up from the garbage bag. She smiled.

"I miss you terribly," Joy said.

The smile faded. "That makes me feel kind of guilty, Mom."

"Would you prefer that I didn't miss you?"

Molly pondered that. "I don't know. Maybe. No."

"Good. Because I do, whether you like it or not."

She watched Molly spray the kitchen table with Fantastik and scrub it vigorously with a sponge, her elbows almost banging into Joy's face.

"Should I move?"

"You're okay."

Joy did not offer to help. Molly did not like help. Joy watched her with growing satisfaction. The chemicals in the spray made her eyes sting, but she said nothing. The sticky circles left by teacups and jam jars disappeared. Molly gave her a quick kiss on the head as she put back the saltshaker, the sugar bowl with one of its handles broken off, the portable radio, then quickly took them off again and scrubbed them, too. She scrubbed the blackened windowsill.

"That will never come off," Joy said.

"I miss you, too, you know," Molly said.

"I should hope so."

Joy listened to the water run as Molly took a shower in Danny's minuscule bathroom. There was life in the apartment, echoes of her old life, echoes of life before she was old.

"Aaron," she said that night as she tucked him in, wrapping her arms around him and pressing her face against the back of his head, "I love you."

He said, "I love you, too, my darling."
The words echoed in the apartment full of echoes.

Joy left for work at 9:30. She never knew what she would come home to, but Aaron tended to sleep during the day and never went near the stove, so she told herself. She was a conservation consultant for a small museum on the Lower East Side that specialized in Jewish artifacts. It was, she had once observed, years ago, not unlike Hitler's Museum of an Extinct Race, but with less stuff. Aaron was shocked when she said this. They were in Prague at the time, entering a museum beside the old synagogue, a museum that was piled with candlesticks and spoons and silver spice boxes stolen from Jews by the Nazis and stockpiled in anticipation of Hitler's museum.

"Joyful, darling, a little perspective," Aaron said.

A museum like hers was a record of the past, not a trophy of genocide, certainly that was true. But Time was so cruel and so thorough. It made her sad sometimes as she examined her own museum's jumble of dented tin *pushkes*, Sabbath candlesticks brought from the Old Country, telegrams, newspapers, photographs, the wheel of a pushcart, a deck chair from the Catskills. Where did they belong now? Nowhere. It was an extinct world that passed through her hands and into the Lower East Side Museum. Joy would examine each item donated to the museum or acquired, each fragment of this lost world, to determine if it deserved to be found or to be lost again, to be tossed back quite literally onto the dust heap of history. This choosing which item lived and which died, so to speak—that was the part of her job she did not relish, separating the wheat from the chaff.

"Who am I to judge?" she said to Aaron. "If the pope said that about his flock, is it any wonder I feel that way about my flock of artifacts?"

"I don't know how to tell you this, my love, but you are not the pope."

Joy wanted to save everything, every scrap, as if it were a soul. A museum was not a warehouse, however, and a conservator was not a hoarder. Collections had priorities, strengths. Every Houdini flyer did not need to be preserved. One Houdini flyer was quite enough. Yet she had been trained to save, not to choose.

A mother of small children with a bachelor's degree in Art History, she had volunteered at the museum two days a week as soon as Daniel started nursery school. It wasn't until that first bank-ruptcy that she'd gone to work there full-time as a secretary, as-sisting the conservator. Both he and the director of the museum encouraged her to go back to school. She couldn't give up her job to go full-time, but she managed, working during the morning, going to school in the afternoon, so she could be home to make dinner and put the children to bed. She worked long and hard for that Ph.D. The museum hired her as a conservator even before she finished. She loved the battered pots and pans, the sewing machines, the Yiddish-to-English primers, liked to handle them. She knew others would like to handle them, too, and so she protected them from the loving caresses that would, as in a myth or a fairy tale, eventually destroy them.

The director had a bit of a crush on her, though he had never bothered her after that one time, and even then she had been able to fend him off with a pretense of utter ignorance and innocence, one of her favorite strategies, no hurt feelings or embarrassment. It had been a long time since she'd had to act as though she had no idea what a man meant when he spoke in a husky voice and happened to rest his hand on her knee. That was one piece of the past she'd been only too happy to consign to the garbage.

The conservator who had encouraged her had died years ago. The director had retired. The field of conservation relied more and more on computers and software and technology, or so she read, she could not possibly employ all the new techniques, it was hard enough for her writing emails. The museum was changing with the times, too, growing bigger and more professional, and Joy had begun to identify with her artifacts, out of date, obsolete, left behind.

Joy had already gotten Aaron dressed. All Molly had to do was bring her father his breakfast and his lunch, and make sure he didn't wander or fall.

"For once I can relax at the office," Joy said. "Goodbye, Aaron. Goodbye, Molly. Don't drive each other crazy. I'm off to the salt mines."

Aaron poked at the lump in his sweatshirt and asked what it was doing there. Molly explained about the colostomy bag at great length, as if a longer explanation would stay in his head longer, but at a certain point he just waved his hand at her, a dismissal, and she left him in his chair and washed his dishes. By the time she was done, he was calling for her mother.

"She went to work, Daddy," she said from the doorway.

"Is that so?"

"Yes, that is so."

He called for Joy ten minutes later, and ten minutes after that, until Molly decided to stay in the bedroom with him.

"No wonder Mom is going nuts," she said to him.

"*Who can from Joy refrain,*" he sang, "*this gay, this pleasing, shining, wond'rous day?*"

By two o'clock, the apartment was driving Molly insane, the banging radiators and stifling steam heat, the television's endless loop of NY1 weather and politics and interviews of off-Broadway dancers. She had to get out.

"You have to get out," she said to her father. She bundled him in his jacket and herded him and his walker to the door. "Come on. It's so hot in here. With the TV grinding on and on. I can't stand it."

"Well, I can."

"You need fresh air."

"You sound like your mother. Where is your mother? Joy! Joy!"

"She went to work."

"Oh, she did, did she?"

He often took on this joshing tone when he was confused. Molly hustled him into the elevator.

"Well, where's your mother, anyway?" His voice had gone from joshing to desperation. "Joy? Joy! Where are you? Where's your mother?"

They made it to the park, and Aaron stared at the evergreen bushes.

Molly sat on a bench beside him. The air was cold and wet. "So," she said. Before the dementia, he had been a kind of genius at small talk, always able to chat and charm. That gift had been lost, gradually, but even so he had continued to enjoy a good attack on the mayor. She mentioned the mayor now, and he said, "All a bunch of crooks," but did not elaborate. Molly moved on to the grandchildren. He liked to hear anything at all about them, laughing and calling them spitfires or *wisenheimers*.

"So Cora and Ruby go to public schools," she said.

"Imagine that."

"I hope they're really good ones."

Her father nodded. "Yes, indeed," he said.

"I thought Ruby would go to private school for seventh grade for sure. Not that anyone asked my opinion. Of course no one can afford the tuition anymore. Except Russian oligarchs."

"Well, now."

"*Are* there any good public middle schools?" she soldiered on. "There weren't when Daniel and I were that age, that's for sure."

"Is that so?"

Molly tried a couple of other topics, but none of them, not the state of the CIA or health care or water quality, sparked more than a nod, an all-purpose phrase: You don't say; imagine that.

Oh, Daddy, Molly thought, and tears came to her eyes. She was a useless, selfish daughter, dragging her father out into the cold against his will so that she could get some fresh air, so that she could breathe, so that she could escape when she knew he could never escape what was happening to him, not if she made him stumble behind his red walker as far as the North Pole. And to top it all off, in these precious moments at what was surely the beginning of the end of his conscious life, she couldn't even think of anything to say to him. To her own father.

She tried reminiscing. Older people loved to reminisce. "Remember when you had to drive up to Vermont to take me home from camp?"

"You don't say?"

"Yup. Twice, actually. Because when you got there the first time, I had already changed my mind and wanted to stay. But by the time you got home again, I had changed it again and wanted to leave. I was so bossy. Why did anyone listen to me? I was eleven, for god's sake."

But her reminiscences were apparently not his reminiscences. He smiled and patted her gloved hand with his gloved hand, his expression blank.

"Now, look, Daddy," she said, "you drove all day. I *know* you remember. You have to. You were so annoyed, but then you just laughed. That got me really upset—that you laughed at me, that my situation was comical and I was just one of a million little girls who did this, just an ordinary, predictable child. You have to remember all that. I got mad when you laughed, and you somehow understood and stopped laughing and pretended to take me very seriously, and then I was happy."

"Imagine that, imagine that."

Then another old man with an identical red walker appeared, and Aaron seemed to come alive. He stood up, with great effort, and offered the man his hand. "How do you do?" he said.

The slow determination of his movements, the difficulty and awkwardness of them, lent them a seriousness, almost dignity. Why don't we revere the elderly? Molly wondered briefly. She knew why. They were difficult and inconvenient. But how brave her father was just by standing up, by insisting on the code of conduct he'd been brought up with, by being, simply, polite. He still tried to open doors for Molly, his hand shaking. At first she told him not to, afraid he'd topple over. But then she saw it mattered. It was what a man did, a man brought up when he was brought up.

Aaron put out his hand to shake the newcomer's and with some formality introduced first Molly, then himself. There was a cookie crumb in his beard. Molly saw it and thought, for a flash, how foolish he looked, then recanted. The cookie crumb was not foolish at all, it was a battle scar from a battle to exist in a world that insisted on changing if he so much as blinked.

The other man introduced himself as Karl. "And this," he said, gesturing toward his plump, red-cheeked caretaker, "is Marta. She is kind, though strict."

"I go coffee," she said in a heavy accent, Polish, Molly guessed.

"Would you like coffee, too?" Karl asked. "Marta, can you get this nice young lady and her delightful father a cup of coffee?"

Molly pulled her wallet out, but Karl put up his hand and said, "My treat."

He was a good-looking old man, silky gray hair nicely cut, beautifully dressed. Molly shot a glance at her father. The cookie crumb had been dislodged. His beard could use a trim, but it wasn't too bad. Her mother took very good care of him. Better than she took of herself, but there are only so many hours in the day, as Joy said when Molly pointed this out to her.

Marta returned with four cups of coffee, and they sat there drinking the scalding coffee in the cold November air.

"Chilly for two old geezers like us," Karl said to Aaron.

"Not like the war," Aaron said, shaking his head.

"I don't know why people call them flying rats," Karl responded. "Listen to them. They coo like doves."

Neither Aaron nor Karl seemed to mind the gaps, the non sequiturs, in their conversation.

47

"We had cold showers in the jungle, but boy oh boy, we sure didn't mind."

"Just listen to them cooing. Like lovebirds. They're pretty, too. Don't you think?"

"*Oh that I had wings like a dove!*" Aaron said. "*For then would I fly away and be at rest.*"

"Dad? That's beautiful. Is that a poem?"

But her father had no answer for her. He smiled and turned his face up to the golden autumn sun. Molly looked on, a little envious, as the two men sat in a companionable silence, side by side, while the pigeons cooed like doves.

9

W hen the groceries arrived on Thanksgiving morning, Joy was astonished. "What are all these boxes? There's no room for them!"

"Don't worry," her daughter said.

"Don't worry," her daughter-in-law said.

Joy allowed them to usher her into the living room. Her original plan was to order Thanksgiving dinner from the coffee shop, but Molly had given her that you-are-crazier-than-I-thought look.

"Don't look at me like that. The kitchen gets too hot when you cook in it."

"I'll take care of everything," Molly said soothingly, as if that were reassuring. But Joy did not want her daughter to take care of everything, she wanted to take care of everything herself. As she always had, but no longer could.

"The coffee shop has wonderful turkey. Moist. And it's sliced."

"That is so depressing, Mom."

Joy knew she should find Thanksgiving turkey from the 3 Guys coffee shop depressing, too, but she found the thought comforting instead. Everything would be done, there would be no banging of pots and pans and oven doors; there would be no grease, no smoke; there would be calm instead of chaos. And she would be in charge.

She said, "I can't take the disorder of cooking a Thanksgiving dinner, the crazy mess, the hot steam in the kitchen, the millions of dishes. It's too much for me, Molly. But I don't want to give up my place as the matriarch, I suppose. What foolishness. But it's true."

Molly looked at her with interest. Then she laughed and said, "So the 3 Guys will be the new family matriarch?"

"I said it was foolish."

It was Danny's wife, Coco, who came up with a compromise. Coco liked to smooth the waters in the family. She was a fidgety intellectual woman who had a fondness for any problem she might be able to solve—her children, for example, presented wonderful puzzles. It was the chemistry teacher in her, Aaron used to say. Coco suggested they order everything ready-made from one of any number of high-end grocery stores. "Zabar's, Fairway, Fresh Direct. We live in New York City, people. We'll get a whole turkey, it's not carved, but you don't have to roast it, and everything else comes with it. You just heat everything up. No cooking."

Joy could not really see the difference between cooking and heating everything up, but she agreed. When there were no problems available for Coco to handle, Joy felt uneasy, almost guilty. Her daughter-in-law's intervention in the Thanksgiving-dinner difficulty provided a rush of satisfaction.

But Joy had not expected so many boxes.

"Where is Aunt Freddie?" Danny's daughter Ruby asked. She had just turned twelve. Her sister, Cora, was eight. Ruby and Cora—Joy never could understand how two nice little Jewish girls had been given such names, the names of women who waitressed in diners in 1932, but then, they thought her own name was odd, so there you were. Such sweet, pretty girls, flowering vines, wrapped around each other as usual, the two of them giggling and tangled on the couch.

"She's coming soon," Joy said. "She took a red-eye."

"A red-eye," Cora said. "Ew."

"It means a flight at night and you have to stay awake all night and your eyes get red," Ruby said.

"Aunt Freddie has blue eyes," Cora said. "So there."

Joy had marveled at first at how blasé the girls were about their Aunt Molly marrying a woman. She still marveled. *It's very strange*, she wanted to say sometimes. *Don't you see?* "Aunt Freddie will be here soon, in plenty of time for dinner," she said instead.

Ruby had recently gone through a Katy Perry phase, mercifully short, when she wanted to dye her hair blue. She settled for a blue wig on Halloween. Then, just a week ago, she'd done an about-face. She still dressed in incomprehensible combinations of sparkly garments. She was wearing such an outfit now, an undersized flared skirt in a strawberry print, each strawberry a collection of layered red sequins, leggings decorated with clown faces, a gold-and-pink-striped lamé T-shirt. But she was now reading *Tom Sawyer* with the same intensity she'd previously reserved for Katy Perry songs and gossip, and she was now intent on getting a pet frog.

"No more Katy Perry karaoke?" Joy asked. It had been cute, Ruby lip-synching the pop songs, until she began shaking her hips in suggestive ways.

"I don't want to be stereotyped," she said.

Daniel flopped down beside his mother. "As what? A teen pop star?"

"Don't tease me," said Ruby. "Mommy said her father teased her about the Beatles and she never got over it."

"Mommy's a stereotype," Daniel said.

Joy listened to the noises from the kitchen. Plenty of banging and crashing, but she found she didn't mind as much as she had anticipated. Still, they didn't know where anything was, those two,

Coco and Molly. Joy got up and went into the kitchen, pointed out the roasting pan, the carving knife. The women smiled at her tolerantly until she went back into the living room. Fine, fine, let them look high and low for platters and gravy boats. If they needed any more of her help, they knew where to find her. She would sit and put her feet up and watch her grandchildren. That was matriarchal, too.

Ruby pushed her younger sister away and kneeled on the floor at the coffee table. She pulled an ornamental wooden box toward her and began to rummage through old photographs that were kept inside. Two years before, Ruby's teacher had asked the class to construct their family trees. Ruby had formed an immediate attachment, bordering on obsession, with the heavy ancestral mustaches, the billowing knickers, the bows and fancy perched hats. She still gravitated to the photographs when she came to see her grandparents. She knew the names of every second cousin on both sides of the family. The old man with a long white beard spread across his chest who was wearing a fur hat was Aaron the First, as she put it—her grandfather's grandfather. He had eyes like an angry crow.

"Why do you like him?" Cora asked. "He's scary. And he's dead."

"So?"

"So he's scary and he's dead."

But Ruby only shrugged and gazed fondly at the old man. He had sent his children to New York for a better life, six of them, holding only one back to take care of him and his wife in their old age. That daughter had died of cholera at sixteen. Tragic, Grandma Joy told her. Ruby thought, *It served him right*, but she said nothing.

"Is the turkey cooked or not?" Joy said, back in the kitchen. "I don't understand."

"Mom, you did plenty. Just sit down and relax. Coco and I can do this part."

Joy had helped set up the extra table and the folding chairs, she'd helped Molly get the good dishes down, the good silverware, all the linens tucked away in boxes lined with tissue paper. That, plus everything she'd done to get Aaron ready—she *was* tired. In the living room, she watched as Aaron trudged in behind his walker. The girls looked up from the box of photographs.

"Do you want to look at your ancestors?" Ruby asked him.

"I'm too old to have ancestors."

"That's silly, Grandpa."

"I'm too silly to have ancestors," he said. He threw two kisses at the children. "Catch!" he said, and they both jumped and raised a hand, as if they were catching a butterfly. "Good," he said. "Sometimes they get away."

Joy helped him sit on his chair. He threw her a kiss, too. "Tough to be an old Jew," he said.

"I'm Jewish," Cora said.

Her sister rolled her eyes.

Cora showed Joy a photo of a man wearing a woman's bathing suit.

"That's my father," Joy said.

"Why did he wear a girl's bathing suit?"

"All the men did."

"There's a girl in my class who used to be a boy. But I've never seen her in a bathing suit."

"Dear god."

"Sometimes people get born in the wrong bodies," Ruby explained to her grandmother.

Joy checked to see if Aaron had been following this, but he appeared to be, mercifully, asleep.

After a while, Cora began her ritual search for spare change, running her small fingers beneath the seat cushions of the sofa. Mostly she encountered grit, but she did come across a few bobby pins. Beneath the cushion of a chair, she discovered a clear plastic bean with a tiny wire. She was so disgusted when she realized that it was her grandfather's hearing aid that she put it back. She moved onto the floor and lifted the sofa's skirt. There, among the dust balls, she saw a ballpoint pen she could not reach.

She moved on to the ashtrays.

"What are ashtrays for?" she said.

Ruby looked at her incredulously. "For ashes."

"For dead people in India?"

"You girls are very odd," Joy said.

"For ashes from cigarettes. And cigars. And pipes," Ruby said. "Don't be so stupid, Cora."

"But nobody smokes cigarettes or cigars or pipes."

"Well, they used to."

"Don't call your sister stupid," Joy said. "How would she know that? How do *you* know that?"

"Hasn't she ever seen a movie?" Ruby said, turning back to a black-and-white photo of her father in the bath as an infant.

But Cora was no longer interested in the conversation. The heavy blown-glass ashtray in the front hall that was full of keys and paper clips was too high up and too heavy for her to lift with any confidence, so she stood on tiptoe and scrabbled through the loose keys and stamps and sample tubes of sunscreen until her fingers felt the cool of silver coins, quarters, quite a few this time. She sat down on the floor and counted them, piling them in towers of four. Nine quarters and then, in a small dish on the dresser in the bedroom, four rather sticky pennies. Her grandmother gave her an eyeglass case with a snap to use as a wallet.

Back in the living room, clutching her eyeglass-case purse, she approached her grandfather in his red chair that looked like a Chinese throne, or what she imagined a Chinese throne looked like after she once heard her grandmother say, "Just sit in it and stop complaining. It's an antique. From China."

Her grandfather looked uncomfortable. He shifted his weight back and forth.

"Grandpa, want to see my money?"

He gave a short laugh. "You rob a bank?"

"I discovered it."

She unsnapped the eyeglass case.

"Whatcha got there? New glasses?" he said.

She thought he was playing with her. She took out two of the sticky pennies and held them over her eyes, the case safely clutched in her armpit.

"Don't do that," her mother said sharply. She had appeared suddenly, the way she often did. "Stop."

"Why?" Cora put the pennies back, her lower lip protruding, sullen. "I was just fooling around."

"Because the Greeks put pennies on dead people's eyes," Ruby said. "To pay the ferryman."

"Coco," Joy said to her daughter-in-law, "your children know far too much about death rituals."

Cora sat on Ruby's lap. "But, Ruby, I'm not Greek," she said. "And I'm not dead."

"*Kaynahora*," Ruby said, looking up from a picture of a skinny elderly couple inside an old-fashioned grocery store. "That means you shouldn't get the evil eye."

"In Greek?"

Now their mother laughed, said, "You two. Honestly," and returned to the kitchen.

"So, Grandpa, you want to see my money?"

He gave another little snort of a laugh, just like the last one, then said, "You rob a bank?" He looked at the eyeglass case. "You wear eyeglasses now?" Then he began to sing: "*My eyes are dim, I cannot see, I have no-ot brought my specs with me-ee-ee . . .*"

"Grandpa, who's this?" Ruby held up a black-and-white photograph of a long-eared dog standing in front of a screened-in porch. She handed it to Aaron.

"That's Prince," he said. "That's my dog Prince."

He brought the photo closer to his face. Ruby thought he was looking at it more closely, but no, he did not bring it to his eyes.

He whispered, "Prince. My dog Prince," brought the photograph to his lips, and kissed it.

When Freddie arrived, Aaron recognized her, but he did not seem to remember her name.

"Look who the wind blew in!" he said.

Molly's son, Ben, got there a few hours later.

"Look who the cat dragged in!" Aaron said.

Ben did look a little like a cat at that moment, a scraggly alley cat. He had gotten a ride from New Orleans with a friend and they'd driven all night. His hair, not very clean, stuck up at unexpected angles in unexpected places. His clothes were wrinkled, even his parka. He had grown a beard, which disconcerted Molly for a moment. She worried about Ben, down there in a violent city with a job that kept him out so late. She worried that he drank too much, that he wasn't doing anything with his life. Sometimes she welcomed the concern about her parents as a distraction from her concern about Ben.

"You look handsome," she said. Ben Harkavy, bartender and handsome alley cat, the kind that rubs against your leg, then hops a fence and disappears.

Ruby and Cora, who loved Ben in a way that reminded Molly of her feelings for her father when she was a child, a reverential physical ownership, threw themselves at him for a double piggyback. Molly gently pushed them aside so she could give Ben a hug. Her arms around his neck, her face on his coat still cold from the outside air, she felt herself relax. Ben was a good boy. Ben was healthy and dear and safe in her arms. And with Ben here as well as Freddie, at last she would be able to make some order in her parents' lives.

"The cavalry," she murmured. "Thank god."

"You miss me?"

"God, yes."

"Don't make him feel guilty," Joy said. "Your mother doesn't like it that I miss her."

Ben hugged his grandmother and said, "You can miss me, too. Instead of missing her. I don't mind."

"I miss you the most," Cora said.

"You're just his cousin," said Ruby.

"So are you."

Ben squatted down and pulled them to him, one in each arm, and the apartment was boisterous and gay. Coco and Molly had used the dessert plates for the salad, but Joy found she didn't mind. The children were playing a game that involved pulling the tablecloth as hard as they could, but she didn't mind that either.

"To Mom and Dad," Daniel said, raising a glass of wine.

Aaron gave a bloodcurdling howl.

"Grandpa," said Ben, jumping up, kneeling beside Aaron. "What happened?"

"What are you talking about?" Aaron said.

Molly saw Ben go white. He had not seen too much of his grandfather in the last year, and when he had, Aaron had always managed to simulate conversation.

"Grandpa forgets sometimes," Ruby whispered to Ben.

He smiled at her. "Thank you." But he was obviously shaken.

"What's going on?" Aaron said, looking around with wild eyes. He swatted Ben away with his enormous white hand. "Off your knees, soldier." He caught Molly's eye. "I'm fine," he said. Then that awful sound, again.

By the time Molly brought out the apple pie, the sound had taken on an alarming volume and pitch.

"What do we do?" Molly said.

"Joy, what should we do?" Coco said.

"Mom, has he ever done this before?" said Daniel.

"Aaron," Freddie was saying, "where does it hurt?"

"I don't know what you're talking about," Aaron said.

Joy had not spoken. The room looked blank to her, as if it had emptied. The sounds were muffled. Except for Aaron's. He was hazy beside her, enormous, ashen, opalescent. But the sounds he was making were not.

"Aaron, eat some pie," she said. How stupid: Eat some pie. But it was all she could think of. She shoveled some pie onto a fork and held it to his mouth. "Delicious pie."

Aaron opened his mouth and allowed her to tip the pie in. He chewed. He smiled. He swallowed. The noise stopped.

Joy looked up at her family and smiled, though she could hardly breathe.

"Pie," she said.

Then the sound began again.

As Molly steered Aaron and his walker through the lobby, the doorman said *Pow! Pow!*, pretending to box. It was his favorite doorman, Ernie, but Aaron did not say *Pow! Pow!* back. Ernie looked solemnly at Molly as he opened the door, then he hailed a cab. Aaron's long, lanky body, always so thin and flexible he seemed to be made of pipe cleaners, was now stiff and unyielding. He sat on the seat of the cab, his legs out, feet still on the pavement. The doorman went around to the other door and tried to pull him over by his shoulders, sliding Aaron across the seat. His legs stuck straight out the door now, feet in the air above the street.

The driver got out, and he and Joy tried to bend Aaron's legs while Molly watched them as if she were witnessing a natural disaster, struck dumb, stuck in place.

"Well, hold my bags, at least," Joy said.

Molly took the three heavy bags.

"No problem, no problem," the taxi driver was saying. "Slowly, slowly."

We are in a cab, Molly texted Freddie. *The coffee is decaf, in case anyone asks.*

Getting Aaron out of the taxi was even worse. The driver, a

wisp of a man who said he was from Bangladesh and had a grandfather and knew how to respect the old, was holding him up beneath his armpits. Joy and Molly each took one arm, but Aaron
began to sink to the ground, slowly, inexorably, the stiffness gone,
as if he were melting.

"I can't, I can't," Aaron said.

"Nice man, do not give up," the taxi driver said. "For the sake
of the nice ladies, do not give up."

Aaron's knees buckled, he was squatting, held up only by the
two women and the determined driver. He sank lower and still
lower, until Joy, shaking beneath the weight, was sure she would
have to let him sink to the ground.

Just at that moment, two enormous arms wrapped themselves
around Aaron, lifting him easily.

The two arms belonged to a security guard who was even
taller than Aaron and far bigger, a muscular giant of a man. He
held Aaron aloft, dangling him, Aaron's feet just touching the
ground.

"We forgot your shoes," Joy said in horror. Aaron was wearing
bedroom slippers. He was out on a cold rainy day in his bedroom
slippers. "Your shoes, your shoes," Joy said.

"Mom, it's okay, he won't need them, it's the hospital . . ."

"Your shoes, Aaron. I'm so sorry." It was all Joy could see, his
large feet, clodhoppers he always called them, brushing the pavement in the wool cable-knit sock slippers with deerskin soles. He
hated them, but they kept him warm and they weren't slippery.
"Oh, sweetheart, you hate these slippers. But why, Aaron? I ordered
them from Hammacher Schlemmer . . ."

"He'll be in bed, Mom. It's okay."

Another security guard came running out with a wheelchair
and Aaron was folded awkwardly into it. He was so weak he was
not even moaning now. But his feet in their warm slip-resistant
slippers were off the sidewalk, placed on the footrests by the two
security guards, one guard per foot. Seeing the men handling the

big feet, seeing each foot on its footrest, made the slippers seem less out of place, and Joy recovered herself.

"There you are, Aaron," she said, holding his hand. "There you are." She ran her other hand along the arm of first one guard, then the second, as if she could gather strength from them, Molly thought. Or for good luck, the way people stroke a talisman.

"You came to our rescue," Joy said. "And on Thanksgiving!" She looked around at the gathering, the first security guard an African-American, the second a giant as pale as Putin, clearly Russian, both towering over the Bangladeshi taxi driver and over her, a Jewish lady, and her daughter, a lesbian lady.

"New York is so cosmopolitan," she said as they wheeled Aaron in after more effusive thank-you's. "Isn't it, Aaron? We've always liked that. Aaron, do you want to be near the window while we wait? We can people-watch."

10

Daniel went to the hospital at lunchtime. He ate a sandwich, a very old-fashioned sandwich, he noticed—bright white bread, a few slices of pink boiled ham, a slice of orange cheese, a piece of pale iceberg lettuce, mustard the vivid yellow of newborn baby poop. The sandwich was a little stale, but comforting, and he wanted to be comforted. His father, the man who sang sea shanties in stormy weather, the tall, skinny father who'd swung his son onto his shoulders as if he'd been a scarf, this man of his childhood was lying in a hospital bed looking like another man entirely. Except for the beard. But even that was uncharacteristically shaggy.

Daniel finished the sandwich in four enormous bites, then answered emails while his father slept. Monday, a workday after the Thanksgiving weekend, so much to catch up on at the office, but his boss said he should stay at the hospital all afternoon if he needed to, working from his phone. If his mother came in, he'd have to put the phone away. She had an aversion to his phone, he wasn't sure why. He hoped she wouldn't come to the hospital, and not just because of his cell phone. He had noticed for some time, months, how tired she was, and this episode with Aaron had really knocked her off her pins. He looked at his father, at the gray beard and disheveled gray hair, the big hawk nose. He turned off his phone.

"Dad," he whispered.

His father twitched, but didn't wake up. His breathing was loud. Sinister red lights blinked above him accompanied by beeps like strangled birdcalls. It was too familiar, the beeping and blinking and labored breathing. Daniel stood up quickly, ready to make for the door.

Aaron opened his eyes.

"You'll be fine, Daniel," he said, reaching out a stringy arm and taking Daniel's hand.

"Me?" Daniel smiled and sat down. "How about you?"

"Where the hell am I?"

"Hospital."

"Don't worry, now. You'll be out of here in no time." Aaron heard the word "hospital," saw Daniel, and put the two together. They had, after all, been a pair, an intimate pair, Daniel and hospital.

"Thank you, Dad. Thank you for worrying about me. But I'm okay. That was thirty-five years ago. Remember that? Bad times."

Aaron nodded. "Terrible."

You were not much help, Daniel thought, in spite of himself. He'd convinced himself he'd put it all behind him, the worst year of his life, the year he was eighteen and developed osteonecrosis out of the blue, a year of searing pain, conflicting diagnoses, the year he couldn't walk, the year he spent in the hospital. His mother had practically moved into his hospital room to look after him. His father had not visited much. He was preoccupied, planning another business, squandering whatever was left of his own father's money. And he didn't like hospitals.

No one likes hospitals, Daniel thought now.

Maybe, Daniel's mother had said, maybe it's just too painful for him to visit. You mean he's too weak? Daniel answered. Yes, said his mother. Yes, I guess that is what I mean. But someone weak can love you, and he does.

"That was a long time ago," Daniel said. "This time, it's you we have to look after. Are you comfortable, Dad?"

"Who knows."

"Well, you, presumably."

"Don't believe everything they tell you," Aaron said.

For a weak man, he was physically strong. His hand still held Daniel's, and Daniel felt the grip tighten.

"Dad?"

Aaron moaned.

"Pain?"

Aaron moaned again. He couldn't speak. He looked pleadingly at his son.

When the nurse arrived, she tipped a pill into Aaron's mouth from a small, pleated paper cup. "Now drink up," she said, handing him a plastic cup of water.

Aaron looked at her with wide-open eyes—eyes full of fright. Did she notice? Daniel wondered.

"It will help the pain," Daniel said.

The moans got louder, a crescendo of misery. Daniel thought he had never heard anyone in such misery.

His father's face seemed to shrink with the pain, his eyes growing wider, fearful, his ears standing out from his head like little elbows.

"Dad, I wish I could do something for you."

The moaning stopped. "You got a stick of gum?"

Daniel put his head in his hands. He waited a few seconds, breathing deeply. "Dad," he said when he looked up, "how is the pain now?"

"Nobody tells me anything," his father muttered, then drifted off into a robust, drugged sleep, snoring deeply.

Aaron was supposed to come home from the hospital soon, and Molly tried to talk to her mother about how she would manage once Molly went back to Los Angeles.

Freddie was gone already, back to her sleepy undergraduates. Her semester started a week earlier than Molly's, and Molly envied her that roomful of hungover boys and girls, students forced to sit and listen. You could test students, grade them, fail them if necessary; you could tell what the correct answer was. Your mother was another story.

Molly tried, she really did. She ran through all the things her father could no longer do, all the things Joy would have to help him with, even writing them down on a large legal pad in broad black letters. Aaron could no longer stand up by himself. He couldn't get himself into bed or out of bed or out of a chair or into a chair. He could not walk by himself, though he often tried, which meant he could not be left by himself for even a minute. Joy would have to dress him, and Joy would have to undress him.

"This is not news to me, Molly."

He needed to be bathed, frequently. And dried. And powdered. He required ointments and unguents. He needed all the attention to pouches and adult diapers that Molly was so queasy about, as well as the rashes and sores they produced, and even so, the bed linens often had to be changed in the middle of the night.

"I can cope. I have *always* coped. Haven't I? Admit it, Molly. Through everything."

"Yes, you cope, but can't you cope with some help? Just keeping him fed is exhausting."

"I order in," Joy said.

Molly had noticed that. In the days leading up to Thanksgiving, her father was given the remains of the same turkey meat loaf dinner from the coffee shop for days, interspersed with the remains of the roast turkey dinner and the turkey burger deluxe, for variety. Joy had tried to feed Molly endless teaspoon-size portions of turkey leftovers, too, but Molly had rebelled and insisted on cooking. Both her parents pronounced her chicken too spicy and her green beans undercooked, then turned rather loftily back to their scraps.

"Next thing I know you'll be sending both of us off to assisted living," Joy said to her now. "To a facility."

"A locked ward."

"In the meantime, I need you to fix the computer. I hate the computer."

She said the words "the computer" with categorical disdain, the way someone might say "Tea Party."

Molly felt the buzz of her phone and went into the bathroom so she could check the text without incurring her mother's rage.

"Help," said the text from Daniel. "Dad thinks I'm in the hospital."

"You are," she responded.

"He thinks I'm the patient."

Daniel was waiting when she got to the cramped café ten minutes later. She swept in, looking harassed, windblown. She always looked harassed and windblown, he thought, even when she was reading a magazine on the sofa or sitting in a restaurant at dinner. Her clothes were always pressed and tucked in and perfectly, overly, coordinated; yet she always appeared to be weathering a great storm. Maybe it was the way she moved—big, jumpy gestures.

"Mom is going to have a nervous breakdown and die," she said.

"Hello to you, too!" He stood up and kissed her. She rested her head on his shoulder for a moment, relaxed and soft. Then he felt her pull herself up. Back on duty.

"Those two are killing each other. What are you eating? I want a panino."

He laughed. A panino, singular. She did like to be correct, Molly did. "I already had a sandwich at the hospital that was prepared in

1958," he said. He ordered an espresso. "A good espresso place in our old neighborhood. Imagine that."

"Imagine that. You sound like Daddy."

Daddy. He liked it when she said that. It made everything seem softer, kinder than it was. "He's in agony one minute, and then the next minute he forgets he was in agony. It's like a backward curse. Or a Greek myth: Dad-alus."

They talked about Coco and his kids for a few minutes. Ruby had turned twelve a couple of months before. Many of her friends were studying for bar and bat mitzvahs. She was not interested. Even the lure of a party and gifts did not entice her. Religions caused wars. Religion was mass hysteria. Like soccer fans, but worse. Cora, on the other hand, was already planning her party, five years to plan it, that ought to be enough, Daniel said, laughing. Then he remembered he should probably ask Molly about Freddie. "How's Freddie?" Molly started to tell him how Freddie was, and he nodded, not listening. Molly said, "Are you even listening? You never listen, Daniel." Molly always told him he didn't listen, and it was true. How else did people get through the day? Daniel's notion of a perfect afternoon was to sit in a garden in the warm sun with bees buzzing lazily around him, his eyes half closed, a battered Panama hat comfortably situated on his drooping head, like the scene in *The Godfather* with an ancient Marlon Brando. Daniel had no interest in being ancient just yet. He just didn't like to rush. He gazed idly at the glass display case and wondered if the cookies were any good. He held his hand up to summon the waiter.

Molly thought, He moves like an old Chinese man on a hill doing tai chi, dignified in the dawn. His expression was serene, self-possessed. But Molly knew he was merely distracted, constantly distracted.

"Wake up," she said. "What are we going to do, Daniel? About Them?"

He shook his head. What, indeed? "I do come up to the apartment every Saturday," he said. "And I bring the girls, too, sometimes. We go to a museum first and then come for dinner. Mom never wants to come with us to any of the museums, though. She doesn't like to leave Dad, although all he does is sleep in front of the TV. I've tried to get him to go in a taxi and then a wheelchair, but he never wants to. Neither of them is very cooperative. They would have such a good time, watching Ruby sketch—she loves Picasso."

"She *would* love Picasso," Molly said, laughing. "But walking around museums at this point . . ."

"Cora is so into the minerals at the Museum of Natural History. Not just the ones that look like jewels. I think she has a scientific bent . . ."

"Come on, Daniel. She's eight. She likes rocks. Which I think is fantastic, I like rocks, too. But what are we going to do when they let Dad out of the hospital? Mommy can't take care of him anymore."

"I don't want them to be old," Daniel said.

"The alternative and all that . . ."

"Maybe."

"We can't put pillows over their faces."

"No," Daniel said. "We would miss them too much."

Joy went to work the Tuesday after Thanksgiving. She was expected, and if she was honest with herself, she could not stand another day sitting in the hospital with Aaron.

The museum was in the process of moving to a new building that week. The little neighborhood museum devoted to preserving a small, vibrant, gritty slice of New York life, the life of pushcarts and sweatshops and vaudeville and Tin Pan Alley, was moving into a new building in a different part of town. It was going to be incorporated into a larger organization, to become a section of the City University system, where there would be more room, more money, more prestige. It was as if the drab middle-aged museum had snagged a rich dentist.

"Dr. Bergman! There you are." The new director was a nervous, suspicious woman with a heart-shaped face instead of a heart, that's what Joy had told Aaron, and he'd laughed. She usually introduced herself as Miss Georgia, as if she were a beauty pageant winner. "Out with the old, in with the new," Miss Georgia was known to say. It was her mandate. It had to do with grants.

"Packed up and ready to go?" she said when she saw Joy. "The new year approaches. The movers wait for no man."

Then, like a schoolmarm or a politician or the Wicked Witch of the West, she shook her finger in Joy's face.

Joy, a little taken aback, recovered and jauntily waved her finger in Miss Georgia's face in response.

By Wednesday, they were in the new building.

"It's big and bulky and it's cement, it's sort of like being inside an inverted swimming pool," she told Aaron. She smoothed his hospital gown. "There are no windows that I can see. The stairs were made by giants for giants. And inside, I couldn't decide whether I was about to be overcome by claustrophobia or agoraphobia. Help! I wanted to say. I'm just an old lady looking for my cabinet of old tchotchkes."

Her new department was called City Collections.

"Like a sanitation-truck company," she said to Aaron.

She had arrived at the new building out of breath and a little confused. Her bags were heavy and she tilted noticeably to the left. Lopsided or not, she thought, here I come.

"But this is a closet," she said when Miss Georgia showed Joy her new office.

"A storage room," the director corrected her. "But it will do nicely. Look at all the . . . storage."

The narrow, windowless room was lined by expensive-looking built-in file cabinets. There was also a table, very white and modern, and a rather worn gray chair on casters.

"But I do need a desk," Joy said. "I mean, after all, a person needs a desk."

"But that is your desk," the director said, pointing to the table.

"But it has no drawers. There isn't even a drawer for a pencil."

"Perhaps you have a nice mug," the director said, patting the table encouragingly. "For your pencil."

"Do you think they're trying to get rid of me?" Joy said to

Aaron. "I don't think they can fire me for being old, so they'll just torment me, right? Until I leave of my own free will."

She spooned some ice cream into his mouth.

"They'll see how easy it is to get rid of me," she said. "They're in for a surprise, aren't they, Aaron?"

Aaron was prescribed various painkillers that teenagers in shrinking Midwestern towns abused. But when asked what the pain was from, the doctors were as canny and cautious as politicians. Molly wanted to shake them. *Tell us what is wrong so we can fix it*, she wanted to say. *He is suffering. And I have to get back to L.A. to teach.* She bombarded the doctors with direct questions, but the doctors always managed not to answer directly. Aaron had bladder cancer—they would concede that much, but everyone already knew that much. Heart failure, colon cancer, bladder cancer, Alzheimer's. Yes, yes, but what was causing this pain?

"Daddy wants a pastrami sandwich," Joy said, coming out of Aaron's hospital room. "Honey, did you hear me?"

Molly had just asked the resident how long her father had to live. The resident said he could die tomorrow. Or not. He could live for a year. Or not. Or more. Or not.

"New York pastrami!" the resident said. "Good sign. A man with an appetite."

In fact, Aaron had eaten nothing but a spoonful of ice cream in days, and when Molly arrived with the sandwich, he said there was a disgusting smell in the room, waved his big hand at her, and made her take it away.

She took the pastrami sandwich, which she had gone all the way to Zabar's to get, to the cafeteria and split it with her mother and brother.

"It shouldn't go to waste," Joy said.

"That doctor said Daddy could come home in a day or two," Molly said.

Joy wagged her head noncommittally.

"So we have to think about that."

"You do need some help, Mom," Daniel said. "Maybe someone to live in. Just for a while."

"Molly's here."

Molly said slowly, clearly, " 'Help' as in 'You can't get good help these days,' not help as in 'My daughter is a great help.' "

"And Molly has to leave on Friday."

"I'll cope," Joy said. "I always have."

"And when you're at work? Do you want Daddy crawling down Park Avenue with no pants on? He needs someone to watch him."

Joy sensed that Molly was right, but she wondered if it was necessary for Molly to bark at her like that. It was certainly ex-peditious, that bark, for even when Molly was not right, people tended to listen to her. But not this time, Joy thought. "I'm not sending him to a home," she said. "Period."

"Maybe we can get a nurse's aide to come in," Daniel said.

"I don't want those people in my house. A different person every day . . . strangers snooping around."

"But it would be so 'cosmopolitan,' " Molly said, her voice full of sarcasm.

"What are you, sixteen years old, Molly? Give me a break."

Molly did not give her a break, how could she? "You have to hire someone, whatever it costs. What have you been saving for all these years? A rainy day? This is the rainy day."

Daniel said, "If it's the money—"

"Of course it's the money."

"—then we can help you out, right, Molly? I mean as long as Ruby gets into a good public high school and Cora gets into a charter school for middle school and . . ."

"Take from my children?" Joy made a disgusted, dismissive sound. "Out of the question."

"Well, then you could always sell Upstate," Daniel said.

A horrified silence.

Then, "Never."

Joy had inherited the little house Upstate when her mother died. She had fought to keep it safe from . . . well, from Aaron. There was no other way to put it, though she had tried at the time. We're putting it in a trust, she had declared. A trust in my name. To keep it safe from creditors, she'd said repeatedly. But they all knew what she meant. Safe from Aaron. The house sat on a hill above a stream in Columbia County, New York. Upstate, Joy's mother used to say. We're going Upstate this weekend. Upstate was where the noise and worry of the city disappeared and the stream gurgled, where the birds sang. Upstate was the fruit of her father's labors, that's what he used to say when he stood on the porch and looked out at the maple tree and the three birch trees and the weeping willow by the stream. It was also the fruit of his frugality, and finally of his generosity. He had worked so hard, supporting every stray uncle or aunt or cousin who wandered through his door, and there had been a mob of them. Then the Depression ended and he was a manager, and then the war ended and he was a vice president. Spend a dollar, save a dollar, he said. And one day he announced that he had a surprise, and they drove out of town and into the country to the white-shingled house. He had saved and he had invested. Upstate was his reward, a reward he left to his wife and she left to Joy.

"I am not selling Upstate. It's all I have. Do you want me to have nothing? Nothing?"

"Yeah, Daniel. Do you want her to have nothing?" Molly said.

"Of course I don't want her to have nothing. I just want her to hire some help."

"So do I. But we can't sell the house. It's our family house."

Daniel noticed that Molly said "we" can't sell the house. But it was their mother's house, not theirs. Molly spent ten days a year in the house, if that. What difference did it make to her? Daniel spent every summer there with his wife and children. He loved the house. But love and sentimentality were two different things, or they ought to be.

"It's part of who we are," Molly was saying. It was true she no longer spent any time there, but she thought about the house all the time. It was an anchor of some kind, an East Coast anchor. It was there, stable and firm, even if she was not.

"Why are you fetishizing this house? Mom and Dad need help, they need money to pay for the help, the house is an asset that can be liquidated. Do you want them to live in squalor so you can idealize a house you never use?"

"Children! Stop it right now."

Molly and Daniel were quiet. They looked at her sheepishly.

"You can argue about the house after I'm dead."

"Mom . . ." they both said.

"You can squabble about it then. I need peace now."

Daniel wondered if the house was even worth anything. But it had to be worth the salary of an underpaid health-care worker.

"We just want you to hire—"

"How can I hire? I have no money! Why are you talking about real estate when your father is so sick?"

Daniel left, wanted to get home before the girls went to bed, and Molly walked with her mother back to Aaron's room. She knew she was being selfish about the house. She did not like to think of herself as selfish.

"You know," she said, "whatever you have to do about the house, I'm fine with it."

Joy said, "Enough, Molly."

"Not that you have to consult me or anything," Molly added. "Or ask my permission."

"I'm not selling the house with or without your permission."

"Well, good, good. But if Daniel is right and you need money . . ."

"I am leaving the house to both of you. It's all I have, and I want to leave it to my children."

"Oh, Mommy," Molly said, her voice tearful. She took her mother's hand and squeezed it. "You know you don't have to leave Daniel and me anything."

"So you *do* want me to die with nothing."

They got back to Aaron's room just as Aaron was being hoisted from the floor beside the bed, soaked and soiled. He had lowered the bed rail. "Get off me," he was shouting at the nurse. White, shaking, he was maneuvered back into bed by Joy and the nurse. Joy wiped him down as gently as she could, but he was a mess.

"Stop bothering me," he kept saying. "Leave me alone, all of you."

Joy helped the nurse attach a clean pouch. When the nurse had gone, she smoothed the sheets and poured some water, which Aaron refused to drink.

"We'll be safer with this." The nurse reappeared with an armful of nylon webbing. She began calmly to strap Aaron to his bed.

"What are you doing to him?" Joy cried.

"Get away from me!" Aaron said.

"Get away from him!" Molly said.

Joy lunged for the netting, trying to pull it off Aaron, but the nurse blocked her and continued with her task, saying, in the same calm way, "It's for your safety, Aaron."

Aaron struggled against the restraints. "Get me out of this!" His eyes rolled like a frightened horse's. "Help! Help!"

"Nurse, please, why are you doing this? I'll stay with him every minute, I'll watch him, I'll hire someone to watch him."

"Maybe if you had arranged that earlier," the nurse said. "But it's too late for tonight. This is for safety, Aaron," she said again as she wrestled him into the restraints. "Your *safety*."

Aaron thrashed and scratched at the orange netting. "You!" he said, poking out a finger and aiming it at Joy. "You can't do anything right! You can't do anything right!"

Joy pulled her hand back from the strap she had been trying to unbuckle. The soiled towels she had used to clean him fell from her other hand to the floor.

"You can't do anything right!" Aaron yelled again. He kept yelling: "You can't do anything right," his face distorted with rage. "You never do anything right! Never!"

"Aaron . . ."

"You did this! *You* did this to me! It's your fault!! You do everything wrong! Everything!" He twisted in the netting like a huge, dying fish. His voice was hard. Spit flew from his cracked lavender lips. "You can't do anything right," he roared. "You can't take care of anything."

"Daddy, stop it. For god's sake . . ."

He sneered at Joy now as he struggled in his webbing. "You can't take care of anything, you know that? You can't do anything *right*. Nothing. You can't do anything . . ."

Molly steered her mother out of the room. Her father's enraged screams followed them down the hall. "Okay," Molly said, holding her mother's arm, feeling the bone of the skinny arm beneath Joy's sweater. "Okay," she said again, but her mother said nothing, and Molly found herself looking away, ashamed, almost as if she'd walked in on her parents having sex. Or something. "Okay."

Her mother turned on her, yanking her arm free. "I've had it," Joy said fiercely, as if Molly were going to argue with her.

"Yeah," Molly said. "Yeah. Jesus."

"Am I not flesh?"

"I know. He's not himself."

"If you prick me, do I not bleed?" her mother continued. She was crazy-eyed now and walking quickly, waving her arms.

"Mom . . ."

"Don't Mom me. After everything I've done. Everything I've lived with all these years. Everything I've had to do. I am a human being!"

Shylock, the Elephant Man. Her mother was pulling out all the stops. And why shouldn't she? Molly felt as if she had just seen a horror film, a monster movie, and her poor father was the monster.

She coaxed her mother to a couch in the waiting room.

"I've had it," Joy kept saying. "I've had it, I've had it."

Then, almost in slow motion, she slumped forward.

She said, "Had I, haa . . . I . . ." She stopped.

"Mom?"

"Haaa daaa. I haa. I, I." She stopped again and looked at Molly in alarm.

12

W hat was that awful smell? The smell was almost a parody of
a fresh smell, a little like chewing gum or floor cleaner,
but sickly and decomposed, as if someone had tried to
cover up the stink of decaying flesh. Was it decaying flesh? Was it
gangrene? Joy thought of wiggling her feet to make sure they were
there, but they seemed far away and she was so tired. She heard
Molly badgering someone. She heard Daniel's voice, too: "But I
thought you said she'd had a stroke."

Oh yes, now she remembered. She was in the hospital visiting
Aaron. Someone must have had a stroke.

"She did, a mild one. But we also think she has a highly contagious antibiotic-resistant infection called Clostridium difficile.
C. diff for short," said a male voice Joy did not recognize.

But who had had a stroke? Who were they talking about?

"C. diff is common in older patients being treated with antibiot-
ics in the hospital or in a nursing home," the male voice continued.
"Has your mother been in a nursing home recently?"

"No," Molly said. "But she practically runs one."

"That's why she's in an isolation room. The C. diff."

"Excuse me, Doctor," Daniel said. "It's just that there's another patient here. In this isolation room."

Daniel was always so polite, using someone's title, his voice soft, though Joy could hear the frustration and anger. She worried about him hanging around a hospital after what he'd been through. He should go home to his family. She would look after Aaron.

"Well," the doctor was saying, "we believe the other patient probably has C. diff, too."

"You *believe*?" Molly said. "They both *probably* have C. diff? What if one has it and the other doesn't? The one who has it will give it to the one who doesn't."

"Then they'll both have it," the doctor said, his voice a little impatient with Molly's absence of scientific method. "That's why they're in isolation."

C. diff. Joy knew she had heard about C. diff somewhere. On the radio, perhaps. Did C. diff cause a terrible odor? The smell, that was what was worrying her.

Molly and Daniel stood together in the blue paper gowns and caps and booties, the white masks and the almost transparent gloves they had to wear in their mother's room. It was hot in her curtained-off portion and rivulets of sweat ran down Molly's back. The woman in the next bed, who may or may not have had C. diff, was small, even smaller than Joy. Her face was caved in around her missing dentures. Her skin was dry and yellow and mottled and tight as a cadaver's. She looked very much like a cadaver. She nearly was a cadaver. A man, Molly presumed it was her son, sat beside her, rocking forward and back, saying, "Mommy, Mommy," and for the first time in her life Molly wondered if it was bizarre that she still sometimes called her mother Mommy, because this man was as old as she was and he was saying Mommy and he was surely bizarre. "Nurse! Doctor! Help! Help!" he would occasionally cry out, running into the hall. He had a disturbing voice, flat and desperate and loud. "My mommy's not answering me," he would say, wringing his hands, when a nurse appeared. "My mommy's not talking!"

The nurses did not like this odd middle-aged man who behaved like a child. And they did not like coming into the room, because of the smell.

"What *is* it?" they asked each time they entered.

"What *is* it?" Molly and Daniel asked each other.

Molly was glad of her paper mask. She got up to check the trash can one more time, but it was still empty.

"What *is* it?"

A strange raspy sound came from the woman in the other bed.

"It's a death rattle!" her son cried. "Mommy, don't die."

He ran out of the room and returned with a nurse, who threw on a gown, snapped on gloves, and examined the emaciated woman.

"It's a cough," the nurse said gently. "Don't worry. It's just a cough." She patted him on the shoulder.

Then she said, "What is that nasty, nasty smell?" She pulled away from him. "No wonder this poor woman is coughing." She sniffed at him, like an unfriendly dog. "Is that your *gum*?"

"Gangrene," Joy said.

"Mom's awake!" Daniel said. "Mom said gangrene! Did you hear her, Molly? Nurse? Hooray! She said gangrene!"

The other woman's son was sniffing at his own arm. "Bengay?" he said.

"Bengay?" Joy said, actually sitting up. "Good god."

"I put it on every morning," the son said, eyeing the nurse warily. "After my shower," he added with sudden defiance.

"You mean like moisturizer?" said the nurse.

"Good god," said Joy.

"Bengay. That's a new one," the nurse said as she left the room.

"Mom, I'm so happy to see you back to yourself," Daniel said.

"Welcome back to the world," said Molly.

"Why are you dressed like that?" Joy asked.

"Isolation," said Molly.

"You can be alone even in a crowd," Joy murmured, and fell back to sleep.

Soon another nurse came in.

"Sir," she said to the man in Bengay. "I'm going to have to ask you to leave. I'm sorry, but the smell of your, um, ointment is disturbing patients and staff and visitors up and down the floor."

"Yes, but do you have the C. diff test results yet?" Molly asked the nurse. "I think both patients deserve to know why they're in isolation *with each other.*"

"Sir?" The nurse ignored Molly. "Sir, please go home, wash it off, and then you can come back. You don't need to use so much, you know. Just a little bit. Why don't you try it at night, before bed? But for now . . ."

"Excuse me, Nurse, but if his mother catches something from my mother," Molly said, "you will have more to worry about than Bengay."

"I use it every day," the man said. "I can't leave Mommy. I can't. Mommy is very sick." He began to cry a little. He covered his face with his hands. "I can't."

Molly patted his back. The smell was less upsetting now that she knew what it was, but it was just as strong. It burned her nostrils. It stung her eyes. She said, as mildly as she could, "You don't want your mother to catch something from my mother, do you?"

He shook his head.

"And if my mother catches something from his mother," Molly said to the nurse, "you should know that my brother is a lawyer."

But it was as if Molly were not there. The nurse, a small, even dainty woman, emanated authority, and she wanted this man, the source of disturbance on her floor, to go away. "Sir?" she said, her hands on her hips. "I really don't want to have to call security."

"I don't think you understand," Molly said. "This man will not be bullied and neither will we. We are in this together." She stood in solidarity beside the unhappy, redolent man. "Aren't we?"

He stopped crying and took his hands away from his face. He

seemed afraid to look at the wee, mighty nurse, but he made eye contact with Molly, brief, furtive eye contact. Then he looked down at his mother. She didn't move. The only sound in the room was her rasping breath. He gazed at her for what seemed a long time, then he squared his shoulders.

"Mommy," he said, "we are calling your doctor."

And he led the way to the nurses' station.

When Molly got back to the room, the Bengay man was headed home and arrangements had been made to separate the two potentially infectious patients.

"Strength in numbers and the desire to get that poor guy off the floor."

Daniel was holding their mother's hand. She was awake again. "Good job!" he said to Molly.

Molly laughed. "That's the voice people use for their kids. And dogs."

"I don't know what you're talking about," Joy said weakly, reminding herself of Aaron, which made her worry suddenly and viscerally how he was. "Daddy! How is Daddy?"

"Dad's doing fine," Daniel said. "He's out of the hospital, how about that? He's home."

"But who's looking after him? What is he eating? How is he—"

"It's all taken care of, Mom," Molly said. "You'll see."

13

The apartment was full of voices, all timbres, tones, and accents. It was like an orchestra. The cushions of the sofa cradled her aching body. She listened to the voices: a deep, male, harsh African musicality; the free-for-all vowels of Portuguese English; the loops of female Polish. And Aaron, his intermittent wailing reaching back to Middle Eastern chanting in its cadences, as if all his ancestors were crying out at once.

Joy opened her eyes. A man the color of ebony smiled at her as he walked past the door toward the kitchen. He stopped to confer with a boxy woman in wide capri pants. And there was Elvira, too, the Bergmans' housekeeper, tall and thin as a daddy long-legs, behind the boxy lady, nodding. It was such a lively group, the three of them speaking together, one more incomprehensible than the next, incomprehensible to Joy, presumably to one another as well.

Joy closed her eyes again and listened to the languages she could not comprehend. It was as though she could comprehend nothing at all, drifting comfortably on the soft outskirts of comprehension. Eventually Danny introduced the compact, quiet black man. His name was Walter. Danny said that Walter came at night. Joy smiled at Walter. How kind of him to come at night to care for Aaron. To care for her. Lovely, she said when Danny introduced her to Wanda, the woman shaped like a UPS package. Wanda emitted a gurgling laugh. Thank you, Joy said. Wanda emitted the gurgling laugh again. She spoke only Polish. Joy said, How kind of you.

"Wanda and Walter are trained in changing the colostomy bag," Danny said. "And they taught Elvira."

"Lovely."

"You absolutely cannot do it anymore. The doctor said you can't even touch it. That might be how you got C. diff."

"C. diff is very, very dangerous." She remembered now, she had heard about C. diff on *The Joan Hamburg Show* on the radio. "Treacherous."

"So you really have to take it easy, Mom. Will you be able to do that? Just rest and let your strength come back?"

"Danny, you're so good to me. You and your sister are so good to me."

"Molly will be back in a few weeks."

"She's a good daughter. I am so lucky."

Daniel smiled. She reminded him of his daughters when they had a low-grade fever. How sweet they became.

"You're okay with not touching the pouch? Molly and I were a little worried. We know you like to take care of everything, especially about Dad, which is admirable, completely understandable. But this is really important. No pouch."

"Lovely," Joy said, closing her eyes. "Lovely."

She could remember, in a soft, foggy way, the motions of taking care of Aaron, gathering his pills, counting them, explaining what each one was, then explaining again, helping him out of his wet pajamas, squatting down to get each of his enormous feet into his pant legs . . . And then the pouch, removing it, emptying it, washing Aaron, drying the hole, affixing the new pouch . . .

Each night Walter helped her to the bathroom. He brought her things to eat and helped her move the spoon from the bowl to her mouth. What a kind, kind man. When he appeared in the room carrying a tray or a basin of water, she was always pleasantly surprised. There was that kind man again.

When it was not night, there were the other kind people. Elvira, wiry and fast as a greyhound, whisking into the room and whisking out again. She had worked for Aaron and Joy for many years, coming every other week for a few hours. But now, Danny explained, she was coming in three mornings a week. She had insisted, he said. She didn't trust the others. Joy smiled when he said this. She smiled when he said anything. She really did not care what he said or what anyone else said as long as she did not have to move, as long as she could lie on the couch and rest. Never had fatigue been this heavy, never had it been this welcome. Lovely, she said when someone spoke to her. Thank you, she said. How kind of you.

"So kind," she said. "Everyone is so kind."

14

Could Molly have ever convinced Freddie to move to New York? Of course she could have. Even though Freddie had a tenured position teaching English at UCLA while Molly had been an adjunct at a community college in New York. Even though Molly had a better position here and was paid more, too. Even though her new Catalina Island investigations, unlike the work she'd been doing in Syria, were not likely to get her kidnapped or beheaded. But she did not want to convince Freddie to move to New York.

She thought guiltily of her mother and father trapped in their apartment. Freddie's father, Duncan, was old, too, as Freddie sometimes had to remind her, but that had not entered into Molly's decision. He did not weigh on Molly's mind as he should have, meaning she often forgot he existed.

But he did exist, he was old, and now he had fallen.

Freddie spoke to the paramedics, who said they'd thought at first that Duncan's hip was broken, but he was standing on it, so it couldn't possibly be broken. "The pain would be unbearable," they said. "Take him to the doctor, though, just to make sure there are no sprains."

The assisted-living facility where Duncan lived was called Green Garden, so Freddie and Molly naturally called it Grey Gardens. When they arrived, Molly waited in the car while Freddie went upstairs and got her father into a wheelchair.

"We going to the track?" Duncan said.

"No. We're going to the doctor. Because you fell."

"I'd rather go to the track."

It turned out you could stand up with a broken hip, after all. Duncan Hughes could, anyway. After the doctor saw his X-rays, Duncan was taken to the hospital in an ambulance. Freddie and Molly followed in the car. Freddie was too shocked to say much. A broken hip for a man in his late eighties. That was pretty much it for her father. Pneumonia would come next, and he would die. That's what always happened.

"He's not like other people," Molly said, as if she'd read Freddie's thoughts. "He'll walk out of there, Freddie. You'll see."

Freddie called her brothers and sisters. One brother lived in Melbourne, one in Hong Kong. Both sisters lived in Rio. They ran a boutique together.

"They all said the exact same thing," Freddie told Molly. " 'Keep me informed.' "

"They came for his eighty-fifth birthday. I guess they think that's enough."

"So then they'll end up coming for his funeral, and it won't make any difference because he'll be dead. People should have pre-funerals."

But Molly turned out to be right: Duncan was not like other people, there was no funeral, and he returned to his room at Green Garden.

"He seems happy to be back. Although he thought the name was Green Goddess. And he still wants to go to the track."

"We should take him. Maybe his luck will hold out. We'll win some money."

Daniel took Ruby and Cora to the Museum of the City of New York. He thought they would like the Victorian dollhouse, but they preferred an exhibit on graffiti. Then they walked down Fifth Avenue, past the hospital, toward his parents' apartment, and the girls insisted on getting ice cream from a vendor although it was windy and cold.

"Let's sit in Grandpa's park," Ruby said. "Maybe we'll see the rat."

They sat on the cold bench and watched pigeons fluff themselves against the wind. There was no one else there. Daniel wondered if his father would ever see the park again, if he would ever leave the apartment again. For all he knew, his father was slipping into a new stage of dementia, leaving the park, the apartment, the entire world. Leaving Daniel forever.

The world without Aaron Bergman was unimaginable to Daniel. Even this pocket park, where he sat on a bench in a swirl of dead leaves with his daughters, was confusing without Aaron. Why was the park here if not for Aaron? Why were any of them in the park if not for its association with Daniel's father?

"It's weird without Grandpa here, isn't it?" he said.

"Do you think raccoons come here?" Ruby asked.

"Or the coyote?"

His father was the embodiment of the word "entitled," Daniel understood that. It was a kind of strength, he understood that, too—Aaron's sense that whatever the world had to offer, it was certainly on offer to him, and deservedly so. Daniel envied him that confidence. Perhaps it arose from being born into a well-to-do family. But it had stayed with Aaron even when he lost his fortune. A small fortune, but Aaron had lost it, lost a profitable, solvent, well-run family business.

My daddy was a gambler, Aaron used to sing, and Daniel would joyously sing along. They listened to Woody Guthrie records while Aaron's business swelled up into a big balloon of impossible debt and then, one day, just like that, popped and shriveled and disappeared. Daniel had been quite young, so young he didn't really remember being well-off. What he remembered were the years afterward, one surefire scheme after another, his mother getting a job, taking any freelance work she could rustle up even as she went back to school. He remembered the need, not for the family to live—there was always, miraculously just enough for that—but the need inside his father, the need for money, and for money to make money, and for that money to make more money, and for the lost money to reappear as borrowed money and the whole thing to start over again.

"*I've been doing some hard travelin', I thought you know'd,*" Daniel sang in a nasal country-Western voice.

"Daddy," Ruby said. She tugged at his arm. Things about him had started to embarrass her.

"*Hard travelin', hard ramblin'* . . ."

"*Hard gamblin',*" Cora joined in.

"You both make me sick," Ruby said. But she joined in eventually, too. There was no one to hear them. Just an old man with the same red walker Aaron had, and by the time he reached the bench, the song was over.

— 16 —

Freddie could not decide whether or not to go to New York for Christmas. She loved going East for the holidays, it was still a novelty for her, it always would be—the snow, the cold, the lights on Fifth Avenue.

"Everything you hate about it," she said to Molly, "like the crowds, for instance—I love that. I love being a tourist there."

"You go to New York and see my father, I'll stay here and see your father. They won't know the difference."

As soon as she said it, Molly wished she hadn't. "I'm sorry. It's so easy to dine out on them. Cheap joke. Why don't we both stay here this year?"

But Freddie knew that Molly's family Jewish Christmas was somehow their most important holiday. They celebrated Hanukkah in a haphazard way, lighting candles on the nights they remembered. But Christmas was a time they all got together, all of them, even Molly's ex-husband and his current wife.

"And Ben will be there," Freddie said. She had said the magic word, the defining word, the name of the son. She watched Molly's face grow almost beatific.

"Ben," Freddie said again, just to see the effect, to see the benignity intensify.

Then Molly caught her at it. "Oh shut up," she said.

Freddie started to laugh. "The idea of you staying here for the holidays—it's pretty funny, Molly. Go see your cockamamie family and I'll stay here and look after my cockamamie father. We will long for each other across the wide continent."

17

In her parents' bedroom, it was dim and cluttered with medical apparatus. Her father sat in his leather recliner, a blanket spread neatly over his knees. He grabbed Molly's hand and motioned for her to lean down, then put his lips close to her ear.

"There's a black man in the house," he whispered, obviously alarmed.

"That's Walter, Mom's nurse's-from-when-she-broke-her-ankle-ten-years-ago's son-in-law's cousin's mother's friend from church. Or some such thing. He's from Ghana." He was a very gentle man with a beautiful smile and a staccato, musical accent. He knew how to change a colostomy bag. He was strong. He was kind.

"What's he doing here? There's a black man in the apartment, I tell you," he whispered again, sputtering now. He pulled on her arm.

"Walter. From Ghana," she said, louder.

"No one from Ghana is named Walter," he whispered. "He's a fraud. Get him out."

She straightened up and looked down at her father. His beard was trimmed. His hair was combed. Even the hairs in his ears had been trimmed. His nails were clean. His shirt was unstained and buttoned properly. And that blanket on his lap—he could have been a gentleman taking in the salt air on an ocean liner.

"Daddy, he's here to help you."

"I don't need help. What are you talking about? Help? I don't need help. You're the one who needs help."

"Well, Mom needs help. You don't want her back in the hospital, do you?"

"Hospital? Nobody tells me anything. Where's your mother?"

"She's resting. Do you want her to drop dead from exhaustion? Then who would take care of you?"

He looked pointedly at her.

"*Me?*" she said. "I wouldn't last two minutes."

"Honey?"

"Yes, Daddy?"

He motioned her to lean down again. "There's a black man in the house," he whispered.

"I knew he was a Republican," she said later to Freddie on the phone. "But he never struck me as any more racist than anyone else his age. The uncomfortable kind of racism, not the suspicious kind."

"He's not himself, though."

"I hope not." That didn't come out right. "Anyway, he's incredibly difficult one minute, then he just switches over to sweetness. When I left the room, he and Walter were sitting side by side eating vanilla ice cream, watching NY1."

"That's the real Aaron, the vanilla ice cream one."

Freddie was a gracious person. It was one of the things Molly loved about her.

"Thank you for being a gracious person, Freddie," she said. "Even in the face of ghastly in-laws."

Freddie laughed. How lovely that laugh was. How close Freddie seemed.

"They could have stopped with the telephone . . ." Molly said. "Who?"

". . . No television, no cars or planes, no computers. Just telephones, the invention that allows me to hear you from so far away, the magical telephone. It would have been enough."

"That and penicillin," Freddie said.

When they hung up, Freddie called her sisters. They were the first and second children, born only eleven months apart. They liked to call themselves Irish twins, though they were not even Irish. Freddie was the youngest, separated from Pamela and Laurel by almost a decade, but they acted like little sisters to Freddie's mind, giggling and teasing each other, trading clothes, trying each other's lipsticks, doing each other's hair. Freddie had never paid much attention to them, two squeaty older girls off on their dates, counting their sweaters. It was no surprise when, both divorced, they opened a boutique together, though why they chose Rio de Janeiro she could not fathom. They must stand out in that city like two sore thumbs, two plump pink sore thumbs, she thought. They resembled Freddie's mother, though they did not remind Freddie of her mother. They were pinker than her mother, who had skin that was soft and blushing, and they were chubby. Freddie's mother had spoken like an adult woman who hoped someone might listen to her now and then. Her older daughters spoke like girls at a slumber party, breathy and secretive, then shrieking with laughter. And now, presumably, in Portuguese. Freddie could not envision them among what she imagined to be the slender, sophisticated bronzed beauties of Rio. They had done well with their boutique, but when Freddie tried to picture them in their store, she saw only the two of them selling clothes back and forth to each other.

She had been closer to her brothers in age and in temperament. But they had grown up and gone their own ways, like her sisters. If any one of them had moved any farther away from Los Angeles, they'd have ended up being home again, the world being round and all.

"I'm keeping you informed," Freddie said when Pamela answered. Laurel immediately picked up another extension. How quaint, Freddie thought. Like our grandparents.

"He's a marvel," Pamela said.

"What are you two doing for Christmas?" Laurel asked.

"Well, Molly had to go to New York to see her mother, so . . ."

"No, I meant you and Dad."

"Oh."

"He won't know what day it is anyway," said Pamela.

"I could take him to the track."

Neither of them thought that was a good idea, but they were sure Freddie would come up with something.

"I picture you two sitting in front of the fire at Green Garden," Laurel said.

"Oh, perfect!" said Pamela. "Drinking eggnog. Just the thought of you and Dad in front of the crackling fire makes me nostalgic."

Freddie did not tell them Green Garden had no fireplace.

She called her brothers next, but she got the time wrong and woke one up, and the other did not answer.

"Molly, I miss you," she texted.

"Never again" said the text that came back.

There were certain things about the Christmas Hanukkah season that Coco did not like. First of all, she felt guilty for having a Christmas tree, not because she was Jewish, but because it was such a waste. A living thing cut down for nothing.

"I understand not eating meat," Daniel had said the first time it came up, when Ruby was two. "I understand being a vegetarian. But you're *not* a vegetarian. And even if you were a vegetarian, you would eat vegetables. Vegetables would die so you could live. Isn't a Christmas tree like a vegetable? It grows out of the ground. It's like a big stalk of broccoli."

"We don't eat Christmas trees. It doesn't die so I can live. It dies so we can decorate it."

"We could eat it. We could chop it up and cook it after Christmas."

"Very funny."

Coco hated waste. It was that simple. The death of the pine tree was not the issue. She was not a fool, she was a science teacher, and she understood the importance and beauty of decomposition, how it brought new things to life. But the planting and cultivating and harvesting of what was essentially a big bauble, a bauble on which to hang other baubles—that was unconscionable.

"It provides employment," Daniel said.

"Those Canadians who drive down every year and sell them on the street?"

"It provides enjoyment!" he said, pleased with the rhyme.

She sniffed her disapproval.

"Ruby really, really wants one."

Then, of course, Coco said "Okay!" instantly. For Ruby, any-thing.

And now she made a big, happy fuss over the tree each year. She did love the smell, the look of them lined up on the sidewalk, the ritual of carrying the tree home. Once it was standing in the living room, though, and opened its fragrant branches, spread-ing the outdoor smell through the house, Coco had to fight off a flicker of sorrow. Like any useless bunch of carnations or daisies, the Christmas tree would shrivel and die. She cheered herself with the thought that the city now had a policy of gathering the trees up and using them for compost.

Choosing presents helped to cheer her up, too. Each potential recipient of a gift presented a puzzle to be solved. This year, she had solved two problems at once—a gift for Ruby, who was so unpredictable and in-between these days, and a more immediate use of the Christmas tree than compost.

She'd been a little unsure about the kit of science projects she'd gotten the girls. It used marshmallows, which of course they would like. It was, however, educational, and educational gifts sometimes fell flat. But when they opened their gifts on Christmas Eve, the science kit was both Ruby's and Cora's favorite. Cora immediately took herself off to watch marshmallow after marshmallow swell prodigiously in the microwave. And because the kit included a slingshot, Ruby, in her new Tom Sawyer phase, was delighted. The rubber tubing, the patch of leather, the plastic Y-shaped stick did the trick. She had been lobbying for a frog for Christmas, but without any real conviction.

"Best of all," Coco said, handing her another package, "you can make a new, stronger slingshot from the Christmas tree!" It was a whittling knife.

"This is the best Christmas we ever had," Coco told Daniel that night. The tree had been put to use, Cora went to bed wearing every wearable gift and clutching a new stuffed dog and a bag of marshmallows, and Ruby went to bed clutching her knife.

"I hope Ruby doesn't cut a finger off in her sleep," Daniel said.

"It's a jackknife. It's all folded up. Would you say that if she were a boy?"

"No. Then I'd be sure there would be cut-off fingers. Don't let my mother see the knife."

"Didn't you have a jackknife when you were a kid?"

"They said I could have a BB gun when I was twenty-one."

"Typical."

"I had a *compass*."

It was too difficult to load Aaron into a taxi this year to go down to Daniel and Coco's, so the family gathered for Christmas Day at the apartment uptown instead.

"Grandpa, look. I made a slingshot. And I'm whittling a new wooden handle for it, too. A slingshot uses kinetic energy."

"That's a dangerous weapon," Aaron said, handling the stick.

"My father would have murdered me if he knew I had a Christmas tree."

"It only shoots marshmallows."

"We always had a tree," Molly said. "Grandpa Bergman didn't mind."

"Like hell."

Ben had been sitting on the floor playing with the Spirograph he'd gotten the girls. Now he examined Ruby's knife. He put it in his pocket.

"Thank you, Ruby. I've always wanted a pocketknife."

She chased him around the apartment and Cora chased her. Joy watched them fondly. But the noise was pounding in her ears, the laughing and happy screaming. Wrapping paper flew around them, ribbons trailed from the girls' shoes, stuck to the soles by tape. Cheerful children, she said to herself. A blessing. She repeated it silently several times to chase away the other things she was thinking, which were, Shut the hell up, Stop it, Why must you be so noisy, You are not on the street, You are driving me crazy.

Ben's father, Doug, came with his wife, Lisa, a sweet youngish person with long, lank hair and a nervous laugh. Who would not laugh nervously, Joy thought, thrown into the bosom of your husband's ex-wife's family? She greeted the woman with as much warmth as she could muster. It wasn't Lisa's fault that Molly had left Doug, it wasn't Lisa's fault that modern mores compelled all these exes to gather together and exchange gifts, it wasn't Lisa's fault that Joy missed Doug and held Lisa responsible, even though it was *not* her fault, it was Molly's, but of course Molly had the right to be happy, of course she did.

Molly threw her arms around Doug when she saw him. I love you, Doug Harkavy, she thought. I will always love you, you are Ben's father and there was a time when we planned our future and our future died yet here we are, and I will always treasure those days and I'm so glad I'm no longer married to you and I bet you're glad you're no longer married to me.

"Whaddya get me?" she said to him. She realized she was a little drunk. Ben had made a cocktail with apple cider and bourbon.

"Where's Freddie?" Lisa said politely.

"Home with her own dysfunctional family. Well, just her father, really. She couldn't leave him. He's been ill. Men-tal-lly ill." Oh dear. She was truly drunk.

"Okay, Mom, sit yourself down right here and drink this big glass of water, that's a good girl."

Molly beamed at Ben. She beamed at Doug and Lisa. Good old Lisa. She beamed at her mother and her brother, at Coco and the two little girls. When her gaze got to her father, she stopped beaming. He was tugging at the colostomy bag.

"Daddy, don't."

He looked up at her. He shrugged.

"You should eat something," Ben said, but Molly was no longer drunk, not even tipsy. She was sad, suddenly and thoroughly sad. She shook her head at Ben, afraid if she spoke she would cry.

"Marshmallows," said Cora. "Eat marshmallows."

"I don't have marshmallows," Joy said. "But I have Mallomars. Would anyone like a Mallomar?"

"Shoot a Mallomar, Ruby," Cora said excitedly.

Ruby said, "I ain't botherin' with suchlike nonsense."

"Ruby is channeling Tom Sawyer," Coco said proudly.

"Sounds more like Slim Pickins," Molly said.

"We used to say '"Ain't" ain't in the dictionary,'" Daniel said to Molly. "Remember? But it turns out it is."

Joy started telling Ben her story of when she had polio as a child.

"They were all so hysterical," she said. "My mother fainted, my grandmother had to tend to her, and for all I know, it wasn't polio at all. Maybe my leg fell asleep."

"But you were in the hospital, Grandma. They put you in the hospital. It must have been something."

"Oh, who knows, they were all so hysterical."

They ate Mallomars while Cora explained Boyle's Law as she understood it, which Coco said was brilliant, until Cora began speculating on volume and pressure in the bowel, at which point Coco interrupted and said the bowel was not a closed system, and Molly involuntarily glanced at her father and thought of his system, definitely not a closed one. He had fallen asleep in his chair, his chin on his chest.

"Do you want to try the experiment, Grandma? You put marshmallows in a syringe."

"Well, I don't have any syringes on hand, sweetheart. Maybe another time. You'll teach me."

Aaron's head jerked up and he said, "You can't teach an old dog new tricks."

"I bet you can," Cora said. "Can we try? Can we get an old dog? From the ASPCA?"

"But what if it really won't learn any new tricks and the saying is true?" said Daniel.

"And we're stuck with an old dog with a low IQ?" said Coco.

"Well, at least it won't live very long," Ruby said. "If it's so old." Cora started to cry.

"Ruby, really," Coco said. "Was that necessary?"

"I'm very sensitive," Cora said between sobs.

"Death is natural," Ruby said. "No dog can live forever, especially an old one."

Daniel rocked Cora on his lap. "Our dog can't ever die, Cora sweetheart, because we don't have a dog."

But that made her cry harder.

On the walk home from the subway, Ruby kicked the snowdrift and waited for her parents and Cora to catch up. Cora was crying and dawdling because she was cold. If Cora would hurry up, she would be warmer, their mother explained, embarking on what Ruby thought was a clear and reasonable, though rather long, disquisition on the relationship between heat and energy. Ruby had tried hugging Cora from behind and duck-waddling along against her to provide some insulation, but there was no satisfying Cora when she was in this mood.

"Hurry up! I'm freezing!" Ruby called.

The snow that had piled up at the edge of the sidewalk was not really a drift. It had been pushed there by snowplows the night before, and it was already specked with black smuts of city dirt. Ruby scooped up a handful of dirty snow and packed it into a ball and took a few steps up the side of the mound of snow. She put the gray snowball in the leather pocket of the slingshot and let it fly, but it fell apart and disappeared into the dusk.

She shuffled her feet on the icy sidewalk. The wind blew and the sky was dark. Cora sniffled and shambled beside their mother. After two more blocks, she again refused to move, demanding a taxi. While her mother and father argued with her, Ruby pushed off and slid on the ice all the way to the next corner. There, the great berm of snow created by the plows took a right angle. She was boxed in by three-foot walls of snow. A narrow path of foot-prints ran up the snowbank. Over the course of the day it had cut into the bank like a mountain pass. It was frozen now, the bumpy pattern of boot soles shining in the street light. Ruby struggled to the top and surveyed her territory. "I'm the king of the world," she hollered into the wind. Nobody heard her.

She bent down and pried loose a small rock that had been plowed up with the snow, then fitted it with frozen fingers into the slingshot.

The hole it made in the plate-glass window of the corner mar-ket was small, like a bullet hole in a windshield in a television show. The cracks around the hole were the cracks around the hole in the ice on the skating pond in a movie and the little girl slips in, mittens flailing above the cold black water, and drowns.

Ruby stood, three feet above the sidewalk in the freezing wind, and stared in surprise at the hole in the window. The hole severed the stem of the letter *T* in the word MARKET. MIKE'S CORNER MAR-KET. Ruby felt her mother yanking on her arm, but did not see her. She saw only the mouth of the man who owned the store, Manuel (not Mike, there was no Mike), a nice man who sold her candy and Doritos. His mouth was moving, his missing tooth appeared and reappeared, a blink of dark space. Like the hole in his window. His face was contorted in mystified rage. He slapped the top of his shiny bald head with an open palm.

"What were you thinking?" That was her mother's voice. "Hand it over this minute." That was her father. They were all inside the store now, all of them in the narrow space between the counter and the racks of chips and boxes of power bars, in a line— Ruby, her father, who was pulling her slingshot from her frozen grip, her mother, her sister, who was white and awed but still wailing, Manuel, and a man Ruby did not know. Manuel's voice was speaking Spanish. Manuel's hand was pointing at the man who stood in front of the cash register. He was a tall man in a navy blue parka. His hair was soft and dark and fell over his forehead like a boy's, but he was not a boy, he was a young man. He was wearing a small beanie, the Jewish beanie, she forgot the name. His eyes were bright and blue. He was holding a Kleenex to his cheek. It was bright red. Red with blood. He was the handsomest man Ruby had ever seen.

The Spanish words and the words of her mother were all mixed together with Cora's wails. The noise was amplified by the constricted space, and the warmth was overwhelming after the windy street, and Ruby was sweating and crying, and her mother was holding her shoulders and shaking her, not very hard, and Manuel was slapping his head with both hands, and Cora was gulping her sobs down.

I'm sorry, I'm sorry, Ruby thought, but no words came out.

And then the handsome man put one hand on Ruby's mother's shoulder and one hand on Ruby's shoulder, the hand with the bloody Kleenex. The blood was so bright. It was the color of the paper stuck in the bottom of the plastic container of raspberries. It was almost pink. The tissue had sucked the color up. It flapped like a flag. A horrible, bloodstained flag. Ruby stared at it, and she didn't even hear herself scream, but she screamed, screamed bloody murder, as her father said later. And everyone else was suddenly quiet, even Cora.

Ruby screamed for quite a while, but eventually she heard what the handsome man was saying. He was kneeling down on the dirty bodega floor, and he hugged her and said, into her cold ear with his warm breath, "You didn't mean any harm. I know that. Accidents are everywhere, just waiting for us, aren't they? This accident is over now. No one was hurt. No one was hurt."

She did not remember her father reassuring Manuel that they would pay for a new window or Cora telling her she would be paying for it from her allowance for the rest of her life.

The handsome man held her hand and walked home with them. He was a rabbi. Call me Rabbi Kenny, he said. That's why he was wearing a beanie, she supposed (yarmulke, that was the name, she remembered). That's why he forgave her. He was a man of the cloth. Manuel had given him a first-aid kit he sold in the shop, no charge, and it had two gauze pads, which the rabbi had unwrapped and placed over the cut. He asked Ruby to apply the Band-Aids to hold them in place. There was no blood coming through them. No more blood, said the rabbi. See?

"You might need stitches," Daniel said.

The rabbi said, "No, I don't think so. Ruby did an excellent job patching me up."

Ruby's mother gave Ruby a cold glance.

"Why did you do that?" Daniel asked for the tenth time.

Rabbi Kenny said, "It was a mistake, a lapse in judgment, and Ruby seems like the kind of person who learns from mistakes."

"Well, that's true," Coco said. "She does. But we're so sorry, Rabbi."

Ruby was thinking how kind it was of the rabbi to refer to her as a person, rather than a little girl. Or a monster.

"I'm sorry, too," she said, the first words she had spoken since what she already thought of as the Incident. "I'm really, really, really sorry." She looked into her victim's lovely blue eyes. She wanted to say, Forgive me, Father, for I have sinned. She had seen it on so many TV shows. It was obviously inappropriate for a rabbi, which seemed a shame, for she *had* sinned and she *did* want his forgiveness.

"People should wear helmets," Cora said.

Rabbi Kenny lived a few blocks away with his wife and two small children. His synagogue was around the corner. They had passed it millions of times, but never gone in.

"We're not exactly observant Jews," Coco said.

"Daddy says monotheism is the greatest disaster to befall the human race," Cora said.

"Well, Daddy said Gore Vidal said that, sweetie," Coco interjected quickly. "I don't know that Daddy thinks that himself."

"He said." She stopped and folded her arms and glared at her father.

"A clever but simplistic sentiment," Daniel said, "and like everything Gore Vidal said, it's a little bit true, that's all I was saying."

"Daniel!" Coco was clearly embarrassed.

"Daddy!" Ruby said.

Cora gave a triumphant "ha" and moved on.

"I still remember my haftorah," Daniel said to the rabbi. "I'm not a complete pagan."

Rabbi Kenny laughed. "Well, if you're ever locked out of the house or something, pop into shul."

18

Molly burrowed into the pillows, eyes closed, a cool scented breeze blowing in through the open window. She listened to the crows in the neighbor's sycamore. The deplorable tree shed darkness and elephantine leaves, but high in its branches there lived a family of crows, an exemplary family, crow sons and daughters from the year before helping out with their new siblings, all sober as a portrait of Queen Victoria and her own mob of children.

There were pomegranates and grapes growing over her neighbors' fences. One house had a garden of neon-colored succulents, another a cheery garden of pink and yellow roses. Molly never argued with anyone who described Los Angeles as a jumbled and incoherent city, a nightmare of traffic bordered by jumbled, incoherent rows of houses in every architectural style known to man. Its flora was jumbled, too, incoherent and abundant palm trees and pine trees, roses and cacti. The place was a foreign country as far as Molly was concerned. And after almost sixty years in New York, years of Manhattan in all its might and frantic momentum, every day felt like a day of blessed vacation in a faraway vacation land. Work did not interfere with this holiday feeling. She could hardly believe her luck. Some sky above her, some sun. Some crows.

She thought of her mother shivering and feeble in the biting January wind. A disconcerting tableau: her lovely mother, her lively mother, bundled and drained, shuffling like a refugee in her own life.

Molly had always thought of her mother as someone sharp and bright, someone light and airy, full of color and warmth and intensity. A kind of maternal sun goddess, always there whether she showed herself or not, always there behind the inevitable clouds of Molly's life, of the family's life. Like Aaron, Joy had been both attentive and absentminded as a parent, but to Molly the periodic negligence was freedom, it was privacy, independence. If Joy worked late or was out of town at a conference and the cupboard was bare like a nursery-rhyme cupboard, Daniel and Molly rejoiced, for that meant hamburgers or pizza or Chinese food or a trip with Aaron to the market to buy the makings of eggplant Parmesan, his specialty. The pressure from such kind and consistently inconsistent parents was negligible. Joy and Aaron held, for reasons the children did not understand but did not question, an unshakable faith in Molly and Daniel. If either child stepped out of line, the line moved accordingly. Even now, Molly could feel Joy trying to forgive her, to understand her act of geographical treachery. But Molly could hardly understand it herself. She had fallen in love. She had been offered a job. She woke up happy every morning. Those were facts. Why did she feel she had to explain them, excuse them; why weren't those facts the explanations in and of themselves?

Molly called her mother every day. She never mentioned the sunshine and the soft breeze. It would be in bad taste to call Joy's attention to the glorious physical reality of Los Angeles. Joy called Molly every day, too, sometimes more than once: she was still so weak from the C. diff, the wind was ferocious, the mayor said something appalling. Sometimes she called to tell a funny story or report on the medical progress of someone Molly had never met, to urge Molly to watch something on television, to discuss her health or Aaron's behavior or a doctor's report or a possible side effect of a pill neither of them was taking. "I told Dr. Moritz he gives me a reason to live," she would say after a dentist appointment. "I have to live many, many years to amortize the cost of these new implants." Molly would laugh. Her mother often made her laugh. Just as often Molly listened annoyed and impatient, yet even then she found herself soothed by the inconsequential drip, drip, drip of the conversation. Her mother's voice made her feel safe, safe from the loss of her mother.

"You're too far away," Joy said.

"So are you," Molly said, but she said it gently, and she meant it.

She also meant to visit every six weeks. It did not work out to be quite that often.

"Don't come, don't come, this is the worst winter we've ever had, it's not even safe to go outside," Joy told her, and Molly pretended she thought her mother meant what she said. She put off her visit for two weeks, three weeks, then a month. The snow fell in New York, then fell again. "The sidewalks are sheets of ice," Joy would say. "Treacherous sheets of ice." The weathermen warned the elderly to stay inside. It was too cold, too windy, too icy. "I went downstairs just to stick my nose out the door, just to get some fresh air, just a walk to the corner, but the doorman wouldn't let me leave the building. Not one step. Far too dangerous."

"The doorman takes better care of my parents than I do," Molly said to Freddie one morning, a beautiful morning, the air brilliant and blue.

Freddie handed her a cup of coffee. "Thank god for those doormen."

"My mother says she has cabin fever. You know, I couldn't do anything about that even if I were there. I can't change the weather. And she won't come out here, even to visit, even for a week. Well, how could she? She can't leave Daddy, and he certainly can't come. So what good would I be there anyway if they can't leave the house? I mean, I spend more time with my mother on the phone now than I ever did in person when I lived in the city."

Molly was talking to herself, Freddie understood that, and she sat in the winter sunshine not quite listening. Her own father had a new girlfriend. It was causing ripples of resentment in the facility, and not only from his former girlfriends. The social worker seemed somehow offended, too. "They're all over each other," she'd said in the last call.

"Am I supposed to leave my job? Leave you? Leave my whole life?" Molly was saying. "Well, maybe she thinks since I did it once, I could do it again, just roll the film backward . . ."

"I don't like the direction in which this monologue is going," Freddie said. "I really don't."

". . . Of course, that's not what she wants, which is good, because it's not going to happen, because how could I even get my old job back, and what job would you be able to get in New York . . ."

Freddie stopped listening again. It was indecent to intrude on such desperate thoughts. She tried not to worry that Molly might someday approach her with a serious plan to leave L.A. A few times when she had taken Molly at her word and thought the guilt outweighed everything else and suggested they move to New York, Molly had been horrified and said, "Can't I feel guilty in peace?"

19

For Joy and Aaron, the months were long and cramped, though not without excitement. The apartment teemed with people in rubber gloves, and the atmosphere was pungent and gurgling with strange cuisines, sausages and beans, African pumpkin and foo-foo, fish heads floating in soup pots, chicken feet protruding from stews. Joy's eyes burned from the spices in the air. She was afraid to look in the refrigerator.

She was still tired, more tired than she had ever imagined a person could be and still rise up and stand on two feet. Her hearing was going, too, she was sure of it. "I'm deaf, Paw," she said to Aaron, and he smiled because he knew he was expected to, not because he thought she was funny, she could tell. There were days when she was glad of losing her hearing, the babel of languages and the sounds of pain thereby muted and dulled. The cold and snow continued morning after morning, afternoons of snow dissolving into snowy nights. Joy and Aaron, trapped inside, migrated from one end of the apartment to the other and back. Aaron could no longer use a walker, and the one time they had tried to push his wheelchair in the snow, before the temperature really dropped, the wheelchair bucked and slid and crashed into a bank of snow.

The wind blew and iced branches fell. The sidewalks dwindled to slippery tracks. The days, short and dark, seemed endless. Joy wondered if Aaron suffered from choking claustrophobia, too. She couldn't ask him. He no longer said more than a few stock phrases. For Joy, the way one indistinguishable hour ran into another was frightening. She came to cherish the arrivals and departures of Walter, Elvira, and Wanda. They were like the chimes of a clock, like church bells, dividing the day into its proper parts.

On one afternoon when the sun peeped out and the temperature rose to just below freezing, and Joy could stand the seclusion no more, she bundled Aaron up in a heavy sweater and the parka she'd gotten him on sale at McLaughlin's, which looked so good on him.

"We have to get out of our cloister, Aaron. We are going to breathe some fresh air."

She adjusted his cap, a tweed driving cap that did not cover his ears.

"Your big ears are going to freeze," she said.

"Watch your language." It was more than he had said in days, and Joy pulled off the hat and kissed his head.

"There."

Sometimes she wanted to put her hands around his neck and squeeze the last lingering pretense of life out of him. More often, she wanted to bury not him but herself—bury herself in her down duvet and never show her face again. She missed him terribly.

She put on her warmest coat. Wanda pushed the wheelchair to the front door and Gregor made a fuss over them, shaking Aaron's hand, then high-fiving him. Though the days of Aaron walking to the park with his little red wagon were gone, every cloud had its silver lining, that's what they said, and Joy, unsteady and weak, took possession of the red walker herself for their outing.

"Won't Coco be pleased, recycling and all," she said to Aaron as she followed him out the door. She leaned down and whispered in his big ear, "I feel like the red caboose of the Old Jew train." She turned to Gregor. "I'm the caboose," she said.

"Good for you, Doctor," Gregor said.

She often wondered if he thought she was a real doctor. He held the door and smiled and nodded encouragement.

The shock of the cold almost stopped her. The snow, banked up on the sidewalk, looked ponderous and old. But the sunlight and the sky, that blaze of blue sky, were miraculous after so many weeks of looking out the window at sky the color of an old nickel.

They turned into the park where Aaron had spent so many afternoons.

"Isn't this nice?" Joy said. "Oh dear god, we're free!"

Aaron, inside his heap of warm clothing, said nothing.

"Okay, Aaron." She sighed, disappointed in spite of herself. "Have it your way."

She sat on a bench blinking in the sunlight like a night creature.

"Koffee?" Wanda said.

Whenever Wanda said coffee, it seemed to Joy that the word began with a *k*.

"No," she said. "Thank you, but I dare not." Dare not. Where had that come from? A book she'd read? Her grandmother? Did all grandmothers use the same phrases no matter what era they lived in? "My digestion," she added primly, as if Wanda did not know their digestive behavior, hers and Aaron's, intimately.

"You go," she said to Wanda. "Go get your koffee. I'll watch Aaron."

And that is what she did, gazing at him with the love of decades past and the angry exhaustion of a sleepless night and the terror of the days and nights to come.

I dare not think that way, she said to herself. I dare not.

The air smelled cold, but the sun gave the illusion of warmth. Snow that had piled on the bushes dripped, just a bit. It was almost like spring, which is just what the man approaching, pushing a familiar-looking red walker, said.

"It's almost like spring!"

He was accompanied by a pink-cheeked woman who immediately began to speak in Polish to Wanda. This must be Aaron's friend, Joy thought. She watched as the man settled himself on the neighboring bench. He adjusted his gloves and his hat and his scarf, then turned to her, obviously about to speak. Instead, he stared.

"Joy?" he said. *"Joy?"*

"Karl? Oh my god. Karl!"

They clambered to their feet and embraced.

"Sixty years? I think that's how long it's been, Karl. I can't believe it. I can't believe you recognized me."

"Sixty-six years," he said. "I would know you anywhere."

They sat down again, on the same bench this time. So this was Aaron's park friend Karl. This was *Karl, her* Karl.

"Karl," she said. "You really are Karl."

He was better-looking, in a way, than he had been as a young man. Old age suited his angular face. His face had been awkward for a young man's face. Now it was distinguished. He wore a beautiful overcoat, and his scarf was elegantly tied. He exuded prosperity and confidence. Even the red walker looked natty. It matched his luxurious silk scarf.

"I wondered if I'd ever see you again," he said.

She had wondered, too. "The world is strange," she said.

"Wondrous strange."

"You have met my husband," Joy said, putting a hand on Aaron's sleeve. "Aaron, your friend Karl is a very old and dear friend of mine."

Aaron nodded affably.

"I've heard about you from Aaron. But I had no idea you were you."

Karl lived right down the block. He was a lawyer, or had been until he retired.

"I'm still working," Joy said.

"It's something you love," Karl said with such assurance that Joy felt buoyed.

"Yes, I do." Must remember that.

They talked until the clouds washed over the sun and the cold could no longer be ignored.

"Very much money," Wanda said to Joy, when they were out of earshot, rolling her eyes toward Karl and his caretaker.

"He was poor as a church mouse when I knew him."

But Wanda's English did not include church mouse or the past tense. She said "Yes" emphatically, and they made their way home.

20

Danny arrived at the apartment for dinner an hour late, but Joy had expected as much. He worked hard, such long hours. But since Aaron had become so sick, Danny made sure to have dinner with her at least once a week, no matter how busy he was. He did it to be nice, she knew. Which both touched and saddened her. We all prefer to have someone visit for our company rather than be kept company, but she must not be greedy, she reminded herself. He was here, and as always when she saw him in the doorway, she was happy, deliriously happy. Sometimes she thought she would swoon with love for him. He put his arm beneath hers to walk her to the dining room, and she felt safe for the first time in days, since he had last been to see her, to be exact. He comforted her, just by being in the same room.

On the other hand, there he sat, expecting to be fed. Thank god for Wanda, because Joy had forgotten to arrange anything for dinner. She tried to remember what exactly she had done all day that kept her from taking care of dinner for Danny, sweet exhausted Danny coming from work in the cold.

Aaron was in bed. He'd had his dinner already, leftover turkey meat loaf from Joy's ordered-in dinner the night before. He used to laugh when Joy fed him from the various dinners they had ordered in, saying she was a genius at assembling and rearranging garbage. Wanda had made stuffed cabbage and a cucumber salad for Danny, which she made him every time he was there, despite the fact that neither Aaron nor Joy could possibly digest that particular meal. Danny never seemed to notice he was the only one eating it. Joy was having the meat loaf left over from the leftover meat loaf she'd given Aaron. She watched Danny wolf down the stuffed cabbage in huge, animal mouthfuls. She really ought to have taught him better table manners. It had somehow not held him back in life: he did have a wonderful wife and wonderful children and a successful career. But his table manners . . . disgusting.

"Mom?" he said, and gently wiped the corner of her mouth with his napkin. "Catsup."

"Dribbling?" she said. "Time to put me out to pasture."

She was excited tonight, Daniel noticed. She folded and refolded her napkin. She absentmindedly picked up a lipstick from the cabinet behind her and applied it at the table using the back of her spoon to make sure it was not on her teeth.

"Going somewhere?" he asked.

"What? No!" She put the lipstick back. "No. Where would I go?"

"Well, it's great you were able to get out to the park yesterday, anyway. Was Dad's friend there?"

"Oh yes. Mmm-hmm. He was there."

"Nice, isn't he?" he said.

"Oh yes."

Joy wondered why she didn't tell Danny who Karl was. She certainly had nothing to hide. "Daddy just lit up when he saw him."

Karl had been so gentlemanly, waiting at the gate to the park to let her and her entourage out first. She thought wistfully of Aaron, what a gentleman he had always been. He still was sometimes, an instinct that had outlived his memory. Joy noticed it when she stood up from the table, the way he tried to stand up, his hand reaching out to help her pull her chair back.

"Good," Danny was saying. "Maybe it will warm up for real sometime soon. This weather is ridiculous. And people don't understand it's a symptom of climate change, just like global warming. They think it counters global warming . . ."

She listened contentedly as he talked about energy, how we squandered it, how there would be no energy left.

"I have no energy. Can you people help me?"

"Mom."

Danny had devoted his professional life to combatting climate change. If he occasionally lost his sense of humor when it came to the environment, you couldn't blame him. She just forgot now and then, forgot not to tease him.

"Danny, I'm sorry. That was glib."

"Sorry, Mom. It's just that I deal with these idiots all day long . . ."

He patted her hand, and she had the urge to put her cheek against his, to press against his cheek, to kiss it, to grab both his cheeks with both of her hands and kiss him some more.

She could see he was getting restless.

"Wanda gave Daddy too much fruit today," she said.

"Did she?"

Joy simply did not want to mention Karl, that was all. It would start up a whole conversation, wouldn't it? All about the past. The past was too alive to her as it was without stirring up memories.

Danny kept looking at his phone, pulling it out of his pocket, staring down at it as he held it below the level of the table, as if that made it somehow more discreet, like holding a napkin in front of your mouth when you picked an annoying bit of food from between your teeth.

"It's very rude, what you're doing," she said. "Is this the way it's going?"

"Is this the way what is going?" Danny asked, still looking at his phone.

"Civilization. Everyone always looking at those electronic things."

He looked up. "Sorry." He looked back at the phone.

"People are going to forget how to talk to each other. That's all."

"I *said* I'm sorry."

Joy could feel the tears welling up. She took a deep breath. Danny was dog-tired, he was overburdened at work, he had so much on his mind. The changing climate, the melting polar ice, droughts and floods, the girls getting into decent schools . . .

"How are the girls?" she asked.

Danny gave her a suspicious look.

"They're very busy, Mom. They have a lot of homework."

And birthday parties, Joy thought. It was mathematically impossible, the number of birthday parties those little girls went to. Homework and birthday parties, a balance of a sort. "I know, sweetheart. They work so hard. So do you."

"Yeah," he said, mollified. "We do."

Joy hadn't seen or heard from her grandchildren in over a month, but that was not why she asked about them. Danny was prickly about his family, as if any inquiry were a veiled criticism. She had asked about the girls because she had suddenly pictured them, like two kittens, their big eyes and silky hair, the way they snuggled into each other like kittens, then batted each other away. They were beautiful, sweet, eccentric girls. It was only natural that she missed them. Only natural that she asked about them. She understood they had their lives and that their lives were imperative and irresistible in that way that a child's life is.

"I'd love if they called. You know, just to say hello."

He laughed unkindly. "You sound like Grandma Bergman. *Your finger broken? You can't dial a phone?* I mean, you can call them, too, Mom."

Joy could not explain this to her son, would have been too ashamed even to mention it, but when she did call his house, everyone there was always so busy. It made her feel awkward and intrusive, out of step.

"Grandma Bergman," she said. "Them's fightin' words."

But there were circles under his eyes, his shirt was wrinkled and his tie rumpled, he'd been up since five, and still he made time for this visit. She got up to spoon out his ice cream herself.

She stood at the door watching as Danny, large and wilted and fiddling with his phone in his pocket, waited for the elevator, and she was glad for once that the elevator was so slow. She could not take her eyes off him.

"Your briefcase is so heavy, Danny. You should get one with wheels."

He laughed, walked back, gave her another hug. Over his shoulder she could just make out the elevator door opening. She said nothing, holding her big, tired son in her arms. The door closed and the elevator began its slow ascent to some other floor. A high floor, she hoped, her face against his chest. Maybe the penthouse.

That night, Joy pressed her back against the cushions of the sofa. It was late, after 3 a.m., but it was not dark. It was never dark in New York, and tonight the cloudy sky reflected the city lights in a pale green glow. It was quiet, though. Those few hours when all the creatures of the city, the screeching, roaring buses, the howling ambulances, all seemed to take their rest, when the garbage trucks had not yet trundled out of their caves. She could hear Walter changing Aaron's colostomy bag. God bless you, Walter, she thought. May the lord bless you and keep you and shine his countenance upon you.

But who will pay you? Not the lord. And there was no version of arithmetic in which Joy and Aaron's social security was sufficient for the parade of helpers each day. It seemed almost Victorian, having caretakers. As if she and Aaron were large estates. She would have to go back to work soon, that's all, maybe go back to full time to help make ends meet at Bergman House. How she would find the strength she did not know. Even with the caretakers there was so much she had to do for Aaron. She wasn't complaining, she told herself stoutly, just being honest, though how she longed to complain sometimes, to let loose and curse the gods. She had tried it out on the children. The response had not been entirely satisfactory.

"I'm lonely," she had said. "Even though Daddy is right here and even though I never feel as though I get to be alone."

"You should get a dog!" Danny had said. "That would be perfect!"

Oh, Danny, another helpless creature to tend to? Yes, dear, perfect. And Molly! When Joy said her head was muddled and she sometimes was so tired she could not breathe, but so worried about the cost of the caretakers that she could not sleep, Molly suggested she go to the 92nd Street Y's poetry readings. Poetry. They meant well, they did. But *they fuck you up, your son and daughter,* Joy thought, pleased with her clever Philip Larkin allusion, 92nd Street Y or no 92nd Street Y. *They may not mean to, but they do.*

21

The light in the synagogue was far too bright for a holy place. The atmosphere was meant to be one of velvet darkness illuminated by sunlight streaming from windows high above, like the church they had visited on their trip to Paris. There were ten rows of chairs divided by a center aisle, six chairs on each side. Sixty in all, but only half of them filled: Rabbi Kenny would be disappointed. Ruby chose the fourth row, the two seats closest to the aisle on the left. She wanted to be able to see.

"Won't the rabbi be surprised to find us here," her mother said. "I'm surprised, too."

"Aren't you glad? Don't you want me to be Jewish?"

"You are Jewish, you know, already."

"That's kind of racist, Mommy."

"Some people think *Huckleberry Finn* is racist. Do you?"

But Ruby was not to be lured back to Mark Twain.

"Tonight is Shabbat," she had said when she got home from school that afternoon. "The service starts at seven, so we should eat early."

"What service, sweetie? Is there a memorial for someone at

school?" Every now and then, a terrible tragedy struck one of the families at school and the other families got together to raise money or protest a law or clean a flooded basement apartment.

"The Shabbat service, Mommy."

Daniel was worried. "Ruby, I know you feel bad about the slingshot, but the rabbi understood it was an accident. He's an awfully nice guy. He wouldn't want you to punish yourself, honey. And Mommy and I would never make you go to services. I had enough of that when I was little, believe me."

"You're not making me. I want to."

"I understand that you feel guilty, but . . ."

"Daddy, I'm going to shul. It's not guilt. It's inclination."

"No one has the *inclination* to go to services," he said to Coco when they were alone in the kitchen. "Especially not a twelve-year-old."

"I had a Joan of Arc obsession. And I was a Taoist."

He groaned. "I can't do it, Coco. I can't sit there and listen to that stuff. I did my time. I had my bar mitzvah."

"It's your ADD. It's a wonder you can sit through a movie." Daniel was constantly jiggling his legs and rattling the change in his pocket. He paced, too, up and down or in tight circles if the room was small.

"Don't blow the candles out, Daddy," Ruby said to him as she left the house with Coco. "You have to let them burn down. I read it."

"Here he comes," Ruby whispered. The bandage was gone and there was no scar that she could see. Rabbi Kenny came up the aisle greeting the congregation on his way to the bimah. "Mrs. Simkowitz, hello, how did Lev's Series Seven exam go? Mr. Krauss, you look so much better. And . . ."

He stopped when he got to Ruby and her mother. He smiled broadly.

"Are you armed, Ruby?"

Ruby held her hands out, empty.

"It is an honor to have you both here. Welcome."

Ruby listened to the prayers. A secret language, a secret alphabet, secret incantations. She could have been in a room of whirling dervishes or monks in saffron robes, it was that exotic, that exciting. Her mother mumbled along with some of the prayers.

"Wasn't it beautiful?" Ruby said afterward. "Did you like the singing? The songs sounded so sad."

"The cantor has a beautiful voice. She seems a little glitzy for a cantor."

"She could be on Broadway. *Les Mis!*"

"Exactly. And I do prefer male cantors, generally."

"Mommy, that's sexist."

"Nevertheless."

They walked around the block to their building. They passed the corner market with its sparkling new pane of glass. Ruby held her breath the way she did when she passed a cemetery.

"Manuel's insurance paid for it," Coco said. "That was a relief."

"Can I have my allowance back?"

"No."

"Mommy," Ruby said as they reached their building, "we need to get another set of dishes."

"I love our dishes. Daddy and I got them on our honeymoon in Italy. They have a few chips, but really, Ruby, why would we want a whole new set, you can be a little extravagant, that's from your father's side of the family . . ."

"You really don't understand anything," Ruby murmured as her mother went on and on. She patted Coco's arm with fond pity. "May god forgive you."

Ruby sat on the floor of her grandparents' living room, her legs stretched under the coffee table. She had spread out the photographs of her ancestors in approximation of her family tree.

"Now she wants to keep kosher," she heard her father say. "With two sets of dishes. I'm all for the bat mitzvah, I'm proud of her, a sudden change of heart, but kosher?"

"I don't think Tom Sawyer kept kosher," Grandma Joy said. "How does she even know about keeping two sets of dishes?"

"The Internet. Google. Wikipedia."

"Aren't there parental controls on those things?"

There was a picture of Grandpa Aaron as a young soldier in the decorative box. Ruby showed it to Cora, who sat on the couch behind her, kicking her gently.

"Dad didn't say anything when I was in there with him," her father was saying.

"Nothing. For days. Almost a week."

There was the muffled sound of weeping. Ruby turned the photos over, facedown, as if they were playing cards, moved them around the table, then guessed which was which, turning them faceup one by one. Cora slid off the couch and cuddled beside her. Ruby felt her breath on her cheek.

"Quit it," she said mildly, and the shove she gave Cora was mild too.

Their mother appeared in the doorway.

"Girls, we're going. I think you should say goodbye to Grandpa."

Ruby and Cora held hands. With the big bed pushed against the wall to make room for a hospital bed, their grandparents' room looked off balance, cluttered, a showroom for things no one wanted to see. The blinds were old venetian blinds, pulled down, a few of the metal slats bent, allowing in shafts of winter light. The bathroom door was open, and a big white booster seat rose up from the toilet. Pajamas hung from a hook on the back of the door, threadbare and limp.

"Do you know a prayer or something?" Cora whispered.

Ruby shook her head. "Not a whole one. Not yet."

Their grandfather's nose was bigger and thinner than ever. It rose up monumentally from his sunken cheeks. His eyes were closed. His lips were almost white and gave a small puff with each breath.

"Grandpa," Ruby said, because she was the older. "Grandpa, it's us, Ruby and Cora."

He did not stir. There were brown bottles of pills and twisted tubes of ointment on a flowered porcelain tray on the dresser. There was a fat roll of gauze and one of white tape, some baby powder, a box of rubber gloves. Cora took out a rubber glove and blew it up like a balloon.

"Udders," she said, handing it to Ruby to tie. They both giggled, then stopped and shifted their feet.

"We have to leave, Grandpa," said Ruby softly.

Cora poked him. "Grandpa!" she yelled.

"Cora!" Ruby whispered. "Shhh."

"Well, what if he's . . ."

"Don't be silly. He's asleep. Look at his mouth. Listen."

They could hear him breathing.

"Grandpa, we're here, we're here," Cora said. She rattled the aluminum bed rail. "Me and Ruby."

"Ruby and I," Grandpa said. He opened his eyes.

"Everyone, everyone! Come quick! Grandpa talked!" Cora pounded down the hall.

Joy rushed to his side. "What is it, sweetheart? What is it, my darling?"

"Chipped beef," Aaron said.

"You're kidding me, Aaron. Aaron, darling . . ."

"In a jar." And he slipped back into silence.

It was three in the morning. Joy went into the bedroom. Aaron had not moved. He was asleep on his back, the covers pulled up to his chin. The only sound he made was a rhythmic quiet groaning.

Walter, who had been in the next room on the pullout bed that would not pull out, appeared at the door.

"Okay?" he said.

She nodded. "Go back to sleep."

There was a kitchen chair beside the hospital bed, and Joy sat down on it. She reached beneath the blanket and found Aaron's hand. His hand was cold. "There, there," she said. A useless, irrelevant comment. "There, there," she said again. Not every comment had to be useful or relevant. Some words were useless, irrelevant, words that meant I'm sorry, I'm so sorry, I wish I could help you, I love you and I have for so many years that I even love you when I don't; words that meant I didn't mean it when I said I was going to put a bag over your head if you asked me one more time where your ice cream was when it was right in front of you. "There, there," she said.

Aaron, eyes still closed, opened his mouth, and through his strained breathing, he said, "There, there," too.

—— 22 ——

When Joy called Molly and said, "It's your father," Molly thought, My father is dead. It was a strangely distant thought, as if it couldn't be true.

"Daddy's dead," Molly said.

"Molly! How can you say that about your own father?"

Daddy was not dead. Daddy was about to start palliative care.

"He's in so much pain," Joy said. "And we can't get him to the doctor's anymore. He's too weak. So now the doctor comes here. Nurses come, too. It's a very good service. Your father is thrilled."

Daniel went to grocery stores all over the city to no avail. He finally tracked down some chipped beef, online. It was frozen, not in a jar, but he ordered a package anyway. Aaron had first eaten creamed chipped beef on toast in the army. They called it Shit on a Shingle. It was one of his favorite dishes. But when the frozen chipped beef arrived from Wisconsin, next day mail, no one prepared it, and no one ever would. His father was dying. He had been dying for a long time, but now he was actively, earnestly dying. Daniel could see it. Aaron's skin was the skin of the dying. His eyes had clouded like the eyes of a fishmonger's fish. He was cold to the touch. He never moved except to raise a hand a few inches from the white blanket, then let it fall back.

"I know what palliative care means," Molly said to Freddie.

"I hope it means he'll be more comfortable."

"It's a euphemism for hospice care."

"Hospice care is its own euphemism."

"It means they can't do anything else for him."

"But you've been saying that for a month."

"But they never said it. Now it means they won't even try to help him."

Freddie put her arms around her and said nothing, another thing Molly loved about her: she said nothing when there was nothing to say.

But within a week, Aaron had gone from palliative care to hospice care. It was snowing in New York when she and Freddie arrived on a red-eye and the dawn didn't really happen; the horizon was too leaden. The ride into town was excruciatingly slow. The sight of the skyline, so grand after the long drab strip of funeral homes in Queens, shocked Molly as it always did, though the buildings were faint, veiled, soft in the storm. Freddie paid the driver and Molly hauled their suitcases across the sidewalk, the wheels leaving tracks in the snow like sleds. She thought back to the snow of childhood, the white hillside Upstate, the wooden sled with red metal runners they waxed with soap, her father seating himself on the sled, then arranging her and all her winter bulk in front of him, the rush of air on her face, the snow whispering beneath the runners, her father's arms around her, his snowy beard against her cheek as he lifted her off the sled, his enormous glove closing around her mitten as he led her and the sled back up the hill. Oh, she was crying now, yes she was, sobbing as the snow landed on her cheeks and her nose, the tears hot, each one identical in the way snowflakes could never be. She was sobbing as she hauled the suitcases through the front door past the doorman, who offered to help and whom she shook off with a quick head motion. The elevator shuddered with her sobs, the melted snow pooled at her feet, her suitcase fell on its side and lay forlornly on the wet floor. Molly kicked it. Freddie kicked it, too, in solidarity, then righted it.

Daniel was sitting in the chair beside the hospital bed. "The hospice nurse said he'll last a day, maybe two."

"Don't say that in front of him, Danny," their mother said. She had appeared in the bathroom doorway.

Daniel was looking at Molly the way he did when he wanted her to tell him what he should do.

"Aaron," Joy said, "look who's here. It's Molly."

Molly stood up straight. She kissed her mother. She kissed her brother. She took her wet coat off and hung it on the doorknob.

"Oh, Molly, really," her mother said, grabbing the coat and taking it out of the room. "You of all people."

"Hi, Daddy," Molly said.

His eyes flickered. Maybe. She took his hand and kissed it.

"It's me, Molly," she said softly. She bent over and kissed his forehead. It was rough and fragile, like cheap paper.

"Speak up, honey," Joy said, back in the room. "He doesn't have his hearing aids in." She began rummaging through drawers. "I'm sure they're here somewhere. You hate them, Aaron, I know, but they do help."

Hearing aids? Don't forget your orthotics while you're at it, both essential components of hospice care. "I don't think he can hear me anyway, Mom. He's kind of out of it, isn't he? All that morphine . . ."

"What do you mean? Of course he can hear you. Of course you can, Aaron."

"It's me!" Molly said loudly.

The eyes flickered again.

"See?" said Joy. "Don't go borrowing trouble, Molly."

That night, Molly straightened the medicine bottles. The hospice nurses had lined them up neatly already. Molly reorganized the reorganization. Molly Mixinovitch, Aaron used to call her when she got like this.

"It's a pick-me-up, isn't it, Aaron? That Molly energy. And her friend Freddie, what a lovely person."

Should she have said wife? "Well, wife, then." She put on her reading glasses and found the ointment for Aaron's lips. "Wife," she said softly. "I am your wife, Aaron. Mrs. Aaron Bergman." She began to say, Till death do us part, but stopped. "Nothing can part us." Even death could not do that after so many years.

They had been Aaron and Joy for a lifetime. Joy contemplated the word "lifetime." How sad that a word meaning a full span of experience, meaning a whole life, should carry within it the end of a life.

Marrying Aaron had been a triumph, the goal of her existence, of any girl's existence in those days. A handsome, well-heeled man, that was part of it. A handsome, well-heeled man who didn't care about money, that had been another part of it—he was an artist, a singer, contemptuous of the grubby world of commerce. On their first date he had lifted her up and carried her through the park singing. It was like a movie. She was swept away. She did not know the difference between carefree and careless in those days. She learned. There were trials and tribulations along the road. "We've had some sickness and health, haven't we, Aaron? Some richer and poorer." She dabbed the ointment on his lips. "Never a dull moment." It didn't seem possible that Aaron's lips were so dry and cracked, lips she had kissed when they were practically a boy's lips, nice well-formed lips, when she and Aaron were both young. Aaron's young lips had been replaced, magically, by these chapped and papery ones. How proud she had been, proud of being in love, of finding love, as if love were a prize on a treasure hunt. Aaron smiled at her as they stood at the altar fumbling with their rings, a crooked smile he never turned on anyone else, until the grand-children were born. It was a dangerous smile, full of promise and play. "That's you, playful and full of promises." He did not keep

his promises, perhaps, but he never stopped making them, and that
had been a different kind of honesty and keeping of the faith.

Molly threw the package of chipped beef away. Joy retrieved the
package when Molly wasn't looking. She put it back in the freezer.

Freddie and Molly took the girls to the Museum of Natural History to get them out of the apartment for a little while.

"They look so real," Cora said. The enormous Alaskan bear
loomed over her, a wounded seal at its feet.

"They are real," said Ruby.

"They're dead."

"They're still real."

Freddie stepped away from the existential discussion to answer
her phone. She backed against the case of the skunks. "Laurel, is
anything wrong?"

"Not that we know of," both sisters said at once. "But we thought
we'd come see Dad in June. It's a slow month for us. It might be the
last time we see him. We have to be realistic."

"He'll be thrilled."

"We have a very good package at the Disneyland Hotel for
three nights, and then the Beverly Hills Hilton. Doesn't it sound
like fun? A night in Palm Springs, a quick trip to Vegas—we've
got it all planned out. You let him know we're coming. We'll send
you our itinerary. And, Freddie, we're gluten-free. Just so you
know."

"Maybe *you* should call Dad and give him the good news. I'm
sure he'd love to hear from you."

"What if he didn't know who we were?" Laurel said. "It would
be so awkward. But you'll know how to tell him. After all, Freddie, you see him all the time. We don't."

Freddie smiled a little at that. When she found Molly and the girls, they were examining the naked Neanderthals. Molly was distracted, worried about her father. Ruby and Cora were hungry.

"I still say the animals are not real."

"Are they fantasies?" Ruby said contemptuously.

"Well, they are in a way," Freddie said. "Nineteenth-century fantasies of everything wild. In their glass cases."

Molly snorted.

Cora said, "Snort again!"

"If I went inside one of those cases and kicked one of those kudus," Ruby said, "I'd hurt my foot. A fantasy wouldn't bang my foot. A real kudu would. A dead, real kudu."

"You refute Berkeley thus, Dr. Johnson," said Freddie.

"Death is the only thing that's real," Molly said softly. Only Freddie heard her. She took Molly's hand and they walked silently home across the park. Cora and Ruby skipped and cried out in English accents, "I'm Berkeley and nothing is real; I'm Dr. Johnson and I refute you thus," kicking stones.

23

This is a general picture, the pamphlet said. Then it said that the skin turns a gray or green or bluish hue. Her father's skin was gray and green and bluish. He is off-color, Molly thought, like a joke. As you hold his hand you may notice that it feels cold. Her father's hand was as cold as ice, as death.

He was dead.

Joy came into the room.

"Oh, Mommy." Molly pressed her face against her mother's shoulder and cried in ugly dry heaving sobs.

"Molly, Molly." Joy patted her back, kissed her cheek. "There, there, Molly. You must be so tired." She turned to Aaron, lying still on his hospital bed. "That terrible jet lag," she said to him.

"But Daddy . . . Daddy's . . ."

"Come," Joy said gently. "Aaron, we're going to get some tea. Back in a minute!"

In the hall, she closed the door to the bedroom and said, "Now, what is it, sweetheart? I don't want to have any sad discussion in front of Daddy."

"But . . ."

"The booklet said you must always act as if he can hear you. Hearing is one of the last senses to go. We have to be careful not to scare him. He can hear what we're saying even if he doesn't seem to."

"But, Mom—"

"The booklet said so," Joy said fiercely. "It's disrespectful to talk about dying in front of him. Do you understand?"

"Mom, his fingers are blue."

"He's chilly."

"Do we get a mirror or something?"

"This is not television, Molly. Go wait in the living room. I want to chat with your father. Just the two of us."

Molly found Daniel and Freddie in the kitchen. "I think Daddy died," she said through her sobs. "But Mommy doesn't want him to know."

She slid down the wall and sat on the floor. She wished she could breathe. She watched Daniel make his slow careful way toward their parents' bedroom. Maybe her father would be alive again by the time he got there. Maybe her mother would have talked him back to life.

"She thinks he's still alive and she's talking to him," Molly whispered.

Freddie slid down and sat beside her. "Is he? Maybe he is."

"But he's green. And waxen."

When he came back a few minutes later, Daniel said, "She's holding his hand. They're having a quiet conversation, she said."

"So he's alive?" Molly asked.

"I don't know." Daniel started to cry.

Freddie and Coco, the in-laws, went in to take a look as more neutral observers.

"He's awfully stiff-looking," Coco said. She emitted a tiny, nervous laugh, then shook her head.

"Is he still green?" Molly asked.

"Bluish green," Freddie said.

"Is he moving?"

"Of course he's not moving. If he were moving they would know he wasn't dead," her brother snapped.

By the time the hospice nurse came for her afternoon visit, rigor mortis had set in. *Rigor mortis*, she said in her rolling Jamaican accent. *Rigor mortis.*

But still Joy could not be sure. Death? How could anyone be sure of something as unlikely as death? Death made no sense. Where was Aaron if not there? Who was that if not Aaron? Why were the children filing in to say goodbyes as if he were about to take a journey on an ocean liner? She sat on the edge of the bed where she and Aaron had slept and looked at the silent, still man in the hospital bed. Who would take care of him now that he was dead? Who would get him his tea and see him sneak three spoons of sugar into it and pretend not to notice? Who would make him wear his hearing aids? Who would buy him warm sweaters? He would be so helpless and so alone now that he was dead and she could no longer look after him.

She supposed she was crying. Her sinuses were swollen and painful. Her face was wet with tears. She heard uneven sounds, hoots of sorrow, and suspected they came from her. She heard sirens and turned toward the window. It had stopped snowing. She stood up and gazed at Aaron on his hospital bed, his arms now crossed over his chest. Perhaps the nurse had done that, because Aaron, she had to admit, certainly had not.

24

There was chaos and urgency in the Bergman apartment. Daniel said, *We have to call a funeral home, don't we?* Molly said, *Well, they aren't going to call us.* Daniel said, *I'll call the one on the West Side.* Joy, with furious conviction, said, *The one on Madison is so convenient.* Molly said, *It's not your health club, it's not the subway stop, you don't have to carry him there yourself,* and she must have been screaming, because Freddie took her hand and squeezed it with what was surely excessive force and, in her annoying Yoga voice, told her to breathe.

"I'm a widow," Joy said. "Show some respect."

"Okay, I'll call the one on the East Side, then." Daniel reached for the phone.

"No! Not yet! Not yet!"

"Rigor mortis," said the nurse.

"Mr. Aaron, Mr. Aaron," Wanda cried.

"Grandpa," the little girls were wailing. "Grandpa!"

Molly marched into Daniel's old room and called the East Side funeral home on her cell phone. She told the man who answered that they would want a Jewish ceremony, as soon as possible, did they have an opening, as if she were calling to have her hair colored. Like the hair salon, the soonest appointment the funeral home had was in two days. But two days was Saturday and you could not have a Jewish funeral on Saturday.

"Of course," said the man. "Well, we do have a spot on Sunday afternoon."

Aaron was zipped up in a black bag and placed on a wheeled stretcher, then steered out by two silent men, the discrepancy in their heights comical, their clothing almost theatrically grim: shabby black suits, white gloves like footmen. One wore a fur cap; the other, the little one, a yellowed straw fedora with a grimy brim and stained brown hat band. Ernie, the doorman on duty, had come up to say goodbye; the grumpy super, too. He was a fine man, said the super. A gentleman, said the doorman. They stood with bowed heads while the family wailed in anarchic waves of hysteria and grief that emanated from every side of the room, then bounced back from the walls, rolling, echoing, as the little girls clutched their mother's waist and Coco said shrilly, desperately, "Who wants cake, I brought cake."

That was how Molly remembered it. Joy didn't remember it at all.

Wanda and the hospice nurse stripped the hospital bed. They pushed it against the wall. Joy refused to go into the room. The room did not exist without Aaron.

She went into the hall bathroom, which Aaron had used as his own. Wipes and pads and pouches in boxes. Creams and lotions and powders. Tubes and rubber gloves. Where would she put them? Aaron was in a refrigerator on Madison Avenue, but what about all of Aaron's supplies? They would not be buried with him, he was not King Tut and they were not treasures. They were garbage. Expensive garbage. How sad that she had all these costly medical supplies and no one to use them. Most of the boxes had not even been opened.

"Daniel, quick! Look on your phone. Where can I donate? I have colostomy pouches. Perfectly good! Someone needs them! Hurry! I have to donate!"

That was what Joy remembered.

She rushed to the phone and said, "Operator! Dial the hospital. I have urgent equipment to donate." Daniel took the phone from her hand gently. "The operators aren't there anymore, Mom. No more operators, remember?"

"She's in shock," Molly said.

"Should I slap her?" Cora asked.

"That will not be necessary," her father said.

Ben came in the unlocked front door and saw immediately that he was too late.

"He's gone," Molly said. "Oh, Ben, he's gone."

He put his arms around her and they both cried.

Joy called her friends to let them know. Natalie first. She always called Natalie when something happened, good or bad. Sixty-five years of good and bad, and now this, which was very bad. She called Natalie to tell her, just as she had called Natalie when she was married to a man who was alive instead of to this man who was dead. She told Natalie Aaron died. She listened as Natalie said such nice things about Aaron. She stopped listening and took comfort in the voice, the same voice, hoarse with cigarettes, that had been bossing her around since college, that had bossed her around during all those days and weeks and months of Daniel's illness, through the depths of Aaron's financial ruin, through chemo appointments, the voice that inevitably called to cancel lunch dates and dinner dates and any date that involved the pleasant, the unnecessary, the routine encounters of a social life, but never failed her when things got tough.

"Oh, them," Natalie said when Joy mentioned the funeral home where Aaron now lay. "They're crooks. They're all crooks. I plan to be cremated and set in a tin box on my own mantelpiece next to my mother and father and dog and two cats in their tin boxes.

Now, let me think. I read something. A nonprofit funeral home on the West Side. Community-based and nonprofit . . ."

Joy imagined a community center, a rec room with Ping-Pong tables and battered metal folding chairs. "That sounds horrible. Like they hand out cheese sandwiches. Oh, I don't care anyway. He's gone. What does it matter?"

As soon as she said it, Joy knew it did matter, that it was all that mattered, there was nothing else. The funeral was Aaron's funeral, the last thing she could do for him. She had to do it properly. Not just properly, but perfectly, in just exactly the way she suddenly and clearly visualized it: "There will be a violinist. The violinist will play klezmer as people file in."

"It's not a wedding," Molly said.

"Never mind your sarcasm, Molly."

"I know what you mean, Mom," Danny said. "Sad, beautiful, Yiddish melodies."

"Why not get a string quartet? They could wear white tie," Molly muttered. "While you're at it."

For a fleeting moment Joy saw the string quartet, three men in evening dress and a woman in a black gown—the violist, probably—before the tone of Molly's voice registered, and Joy began to cry.

Molly made up with her mother within minutes. Of course she did, and she didn't need Freddie to open her eyes in that exaggerated way to get her to apologize, either, for heaven's sake.

Joy was now in a terrible state, trying to decide whether or not to change funeral homes. Another friend had been to the rec-room funeral home and said it was lovely, the downstairs chapel in particular, all wood, like a Reform synagogue from the sixties.

She decided to move Aaron. They had been so happy on the West Side. When the Madison Avenue funeral home told her what they would charge even if the West Side funeral home came and got Aaron that afternoon, Joy said, "That's highway robbery. I would not bury a fly at your funeral home," and arrangements were made to strike camp and head to the West Side.

The funeral director on the West Side extolled the virtues of a nonprofit funeral home just as if he were selling them a fur coat. Ladies, ladies, he said, when Molly took Joy there to take a look, we will take care of everything. Our reputation is how we survive. A plain pine coffin? Of course, of course, every size, immediately available. A rabbi? Naturally a rabbi, and not just any rabbi, a wonderful man, tops, a top rabbi.

"It was very sudden," Joy said, "and yet not sudden at all. Do you understand?"

The funeral director sighed and looked at that moment not like a funeral director or a furrier but like a human being. "I do," he said. "I'm afraid I do." He put his hand across the desk, across the price lists to be perused and the papers to be signed, and he patted Joy's hand.

Her eyes full of tears, Joy gave a small smile. "You *will* have a coatrack," she said, "in case it rains?"

25

Some people had implied, even said outright, that it would be a relief for Joy when Aaron died. Tactless, Molly had thought then. But now that her father was gone, she wondered. The stress of looking after Aaron had been so fierce. Without it, Joy seemed calmer, softer. Even on the phone from California, Molly could sense it, as if her mother's voice, her whole temperament, were gently muted.

Daniel, who went to see Joy every day after work, confirmed this.

"How is she?" Molly asked him. She often called when she knew he would be at the apartment.

Daniel, phone to his ear, poked his mother, who sat beside him at the dining-room table. "Mom," he said, "Molly wants to know how you are."

"As well as can be expected," said Joy.

He nodded. It had been three weeks. "As well as can be expected," he said into the phone.

"Oh good!"

He wasn't sure what was to be expected in three weeks, but he did not say that to Molly. It was hard for her, being so far away. It was hard for him, too, being so close.

Joy had been quiet in those three weeks. She didn't complain. It was almost as if Aaron's death were a liberation, once the funeral and all the hubbub associated with it were over, if a sad smile and general acquiescence to everything Daniel said or proposed meant liberation. He hoped it did. Yes, he was sure it did.

When he told his mother he had to get home, he saw her panic for a second. Then she said, "Off you go."

"Sorry I can't stay for dinner."

Joy looked confused, as if dinner were a rarely performed ritual.

"Maybe tomorrow," Daniel said.

"Tomorrow?"

Joy shuffled in her slippers to the front door.

"Mom, are you okay? Really?" He held both her hands and kissed the top of her head from what appeared to him a great distance. She seemed to have decreased. Not just in height, but in volume.

"Absolutely."

"Oh. Okay. Good. You're a trooper."

"Absolutely," she said.

26

Molly called her mother every day, which was admirable, Freddie thought, and often inconvenient, happening when they both got home from work and should, theoretically, have been talking to each other. Freddie called her father, of course, but not as frequently. Often, when she did call, he wasn't in his room. He was a social person and he had found several of the ladies of Green Garden willing to be social with him. Her father was so social, Freddie told Joy, that the social worker at Green Garden seemed to devote a good portion of her working life to him. So when Freddie got a call from the social worker telling her that Duncan was feuding with a woman in a room down the hall, Freddie was not surprised.

"He's become verbally abusive," the social worker said.

"Oh, that." Freddie breathed a sigh of relief. "Yes, he told me there's a lady who shouts at him when he walks by her door."

"His language is out of bounds."

"Did he call her a crusty botch of nature? That was always one of his favorites."

"I don't think you understand how serious this is. It's disturbing the entire facility."

"But that's from *Troilus and Cressida*."

"It was very upsetting for Mrs. Barsky."

"Mrs. Barsky?" Mrs. Barsky had been his regular dinner partner some weeks back. Now he was sharing his table with another lady. Freddie suggested to the social worker that this shift in dining companions might have something to do with the arguments, but the social worker kept coming back to her father's elaborate curses.

"He called Mrs. Barsky the slander of her heavy mother's womb and, let me see, I wrote it down somewhere, here it is: a swollen parcel of dropsies."

"*Henry the Fourth*, Part I. You know that's why I became a Shakespeare scholar? To keep up with him."

"They're revving up to kick him out. I can feel it," she said later to Molly. "He's making trouble again."

"At least he enjoys himself."

But when Molly spoke to Daniel that night, she said, "I know he has a good time, but still, I'm glad Mom's not a sex maniac like Duncan. She's so dignified. It does my heart good."

"We're lucky we have such a reasonable, levelheaded mother."

"You've done so much, Daniel, to help her get to this point. Going over there every day and everything."

"Well, so have you. You arranged for Wanda to stay on, you got the Life Alert, you took care of the banking stuff."

They both smiled, thinking of their mother safe, clean, and comfortable in her apartment, her Life Alert wristband securely fastened.

27

Joy woke up and, as usual, Aaron was dead.

What was coming was clear to her, and it was a vast emptiness, a blank, much like the winter with its white horizon, dense and low, no distance to the sky at all. The emptiness was everywhere, in every room at every hour. She could feel it draining the life out of her until she, too, would be empty. In the shower, she cried because, there, no one could hear her, though she knew there was no one to hear her anywhere.

Molly had gotten her a medical-alert contraption that came with a wristband with a button on it. Sometimes she pushed the button by accident and a man's voice from the machine asked her if she was all right. It was company.

Wanda stayed on, going home only on the weekends to tend to her alcoholic husband. She made breakfast for Joy. She practically fed it to her with a spoon. Wanda missed Aaron, too. Sometimes they cried together. Sometimes they cleaned drawers.

Walter appeared once to pick up a sweatshirt he'd left behind. He helped her change two burned-out lightbulbs in the kitchen ceiling fixture. He said he would come back and make Foo-foo for her one day. When he left, his absence was acute.

On the weekends, Elvira came at night. Joy would not stay alone. Alone was impossible, it made her shiver, it made her head swim, it made her heart pound, it made her knees buckle, it made her ears ring.

Her children lived in some other world, one that she could see but had left behind, like the wake of a ship. Their lives foamed and splashed while she hurtled forward, away from them, but toward nothing. Well, toward something, and they all knew what that something was.

There wasn't enough money for Elvira or Wanda. She was spending like a drunken sailor, an old decrepit drunken sailor. The children offered to help pay, which was kind but humiliating. And she knew they couldn't afford it. An archaeologist and an environmentalist? They were hanging on by a bourgeois thread. She understood she would have to stay alone eventually. She listened to the wind rattle the windows and knew she was abandoned. She told Molly and Daniel she would not be on the dole.

—— 28 ——

The first night alone was long and she paced from the living room to the bedroom in her nightgown, like a ghost, a skinny, crabby old ghost. The sirens wailed outside, and she paced and wept and took her own pulse and used the toilet and ate crackers and knew she would faint. She paced some more, and the streets became quiet, even the sirens stopped, and she took her pulse again, as if her pulse might account for the silence, and paced some more and waited.

What am I waiting for? she wondered. Whatever it was, it was crucial and elusive. She could hardly breathe. She tripped on the edge of the rug in the hall, but did not fall. She lay on the couch and cried, bitterly and loudly. "I don't care who hears me," she called out to the empty house.

In Los Angeles, it was January and it was springtime. Molly saw a hermit thrush. Hummingbirds flitted in and out of white flowers shaped like bells. Pink buds of jasmine hung over the fence ready to burst into bloom. At the beach, surfers slid into the waves with the garish sunset behind them. Finches began to sing. She took one class to Catalina each week to photograph a cave painting and map the area around it. They used a software program that had originally been developed by NASA for the study of photographs of Mars.

"Mars," her mother said when Molly told her about the project. "Well, well. Digital tracing. Isn't that nice."

"I knew you'd be interested."

"Oh, of course."

Molly told her about the bits of ocher the digital tracing had connected, and if her mother sounded less enthusiastic than Molly had expected, Molly attributed that to the weather. The weather was terrible in New York. It snowed and the bitter wind blew, and Joy could not leave her building.

"Well, this will cheer you up, Mom. One of the grad students in engineering built a drone and we attached a 3-D camera and . . ."

Joy drifted from room to room, listening, aimless, trapped.

It wasn't that Joy expected her daughter, and certainly not her son, to come live with her. They had their own lives, just as she had once had her own life. She did expect something from them, though, something they were not providing, she couldn't put her finger on it. Danny was coming once a week for dinner now, Molly planned a trip to New York in the near future, and Joy waited eagerly for their visits. But visits predicted their own end, and an end to a visit meant she would be alone again.

There is a difference between solitude and loneliness, she thought, and wondered what it was.

She should have spent more time with her own mother. She should have moved in with her mother to take care of her, she saw that now. So what if her mother's apartment had been an L-shaped studio? So what if her mother kept it at 102 degrees and could not stand the smell of any food cooking except white rice, and so what if she talked and talked and talked and lived in the past? Now that Joy was older, she understood her mother. It was *cold*, that was why the heat in the apartment was turned up so high. Her mother's ceaseless talking was an *activity*, a way for her to be alive. As for living in the past, the past was all that was real.

Joy would move right in with her mother now, if she could. Daniel and Molly were not old enough, not lonely enough, not cold enough to understand. And what would they do with their wives? And how was it that she had a daughter and a son and they both had wives, anyway?

No one, not even an old lady, wants to live in someone else's house. Both Molly and Daniel had asked her to move in with them, naturally, just as she had asked her own mother to move in with her. They were good, devoted children, just as she had been. They didn't really mean it, just as she had not really meant it.

Rich or poor, her mother used to say, it's better to have money.

Aaron, you were not a prince among men. You were not. You were a weak man. You squandered your fortune like a prince, but you were not a prince. She thought fondly of his affectations of dress, the tweed cap when other men wore brimmed hats, the custom-made English shirts and shoes. How handsome he was, his beard groomed, his hair tousled. It had been so long since she had thought of him as handsome. But now she had trouble picturing him when he hadn't been handsome, when he'd grown bent and stiff and hollow, when his lips were chapped and his teeth dulled, when his eyes went blank, when his clothes devolved into the clothes of a small child, the elastic-waist sweatpants, the hooded sweatshirt that he could not zip himself. Those images were fading. Instead, she could feel her head on his shoulder and his hand running through her hair. She could hear his breath in her ear, feel it, soft and warm. As she tried to fall asleep each night, she saw him as she had first seen him, a young man with no beard, his eyes a watery blue, his jacket handmade in Scotland, she later discovered, his large hand held out as he asked her to dance.

The memories did not comfort her. They made her feel the years that had passed and that, like Aaron, would never return. They made her old. Sometimes, when she got up to go to the bathroom, she caught sight of herself in the mirror and thought it was her grandfather. All she had to do was spit some tobacco. The smell of her grandfather and his chewing tobacco came back to her, and she got back into bed, sleepless and sick to her stomach.

When Danny came to dinner, he always said, "I'll bring a roast chicken from Gourmet Garage so you won't have to cook."

Cook? She could barely recall when she had last cooked. She did make toast. She sometimes boiled an egg. But she would not be cooking Danny a nice dinner like a proper mother, like a proper hostess, she didn't have the strength, he was right about that. She decided she would make the table look pretty. She would use the silver. She would light candles.

She bent down and pulled out the bottom drawer in the kitchen cabinet, where the tablecloths were kept, then stood up holding a fresh bright white embroidered cloth and banged her head on a cabinet door she'd left open. She cried from pain and frustration, but forced herself on, into the dining room, to spread the cloth. But how could she spread the beautiful white cloth? The dining-room table was covered with mail and file folders; there was a tray with an egg-stained plate and a pink jammy crust of bread; large bottles of pills dozed on their sides like sea lions; magazines and catalogues and unread newspapers had slithered out from piles that had then collapsed and fanned across yet another egg-stained plate. A pile of bills, three piles of bills, each topped with a yellow Post-it that said *Urgent*. Joy sat at the table crying and trying to decipher the bills. They made no sense. She began to dial Molly's number to tell her the dining-room table was a mess, as if Molly should fly in from California to straighten it up, then caught herself and hung up.

She choked when Danny came to dinner. A piece of chicken flew out of her throat and landed on her plate, slimy and colorless.

The sounds were hideous, like a crow's, like a gasping dying crow's. KEH-KEH-KEH. She tried to drink water. No air came in, no air went out, her throat was closed and squeezing and pushing, and out came the piece of chicken in a gush of unswallowed liquid. It lay there in a pool of water like a tiny dead baby.

Danny had been pounding her on the back. Now he stood beside her staring at the lump of flesh in its little pond. "Jesus."

Joy patted her mouth with her napkin, then spread it over her plate, covering the chicken.

"Jesus," he said again. He stroked her hair. "Mom, can you talk?"

Joy put her head in her hands. She could talk. But what was there to say?

"So how's Mom?" Molly asked Daniel later that night.

"She says she's okay. She got a piece of chicken stuck in her throat. It was disgusting. And scary."

"But she's okay?"

"Yeah, yeah. You know her. She's a trooper."

"Daniel said you seemed pretty good," Molly said to her mother the next day.

"We had chicken."

"Are you getting out at all? You need to get out, see your friends."

"Oh no. Not in this weather."

"Aren't you going stir-crazy?"

"You know, I'm a very busy person, Molly." Joy gazed at the datebooks splayed in front of her on the dining-room table, one of them so old the cover hung off like an empty sleeve, an amputee's empty sleeve. "Between losing things and looking for things I've lost and going to the bathroom," she said, "well, the day just isn't long enough."

"You're funny."

"I'm not trying to be."

Molly laughed. "You really are funny. Now make a date with a friend. With Natalie. Go to the 92nd Street Y the minute it gets warm enough, okay? I'm so proud of you, Mom! Daniel's right. You really are a trooper."

"She's so strong," Molly and Daniel told each other.

"Of course she misses Dad," they added, "we all do, but what a terrible weight she's been carrying all these years. Now, finally, she can have some time for herself."

"I can talk to her now, really talk to her," they said. "About me."

She seemed to need them more than ever, which was gratifying, but she didn't seem to need them too much, which was more gratifying still.

When the weather warmed up and the ice turned to broad rivers of slush, Joy did try going to the 92nd Street Y, to a poetry reading.

"Count me out," said Natalie. "Poetry is depressing at our age."

"Why at our age particularly?"

"Because everything is depressing at our age."

The Y was dark and frequented by women who did not bother about their hair. The screaming children running in and out, who should have cheered her (that had always been one of her theories, that the generations should mix), were unsettling. She could feel her irregular heart beating more irregularly than usual and she went home.

When Daphne got back from Florida, Joy went out again to meet her at the coffee shop. They had not seen each other since Aaron's funeral.

Joy said, "I miss Aaron. And I don't like being alone."

"The first year is the worst. Then it calms down to a dull roar."

"How's your boyfriend from down there?" Joy asked.

"Dead."

Daphne had two other men she "went to dinner with": one she had picked up at a coffee shop farther downtown near her apartment, the other the widower of an old friend. But it had been a hard winter for them, and for Daphne, too: "All my boyfriends are dead."

Joy felt dizzy. Maybe matzo-ball soup and waffles was a bad idea. "I'm sorry," she said.

"My kids think I should consider going into assisted living."

"*Do* they. Well, what do *you* think?"

"They worry because they're not here. They want me to come

to them in Cincinnati. Well, to a place near them in Cincinnati. I understand. But I can't go to Cincinnati. I told them I'm staying, and it's called 'Aging in Place.' That's what the social workers call it."

"You saw a social worker?"

"No, of course not. In Florida they talk about these things. It's all the rage in the world of gerontology, otherwise known as Florida. Aging in Place."

"Like running in place."

"Going nowhere fast." Daphne laughed.

"Whatever they call it, it's better than a nursing home . . ."

". . . In Cincinnati!"

"I read somewhere that Cincinnati is a very nice city. Or was it Charlotte?"

"The assisted-living place on Eighty-sixth Street is supposed to be beautiful," Daphne said. "Leonard's children sent him there, you know."

"Leonard?" Leonard, their handsome classmate in college, Leonard who had proposed to her all those many years ago. A lot of men had proposed to her. Men did that in those days, proposed. Why? What was their hurry? Oh yes, the Korean War, that was it. She had expected Karl to propose, but he was more sensible than the rest of them, he was waiting until he had a decent job, that's what he said when she told him she was going to marry Aaron. "I saw Leonard about a year ago. He drove past in a red Cadillac convertible with a woman half his age. If that."

"He picked her up in a bar. They went to Bermuda together, and he had a heart attack and wound up in the hospital. His daughter had to fly down, and that, as they say, was the end of that."

"He took her to Bermuda?"

Daphne nodded.

"Who goes to Bermuda?"

Joy got a bad cold after that outing. She stayed in the apartment for a week, ten days, twelve, ordering chicken soup from the coffee shop. The cold turned into bronchitis.

"Whatever you do, *don't* get pneumonia," Molly said.

Joy promised that she would not.

She wondered what her children would do if she did get pneumonia. Put her in a home? Just until you get better, for your own good. What if they decided to leave her there, for her own good? The thought kept her up that night and woke her up many nights after. They had never said anything about sending her off to an assisted-living place. They couldn't send her against her will. They wouldn't send her anywhere against her will! And she didn't even have pneumonia! She told herself these things. But you never know. That was one thing she had learned over the years. You really never know anything.

— 30 —

Ruby went to Hebrew school three times a week after school. She babysat for Rabbi Kenny every Thursday night when he and his wife went out to dinner and to the movies. He had five-year-old twin boys.

"The only problem," Daniel told Molly, "is that she wants to change her name to Rachel."

Daniel talked about his daughters incessantly. There had been a time when his fascination with his own offspring had annoyed Molly, but since she'd moved to Los Angeles, Ruby and Cora had become like fantastical figures in a storybook, characters in a book about a magical, faraway place: Home. Now she encouraged Daniel. When he talked about his children, she felt she could safely relax and indulge herself in nostalgia and love for the city she left behind.

"She gave the rabbi's kids all her old Pokémon cards."

"Very generous."

"Well, I guess she kind of outgrew them. And Cora didn't want them. Not that she actually asked Cora."

"I miss everyone so much," Molly said.

"Did you talk to Mom today?"

"I did. She said she was very tired and the doctor told her to use her asthma inhaler thing, and she fell asleep reading the paper and woke up and thought it was morning. She was feeling a little better, so she ordered a turkey burger for dinner and she ate half of it."

They hung up happy in the knowledge that their mother was thriving.

31

Joy began to feel that there was another person in the apartment, a stranger, and it was her. She had to watch over this person, this boring, fearful, sickly person. She had to make sure it took its pills. She had to watch its step so it didn't fall. She made sure it chewed its food so it didn't choke. She worried about the person constantly; the worry was a weight heavy on her shoulders, on her mind, on her heart. It followed her as she followed this person from room to room, this awful, needy person who was herself.

"I don't know what to do with her. *And* she's an *irritating* person. What a responsibility!" she said to Molly.

She had begun timing herself in the morning to see how long it took her to get dressed.

"It feels like two hours, and it is."

Sometimes she didn't bother to get dressed.

"It saves so much time. Some days I don't even want to take a shower, but then I think, Well! I'll do it for my children. I don't want them to have a filthy old mother with fuzzy gray hair."

"You're funny," Molly always said, laughing, relieved—Joy could hear it in her voice. That was another of the responsibilities Joy had, relieving her children of worry. She did not want them to be upset. And she did not want them to send her to an assisted-living facility in Cincinnati. Or anywhere else.

32

J oy looked out her window and felt an affinity for the ugly March street and the ugly March sky. Even her heart felt ugly, especially her heart, dusty and empty except for the shaky memories scattered around like sticks of broken furniture. She was physically ugly, too, listless skin sagging at her jaw, red-rimmed eyes—she examined her face in the mirror and took a certain satisfaction in its fall from beauty. It was the only power she seemed to have anymore—the power to deteriorate. Her hair was too long, too thin, scraggly and white like a witch's hair, and there was a long white hair on her chin. Her clothes, which had once charmed and fascinated her, now sulked in the closet, a closet that had no light. She tried a flashlight. It was too heavy for her, twisting her wrist so painfully she grabbed at the doorframe to keep her balance. Everything was too heavy for her these days, even the clothes themselves. Those she extracted were random and old, decades old. Excellent quality, she could still appreciate that. Pity they didn't fit, pity about the moth holes, pity about so many things. She lost weight, something that automatically pleased her, until she remembered that she'd lost the weight because of illness, stress, old age. Her good Italian knit pants fell right down to her feet, like a clown's pants in the circus, like Aaron's pants, a thought that made her sit on the edge of the bed, that made the room spin. Usually she ended up wearing the same gray sweatshirt, the one Aaron had worn, and a pair of black jersey pants she'd gotten at the Gap, although the drawstring was tied in an inextricable knot.

She sat at the table not even bothering to look at the car lights outside. Lou Barney, Lou Barney, who the hell was Lou Barney? The iPad only wanted to play Lou Barney, flashing his name on the screen. Joy had never heard of him. Why did Molly and Danny ever get her this thing? It was very generous of them, but it always wanted to play Lou Barney, and then wouldn't even play him, whoever he was. Joy shook the iPad. She was just about to call Molly when she decided to try one more time. She changed glasses and tapped the screen.

It wasn't Lou Barney. It was Low Battery.

I really cannot take much more of the modern world, she thought. I really cannot.

Soon after Lou Barney, Molly came for a week, by herself. Joy was still coughing, but the bronchitis was mostly gone. She had not gotten pneumonia.

"That's wonderful, Mom. You look so much better than I expected. You're so independent."

Joy said, Yes, I am. She did not say, Thank god you're here, Molly, I could not have taken one more minute on my own, I'm so weak I can hardly lift my toothbrush.

She took a walk with Molly and tried not to lean on her arm.

"Mom? Are you okay? You look a little pale."

"It's the weather," Joy said.

Molly took her arm gently. "I'm glad you've taken such good care of yourself."

"Danny did what he could," Joy said. "And now you're here."

She felt Molly stiffen, for just a split second. Then Molly stopped and wrapped her arms around her. Joy's face was pressed uncomfortably against the zipper of her daughter's coat.

"I don't want to be a burden," Joy said.

Molly laughed. "I should hope not."

It was about a month later that Joy was finally able to force herself to go back to work. She took a cane. Her bags seemed heavier than ever, but the weather was better, no snow, no rain, just a vicious wind. Gregor got her a cab. She immediately began to worry about whether she'd be able to get a cab home. It would be too windy to wait for the bus even with the cane. The cane had four little feet and a dirty white stripe where someone had torn off the adhesive tape on which the name Aaron Bergman had been scrawled in black Sharpie. I should have gotten him a nicer cane, she thought. How could I have let him walk around with this?

She typed some figures into the computer. The screen shuddered and suddenly there was something different on it. What had she done?

What had she done? What was she doing? Why was she here? These were vast questions that had become horribly small and specific to her. It was hard to remember exactly what she had done earlier in the day. It was hard to focus on what she was doing at that moment. It was hard to understand why she was in this windowless, airless closet.

She tried to concentrate on the report on the air quality necessary for new display cases. She pulled a bottle of water from one of her bags, but she could not unscrew the cap. She glanced at a study of formaldehyde in enclosed environments. She wondered if she was breathing formaldehyde in the enclosed environment that was her office.

She leaned back and looked up. There were several missing ceiling tiles near the light, as well as some wires left hanging from a wall socket. She had filled out all the forms for maintenance, but then she'd been told it would take weeks for anyone to get to it. "Volatile Organic Compounds," she typed, a term for hydrocarbon gases.

When a workman passed she went to the door and hailed him like a cab. He was a lovely man, happy to help her, very sympathetic, even when he had to go and get a ladder. The room had such high ceilings—it was higher than it was wide, higher than it was long. He came back and set up his ladder and fixed everything just like that, one, two, three. He had a daughter in high school. They chatted about the cost of college as he hung her posters.

Then Miss Georgia whisked by the open doorway and, like a character in a cartoon, backed up, demanding to know what was going on. The workman, whose name was Marlon, winked at Joy and slid out the door. Miss Georgia watched him go with a disapproving look, then turned to Joy. "Chop-chop," she said. "We have work to do."

"Excuse me?"

Miss Georgia clapped her hands together like a kindergarten teacher. "Chop-chop."

"Chop-chop?" Joy said, thinking of all the years she had worked to get her master's degree and then her Ph.D., thinking of her training and all her experience, all the years she had worked at this museum before Miss Georgia even knew how to spell museum. Chop-chop? "I'm sorry, but what is it you think I'm doing if not working?"

It was the slight smirk that appeared on the director's face that pushed Joy over the edge.

"Why don't I just stick a broom up my ass and sweep the floor, too?" she said.

Now she lowered her head to the shiny white top of the drawerless desk and did not move for what seemed like a long time. She pictured the director's face after her outburst: truly shocked. Joy wanted to laugh, but she was too tired. The surface of the table was cool and soothing on her forehead. When she lifted her head, the windowless room spun around her like a merry-go-round and the director seemed to be back in her doorway, a file in her hand.

"I've been knocking for quite a while," Miss Georgia said.

Joy stared at her.

When Joy still did not speak, Miss Georgia added, "Yes. The less said the better." Miss Georgia held up a hand, traffic-cop-like, then dropped a thick manuscript on Joy's desk. "Your recommendations for the photographic collection."

Joy pulled it toward her.

"Because you were ill," Miss Georgia said, "we decided to help you out."

Joy started to ask why they thought she needed help on that particular report, which was, after all, finished.

"No, no, don't thank me," Miss Georgia interrupted. "Not necessary. We got some excellent outside help on the project."

"But I—"

"Say no more." Miss Georgia put her finger to her lips.

Joy flipped through the manuscript, a comprehensive guide to protecting the museum's photographs in their new location that she'd worked on for months before the move.

"We read your report, of course," the director said. "But under the circumstances, we felt it would be prudent to hand the project over to outside sources."

Joy's bags were even heavier going home. The report was hundreds of pages long. She put it in the red bag and clutched it to her side. When she finally got a cab, the thought of going home to her empty apartment was too grim. She got off at the coffee shop wondering if they would force her to sit at one of the sad little tables against the wall where all the old widows and widowers sat. She wanted a booth. She wanted to be near a window. She was breathing heavily. It was from anger, of course. Unless she was having a heart attack.

"Joy!" a voice cried out when she got inside, and it was Karl.

She hadn't seen him since before Aaron died. He had been so kind, sending a lovely note on thick creamy stationery. Beautiful old-fashioned fountain-pen handwriting. It had disturbed her, that familiar handwriting from long ago.

"Joy, I'm so sorry about Aaron. I lost a good friend," he said when his attendant had lurched out of the booth, offered her seat to Joy, and disappeared into the night. When her waffle came, Joy pulled a brown glass bottle out of one of her bags.

"Maple syrup," she said. "*Real* maple syrup. No one serves real maple syrup anymore."

They talked about Aaron, about his reminiscences about the war, about the pigeons. Joy cried, just for a minute, and Karl handed her a large, clean white handkerchief with his initials monogrammed on it. She hesitated before handing it back and had a flash of memory, another large, clean white handkerchief, no monogram in those days, a fit of sneezing, the embarrassment of handing it back. She looked up. Karl was smiling.

"I remember," he said.

"Were we on a sailboat?"

He nodded.

"I thought you were very brave to take it back after all that sneezing."

"I didn't have much choice."

She laughed. "I remember thinking it would be very forward of me to keep it. That was the word. 'Forward.' Why didn't I have my own handkerchief? And why do you still use a handkerchief? They're very unsanitary."

"You can keep that one."

"Oh no," she said. "I couldn't. It's too beautiful." She wrapped it in a paper napkin and gave it back to him. Then she ordered a cup of soup, and suddenly, as if she'd known him all her life, which she very nearly had, she began confiding in him, telling him about going back to work, about how awful Miss Georgia had been. She took the report out of the red bag.

"It's a perfectly good report," she said. She began leafing through it, nodding approval at her own conclusions. "An excellent report, actually."

"Joy?"

She had stopped turning the pages. She was staring, riveted, at one page. Then she grinned. "Oh dear," she said, still grinning. "Oh dearie dear." Surely that was supposed to say CUNY facilities. Surely that was not supposed to say CUNT facilities.

"Something wrong?" Karl said.

"Oh no," Joy said. "Just a little typo."

33

Hi, Grandma," Ben said. "Would you like a visit? I have a week off."

In fact, the bar Ben worked at had gone out of business and he had Airbnb'd his apartment out for the month. He wasn't sure why, but he admitted it to his grandmother as soon as he arrived.

"I won't stay for a month or anything, but I didn't know where else to go. Please don't tell Mom. She'll freak out."

Joy found Ben fascinating. He was so sweet and so difficult in such a sweet way, drifting without bothering anyone, unproductive and undemanding, working at what in Joy's day were considered summer jobs for a college man—construction, bartending, temporary doorman. It was not a philosophical choice, this drifting, not like Dolores's granddaughter, who was a Dumpster diver, god help her. Molly worried too much about him, he was a good boy finding his way.

And now he needed her, Joy. She wondered if Molly had put him up to this, part of her plan to keep her relevant.

"As long as you like," she said.

She wanted to dance, she was so relieved. She would not have to sleep in the apartment alone.

Uncle Daniel's old bedroom, a.k.a. the maid's room, was fusty and weird—childish and elderly at the same time. The carpet was as old as his uncle, the paint had once been a lovely shade of blue, he'd been told, but was now a sad colorless shade of nothing, and the window needed no curtains or blinds because it was darkened by grime. The built-in shelves, once so enviously shipshape (at least according to Ben's mother), were claustrophobic and warped. The sink dripped, not too much, just enough to catch you by surprise.

"Honey, do you want some tea?" his grandmother called out.

Yes, he did want some tea, and how comforting to have his grandma make it, though she made the worst tea he had ever tasted, weak and lukewarm. But just the sound of her voice made the little room feel much nicer, more like home. Ben had always loved coming to her apartment. She'd made him cracker sandwiches: buttery orange Ritz crackers and peanut butter. There were toys she'd kept there just for him and interesting junk retrieved from the museum she worked at. There was a Betty Boop videotape he had always loved, it was so sexy and so peculiar—especially when she told him that Betty Boop was Jewish. Sitting on her bureau in her bedroom, there was still a wooden puzzle box in the shape of a butterfly he had gotten her for Christmas when he was a little boy. He'd bought it at a street fair and thought it was the most beautiful and original object anyone had ever given anyone as a gift. One of his paintings from kindergarten was framed in Lucite and hung in the foyer.

The kitchen was long and narrow, a tunnel, really, and at the end was a window. His grandparents had jammed a small square table there. It had two chairs, and you could not open the oven door all the way even if the second chair was pushed in. He sat there with Joy and looked out the window and drank his tea.

"Grandpa and I used to sit here," she said.

"I can see all the flowering trees. It's really pretty."

"Yes. You're in Grandpa's seat."

Oh god. How awkward. "Oh. Right," he said. "Good seat to be in."

His grandmother smiled. "You're a fine person, Ben."

"Like Grandpa."

"He was all right," said Grandma Joy. "Up to a point."

She continued to smile, reaching behind her to grab a package of Oreos. She funneled several cookies into her hand.

"Enjoy," she said absently, rattling the package at Ben.

She could remember so clearly the first time Ben stayed at her apartment. He had been eighteen months old, jabbering quite coherently, with the bottle hanging from the side of his mouth like a cigar. She and Aaron had set up the old crib, a beautiful, highly decorated wooden crib that had originally been Aaron's, then taken it apart again the minute Molly saw it.

"The spokes are too far apart!" she said. "Are you trying to kill him? He could get his head caught. You put us in this? Unbelievable."

So they had moved the beautiful crib from the 1920s back into the cedar closet and bought an ugly blue nylon playpen that could double as a crib. Ben ended up sleeping in their bed, anyway, whenever he stayed with them. Joy could hear his small, even breath; she could smell the warm, bathed skin; she could see his eyelids flutter, his fingers clutch his bear. When she looked at him now, a skinny young man who needed a shave, he was the same to her, her first grandchild.

In the morning, Joy put some sort of clothes on so she wouldn't scare the horses, then staggered weakly to the kitchen to make Ben his breakfast. Standing over the stove to stir the Cream of Wheat, she eliminated the lumps in the cereal with solemn determination.

She put the two bowls of cereal on the kitchen table with two spoons and two cheerful cloth napkins. She put the kettle on and forgot it until its whistle startled her and woke Ben.

"You're the best," he said.

She could feel him watch as she shoveled sugar into her Cream of Wheat.

"Grandma, are you okay with sugar?" he said the first morning. "I thought . . ."

"Oh yes," she said. And to his credit he dropped the subject. He must have gotten that from his father, discretion. Certainly not from his mother. Joy missed his father. Doug Harkavy was such a nice man. Molly was lucky to have married him. Freddie was wonderful, too, of course. But what was the point? Well, the world was upside down, that's all.

"How is your father, Ben?"

"He's great. He has a grandchild. Well, she does, so he does. It's cute, too."

When Molly had announced she was leaving her husband for Freddie, a woman named Freddie, Joy had not fainted, though her heart was pounding and the room began to darken. She had smiled and said she wanted Molly to be happy, to be herself, and it was true, but she'd been thinking, *What about Ben?* He might be shunned by other children, he might be stunted in some Freudian path to maturity. She had worried, Aaron had worried, and then it turned out there was nothing to worry about, after all. Ben's friends—well, it was a different generation, wasn't it?—seemed to take the situation in stride. Ben was miserable about the divorce, but he didn't seem unduly upset about his mother and Freddie. Of course, he was in college. And this is New York City, anything goes, she had said to Aaron. All that worrying for nothing. It had been a great strain, worrying so much and hiding it from Molly.

"Worrying is inefficient," she said to Ben, smiling at him. "Look at you. You're a fine person, Ben."

Ben looked surprised. "Do you worry about me?"

"Not anymore."

"I worry about me. I wish I knew what I really wanted to do."

"Don't you want to go to law school?"

"Sort of. It seems interesting. But what if I have to get a job doing, like, contract law or something? I wish I were, I don't know, passionate about something."

He gazed at her so confidingly. He was very good-looking, and when his eyes shone with emotion like this, he was irresistible. She thought of saying, Passion is for the bedroom! Get a job! Get a job with health insurance! That's all that matters! Don't be like your grandfather, always looking to be happy in his work, excited, creative (English translation: broke). Independence is overrated. It leads to dependence. Get a job in a nice steady corporation and keep your head down, and do your dreaming on the weekends and pay your bills.

Of course there were no nice steady corporations anymore, not the way there used to be. And Aaron's problem had not been independence, it had been entitlement. And why shouldn't Ben try to find something he loved doing? He was young and bright and earnest.

"You'll find what you want," she said. "It may not be what you think it will, it may find you when you least expect it, it might even be law school. And if you're drifting, you might just drift into the right thing. Or if it's the wrong thing, you'll figure out how to turn it into the right thing. Sometimes you have to create your passion. I have great confidence in you. You're young. You have time. You're a fine person, Ben."

He sighed and finished his Cream of Wheat. Then he said, "Thank you." He smiled and got up and kissed her cheek and put his bowl in the sink. It amused her to see that he did not put it in the dishwasher or even rinse it, that he just left it there. "Thank you, Grandma," he said again. "You've always helped me a lot, you know that?"

No, she didn't, but she was extremely happy to hear it now when she felt she was about as useful as one sock.

"You have time," she said again.

They went for a walk every day and sat on the same bench in Central Park watching the dogs parade by. They ate lunch in the coffee shop, and when Ben wasn't seeing his old friends, they ate dinner there, too. They bumped into Karl twice, but they didn't sit with him.

"He was Grandpa's friend in the park."

"Yeah?"

Ben didn't seem interested and Joy had no desire to tell him more. There was nothing to tell, anyway.

She was none too steady on the walks back and forth to the coffee shop. Sometimes her feet just sort of slid forward instead of lifting up and moving the way feet are meant to do.

"I'm shuffling," she said. "I'm going to shuffle right onto my face if I'm not careful."

"You can lean on me," said Ben.

That made Joy smile. She remembered holding his little hand to cross the street, lifting him onto the bus's high step. He used to wear tiny navy-blue sneakers and overalls.

"Yes," she said. "All right, I will."

His arm was wiry and strong. He slowed his step and shortened his long stride.

Ben stayed for six nights before he heard about another job in New Orleans and decided to sleep on a friend's couch down there until he could get his apartment back. But before he left, he asked his grandmother for a favor.

"It's kind of private," he said.

"Do you need money, sweetheart? Of course you do. Here's a twenty. No, that's not enough. Here, I've got eighty bucks."

Why is my grandmother carrying a purse around her own house? Ben wondered. He knew that if he asked her she would tell him a long complicated story that would make no sense to him, so he didn't ask her. But he put his hand out to stop her rummaging in the big shoulder bag.

"No, Grandma, no. It's not money. And you gave me a really generous Christmas present. Really."

She'd had to be creative at Christmas. So much had been going on. There was no way she could have gotten out to go Christmas shopping. A card with nice crisp bills for Ben had done nicely, five twenty-dollar bills. She thought of the two beautiful teacups (they'd been her mother's, just a small chip on one, and she had three more) she'd given Molly and Freddie, plus an opal and silver ring she'd found that Molly had liked as a child, she told them they could share it, there had to be some advantage to having your daughter marry another woman. But money had been fine for Ben.

"Then what can I do for you, Bennie?"

He blushed and reached into the breast pocket of his shirt. It was a nice shirt. Had she given it to him for his birthday last year?

"Did I give you that shirt?"

"Yeah, I think so." He handed her a crumpled wad of pink paper.

"Ben! A traffic ticket? You don't even have a car."

"Don't tell Mom, okay? It's kind of embarrassing."

He did look embarrassed, that was certain. His cheeks were as rosy as a little English choirboy's. It made him even more appealing. He was such a handsome boy. He was such a good boy, staying with her like this. She felt sick at the thought of him leaving. Maybe it would have been better if he had not come at all, then she wouldn't have minded his departure.

"And the problem is, there's a court date," he was saying. "And I won't be here because I'll be back in New Orleans, and so I was wondering . . ."

Joy nodded and smiled. Ben needed her. This strong young man needed her, and it made her feel a bit strong and a bit young herself. A bit manipulated, too, but that was a grandson's god-given right, to manipulate his grandmother.

"I'll pay you back the money for the fine," he said with the generous confidence that his offer would not be accepted.

"But how did you get a parking ticket without a car, Ben?"

"Oh," and he said something in that soft, barely comprehensible mumble young people so often employed.

"What? I hate it when you people mumble. Even your mother does it sometimes."

"You know, um, public urination."

Joy looked down at the piece of pink paper in her hand, then gingerly dropped it onto a paper napkin she pulled out of her pocketbook. "*What?*" she said. "That is disgusting, Ben. What is the matter with you? Is this what people do in New Orleans? Are you insane? . . ."

She went on and on, making her way to the bathroom sink to wash her hands, Ben following like a shamed dog, which is just what he had behaved like, a dog. On the street. Public urination? There was a ticket for that, that specifically? How much urine was on the public street if they had to maintain a special traffic violation category for it? "Why on earth did you pee in the street? In public?"

"It was really late at night. Everything was closed. And, you know, New York has no public bathrooms. In Paris they have public toilets."

She paused. She said, "Ah." She said, "Well."

He knew the word "Paris" would do it. She had taken him to Paris once, when he was quite young. Just the two of them. She had gone to do some research for the museum, and she brought him along. She made him go to a ridiculous number of museums, but mostly they ate and walked.

"Oh, Ben," she said. "What is to become of us?"

"I didn't pee on the ticket, Grandma."

She picked it up and folded it neatly and zipped it up somewhere in her bag. "Our secret," she said.

34

Molly's department had gotten a request to excavate a race-horse that had been buried in the 1960s at a racecourse that was closing. The owners of the horse wanted him and his memorial moved to another racecourse intact. Molly had never heard of the horse, but Freddie told her he was quite famous in California. Her father had been a fan.

Molly called Ruby in New York and said, "I don't know why, I thought it would interest you."

"Do you think I'm morbid, Aunt Molly?"

"A little."

"Yes, it does interest me. Is the horse in a casket?"

"No. Afraid not. A canvas sack. We may not find much. But the shoes should be intact."

"Can I have one?"

"No."

"Can I come?"

The excavation of the racehorse happened to coincide with Ruby's vacation, and after a relentless campaign of whining, Ruby convinced her parents to allow her to go to Los Angeles to stay with her aunts.

Joy was horrified. "We just buried Daddy," she said when Molly phoned to tell her. "Don't you think it's too upsetting for a little girl to dig up a dead body so soon? It's too upsetting for me, that I can tell you. I'm sorry, Molly, but I do not want to hear any more about horse corpses. Goodbye."

"I didn't even think of my father," Molly told Freddie. "My mother said it's a lack of imagination."

"Well, good. You remember him as he was. I remember my mother as she was. It's more realistic, in a way. We don't live in a horror movie, after all."

"No," Molly said. "Do you think my mother does?"

Freddie chose to say nothing, which Molly seemed to find reassuring, because she smiled as if at her own foolishness and said, "Of course not. Of course she doesn't."

At first, Cora did not want to be left behind.

"Do you really want to watch Aunt Molly dig up an old dead horse?" her father asked.

She thought about it. The horse might smell. It was probably a skeleton, which was bad enough, but it might look like the Mummy or a horse zombie. And the digging was slow, which could be boring. "Joanie and I were going to have a lemonade stand outside the building. It's not very warm yet, but you can do good business that week because of tourists."

"So you'd rather stay home?"

Cora nodded. "You write the e's on the sign backward. To make it look childish. It draws customers."

He was glad at least one of them would be home. Daniel had never understood that you could love anyone as much as he loved Ruby and Cora. This love was new, born when they were born. Now life without that love coursing through him was unimaginable. Their voices were like birdsong, their movements like dance.

"Every morning when I see them my heart sings, it really sings," he said to Molly. "I don't want Ruby to visit you. I'll miss her too much."

Molly felt a pang of longing for Ben. "It never goes away, missing them."

"Like Mom and you."

"Not what I was thinking of."

"I, on the other hand, am the good sibling who stayed home," he said happily.

"The oceans are rising," she replied.

Molly stood with Freddie and Ruby waiting for Ruby's suitcase.

"In Japan they have sushi that goes around just like this, on a conveyor belt, but smaller, obviously," Ruby said.

"You've been to Japan?"

"No. But I like sushi. But Daddy says overfishing is ruining the ocean."

"We'll get you some sushi."

"Thank you, Aunt Freddie. And thank you, Aunt Molly, for inviting me to your dig."

"It's not the walls of Troy," Molly said. "But it's good practice for the students. The horse died of colic very suddenly. They didn't even mark the grave properly, so we'll have a bit of a search."

"Did they shoot him?"

Ruby did not look like a morbid child. She was dressed in pink and sparkles and frayed denim like every other little girl in the airport.

"I don't think so. I think they give them shots or something."

"Cora's scared of dead things. But I don't see why. They're dead. I don't mind them. I like to know that things happened before I came along. I don't know why, but I do."

The purple camouflage suitcase appeared on the belt.

"Maybe it helps you realize that things will come along after you, too."

"I think I'm too young to think that."

They found the rib cage first. Ruby dusted off the dirt with a paintbrush, following the curves that outlined the commanding chest. The mighty horse's legs seemed to be galloping even now. The students were silent when they saw all of him, a bas-relief of bones rising from the sandy soil.

Ruby lit a candle for him when they got back to the house. "*Yitgadal v'yitkadash,*" she said. She shrugged. "That's all I know of that one by heart. You're supposed to have ten people, and I'm sure you're not supposed to say it for a horse, but I don't care. And I say it every night for Grandpa." She looked at them defiantly.

Molly wiped away a few tears. She did not sleep that night. Her mother was right, it was too soon after Aaron's death to dig up a body. Ruby was fine. It was Molly who had nightmares.

"You were crying in your sleep," Freddie said. "I couldn't wake you."

Molly didn't want to talk about it. And she certainly didn't want to talk about her bad dreams to Ruby, who looked as chipper as ever when they went into the kitchen. She had helped herself to a large bowl of the neon-colored cereal her parents forbade her.

"Guess what my father said to his ex-girlfriend," Freddie said. She read aloud from an email sent by Green Garden: "'Thou wouldst eat thine dead vomit up and howlst to get it.'"

Ruby looked up happily from her cereal bowl. "Dead vomit! Can I meet him?"

They went to Santa Anita. Molly and Ruby sat in the backseat, Freddie and her father in the front. Ruby nudged Molly, then pointed to the back of the father's head and the back of the daughter's head. They were shaped identically.

"Molly and her students and Ruby dug up a racehorse and moved him to Santa Anita, Dad."

"Your friends always were peculiar."

"We didn't move him, actually. Just dug him up. Not too many opportunities to dig things up in Los Angeles. It's great experience for the students."

"Students?" Duncan said. "Students of what? Grave-robbing?" He chuckled. Then, "Don't go digging me up, you girls." Then, "Where are the flowers?"

"What flowers?"

"For your mother. I always bring flowers."

"Dad, we are not going to the cemetery. We're going to the track."

"Yeah? Why didn't you say so?"

They ate pastrami sandwiches and bet ten dollars on a horse named Madeira My Dear, who won.

Freddie's father made Ruby promise to go to the track with him again. "You bring luck."

"I'm not superstitious."

"That's okay," he said. "I am."

35

The thought of an outing excited Joy. The brick buildings glowed, genial and rosy in the sun. What a beautiful day and she'd woken up feeling strong. Oh, this was very nice! She began the search for her wallet, her bags, her sunglasses, her gloves.

She bought a tuna-fish sandwich and a ginger ale at the little deli on the corner and watched the man behind the counter wrap the sandwich in white paper, then cut it diagonally. That was nice, too. She liked her sandwiches cut diagonally. This is what she would do when she retired. Go on outings with tuna-fish sandwiches cut on the bias. You couldn't do that in an assisted-living facility, not like this, spontaneously. You probably had to check out at the desk, sign an attendance sheet, get permission, like the loony bin.

She didn't have to ask anyone for anything.

She carried her brown bag out to the street and the wind nearly knocked her down. It was chillier than she'd thought. The tulips planted on the meridian of Park Avenue were bright orange this year. The cherry trees above them were in full pink bloom. The wind would take care of that, soon enough, she supposed. The petals would blow around like bright pink snow, then settle into colorful drifts, then turn brown and rot like all flesh, even flowered flesh. But for now, they danced gaily against the blue sky.

She turned into Aaron's little park and sat on a bench. The sun was glaring. The bread of her sandwich was dry. The wind was cold. This was a mistake. She was not ready. She felt her heart beat unevenly. Atrial fibrillation. Right now, the blood could be languishing, clotting during a skipped beat, and then, wham, a clot could be thrown up to her brain and she would be dead. Or worse.

Karl came into the park just as she was balling up the wrapper from her sandwich.

"Joy!" He pushed his red wheeled walker aside and sat next to her on the bench. "You're a sight for sore eyes."

"You want coffee?" said his attendant, Wanda's friend Marta.

Karl shook his head. "Go, go," he said. "Enjoy."

Joy and Karl sat silently awhile. Joy pulled her hood up. She stood to dump the remains of the sandwich in the trash can, but Karl took it from her and tossed it like a basketball.

"You have good aim," Joy said. "We never went to a basketball game, did we, you and I?"

"Baseball. You're a dirty rotten Yankees fan. I remember."

Did he remember the ride home on the subway, hand in hand?

"Are you still a dirty rotten Yankees fan?" he asked.

She laughed. "I don't pay much attention to sports."

"My wife was a dirty rotten Yankees fan. She died two years ago. It's terrible, Joy. I know it's terrible."

They looked at each other. Why, his eyes were the same, the same eyes they had been when they were young, hazel eyes specked with green. There were tears in them.

"It's so windy," she said.

"My children want me to move."

"Oh, that," Joy said. "Pay no attention."

But sometimes she did worry about her own situation. She did not want her children to send her away to a home. If she became weak enough . . . well, stranger things had happened. They watched her like hawks to make sure she was okay, and like a field mouse she scuttled and hid. Yes, I'm doing quite well, she would say. Nothing to report. They seemed to believe her. They wanted to believe her. They told her she was a good sport.

But the illusion of good sportsmanship was becoming more and more difficult for her to pull off. She did not want to burden them with her problems. That might push them over the edge. She didn't want assisted living; just, sometimes, a little assistance.

"There's so much paperwork," she said to Karl. "In life."

He nodded sympathetically, but he continued to talk about his son who wanted him to move to Rhode Island and his other son who wanted him to move to Denver. "I can't move. I mean, look at me. I, literally, can't move."

The papers accumulating on Joy's dining-room table had begun to haunt her, zombies from another life, infinite and unfinished though Aaron was finite and gone, as if the magazine subscriptions addressed to him were more important, more vital than he had ever been. He lived only in the gruesome form of debts and appointments, doctors' bills.

"I have enough money, I have a nice apartment, I have Marta, who's a godsend. Why don't they leave me alone?"

"Who would want to live in someone else's city?" Joy said. But she was thinking about the piles of papers waiting for her. The papers oozed across the table, an accusing slop of obligation, neglect, pressure, the pressure of a hostile world to pay attention and to pay, pay, pay. She was old and she was alone, and the papers took no pity.

"They mean well," Karl said.

The papers had begun to take on a mythical quality. They were an angry god of chaos who never stopped reproducing himself, growing bigger and stronger, tentacled, menacing, choking her to death.

"I don't understand how they pile up so fast, the papers," she said.

"Maybe it would be nice to move away, just leave all the mess behind. I never thought of it like that."

"Absolutely not," Joy said. "That mess is your life. Don't ever let 'em tell you any different."

Then she hobbled back to her apartment. There it all was, her mess, waiting, turrets and towers of files and mail, its banners of Post-its and crumpled tissues. It was an eclectic collection. Everything had been or was to be filed, but the names on the files had little to do with their contents and few hints for what should be added. There were multiple files labeled, for example, *Urgent!!*, though some were labeled URGENT, all caps, and a few *Urgent!* with just the one exclamation point. There was a *Pay Today* file and a *Pay Immediately* file, a *Miscellaneous* file and a *Miscellany* file. There were *Medical, Medicine, Health, Health Care, Health Insurance, Doctors, Doctor Bills, Medicare*, and there were files by illness as well: *Diabetes, Cancer/Joy*, and *Cancer/Aaron*. Inside were flyers for Roundabout Theater and YIVO, Time Warner, DirecTV, AT&T, Verizon, and free shingles shots from CVS. There were unopened envelopes with requests for money from starving children, dogs, cats, and abandoned farm animals; newsletters from Israel and Trader Joe's; literature from city council candidates, mayoral candidates, cemeteries, the Neptune Society, and juice fasts. Bills and tax returns, X-rays and lab reports showed up, too, here and there, as well as clippings of art reviews by Adam Gopnik from the 1980s.

She adjusted a stack of unopened envelopes, tilting her head at them, like a curious dog. She opened one envelope and carefully read the marketing materials for a service she would never need or want. She put the torn envelope on the table, placed the glossy marketing pamphlet beside it. She shuffled through the stack of unopened envelopes again. She spread them out like a deck of cards on the table. She touched them, moved them slightly, piled them up again. She sighed. She began to read yesterday's paper, which was on the chair next to her. She reached for her scissors. She intently cut out an article and laid it on the table. A crumpled tissue fell from her sleeve. She carefully removed the cellophane from a lemon drop, which she then popped in her mouth, placing the sticky cellophane between the torn envelope and the tissue. She spread the pile of unopened envelopes out like a deck of cards on the table again.

She finally broke down and called Danny. "I think someone has to help me. But no one can help me. What should I do?"

"Close the door," Danny told her. "And never go in again."

When she called Molly, in tears, Molly said, "That's all? God, you scared me."

To them, it was a pile.

To Joy, it was the past and the future jumbled together.

Someday they would understand. They would feel sad the way she felt sad about her own mother, about all the ways she had not been able to understand until she, too, was old. If only everyone could be old together.

"Natalie!" She called her friend immediately. "I just had the most ghastly thought . . ."

Joy ran into Karl at the coffee shop regularly now. As soon as Marta saw her, she hauled herself up, said, "Errands," and lumbered out of the restaurant. It was pleasant for Joy, having someone to sit with, to confide in, someone her own age. And, she admitted this to herself, it was pleasant to spend time with a man.

She ordered her soup and listened to Karl tell one of his stories. She occasionally had to hold her hand up. "Karl," she would say, "my turn to speak."

"He has so many stories," she told Danny that night on the phone. "Very entertaining."

"You knew him in college? How come I never heard anything about him?"

"Oh, we lost track when I got married. You know how it is."

Molly called Daniel every Wednesday after his weekly dinner with their mother. She told Freddie she wanted to be supportive, but Freddie suggested she was just trying to cling to Daniel's devoted-child shirttails.

"Did you have a good time with Mom tonight?" Molly asked her brother. "Did you have a nice dinner?"

"I didn't go. She said she was too tired."

"She told you *not* to come? That doesn't sound good. Is she sick?"

"No. She said she had lunch with a friend and they walked in the park and she got tired."

"Yeah? Natalie?"

"No."

"Well, who, Daniel? You're being weird and mysterious."

"That guy. That Karl guy."

36

Molly called her mother to tell her the plans she and Daniel had made for Passover. Their first Passover without their father.

"We're all going to come. We'll have a real family Passover."

"At the apartment? Without Daddy?"

"It will give us a chance to be together and honor him," Molly said. "As a family."

Joy tried to picture the family gathered around the table without Aaron.

"No, no," she said. "No. Not this year. Not yet."

"Daniel and I worked it all out. We'll take care of the food, of course. You won't have anything to worry about."

"It will be too sad," Joy said. "I think it will be too sad. Everyone there but your father."

"We'll all be *together*, Mom."

At the coffee shop that night, Joy saw Karl, as she had hoped she would.

"I don't want this seder," she told him. "It's just too soon. Why can't they wait till next year?"

"Who knows if we'll be here next year," Karl said.

"That's cheerful."

"Well."

Joy tried to explain it to him. "Just picture it," she said. "The whole family. Picture the whole family, picture Danny, Molly, the wives, the grandchildren, me. And no Aaron. It's like one of those photographs from Russia where they scratch out Trotsky."

"I guess you could invite more people," he said. "Dilute it a little, like soup. Invite other people."

"Other people," Joy said. It was a brilliant plan. "Other people!"

The brilliant plan required a good deal of work. Just the thought of the preparations tired her. She was still not herself. She wondered if she'd ever be herself again, but no one must realize how tired she was. It was an effort to get her socks on, to tie her shoes. Her mugs were too heavy to lift. She now drank her tea in her mother's remaining china teacups.

She still went to work, however. She could not imagine retiring. If she stopped working, her world would screech to a halt, that's what it felt like to her. And she did enjoy the perplexed expression of Miss Georgia each time Joy plodded into the office, slowly and laboriously, leaning on her ugly cane. Then there was the issue of assisted living. If she had no job, it might seem as though she had no reason to remain in New York, in her apartment. She did not want her children to think it was time to move her. They never would, of course.

Unless they thought it would be better for her. She could hear their concerned voices: She'll have more company, you know how social she is; She'll have all her meals taken care of, no more ordering in from that greasy diner; Someone will change the linens; And if she falls . . .

Joy trudged up the miles of steps at the new building. She unlocked the door of her stunted new office. No, no one would be getting rid of her so easily. There would be no excuse to put her out to pasture. The trip on two buses was far more than she could manage, so she took a taxi to work. The cab fare added up to a good portion of her salary. But every little bit helps, she thought. And it's my every little bit, I earn it, I work for it. I am a working woman.

She pushed open the door.

There was another person sitting at her computer, at her desk.

"There's no drawer," Joy said.

The young woman in Joy's desk chair looked confused.

"For pencils," Joy said.

"Can I help you?" the young woman said. She had the sleepless, unkempt, poorly paid aspect of a graduate student. Joy's heart went out to her.

"I'm Dr. Bergman."

A blank look.

Joy tapped the nameplate on the door.

"Oh!" the young woman said, smiling. "Did you come to get your things?"

The graduate student, borrowed from CUNY's student work program, was under the impression Dr. Bergman had retired. She was terribly sorry. She'd just been told to use this office to do conservation work for the museum, though she was actually studying anthropology.

When confronted about the budding anthropologist in Joy's office, Miss Georgia did not have much to say, other than to assure Joy that the museum was operating with much more efficiency than it ever had before and she knew how loyal Joy was to the institution, which was why she had not hesitated in making these changes for the vitality and energetic future of the conservation department, knowing that Joy would welcome the chance to add to the viability and vigor of the museum.

"By retiring?"

Miss Georgia knew she would understand. She could gather up her boxes and books whenever it was convenient for her.

Joy had the taxi drop her off at the coffee shop. Karl was there, thank god.

Marta jumped up in her lumbering way, patted Joy's arm with what seemed like relief, and disappeared out the door.

"Loves her work," Karl said, laughing.

"I was *retired* from *my* work today. I was fired. Behind my back."

She ordered mashed potatoes and scrambled eggs and a lemon meringue pie. She tried to eat, but could manage only the pie.

"You can sue them for age discrimination."

"I'll be dead before it goes to court."

Karl nodded. "True." He was sympathetic, though. He'd been eased out of his law firm, his own firm, by the younger partners. "Experience? They're not interested."

"It's true I missed a few months when I was so sick."

"Months. What's a month?"

"I was a little fuzzy when I got back. The new building is like a railroad station, it's so big."

"They change things just to change them."

"I don't like change. They say you don't like change when you get old, and they're right."

Karl shrugged. "But some change is good." He smiled at her. "It's good we bumped into each other again, isn't it?"

"That's not change," Joy said. "That's continuity. I like continuity."

Karl did not want a bite of her pie. One more thing in his favor, she thought, finishing it with relish, scraping her fork against the plate to get the last lacquer-yellow traces.

37

Molly watched her mother opening folders, closing them, stroking, piling, opening them again. Each time Molly tried to pick one up, her mother swatted her away. It was hopeless. She headed for the kitchen to make some tea.

"What are you doing, Molly? You came all this way to help me clean up for the seder. Now please help me!"

Molly scooped up some mail from the other end of the table and began to sort it, but the sound of envelopes being torn open drew her mother's attention, the way the flutter of wings draws a cat, and Joy abandoned her files to touch each piece of mail, to finger the envelopes as if they were silken Chanel or velvet brocade beaded with seed pearls.

When Joy finally went to lie down on the couch for a rest, Molly furiously extricated the bills from the slippery towers of junk mail, sorting, filing, labeling the files and sliding them, quickly, quickly, before her mother could wake up, into new blue plastic file boxes she had ordered from Staples. She labeled the file boxes. She stuffed the junk mail into kitchen garbage bags and took them out to the back hall, where her mother would not find them.

Out of breath, gathering up the last bobby pin, the matchbooks, doctors' business cards, the coffee shop delivery receipts, Molly heard a horrified gasp behind her.

"My papers. Oh, my papers . . ."

Joy stared at the table, now empty. She sat down in Aaron's chair, her small frame hidden in a voluminous silk bathrobe she had found deep in the cedar closet, a burgundy paisley bathrobe that had been Molly's grandfather's. Heavy fringe hung from the sash. On the lapels was a braided border. She looked like a diminutive general of the Empire in her exotic silk robe and Oriental chair, her delicate little face pale and weary, relieved to hear that the native rebellion had been put down, though at what cost?

"I think I have to lie down again. Or eat something." Joy leaned her head back and closed her eyes.

"Listen, I have an idea. *I* can take care of all your bills from now on, Mom."

"I'm not senile." Eyes still closed.

"I can get everything on the computer and do it for you from L.A."

"I'm certainly not ready for that, thank you very much." Her voice had become rather severe.

"But I could—"

"Molly." Joy stood up, the hem of the silk robe pooling at her feet.

"What?" Molly said, sulky now.

"Let's face it."

"What? Face what?"

"The buck," Joy said, "stops here."

Karl arrived at the apartment exactly on time. Joy opened the door for him and noticed again his eyes, hazel with flecks of green, slightly protruding. She could remember being young and troubled by how earnest those eyes were. He carried flowers, a burst of tulips in many different colors.

"Look who's here," Joy called out to her family.

"That's not Elijah," Cora said. "Is it?"

"This is a very old friend of mine and a dear friend of Grandpa Aaron's," Joy said. "This is Karl."

Molly pulled her aside. "Mom," she whispered, "this seder is for family. Our family."

"One who locks the doors of his courtyard and eats and drinks together with his children and wife and does not feed and give drink to the poor and embittered—this is not the joy of a mitzvah but the joy of his stomach," Ruby said. "Maimonides."

"Oh Christ," said Molly.

"I read it on Chabad.org."

Molly shook her head and walked away. Joy kissed Ruby and said, "That's very wise. But I don't think Karl is either poor or embittered."

"You never know," Ruby said. "I mean, just in case, right?"

Joy nodded. "Just in case. But, Ruby, promise me, no more Chabad."

"Don't worry. I'm a feminist, Grandma."

Joy hurried away to answer the door and let Natalie in.

"Are you poor or embittered?" she asked.

"Embittered."

"Then you may enter."

"I'm poor, Grandma," said Ben, who stood right behind Natalie.

Joy hugged him and kissed him and thanked him for coming so far.

There were two more, Trevor and Melanie, a young couple from England who had just moved into the building.

This time it was Danny who pulled her aside. "Mom, what are you doing? This is a family thing. How many other people are coming? Hi, Natalie! Welcome!"

"This is so kind of you," Melanie said. "We've never been to a seder."

"Americans are so welcoming," said Trevor.

Joy smiled. She wanted to lock herself in the bathroom and never come out. She wanted to sit by herself and think about Aaron and watch the traffic from the kitchen window. She forced another smile and took a seat beside Ben and grabbed his hand and kissed it. His beard had grown in. "You look like Grandpa." Then she did get up and lock herself in the bathroom for a cry, but just a short one.

Looking down the table, Daniel realized that he, Daniel, was expected to lead the service. He cleared his throat and dinged a spoon against his wineglass. "Ahem," he said, and there was a slight diminution of noise. They got through to the first glass of wine without too much commotion. There was an empty place for Elijah, but it looked like a chair waiting for Aaron. Daniel tried not to stare at it. Ben kept filling up the wineglasses. It was thick, viscous stuff, but Daniel had downed several glasses before they got to the part where you raise your second glass. When they finally did, he made a toast to his father and realized he was singing Bob Dylan's "Forever Young." "May your heart always be joyful . . ."

"Daddy called me Joyful," his mother said. She sniffled. "It was ironic."

"Daddy wasn't ironic," said Molly.

"Well, wrong, then. He was wrong."

Ben had to finish the service. Uncle Daniel was lying on the couch by then, staring at the ceiling. Aunt Coco was handing out sticky flourless baked goods, her mouth set in a hard, furious line. Wine made her angry, especially at those who drank too much wine and lay on the couch.

"When do we sing the goat song?" Cora asked.

Ben led the diminished group through a few verses, the children belting out the chorus.

"What's a *zuzim*?" Cora asked. "A penny? Or a dollar, or what?"

Molly had opened a bottle of decent wine. She and Freddie were well on their way to having to join Daniel on the couch, Ben thought.

"Mom," he said, "easy does it."

His mother leaned back in her chair and put her glass to her lips, defiant, like a child. Freddie said, *"Dayenu!"* and drained her glass.

"Your mother drinks like a goy," Joy said.

"Well, you're supposed to drink wine on Passover," Ben said.

"It's okay for me to criticize her, Bennie. I'm her mother."

"Also, that's kind of a stereotype, Grandma." He smiled when he said it. He had noticed his grandmother had become quite sensitive to criticism.

"I love the word 'dipsomaniac,'" Karl said.

Natalie said, "Other people's families are so much less trouble."

Trevor and Melanie seemed content, turning redder with each glass, gamely crunching matzoh. "Brilliant," Trevor said each time Ben poured.

"Brilliant," Cora repeated.

Ruby began reading the four questions in pig Latin, Cora disappeared under the table, and Joy was eating macaroons dipped in chocolate, one after the other.

"Mom, easy does it," Molly said.

Ben laughed, then saw on his mother's flushed face nothing but earnest concern. You're not ironic either, Mom, he thought, but kept it to himself.

"I'll pay for this later," Joy said, licking her fingers. "Oh boy, will I."

Ben wondered if he could sneak away to watch the ball game. It was opening day. It was then that he felt the stab of absence, the moment that he glanced around to ask his grandfather if he wanted to watch, too, and remembered that his grandfather was gone.

———

The next morning, Molly woke up with a headache. She and Freddie were on a single blow-up bed wedged between the pullout couch that did not pull out and the bookcase.

"It's morning," she said, but Freddie groaned and did not move.

In the bathroom, the door locked, Molly called her brother.

"What the hell was that all about?" she said.

"Okay, I drank too much. I'm sorry I passed out on the couch. Please don't give me a hard time, Molly. Coco has already done that. Several times. And it's not even nine o'clock yet."

"Not you. *Mom*. What was with all those *people*? What was *Karl* doing here? Who is he, anyway? Some random guy from the park? At our first family gathering without Dad? What was she thinking?"

"She knew him in college. But I never heard her mention him until a few days ago. Do you think he was an old boyfriend?"

"Well, he's sure an old boyfriend now."

They both laughed.

"At least no one ended up in the ER after this holiday dinner," Daniel said. But he had been shocked to see Karl there, and hurt. He couldn't admit it even to Molly, but there was a moment when he walked into the apartment when he'd thought, I am the man of the house now, an unworthy thought that filled him with unworthy pride, until it dissolved into sadness and guilt. And then to have Karl appear—it was all wrong. Still, what was an old geezer like that going to do? Switch walkers with Joy when she wasn't looking? Daniel thought of himself as a calm, thoughtful, and reasonable person and he was determined to behave like one, but really his mother could have shown a little more consideration. And the man had brought his mother flowers.

"At least he didn't try to run the seder," he said, calming himself down. "Although it might have been better if he had. But I'm sorry, there was just something about him being there when Dad wasn't. It's only been a few months, for god's sake."

"Is this what Mommy wants?" Molly was saying, talking over him. "Every holiday dinner at the Mount Sinai emergency room with an old sick man who isn't even Daddy? This guy is bad news, Daniel."

"Bad news."

"The man wants a nurse, a *loving* nurse, not a paid companion. That's what they all want. And we can't let Mommy fall into that trap."

"It's like she's not thinking clearly. She's like in shock."

"Look," Molly said. "We have to face facts. Mommy's got nothing left in her life. Nothing. No job to go to. No sick husband to take care of. Her life is empty. She's very vulnerable."

Daniel said, "It's us she needs now."

"It's up to us to protect her."

38

Daniel pulled his mother's suitcase out of the closet. The sting of mold came with it.

"Oh dear," said Joy, sneezing.

"Yeah, it's pretty bad, Mom."

"It's a little like being in the country, though, that smell and the green. It makes me nostalgic."

The suitcase had been a gift from Daniel and Coco ten years ago. He wondered if she'd ever used it.

"Why don't you ever use this when we go Upstate?"

"Danny, honestly, it's full of mold. How could I possibly use it to go anywhere?" She sat on the bed. "Well," she said, "now that we see how the land lies, mold in the suitcase, very unhealthy, I'll just have to stay put in New York. In my own apartment."

Daniel took the suitcase down to the basement and left it by the garbage cans. That was on Saturday. On Sunday, he returned with a new suitcase. At first he'd gone to look for a cheap one in a crummy shop in Chinatown. He found a flimsy roller bag with zebra stripes for eighteen dollars and was about to buy it, thinking,

It doesn't have to last too long, she won't be making too many more trips at her age, then immediately felt so guilty that he left the zebra stripes behind, took the train up to Bloomingdale's, and got her an expensive roller bag in a respectable shade of blue with wheels that swiveled in all directions.

"You shouldn't have done that," Joy said when he spun the bag in graceful circles to demonstrate.

"You can't go to California with your stuff in garbage bags."

"California is not for me, Danny. I've never been there and there's a reason—it's not for me."

In the airport, Joy dropped her boarding pass, not on purpose, but she was not sorry to have lost it. The man pushing her wheelchair went back to look for it while Danny tapped his foot and forced a smile. She hated being a burden, but since she was, she wished people could shoulder her with more grace.

"I'm sorry to gum up the works," she said.

Danny shrugged, not very gallantly. Could you shrug gallantly, she wondered.

People were rushing past her in every direction. Little children were outfitted like their parents, wearing miniature backpacks, pulling little suitcases. Too many people from too many places traveling to too many other places.

How would she bear it? Two months in L.A.

"When you come back, the kids will be out of school and we'll all go Upstate," Danny said.

She was weary and she had not even gotten into the airport proper, much less the plane. People wheeling luggage the size of coffins rumbled past her. She heard a sparrow chirping high above in the rafters. Poor little bird, lost in a vast edifice, trapped, just like me.

"Let's go home," she said.

Danny pretended not to hear her.

"I don't belong here," she said.

"*No one* belongs here. It's an airport."

The wheelchair man had reappeared, victorious, waving the boarding pass. "Okay then, Madame." He spoke with a lilting Caribbean accent. He was almost as old as she was. Had his children made him leave his comfortable home and come to New York City because they were afraid he'd slip and fall?

"I'm supposed to age in place," she said to Danny.

"It's a vacation, Mom, in a warm place with people who love you."

"I don't really need a wheelchair," she said to the wheelchair man, turning, twisting her neck so she could see him. "My children are overly cautious."

"They love you," the man said.

"I'm going to stay with my daughter. In California." She did not mention Freddie. Perhaps that was wrong, but she could not come up with a way to explain Freddie, not on the spur of the moment to the wheelchair man.

"That's beautiful," said the man.

"Yes, I suppose it is."

Danny set off the beeping alarms as he went through security.

"Hips," he said apologetically to the guard. "And knees."

"I am free of prosthetics," Joy said. "I am also free of most of my large bowel, my gallbladder, my uterus, ovaries, and appendix. I have my tonsils and most of my teeth. Check on your machine. You'll see. Go ahead, check."

39

When she had been in Los Angeles for three days, she knew two things for certain. One: she could not spend two months with her daughter. Two: she could not spend two months with her daughter in California. The California sun was blinding, much brighter than the friendly East Coast sun. This sun was used to shining on a desert, harsh and unrelenting.

"Isn't it beautiful, Mom? Do you see why I love it here?"

"Very nice," Joy said.

Then there was Molly herself, as bright and unrelenting as the sun. Every time Joy put a glass down, Molly picked it up and put it in the dishwasher. The temperature was constantly shifting, depending on where that sun was and at what angle it was hitting the house, and Joy put on and took off sweaters all day long, but each time she reached for a sweater she had removed, it was gone, gone to its closet, hung up there by Molly. Books, magazines, sandwiches—they disappeared practically from Joy's hand. Her toothbrush, which she left on the side of the sink, immediately hid itself in the medicine cabinet. Sometimes, when Joy lifted her coffee cup, a hand with a sponge swiped the spot where it had been on the table before Joy was able to take a sip.

"This is so relaxing, isn't it, Mom?"

"Very nice."

"Are you comfortable, Mommy? We got you a memory foam pad for the bed."

The two girls were so thoughtful, but the bed was so high Joy had trouble getting into it. It loomed before her at night, a great bulbous affair piled with pillows, six, seven, eight pillows. The box spring and mattress and memory foam mattress pad and the down mattress pad on top of that looked like a big billowy hat that might topple off its head at any moment. It might cushion the fall in an earthquake. Then she thought, Earthquake, and could not sleep.

The jasmine bloomed, and it made her eyes water.

She uttered not a word of complaint. Molly was so happy to have her. Even Freddie seemed happy to have her here. Were they insane, both of them? She was a nuisance. Even at her best these days, she was a nuisance.

"I'm very annoying," she said.

"No, you're not," said Molly.

"No, I am. I really am. I'm annoying. I annoy myself, even."

Molly laughed and hugged her. Joy, hugging her back, felt the sturdy flesh of Molly's back. "You certainly are strong."

Molly rolled up her sleeve and made a muscle, like a man. Joy dutifully touched her daughter's biceps and wondered when it was that muscles on women had become fashionable. "Okay, Popeye," she said.

Molly was heading out for a walk. She walked very fast and very far every day. Stop and smell the roses, Joy had said once, but Molly said the roses in California did not have much smell.

"I'll walk you to the gate." Pretty much all she did. There were no doormen to gossip with, no coffee shop to walk to, no park, no friends to have lunch with, no Karl to bump into. "Just let me find my sunglasses."

She looked first through one bag, then through another bag. As she pushed the packages of Kleenex and lipsticks and tubes of moisturizer aside, she began to panic. Her sunglasses had to be in her pocketbook, in this brown eyeglass case perhaps, but no, the brown one was empty, and this one, the turquoise, held her reading glasses, the old ones that worked better than the new ones, she had been searching for them all day, and another glasses case, a hard case, white, this had to be the one with the sunglasses, but these were a pair of glasses she had never seen before, where on earth had *they* come from?

"Here, Mom. I found them. They were in the pocket of your jacket. In the closet."

"Oh thank god. Now I'll just put my shoes on."

Before she could put her shoes on, she had to put on her special elastic stockings that helped her circulation. The special rubber gloves she needed to put on the special stockings were somewhere in the guest room where she slept, which was also Freddie's home office, poor Freddie. She shuffled into the guest room, fumbled through several drawers until she found the rubber gloves.

"Mom, I don't have that much time before I have to get to work." Molly was pacing up and down the hall, all decked out in her sneakers and Lycra. A uniform to take a walk. Joy smiled. Molly had always liked uniforms. She had taken up skating just to get the skates and the silly skirt, horseback riding just to get the breeches and the ratcatcher shirt and the white stock and the shiny black boots; skiing, tennis—she had been very good at sports, but it was all about the equipment.

"You were such a good little tennis player."

"Mom?"

"Yes, all right, but don't rush me," Joy said. "I get flustered."

"Oh, for god's sake. Why didn't you get ready half an hour ago when I said I was going out?"

Joy looked up from her sneaker, the lace of which she was

trying to untangle. "See?" she said, beaming. "I was right! I *am* annoying!"

Molly and Freddie tried, they did try. They took Joy to the beach to watch the sunset. They took her to dinner. They made her dinner. They walked her up and down the street like a much-loved dog. In the evening they sat outside and had their glass of wine and Joy sat with them, but she was alone in those moments, she was alone in every moment. How could she have explained that to the two girls? That's how she had come to think of them, as the two girls. Not The Girls. The Girls were her friends back in New York. The Two Girls were here, attentive, dutiful, insufficient.

I have no life, Joy thought. I belong nowhere. I am residing in someone else's life, in the Two Girls' life.

The days passed, many days, Joy was sure, though she began to lose track of them.

"Give it a little time, Mom. It's only been a week," Molly said.

"It seems like a year. Fish and guests, you know what they say."

Molly looked crestfallen, a word Joy was sure she had not thought of in years. She could not stand to have her daughter look crestfallen. It broke her heart.

"It's lovely," she said quickly. "You two girls are wonderful to me. But what am I doing here, honey? I don't belong here. I'm in your way and I do have my own home. At home."

"It's a change," Molly said. "A change of scenery."

Joy tried to smile appreciatively. She must stop complaining or she'd end up with yet another change of scenery, she thought, the parking lot out of a nursing home window.

That night in bed, Molly whispered to Freddie, "I think she misses him."

"Of course she does, honey. So do you," Freddie whispered back. "So do I. It's been just a few months."

"No, I mean Karl."

Freddie started to say that was unlikely, but then wondered. "You think she's like my father?"

Molly, obviously offended, said, "She's lonely and vulnerable. That's all."

"It's probably pretty boring for her here."

Molly had tried to interest her mother in gardening. She offered to get raised beds if Joy wanted to grow vegetables. Molly did not like gardening, but she saw no reason that her mother shouldn't, and if that meant fresh Tuscan kale and artichokes on Molly's table, so much the better. "It's very spiritual, Mom," she'd said. "Working with the soil." She wished her mother had shown even a little initiative, if not with vegetables, then with flowers. They had a rosebush out front that was not doing at all well.

"She's always on the phone," she whispered to Freddie. "And she's secretive."

She thought it was usually Daniel, sometimes Natalie or one of the other girls. But it could be Karl, for all she really knew.

"She probably misses her cronies, her routine. Old people like routine. That's what they keep telling me at Dad's place. That's one of the things they can't understand about him. He hates routine."

Molly kissed Freddie. "That's it! You are a genius. We'll take her to visit your father. She'll see her peers and feel less lonely. We'll take her to Green Goddess!"

Joy sat glumly in the backseat. The thin end of the wedge. The way they talked this place up, as if it were a resort in the Caribbean—it had happened to her friends, but she had not really expected this from Molly, her own daughter.

"I plan to go back to work in the fall," she said.

"One day at a time," Molly answered.

The parking lot seemed to be home to a number of cats.

"Pets are allowed," Freddie said, "but the cats are feral."

The building was pink stucco. The rooms had small balconies. In the center of an inner courtyard a fountain bubbled, and there was a front desk like a hotel. The whole place felt like a hotel, actually, a small hotel just a bit down at the heels.

"Not bad, right?" Freddie said.

Joy gave a weak smile.

They had lunch in the dining room. Joy was alarmed by the bibs the residents wore, but the food was quite good. She had never met Freddie's father before this, which struck all of them as odd.

"Where have they been hiding you?" Duncan asked.

"I live in New York City." It felt good just to say that: I live in New York.

"What are you doing here with these two harridans?"

"We thought it would be nice for you two to meet, that's all," Freddie said.

Joy felt something on her knee. A hand.

"Well, it's about time, says I," the owner of the hand said. He gave Joy his handsome smile.

Joy shifted, freeing her knee. "Oh yes."

A woman at a nearby table was glaring at her. Joy took a bite of her tuna-fish sandwich. The hand returned to her knee. She felt her throat closing and thought, What if I choke and die with my daughter's father-in-law's hand on my knee?

"So when did you move into Green Acres?" Duncan said.

"Excuse me?"

"She doesn't live here, Dad. She's staying with us."

"Green Acres? That's a good one," Molly said.

"Remember Zsa Zsa Gabor?" Joy said. "Those were the days."

"That was Eva Gabor."

"Sweet girl, Zsa Zsa," said Duncan. "We worked together. Years ago, years ago."

As Duncan described an obscure movie in which he had an even more obscure part, Joy noticed Freddie raising an eyebrow at Molly. They exchanged just noticeable smirks. Joy kicked Molly under the table, which had the advantage of also dislodging Duncan's hand.

"A little respect," Joy said, first to Molly, then to Freddie's father. "A little respect."

"Nothing will come of nothing," said Duncan in his rich and sonorous voice. He tried his smile again.

"Wasn't that fun, Mom?" Molly asked as they drove home. "Jesus, Freddie, do you actually aim for the potholes?"

Freddie laughed.

Freddie really was good-natured, Joy thought. "Your father is a ball of fire," she said. She would not mention the hand. What would be the point?

"Never underestimate a minor character actor," Freddie said. "It's already been done. Their whole life."

"Who was that woman who tried to trip us with her walker?" said Molly.

Freddie shrugged. "One of his girlfriends?"

"I'm sure that was an accident," said Joy. But Green Garden was even more frightening than she had imagined.

Joy leaned on the grocery cart, weary in body and soul. It was an expensive, trendy grocery store, the kind of grocery store in which half the children were probably not vaccinated against measles. Molly examined a small ugly root vegetable.

"I think you girls deserve some privacy," Joy said. "You've been so hospitable." She had tried this before but gotten nowhere, and this time, too, Molly smiled an abstracted smile and said, "Don't worry about it, Mom."

Joy pushed the cart to the fish counter and waited for Molly to catch up. She missed her apartment, her lonely apartment in which she could roam and mourn at will. She missed the doormen. She missed her friends. She missed the park and Karl.

"I'm homesick, Molly. I keep trying to tell you nicely. I want to go home."

"I understand that you're not completely adjusted—"

"Adjusted? No, I'm not adjusted. I don't want to be adjusted." Joy realized she was speaking loudly and the mothers of unvaccinated children were glancing at her suspiciously. Careful, Joy. Don't rile up the natives, don't rile up Molly, especially. "Sweetheart, you and Freddie have been absolutely wonderful, but put yourself in my position."

"That's just what I was talking to Daniel about, and we decided that even more than the change in scenery, even more than the warm weather, that what you need is to be useful."

"Yes," said Joy, suddenly jubilant. At last her son and daughter understood.

"Everyone needs to be useful."

"That is so true." She would go back to work and insist on getting her projects back. She would call Norman, that fellow on the board, the one who Aaron used to play poker with, why hadn't she thought of it before . . .

"We thought you could do something at the Getty, maybe."

"The Getty?"

"Yeah, you know, like volunteer. Or the Skirball. The training for docents is pretty rigorous, but still . . ."

Molly prattled away about Los Angeles museums and their volunteer programs as they loaded the cart with healthful food that Joy could not digest. Joy searched the shelves for Cream of Wheat and said, now and then in hopeless punctuation of Molly's recitation, "Such good ideas! If only I did not already have a museum. In New York."

One evening when Molly was at a meeting and not coming home until late, Joy and Freddie went out to dinner, just the two of them. It was the first time they had done anything like that, and they were both a little nervous, Joy's discomfort manifesting itself in silence, Freddie's in chatter.

"Molly doesn't like this place, she thinks it's boring, but I love it and I think you might like it, too. The traffic will be impossible on the 10, even in this direction, so I think I'll take Venice, oh my god, look at them trying to get to the 405 . . ."

Joy opened the window and let the cool air in. It smelled like flowers even on this busy street. She braced herself for yet another restaurant with painfully loud music, painfully hard benches, women in painfully high heels and men comfortable in sneakers, all of them eating spicy, fishy fragments of raw things on little saucers. It was the same in New York, she supposed, but she never went to restaurants like that in New York. She was in the mood for spaghetti and meatballs.

It seemed like a long time before they finally pulled into a parking structure, then spiraled down several levels until they found a space. Disoriented, Joy squeezed out of the car and followed Freddie to an elevator that took them back to street level. Freddie was still talking. Something about her department at the university trying to screw someone over in a fourth-year review and a committee that never met. Joy thought of the museum, of Miss Georgia, of all the orphaned artifacts she could no longer tend to. She was grateful to Freddie for talking, for trying. Freddie was a good sport. Joy remembered being a good sport. It required energy and optimism and faith, and it had been quite rewarding. Really, she had spent her entire life being a good sport. But to what end? She had grown old and uncomfortable, just like a bad sport. And now she *was* a bad sport. There was no protection in good behavior. She felt suddenly compassionate toward Freddie, struggling on in a unilateral conversation that would not protect her from the disappointments of old age.

"You're a good sport, Freddie," she said.

Freddie's face lit up, that tan, weathered face, into an almost goofy smile. How charming, that large unconscious grin. Freddie's was not a beautiful, womanly face by any stretch of the imagination, more a wary, taut look to her, but when she smiled, the contrast was overwhelmingly pleasant. It made Joy grin back at her. It was like a happy slap on the back, that smile, an arm thrown joyfully around your shoulder. It was as friendly a smile as Joy could remember seeing. It was irresistible. No wonder Molly fell in love with this person. Joy marveled that she had never noticed the warmth of that smile, of everything about Freddie, really. Then she realized she had never really looked at Freddie's face before. It had been an indistinct oval, an unwelcome blur from the dreaded California.

"This is very nice of you," Joy said.

They walked a quarter of a block, then turned into a small strip mall. There was a sushi restaurant, a Korean barbecue, a nail salon, and an Italian restaurant. Freddie opened the door of the Italian restaurant.

"It's so quiet," Joy said.

"It's so comfortable," she added, sliding into a padded booth.

"Spaghetti and meatballs," she told the waiter happily. "Just what I wanted."

"This place has been here forever," Freddie said. "My father used to take us when I was a kid. I bring him back once in a while, but he doesn't remember it, so it's kind of sad."

Joy reached across the table for Freddie's hand. "It's awful when they don't remember what you remember, even when you're right there with them. It's like nothing exists anymore."

Freddie was crying, just a few tears. Joy had never seen her cry. She was such an odd little thing, ebullient and tough all at once. Poignant tears, not like me, Joy thought, with my weeping and wailing every minute. Not like Molly, either.

"No one really understands this particular abyss," Joy said. "Our abyss."

"No, they don't. But why should they, I suppose."

"We're an exclusive club."

"The Abyss Club," Freddie said, laughing. She took her hand back, wiped her eyes with the big cloth napkin.

They had ricotta cheesecake and cannolis for dessert.

"I'll pay for it later," Joy said. "So I always say. But it never stops me."

Molly and Freddie disappeared the next morning and came home with a very small dog.

"You can walk it," they said.

"Step on it is more likely."

"Listen, it's perfect: Freddie and I went to the pound and rescued this little fellow. Now we have a dog, right?"

"Apparently."

"But we both have jobs, right?"

"Thank god. I don't care what the 'experts' report about the economy, people are suffering, that's all I can say."

"We have a dog, but because of our jobs we don't have time to walk the dog. So, Freddie and I really need you, Mom. We need you to walk our dog."

"It would be a big help to us," Freddie said. She smiled, and Joy of course smiled back and took the new plaid leash attached to the tiny dog.

They were such nice girls, and she appreciated the thought and effort that had gone into the plan. It was creative of the girls, she had to give them that. And she was touched that they cared enough about her mental health to go to such lengths to give her something to do. It was not their fault that the dog refused to cooperate.

The dog was named Gatto, which was amusing. But Gatto did not like to take walks. Gatto hated to take walks. The size of a large rat, he was part Chihuahua, part poodle, part parrot, Joy thought, for he was a very vocal little dog, making his wishes known with a remarkably varied vocabulary of squeaks and yelps, and his wishes were to stay home, curled on Joy's lap.

"Gatto, indeed," she said. Gatto squeaked, snorted, stretched, and balled himself up again. Joy patted his head, the size of a nectarine, and dozed uncomfortably. She was afraid to move. She did not want to disturb him.

The days went by, blue skies and pretty smells. She carried Gatto with her on her strolls, mostly as a way of starting conversations. She was uneasy talking to the girls, noticing their impatience, how they interrupted with unnecessarily big smiles to change the subject. Was she talking too much? Had she become boring? She supposed she was and she had. She became more and more quiet at home. But on her walks all kinds of people stopped her to admire the dog. They laughed when she told them his name.

"My daughter got him for me so I could take him on walks, but he doesn't like to walk," she would say, and they would laugh again.

Aaron, she thought, you would not like it here. There's no normal place to get coffee, no normal barber, just an overpriced coffee place where people sit on uncomfortable, oversized wooden boxes, just hair salons for skinny young men. You would not like it here, but you are gone. She sometimes thought he was there beside her, shaking his head at the young people riding bicycles, no helmets, carrying surfboards under one arm.

"Where are all the old people?" she asked.

"It's gotten sort of gentrified," said Freddie. "A lot of tech companies moved in."

"But where are the old people?"

Molly shrugged. "Assisted living?"

Joy did not ask again.

Because Gatto did not like to walk and Joy had gotten so much stronger, Molly and Freddie revised their plans for Joy to be useful. They got her a tricycle.

"It's red," she said. She did not know what else to say. What is there to say when presented with an adult tricycle? It had a basket for Gatto. It had an old-fashioned bell. It was gigantic. It was a tricycle. It was red.

"You can ride on the boardwalk. It's great exercise."

"You can do errands," Freddie added. "Which are so . . ."

"Useful!"

Molly often finished Freddie's sentences, and vice versa.

"Useful." Joy wanted to be useful. She wanted that almost as much as she did not want to be lonely. But was a tricycle really the road to relevance? Were errands the answer? And she would look like a kook.

"Wear a hat for the sun, Mom."

A kook in a hat.

"We got you a water bottle," Freddie said.

Joy had ridden just such a red tricycle when she was a child. It was not dignified then. It was not dignified now.

"I know they mean well," she said to Natalie one morning when both girls were off at work and she could speak freely on the phone.

"Don't you know how to ride a two-wheeler?"

"Of course I do. They wanted me to ride it to the grocery store to get milk yesterday."

"I thought you were lactose-intolerant."

"I am, but I don't want to hurt their feelings. But luckily, I had a terrible bout of diarrhea and couldn't go. At least it's flat here. But they really are making an effort, they're trying."

"Trying to what? Turn their mother into an errand boy?"

"They think I'll feel useful, that they've given meaning to my life."

"Ridiculous. Just ridiculous. Don't they have a car?"

"I just realized something. People will think I lost my license."

"They'll think you're a drunk, an old, eccentric drunk with a DUI."

They laughed at that.

"Okay," Natalie said. "Time to come home."

Joy poked through the bookcase looking for something to read. Molly and Freddie did not get a newspaper. They read it online. What difference did it make, her eyes were terrible anyway. She could read a little if the light was right and she tilted her head and the print was dark. She picked up an old *New York* magazine from a pile in a basket. Interesting that Molly still got *New York* magazine. She must miss New York. Joy caught her breath. Perhaps that meant she would move back. She could get an apartment nearby. They could see each other for lunch. And dinner.

She spent some time searching for her striped bag, then searched through it for her sunglasses. Maybe they were in the green bag. The dog followed her wherever she went. She wondered if he would follow her outside, if it was the leash that made him refuse to go on a walk.

"That way you could get a little exercise, fatso," she said. He really was getting tubby, and so quickly, too. Molly said it was not healthy for him to be so heavy, that Joy should stop feeding him bits of her own food. "We'll show her," Joy said. "You deserve every bit of food you can get after the life you lived, whatever it was." She imagined him on the street, fighting with the crows for pizza crusts.

She put on her sunglasses, got her cane, opened the door, and called Gatto. He made some inquiring noises, then slunk to the door on his belly. Joy went out and down the steps to the street. She called him again. "Come here, come here, Gatto. Cardiovascular activity! Come on!" He looked at her dubiously, then darted out the door and stood beside her. "Good boy." Now she walked down the street, stopping periodically so he could catch up. He lay down on her feet after each of these sprints, but they made it all the way down the block before Joy turned around to go back.

And then, from nowhere, a giant of a dog galloped around the corner, gave a deep thunderous growl, a deeper more thunderous bark, and Gatto was hanging from the beast's jaws like a rag toy.

Probably she hit the dog with her cane. That would account for the owner pushing her out of the way and screaming. Unless the screaming was Joy's, which it may well have been. She grabbed the animal's jaws and tried to pry them apart, that she was sure of. She was sure she ultimately shoved her cane in its mouth and yanked down until Gatto flopped out onto the ground and the beast's owner dragged it away by its collar.

Joy carried Gatto into the house. He was alive. His heart was beating, fluttering like hummingbird wings. There was blood on his belly. Joy wrapped him in a towel and put him in the basket of the tricycle. She pushed open the back gate and pedaled as furiously as an eighty-six-year-old can pedal a tricycle. There was a main thoroughfare one block away, a street with stores and malls and an animal hospital. She pedaled and pedaled and crossed the street against the light and heard cars honking and screamed an obscenity and pedaled some more until she saw the vet's office and pulled the tricycle onto the sidewalk.

Gatto was stitched up and given some shots. The vet was a young woman with freckles sprinkled across her nose who treated him like a VIP, Joy thought. A VIP, she said to Gatto as she pedaled him home. That's what you are, a VIP.

When Molly came home, she found her mother in bed, Gatto beside her, shaved and stitched, both of them fast asleep. The gate to the alley had been left open, and when she went to close it, she noticed the tricycle, in its basket a bloody towel.

"This is a dangerous city," Joy said when she woke up. "I'm taking Gatto home where it's safe."

40

The sadness was there, waiting for her in the apartment. I'm sorry, Joy said to the sadness. I'm sorry I had to leave you behind for so long. But, believe me, the blue skies never fooled me, you were in my thoughts, in my heart, every minute. She looked out the window at the rain and the wet trees and the bleary spots of red taillights and white headlights. I'm home, she said, with relief, to the emptiness.

She sat at the kitchen table and Gatto leaped onto her lap, his nails scratching her leg. He was a good traveler. He hadn't made a peep, zipped up in his bag beneath the seat. She had forgotten he was there, had almost left him behind, abandoned a dog that had already been abandoned, it would have been terrible, and she wondered who would have found him, a flight attendant or one of the cleaning crew, perhaps, and whether they would have taken him home and given him a good life.

"But I didn't abandon you," she said aloud. She petted his hard little head and wondered why *she* felt abandoned. No one had left her behind under an airline seat, it was she who had insisted on leaving California and Molly, but it had taken only a moment for the abandonment to rise up, like a cold flame; it had taken only the sight of Molly turning her back after she got her settled in her JetBlue wheelchair.

Joy pulled the dog up to her face, letting his warmth muffle the silence. "But we didn't belong there, did we?"

Gatto jumped down and lifted his leg against the leg of the table.

Joy watched him blandly. "You think you can scare me with a little pee? Think again, dog. I've been worked over by an expert. With a colostomy bag."

She wiped up the dog pee. She mourned her husband. She mourned her life, which seemed so far away, lost in time. She longed for her daughter and her son, the sounds of their voices, the strength of their arms, and the loving condescension of their hearts. She longed for Aaron.

She didn't seem to belong anywhere anymore. But it was good to be home just the same.

"Promise you'll call me every day and tell me how you're doing," Molly had said before Joy left.

Joy took her promise to heart. She called every day, eagerly, hesitant to disturb Molly, but not hesitant enough to stop dialing. Sometimes she called twice a day, sometimes more. It was dangerous to call so much, signaling need and helplessness, she knew that. She made sure to sound happy and engaged, made sure to share only what bits of information she believed shed a pleasant light on her and her days. The deliveryman from the coffee shop looked cold, she told Molly, so she gave him one of Aaron's scarves, he was so grateful.

"Mom, it's June. How could he be?"

"The point, Molly, is how nice it is to be able to make a gesture like that and have it mean something to someone."

"Which scarf? I hope not the gray cashmere."

Joy tried to monitor her voice and conversation, to weed out any petulance and grievance of tone, but it was difficult. No matter how hard she listened to herself and monitored herself, what she heard was an indolent, wide-ranging, rolling report of the minutiae of a disgruntled old woman's existence: the chronology of meals, of courses within meals, the digestive consequences of meals; the frequency of sleep and sleeplessness, the details of other phone calls, phone calls with people Molly did not even know. She couldn't change the course of her words, they rushed along like a flooded river. She talked about her grandchildren and their bad colds, but also the grandchildren of friends and neighbors with colds that were even worse. Those grandchildren, the grandchildren of friends and neighbors, had cousins, too, whose troubles and triumphs she found herself confiding to Molly. Her voice droned on and she was mesmerized by it, helpless to stop, unwilling to hang up. Not that long ago she had been lying on Molly and Freddie's couch watching television, her daughter giving her a foot massage, and Joy had been longing to be alone with her loneliness. Now she experienced every phone call to Molly as essential, something she could not let slip away.

"I take the dog out every day."

"Yes, you told me, that's great for you, to get out."

"I still have to carry him. It's good he only weighs a few pounds. I'm not as strong as I once was. But yesterday it was so windy the doorman, that nice Ernie who Daddy liked so much, he wouldn't let me out the door. I called the hardware store, Feldman's, the one with all the tchotchkes, and they suggested Wee-Wee pads, but I had to call a pet store to get them. My neighbor upstairs, the man who was always such a sourpuss until he got his poodle, well, he gave me a number, left it with the doorman, actually, and I called . . ."

"Mom? I'm sorry, but I'm in the middle of cooking dinner. I really should get off the phone."

"Oh! The time difference. And why am I rattling on like this? It's a mild form of senility. Good night, sweetheart."

"I wish Mom would get hearing aids," Daniel told Molly after one of his own conversations with their mother.

But Molly didn't think it would make much difference. Their mother wanted to talk, not to listen. It was an exhalation of words, no intake of breath, no pauses, a stream of consciousness into which no one else could dip a toe, an incompleteness so complete there could be no natural end to a conversation. Molly often found these monologues strangely soothing. She wondered if that was what meditation was all about, that absence of meaning, that sense of eternity. She was almost as helpless in that cocoon of superfluous information as her mother. The truth was, she craved the sound of her mother's voice. It calmed her, reassured her. Ah yes, the twins' First Communion. Whose twins? she would wonder idly. But it didn't matter. They were the twins created by her mother's voice, created by her mother.

There was little chance for Molly to interrupt, and she stopped trying. She did not say, for example, *I miss Daddy at the oddest times.* She missed him whenever the fog came in. He used to quote Carl Sandburg when there was fog, little cat feet, silent haunches. She missed him when she made gravy because he hated giblets, or when she made lima beans because he hated lima beans, or pea soup because he loved pea soup. She missed him when she got an ingrown toenail and cut a V in the nail the way he'd taught her. She rarely had a chance to say any of that to her mother, and the few times she tried, she felt intrusive and loud. She didn't say much and she didn't listen carefully. Her mother's voice washed over her, intoxicating.

"Until I can't stand it anymore."

"Well, an hour on the phone is a lot," Freddie said sympathetically.

"It's no skin off your nose," Molly said. "Why do you care?"

Freddie shook her head and laughed. "You're impossible."

"A hundred years ago we would have had to write letters, which would have taken days to get across the country. And I would not have heard her voice. I love her voice. I love to hear it. Until I can't stand it anymore! And then I hang up, and then I miss her and want to listen to her talk more."

Freddie tried to remember her own mother's voice. She could feel it, in her thoughts and in her body, high and fluty, but she couldn't hear it. That night she dreamed about her mother: her mother had been alive all this time, Freddie was surprised and overjoyed to see her, to hold her hand and kiss her and cry with relief.

"The apartment is a shambles," Daniel told his wife. "And there are Wee-Wee pads all over. And my mother is in her pajamas and bathrobe. She never goes out. It's like she's become a recluse in two weeks. The dog is a fat pig."

Coco asked cautiously if he wanted Joy to stay with them.

"Oh, I don't think we're there yet."

"She's so independent," she said, with obvious relief.

"And California was not exactly a success."

"But we would be less intrusive," Coco said. "We would let her go her own way. Your sister and Freddie, well . . ."

"They can be a little . . ."

"Overbearing."

Daniel laughed. He sat next to Coco on the couch and put his arm around her.

"But I hate to think of her in that big old apartment all by herself," Coco said.

"Big? Not for her. She's covered every surface with papers and clothes. She needs more rooms to clutter. Anyway, she's not alone. She's got the obese dog."

He tried to imagine his mother in their loft. They would have to box her in, the way they had the kids. But the kids' little box rooms had the only windows in the back. They could always give

Joy a windowless closet, the way the museum did. He remembered the younger Joy, funny and full of eccentric energy. The first day of moving in, she would have had the whole family out bird-watching or making rubbings of manhole covers. Now, though, she spent most of her time shuffling through her apartment looking for her glasses, the dog shuffling after her, or making toast on which she slathered something yellow and glistening that was not butter.

"Oh god, Coco, why are we even thinking about this?" But he was grateful she had brought it up. He wondered what she would have done if he'd said, Yes, that's a splendid idea, let's move her in as soon as we can.

"But, Daniel, we're so lucky to have Cora and Ruby around, I feel almost selfish. They would make things so much more cheerful for your mother."

Daniel could not argue with that. Both he and Coco considered their children an indisputable addition to any situation. They were always surprised when the girls were not included in wedding invitations or cocktail parties. Again, Daniel tried to picture his mother in the loft. It's so drafty, she would say. The lighting is so harsh. He knew she would say those things because she had already said them when they once had Thanksgiving there. I just feel uncomfortable, in my head, the proportions are off, Danny, but at least they fixed your elevator. "Maybe we could just lend the children to her."

Coco said nothing. She was thinking of her own old age. Would Cora or Ruby want her to come and live with them when the time came? She would have to set a good example. "We could make her feel much more at home than Freddie and Molly did."

Daniel suspected her generosity of spirit was propped up just a bit by her certainty that he would not agree. Even though his mother had been so good to him all his life, especially when he'd been sick, coming to the hospital every day before and after work. In so many ways, Daniel had modeled himself on her, trying to do good, to be generous, to repay the world with some of the care she had shown him. Maybe, it occurred to him, he should be repaying *her*, not the planet. Maybe Coco was right and they should share their lives with her the way she had devoted so much of her life to him.

The girls came running into the living room at that moment and demanded ice cream.

"You girls could share a room if Grandma came to live with us," Coco said.

Share? Horror-stricken faces. Pushing. Kicking. Squeals of aggression, squeals of pain.

"Go to your rooms this minute!"

"Yeah, and stay out of my room, too," Cora said to her sister, delivering one last blow.

"Stay out of my room first," said Ruby.

"I'm already out of your room. I win."

Daniel shepherded them into their rooms and shut their doors.

When he came back with two glasses of Scotch, Coco took hers gratefully and said, "I guess that won't work, sharing a room."

"No."

She determined then and there always to have two extra bedrooms when she was old, one for each of her daughters to move into.

Daniel asked his mother if she was depressed. She said, "Naturally."

Molly had often wondered, too often to tell anyone, even Freddie, what it would feel like to jump off a building, what your thoughts would be. Would your thoughts be narrowed to a simple unthinking scream? Would you think of all those you would miss? Would you wonder if they would miss you? Would you think, What in the world am I doing, falling, falling, no way to stop, no way to go back? Would you think, Why did I do this? Or would you think, Why didn't I do this long ago? That, all of that, was what she felt her mother must be feeling. Her mother was falling through the air of her life. Molly had tried hard to ignore it, but she could hear it in her mother's voice.

And Molly was doing nothing to help her. Nothing.

She sat in the dappled shade of a small garden, admiring a spider's web that ran from the tea tree branch up to the trunk of the apricot tree, a marvel of fantasy engineering, beautiful in the soft afternoon light, ugly as a weapon, a large beetle imprisoned in its lace. She was sitting, staring at a cruel bit of silver embroidery while her mother floated helplessly in her loneliness, stunned and airborne, not even caught in her fall like the beetle. Molly was watching a hummingbird, listening to the whir of its movement, catching the colors of its throat as they changed, and they were dazzling, and the sound of a finch was musical and a flock of noisy parrots flew high above. The flowers of the succulents were blooming, minuscule, stunted, almost invisible. Everything was soft and green and serene. Molly was comfortable and the neighbor's cat stretched beyond the fence, a calico cat, and—she couldn't help herself—she was filled with joy and a sense of wonder. Her happiness made her sad, because it wasn't fair, it couldn't be fair to be happy when her mother was falling from a building toward the cold gray sidewalk.

43

Joy took Gatto and a sandwich to the park.

"I went all the way to Daddy's park," she told Molly. "I bought a turkey sandwich, low sodium, and ate it on a bench."

"I went to Daddy's little park," she told Danny. "It was very peaceful."

She'd been looking for Karl, but he wasn't there. He wasn't at the coffee shop at his usual time, either. She had missed Karl more than she expected when she was in California. She hoped he wasn't dead. She considered walking to his building to ask the doorman if Karl had died while she was in California, but if he had, she would be devastated, and if he hadn't, she would be embarrassed.

"She's seeing that guy again, I'm sure of it," Daniel told Molly. "She went to Daddy's park. That's like code. She's very vulnerable right now. In more ways than one." Daniel had finally worked out where all her bits and pieces of money had been squirreled away in different bank accounts to confuse Aaron, and there wasn't much left. "The good news is, he's a fool if he's after her money."

"She does *not* want to sell Upstate."

"She's running out of dough, Molly."

"We'll help her."

"What if she gets sick again? We can't afford all those aides. She spent everything on Daddy. She's broke."

Molly said, "She's got the house."

"My point exactly."

And so the argument went, round and round and back again. For Molly, Upstate was a tie to home. For Joy, the house was both her past and what she would give to her children's future. Daniel understood all of it. He felt the same way, really.

"But we have to be realistic, Molly. If she sells Upstate, she'll be able to plan properly, plan how much she can spend each year."

"She can't plan," his sister said slowly, clearly, as if talking to someone else's backward child, "because she doesn't know how long she will live. Why are we pretending she can make plans? Why can't she just live her life?"

"Because," he said, just as slowly and clearly, "she has no money."

Joy knew they spoke to each other about her. She didn't like it, but she didn't want to know what it was about, either, because she already did: it was about what to do with her.

They were always coming up with electronics that were meant to make her life easier but ran out of batteries.

"They mean well," she said to Karl. He had not died, but he had suffered from a long bout of flu. This was his first day out.

"I'm sorry I worried you," he said. "Why didn't you call?"

"No news is good news, Karl." They were sitting in Central Park on a bench facing a noisy playground. "Molly and Daniel want me to be happy, but they're driving me crazy. I think someone of my age and experience should be allowed to feel exactly the way she wants."

"Hear, hear."

"Which is miserable."

"Hear, hear."

It was pleasant to have someone to meet in the park, to meet at the coffee shop, someone who knew her when she was young and beautiful, someone who remembered the things she remembered. Karl began to tell her a story about an uncle who had been a boot-legger but got the flu and missed a meet-up at which everyone else got shot. She'd heard the story before and closed her eyes. Oh, Aaron, she thought, her attention drifting comfortably, I do miss you. You should be here with us. You loved this story.

"Are you married?" she asked Marta as the three of them walked slowly across Fifth Avenue. Joy wondered if men still married their nurses, the way they did in World War I novels. No, now it was just doctors who married their young nurses, married doctors who left the wives who had put them through medical school.

"Don't like," Marta said.

"I think marriage is a fine institution." Karl stopped to catch his breath when they reached the sidewalk.

"Institution" is a funny word, Joy thought, like a mental hospital.

"Why don't like?" she asked Marta.

"Husband drink."

"Well, *I* don't drink," Karl said. "Not excessively."

"*Or,*" Marta added pointedly, "husband *old.* Get sick."

Joy repeated the conversation to Danny, laughing, but he seemed quite serious and said, "Well, she's right. Terrible to get stuck with an old invalid. At least Marta gets paid for all she does to take care of him."

"Well, of course she's right, in a way, but it never stops anyone, does it? You should hear what goes on in Florida."

"I think I'd rather not."

"I think it's nice she has a friend," Coco said. "Someone she can talk to."

"She can talk to me."

Coco suggested he might be jealous.

"She doesn't understand," Molly said when he told her. "She doesn't understand us," she said to Freddie.

Freddie understood. The clan was pulling together just as they had when Daniel was in the hospital, when Aaron went bankrupt. The Bergmans against the world. There was no room for an outsider. The emptiness left by Aaron's death was not a space to be filled; it was a bond to be protected.

44

Ruby's bat mitzvah was months away, but Joy began going through her clothes, looking for something suitable to wear. It was a tiring business, trying on clothes. She made sure to do it in the morning before her afternoon fatigue set in. The discarded dresses and trousers and jackets and blouses were strewn around her bedroom, colorful, fluttering like flags when she passed.

"What in god's name happened?" Daniel said when he saw her bedroom.

"I'm looking for an outfit."

He pushed some clothes aside and sat on the edge of the bed. "Where do you sleep?"

"On the couch. In the living room."

The dining-room table was again covered in papers. And now that Walter and Wanda were no longer coming and Elvira was back to once every two weeks, the kitchen was a mess. Daniel washed the dishes in the sink, then opened the refrigerator. It was filled with demitasse saucers, some covered with plastic wrap, some with aluminum foil, some with paper towels, some uncovered. How many demitasse saucers could one person own? There had to be thirty diminutive saucers, and beside them was a jumble of plastic containers used for condiments at coffee shops.

"Hungry?" his mother asked. "I have half a hard-boiled egg somewhere, and a little bit of applesauce. There's a bit of chicken soup . . . Oh no, don't touch that dish, that's food for Gatto . . ."

Daniel said he was not hungry. He sat at the kitchen table, his head in his hands.

"Are you all right, sweetheart?" his mother said. "Tired? You work too hard. You need a vacation. You're the one who should have gone to California, Danny, not me." She came over and rubbed his head. He still had all his hair. Just like his father. "Poor dear."

Daniel stared at the floor, at his own big feet, at his mother's feet in scuffed slippers.

"Mom," he said softly. He did not want to alarm her. "Mom, a mouse just ran across your foot."

His mother laughed. "Oh, him again."

Daniel telephoned Molly from the subway platform. "Do you realize how much an attendant will cost?"

"She doesn't need an attendant."

"Oh, but she will. And soon, believe me."

"How do *you* know?"

"Molly, a mouse was standing on her foot."

That was an alarming development, Molly had to admit. "But I don't see how an attendant would help with mice," she said. "Did you call the super?"

"Of course I called the super. The exterminator is coming to-morrow. But that is not the point and you know it. She has to have some help. Which means she has to spend money. Which means she has to get some money. She won't take it from us, and we don't have enough to cover it, anyway, which means she has to sell the house."

———

"How would Daniel and Coco like it if I told them to sell their loft," she said to Freddie. "How would they like it, the loft they bought so many years ago when no one wanted to live in their disgusting neighborhood, the loft they so lovingly restored bit by bit until now it's worth millions of dollars, how would they feel about *that*?"

"But the point is to keep your mother in her apartment," Freddie said gently, "to keep her independent and, and . . . mouse-free."

"Yes, but—"

"Daniel's just trying to figure things out, honey."

Molly grunted a thank-you, but no one understood about the house. Freddie thought it was a dump, anyway. It wasn't a dump. It was rustic. If by rustic you mean uncomfortable, Daniel once said. No one understood.

45

Joy thought of asking Karl to dinner. Boeuf bourguignon, a baguette, a salad—she could see the meal, it looked lovely, civilized, and Joy would have given a lot to feel civilized. Instead, she felt lurching and matted, like a wild dog. She hadn't made boeuf bourguignon in twenty years. She'd barely eaten boeuf in twenty years. The thought of it, the fat as it browned in the pan, was sickening. And she was no chef these days, scuffing around the kitchen tugging weakly at the recalcitrant refrigerator door, burning toast.

"We'll order Chinese," Karl said when she told him her problem.

"We'll eat on paper plates!"

"Like young people when they move into their first apartment and haven't unpacked the boxes."

Joy wondered what it would have been like to be young in a first apartment with Karl, no money, boxes of books, and a scratched desk from home. Joy and Aaron had furnished their first apartment with a decorator, Danish modern, she had gotten rid of most of it, uncomfortable stuff, though it was worth a fortune now, judging by *Antiques Roadshow.*

"Where was your first apartment?" she asked Karl. "After college?"

"I lived with my parents for a couple of years. Saved money. Then Joan and I got married and we bought the place I'm in now."

"You were always careful."

"And dull."

"No, I mean it in a good way. You were always not careless."

"You were always glamorous."

"And ditzy."

"I mean it in a good way, too. You were like sunshine, that kind of glamorous. Bright and shining and warm and cheerful. And unattainable."

Maybe I'll put out real plates, Joy thought.

The dining room looked pretty. Joy had stacked all her files in shopping bags that were pushed into one corner of the room. At the florist she bought a petite arrangement of small flowers gathered into an old-fashioned bouquet. There were candles, unlit; she could not find a match.

"I go," Marta said when she had helped Karl off with his coat and settled him into a chair. Gatto jumped in his lap.

Joy said, "Just what I needed, right? A dog."

"I had a dog as a kid. I loved that dog."

"Never got one for your own kids?"

"No. Joan couldn't bear it."

"The mess, the walking, and the kids promise to take it out, but then they have homework . . ."

"No. It was just she loved her childhood dog so much, and when he died she was heartbroken, and well, if we had gotten a dog, they don't live that long, it would certainly have died in her lifetime, and she said it was just too painful. She just didn't want to go through that again."

Joy brought the containers of Chinese food out on gaily patterned trays. It was a picnic, the takeout containers right on the table. She noticed Karl did not bother with chopsticks. Aaron had insisted on them when they had Chinese food, saying forks changed the flavor. But Joy was never very handy with chopsticks.

If Karl got a dog, she thought, they could walk their dogs together, if his dog liked to walk. Otherwise they could carry them together. People would stop them to ask about the little dogs. Karl could get a basket for his walker.

"I can't think that way," he was saying.

"About what?"

"Worrying about getting attached, about the pain of losing someone. I can't live like that. Not anymore. Too old . . ."

Joy did not bring up her idea of a basket for Karl's red walker. He didn't seem to be talking about dogs anymore.

46

Thank god it's almost time to drive Mom Upstate, away from that man and into the bosom of her loving family in her own little house."

"You're a little prudish about your mother," Freddie said. It just came out.

"I don't want her to be taken advantage of, that's all."

"I'm not sure what you and Daniel think Karl is after. Her virginity? Isn't it possible he just really likes her?"

Molly had assumed her sullen face, an expression so infantile and so obvious that Freddie was always tempted to laugh. Instead, she said, "You just don't like it that your mother has a boyfriend. Admit it."

"He's not her boyfriend."

"Whatever that would mean, anyway." But Freddie was happy to drop the subject. She had her own relatives to worry about. Her brothers and sisters would soon be there, though not for long.

"They'll be in L.A. for three days, that's it, three lousy days. It's probably the last time they'll see my father, the last time we'll all be together, and I can't decide if I wish they'd stay longer or leave after one night or not come at all. I have a fucked-up family."

"He's *not* her boyfriend."

"I'll miss you," Karl said.

He was wearing a cashmere blazer. Joy patted his arm. Aaron had favored hearty tweed. She'd always loved his custom-made jackets and suits. Now they called them bespoke. Aaron had looked like a country gentleman, what country she could not have said, but she would have followed him there, she knew that much. She had followed him there, she supposed. The sleeves of his sweaters and tweeds had always been rather itchy to her touch. She ran her hand along Karl's arm again. "Soft," she said.

Karl was someone you could call dapper and mean it as a compliment, not a suggestion of fussiness. Marta did right by him. He looked marvelous today, Joy thought, in the spring sunshine, his shoes polished, his blue shirt pressed, his tie a deeper blue paisley.

"It's a little too wide to be fashionable," he said when she complimented it. "But I've always loved it, so I just keep on wearing it."

He had admitted to her that he kept most of his clothes for decades, that he had shoes from his college days. He took good care of everything. Shoe trees, cedar closet, sweaters wrapped in tissue. His wife had teased him about it.

"You look very good in blue," Joy said.

"You look good in every color."

Joy laughed. They were walking beneath the trees on Fifth Avenue, beneath the fresh new leaves, beneath the sweetness of the air. "The wreck of the *Hesperus*. That's what I feel like. In every color."

Karl pushed his red wheeled walker and Joy kept one hand on it to hold herself steady. In a few days he would be off to stay with his son in Rhode Island. She would be off to her house Upstate.

"I've been thinking," Karl said.

Joy said, "Stop." She had to catch her breath.

In the park, a group of girls wearing headscarves were playing softball. She watched while the banging in her chest slowed. She took a deep breath. "I don't know if it's pollen or my heart. Who can tell anymore?"

"It's the exciting company you keep."

"I used to love softball," she said. The pitcher was winding up. A strike. "Brava."

Karl laughed. "Is that what they say at Yankee Stadium?"

They started walking again. Joy wished that Marta had stuck around. She was feeling a little strange. She had hung two of her bags on Karl's walker, but the third one, with Gatto peering out of it, was weighing her down.

"So," Karl said, "I was thinking."

"Karl, would you mind if we sat down for a minute? I'm feeling wobbly."

They made their way to a bench, backs to a stone wall that separated them from the park, but Joy could hear the park sounds clearly, the high-pitched pleasure of children, the squeak of swings, dogs barking, the ping of bicycle bells, whoops and cheers and chattering squirrels. Gatto emerged from the bag and stretched out in a patch of sun on the ground. Joy closed her eyes against the glare of the afternoon sun reflected from the apartment windows across the street. Someone with a French accent asked Karl where the Guggenheim was. The smell of spring was everywhere. And the faintest smell of urine.

"Oh my god," Joy said, her eyes open. Urine. "I forgot my court date!"

She began to dig frantically in the bag next to her on the bench. "Oh Christ. Oh, how could I do that?"

"Court date?"

"Nothing, nothing, a ticket, nothing . . ." The dog began barking and scratching at her leg. She pulled the other two bags from the handles of the walker and emptied them onto the bench.

"You're sure? Can I help . . . But how did you get a traffic ticket? You don't have a car."

"Don't ask. Gatto, shoosh, not everything is about you." Joy pulled out lipsticks and applesauce containers. How could she have failed Ben like this?

"Well then, listen, Joy, as I said, I've been thinking—"

"Good. Thinking. Good, good." She was pawing through papers and receipts now, candy wrappers, pamphlets.

"Look, we've known each other a long time." Karl hauled the screeching dog onto his lap and stroked him. "Quiet, Gatto. That's right. Good boy. A long time, Joy. Practically our whole lives, give or take a few decades when we lost touch . . ."

Joy saw a yellow piece of paper that she thought might be it. But Ben's ticket was pink, it was pink. What if she had missed his court date? What would happen to him? Some awful permanent mark on his license or his credit rating. It was not as if they'd throw him in jail. Was it? But a fine, there would be a fine . . . He would never trust her again with something important. He would think she was old, senile, useless.

". . . I think it could be good for both of us, and it just makes sense, don't you think?"

In the inside zipper pocket of the largest bag—a black-and-white-striped bag she had gotten on a trip, which trip? Oh, it didn't matter which trip, Joy, for heaven's sake, all that mattered was the court date—she felt something, paper, wadded-up paper.

"Joy?"

She pulled it out. It was pink. She unfolded it.

"What do you think, Joy?"

"I found it! It's not until September!"

"No, I mean about us moving in together."

Joy folded the summons carefully and put it back in the zippered inner pocket. She put everything back in her bags, the thermos, the flashlight, the pads and adult diapers that were, thank god, in an opaque plastic bag. She was nearly panting. So much excitement.

As she went to put her atomizer back in the smaller bag, she took a few puffs, just in case. And finally the dog, into the striped bag.

Living with Karl. What would that mean? The end of loneliness? The echo of another person's footsteps in the house. Someone to pretend to listen to you as you read out loud from the newspaper, with whom to discuss what to have for dinner, someone with whom to chat about the weather, someone with whom to share a life.

"I've been in love with you for sixty-five years," Karl said. "How corny that sounds. But it's true. It's not that I thought of you every day. I didn't. But there was an impression of you, I suppose you could say that. An impression on my heart."

Tears came to Joy's eyes. She was staring blindly down at the pavement. She could not look at him. She wondered what Aaron would think when she told him. But she could not tell him. Aaron, Aaron, how can I know what I feel without you here?

"I'm sorry," Karl said. "Bad idea."

"No, it's a wonderful idea, Karl."

"But?"

She shook her head.

"Your children? I thought that might be a problem."

"No, no. Not them." Although they might not like it, he was right. In which case, she thought, they could lump it.

"It's too soon," Karl said.

"Well, yes, it is too soon."

Karl made a disgusted sound. "I was afraid of that, I understand, but when you think about it, nothing is too soon when you're our age."

"It's not just that, Karl. Although it is too soon for me, even if I'm old. But there's something else. It's my apartment. I can't leave my apartment. I just can't."

"Too many memories, the place where you raised your children, yes, I see."

"No, not that."

"Well, what then?"

"The apartment is . . . rent-controlled."

They both burst out laughing.

"I can't give it up. I mean I just can't," she said, laughing still.

Then Karl took her hand, kissed it. "We are star-crossed lovers," he said good-naturedly.

Joy took his hand now and squeezed it. "Star-crossed lovers." She liked the sound of that. She liked the idea of being any kind of lover at all. She finally looked at him, his clean-shaven face a little pink in the spring air, his heavy eyelids and serious eyes, his fine silver hair shining. He loved her. He had loved her all along. She wondered if she loved him. A shiver of something that could have been love passed through her. Or it could have been simple pleasure. Or vanity. Or was it gratitude? She tried to remember what she had felt like when she had fallen in love as a girl. She remembered the sunlit giddiness, the dizzy confusion of falling through air without moving, the conviction that roared like an animal inside her. She remembered trembling and touching and knowing. She remembered Aaron scooping her up in his long arms. She remembered Karl, too, pushing the hair from her face before he kissed her. She remembered parties and dancing and being held close, her face against Aaron's cheek. Unless it was Karl's. But, no, it was Aaron's, before he grew his beard, she could hear him singing along to the music, his breath in her ear. She could not remember the song. She wished she could remember the song.

"It was all so long ago," she said. "And it's still too soon."

47

For weeks, thick, heavy invitations had been arriving for Ruby, a glory of colors and raised types and complicated inserts. One had a pop-up basketball net and ball, another a locker opening to reveal "baseball cards" featuring the bar mitzvah boy, a cute little boy disfigured by a wad presumably of gum meant to look like chewing tobacco, at bat and leaping for a fly ball. One was a flat pink satin box that opened to reveal not only the invitation but also a string of fake pearls.

Coco collected the mail each day with increasing dread. What origami of excess would fly from the mailbox next?

"Aren't there any nice little gentile children in your school? This is crazy. I guess we better send out our invitations soon," she said.

"Mommy, it's months from now."

Coco fingered the flowered chiffon of one invitation and marveled at it. She had no idea what kind of invitation Ruby would want. A sparkly corncob pipe in honor of Tom Sawyer? Pop-up Dead Sea scrolls to show her seriousness?

"But you will have to have a party. And you'll need party clothes."

"Yes, Mother, that does follow."

Ruby refused to partake in either the excitement or the dread of the social aspect of her coming-of-age.

"As if it all just happens by itself," Coco said to Daniel one night. "I don't know what to do. I'm not a party planner and I'm not a mind reader." She had gone to Sunday school at a Reform temple. She could not remember a single bar or bat mitzvah growing up. "I'm out of my depth."

"Well, just Google it, I guess."

When she did Google "bat mitzvah," she saw dresses that looked to her like figure-skating costumes on thirty-year-old prostitutes. She saw professionally produced videos of little girls dressed as rainbow-hued rappers lip-synching hip-hop songs.

"Daniel, we are in big trouble."

Whenever Coco tried to get Ruby to discuss plans for the bat mitzvah, Ruby was busy doing her homework or studying Hebrew.

"Can't have a party if I can't do the service, Mother," she would say in her new sarcastic way. Mo-ther: Coco noted how ludicrous a status the word suggested.

Finally, Coco ambushed her as she came in from school. "Ruby, sit down. Now."

Ruby slammed herself down on the couch and crossed her arms. "Hello to you, too, Mo-ther."

"About your bat mitzvah . . ."

"You can't talk me out of it, so don't even try."

"I don't want to talk you out of it. What makes you think I want to talk you out of it?"

In truth, though she would never have admitted it to her mother, Ruby was getting a little worn down by Judaism. There were an awful lot of rules. And poor old God was always so annoyed with his chosen people. Rabbi Kenny explained the historical context of the rules and explained the relationship between

God and his people as a dynamic one. She liked talking to Rabbi Kenny. She was still mesmerized by his physical beauty. His eyes were the color of sapphires. And she liked learning the alphabet, the sounds of the language, ancient and secret. She liked to chant, and she liked to think about Genesis and the big bang. All in all, it had been a satisfying hobby. But it was nearly summer. Her best friend, Alexandra, went to a stable in Riverdale twice a week to go horseback riding. Ruby started to go with her. In August they were going to riding camp together.

"I study my Hebrew," Ruby said. "I go to services. What do you want from my life? I'm very assiduous."

You are very supercilious, Coco thought. Put that in your adolescent vocabulary book. But she took a deep breath, reminded herself of the angst of being twelve, an angst she could still remember all too well, and she looked lovingly at the skinny girl sucking on her braces and said, "The party, honey. The invitations. The, you know, the theme. Like the girls on YouTube . . ."

"Mommy!"

". . . I suppose you could make a Katy Perry video. You like her."

"Mommy, stop! I don't want to be on YouTube. That's, that's . . . suburban."

Relieved, infinitely relieved, Coco silently thanked the heavens above. "No Katy Perry, then?"

"Mommy, Katy Perry is for babies. Honestly, Mother."

"Oh."

"Katy Perry," Ruby was muttering with disdain. "God, Mommy, you should know me better than that."

"You don't want a Tom Sawyer party, I suppose."

Ruby burst out laughing. Her braces sparkled in the lamplight. "You're hilarious," she said, leaning companionably against her mother.

They sat like that for a few minutes, enjoying the contact. Don't grow up, please, Coco thought. Just don't do it. Just don't.

—— 48 ——

Joy checked the gigantic calendar she had gotten for Aaron to help him keep track of passing time. She allowed herself a moment of pathos: Time is no more for Aaron Bergman. Time has passed him by. Then she lay down on the couch and elevated her legs and prayed for time to pass a little more quickly for herself. Only a few days until she could escape to Upstate. She was rattled by Karl's proposition. A temptation, there was no doubt about that.

The pleasure of existing in a man's memory as someone young and beautiful and alluring, and the place Karl held in her own memory, a young man besotted and devoted—those were powerful forces that rose delightfully to the surface whenever she saw him, when she thought about him, too. There was also the physical frisson, it was still there, the few ancient remaining hormones rearing their heads like old warhorses at the sound of a trumpet.

Standing beside Karl beneath an awning on Fifth Avenue during a sudden rain shower, close, their shoulders pressing.

Just the two of them.

And the red walker. And Marta.

Well, a nice diversion from bereavement and lamentation, that's how she put it to herself. And added to that was the thought of not being alone. Solitude is not my thing, she said out loud. But was living with a new old man her thing? She didn't know, and all she wanted to do was to see her house in Upstate New York, her white-shingled house with its wavy asphalt roof and rusting porch swing, her own house, nestled among its trees on top of its hill, the stream running merrily below. Someone like Karl, a man who had made his fortune and kept it, might not think much of a house like hers. But it was hers, her own house, unencumbered; she had fought to keep it safe, and now, she thought, it would keep her safe.

She wished she had named it the way people do in English novels. The Remedy, she could call it.

But they all just called it Upstate, and she loved it whatever its name. Every room looked out at different trees she had watched grow over the years, maple trees and birch trees and a weeping willow. The floors squeaked exactly where she expected them to.

She wanted to be in the house immediately, almost feverishly. She could feel the give of the noisy floorboards beneath her feet. She would yank open the windows and let the breeze in, let in the sound of leaves rustling.

Everything in her life had changed when Aaron died. But not the house. The house was not shaken by Aaron's death, it had been through death already, her father's, then her mother's, and it had survived. Once she got to the house, Joy thought, she would finally feel at home again.

For the last decade, ever since Aaron had begun to fade, Joy had hired a car to drive them and their stuff to the house Upstate for the summer, always the same car and driver, an aging Vietnam vet from the town nearest their house. The car, a resplendent used limousine he had gotten from a national limo service when it was a mere six years old, was close to twenty now. The driver, Mr. Bailey, was in his seventies.

"I hope you don't mind that I brought Mother," he said, nodding toward a small white-haired head just showing above the passenger seat. The ancient limousine rocked and swayed. The two heads swung back and forth, rhythmic and synchronized. "But she likes an outing, don't you, Mother?"

Mother did not answer.

"Very thoughtful of you," Joy said. She glared at her children, one on either side of her, both giggling like infants. Daniel hummed the *Psycho* shower music under his breath. In the enormous well of the car were a pile of black garbage bags, like so many lumpy corpses—Joy's luggage.

"Thank you for taking the dog," Joy said.

"Oh, we love dogs, don't we, Mother?"

The traffic was heavy. Where were they all going? Why couldn't they stay home and tend to their business? "This is a disaster, darling," she said to the dog.

Daniel looked at the trees, so green and full. "Traffic or no traffic, the house will still be there."

"You're too complacent, Danny."

"I wonder if anyone can be too complacent. Complacent seems like a good thing to be, Mom. Maybe you're not complacent enough."

"Don't you start with the Prozac. I am not taking any of your pills."

"I didn't say anything about Prozac."

"Well, your sister did."

"No, I didn't. Not today."

"I know it's what you're both thinking. But forget it. I'm in mourning."

"So am I," Daniel said.

His mother said, "Oh, sweetie, of course you are," and gave him a package of peanut-butter crackers.

Daniel wished he could wear a crepe hatband, he wished wearing black meant something these days, meant mourning instead of fashion. His father's death had taken some layer of earth out from beneath his feet. He thought of his father more than he ever had when Aaron was alive. He thought of him when he shaved, remembering watching his father shave the two patches above the beard on each cheek, the neck beneath the beard. Daniel had never wanted a beard, never liked his father's fussy attention to its shape and fullness. Now, all of a sudden, he thought about growing one. He thought of his father when he ate. Dad liked bratwurst, he would think. Dad loved smoked whitefish. Dad hated beets. And yogurt. He thought of his father whenever he paid his credit card bills, too. Daniel always paid them on time, the full amount. Dad ran up huge debt, he would think. And along with the anger that had plagued him for so many years, he would think, Poor Dad, poor Dad, always in debt. Daniel had a strong, easy-to-access financial plan. What would Dad do? he would think, and then he would do the opposite. He was not rich, but he was not gambling his family's life away on one lousy business venture after another. But poor Dad, now that poor Dad was dead. His father had always been hopeful, cheerful, sure his next venture would make him a fortune. There was strength in that, he supposed, and he missed his father's strength.

Joy began to rummage in a shopping bag. She extracted aluminum foil packages. "Want one, anyone?" she asked, pulling the foil off a hard-boiled egg. The smell of hard-boiled eggs filled the rocking car.

"No," Molly said, turning away quickly.

"Protein," Joy said. "Yummy protein." She pinched a piece off for Gatto.

Daniel shoved the rest of the egg, whole, into his mouth.

"Is it okay if I open the window?" Molly asked.

"It's very noisy," said Joy. "And with the dog . . ."

"Just for a minute. I feel kind of sick."

"You should eat something," Joy said. She unwrapped another egg.

"Oh, how your father loved this house," Joy said as they pulled in the driveway.

"No, he didn't," Daniel said.

"Yes, he did," said Molly.

Molly stepped out of the car and took in the familiar trees, the warm summer light, the clean white clouds against the rich blue of the sky. She had been going Upstate every summer since she was born. Her mother had spent summers there before that when she was a child. How many people could say that? How many families were that lucky? It was a wonderful house, a family house, full of family memories and full of family every summer. Molly felt the ground beneath her feet, felt it hold her weight, felt its solid, gentle welcome.

Her mother's little dog flew out of the limousine and began to sniff the ground.

"He's happy," Joy said.

Molly sniffed the air, light with honeysuckle and privet.

The house had a front porch, which was already piled with stuff. Coco and the girls had come earlier, the car packed to the roof with toys, all toys and electronics, as far as Joy could tell. She got out of the car with some difficulty, she got so stiff these days, and walked up the flagstone path to the house. She put her hand on the doorknob and waited to be as happy as the dog. A breeze blew. The smell was there, that mixture of humid earth and humid air, of wet bark and grass. She could hear the children calling to each other, her children, but of course they were Danny's children, her children were no longer children. She opened the door to the slight sting of mildew. The dog rushed past her, brushing against her legs, a butterfly of a dog. He was wet, he was fast, he was gone. She held the doorjamb to steady herself. The girls ran past her. Hi, Grandma, they called. They did not stop. They were gone.

"Mom?"

Joy opened her eyes. She hadn't realized they were closed.

"Mom, sorry, I just have to squeeze in here . . ." Molly pressed against her, trying to get inside. "Mom, come on . . ."

"Okay, okay, sorry."

Molly darted past her to the bathroom.

Coco had already unloaded most of the contents of the station wagon: the bicycles and scooters, the computers and Wii console, the electric piano, the stuffed animals, the toy wheelbarrow, and the puppet stage. The volume of child equipment was incomprehensible to Joy. She remembered Daniel's and Molly's toy box when they were growing up. It was yellowy unfinished wood with a top that crashed down on their fingers if they were not quick enough. It was a good size, or so they all thought at the time, the size of a small steamer trunk. What was in it? A truck, some blocks, a doll, a robot, a stuffed monkey, toy pistols and holsters, boxing gloves, a cowboy hat, maybe. She looked at the mound of possessions on the porch of the house.

"Is this really all yours? All that stuff?"

Danny gave her a look, a warning look, as he dragged her black garbage bags into the house.

"Matching luggage," Joy said to the girls.

They barely acknowledged her. "Gatto! Gatto!" they cried, running out the door, this time followed by the clatter of the dog. They ran in circles around the maple tree, then the girls rolled down the hill, getting themselves dizzy, the dog chasing after them. Joy remembered doing that. Now she got dizzy without any rolling.

"Goodbye!" she called to Mr. Bailey as he backed out of the driveway. "Goodbye, Mother!"

Joy wondered what she had packed in all those bags. They looked so anonymous and lumpy. Each July, she would take the bloated garbage bags to the house, and each September she would drag them back, most of them undisturbed since their arrival.

"Upstate is perfect," she said, running her hand along the back of the sagging sofa. "It never changes."

"Everything changes," Danny began in his environmental voice.

Please don't start with climate change, Joy thought. She felt as if the house had taken her hand and said, Welcome home. "Welcome home," she said. "That doesn't change."

She sat on the porch swing and listened to the stream that ran behind the house. Sunlight floated through the maple leaves above. The sounds of decades of summers surrounded her—the robins, the peepers.

She wondered what her life would have been like if she'd married Karl instead of Aaron. She probably would never have had the career she'd had. It would not have been necessary. That would have been a loss. On the other hand, there would have been enough money for them to survive without her scrabbling for work. What a luxury, not to worry about money. She wondered if anyone really had that luxury.

"I'll miss you," she had said to Karl before leaving. She touched his old hand with her old hand. And when she'd said it, she didn't realize how true it was. She missed him already. She could see his earnest eyes, his face opening up into a smile. She could feel his close-shaved cheek as she gave him a kiss goodbye. His cheek was soft, old, but it was new, too, unfamiliar, exciting. Maybe his poor dead wife was right, maybe it was better to let sleeping dogs, dead dogs, lie. It was enough to lose Aaron, to miss Aaron. She didn't need to miss Karl, too. She was too old. She was too tired.

And now at least she was not alone. She was surrounded by the ones she loved. Although they made so much noise. Coco was already banging pots and pans around. Daniel was bumping suitcases up the stairs. The girls were screaming, and Molly was somehow talking to Freddie on the computer she'd brought with her.

But this was the place Joy knew best. She had grown up in the city and lived her entire adult life in the city, but this was where she belonged. The air was her air, as if it had been made for her, air that revived her and soothed her. The light was her light, changing in ways she knew and anticipated and loved. There was nowhere on earth in which she felt more at home. Even the sounds seemed to welcome her, to know her, to greet her. There had been rain and the stream was high and rushed noisily by. A finch sang its chortling musical song. She listened for the cows from the pasture across the road. She heard something low and rumbling, not cows. A tractor plowing a far-off field.

But it was not a tractor, and it was not far off. The sudden crash of rocks reached her, the beeping of heavy machinery backing up, muffled shouts, a jackhammer.

"What are they doing, Grandma?" Cora asked. She climbed onto the roof of the car and looked across the street. "They're digging up rocks with a steam shovel."

Gatto jumped into Joy's arms.

Molly stormed out of the house. "What the hell is going on?" she said, and stomped down the hill, yelling, "Hey! Hey!"

"Well, we're not building this swimming pool for the cows," the foreman said cheerfully when they had all followed Molly to the field.

Joy heard herself say with what she knew was irrelevant conviction, "I am a widow."

The foreman was named Bill. He reached over to pet Gatto and Joy felt the growl building in the dog's chest, but to her disappointment it quickly shifted into a friendly whimper and he licked the foreman's hand.

"How long will you be doing this?" Molly said.

"And what exactly are you doing?" Daniel asked.

"Well, let's see, building a road, of course, and houses. Nine. So yeah, we'll be here awhile, I guess. Beautiful houses, pretty high-end. Pools, too. Hey, little puppy, what's your name?"

There was an unpleasant discussion that night. Daniel said, "With this development going up, someone might actually want to buy our house."

"This is my ancestral home," Joy said. "And yours."

He explained again that Joy was running out of money. "Anyway, our ancestors lived in shtetls."

Molly told him he was morbid. Joy said perhaps she would die and solve everyone's money worries. All of this had to be conducted in whispers, because the girls were asleep.

"Let it go," Coco said to Daniel in bed that night. "Give your mother a summer off."

"I'm just trying to be responsible."

"Let it go."

"Where's Aunt Freddie, anyway?" Cora asked at breakfast.

Aunt Freddie always slipped her a crisp dollar bill when she saw her.

"You're a miser," Ruby said.

"I'm not."

"It means you love money."

"Oh. Then I am. So what?"

"Why do you love money?" Joy asked.

"I collect it."

Joy nodded. Better than fingernail clippings. Molly had collected fingernail clippings.

Molly grabbed Cora and kissed her. She was touched that Cora thought to ask where Freddie was. Sometimes she wondered if any of them remembered Freddie existed when Freddie wasn't standing directly in front of them. Particularly Joy. Since Molly's divorce, her life had become less and less real to her mother. Molly knew her mother was proud of her, knew Joy liked Freddie, but she knew also that she existed in a different way for her mother now, that the new reality was perceived dimly, as if the lights had gone out when she got divorced and her mother had never turned them back on. Molly plus a husband plus a child to raise had made sense to Joy. That was a discernible unit, that family of three. But Molly and Freddie in California? That was not a unit. It was an absence.

"I wish Aunt Freddie were here," she said to Cora.

"Yeah, why isn't she?"

"Good question. Why isn't she?" Daniel asked, as if this were the first moment he'd noticed her absence.

"Daniel, she's with her father," Coco said. "All her sisters and brothers are coming to L.A., remember?"

"That Freddie is a fine, fine person," said Joy.

Molly looked at her in surprise.

"I could see that when I stayed with you. A fine person."

Molly smiled, a grin really. "Thank you, Mommy."

"Why are you thanking me?" Joy asked fondly. "I didn't say you were a fine person. You're lucky Freddie puts up with you."

50

Freddie let her father open the barbershop door for her, discreetly helping him. It was the third time they had been to that barbershop in three days.

"Mr. Hughes! Good to see you."

"I need a haircut, my good man."

The barber caught Freddie's eye. She nodded slightly.

"Okay, Mr. Hughes! Sit right here."

Ever since Freddie told her father about the impending visit of his four other children, he had been insisting he needed a haircut. The insistence continued, the two haircuts in the last two days notwithstanding.

The barber was a stolid middle-aged man whose father had cut Duncan's hair until his retirement ten years ago.

"How's your father?" said Duncan.

"The same. How are you?"

"Still here."

They'd had the same exchange the day before and the day before that.

"Thanks, Mel. Dad was really eager to come in," Freddie said.

"Oh yeah, we're always happy to see Mr. Hughes."

Duncan hummed a little, then faded away for a moment, then caught his own eye in the mirror. "Hello, handsome."

"You do look sharp, Dad."

He was pleased, and as they drove back to Green Garden, he read the signs they passed out loud as if they were lines in a dramatic play. It had always been one of his car trip games. He seemed like his old self and Freddie said nothing, not wanting to break the spell.

51

S ometimes, Joy almost missed the red tricycle.

   "Maybe I'll come with you," she said when Coco and the girls set off to the market.

But the market was about to close and they could not wait for Joy to get herself together to go. No one asked her to do errands at the house Upstate. No one asked her to do anything at all. She could have been another cushion on the old sagging couch, she thought, as everyone came and went, busy with things that had once been the things that had busied her, though even the cushions, covered by her mother's petit point, were more useful than she was. No one leans on me, she thought.

At least she could listen to the radio, now that everyone was out of the house. They hated the scratchy sound of her old portable radio. She turned it on, but it was out of batteries. The extra batteries were not in the drawer where she had always kept them. That drawer was filled with coffee filters for Coco's complicated machine. The days were long for Joy, longer than even a summer day should be.

There was some excitement when Ben showed up. He surprised them, arriving on the same train as Daniel. The girls introduced him to the dog, who leaped in the air and shrieked in uncanny, high-pitched glee. Ben patted Gatto, and Molly patted Ben.

"Dinner!" Coco said, and rang the cowbell outside even though they were all already together.

At the table, Ben said he had an announcement to make. No, Grandma, I'm not pregnant. The little girls laughed and pushed each other. Not pregnant, but moving back to New York for August, a job as a paralegal, enrolled in an LSAT study course at night, signed up to take the exam at the end of the month.

"You can stay in my apartment," Joy said. "Would that be helpful?"

Ben gave a sheepish smile. "Well, as a matter of fact, I knew you wouldn't mind, so I kind of already left my stuff there. The doorman let me in."

"But you won't get to be in so many parades if you leave New Orleans," Cora said. "And wear costumes."

"Maybe that's a good thing," said Molly.

Ben's genial smile disappeared. "Why?"

Because it's infantile, she wanted to say. Because all you ever do down there is drink and play dress-up. "Just time for something new."

"New is overrated," Joy said, but no one responded. It was a noisy table and she thought again about getting hearing aids; perhaps she had spoken too softly. It was sometimes hard for her to gauge these days.

"I'm very proud of Ben," she said in a louder voice. "It's difficult to change anything in this life."

Still no one looked her way. They were lost in their excitement and chatter. But Ben must have heard her, for he kissed her cheek and whispered in her ear, "Thank you."

They were sitting outside at the long picnic table. Daniel took in the scene before him with satisfaction: his wife and children, his sister and his nephew, his mother; the corn on the cob, the first corn of the year, the butterflied leg of lamb he'd grilled perfectly, not gray, not blue.

But Ben then announced he was a vegetarian and refused the perfectly grilled lamb. Ruby asked if the lamb was butchered by a kosher butcher, and Cora, horrified at the thoughts brought on by the word "butcher," said she was vegan as of that moment and refused her plate of lamb, too.

Daniel sat in the gloaming, swatting mosquitoes, morosely chewing the perfect lamb, aggrieved by his family and their vegetables, when his mother cleared her throat and said in an uncharacteristically formal voice, "I'd like to invite Karl to Ruby's bat mitzvah."

"What?" he said. "Why?"

"*Why?*" said Molly.

"Who's Karl?" Ruby asked.

"You remember, Ruby," Ben said. "Old guy with the red walker like Grandpa's?"

Joy wasn't sure she liked that description, but she nodded. "You met him at Passover," she said. "He was a friend of Grandpa's."

"I'm sorry, but this is not appropriate," Daniel said. "He's practically a stranger. Ruby's met him exactly once. Why would he come to her bat mitzvah?"

"He and Grandpa became good friends," Joy said. "And I would like to invite him. Period." She was a little red in the face. Daniel could see the color rising even in the dusk.

"But why do you want him to come," Ruby said, "if he's Grandpa's friend? He won't be able to see Grandpa."

"Ruby," her mother said sharply.

Joy said, "I thought it would be nice, that's all."

"Oh, okay," Ruby said. "Since Grandpa can't come, like a representative."

"Like *instead* of Grandpa," said Cora.

For a moment there was silence, then Coco boomed, "Salad! I forgot the salad," and dashed inside.

"No one can take the place of Grandpa," Daniel said.

"Yeah," Ruby said, giving Cora a punch in the arm.

Cora began to cry, Ruby called her a crybaby, Joy excused herself with a headache, Ben cleared the table, Ruby punched Cora again and said it was her fault that Grandma had a headache because she was such a crying crybaby, Daniel yelled at them both, Coco yelled at Daniel for yelling at the children, Molly filled her glass with wine and downed it, and dinner was over.

"I really think it's, I don't know, unsuitable," Molly said to Daniel as they sat in the lawn chairs in the dark a few hours and a few bottles of wine later. "It's, it's unseemly." She knew she'd had far too much wine, but when your octogenarian mother announces her intention to betray your recently deceased father with her college boyfriend in public, there's not much choice but to drown your sorrow and humiliation in drink, that's what she told Freddie when Freddie called earlier.

Molly looked up at the stars. They were revolving. Stars did revolve, didn't they? No, they didn't. The earth revolved and it looked like stars revolved, she could almost hear that little pedant Ruby correcting her, but these stars were revolving so fast. "Unseemly," she said again. "It's like she's bringing a date. A *date*. To Ruby's bat mitzvah." Molly closed her eyes, but the stars kept spinning.

"Okay, so she has a new friend, okay, fine, good," Daniel said. "But you don't have to bring him to a family thing, right? I think it's disrespectful. To Dad."

"And us."

"The body isn't even cold yet."

"No boundaries," Molly said. "I mean, she's *our* mother."

There was silence, except for the stream.

Then Daniel said, "Do you think they . . ."

"What? Do I think who what?"

"You know. Mom and Karl."

"Daniel! You're, you're a . . ." She wanted to say pervert, but she was overcome by a wave of nausea.

"Molly, oh god, that's disgusting." He moved out of the way as she retched.

"Thank god Ben didn't see that," she muttered, still leaning over the side of the chair.

The next morning was a Saturday and Coco took Cora to a mall an hour away as compensation for too much nature, Ben and Ruby went out on a bike ride, and Molly and Danny were both still asleep. Joy made herself a soft-boiled egg that was too hard and a piece of toast. The house was unusually quiet, no construction equipment grinding next door, no grandchildren squabbling. Even Gatto was silent, asleep in a patch of sun in the kitchen. Joy drank her tea and thought how serene it was.

Alone at last.

That was meant to refer to a couple, surely. Two lovers, alone at last.

Nevertheless.

She and Aaron had lived together for so long they had barely noticed each other, like two old dogs asleep before the fire. Without him, the room was empty, any room. Yet it was wearing to be around other people. That was something she realized more and more. People you love, they wear on you, too. Molly and Danny and Coco and the girls, she wanted them to be near every minute of every day—it was wearing, that was all. Lovely. And wearing.

She looked for the jam in the refrigerator, but then remembered Coco kept it in the cabinet. But she kept peanut butter in the fridge instead of the cabinet. It was aggravating, all this change. Coco and Danny put knives in the dishwasher, they left the bathroom door closed when no one was in it. There were so many things here, Upstate in *her* house, that were done differently now. The television remote was new and made no sense to her, but then, she was not allowed to watch television, anyway, she made it too loud and disturbed everyone. The toilet paper was the wrong brand, as were the paper towels and the dishwashing liquid. The towels were folded oddly and put in the wrong closet when they were clean or, when they had been used, hung wet and moldering on hooks she had never installed in the bathroom. The place had become almost foreign to her, as if she were a stranger, a stranger in the house her mother gave her, the house she had nurtured and protected for so many years.

She wondered what would happen if she agreed to live with Karl. It was possible he would turn out to be another comfortable old dog, just like Aaron, just like her, but it was more likely he would be wearing. New, unfamiliar, and wearing.

Of course she would bring him to Ruby's bat mitzvah. Her children were behaving like children. They should be happy she had a new friend. She hadn't mentioned Karl's proposal that the two of them live together, but even that should make her children happy. Would they prefer she be sent off to a nursing home, by them? Like Freddie's father? To fend off some senile old goat? Like Freddie's father? Molly and Danny were probably worried about their inheritance, that's what it was. She was doomed to rot on a urine-stained sofa like Mrs. Astor. Except there was no inheritance. Except the house. Which they wanted to sell. Where she no longer belonged.

She tried to shake off this feeling that she was an intruder, the sense that even this timeless place had moved on and left her behind. She went outside and sat in one of the Adirondack chairs. Such an unpleasant smell. The dog must have vomited. She moved to the porch swing and breathed in the wet summer air, so familiar, her summer air. But it felt all wrong, even the air was wrong, heavier than she remembered it, stickier. The fresh smell of grass and soil and the damp living smell of the stream evaded her. She had hoped, she'd been sure, that Upstate was where she would get her bearings again. She would walk along the road and pick wildflowers, wade in the stream to cool off from the summer heat, pick raspberries from the thorny hedges at the bottom of the hill.

But everything had gone awry. The weather had gone wrong first, hotter and rainier than any year Joy could remember, but that was just the beginning. There was the construction on the other side of the road, which got worse and worse, puffing out clouds of dust when it didn't rain, oozing mud when it did. And that rain, forcing the field mice to take refuge in the house, the lightning knocking out the power every week. There was a coyote, too, which prowled the property and howled at night. She worried about Gatto, so small, so urban in his experience of the world. Bad enough he'd been attacked by a brute in Los Angeles. What if he wandered out one night and was attacked by a coyote? She wouldn't be there to save him. She'd be inside, asleep. She had become attached to the dog. He was the only one who didn't tell her what to do.

The swing creaked as she stood up. She could not wade in the stream this summer. It was rushing full speed ahead, carrying fallen branches, no time to wait for an old lady and her poor balance. She could not pick raspberries, either. The bulldozers had ripped the bushes out of the ground. And the wildflowers had been crushed beneath enormous tire treads.

She walked out onto the lawn and looked back at her house. Perhaps she should sell it, after all. It stood on the hill, dim and weather-beaten, her own house, a house she loved and had loved for almost as long as she could remember. But at that moment, in the gray morning heat, this wonderful place, this house that had given itself over to the happiness of so many generations of children, seemed to feel as out of place as Joy did.

The sky was suddenly dark, thunder grumbling in the distance. Poor Ben and Ruby. They'd get soaked. What if they went under a tree to get out of the rain? What if they touched a wire fence? They could be electrocuted. Joy felt herself tilting, listing to one side. The bottom of the earth shot away from her, from beneath her feet, then came back. Vertigo, a new plague, thank you very much. And her eyes, so unreliable. There had been several trips to the ophthalmologist in the city and an emergency repair of a cataract lens that was far from successful. She closed one eye, but the sky still threatened rain.

She wished Ruby was not going off to sleep-away camp. She wished Cora would not be going to day camp every weekday. She wished Danny didn't have to go to the office. She wished Aaron were not dead.

It's your fault, damn you, she thought. All your fault, Aaron.

What was the point of everyone being together if people went away?

If the black clouds above had not spelled certain death for Ruby and Ben, she would have welcomed the darkening sky and thought it beautiful, much more beautiful, certainly, than the dingy clouds of dust, the dun-colored fog, that was usually lurking in the sky from the building site. The digging had done something to the septic tank as well, something obstructive, and there had been over-flowing toilets. The fireflies had given way to houseflies and bees and wasps and, with all the rain, a burgeoning crop of mosqui-toes. Inside, the air conditioners labored noisily and the doors and windows were kept shut.

The girls sometimes sat on her lap, smelling of dirt and child-hood, and she would say, "I'm so lucky to be able to spend so much time with you."

"Yes, you belong here with us, Mom," Danny would say, benevolent, as if the house were his and Joy were his guest.

And Joy would think, I don't belong anywhere. Then: Joy! Are you such a delicate flower? Get a grip.

"Mom!" Danny said, pushing the screen door open, still in his pajamas.

He was angry, Joy realized with surprise. He was so rarely angry about anything that did not have to do with climate change. Maybe another glacier had melted.

"We have to talk," he said. "Right now."

"Don't come out here barefoot, Danny. The deer ticks . . ."

261

"Come in, then." He gestured impatiently.

As she sat at the kitchen table, Joy allowed herself to feel just how tired she was. Then she sat up straight and smiled at her son. "We'll sell it, that's all," she said.

"Sell what?"

"The house. This. The house, the house."

"No. Karl. We have to talk about this Karl guy."

"This Karl guy? Is that how you think of your father's friend?"

"Oh come on, Mom, let's cut the 'Daddy's friend' crap."

Joy was stunned. Danny never spoke to her like that.

"What is the matter with you?" she said. "Good lord."

Joy went outside again. It was raining now. Good. She would catch pneumonia and die and everyone would have to stop lecturing her.

The raindrops were enormous. She could almost hear them as they hit the ground. They were cold on her arms, on her face, a shock in the steaming heat of the day. Her clothes were soaked through immediately, her pants sticking to her legs.

"Mom, come inside. What are you doing?" It was Molly. She ran outside.

"You're barefoot! You'll get a tick!" Joy said.

Molly pulled her inside and threw a beach towel around her.

"It's only water," Joy said. Her teeth were chattering. She let Molly rub the towel on her hair, her back, her arms. She obediently went into her room and put on dry clothes. When she came out, Molly handed her a mug of coffee.

"I can't drink coffee. My digestion . . ."

Molly snatched it back. "Fine."

"Where's Danny?"

"Sulking in his bedroom."

"He was very rude to me. I'm eighty-six years old and I deserve some respect." Joy felt the tears and willed them back.

Molly sat across from her at the table, bedraggled, her hair wet and matted, dark circles under her eyes. "Yes, let's talk about respect," she was saying. "Respect for your husband, my father, Daniel's father. Let's talk about that. Since we're talking about respect."

"Why did you make such a fuss about the rain? It's about a hundred degrees out."

"Mom, it's disrespectful to Daddy to invite Karl to Ruby's bat mitzvah. That's what Daniel is upset about. And so am I."

"That's ridiculous. Karl was your father's friend."

"He's *your* friend."

"Am I not allowed to have friends now? What is wrong with you two?"

Molly offered her mother a cup of tea, which Joy accepted. She did not want tea. It would make her have to pee. And the kitchen was humid and hot. But she could see Molly trying to be civil. It was important to be civil. She had tried to teach her children that.

"Look, Mom, you can't bring him to the bat mitzvah, okay? You just can't. It wouldn't look right. I mean, it's only been a few months. It might, you know, embarrass Ruby."

"Ruby? You mean it will embarrass you two, although god knows why."

"You think he can take Dad's place?" Molly said, all pretense at civility gone. "Well, he can't. Ever."

She was shouting now, and Daniel stomped down the stairs to join in: "The body is not even cold. How can you do this to us?"

Joy looked away from them, her two beloved children, yelling and stamping their feet like toddlers. Graying toddlers. She tilted her head back and looked at the ceiling and wondered if it might fall in and shut them up.

"What has Karl ever done to you?" she said softly.

There was silence, just the thunder, closer now, and the rain on the roof.

"Did you know that Karl asked me to live with him?"

"See?" Daniel said to Molly. "See? I told you."

"Mommy! You can't. You'll turn into a caretaker."

"Your father liked Karl. Your father would have wanted me to have some companionship. Your father would be ashamed of you both."

They shifted uneasily.

"Yeah, well, still, it's just . . ." Daniel's words trailed off.

"And whether I choose to live with Karl or not," Joy continued, "one thing I can see clearly now. I cannot stay in this house one day longer. I am not welcome. I do not belong."

And she marched out, slammed her door, and began packing.

52

Duncan smiled and smiled, but he did not say much. If he was overwhelmed, he could hardly be blamed. His family had gathered around him from the four corners of the earth, as Gordon put it. There were grandchildren, too, Gordon's kids, now quite grown up: one of them, the daughter, in college; the son engaged and holding the hand of his fiancée. Freddie was overwhelmed, so why shouldn't her father be? None of it seemed quite real. Laurel and Pamela wore colorful sundresses, not identical in pattern, but complementary, and identical enough: four spaghetti straps cutting into four plump white shoulders. Freddie, who was wiry and always had been, who wore gray and always had, knew she looked a little dreary beside them, a caterpillar beside two butterflies. Her brothers were somewhat more soberly attired, but still in vacation costumes—and they did seem like costumes to Freddie, the golf shirt and white pleated Bermuda shorts of her brother Gordon, a similar golf outfit on his wife; the jeans and big silver belt buckle, the chestnut-colored cowboy boots Alan wore. But they probably thought she was in costume, the same costume she'd worn since the age of six. Jeans and a T-shirt. Only the grandchild generation looked right. Perhaps because they were at the Third Street Promenade in a pedestrian mall filled with other young people.

Freddie wearily followed the group into another shop. They seemed to be drawn to chain stores that also had outlets in their own countries. Duncan was a bit pale, but he shambled along behind them.

"Are you okay, Dad?"

He did not answer, but smiled, grabbed her arm to steady himself.

"Well, *I'm* exhausted," Freddie said. "Maybe we should go sit down somewhere," she said to her siblings, all of whom were trying on sunglasses.

They wanted to sit outside. It was winter where they lived. Wasn't the sun beautiful and warm here in Los Angeles?

The beautiful warm Los Angeles sun beat down upon them. Freddie never sat in the sun as a rule, and certainly not in July. The air, even in Santa Monica, so near the beach, was blazing hot, dry as dust, and still. But her siblings were ecstatic. What a good time of year they had picked. What a perfect vacation. They began to trade tales of vacations that had gone wrong. Food poisoning, sharks, terrorism, cyclones, earthquakes.

They did not mention heart attacks. But that's what Duncan had. The paramedics came and hustled him away in an ambulance. Freddie sat next to him, holding his hand. The rest of the family followed in a caravan of rented cars.

53

Joy was dressed and packed. The garbage bags, undisturbed since their arrival, could stay and rot for all she cared. She had stuffed her clothes and pills and creams into her California roller bag. She had called Mr. Bailey and he said he and Mother would be right over to drive her to the station.

She waited on the porch swing and pictured her apartment, dim, stuffy, mail piled high, Ben's dirty dishes in the sink, though he had not even stayed there yet. It didn't matter. It had to be better than staying here, where no one wanted her, where no one made room for her, and where, she now realized, no one trusted her.

"This is ridiculous, Joy," Coco said. "You don't have to go, and you certainly don't have to take a car service. If you insist on leaving, let me drive you. I'm driving Molly to the station anyway."

Molly was going back to California to be with Freddie, whose father was in pretty bad shape in the hospital.

"That's quite all right."

Coco stood in the doorway. Danny appeared behind her.

"Mom, come on. You're acting crazy."

Joy narrowed her eyes. "Don't you dare call me crazy. The first step to sending the elderly to a home is saying they're crazy. Well, just forget it. I'm not going to a home. I'm going to *my* home in New York. Since you've taken over this one."

"Now you're being paranoid."

"Me? You're the one who is paranoid, all this fuss about a simple invitation to a bat mitzvah."

"She has a point," Coco said. "What is the big deal?"

Danny stormed back inside, followed by Coco saying, "Well, really, Daniel, you're being silly . . ."

"I have choices," Joy yelled after them.

"She's moving in with him," Danny was shouting inside. "You didn't believe me, but you hear her."

"Oh, so what?" Coco said.

Joy dreaded the arrival of Mr. Bailey and his car. Her heart was hammering and her vertigo was sweeping in like nauseous fog. She was arguing with Danny, her dear sweet Danny. Why? Over Karl? I don't want to live with him, she wanted to call out. I just want to invite him to my granddaughter's celebration. I want someone there I can lean on, literally lean on the red walker that is just like Daddy's walker; I want to smile at someone and be proud and have him see how proud I am instead of seeing a problem who has to be taken to the ladies' room, who has to be helped down the stairs to the street, who has to be transported the three blocks from the synagogue to the restaurant.

Cora and Ruby came outside and settled themselves on the swing, one on either side.

"You can invite whoever you want," Ruby said.

"I'm inviting a friend," Cora said, "so I don't see why you shouldn't."

"Yeah, Daddy's being silly." Ruby sounded like Coco, dismissive; even her gesture, hands held up in mock surrender, reminded Joy of Coco. Without thinking, Joy said, "He is not."

Molly was the next to perch on the swing to try to talk her out of going back to the city.

"You're one to talk," Joy said. "*You're* leaving. I don't see why. You're not a doctor. It's not as if you can do anything for the old goat."

Molly gave her a baleful look.

"Oh, I didn't mean that. Of course you have to go back to be with Freddie. I'm selfish, I admit it, but I look forward *all year* to spending this time with you, Molly."

"But if you're not even going to be here, what difference does it make if I go home to L.A.?"

"I have to be honest," Joy said.

Ben climbed into Mr. Bailey's old limo next to his grandmother and Gatto.

"Stay here, Bennie. You have a whole day before you have to be back. I don't want to cut your time in the country short."

He shrugged. "Mom's leaving, you're leaving, it's awkward now anyway. Everyone is so upset."

He carried her bag up the steps to the platform.

"You're a good boy," she said, but she might have been talking to the dog.

She was silent then, until they were on the train. "I was having a temper tantrum," she said. "That's all."

"So was Uncle Daniel. And Mom, too."

Ben thought back to his own temper tantrums.

"Do you see red when you get angry?" he asked.

"I think that expression has to do with bulls and the red cape the toreador swishes around."

"But I see red. I always saw red when I had temper tantrums when I was little." A soft dark red screen, behind it the grown-ups above him talking and talking, hollering, but no sound coming through, just the rush of blood in his ears, red blood—that's how he remembered his childhood tantrums. And he'd had quite a few of them.

"At least your father and I don't kick," his grandmother was saying. "You were a kicker."

He sensed that she had started to cry and he turned away, staring out the window at the weedy cliffs rushing by. Then he turned back and wrapped her in his arms and let her weep against his chest. He wondered if this was what it meant to be an adult, to be on the other side of the tantrum.

54

Joy decided she was not speaking to either Danny or Molly.

"I have never played favorites," she told Natalie proudly when she got back to New York. "I'm not going to start now."

Natalie was the only one of the girls in town. She never left New York City, nor could she understand those who did. But since neither Joy nor Natalie wanted to venture out in the heat, they might as well have been in different countries. They were speaking on the phone, each in her air-conditioned bedroom.

"I'm surprised they didn't follow you into town. As chaperones."

"First they want me to stop grieving. Then they think I'm not grieving enough."

Joy was angry, but the silent treatment was difficult for her to maintain. She wondered how Freddie's father was. And she wanted to tell Molly about the deliveryman (the turkey burger she ordered was too dry, but she put sliced tomatoes on it and microwaved it and it was delicious), the same deliveryman she'd given the scarf to. She'd asked if he was cold and wanted another scarf, and they had laughed and laughed. Then, too, she wanted to call Danny to tell him about the letter Ruby had written her and stuffed in her suitcase begging her to send candy to camp immediately, it was an emergency, this way it would be there when Ruby arrived, and it should be flat and hidden inside a magazine or book. Danny had done the same thing when he went to camp. Some things never changed.

Joy gave the telephone a poisonous glance. Never mind. Let them stew.

"She needs space?" Molly said when Ben answered the phone. "What does that mean? She's not my boyfriend. We're not twenty."

"Mom," Ben said, "she needs some time on her own."

"*You're* there."

"Just give her some time. It's hard to be an old Jew, remember?"

Daniel called a few minutes later.

"She's so sensitive. Honestly," he said when Ben said she could not speak to him because she was too upset, and he hung up, his feelings hurt.

Joy was relieved that Karl was still in Rhode Island with his son. She could not imagine speaking to him, either. She was happy when Ben went out. She spent the day quietly, adjusting the air conditioners, looking for her glasses, reading the newspaper, petting the dog. The coffee shop delivered her meals. In the late evening, when it was less hot, she took a short, careful walk, Gatto under her arm. She could not remember the last time she had spent a summer day in the city. She could see the sunset between the buildings.

Coco called to try to make peace. Joy told Ben to tell her she would let her know if and when she was ready to negotiate.

When Freddie called, though, Joy got on the phone.

"I'm so sorry, dear. I hope your father recovers very quickly. It must be a nightmare for you. All that family. Family is a nightmare, isn't it?"

She pictured Freddie surrounded by all her brothers and sisters.

And nieces and nephews. And Molly. Was Molly standing right beside her?

"Is Molly there?"

"Yes. Do you want to talk to her? She's very ashamed of herself. Aren't you, Molly?"

Joy heard a mumbled assent.

"Very," Freddie added.

"Well, then."

"And she misses you. She can't stand it that she hasn't spoken to you."

"She just got off the plane."

"True. We're going straight from the airport to the hospital to see my father."

Joy sat down in the kitchen. There were so few cars on the street. No sirens. She thought of Freddie's father in the hospital, in a coma, unable to speak to his daughters or his sons. And Freddie and Molly going to see him, to stand silently at his silent bedside.

"That's good," Joy said. "Good girls."

And the feud was finished.

55

In the weeks that followed, Duncan's grandchildren and sons and daughters-in-law all returned home, but Pamela and Laurel stayed on. Their father lay unconscious in a hospital bed, and they sat every day, one on either side of him, discussing the disposition of his property. Freddie explained to them that he had no property to speak of, but they spoke of it anyway. There was the jewelry, their mother's jewelry, which had never been distributed. It was costume jewelry, but you never knew. And there were Duncan's watches, vintage watches that had become valuable. Not to mention his life insurance, which was all paid up years ago, and his car.

"He sold the car after his last accident," Freddie said.

"Well, then, the proceeds . . ."

"For scrap. He sold it for scrap. Can we discuss this somewhere else? Or not at all?"

"Oh, he can't hear a thing, can you, Dad?" said Pamela. "And if you could, you wouldn't mind, would you? He certainly can't take care of all these details himself, Freddie."

"We're being practical," Laurel said. "Someone has to."

Freddie went to the hospital every day, too, but one day slid seamlessly into the next, her father the same, his chest moving up with great effort and, then, with equal effort, down. His cheeks had sunk into his skull, he got no better, he got no worse. Her sisters had moved out of their hotel room into his room at Green Garden.

"I know they're going through his things," Freddie told Molly. "It's ghoulish."

Molly was kind and distracted, the distraction perhaps making her kinder than she would ordinarily be. The argument with her mother had shaken her.

"It was only a day, only a little quarrel, I know, but it was almost as if she had died. I don't want her to die. I don't want your father to die. It's a very messed-up system, death. I don't like it at all."

She was gone a lot of the time, too, taking her summer field session students to Catalina Island to drag sensors behind kayaks, measuring the temperature, looking for fresh water feeding into the ocean. The first year she taught this class, one of the students had asked her which ocean it was. This year the group was smart and dedicated, although when she pointed out the bay where Natalie Wood drowned, they asked who Natalie Wood was.

"It made me feel so old," she said.

But she and Freddie both knew that until their parents died, they would still be the children.

— 56 —

Joy discovered that she rather liked Manhattan in August. She could see the lightning and hear the thunder and not worry that her power would go out. She could watch the raindrops stain the pavement from six stories above and not wonder if the basement would flood. The early mornings were bearable, and she took Gatto in her bag in one hand, the other bags hooked on Aaron's walker, just to be safe, you never knew, and made her way to Aaron's park to mourn him and, now and then, to silently rail at him as the pigeons cooed and the sparrows chirped. No other people were there, in the park, or on the streets. The city was as quiet as a small town.

The invitations to the bat mitzvah had been sent out last month, but Danny made sure to tell her that one had now been sent to Karl, too. "My response was a little out of proportion" was his way of apologizing. Joy said, "We all mourn in our own ways, Danny. Some of us regress, that's all."

Karl had called her from his son's house. They did not stay on the phone. Men so rarely did. He asked her if she had thought any more about what they talked about. She said she had, and that was true. She had thought about it a great deal. And the more she thought about living with Karl, the more she enjoyed living with Ben. Ben was never there. He went to work during the day and to class in the evening. At night, he was out until the wee hours. Joy saw traces of him, reassuring traces. A mug in the sink. An empty carton of milk put back in the refrigerator.

So when he arrived at the apartment unexpectedly early one afternoon, Joy was surprised but delighted.

"Did you get the afternoon off? We can go out to the early-bird special!"

"My life is ruined," he said, flinging himself onto the couch. He thrashed around a bit, then said, "They want a urine sample."

"For DNA? But they saw you, Ben. The police know it was you. What a waste of city resources."

"No, Grandma, not the city. The law firm. They want a urine sample."

"You and your urine, Ben. Really."

"I have to give it to them today, and you know, I was out last night and so there might be, you know, traces. Of stuff. They'll fire me and I'll never get into law school."

"Stuff? Like drugs? You take drugs? Bennie, Bennie . . ."

"Just weed, Grandma. But it's against their policy and . . ." He took an empty plastic specimen jar from his pocket and looked at it sorrowfully. "I'll have to be a bartender forever."

"Oh, for heaven's sake," his grandmother said. "Give me that." She went in the bathroom and filled it up.

"Here, take this." She was really angry. "Marijuana! As if it's any business of theirs."

57

In the baking, desiccated air of September, Duncan sat up. He demanded to see all his children just once more before he died.

"Die? You just woke up. Slow down, Dad." Freddie was so happy she felt almost sick. She had not expected to hear her father's deep, smooth voice ever again.

The doctors were stunned. He's a tough nut, they kept saying. A tough nut.

"Do this for me so I can die in peace."

Freddie had already called her sisters, still encamped in Duncan's room at Green Garden, and they were on their way.

"They're coming, Dad. Laurel and Pamela are coming from Green Garden."

"The traffic," he muttered, looking at the clock on the wall. "I could be gone before they get here."

As for her brothers, the best Freddie could do was FaceTime them.

Duncan sat up in his hospital bed when they all assembled. He stretched out one pallid skinny arm, tubes dangling from it.

" 'Howl, howl, howl, howl! O! you are men of stones.' "

Someone, one of the brothers on FaceTime, muttered, "This really cannot be happening."

"*'Had I your tongues and eyes,'*" Duncan continued, his voice low now, "*'I'd use them so that heaven's vaults should crack.'*"

"It's his last performance," Pamela whispered. Laurel nodded, eyes wide.

"*'A plague upon you, murderers, traitors all!'*" Duncan roared.

It was a disjointed piece of theater, he spoke only Lear's lines, but it was moving nonetheless. Freddie was tempted to fill in the missing dialogue, but stopped herself. She saw that this was her father's show, and a show it was, Duncan's voice rising and falling with emotion, his arms flung out, then pulled back to his heaving chest.

"*'No, no, no life!'*" he cried, turning first to Pamela, then Laurel, to each son's face, one on Freddie's phone screen, one on Molly's. At last he turned to Freddie herself. "*'Why should a dog, a horse, a rat, have life, and thou no breath at all?'*"

"I'm breathing, Daddy," she reassured him softly.

But suddenly, it appeared, Daddy was not breathing. He dropped back on his pillows, his mouth agape, his arms hanging from either side of the bed.

There was a hush.

Then Lear opened an eye.

Lauren gasped. "He's not dead."

"Rotten trick, Dad," said Gordon's FaceTime voice. "You scared the living daylights out of us."

Duncan, though pale, trembling, and clearly exhausted, smiled through the fatigue, sat up, and bowed from the waist, first to the left side of the room, then the right, then straight ahead.

Freddie began to clap. What else was there to do? It had been a brilliant performance.

58

The great day arrived. Ruby sat nervously waiting to be called to read her Torah portion. It was a portion full of curses cast on the people, but she could not really blame God—the Israelites were always straying. She had recently seen an old black-and-white movie in which Lassie, actually Lassie's son Bill, a perfect and brilliant collie sheepdog belonging to a young Elizabeth Taylor, accidentally goes off to World War II and comes home with Post Traumatic Stress Disorder, growling at and biting anyone who comes near him, raiding chicken coops, until at last he is reunited with Elizabeth Taylor and regains his calm and loving nature. Ruby had, in the last few days of frantically practicing her Haftorah, begun to confuse the behavior of God and of Bill, both of them essentially good, both of them driven to violence by the misbehavior of human beings. She sensed this must be sacrilegious, the comparison of a dog, however regal, and the god of the Israelites, but the thought was hard to get out of her head once it had planted itself there.

Her sister had wanted to wear a matching dress. Ruby had not had to throw a fit, though she was prepared to do so. Their mother had pointed Cora to a frilly dress she knew Ruby would never have worn, and Cora had fallen for the bait. Ruby was content in a dress her grandmother called elegant. Her mother had been willing to spend quite a bit of money on it, she was so relieved it was not a bejeweled ice-skating costume. "Sophisticated" was the word Ruby used to describe it, and herself, to herself.

She looked down at her grandmother, in the first row, who was rather violently slapping her legs together, then moving them apart, then slapping them together again, staring meaningfully at Ruby. Maybe Grandma Joy had to go to the bathroom. But it was very distracting.

"Why won't Ruby put her legs together?" Joy whispered to Danny. She slapped her own closed again, instructively. "She looks like Sharon Stone, for heaven's sake."

Ruby could not remember much of the actual ceremony. She was aware of the rabbi, her wonderful rabbi, right beside her, a strong and comforting presence. The cantor was wearing perfume, which made Ruby sneeze once. She had no love for the cantor, a cold, shrill taskmaster in soft feminine sheep's clothing. The Hebrew letters of the sacred yellowed scroll came in and out of focus, but the words were there, in her head, in her soul, she realized, and she chanted a little louder, her voice firm and high and only occasionally off pitch.

Karl sat on Joy's other side, murmuring along with the prayers. Danny had insisted Karl sit there, right in front, and that was nice, but Joy's escort was someone else, someone not there; she felt Aaron's absence as if it were a physical presence beside her. She wore sunglasses and cried freely. Aaron, she thought, you would be so proud. Aaron had not been religious, not at all; he had not been brought up with any Jewish education and he claimed to think all religion was superstition. He did not in the least mind singing about Jesus Christ when Purcell or Handel wrote about him, he was as comfortable in a church as in a synagogue, but he would have been happiest now, proud of his granddaughter up there, so brave, so learned. Joy pressed the damp Kleenex to her cheek. Danny was grinning and crying, too. Cora was kicking her feet, but they were in the front row, so she wasn't bothering anyone. Joy wished she believed she would see Aaron again in heaven, but since she did not, she was grateful to think of him here in this place, at this moment, when he would have been so gloriously happy.

The party had no theme. It was a party, a celebration, pure and simple. There were about sixty of them in the restaurant, an old neighborhood Italian place that Ruby had loved since she was a small child. They filled the restaurant. Ruby made sure to thank Manuel, the owner of the corner store she had defaced, for coming. She introduced him and his wife to her Aunt Molly and Aunt Freddie. "I introduced Ruby to the rabbi," Manuel said. He grinned and looked proud, and Ruby made her retreat before he said any more. She took a sip from her mother's glass of champagne and was brushed gently away. Then Ben grabbed her and she was placed on a chair and lifted high in the air, waving regally. It wasn't a horse, and she had been assured by both parents that she would never be getting a horse, but, she thought, up there on the wobbling chair, it was an awfully good ride.

In the car that was driving them back to the Upper East Side, Joy and Karl sat quietly side by side.

"You have a wonderful family," he said.

"I do." She gazed out the window. The Pepsi sign was cursive and bright, the river sparkled with the reflection of the city. Queens. Even Queens was no longer affordable, that's what the young people at the party had been saying.

"I told my sons about you, Joy."

She looked at him in surprise. "Really? What did you say? They were not too pleased, if my children are anything to go by."

"I said I wanted to marry you."

"Oh boy. I bet they didn't like that."

"No, they didn't. They think I've lost my marbles. They were furious." He started laughing. "It was worth it just to hear them sputtering, trying to come up with reasons it would be a bad idea. I told them we would have a prenup of course, and that calmed them down."

"But, Karl honey, did you tell them that I don't want to marry you?"

He shifted, took out his handkerchief, blew his nose, shifted some more. "No."

"Oh."

"Joy, I know it's too soon, and we'll probably both drop dead before it's not too soon . . ."

". . . carried to the altar feetfirst."

Karl laughed and said, "But you never know. In this life you never know."

Outside, on the river, a tugboat pushed a barge. "You know certain things," she said.

"It was very satisfying, at any rate, telling the kids," Karl said. "Put the fear of god into them."

Joy nodded. "Good. That's good. Poor things."

Then she had an idea.

She didn't want to marry him, and she didn't want to live with him, it was true. They were both too old and set in their ways, and her apartment turned out to be just big enough for her and all her mail, and now that she had the dog, she didn't mind staying there alone. But, well, she had feelings for Karl. She did. Strong feelings. She loved being with him, having dinner or sitting beside him in the park. She missed him when they were not together. Karl bracketed her long love for Aaron—on the one side hovered the youthful, passionate Karl and the foggy memories of a college beau, on the other this new foggy tolerant affection for a man in old age.

Marriage, however, even living with him—that was a time together they had missed, a time that could not be recovered.

"No wedding," she said. "No oldies shacking up."

"I know, I know."

But their children, they'd gotten her back up. Who did they think they were, those sons of his, telling Karl he shouldn't marry someone if he wanted to? As for Molly and Daniel, had Karl's presence at the bat mitzvah hurt anyone?

"The children mean well," she said. "But it can be a bit much."

He said, "Amen."

"Well, here's my idea," she said. "We'll get engaged. Just engaged. Nothing decided, nothing certain, no plans, but always that possibility. It's very existential. *And* it'll keep those kids all on their toes."

Karl laughed. He lifted her hand and kissed it. "Joy," he said, "you take my breath away."

$$59$$

A ticket window and a growl from the female functionary. The paint was thick and tired on the walls. The trip down to 2 Washington Street had been a tiring fuss of bumps and jerks, horns, the sputtering of the taxi TV that would not turn off, the smell of the driver's lunch, which he ate as he swore automatically and without passion in his second language. The fare was a shock, and Joy tried to put it out of her mind as she waited for the elevator, waited and waited, then forgot what floor she was going to and guessed the fifth. She was right, there was a sign, and she turned and stood before a counter that had obviously emigrated from Eastern Europe well before the Velvet Revolution. Joy gave Ben's name and handed over the rumpled pink traffic ticket.

"Is this where I belong?" she asked the clerk.

The woman nodded, and Joy said, "But I don't really. I'm here for my grandson. He's back in New Orleans tending bar while he applies to law school. He did very well on the LSATs. So he's not here. But I am his emissary."

The clerk handed her a card with a number and name scribbled on it.

"Where do I go?" Joy asked.

The clerk pointed to a hallway.

In the courtroom, Joy walked down the center aisle. On either side were long benches crowded with people, like a well-attended church, although a round-shouldered resentment permeated the space, a communal almost penal resentment and resignation. Joy found a space far in the back and settled on the hard bench. She was out of breath. She was out of her element. She was out of her mind. She could have been married to a nice old man who loved her and had enough money to keep her safe and warm and fed and to hire someone to wipe the drool from her chin. Aaron, she thought, don't you think I should have said yes? I still could, though it would be so undignified. What do you think, Aaron? But Aaron had no answers for her. Why should he? He was safely out of this vale of tears. Well, enjoy, she said to him. Don't worry about me, left behind in this place where I have no place. Enjoy.

There was a judge in the room, though he was not seated high above them on an elaborate wooden platform as Joy had expected. The bench in this case appeared to be a metal folding chair. In front of the judge, a lawyer stood and seemed to interview each defendant, reading out their names and crimes in a loud ringing voice, asking them questions, then repeating it all to the judge, who sat not more than two feet away.

Joy had dressed for a civic appointment. Her outfit did not fit her as well as she would have liked, that's how much weight she had lost since Aaron's death, but it was respectable, and with her silk scarf, it was quite elegant, she thought. The other traffic offenders had been somewhat less exacting about their clothing. Most of the men were wearing tank-top undershirts, and it was hot for a September day, Joy had to admit. There weren't too many women present, but the ones who were there were also, for the most part, wearing tank tops, though theirs were brightly colored. So many young people had tattooed their arms and shoulders and necks. Joy could see tigers and winking eyes and dragons and flags and long-tailed birds. She was wearing a long-sleeved shirt. She had not a single tattoo. She could not imagine what tattoo she would wear if she chose to wear a tattoo. Her grandchildren's initials? Betty Boop, perhaps.

She was overcome with self-consciousness. I do not belong here. I have no tattoo. I am out of place. My clothing is wrong. No, their clothing is wrong. How dare people come to a public hearing dressed for the beach? But that's how it's done these days, that must be how it's done. I have lost touch with normal social behavior. I no longer know what is expected. And when I find out what is expected, undershirts and tattoos, I do not like it.

I do not belong here. I do not belong anywhere.

A gust of the place's generalized resentment wafted over her for a moment, becoming her own resentment, resentment toward Ben for peeing in the street, resentment toward New York City for giving him no alternative, resentment toward the courtroom full of sweating people in shorts and flip-flops. Then the resentment eased into resignation, the room's other mood, heavier, oppressive. Here I am, she thought, where I don't belong. One more place in which I do not belong. A great spinning globe of places revolved beneath her feet, and not one patch of it was the right patch for her, Joy Bergman.

She thought of the museum, of her job, of Molly and Freddie and their house in California, of her own house Upstate, of her apartment with the windows looking over the white headlights and the red taillights and no one to sit beside to watch them.

The judge, who may or may not have been listening to the lawyer hollering information in his direction, perhaps he was deaf like Joy and all her friends, spoke softly into the lawyer's ear, leaning forward, his hand cuffed over his mouth. He was no spring chicken. There were young men and middle-aged men in the pews, young women and middle-aged women, but there was no one, neither man nor woman, who approached Joy's age, not even the elderly judge.

The big clock on the wall behind the judge proclaimed the time was now 3:39. Three thirty-nine p.m., Eastern Standard Time, Joy thought. Or was it Eastern Daylight Time? When young people said, "This is my time," they meant it was the portion of their lives to treasure and to live fully. When old people said, "This is my time," they meant it was their time to die.

Joy took a juice box from one of her bags, but a guard in a brown uniform shook his head and she put it back. She had already inserted the straw. It would leak.

She waited and watched the tattoos that went by. Some were so elaborate and colorful. She wondered if Ben had a tattoo, a hidden tattoo. So much about a young person's life is hidden. So much about anyone's life. That was a blessing. Other people's secrets were so often tawdry and so rarely surprising, even the most extravagant gossip. Gossip was not what it used to be, which was to say, shocking.

Nothing was shocking anymore because everything was shocking. Public urination. Public urination certainly existed when Joy was young. It must have. But no one knew about it, or talked about it, or asked their grandmothers to go to court about it.

The room was hot and the air was stale. Joy noticed it blurring, first the heads of the people in front of her, then the walls. There was a golden light. Fluorescent light, yellow walls. A blurry room. Oh, a blurry room was never a good sign.

The man next to her said, "You okay, Mommy?" He smiled and fanned her with his *New York Post*.

For a moment she thought he was Danny. Who else would call her Mommy? But he was short and thickset and had a perspiring bald head, and the hand that held the newspaper was hairy and loaded with chunky gold rings. How beautiful that hand looked to her, bringing the gentle breeze.

"You are so kind," she said. "Oh, thank you."

The man on the other side of her offered her a Life Saver. Mint. Perfect. "You feel better, Mommy?" he asked.

"Yes, I do," she said. "You are such gentlemen. Old-fashioned gentlemen."

The room straightened itself out slowly.

Joy sucked on the Life Saver, felt the rim of the circle sharpen, sucked on it until it was a paper-thin sliver.

A man in front of her was called up for a broken taillight. A woman was called for no signal lights.

Oh, Ben, Joy thought. Public urination? Was that really necessary?

A missing muffler.

Bennie, Bennie, Bennie.

The nice man who had given her the mint Life Saver was called up. He squeezed apologetically past her. A missing headlight.

A missing headlight, Ben. A missing headlight. But Ben had always been a difficult child. Sweet. But difficult.

"I'm here for my grandson," she whispered to the gentleman with the *New York Post*.

He smiled.

And then she heard a name. Bea Harkavy. Harkavy was Ben's last name. Bea Harkavy, the clerk said again, even louder. Joy looked at the card the Cold War clerk had given her. There it was. Bea Harkavy.

"No, it's Ben," she said, standing up.

"Bea Harkavy," the clerk called again.

Joy made her way to the center aisle.

"Public urination," the clerk called out loudly.

"It's not me," Joy was saying. "It's my grandson . . ."

And then she looked around at all the men and women whose cars did not have taillights or headlights or side-view mirrors, all the men and women who had made mistakes on their registration papers or had read a form wrong or who had forgotten to mail some paper or who'd just never gotten around to going to the garage to get the muffler fixed, and she thought, This is humanity, all these people with shining sweaty bare shoulders and Life Savers and *New York Posts* folded into fans and excuses and worries and troubles and fines, and here they were all together. Everyone was so kind. Everyone was so helpful. It was really very cosmopolitan. Here she was surrounded by her fellow citizens, part of them, one of them.

"Bea Harkavy," the voice boomed. "Public urination."

"Is that correct?" the lawyer asked Joy.

"Oh yes," said Joy. "This is exactly where I belong."

Acknowledgments

I would like to thank Lynn Swartz Dodd and the USC Wrigley Marine Science Center for sharing Catalina with me; my friend Elizabeth Strout; my editor, Sarah Crichton; my agent, Molly Friedrich; my dearest Janet; and my entire endlessly indulgent and good-humored family.

A Note About the Author

Cathleen Schine is the author of *The Three Weissmanns of West-port*, *The Love Letter*, and *The New Yorkers*, among other novels. She has contributed to *The New Yorker*, *The New York Review of Books*, *The New York Times Magazine*, and *The New York Times Book Review*. She lives in Los Angeles.